Acclaim for Yu Hua's

BROTHERS

"Sensational, sweeping. . . . Tremendous. . . . In recognition of this ter-rific literary achievement, I think that, instead of the Year of the Ox, this should be the Year of Yu Hua."
—Maureen Corrigan, *Fresh Air*, NPR

"Impressive. . . . A family history documenting four decades of pro-found social and cultural transformation in China. . . . [An] irreverent take on everything from the Cultural Revolution to the capitalist boom. . . . [A] relentlessly entertaining epic." —*The New Yorker*

"A work of rare scope and grandeur. . . . [Yu Hua's] sharply unadorned language is all his own, carrying a ripe and pungent tone. . . . This is the epic as plainspoken brawl, one with blood on its face, a tear in the eye, and a grin on the lips. Ten out of ten stars." —*Pop Matters*

"For their translation Eileen Cheng-yin Chow and Carlos Rojas receive high marks, giving their narrator a consistent voice with palpable wit and visible verve, shortening Yu Hua's sentences to fit English expecta-tions but maintaining fidelity to the length and pace of his clauses, the real seat of an author's prose style." —*Rain Taxi Review of Books*

"Yu Hua's epic novel—a bestseller in his native China—is a tale of ribaldry, farce and bloody revolution, a dramatic panorama of human vulgarity. . . . At once hyperrealist and phantasmagorical. . . . We can see a true picture of the country refracted in this funhouse mirror."
—*The Washington Post*

"Vigorous and racy. . . . This wide-ranging and ironic portrait of modern China evokes the very feel of the place, with its popular Korean TV soaps, Eternity bicycles, factory labor, Big White Rabbit candies, neon lights and raucous music. . . . A major achievement by any standard."
—*Taipei Times*

ALSO BY YU HUA

Cries in the Drizzle

Chronicle of a Blood Merchant

To Live

The Past and the Punishments

YU HUA

BROTHERS

Yu Hua was born in 1960 in Zhejiang, China. He finished
high school during the Cultural Revolution and worked as
a dentist for five years before beginning to write in 1983.
He has published four novels, six collections of stories,
and three essay collections. His work has been translated
into French, German, Italian, Dutch, Spanish, Japanese,
and Korean. In 2002 Yu Hua became the first Chinese
writer to win the prestigious James Joyce Foundation
Award. His novel *To Live* was awarded Italy's Premio
Grinzane Cavour in 1998, and *To Live* and *Chronicle of a
Blood Merchant* were named two of the last decade's ten
most influential books in China. Yu Hua lives in Beijing.

Eileen Cheng-yin Chow and Carlos Rojas both teach modern Chinese cultural studies, Eileen at Harvard University and Carlos at Duke University. They are also the editors
of *Rethinking Chinese Popular Culture: Cannibalizations
of the Canon.*

YU HUA

BROTHERS

Yu Hua was born in 1960 in Zhejiang, China. He finished high school during the Cultural Revolution and worked as a dentist for five years before beginning to write in 1983. He has published four novels, six collections of stories, and three essay collections. His work has been translated into French, German, Italian, Dutch, Spanish, Japanese, and Korean. In 2002 Yu Hua became the first Chinese writer to win the prestigious James Joyce Foundation Award. His novel *To Live* was awarded Italy's Premio Grinzane Cavour in 1998, and *To Live* and *Chronicle of a Blood Merchant* were named two of the last decade's ten most influential books in China. Yu Hua lives in Beijing.

Eileen Cheng-yin Chow and Carlos Rojas both teach modern Chinese cultural studies. Eileen at Harvard University and Carlos at Duke University. They are also the editors of *Rethinking Chinese Popular Culture: Cannibalizations of the Canon.*

BROTHERS

YU HUA

Translated from the Chinese by
Eileen Cheng-yin Chow and Carlos Rojas

ANCHOR BOOKS
A DIVISION OF RANDOM HOUSE, INC.
NEW YORK

FIRST ANCHOR BOOKS EDITION, JANUARY 2010

Translation copyright © 2009 by Eileen Cheng-yin Chow and Carlos Rojas
Translators' preface copyright © 2009, 2010 by Eileen Cheng-yin Chow and Carlos Rojas

The Library of Congress has cataloged the Pantheon edition as follows:
Yu, Hua, [date]
[Xiong Di. English]
Brothers / Yu Hua : translated from the Chinese by Eileen Cheng-yin Chow and Carlos Rojas.
p. cm.
1. Yu, Hua, 1960–Translations into English.   I. Chow, Eileen Cheng-yin.
II. Rojas, Carlos.   III. Title.
PL2928.H78x5613 2009
895.1'352—dc22
2008021617

Anchor ISBN: 978-0-307-38606-9

Book design by Iris Weinstein

www.anchorbooks.com

Printed in the United States of America

CONTENTS

CONTENTS

TRANSLATORS' PREFACE

THE YEAR 2008 has been a watershed for modern China, for reasons both anticipated and unanticipated. From the agonizing spectacle of digging children's corpses out of the rubble of collapsed school buildings following the Sichuan earthquake, to the spontaneous outpouring of communal support and goodwill that ensued; from the international controversies that have surrounded the preparations leading up to the Beijing Olympics, to the nationalistic pageantry that was the Olympics itself, the Chinese people have experienced a year of remarkable highs and lows. As such, this past year has appeared to contain in concentrated form many of the contradictions that have characterized China's multidecade transition from high Maoism to hypercapitalism.

Published in 2005 and 2006, Yu Hua's *Brothers* spans many of these same emotional extremes. Though he originally conceived of the idea for the novel as early as 1995, Yu Hua was inspired to revisit the project during a seven-month sojourn in the United States and France that he began in late 2003. The China he left behind, meanwhile, was in the grip of a pre-Olympics beauty-pageant fever. In September of that year, for instance, a national beauty pageant was held on Hainan Island as a prelude to China's first time hosting the Miss World competition two months later. Having banned beauty pageants for the entire latter half of the twentieth century, China dove back into the pageant habit with a vengeance, and over the next few years proceeded to host a wide variety of regional, national, and international pageants—including a Tourism Queen International pageant, a Top Model of the World competition, a National Contest of the Beauty of the Gray-headed for contestants over fifty-five, a Miss Artificial Beauty pageant for plastic surgery recipients, as well as three out of the next four Miss World competitions. Inspired quite possibly by the perspective he gained from his trip abroad, together with the melding of sexual display and regional pride found in the pageant fever that was simultaneously sweeping China, Yu Hua returned to China in March 2004 and immediately began writing *Brothers*, his first novel in a decade.

Completed over a two-year period, *Brothers* is a two-volume, half-million Chinese-character behemoth that traces modern China's past four decades of social and cultural transformations through the lives of the stepbrothers Baldy Li and Song Gang. The first volume, which covered the brothers' childhood during the tumultuous years of the Cultural Revolution, was an immediate national sensation when it appeared in 2005. Published the following year, the highly anticipated second and final volume brought the narrative of *Brothers* through the post-Mao period and the first giddy years of a new capitalist China.

Brothers presents a unique perspective on contemporary Chinese history, viewing it through a gaze that is precariously balanced between beauty and perversity. The object of this narrative gaze is often the female body (together with its various substitutes), but just as often it is the Chinese body politic—the deeply schizophrenic national history that Yu Hua has lived through, and to which he attempts to give life in the pages of the novel.

Like a beauty pageant, *Brothers* is flashy, blunt, and often deliberately repetitive, yet has moments of sublime beauty and gut-wrenching pathos. It uses a combination of subversive humor and haunting sentimentality to chronicle contemporary China's transition from socialist austerity to capitalist hyperbole. Featuring frank descriptions of sexual perversity and unthinkable political violence, not to mention detailed accounts of gender-bending cosmetic procedures and harebrained confidence schemes, *Brothers* presents a highly idiosyncratic account of China's transition from Maoist state into that curious socialist-capitalist hybrid that Deng Xiaoping euphemistically called "socialism with Chinese characteristics."

The tenor of the work is established unapologetically in the opening pages. First, the protagonist, Baldy Li, sitting on a gold-plated toilet, imagines himself on a Russian Federation space shuttle, peering down at the Earth below. Almost immediately, the narrative jumps back three decades to another toilet scene, in which fourteen-year-old Baldy Li was caught peeking at women's naked posteriors in a public latrine. Although he doesn't realize it at the time, it is revealed that the teenager is actually following in the footsteps of his father, who, on the day of Baldy Li's birth, lost his balance while also sneaking a peek in the public latrine and, as a result, drowned in the cesspool below. At the same time, this scene anticipates Baldy Li's subsequent lifelong obsession with women's nether regions, and specifically their hymens—an obsession that will culminate decades later in his hosting a hilarious national beauty pageant for virgins.

Like conventional beauty pageants, this Inaugural National Virgin Beauty Competition comments on issues of sexual purity, the lure of celebrity, and national pride, as well as processes of self-commoditization. The twist is that it is quickly revealed that none of the contestants is actually a real virgin; instead, they all rely on a combination of artificial hymens and hymenorraphy, or hymen-reconstruction surgeries, to create an illusion of virginity (an echo of the Miss Artificial Beauty competition that was held in December 2004, while Yu Hua was writing his novel). The pageant's motifs of personal self-reinvention and the creation of a veneer of sexual purity also suggest the ways in which Beijing attempted to refashion itself in the eyes of the world in preparation for hosting its first Olympics, in summer 2008. China, Yu Hua seems to imply, is presenting the international community with an illusion of refurbished purity, while *Brothers*, by contrast, attempts to plumb the depths of the nation's soul.

We saw Yu Hua and his family when they visited Cambridge, Massachusetts, in November 2003. We were, of course, already very familiar with his works, but what struck us most during the few days spent together was not Yu Hua the literary bête noire, but Yu Hua the doting, proud father to his ten-year-old son, Yu Haiguo. Yu Hua marveled at how quickly Haiguo, after only a few short months in the United States, was adapting to his new environment, and he took obvious delight in Haiguo's many quirky observations of their shared adventure. In addition to everything else, *Brothers* is about parents and children, and the lengths to which parents will go to protect their children from a world gone mad. We ourselves have come to appreciate that aspect of the novel more as we have, in the interim, found ourselves proud parents to a little Baldy Li of our own.

ADDENDUM TO THE ANCHOR BOOKS EDITION

One of the pleasant challenges of literary translation involves the question of voice. Not only does a translation, by definition, involve the melding of the respective voices of the author and translators (and often includes many additional layers of editors and copy-editors), but furthermore every literary tradition has its own conventions for how a text's narratorial point of view may be articulated. Classical Chinese, for instance, typically uses very few personal pronouns, and consequently the identities of the speakers and subjects often must be inferred from context. Late imperial fiction draws on a narrative storytelling tradition that frequently includes second person addresses to the reader, though the implied speaker is not explicitly identified. In some contemporary literature, meanwhile, the problem is instead an *excess* of pronouns and corresponding points of view. For example, Gao Xingjian, the first Chinese-language Nobel laureate in literature, notoriously splits the narrative voice of his fictional works into a second person "you" and a third person "he"—with these two voices sometimes even entering into a dialogue with one another within the same text.

Brothers is written in a distinctive "voice of the village," with virtually every reference to Liu Town in the text being preceded by an obligatory "our": "our Liu Town." This is clearly a very deliberate gesture on Yu Hua's part, and he has remarked that it was his discovery of this narratorial technique that permitted him to write the novel in the first place. The precise antecedent of this "we" is never specified in the text, and Yu Hua sought to capitalize on this strategic ambiguity to capture the cacophony of disparate voices and perspectives that make up the novel. As he puts it:

> This work uses a direct narration to articulate two different historical eras, and therefore I've found that the use of a collective "our Liu Town" perspective allows me the greatest freedom by reassuring me that the story is being narrated collectively by many of the townspeople of Liu. Sometimes, this "we" refers to just one or two individuals, while at other times it represents dozens or even several hundreds of townspeople, thereby allowing me to express comprehensively the insanity of these two respective historical eras.

In the process of translating *Brothers* into English, we decided that, in the interest of readability, it would be impractical to preserve *all* of the hundreds of "our Liu Towns" that saturate the original text, though we felt strongly that the translation should at least retain a representative sampling in order to remind the reader of this ever-present collective narrative voice. Our editors, however, argued that the "our Liu Town" formula read awkwardly in English, and firmly recommended that we delete the first person pronouns altogether. We reluctantly agreed, though insisting on at least retaining the initial "our Liu Town" in the opening line of the work. With this printing of the American paperback edition of the novel, however, we are delighted to have the opportunity to restore to the translation our original sampling of these collective first person pronouns. In addition, we also add this addendum to explain this single revision to the text, and also to serve as a reminder of the collective "we" that inevitably lies hidden just below the surface of any translation.

June 2009

PART ONE

PART ONE

CHAPTER 1

BALDY LI, our Liu Town's premier tycoon, had a fantastic plan of spending twenty million U.S. dollars to purchase a ride on a Russian Federation space shuttle for a tour of outer space. Perched atop his famously gold-plated toilet seat, he would close his eyes and imagine himself already floating in orbit, surrounded by the unfathomably frigid depths of space. He would look down at the glorious planet stretched out beneath him, only to choke up on realizing that he had no family left down on Earth.

Baldy Li used to have a brother named Song Gang, who was a year older and a whole head taller and with whom he shared everything. Loyal, stubborn Song Gang had died three years earlier, reduced to a pile of ashes. When Baldy Li remembered the small wooden urn containing his brother's remains, he had a million mixed emotions. The ashes from even a sapling, he thought, would outweigh those from Song Gang's bones.

Back when Baldy Li's mother was still alive, she always liked to speak to him about Song Gang as being a chip off the old block. She would emphasize how honest and kind he was, just like his father, and remark that father and son were like two melons from the same vine. When she talked about Baldy Li, she didn't say this sort of thing but would emphatically shake her head. She said that Baldy Li and his father were completely different sorts of people, on completely different paths. It was not until Baldy Li's fourteenth year, when he was nabbed for peeping at five women's bottoms in a public pit toilet, that his mother drastically reversed her earlier opinion of her son. Only then did she finally understand that Baldy Li and his father were in fact two melons from the same vine after all. Baldy Li remembered clearly how his mother had averted her eyes and turned away from him, muttering bitterly as she wiped away her tears, "A chip off the old block."

Baldy Li had never met his birth father, since on the day he was born his father left this earth in a fit of stink. His mother told him that his father had drowned, but Baldy Li asked, "How? Did he drown in the stream, in the pond, or in a well?" His mother didn't respond. It was only later, after Baldy Li had been caught peeping and had become stinkingly notorious throughout Liu Town—only then did he learn that he really was another rotten melon off the same damn vine as his father. And it was only then that he learned that his father had also been peeping at women's butts in a latrine when he accidentally fell into the cesspool and drowned.

Everyone in Liu Town—men and women, young and old—laughed when they heard about Baldy Li and couldn't stop repeating, "A chip off the old block." As sure as a tree grows leaves, if you were from Liu Town, you would have the phrase on your lips; even toddlers who had just learned to speak were gurgling it. People pointed at Baldy Li, whispering to each other and covering their mouths and snickering, but Baldy Li would maintain an innocent expression as he continued on his way. Inside, however, he would be chuckling because now—at that time he was almost fifteen—he finally knew what it was to be a man.

Nowadays the world is filled with women's bare butts shaking hither and thither, on television and in the movies, on VCRs and DVDs, in advertisements and magazines, on the sides of ballpoint pens and cigarette lighters. These include all sorts of butts: imported butts, domestic butts; white, yellow, black, and brown; big, small, fat, and thin; smooth and coarse, young and old, fake and real—every shape and size in a bedazzling variety. Nowadays women's bare butts aren't worth much, since they can be found virtually everywhere. But back then things were different. It used to be that women's bottoms were considered a rare and precious commodity that you couldn't trade for gold or silver or pearls. To see one, you had to go peeping in the public toilet—which is why you had a little hoodlum like Baldy Li being caught in the act, and a big hoodlum like his father losing his life for the sake of a glimpse.

Public toilets back then were different from today. Nowadays you wouldn't be able to spy on a woman's butt in a toilet even if you had a periscope, but back then there was only a flimsy partition between the men's and women's sections, below which there was a shared cesspool. On the other side of the partition the sounds of women peeing and shitting seemed disconcertingly close. So instead of squatting down where you should, you could poke your head under the partition, suspending yourself above the muck below by tightly gripping the boards with your hands and your legs. With the nauseating stench bringing tears to your eyes and maggots crawling all around, you could bend over like a competitive swimmer at the starting block about to dive into the pool, and the deeper you bent over, the more butt you would be able to see.

That time Baldy Li snared five butts with a single glance: a puny one, a fat one, two bony ones, and a just-right one, all lined up in a neat row, like slabs of meat in a butcher shop. The fat butt was like a fresh rump of pork, the two bony ones were like beef jerky, while the puny butt wasn't even worth mentioning. The butt that Baldy Li fancied was the just-right one, which lay directly in his line of sight. It was the roundest of the five, so round it seemed to curl up, with taut skin revealing the faint outlines of a tailbone. His heart pounding, he wanted to glimpse the pubic area on the other side of the tailbone, so he continued to lean down, his head burrowing deeper under the partition. But just as he was about to catch a glimpse of her pubic region, he was suddenly nabbed.

A man named Victory Zhao, one of the two Men of Talent in Liu Town, happened to enter the latrine at that very moment. He spotted someone's head and torso burrowing under the partition and immediately understood what was going on. He therefore grabbed Baldy Li by the scruff of his neck, plucking him up as one would a carrot.

At that time Victory Zhao was in his twenties and had published a four-line poem in our provincial culture center's mimeographed magazine, thereby earning himself the moniker Poet Zhao. After seizing Baldy Li, Zhao flushed bright red. He dragged the fourteen-year-old outside and started lecturing him nonstop, without, however, failing to be poetic: "So, rather than gazing at the glittering sea of sprouted greens in the fields or the fishes cavorting in the lake or the beautiful tufts of clouds in the blue sky, you choose instead to go snooping around in the toilet. . . ."

Poet Zhao went on in this vein for more than ten minutes, and yet there was still no movement from the women's side of the latrine. Eventually Zhao became anxious, ran to the door, and yelled for the women to come out. Forgetting that he was an elegant man of letters, he shouted rather crudely, "Stop your pissing and shitting. You've been spied upon, and you don't even realize it. Get your butts out here."

The owners of the five butts finally dashed out, shrieking and weeping. The weeper was the puny butt not worth mentioning. A little girl eleven or twelve years old, she covered her face with her hands and was crying so hard she trembled, as if Baldy Li hadn't peeped at her but, rather, had raped her. Baldy Li, still standing there in Poet Zhao's grip, watched the weeping little butt and thought, *What's all this crying over your underdeveloped little butt? I only took a look because there wasn't much else I could do.*

A pretty seventeen-year-old was the last to emerge. Blushing furiously, she took a quick look at Baldy Li and hurried away. Poet Zhao cried out for her not to leave, to come back and demand justice. Instead, she simply hurried away even faster. Baldy Li watched the swaying of her rear end as she walked, and knew that the butt so round it curled up had to be hers.

Once the round butt disappeared into the distance and the weeping little butt also left, one of the bony butts started screeching at Baldy Li, spraying his face with spittle. Then she wiped her mouth and walked off as well. Baldy Li watched her walk away and noticed that her butt was so flat that, now that she had her pants on, you couldn't even make it out.

The remaining three—an animated Poet Zhao, a pork-rump butt, and the other jerky-flat butt—then grabbed Baldy Li and hauled him to the police station. They marched him through the little town of less than fifty thousand, and along the way the town's other Man of Talent, Success Liu, joined their ranks.

Like Poet Zhao, Success Liu was in his twenties and had had something published in the culture center's magazine. His publication was a story, its words crammed onto two pages. Compared with Zhao's four lines of verse, Success Liu's two pages were far more impressive, thereby earning him the nickname Writer Liu. Liu didn't lose out to Poet Zhao in terms of monikers, and he certainly couldn't lose out to him in other areas either. Writer Liu was on his way to buy rice when he saw Poet Zhao strutting toward him with a captive Baldy Li, and Liu immediately decided that he couldn't let Poet Zhao have all the glory to himself. Writer Liu hollered to Poet Zhao as he approached, "I'm here to help you!"

Poet Zhao and Writer Liu were close writing comrades, and Writer Liu had once searched high and low for the perfect encomia for Poet Zhao's four lines of poetry. Poet Zhao of course had responded in kind and found even more flowery praise for Writer Liu's two pages of text. Poet Zhao was originally walking behind Baldy Li, with the miscreant in his grip, but now that Writer Liu hustled up to them, Poet Zhao shifted to the left and offered Writer Liu the position to the right. Liu Town's two Men of Talent flanked Baldy Li, proclaiming that they were taking him to the police station. There was actually a station just around the corner, but they didn't want to take him there; instead, they marched him to one much farther away. On their way, they paraded down the main streets, trying to maximize their moment of glory. As they escorted Baldy Li through the streets they remarked enviously, "Just look at you, with two important men like us escorting you. You really are a lucky guy."

Poet Zhao added, "It's as if you were being escorted by Li Bai and Du Fu. . . ."

It seemed to Writer Liu that Poet Zhao's analogy was not quite apt, since Li Bai and Du Fu were, of course, both poets, while Liu himself wrote fiction. So he corrected Zhao, saying, "It's as if Li Bai and Cao Xueqin were escorting you. . . ."

Baldy Li had initially ignored their banter, but when he heard Liu Town's two Men of Talent compare themselves to Li Bai and Cao Xueqin, he couldn't help but laugh. "Hey, even I know that Li Bai was from the Tang dynasty while Cao was from the Qing dynasty," he said. "So how can a Tang guy be hanging out with a Qing guy?"

The crowds that had gathered alongside the street burst into loud guffaws. They said that Baldy Li was absolutely correct, that Liu Town's two Men of Talent might indeed be full of talent, but their knowledge of history wasn't a match even for this little Peeping Tom. The two Men of Talent blushed furiously, and Poet Zhao, straightening his neck, added, "It's just an analogy."

"Or we could use another analogy," offered Writer Liu. "Given that it's a poet and a novelist escorting you, we should say we are Guo Moruo and Lu Xun."

The crowd expressed their approval. Even Baldy Li nodded and said, "That's more like it."

Poet Zhao and Writer Liu didn't dare say any more on the subject of literature. Instead, they grabbed Baldy Li's collar and denounced his hooligan behavior to one and all while continuing to march sternly ahead. Along the way, Baldy Li saw a great many people tittering at him, including some he knew and others he didn't. Poet Zhao and Writer Liu took time to explain to everyone they met what had happened, appearing even more polished than talk-show hosts. And those two women who had had their butts peeped at by Baldy Li were like the special guests on their talk shows, looking alternately furious and aggrieved as they responded to Poet Zhao and Writer Liu's recounting of events. As the women walked along, the one with a fat butt suddenly screeched, having noticed her own husband among the spectators, and started sobbing as she complained loudly, "He saw my bottom and god knows what else! Whip him!"

Everyone laughed and turned to look at the husband, who was standing there motionless, flushed and frowning. Poet Zhao and Writer Liu stopped Baldy Li and, gripping his clothes, dragged him up to the unfortunate husband, as if presenting a meat bone to a dog. The fat woman continued to wail, urging her husband to beat Baldy Li up: "My bottom is for your eyes only, but now this hooligan has seen it, too. What am I going to do? Whip him! Scratch out his eyes! Why are you just standing there? Aren't you ashamed?"

All the spectators burst out laughing, and even Baldy Li tittered. He was thinking that this man was losing face, not on Baldy Li's account but, rather, because of this wife of his. The wife started shrieking again, saying, "Look at him, he even has the gall to laugh! He took advantage of me, and he's happy about it! Why won't you beat him? He's humiliated you, and you still won't take action?"

This man was Liu Town's famous Blacksmith Tong. When Baldy Li was a young boy, he would often go to Tong's shop to watch him work, and admire the sparks shooting off hammered metal. Now Tong was so furious that his complexion became darker than molten steel. He slapped Baldy Li across the face as if he were striking metal, slamming the teenager to the ground and knocking out two of his teeth, thereby filling his eyes with shooting stars and making his ears buzz for the next 180 days. This slap upside the head made Baldy Li feel that he had paid heavily for his transgression, and he swore to himself that if he ever encountered the blacksmith's wife's butt again, he would keep his eyes tightly shut and wouldn't take a single look, even if he were offered all the gold and silver in the world.

After Baldy Li was smacked, Poet Zhao and Writer Liu continued to parade him through the streets with a black eye and a bloody nose. They circled Liu Town's streets over and over again, walking right past the police station three times. By the end, even the police were standing outside their front door watching the show, but Poet Zhao and Writer Liu still refused to turn Baldy Li over to them. Zhao, Liu, and the remaining two women paraded Baldy Li around town until eventually the fresh pork-rump butt didn't want to follow anymore and the dried-jerky one also lost interest. After the two of them went home, Poet Zhao and Writer Liu took Baldy Li through the town one last time, until their own legs and backs were sore and their throats dry. Only then did they deliver him to the police.

At the station, all five policemen rushed up and started questioning Baldy Li at once. After ascertaining the five women's names, they started asking about each of them in detail, skipping over the little butt. They didn't appear to be following police procedure at all but, rather, seemed more intent on getting the lowdown on the various butts. When Baldy Li started explaining how he had peeped at the just-right, not-fat-not-skinny, so-round-it-curled-up butt, the policemen looked as though they were listening to a spine-tingler. This round-bottomed maiden, named Lin Hong, was a well-known beauty of Liu Town, and the policemen had often checked out her pretty little ass as she walked down the street. There were plenty of men who had examined her rear end with clothes on—but only Baldy Li had seen it in the flesh. The policemen realized that Baldy Li's arrest presented them with a golden opportunity and therefore asked him about her bottom over and over again. Whenever he started describing the taut skin and slight rise of her tailbone, the policemen's eyes all lit up like lightbulbs, but when he noted that he didn't see much more, their eyes immediately dimmed as if the electricity had suddenly been cut. Their faces full of disappointment and frustration, the men pounded the table and shouted, "A full confession brings leniency, and holding back will only result in severe punishment! Now think carefully: What else did you see?"

With his heart in his throat, Baldy Li recounted how he had lowered himself a bit farther, trying to glimpse Lin Hong's pubic area. His voice dropped to a whisper, and his listeners all held their breath. It was as if Baldy Li were back to his ghost story, but just as the ghost was about to appear, the story abruptly ended. Baldy Li explained that just as he had been on the verge of seeing Lin Hong's pubic area, Poet Zhao had grabbed him by the collar and pulled him up, and as a result he hadn't seen anything at all. Baldy Li said regretfully, "I missed it by just a hair. . . ."

When Baldy Li stopped, the five policemen at first couldn't catch their breath and continued staring at him. Only when they realized that his lips had stopped moving did they finally understand that this was yet another story without an ending. They all had peculiar expressions, looking like five starving dogs who had just seen a freshly roasted duck fly out of their reach. One of them blamed Poet Zhao, saying, "This Zhao fellow—shouldn't he have been sitting at home writing poetry? What was he doing in the latrine?"

Once the policemen realized that they couldn't get anything more out of Baldy Li, they agreed to let him go home with his mother. Baldy Li told them his mother's name was Li Lan and that she worked at the silk factory. A policeman walked out the main door of the station and started yelling out to people on the street, asking if any of them knew Li Lan: "You know, the one who works at the silk factory." After hollering for five minutes or so, the officer finally found someone who was on his way to the factory. The passerby asked the policeman why he was looking for Li Lan, to which the policeman replied, "Just tell her to come to the station to pick up her hooligan son."

Baldy Li stayed at the police station all afternoon, like a lost item waiting to be reclaimed. He sat on the long bench, watching the sunlight streaming in through the open front entrance. At first the ray of light on the cement floor was as wide as the door frame but then it became narrower and narrower, and eventually it disappeared altogether. Baldy Li didn't realize that he had already become famous and that everyone who walked by the station would come in to take a look at him—men and women, all tittering as they strained to see the guy who peeped at women's butts in the public toilet. When no one happened to be gawking at him, one policeman after another would walk over, still hoping against hope, and slam his fist down on the table, asking sternly, "Think carefully, is there anything you forgot to report?"

It was night by the time Baldy Li's mother finally showed up at the station. She hadn't come earlier because she was afraid of people in the street pointing and talking about her. Fourteen years earlier Baldy Li's father had brought her excruciating shame, and now her son had exacerbated her humiliation. Therefore, she waited until after dark, then put on a head scarf and a surgical mask and crept to the station. When she entered the front door, she took one look at her son and immediately averted her eyes. Cowering in front of the lone remaining policeman, she explained in a trembling voice who she was. The policeman, who was supposed to have already gone off duty, blew a gasket, shouting, "Do you realize what fucking time it is? It's already eight o'clock and I haven't even eaten yet, and furthermore I was supposed to see a movie tonight. I had to push and shove at the ticket booth just to get a ticket, and now what the hell am I going to be able to see? Even if I took a plane to the theater, I'd only get to see 'The End' flash on the screen." Throughout this tirade, Baldy Li's mother stood there cowering in front of the policeman, nodding at every curse, until finally he said, "Stop nodding your goddamn head and get the fuck out of my sight. I'm going to lock up."

Outside the police station, Baldy Li's mother walked silently, head bowed, along the dark side of the main street. He followed behind her, strutting and swinging his arms blithely, as if she had been the one caught in the latrine and not he. When they got home, Baldy Li's mother walked into her room without saying a word, shut the door, and didn't make another sound. Late that night, in his half-asleep state, Baldy Li thought he sensed her walk up to his bed and, as on other nights, replace the blanket he had kicked off. Li Lan didn't speak to her son for several days, until finally one rainy night she tearfully uttered a single phrase: "Chip off the old block." She sat in the shadow of the dim light and recounted to Baldy Li in an even dimmer voice how his father had drowned while peeping at women's butts in the public latrine. At the time, she had felt so ashamed that she had considered hanging herself, but she had resolved to live on only thanks to her newborn's tears. She said that if she had known then that he would turn out the same as his father, she would have gone ahead and killed herself.

Helen, and now what the hell am I going to be able to see? Even if I took a plane to the thousand-kilometer-high sky. The bird flesh on the screen." Throughout this tirade, Baldy Li's mother stood there, cover-ing in front of the police, nodding at every curse, until finally he said, "Stop nodding your goddamn head and get the fuck out of my sight. I'm going to lock up."

CHAPTER 2

BALDY LI'S peeping ruined his good name but at the same time guaranteed that everyone in our Liu Town would know that name for years to come. Out on the street, women shied away from him—even little girls and old ladies avoided him. Baldy Li was indignant, thinking that though he had spent less than two minutes try-ing to catch a glimpse of some naked bottoms, he was being treated as if he were a serial rapist. But, at the very least, he had gotten to see Lin Hong's bare bottom. Lin Hong was the preeminent beauty of Liu Town, and all the town's men—including old men, young men, and even little boys—stared at her with googly eyes and drooling mouths. Some even got so worked up that blood started running from their noses. It was impossible to calculate how many of these men were lying in bed at night masturbating as they fantasized about two or three key parts of Lin Hong's figure. These poor saps were overjoyed if they had the good fortune to run into her once a week, but even then they'd only see her face, neck, and hands. In summer, they might have a bit more luck and glimpse her sandaled feet and her calves peeking out from under her skirt but not an inch more. Only Baldy Li had seen her bare bottom, and this aroused the envy and admiration of all the men of Liu Town, leading them to conclude that Baldy Li must have done some-thing spectacularly virtuous in a past life to have earned his present-day erotic karma.

Baldy Li became a celebrity. Though women hid from him, the men would invariably greet him with warm and knowing smiles, throwing an arm over his shoulder when they ran into him in the street. When they were sure that no one was within earshot, they would quietly ask, "So, kid, what did you see?"

Baldy Li would answer in a ringing voice, "I saw naked butts!"

The man in question would then flinch and grip Baldy Li's shoulder, saying, "Damn, lower your voice." Then, after looking around once more, he would whisper, "Hey, so what's Lin Hong's like?"

Even at this tender age, Baldy Li fully appreciated his own worth. He understood that though his reputation reeked, it reeked like an expensive dish of stinky tofu—which is to say, it might stink to high heaven, but damn, it sure tasted good. He knew that out of the five butts he saw in the public toilet, four of them were completely worthless while the fifth—Lin Hong's—was a priceless, five-star view. The reason Baldy Li would later become Liu Town's premier tycoon was that he was a born entrepreneur. At age fourteen he started using Lin Hong's butt to do business, knowing instinctively how to drive a hard bargain and adjust for inflation. The moment he saw those lecherous men grinning at him, grabbing his shoulder and slapping him on the back, he knew they were after one thing and one thing only, and that was the secret of Lin Hong's butt. When the five policemen at the station had tried to extract that same secret from him during his questioning, Baldy Li had told them everything, not daring to hold anything back. But after that initial interrogation, he wised up and resolved to stop providing free lunches. From then on, whenever he encountered one of these insincerely buddy-buddy fellows, Baldy Li remained tight-lipped and wouldn't sketch even the shadow of a single pubic hair. Instead, he would only utter the single word *Buttocks*, and those men who had come forward to unlock the mysteries of Lin Hong's butt would go away empty-handed.

Writer Liu, who was originally a lathe worker at the metal factory, earned the favor of the factory head thanks to his ability to whip up a fancy phrase and talk up a storm, and as a result was promoted to sales manager. He already had an average-looking girlfriend, but as soon as he received his promotion and had his story published, he decided that his girlfriend was no longer good enough for him. He therefore started having designs on Lin Hong, since she represented the ultimate fantasy of all Liu Town's men, unmarried and married alike. Writer Liu tried to dump his girlfriend, but she absolutely refused to be let go of. She went and stood outside the police station and started wailing that she had been bedded by Writer Liu, tearfully holding out all ten fingers. Everyone assumed that she meant that Writer Liu had slept with her ten times; they therefore were flabbergasted when they realized she was counting by tens, meaning that the two of them had slept together more than a hundred times. After this performance, Liu didn't dare dump her. In those days, if a man and a woman slept together, they had to get married, so the factory director summoned Writer Liu and chewed him out, telling him that he had two choices: He could marry his girlfriend and keep his job or dump her and settle for cleaning toilets. Weighing these two options, Writer Liu concluded that his career trumped romance and so crawled back to his girlfriend, apologizing abjectly. Soon the two of them were as good as ever, taking strolls together, going to movies, ordering furniture, and even making preparations for their wedding.

Whenever Poet Zhao happened upon someone, he expressed deep sympathy over Writer Liu's travails, feeling that Liu had handed over his life to a shameless hussy. Lust had gotten the better of him and had ruined his life. He would conclude, "This is an example of the proverbial *single misstep leading to regret of a thousand ages.*"

The townspeople did not agree with Poet Zhao's choice of literary allusion here and retorted, "How was this a single misstep? He bedded her a hundred times, so at the very least that would make it a hundred missteps."

Poet Zhao was left momentarily speechless, so he tried a different literary nugget, intoning, *"Even the mightiest hero still falls at the hands of a beauty."*

The crowds still begged to differ, asking, "How is he a hero? And she certainly is no beauty."

Poet Zhao had to nod in agreement, thinking that it is indeed true that The People see all. If Writer Liu couldn't even survive a non-beauty, what *could* he survive? So Poet Zhao no longer expressed his sympathy and regret at his compatriot's downfall. With a dismissive wave, he sniffed, "Well, he could never amount to much."

Even though Writer Liu was in the thick of his wedding preparations, he was still dreaming of greener pastures. Every night before going to bed he would get all worked up fantasizing about each and every detail of Lin Hong's body, hoping at least to be united with her in his dreams. Though it was Writer Liu who, along with Poet Zhao, had paraded Baldy Li through the streets of Liu Town, he was rather awed by the fact that Baldy Li had glimpsed Lin Hong's naked behind. In order to increase the authenticity and realism of his fantasized couplings with Lin Hong, Writer Liu urgently wanted to know the remaining mysteries of her body. So now every time he saw Baldy Li, he greeted him like an old friend. However, he was sorely disappointed by Baldy Li's refusal to utter more than the single word *Buttocks*. One day Writer Liu good-naturedly slapped the back of Baldy Li's head and asked, "Can't you spit anything else out of that mouth of yours?"

Baldy Li asked, "Like what?"

Writer Liu replied, "The word *buttocks* is a bit too abstract. Can you give me something more concrete . . . ?"

Baldy Li asked in a ringing voice, "How do you make buttocks concrete?"

"Hey, hey, stop hollering!" Writer Liu looked about him, then continued, gesturing wildly: "For instance, how big or little the butt was, how plump or bony. . . ."

Baldy Li reflected on the five bottoms he had seen in the latrine and then announced delightedly, "You're right! Butts *do* vary in size and shape."

But then he became tight-lipped again. Writer Liu thought that he needed further guidance, so he patiently prompted: "Buttocks are like faces. Everyone's face is different; some have moles and some don't. So how was Lin Hong's?"

Baldy Li thought carefully, then replied, "Lin Hong doesn't have a mole on her face."

"I know that she doesn't have a mole on her face," Writer Liu said. "But I'm not asking about her face. What was her butt like?"

Even at this tender age Baldy Li had already mastered his poker face. He quietly asked Writer Liu, "So what will you give me in return?"

Writer Liu had no choice but to try to bribe him. Reasoning that Baldy Li was still a kid, he had brought along a few pieces of hard candy. Baldy Li gnawed on the candy and gestured for Writer Liu to lower his head. Then, with considerable gusto, he launched into a detailed description of the worthless little butt. Writer Liu asked dubiously, "That's *Lin Hong's* butt?"

"Nope," Baldy Li replied. "That was the puniest one."

"You little bastard," Writer Liu cursed. "I'm asking about Lin Hong's butt."

Baldy Li shook his head. "I can't bear to talk about it."

"Damn." Writer Liu continued to curse. "She's not your mom, and neither is she your older sister."

Baldy Li decided that he had a point. "You're right, she's not my mom, nor my sister. . . ." But then he shook his head again and added, "But she *is* my dream lover, so I can't bear to talk about it."

"What kind of dream could you have, you little bastard?" Writer Liu asked impatiently. "So what would it take for you to be able to bear talking about it?"

Baldy Li frowned and pondered for a long time. "Why don't you treat me to a bowl of noodles? Then perhaps I could bear it."

Writer Liu hesitated, then gritted his teeth and agreed. "Okay."

Swallowing hard, Baldy Li went in for the kill. "I don't want a nine-cent bowl of unseasoned noodles. What I want is a thirty-five-cent bowl of house-special noodles—the kind with fish, meat, and shrimp flavors mixed together."

"Three-flavored house-special noodles?" Writer Liu bellowed. "You little bastard. Even I can't afford to have house-special noodles more than a few times a year. If I can't bear to buy them for myself, why would I be willing to buy you a bowl? Keep on dreaming, kid."

Baldy Li nodded earnestly. "Yeah, if you can't even bear to buy house-special noodles for yourself, how could you possibly treat me to some?"

"Damn right." Writer Liu was very pleased with Baldy Li's attitude. "So you'll have a bowl of plain noodles."

Baldy Li swallowed and said with an air of regret, "But for unseasoned noodles, I don't think I could bear to part with my secret."

Writer Liu gnashed his teeth in fury. He wanted nothing more than to smack Baldy Li in his face until it was a bloody pulp. But in the end he agreed to treat Baldy Li to a bowl of house-special noodles. He cursed again, adding, "Okay, here's your house-special noodles. Now give me all the details."

Blacksmith Tong also came to hear about Lin Hong's butt. After discovering that Baldy Li had glimpsed Tong's own wife's plump butt, Tong had given him a good thrashing. But Blacksmith Tong was also a "greener pastures" sort of guy, and each night as he went to bed with his plump wife in his arms, he closed his eyes and fantasized about Lin Hong's slender figure. Unlike Writer Liu, Tong went straight to the point. When he spotted Baldy Li in the street, he blocked the boy with his massive figure and peered down, saying, "Hey, kid, you remember me?"

Baldy Li looked up. "I'd recognize you even if you were a pile of ashes."

Blacksmith Tong glowered. "So you wish me dead, kid?"

"No, no, no," Baldy Li quickly answered, thinking that he had to avoid those big hammer fists at all costs. He pried his mouth wide open with his hands, showing Blacksmith Tong. "You see, you see? I'm short two teeth because of you."

Then Baldy Li pointed to his left ear. "It's like a beehive in there with all the buzzing."

Blacksmith Tong laughed and proclaimed for the benefit of the passersby, "Well, since you're just a kid, I'll treat you to a bowl of noodles to make up for it."

Blacksmith Tong strutted toward the People's Restaurant, with Baldy Li closely following, hands behind his back. Baldy Li thought to himself that Chairman Mao was right when he said that there is no such thing as unmerited love or hatred. So if Blacksmith Tong suddenly wanted to treat him to a bowl of noodles, it must be because he wanted to find out about Lin Hong's butt. Baldy Li scurried forward and quietly asked him, "So you're treating me to a bowl of noodles to find out about buttocks. Right?"

Tong laughed and nodded. "You're a smart kid."

Baldy Li said, "But you already have some ass at home. . . ."

"You know how men are," Tong confided. "They're always peering into the pot even when they're eating out of the bowl."

Tong walked into the People's Restaurant with the air of a big spender, but the moment he sat down he became a cheapskate and only bought Baldy Li a bowl of plain noodles. Baldy Li *hmmph*ed to himself but didn't say anything. Once the bowl was on the table, he dove in with his chopsticks and slurped away until he was covered in sweat and his nose was running. Blacksmith Tong watched as Baldy Li's snot ran down to the edge of his lips and was sucked back up, again and again. After watching four rounds of this, Tong suddenly noticed that half the noodles had already disappeared, and he became impatient with Baldy Li's reticence. He said, "Hey, hey, don't just sit there and eat. Time to talk."

Baldy Li stopped slurping, wiped away his sweat, looked about, and then started to speak in a low voice. He described not Lin Hong's bottom but, instead, a plump one. When Baldy Li was done, Blacksmith Tong looked at him suspiciously. "How come that sounds a lot like my wife's?"

"It *is* your wife's butt," Baldy Li replied earnestly.

Blacksmith Tong flew into a rage and raised his hand, bellowing, "I'm going to whup you good, you little bastard!"

Baldy Li quickly leapt up to avoid Tong's huge palm. At that moment, everyone in the restaurant turned around to look at them, so Blacksmith Tong had to convert his whupping gesture into a wave. He pointed to Baldy Li and said, "Sit back down."

Baldy Li smiled and nodded at the other patrons in the restaurant, calculating that as long as they were paying attention, Blacksmith Tong wouldn't dare beat him. He sat down again across from Blacksmith Tong, who glowered at him. "So come on, hurry up with Lin Hong's. . . ."

Baldy Li looked around and, seeing that everyone was still watching him, smiled in relief and continued in a low voice. "Every butt has its price. A bowl of plain noodles will buy you your own wife's butt, but Lin Hong's calls for a bowl of house-special noodles."

Blacksmith Tong was so furious that for a long time he couldn't even muster up a response. Seeing Baldy Li nonchalantly returning to his noodles, Blacksmith Tong snatched the bowl out of his hands and spat out, "I'll eat them myself."

Baldly Li turned around to look at the other patrons in the restaurant, who seemed perplexed by this transfer of noodles. Baldy Li smiled and explained, "It's like this: First he treated me to half a bowl of noodles, then I treated him back with the remaining half a bowl."

From that point on, Baldy Li's asking price was public knowledge: one bowl of house-special noodles for the secrets of Lin Hong's butt. In the six months while Baldy Li's ears were still ringing, he was treated to fifty-six bowls of house-special noodles, systematically eating his way into his fifteenth year and gradually transforming his skinny, sallow body into a ruddy, plump one. He thought that being able to eat so many house-special noodles was truly a case of bad luck begetting good. At that point, Baldy Li had no idea of the vast fortune he would subsequently amass and no inkling that he would ultimately grow bored with even the most extravagant feasts. Back then Baldy Li was still a poor lad and felt that having a bowl of house-special noodles was like taking a stroll in paradise—a stroll that he took fifty-six times during that half year.

Baldy Li's designs on a bowl of house-special noodles didn't always go smoothly, and sometimes he would attain it only after a certain amount of struggle. Countless people hoping to learn the secrets of Lin Hong's butt would try to get by with just plain noodles, but Baldy Li wouldn't fall for it and would patiently bargain until he got what he was after. As a result, each of these clients looked at him with new respect, remarking that this fifteen-year-old little bastard was sharper and drove a harder bargain than a fifty-year-old seasoned salesman.

Across from Blacksmith Tong's shop was a scissor sharpener's shop belonging to Old Scissors Guan and his son, Little Scissors Guan, who began learning his craft from his father when he was fourteen. Now in his twenties, Little Scissors Guan had neither wife nor girlfriend but had long admired Lin Hong; therefore he too wanted to learn the secrets of her bottom. He waved at Baldy Li and suggested that his good times were almost over, since Lin Hong would soon have a boyfriend, after which no one would have to treat Baldy Li to any more noodles. Therefore Baldy Li should take what he could and make do with the bowl of plain noodles, because soon he would be lucky to get even a bowl of broth.

Baldy Li was perplexed and asked, "Why is that?"

Little Scissors Guan explained: "Just think about it. Once Lin Hong has a boyfriend, certainly he'll know more about her posterior than you. So everyone will go to him to find out about it, and then who'll pay any more attention to you?"

At first Baldy Li thought this made a lot of sense, but upon further reflection he noticed the fault in Little Scissors Guan's logic and asked with a chuckle, "But would Lin Hong's boyfriend tell you these details?"

Baldy Li then raised his head, closed his eyes, and said dreamily, "If one day I were to become her boyfriend, I certainly wouldn't tell anyone anything. . . ."

He then turned to Little Scissors Guan and said shamelessly, "So you should seize the moment and treat me to a bowl of house-special noodles before I do become Lin Hong's boyfriend."

Though Baldy Li never yielded an inch on his asking price, he was a man of his word, so once he did get treated to a bowl, he never held back a single detail about the secrets of Lin Hong's butt. As a result, he enjoyed a steady stream of customers and almost more business than he could handle. There were even repeat customers, including one particularly forgetful person who came back three times.

When Baldy Li described the shape of Lin Hong's buttocks, his audience listened rapt with attention, their mouths hanging open, not even aware that they were drooling. But when he finished, they would look thoughtful and say, "It sounds a bit off."

Thanks to Baldy Li's detailed descriptions, these men understood that the Lin Hong they fantasized over every night was in fact a bit different from the actual person.

Poet Zhao also tracked down Baldy Li. One of the fifty-six bowls of house-special noodles that Baldy Li received was from Poet Zhao. As

Baldy Li enthusiastically gulped it down, he remarked that this bowl of noodles, for some reason, was tastier than the others. Beaming with satisfaction, he patted his chest and said to Poet Zhao, "There's only one person in all of China who has eaten more house-special noodles than I."

Poet Zhao asked, "Who would that be?"

"Chairman Mao," answered Baldy Li solemnly. "Of course, our venerable Chairman Mao can eat whatever he wants. Besides him, there's no one who can match me."

Poet Zhao had often gone to peep at women's butts in the same latrine where he caught Baldy Li, but after a whole year of surveillance he hadn't caught a single glimpse of Lin Hong's. Baldy Li had merely been poaching on Zhao's turf, but he had managed to snag a prime butt his first time out. If Baldy Li hadn't beaten him to it that day, Zhao would have been the first person to glimpse Lin Hong's butt. Poet Zhao felt that Baldy Li must be truly blessed to have lucked out this way. That day Poet Zhao had been planning to peep, but when he nabbed Baldy Li, his face flushed with excitement, Zhao suddenly lost interest in butts and directed all his attention to Baldy Li.

Now Poet Zhao, not wanting to be left out of the loop, planned to learn the secret of Lin Hong's butt from Baldy Li. But Zhao wasn't even willing to treat him to a bowl of plain noodles, much less house-special noodles. Though Poet Zhao was the one who had paraded Baldy Li through the streets and wrecked his reputation, he had also single-handedly made Baldy Li the recipient of over fifty bowls of house-special noodles. Baldy Li's increasingly ruddy complexion was all thanks to him, so Zhao felt that Baldy Li should express his gratitude. Poet Zhao took out the provincial cultural center's magazine, with pictures of Li Bai and Du Fu on the cover, and flipped to the page containing his magnum opus. When Baldy Li reached out to take the magazine, Poet Zhao tensed up as if he were being mugged and immediately whacked Baldy Li's hand away. He wouldn't let Baldy Li handle his magazine, telling him that his hands were too dirty, and therefore Zhao insisted on holding it as Baldy Li read.

Instead of reading the poem, Baldy Li merely counted the characters and exclaimed, "So few? There are just four lines, with seven characters to a line—that makes only twenty-eight characters."

Poet Zhao was extremely annoyed and said, "There may be only twenty-eight characters, but each of them is a pearl!"

Baldy Li said he understood Poet Zhao's love for his own work. Speaking like an old-timer, he commented, "There are two things that one always prizes: one's own writing and someone else's wife."

Poet Zhao answered dismissively, "What would you know, at your age!"

Then Poet Zhao got to the point. He said that he was writing a story about a youth who was nabbed while peeping at women's bottoms in the public latrine, and he wanted Baldy Li's help with a few of the interior psychological descriptions. Baldy Li asked, "What sort of descriptions?"

Poet Zhao prompted, "What was your state of mind when you caught your first glimpse of a woman's bottom? For instance, when you saw Lin Hong's . . .?"

Baldy Li suddenly understood. "So that's what you're after, Lin Hong's butt? That'll be one bowl of house-special noodles."

"Rubbish," Poet Zhao answered indignantly. "Do I seem like that sort of person? Let me tell you, I'm not Writer Liu. I'm Poet Zhao! I've already dedicated myself to the altar of literature. I've already made a vow that until I publish in one of the nation's top literary journals, first, I won't look for a girlfriend; second, I won't get married; and third, I won't have children."

Baldy Li thought the logic of Poet Zhao's statement seemed a bit off and asked him to repeat his vow. Poet Zhao thought that his words had moved Baldy Li, so he repeated himself, emoting heavily. Baldy Li finally figured out the problem and remarked smugly, "Your reasoning makes no sense. If you don't find a girlfriend, how could you get married or have children? So really you just need the first vow, because the other two are redundant."

Poet Zhao was speechless. After opening his mouth several times, he finally spat out, "You have no understanding of literature. Just forget it, and tell me about your state of mind."

Baldy Li held up a finger. "One bowl of house-special noodles."

Poet Zhao couldn't believe anyone could be so shameless. After gritting his teeth for a while, he finally smiled and resumed his entreaties. "Think about it. You are the protagonist of my novel. Once my novel is published and becomes famous, won't you be famous, too?"

Poet Zhao saw that Baldy Li was listening earnestly, so he continued. "And won't you have me to thank for your future fame?"

Baldy Li cackled, "So you're going to make me a villain, but I should be grateful?"

Poet Zhao was taken aback. He thought to himself, *This little Baldy Li is sharp. No wonder everyone says this fifteen-year-old bastard is a tougher nut to crack than some old farts.* Zhao tried his best to continue smiling. "At the conclusion of the novel, the youth sees the error of his ways."

Baldy Li had zero interest in Poet Zhao's novel. He held up one finger and said firmly, "I don't care if it's my state of mind or Lin Hong's butt. My price is one bowl of house-special noodles."

"How hard it is to reason with a barbarian!" Poet Zhao looked up into the sky and heaved a great sigh. With panged reluctance he gave in. "It's a deal."

Poet Zhao and Baldy Li arrived at the People's Restaurant. As Baldy Li slurped away at the noodles Poet Zhao was paying for, he started to describe what he had been thinking when he saw the women's butts, recalling how he had trembled all over. Poet Zhao asked, "You mean your body was trembling, or your heart?"

"Oh, my heart was trembling, too."

Poet Zhao thought that this was a marvelous description and hurried to write it down in his notebook. Baldy Li, wiping away the sweat and snot generated from eating the noodles, paused awhile, then continued. "Then I stopped trembling."

Poet Zhao didn't understand. "What do you mean, you stopped trembling?"

"I just stopped, that's all," Baldy Li explained. "Once I saw Lin Hong's butt, I was completely mesmerized. I couldn't see or feel anything— only her butt and the desire to see it more clearly. I couldn't hear anything around me. Otherwise how could I have not heard you come in?"

"You have a point there." Poet Zhao's eyes glistened. "When silence trumps sound, that's really the pinnacle of art!"

As Baldy Li continued, describing Lin Hong's taut skin and the slight protrusion of her tailbone, Poet Zhao's breathing thickened. Baldy Li described how he'd tried to lower his body just a little more to be able to see Lin Hong's pubic area. Poet Zhao's face filled with tension, as if he, like the policemen at the station before him, were waiting breathlessly for the climax of a ghost story. Suddenly he noticed that Baldy Li's lips had stopped moving. He asked anxiously, "And then?"

"And then nothing," Baldy Li answered angrily.

"Why nothing?" Poet Zhao was still lost in the reverie of Baldy Li's words.

Baldy Li banged the table and said, "Because at this critical juncture, you, you fucking pulled me up!"

Poet Zhao shook his head again and again. "If only I had gone in ten minutes later."

"Ten minutes?" Baldy Li grumbled. "If you had arrived ten seconds later, even that would have been enough, you bastard."

CHAPTER 3

BALDY LI'S real name was Li Guang. In order to reduce hair-cutting expenses, his mother always told the barber to shave him bald. Even after his hair grew out like a wild bush, the nickname stuck. When Baldy Li grew up, he reasoned that since everyone would always know him as Baldy, he would shave his head to live up to his nickname. Back then Baldy Li was not yet our Liu Town's premier tycoon but, rather, one of its poorer citizens, and he discovered that maintaining a bona fide bald head was no simple matter—it actually cost twice as much as growing his hair out. He bragged about how it cost a lot to be a bona fide poor person! His brother, Song Gang, got his hair cut only once a month, but Baldy Li had to go at least twice a month to have the barber run his bright, shiny blade again and again over his pate, as if he were shaving someone's face. Only when his head was as smooth as a piece of silk and shinier than the blade itself, and only then did he live up to the name Baldy Li.

Baldy Li's mother, Li Lan, passed away when he was fifteen. He said she was afraid of losing face, while he and his father were shameless bastards who couldn't care less. Raising a single finger, Baldy Li would say that, while there might be a handful of women in the world whose husbands were murderers and whose sons turned out to be murderers as well, there was probably only one woman who had the misfortune of having both husband and son caught spying on women's butts in the public latrine—and that would be his mother.

In those days countless men spied in the public latrine, but nothing ever happened to them. When Baldy Li tried it, however, he was caught and paraded down the street; and when Baldy Li's father did it, he fell into the cesspool and drowned. Baldy Li felt that his father must have had the most boneheaded bad luck imaginable to have kicked the bucket for a glimpse of ass. Even if someone were to, as the proverb has it, *pick up a sesame seed only to lose a watermelon,* he would still get a better deal than Baldy Li's father had. Meanwhile, Baldy Li felt that he himself was the second-unluckiest person in the world. But at least he didn't lose his life in the process, and furthermore, he had

managed to turn a profit with those fifty-six bowls of house-special noodles. As they say, *as long as you own the mountain, there's no need to
worry about firewood.* Baldy Li's mother, however, had neither a
mountain nor firewood, and in the end all the father's and son's bad
luck fell on her innocent shoulders, making her truly the world's
unluckiest woman.

Baldy Li didn't know how many butts his father saw that time, but
according to his own experience, he figured that his father must have
crouched down too low. He must have wanted to see the women's
pubic hair and therefore lowered his body farther and farther down,
until his legs were almost suspended in midair while the entire weight
of his body rested on his hands. His hands would have tightly gripped
the wooden slats, over which untold numbers of butts had once squatted, polishing them smooth and slick. This unlucky man may very well
have glimpsed the pubic hair that he had dreamed about, his eyes bug-
ging out like birds' eggs. The nauseating stench of the cesspool would
have made his eyes tear up and become unbearably itchy, but at that
moment he certainly wouldn't have dared to blink. Excitement and
trepidation would have made his hands slick with sweat, and that sweat
would have made the boards he was grasping even more slippery.

Just at that moment, a man more than six feet tall had rushed into
the toilet, frantically unbuttoning his pants with one hand. All he saw
when he entered were two legs sticking straight up in the air, making
him scream as if he had seen a ghost. This scream scared the living day-
lights out of Baldy Li's father, making him lose his grip and fall headfirst into the thick, viscous goo below. In seconds, the excrement filled
his mouth and nose and then his lungs, and that was how Baldy Li's
father drowned.

The man who let out the cry was Song Gang's father, Song Fanping,
who later became Baldy Li's stepfather. As Baldy Li's birth father fell
into the cesspool, his future stepfather watched in shock. It appeared
to Song Fanping that the pair of legs had disappeared in the blink of an
eye. Beads of cold sweat covered his forehead as he contemplated the
possibility that he might have seen a ghost in broad daylight. At that
moment, a shriek was heard from the women's side of the toilet: Baldy
Li's father had hit the cesspool like a cannonball, and now the women's
backsides were all covered in shit. They jumped up, startled, and when
they looked down, they saw that there was a man lying in the cesspool
below.

Utter chaos ensued. The women cried out repeatedly, like summer cicadas, attracting a curious crowd. One of the women ran out of the toilet without remembering to pull her pants up, but when she saw the men in the crowd staring at her lecherously, she let out another scream and ran back in. The women with their backsides covered in shit discovered that they didn't have enough toilet paper to clean themselves off and started begging the crowd to gather some leaves for them. Three men immediately climbed up a wutong tree and collected at least half of its broad leaves, then asked a young woman to take them inside.

In the men's section, at the other end, crowds of men stood around engaged in animated discussion. They peered down through the eleven toilet holes at Baldy Li's father, debating whether he was dead or alive and how to retrieve him. Someone suggested using a bamboo pole, but someone else pointed out that while bamboo might suffice for lifting a chicken, for a grown man they would need a metal rod. The question was where they would find a rod long enough.

At that moment, as everyone was standing around chattering, Baldy Li's future stepfather, Song Fanping, walked up to the cesspool opening where the sanitation workers siphon off the waste and proceeded to jump right in. Is this why Li Lan would come to love this man so deeply? Buried in human waste up to his chest, he held up his arms and slowly dragged himself through the muck. Maggots crawled up to his neck and face, but he still moved forward with his arms over his head. Only when the maggots climbed up to his mouth, eyes, nose, and ears did he reach down to sweep them off.

Song Fanping moved through the cesspool, picked up Baldy Li's father, and slowly made his way back out again. He lifted Baldy Li's father out of the pit and then climbed out himself.

The crowds around the latrine quickly moved away. When they saw Baldy Li's father and Song Fanping, both covered in shit and maggots, they felt their skin prickle with revulsion. They held their noses and covered their mouths, complaining incessantly. After Song Fanping climbed out, he squatted near Baldy Li's father's body and held his finger under the man's nose, then felt his chest. Eventually he stood up and announced to the crowd, "He's dead."

At that point, the tall and muscular Song Fanping hoisted Baldy Li's father onto his back and walked away. The sight of the two of them caused an even greater commotion than Baldy Li's parade would years later: a live man walking down the street with a dead man, both of them completely covered in excrement, with filth sloughing off them, leaving behind a stream of stench extending several blocks. About two thousand people came to watch the spectacle; of these, a hundred or so yelled that their shoes had been stepped on, a dozen women shrieked that they were being felt up, and a few men cursed that their cigarettes had been picked from their pockets. It was through this sea of humanity that Baldy Li's once and future fathers both arrived at his doorstep.

Baldy Li at this point was still in his mother's belly. She had heard the tragic news and was standing in the doorway with her huge belly, supporting herself by leaning against the door frame. She saw her husband being lowered from a man's back and placed, motionless, on the ground. Her dead husband looked like a stranger lying there. To those who saw her, Li Lan's eyes appeared utterly vacant. This sudden blow left her dazed, and she seemed not to grasp what she was seeing or even understand where she was.

After placing Baldy Li's father down, Song Fanping proceeded to the well, where he lifted pail after pail of water to rinse himself. It was May, and the icy well water ran down his neck onto his clothes, making him shudder uncontrollably. After he finished rinsing himself off, he turned to take a look at Li Lan, whose blank gaze convinced him to stay a little longer. He used the well water to rinse off Baldy Li's father, turning the body over several times, then stood up and looked at Li Lan, whose wooden expression made him shake his head. Song Fanping lifted Baldy Li's father and walked to the door, but Li Lan still stood there motionless, so he had to carry the corpse in sideways.

Song Fanping saw that the pillowcases, bedspread, and blankets in the inner room were all embroidered with a big red Double Happiness character, indicating newlyweds. He hesitated for a moment, but in the end he didn't place Baldy Li's father's wet corpse on the ground but, rather, on the newlyweds' bed. When he turned to leave, Li Lan was still standing motionless and leaning against the door frame. Song Fanping saw the people outside, all looking as if they were watching a show, and in a low voice he urged Li Lan to come inside and close the door. She acted as if she hadn't heard him. Eventually Song Fanping had no choice but to walk out, dripping wet, into the crowd. When the people saw him coming toward them, they immediately opened up a path, as if he were still covered in shit. In the resulting commotion, it seemed that there were more people who lost their shoes and more women's butts that got felt up. The icy well water made Song Fanping sneeze repeatedly as he walked out of the narrow alley and into the street. The crowds returned, continuing to watch the pitiful Li Lan.

Li Lan slowly slid down the door frame, her wooden expression suddenly transforming into one of anguish. She lay on the floor, legs spread and fingers digging into the ground. Beads of sweat covered her forehead, and her eyes opened wide to take in the crowds of people around her. Someone noticed that there was blood coming from between her legs and screamed, "Look, look, she's bleeding!"

A woman who had had a child recognized what was happening and shouted, "She's giving birth!"

CHAPTER 4

BALDY LI'S birth marked the beginning of Li Lan's migraines. For as long as Baldy Li could remember, his mother wore a scarf wrapped around her head, like a peasant woman in the fields. The dull, steady ache and the sudden onslaughts of sharp pain caused her to weep all year long. She often rapped her head with her knuckles, and her knocks grew ever crisper and louder, like the steady drum of a temple clanger.

After losing her husband, Baldy Li's mother then lost her mind. But as she gradually recovered she felt no pain or fury, just shame. Baldy Li's grandmother came from the countryside to help take care of them. During Li Lan's three-month maternity leave from the silk factory, she never once left the house. She didn't even want to stand near the window for fear of being seen by someone. After the third month, Li Lan finally had to return to work. Trembling all over, her face pale, she opened the front door and stepped out as if she were about to jump into a vat of boiling oil. But she had no choice and so timidly walked into the street, her lead lowered to her chest. While hugging the sides of the buildings as closely as she could, she felt that the stares of people on the street were like needles stabbing her all over her body. An acquaintance called out her name, and she reacted as if she had been shot, nearly falling to the ground. Heaven knows how she managed to walk into the silk factory. How she managed to work the silk shearing machines all day. And how she managed to walk down the street to return home. From that point on she became mute, and even in her sealed-off house she scarcely spoke, even with her own mother and son.

The infant Baldy Li also became the object of the town's derision, and whenever his grandmother carried him outside, people would point and stare at him and say horrible things. They said that Baldy Li belonged to that man who drowned in the latrine while peeping at women's butts. Their comments were completely illogical, seeming to implicate the baby in the episode. They would say that this little rascal was just like his father, often dropping the "just like" and saying instead that the two of them were actually identical. This made Baldy Li's grandmother turn both pale and livid and left her unwilling to take him out again. Occasionally she would carry him to the window to let him get a bit of sunlight, but if anyone passed by outside, she would quickly move away. As a result, Baldy Li's once cherubic face became gaunt and sallow from spending day after day in a dark room.

After her husband died so shamefully, Li Lan never again lifted her head to look at anyone and never cried out—the head-splitting pain of her migraines audible only through the anguished grinding of her teeth and her soft groans as she slept. Whenever she held her son in her arms and saw his pale face and thin limbs, she would weep abjectly. Even so, she lacked the courage to walk outside with him during the daytime.

After more than a year, Li Lan finally took Baldy Li outside on a clear moonlit night. Her lowered head tight against her son's face, she walked quickly along the sides of the buildings. Only after having made sure that there were no other footsteps did she slow down and lift her head to look at the clear moon in the sky, enjoying the cool night breeze. She liked standing on the deserted bridge, gazing into the water and the steady waves of moonlight reflected on its surface. When she lifted her head, she saw that the trees by the river were still, as if they were asleep, their tips painted with moonlight and swaying slightly like the water. There were also the fireflies leaping and darting in the dark night, like an undulating melody.

Li Lan held her son on her right side and with her left hand pointed out the water under the bridge, the trees by the river, the moon in the sky, the dancing fireflies, explaining to him, "This is a river, this is a tree, this is the moon, these are fireflies. . . ."

Then she sighed contentedly. "The night is so beautiful."

From that point on, sunlight-deprived Baldy Li would bathe in the moon's rays every night, wandering the streets while all the other children in town were sound asleep. Late one night, without realizing it, Li Lan walked until they reached the edge of town, to the south gate, where the fields under the moonlight seemed to extend forever. She let out a soft gasp. Now that she had become familiar with the peaceful silence of the houses and streets in moonlight, she was caught by surprise at the majestic beauty of the wide open fields under the same moonlight. In her arms Baldy Li also became excited, reached his arms toward the wide expanse of field, and uttered a mouselike *eek*.

Many years later, when Baldy Li would become Liu Town's premier tycoon and decide to take a tour of outer space, he would close his eyes and imagine himself high in orbit peering down at the earth below, whereupon this impression from his infancy would miraculously return. When he imagined the beauty and majesty of Earth, it was the same as the sight of the endless fields under the moonlight, the time his mother first took him down to the south gate. The infant Baldy Li's gaze passed over the scene like a Russian space shuttle.

So it was under the cool, bright moonlight that Baldy Li learned from his mother what a street was, what a house was, what a sky was, and what a field was. Baldy Li was not yet two, and he gazed out with wonder at this cool, bright world.

Once when Li Lan was walking in the moonlight with him, she ran into Song Fanping. As Li Lan walked with her son in her arms along the deserted street, she saw a family chatting and walking in the other direction. This was Song Fanping's family, and the tall Song Fanping was leading his son, Song Gang, who was a year older than Baldy Li. His wife was holding a basket in her hand, and their voices rang clearly through the quiet night sky. Upon hearing Song Fanping's voice, Li Lan suddenly lifted her head, recognizing instantly who this tall man was—he was the man who had carried her husband back to her, all the while covered in filth. At the time Li Lan had merely leaned dazedly against the door frame, but she had always remembered the sound of the man's voice and how he used the well water to rinse down not only himself but also her dead husband. So now she lifted her head, her eyes perhaps flashing when she saw him. Then, when she saw him pause and say something to his wife in a low voice, Li Lan lowered her head again and scurried away.

Li Lan ran into Song Fanping twice during those late-night strolls with Baldy Li. Once he was with his entire family, and the other time he was alone. The second time Song Fanping suddenly used his large figure to block the mother and son's path. His big, rough hands touched the child's upturned face, and he said to Li Lan, "This child is too thin. You should let him get more sunlight, since there are vitamins in sunlight."

Poor Li Lan didn't even dare to lift her head to look at him. She trembled as she held Baldy Li, and Baldy Li was jostled in her arms as if by an earthquake. Song Fanping smiled and walked away, brushing past them. This particular night Li Lan didn't linger to enjoy the moonlight, instead hurrying home with Baldy Li. The grinding noise from her teeth sounded different than usual, because perhaps this time it didn't come from her migraines.

When Baldy Li was three, his grandmother left her daughter and grandson and returned to her hometown. By this point, Baldy Li had learned to walk but was still very thin, even thinner than he had been as a baby. Li Lan's migraines had their good and bad days, but she had developed a slight stoop from walking around with a perpetually bowed head. After his grandmother left, Baldy Li started having the opportunity to walk in broad daylight. When Li Lan went to the market, she would take him along. She walked quickly with her head lowered, and Baldy Li would stumble along behind her, holding on to the hem of her clothes. By that time no one pointed them out anymore—in fact, no one even looked at them—yet Li Lan still felt the public's gaze like daggers in her back.

Every other month Baldy Li's frail mother went to the rice store to buy forty *jin* of rice. These would be Baldy Li's happiest times, because when she hoisted the forty-*jin* sack of rice on her back, he no longer needed to hurry and stumble after her. She panted as she walked with her sack of rice—by that point even her breath began to sound like the grinding of her teeth. She would walk and pause, walk and pause, and Baldy Li would have time to take a look around.

One autumn day around noon, the tall Song Fanping walked up to them, and just as Li Lan lowered the sack down to wipe the sweat from her face, she saw a strong hand suddenly lift the sack of rice from the ground. Startled, she looked up to see this man smiling at her, and saying, "Let me carry this home for you."

Song Fanping carried the forty-*jin* sack as easily as if he were carrying an empty basket. With his left hand he scooped up Baldy Li and hoisted him onto his shoulders, telling the boy to hold on to his forehead. Baldy Li had never seen the world from this height. He was always lifting his head to look up—this was the first time he had ever been able to look down at the passersby in the street. He couldn't stop giggling as he sat on Song Fanping's shoulders.

This well-built man carried Li Lan's rice sack with her son on his shoulders and spoke in a ringing voice as they walked down the street. Li Lan walked alongside him, her head lowered, pale and drenched in cold sweat. She felt that everyone was laughing and staring at her, and she wished she could simply disappear into a crack in the ground. Song

Fanping asked questions as they walked, but Li Lan would merely nod or shake her head, her teeth still making that grinding sound.

They finally arrived at her front door. Song Fanping placed Baldy Li on the ground and emptied the cloth sack into the rice barrel. He glanced at the bed, made up with the same coverlet and sheets that he had seen three years earlier. The Double Happiness character on them had faded, its embroidery frayed. As he was about to leave, the man told Li Lan his name was Song Fanping and he was a teacher at the middle school, adding that if they ever needed help with anything, she should let him know. After he left, Li Lan let her son play outside by himself for the first time and locked herself in her room, doing who knows what. She didn't open the door again until after dark, by which time Baldy Li had fallen asleep leaning against the door.

Baldy Li remembered how, when he was five, Song Fanping's wife died of an illness. After Li Lan heard the news, she stood at the window for a long time, her teeth chattering, until the sun had set and the moon had risen. Then she took her son by the hand, and together they walked silently under the night moon to Song Fanping's house. Li Lan didn't dare enter his home; instead she stood behind a tree watching as people sat and walked around under the dim light inside. A coffin sat in the middle of the room. Baldy Li held on to the hem of his mother's clothes and listened to her chattering teeth. When he lifted his head to look at the moon and stars, he saw that his mother was crying and wiping away her tears with her hand. He asked her, "Mama, are you crying?"

Li Lan nodded and told her son that someone in their savior's family had died. Li Lan stood there a little longer, then took Baldy Li by the hand again and walked silently home.

When Li Lan came home from the silk factory the next evening, she sat at the table making paper coins. She made a great pile of paper coins and paper ingots, stringing them onto two strands of white thread. Baldy Li sat by and watched with great interest as his mother first cut the paper into squares and then folded the paper ingots one by one. She wrote GOLD on some of them and SILVER on the others. She took a "gold" ingot and explained to Baldy Li that at one time this would have been enough to buy a mansion. Baldy Li pointed at a "silver" ingot and asked her what you could buy with this. Li Lan replied that you could also buy a mansion, but perhaps a smaller one. Baldy Li looked out at the "gold" and "silver" ingots piled up on the table and calculated how many mansions you could buy with all of them. Having just learned his numbers, he counted the ingots one by one; but he knew how to count to only ten, so every time he reached ten, he would have to go back to one again. As the pile of ingots on the table grew he worked up a headful of sweat but still couldn't come up with a total. Nevertheless, he continued struggling until his counting even brought a smile to his mother's face.

Once Li Lan had a huge pile of paper ingots, she started making paper coins. First she cut circles out of the paper, then cut little holes out of the centers. Finally, she carefully drew lines on the paper circles and wrote a line of characters on each. Baldy Li felt that making a paper coin was much harder than making a paper ingot, so he wondered how many houses you could buy with a paper coin? Could you buy an entire row of houses? His mother dangled a long string threaded with paper coins and said, "You could probably buy only a piece of clothing with this." Baldy Li fretted over this until he had worked up another headful of sweat trying to figure out how clothing could cost more than a mansion. Li Lan explained that even ten strands of coins would not come close to equaling one ingot. Hearing this, Baldy Li was confounded yet again. If ten strands of coins couldn't equal one ingot, then why was his mother going to such efforts to make coins? Li Lan said that this money was not to be spent in this world but, rather, in the next; it was travel money for the deceased. Baldy Li shuddered at the word *deceased,* and shuddered again when he glanced at the darkness outside. He asked his mother which dead person this money was for. Li Lan put down what she was working on and replied, "It's for our savior's family."

On the day Song Fanping's wife was to be buried, Li Lan placed the strands of paper money and ingots into a basket. Then, holding the basket in one hand and Baldy Li's hand in the other, she stood waiting on the street. That morning was the first time Baldy Li could remember his mother lifting her head in public. As she stood there waiting for the funeral procession, some of her acquaintances passed by and peered into her basket. One of them even lifted out the strands of ingots and coins and complimented her on her craftsmanship, then asked, "Did someone else in your family die?"

Li Lan bowed her head and softly answered, "No, not in my family. . . ."

There were only a dozen or so mourners in the funeral procession.

The coffin had been placed on a cart, which creaked and rattled over the cobblestone road. Baldy Li observed that the dozen or so men and women in the procession all had white cloths tied around their heads and waists, and they wept as they walked by. The only person he recognized was Song Fanping, from whose shoulders he had once looked down at the whole world.

Song Fanping walked alongside Song Gang. As they walked past the Lis they paused, and Song Fanping turned to nod to Li Lan. Song Gang imitated his father and nodded to Baldy Li. Li Lan then took Baldy Li by the hand and followed along at the end of the funeral procession, which marched slowly down the stone paved roads out of Liu Town and onto the dirt road in the countryside.

Baldy Li and his mother followed those weeping people for a very long time, until they eventually arrived at an open grave. As the coffin was lowered into the ground the soft weeping became loud wails. Li Lan stood with her basket and Baldy Li to one side and watched while the mourners shoveled the dirt into the grave until it became a mound. The wailing once again became soft weeping, whereupon Song Fanping turned around, came toward Li Lan and Baldy Li, and gazed at Li Lan through tear-filled eyes as he took the basket from her hands. He then returned to the grave and placed the paper ingots and coins on top of the fresh grave and lit them with a match. Once the paper money started burning brightly, the weeping broke out again. Baldy Li saw that his mother was also weeping, as though her heart were broken, as she remembered her own misfortunes.

Then they all walked a very long way until they finally got back to town. Li Lan was still carrying her basket and holding her son's hand, following behind everyone. Song Fanping, up front, repeatedly turned around to look at the mother and son. When they neared Li Lan's alley, Song Fanping paused and waited for Li Lan and Baldy Li to walk up. He spoke to Li Lan in a low voice, inviting them to come to his house for a tofu meal in memory of the deceased. This was a custom of the town.

Li Lan shook her head hesitantly, then walked with Baldy Li down their alley and into their home. After having walked for almost the whole day, Baldy Li fell asleep the moment his head hit the pillow. Li Lan sat alone, staring out the window. At dusk someone knocked at the door. Waking from her reverie, Li Lan went to open the door and found Song Fanping standing outside.

His sudden appearance startled Li Lan. She didn't notice the basket in his hand, and even forgot to ask him to come in. Out of habit, she lowered her head. When Song Fanping took food out of the basket and handed it to her, she saw that he had brought them the tofu meal. She timidly accepted the dishes that Song Fanping placed in her hands and deftly poured the food into her own bowls. She quickly rinsed out the dishes, but when she returned them to Song Fanping, her hands began to shake again. Song Fanping put his plates in his basket and turned to leave, and once again Li Lan bowed her head. Only when Song Fanping's footsteps could no longer be heard did she realize that she hadn't even asked him in. By the time she lifted her head, Song Fanping had disappeared from sight.

CHAPTER 5

BALDY LI didn't really know how Song Gang's father got together with his mother. By the time he learned that this man's name was Song Fanping, he was about seven.

One summer evening, Li Lan led Baldy Li to the barbershop, where he was shaved to the proper degree of baldness. Then she took him to the basketball court across from the movie theater. This was the only lighted court in our Liu Town, and everyone called it the Light Court. That evening, Liu Town was playing a neighboring town, and more than a thousand men and women shuffled in in their slippers to form concentric circles around the court, looking like mounds of dirt around a giant ditch. The men were smoking, and the women were cracking watermelon seeds. The nearby trees were full of screaming children, while foul-mouthed men crowded the wall behind. There wasn't a spare spot along the entire wall as the people below struggled to climb up and the people on top kept kicking them back down.

It was here that the two boys spoke to each other for the first time. Song Gang was wearing a white sleeveless shirt and blue shorts, had a runny nose, and was holding on to Li Lan's clothes. Li Lan caressed the top of his head, his face, and his slender neck, looking as though she wanted to eat him up. Then she pulled the two kids together and chattered on and on, but it was so noisy the boys couldn't make out a thing she was saying. Watermelon seeds and cigarette smoke were flying everywhere, and a fight had broken out over by the wall, where one of the tree branches had snapped and dumped two kids to the ground. Li Lan was still chattering at them, and finally they were able to make out what she was saying.

Li Lan pointed at Song Gang and said to Baldy Li, "This is your older brother. His name is Song Gang."

Baldy Li nodded to the boy and repeated, "Song Gang."

Li Lan then pointed at Baldy Li and said to Song Gang, "This is your younger brother. His name is Baldy Li."

When Song Gang heard Baldy Li's nickname, he broke out into

peals of laughter as he stared at the younger boy's shiny bald head. "Your name is Baldy Li? That's hilarious!"

But suddenly Song Gang started to bawl as a man burned his arm with his cigarette. When Baldy Li saw Song Gang bawling, he was amused and almost laughed out loud, until another man's cigarette burned him on the neck and he started bawling as well.

At that point the game began. Under the brilliant lights of the court and amid the cyclones of sound, Song Fanping shone. Li Lan was astounded by his height, strength, jumps, and skills. She yelled until she was hoarse and her eyes were bloodshot. Every time Song Fanping made a basket, he would run past them, his arms extended as if he were flying. Once he even dunked the ball. In his entire life he managed to dunk only once, and this was that time. For the thousand spectators crowded around the court, this was also the first and only time they witnessed a dunk. The deafening roar suddenly died away, and people stood slack-jawed, looking at one another as if trying to confirm what they had just witnessed. Then the waves of human voices roared back all around the court. It hadn't been this loud even back when the Japanese invaded.

Stunned by his own dunk, Song Fanping stood frozen for a moment under the net. After he realized what he had accomplished, he ran toward Li Lan and the kids, flushed and wide-eyed. He spread his arms and lifted Song Gang and Baldy Li high into the sky, then he ran with them toward the basket and would have joyfully tossed them in if they hadn't been crying so loudly. Fortunately, he eventually recalled that they weren't basketballs and, chuckling, ran back and set them down. Still lost in the moment, he then lifted Li Lan. In front of a thousand people, he lifted her up as waves of laughter washed over them. Every variety of laugh could be heard: bellows, titters, shrieks, chuckles, guffaws, cackles, dry and wet laughs.

In those days, to see a man embracing a woman was tantamount to watching an adult film today. After Song Fanping put Li Lan down, he ran with arms extended back into the game. Now that she had starred in her adult film, Li Lan was perceived in a completely different light, and for the rest of the game half the spectators watched the match while the other half stared at her curiously. They recalled the man who had died while peeping at women's naked bottoms, and they pointed out that she had been his wife. Li Lan, meanwhile, was lost in her own happiness. Tears in her eyes, lips trembling, she no longer cared what anyone else said.

After the game, Song Fanping removed his sweat-soaked jersey and Li Lan held it up to her breast, as if it were something precious. The four of them then walked over to a soda shop. By the time they were seated, the sweat from Song Fanping's jersey had soaked through Li Lan's white blouse, but she was blissfully unaware that her breasts were now completely visible. Song Fanping ordered two bowls of mung bean ice and two bottles of soda. Baldy Li and Song Gang both dug in. Song Fanping opened the cold bottles of soda and passed one to Li Lan as he gulped down the other. Li Lan didn't drink hers but instead pushed it back to Song Fanping, who paused for a second, then picked it up and gulped it down, too. The two of them sat gazing at each other, no longer paying any attention to their children. Song Fanping couldn't help staring at Li Lan's breasts, and she kept looking at his bare chest—his wide shoulders and cut muscles making her blush.

Baldy Li and Song Gang didn't pay attention to them either. This was the first summer the two kids had enjoyed this sort of icy treat. Previously, the chilliest thing they had tasted was a bowlful of well water, but now they were eating an icy mung bean treat, with sugar sprinkled on top like snowflakes. They lifted their bowls, and the mere chill of the bowls was more pleasurable than drinking well water. With the sugar on top dissolving like melting snow, each spoonful was sheer ecstasy. After the first few bites, their mouths became revved-up engines that couldn't be shut down. They slurped mouthful after mouthful of the ice-cold treat, freezing their tongues and lips. They would pause and let their mouths open as if they had been scalded, and then would start up again, rolling the icy mung beans around on the tips of their tongues. Eventually they finished their bowls and licked them clean, then continued licking, savoring the lingering chill of the bowl. They licked until their bowls were warmer than their tongues, and only then did they reluctantly put them down. They raised their heads, looked at Song Fanping and Li Lan, and asked, "Could we come back again tomorrow?"

Song Fanping and Li Lan answered in unison, "Sure!"

CHAPTER 6

BALDY LI and Song Gang didn't realize that their parents were getting married in a few days. Li Lan bought two pounds of hard candy from Shanghai, roasted a big pot of fava nuts and another of watermelon seeds, and then poured everything into a barrel and mixed it together. When she was done, she gave a handful of the mixture to Baldy Li, who spread it out on the table and counted: only 12 fava nuts, 18 watermelon seeds, and 2 pieces of hard candy.

On the day of the wedding, Li Lan got up before dawn. She put on her new blouse, her new pants, and a pair of shiny new plastic sandals. She sat on the edge of the bed and watched the darkness outside her window dissipate as the rosy dawn light shone in. Her teeth were chattering. This time, though, it wasn't because of a migraine but, rather, because she was breathless and flushed at the prospect of another wedding. Li Lan hated the darkness with all her heart, and as the dawn arrived, she became more and more worked up, making her teeth chatter louder and louder and waking Baldy Li from his dreams three times. The third time he woke up, Li Lan didn't let him go back to sleep but told him to hurry up and get out of bed, brush his teeth, wash his face, and put on his new shirt, shorts, and plastic sandals. As she knelt in front of Baldy Li to fasten his sandals she heard the rumbling of a cart outside her door. She leapt up and dove to open the door and found Song Fanping, who was pulling the cart, standing there beaming, and Song Gang, who was seated on top, laughing and calling out, "Baldy Li!"

Song Gang chuckled and said to his father, "That name is hilarious."

Li Lan's neighbors gathered around them. They watched with surprise as Song Fanping and Li Lan loaded the cart with assorted housewares. Among the neighbors were three middle-school students. One, Sun Wei, had a headful of long hair, while the other two were our Liu Town's future Men of Talent, though back then they were only a couple of students named Success Liu and Victory Zhao. After becoming Writer Liu and Poet Zhao, they would parade the Peeping Tom Baldy Li through the streets of Liu. These three students crowded curiously around the cart. They nudged one another, chuckling, and leered at Li Lan, saying, "Are you getting married again?"

Li Lan, blushing bright red, went over to her neighbors and started passing out handfuls of fava nuts, watermelon seeds, and hard candy. Song Fanping also left the cart and followed behind Li Lan, handing out cigarettes to the men in the neighborhood. The neighbors munched on nuts, seeds, and candy and laughed as they watched Song Fanping and Li Lan load her possessions onto the cart.

Then they started pulling the cart along the summer streets. This was a cobblestone street, and when the wheels of the cart rolled over them, the stones would shift and the wooden electrical poles would creak. The cart was full to the brim with clothes and blankets from Li Lan's house, as well as tables and chairs, washbasins, pots and knives, and spoons and chopsticks. Baldy Li's mother and Song Gang's father walked in front, and the tagalong children followed behind.

Li Lan grabbed two handfuls of nuts, seeds, and candy and stuffed them into Baldy Li's and Song Gang's hands. The boys followed behind with their hands full of treats. Their mouths were watering in anticipation, but since they didn't have a third hand to open the candy wrappers and crack the seeds, their mouths remained empty.

A few hens and roosters trailed the two boys. Clucking as they fought over the nuts and seeds that slipped through fingers, they passed through the boys' legs and flapped their wings, trying to reach the treats. As the boys tried to avoid them, they dropped more and more of the nuts and seeds in the process.

Song Fanping pulled the cart and Li Lan held the wooden barrel and walked along the increasingly crowded streets. The two of them were beaming. Many people who knew them stopped in their tracks and looked curiously at this couple and the two boys trailed by chickens. They pointed and asked, "What is this?"

Periodically, Song Fanping would put down his cart and hand out cigarettes to the men, while Li Lan distributed handfuls of nuts and candy to the women and children. Flushed and beaming, they explained in tremulous voices that they were getting married, to which everyone nodded and said, "Ohhh." They looked at Song Fanping and Li Lan, then at Song Gang and Baldy Li, and chuckled: "Getting married. Ohhh, getting married. . . ."

Song Fanping and Li Lan walked along, smiling and telling the passersby about their wedding as everyone along the street smoked their auspicious wedding cigarettes, chewed their auspicious candy, gnawed on their auspicious nuts, and cracked their auspicious melon seeds. But Baldy Li and Song Gang didn't even get an auspicious fart, so busy were they protecting the treats in their hands while being chased by the chickens. Their mouths watered as they watched everyone else eat, but they could do nothing but gulp down their own drool.

All along the street, people pointed at Baldy Li and Song Gang, debating which of the kids would be considered the proverbial *excess baggage* in the new family. After much discussion, they eventually concluded, "Both of them are excess baggage."

Then they said to Song Fanping and Li Lan, "You two make a real good match."

Finally, the newly melded family arrived at Song Fanping's house, and with that the wedding parade reached its destination. Song Fanping moved the stuff on the cart into the house while Li Lan stood at the door with her wooden barrel, passing out handfuls of treats to the neighbors. Not much was left in the barrel, and Li Lan's handfuls became progressively smaller.

Baldy Li and Song Gang both rushed inside and dumped all the treats in their hands onto the bed. The fava nuts and melon seeds were all soggy with sweat, but the boys were so famished that they immediately stuffed their mouths full of nuts, seeds, and candy until their cheeks were round like buttocks. Finally, unable to move a muscle, they discovered that they couldn't eat another bite. From the living room, Song Fanping called out for the boys. A crowd had gathered outside, and now that they had examined the second-time-around newlyweds, they wanted to examine the two sons.

Baldy Li and Song Gang rushed outside, their mouths stuffed so full that their eyes squinted and their cheeks puffed out, making everyone burst out laughing. "What treasures do you have in there?"

The boys first shook and then nodded their heads, but they couldn't utter a word. One man said, "Don't think that just because their mouths are as full as balloons they won't be able to stuff more in."

The man walked into Song Fanping's house and rummaged around until he found two white porcelain teacup lids. Then he made Baldy Li and Song Gang latch onto the nibs on their lids as if they were nipples. The kids did indeed manage to latch on, prompting everyone to burst out laughing again. They laughed until their bodies shook, producing tears, snot, saliva, and even an occasional fart, remarking on how it looked like the boys were latching onto Li Lan's nipples. Li Lan blushed furiously as she turned to look at her new husband. Appearing completely discomfited, Song Fanping walked up to the two boys, removed the lids from their lips, and suggested, "Why don't you go back inside?"

Baldy Li and Song Gang returned to the room and climbed up once again onto the bed. They exchanged despairing glances—their mouths were full of treats, but they couldn't swallow. Baldy Li was the first to think this through and quickly started to dig out a bit at a time from his mouth. Song Gang followed his lead. They spread out the newly extracted nuts, seeds, and hard candy on the bedsheet. The treats were gummy and sticky and glistened like snot, and they made an absolute mess of their parents' bed. Having had their jaws propped open for too long, the boys now found that they couldn't shut them. They stared at each other's cavelike mouth, both at a complete loss. Meanwhile, they could hear Song Fanping and Li Lan outside calling for them again.

Li Lan's old neighbors had brought along their children and had walked through the alleys looking for Song Fanping's home. When they showed up, Li Lan felt a wave of pleasure that lasted only as long as a sneeze and then immediately fell into disappointment. It turned out that the neighbors weren't here to congratulate them on their marriage but, rather, to look for their missing chickens. The birds had trailed Baldy Li and Song Gang through the streets, but after that no one had any idea where they had gone. The neighbors started making a ruckus, cursing at Li Lan and Song Fanping: "What about our chickens? Where are our goddamn chickens?"

The newlyweds had no idea what they were talking about. "What chickens?"

"Our chickens. . . ."

In a hubbub, they tried to describe what their chickens looked like. They said that lots of people had seen the chickens follow Baldy Li and Song Gang into the street. Song Fanping was perplexed. "Chickens aren't dogs. Why would they follow people into the street?"

The neighbors insisted that lots of people had seen Baldy Li and Song Gang dropping a trail of seeds and nuts, and the chickens had followed behind them and ended up in the street. Song Fanping and Li

Lan called out to the boys and asked them, "Chickens? Did you see any chickens?"

Their jaws still locked open, the boys could only shake their heads.

The chicken search party consisted of a trio of men, a trio of women, and a trio of middle-school students, as well as a couple of boys slightly older than Baldy Li and Song Gang. The eleven of them surrounded Song Gang and Baldy Li, clucking at them angrily, "Where are our chickens? Did they follow you?"

Baldy Li and Song Gang nodded, and the mob turned back to Song Fanping and Li Lan. "See! The little bastards admit it."

They turned again to Baldy Li and Song Gang. "Where are our goddamn chickens?"

The boys shook their heads, which angered the mob. "You little bastards, you just nodded, now you're shaking your heads. . . ."

The crowd insisted that roosters and hens were not fleas and ticks, and therefore they had to be somewhere in plain sight. They walked into Song Fanping's house, searching, opening cabinets, looking under the bed and into pots. The long-haired middle-school student, Sun Wei, even started sniffing Baldy Li and Song Gang's open mouths to see if he could detect any chicken on their breath. Sun Wei sniffed for a while but couldn't decide, so he called Victory Zhao over. Victory Zhao also sniffed for a while but couldn't tell either, so he asked Success Liu to come take a whiff. Success Liu smelled for a while and also concluded, "I don't think so."

After failing to find so much as a single feather, the search party came back outside, cursing and swearing. Song Fanping was no longer beaming with pride but, rather, had turned steely-faced. His bride was pale with terror and tugged at his clothes to hold him back, afraid that her new husband would start a fight. Song Fanping had been suffering silently, and even when these people barged out of his house saying all sorts of foul things, he still restrained himself, just glaring at them with firmly set eyes.

The search party started looking around the outside of the house. A few of them even took turns peering into the well, but they didn't see any hens and roosters, just the reflections of their own faces. The three middle-school students clambered up the tree like monkeys to see if the roosters and hens were hidden on the roof. They didn't find any chickens, though they did see a few sparrows.

Unable to find anything, the search party continued uttering profanities, whereupon one suggested, "Maybe they fell into the toilet and drowned while sneaking a peek at women's butts."

"Chickens also look at women's butts?"

"Roosters."

The men guffawed and the women tittered. By this point Li Lan was shaking all over. She no longer dared to even hold on to Song Fanping's clothes, feeling that she was bringing her own misfortunes onto her new husband. Song Fanping couldn't bear another word, and these people were still chattering as they walked away, "How about the hens?"

"The hens wait till the roosters drown and then remarry."

Song Fanping pointed to the man who was talking and bellowed, "Get back here!"

All of them turned back. Three men plus three middle-school students, three women and two boys. Song Fanping saw that they had stopped in their tracks, and he yelled again, "Get back here!"

All of them started cackling. The three men and three middle-school students walked up to Song Fanping and surrounded him, while the three women took the two boys and stood to one side, as if watching a good show. They knew they had him outnumbered and sneeringly asked him, "Do you want to treat us to a wedding banquet?" Song Fanping retorted, "No banquet, just my fist." He then pointed to the man in the middle and demanded, "Repeat what you just said."

The man sneered, "What did I say?"

Song Fanping hesitated, then said, "You were saying something about a hen. . . ."

The person said, "Oh!" as he remembered, then asked, "You want me to repeat that?"

Song Fanping said, "If you dare say it again, I'll smash your mouth."

The man looked at his companions and the three students. "And what if I don't?"

Song Fanping, stunned for a moment, eventually sighed. "Get out of here."

The group started laughing. The three middle-school students blocked Song Fanping and chanted in unison, "After the rooster drowns, the hen remarries?"

Song Fanping raised his fist, then lowered it again. He shook his head at the three students and pushed them out of his way. He was going back in when the first man said, "What does the hen remarry? Another rooster!"

Song Fanping turned around and punched him. His punch was swift and devastating, and the man promptly toppled over like an old blanket being tossed aside. Baldy Li and Song Gang's mouths suddenly both snapped shut.

When the man got up off the ground, his mouth was full of blood, and he spat out a mouthful mixed with saliva and snot. After Song Fanping threw his punch, he leapt out of the circle the group had formed around him. When they came at him, Song Fanping crouched down and kicked his right leg straight out. Baldy Li and Song Gang at that moment learned what a "sweeping leg kick" was; Song Fanping knocked down the three men with his one leg and made the three students stumble over one another.

When they got up to leap at him again, Song Fanping shot out his left leg, catching one man in the stomach. The man fell back to the ground with a howl and also dragged down the two men behind him. The men and middle-school students stared at one another in astonishment, trying to absorb what had just happened.

Song Fanping stood facing them with clenched fists. One of the men started hollering that they were going to surround him. The six of them immediately crowded around and started pummeling him. The moment he rushed out of the circle, he would be trapped in the middle again. It became a mêlée. No one could see what they were doing anymore. Sometimes the men seemed squashed together like steamed buns, and at other points they scattered like popped corn.

The two boys, who were about three or four years older than Baldy Li and Song Gang, then took the opportunity to grab the brothers and slap their cheeks, kick their shins, and spit in their faces. At first Baldy Li and Song Gang didn't give an inch and tried to slap, kick, and spit back. But they were short and couldn't reach the faces or the legs of their tormentors, and furthermore they had less spittle to spit out. After a few rounds, Baldy Li and Song Gang realized they were done for and started wailing.

Song Fanping heard their cries, but he was fighting one against six and couldn't get over to help. Baldy Li and Song Gang had to hide behind Li Lan, who at this point was crying even harder than they were. She appealed to Song Fanping's neighbors and to the passersby who had gathered around to watch the show, begging them to help her new husband. She appealed to them one after another, as Baldy Li and Song Gang clutched at her clothing. The two older boys followed behind, continuing to slap, kick, and spit. Baldy Li and Song Gang wailed for Li Lan to help them as Li Lan begged the spectators to help her husband.

Eventually, a few of the neighbors and spectators rushed up and separated Song Fanping and his six tormentors, pulling them off to either side as they themselves stood in the middle. Song Fanping's eyes were swollen, blood was dripping from his mouth and nose, and his clothing was in tatters. The other six were equally bad off, though at least their clothes were still intact.

The peacemakers started to work on both fronts. They reasoned with Song Fanping, explaining that anyone would naturally be upset if they had lost their chickens, and when people are upset they can't help but say ugly things. They also reasoned with the tormentors, explaining that today was not just any day but, rather, was Song's and Li's wedding day, and that they should take that into consideration. The peacemakers pushed Song Fanping into his house and the others back into the street, urging them, "Forget it, forget it. It's easier to make friends than enemies. Song Fanping, go back to your house, and everyone else go home."

Though he was bruised and battered, Song Fanping proudly held his ground, while the others were equally unwilling to leave. They felt that they had strength in numbers and were not about to give in. They said this wasn't over and insisted on getting something before they left: "At the very least we need compensation and apologies."

Eventually, it occurred to one of the peacemakers to propose to the tormentors that they each accept a cigarette from Song Fanping. According to the code of the time, to offer a cigarette after a fight was to admit defeat. The others considered this and agreed that it would be a good way of saving face. They said, "Fine, then we'll let him off the hook."

The peacemaker then walked up to Song Fanping. He didn't say the cigarettes were for admitting defeat but, rather, suggested that Song should pass out some auspicious wedding cigarettes. Song Fanping knew what cigarettes would signify and shook his head. "No cigarettes. All they'll get is my fist."

After saying this, Song Fanping looked over at Li Lan's tear-swollen eyes and at Song Gang and Baldy Li's faces covered with their own tears and other people's spit. Suddenly he was filled with sadness. He stood for a while, then walked into the house, his head bowed. When he returned, he had a pack of cigarettes. Ripping it open, he walked over to the three men and three middle-school students and took out one cigarette after another, handing one to each of them. After he was finished and turned to walk away, the men called out, "Not so fast! Light them for us."

Song Fanping's sadness was immediately transformed into fury. He threw the cigarettes to the ground and was about to turn back and hurl himself into battle again when Li Lan leapt up and restrained him. She pleaded with him, "Let me do it. Let me go light them."

Li Lan went over to the men. She initially stood there wiping her eyes, then lit the match and used it to light the cigarettes dangling from their mouths. The middle-schooler named Sun Wei took a drag and then deliberately blew smoke into her face.

Song Fanping saw this, but this time he didn't fly into a rage. Instead, he simply lowered his head and walked into the house. Baldy Li saw that his stepfather was weeping as he walked in. This was the first time that Baldy Li saw Song Fanping cry.

After Li Lan lit their cigarettes, she placed the matches back in her pocket and walked over to Baldy Li and Song Gang. She used the corner of her blouse to wipe the tears and spittle off the boys' faces. Taking them both by the hand, she walked inside, then closed the door behind them.

Though he usually didn't smoke, Song Fanping sat on a bench in the corner of the main room and smoked five cigarettes in a row. His coughing sounded like retching, and he spit blood-tinged saliva and phlegm all over the ground. This terrified the boys as they sat huddled on the bed, their legs trembling as they dangled off the edge of the bed. Li Lan covered her face with her hands and stood by the door. She was still weeping, her tears leaking through her fingers. After he finished smoking the five cigarettes, Song Fanping finally stood up. He removed his tattered clothes, wiped the blood off his face, and then with his sandaled foot he smudged the bloody spittle on the ground and proceeded into the inner room.

After a while Song Fanping emerged looking like a new man. He was wearing a clean white shirt, and although his face was bruised and swollen, he was smiling. He thrust out his fists toward Baldy Li and Song Gang and said, "Guess what I have?"

Both boys shook their heads. Song Fanping opened his hands, and when he had spread his fingers, they saw two hard candies in his palms. They laughed with delight as Song Fanping unwrapped the candies and placed them into their mouths. How sweet they were! The boys had been wanting to sweeten their mouths since this morning, but only now that the sun was almost setting were they finally able to savor the sweetness.

Song Fanping walked up to Li Lan, a smile on his swollen face. He patted her back, caressed her hair, and leaned over and whispered in her ear for a long time. Baldy Li and Song Gang sat on the bed eating the sweet hard candy. They didn't know what Song Fanping said to her, but after a while they saw that Li Lan was smiling, too.

That night the four of them sat together. Song Fanping cooked a fish and stir-fried a plateful of greens, and Li Lan brought out of her bag a bowl of braised pork that she had cooked earlier. Song Fanping got a bottle of yellow rice wine, pouring a cup for himself and another for Li Lan. Li Lan protested that she didn't drink, but Song Fanping replied that he didn't either and that after today no one would drink, but tonight they had to. "This is our auspicious wedding wine."

Song Fanping lifted his wine cup and waited for Li Lan to lift hers. He tapped his cup against hers, and she smiled bashfully. Song Fanping downed the yellow wine in one gulp, and the wounds in his mouth caused his face to contort in pain. He fanned his open mouth as if he had eaten a very hot chili pepper, then told Li Lan to drink up. She also drained her cup, and he waited until she put it down before setting his down as well.

Baldy Li and Song Gang sat next to each other on a long bench, their heads barely reaching the table. They rested their chins on the table-top, level with their parents' elbows. Song Fanping and Li Lan piled the boys' rice bowls high with meat, fish, and greens. Baldy Li took a bite of meat, a bite of fish, and a bite of greens and rice, then decided he didn't want any more. He turned to look at Song Gang next to him and said softly, "Candy."

Song Gang was relishing his mouthful of fish and meat, but when he heard Baldy Li, he decided he didn't want any more either. He also said softly, "Candy."

The children were already acquainted with the wonderful taste of fish and meat and enjoyed them a few times a year. But what they wanted now was candy. The sweetness in their mouths had disappeared quickly, so now they started to repeat over and over—first softly, then loudly, and finally at the top of their voices—the single word: "Candy, candy, candy . . ."

Li Lan explained that there wasn't any more, that she had already passed out all that she had. Song Fanping chuckled and asked the boys what kind of candy they wanted. The boys took up the wrappers on the table and said together, "This kind."

Song Fanping made a big show of reaching into his pockets, asking the boys, "So you want some hard candy?"

They nodded vigorously and craned their necks to peer into his pockets. But Song Fanping shook his head and said, "There isn't any more."

Both kids were so disappointed they almost wept, whereupon Song Fanping said, "There isn't any more hard candy, but there is soft candy."

The boys' eyes opened wide. They had never heard of something called *soft candy*. They saw Song Fanping stand up, feeling through all his pockets as if looking for the soft candy, and their hearts pounded with excitement. He emptied each pocket in turn, saying, "Where's the candy?"

When Song Fanping emptied his last pocket and there was still nothing, the boys both burst into tears. Slapping his forehead, Song Fanping exclaimed, "*Now* I remember!"

Song Fanping turned and tiptoed into the inner room, as carefully as if he were about to go catch a flea, making Li Lan giggle. When his bruised and swollen face reemerged, Baldy Li and Song Gang saw that he was carrying a bag of milk candy in his hand.

The boys cried out in surprise. This was the first time they had tasted soft candy—chewy, cream-flavored candy. The wrapper had a picture of a big white bunny, and the name was White Rabbit. Song Fanping explained that his sister in Shanghai had sent these as their wedding present. He let Li Lan have one and took another for himself. Then he gave Baldy Li and Song Gang five each.

The two kids placed the milk candy in their mouths, slowly licking, chewing, and swallowing their saliva, which was now sweetened with candy and tasted like cream. Baldy Li put some rice into his mouth and chewed it along with the candy, and Song Gang did the same. The rice was now as sweet and creamy as candy. Now the grains of rice in their mouths also became White Rabbits. As he savored every bite, Song Gang cried out affectionately, "Baldy Li, Baldy Li."

Baldy Li also cried out, "Song Gang, Song Gang. . . ."

Song Fanping and Li Lan smiled contentedly. Looking over at Baldy Li's shiny pate, Song Fanping commented to Li Lan, "We really should call him by his name, not his nickname." Song Fanping scratched his head. "I only know him as Baldy Li, I don't even know his real name."

He asked Li Lan, "What is Baldy Li's name?"

Li Lan couldn't help but smile. "You just said not to call him by his nickname, but you just did."

Song Fanping raised both hands in surrender. "So from this day forward, what should we call him if we don't want to use his nickname?"

Li Lan burst out, "Baldy Li's name is—"

She covered her mouth before she finished, realizing that she had used his nickname. She couldn't help giggling. "His name is Li Guang."

"Li Guang." Song Fanping nodded. "Now I know."

Then Song Fanping turned to the two boys and said, "Song Gang, Baldy Li, I have something to say to you—"

Song Fanping saw that Li Lan was suppressing a giggle and asked carefully, "Did I call him by his nickname again?"

Still smiling, Li Lan nodded. Song Fanping scratched his head and said, "Well, okay, let's use the nickname then. It's impossible not to call him Baldy Li."

He burst out laughing and turned to the two boys again. Once his laughter had subsided, he said, "From this day forward, you will be brothers. You must treat each other like your own blood, look out for each other, and stick together in sickness and in health, in happiness and in misfortune. You must study hard and strive to improve. . . ."

Song Fanping and Li Lan became husband and wife, and Song Gang and Baldy Li became brothers. Two families became one. Baldy Li and Song Gang slept in the outer room, and Li Lan and Song Fanping slept in the inner room. That night, the children lay in bed cradling their White Rabbit wrappers, sniffing the remaining traces of creamy sweetness and thinking about how they would encounter more White Rabbits in their dreams. Before he fell asleep, Baldy Li kept hearing the creaking of the bed inside and heard his mother sigh and moan, sometimes even bursting into a wail. But Baldy Li felt that this night his mother's cries sounded different from before, as though she weren't really crying. In the creek outside the window, a small boat floated by, and the rhythmic stirring of the oars echoed Baldy Li's mother's voice from the inner room.

CHAPTER 7

SONG FANPING was a happy man. Although his face was covered in bruises and it hurt to smile, he would still laugh heartily. On the second day of his marriage he made a big show of washing Li Lan's hair outside the house. His face was swollen like one of those pigs' heads hanging in the window of a butcher shop, but he paid no heed to the snickers of his neighbors. He poured well water into a face pail and helped Li Lan wet her hair. Then he applied soap and started to massage her scalp like a professional barber, until her entire head was covered in soapsuds. Finally, he brought another pail of well water to rinse her hair out, then used a towel to dry it and a wooden comb to comb it through, refusing to let her do anything herself. When Li Lan looked up, she saw that there was a crowd of a dozen or more adults and children gathered around her. She flushed bright red but also beamed with happiness.

Song Fanping announced that he wanted to take a stroll. Li Lan's hair was still dripping, and she looked hesitantly at Song Fanping's swollen face. He knew what she was thinking and assured her that his face was just fine. He turned to lock up the house, then took Baldy Li and Song Gang by the hand and walked ahead, leaving Li Lan with no choice but to follow.

The four of them walked down the street hand in hand. Passersby watched them and tittered, knowing that this was a second marriage for both of them, and that the groom had gotten into a fight with six people the day of his wedding. They simply couldn't believe that this bruised and swollen groom was now sauntering down the street, beaming with contentment. Whenever he saw someone he knew, he would greet them and happily introduce Li Lan: "This is my wife." Then he would point at the children: "And these are my sons."

Everyone looked very pleased, but their pleasure came from different sources. Song Fanping's was that of a groom, while the crowd's pleasure derived from the freak show they felt they were witnessing. Li Lan knew what their snickers meant and what they were saying as they pointed at her family, and therefore she lowered her head. Song Fan-

5 3

ping also knew what the snickers meant but nevertheless told Li Lan, "Lift your head."

The family strolled down two main streets. When they walked past the soda shop, the children looked longingly inside, but their parents dragged them along until they arrived at the photography studio. Song Fanping stopped and announced that he wanted to take a family portrait, having completely forgotten about his swollen face. Li Lan suggested that they could come back later, but Song Fanping had already walked inside. He turned back and saw Li Lan standing with the boys outside the door, so he enthusiastically waved them inside. But Li Lan held on to the boys and refused to go in.

When Song Fanping explained to the photographer that he wanted to take a family portrait, the man looked at him with astonishment. It was then that Song Fanping realized that today might not be a good day to have his picture taken. Cocking his head, he saw his face reflected in the studio's mirror and said to the photographer, "Well, perhaps not today, then. My wife says we can come back later."

Song Fanping walked happily out of the studio, still chuckling to himself. His happiness infected Li Lan, and both of them chuckled as they continued their stroll, until soon Baldy Li and Song Gang were giggling too, though they had no idea why.

The newly remarried Li Lan was aglow with happiness. For the past seven years, ever since her first husband drowned in the public latrine, she had endured a life worse than death. Her hair had become tangled like a bird's nest, but now she resumed the girlish braids of her youth and even tied two red bows at the ends. Her complexion was suddenly blooming as if she had eaten ginseng, her migraines disappeared, and she started humming again. Her newly remarried husband's gestures became expansive with pleasure. When he walked about the house, his steps would ring, and when he pissed against the wall outside, the urine would splatter like a thunderstorm.

This newly remarried couple stuck together like honey throughout their honeymoon. Whenever they had a free moment, they retreated to the inner room and shut the door tight. Baldy Li and Song Gang could only imagine what was going on inside. They heard loud smacking sounds and were firmly convinced that their parents were hiding inside to eat from that bag of White Rabbits. The sounds could be heard not only throughout the day but late into the night. Before it was even dark, the two of them would force Baldy Li and Song Gang to go to bed and then would lock themselves in their room, their lips smacking away. Neighborhood children were still running around outside, but Baldy Li and Song Gang were forced to go to bed. Listening to the smacking sounds, they would fall asleep with tears in their eyes and drool on their lips. The next morning they would wake up and find that their tears had dried up but their saliva was still flowing.

Baldy Li and Song Gang became insanely gluttonous. One day after finishing lunch, when their parents started smacking lips again in the inner room, Baldy Li stood by the door and peeked inside, with Song Gang right behind him, eager for an update. Baldy Li saw through the crack in the door that there were two pairs of legs on the bed, with Song Fanping's on top gripping Li Lan's below, and he whispered to Song Gang, "They're eating on the bed."

Baldy Li shifted to the other crack in the door. He saw that Song Fanping's body was on top of Li Lan's, his hands encircling her waist. He whispered, "They're eating while hugging."

From the third crack in the door Baldy Li saw that that Song Fanping and Li Lan were kissing passionately. Baldy Li initially giggled, thinking they looked funny, but then he quickly became mesmerized by what he saw. Song Gang, standing behind him, nudged him several times, but Baldy Li didn't notice. Song Gang whispered to him again and again, "Hey, hey, what are they eating?"

Baldy Li, in the midst of watching, turned around and said mysteriously, "They're not eating candy. They're eating lips."

Song Gang was confused. "Who's eating whose lips?"

Baldy Li answered mysteriously, "Your father is eating my mother's, and my mother is eating your father's."

Song Gang was startled, imagining Song Fanping and Li Lan gnawing away at each other like two wild beasts. The door to the inner room suddenly opened, and Song Fanping and Li Lan stood in the doorway staring at the boys in astonishment. When Song Gang saw that their lips were still attached to their faces, he was immensely relieved. He pointed at Baldy Li and said, "He tricked me. He said that you were eating each other's lips."

Song Fanping and Li Lan grinned, blushing, and then left to return to work without another word. After they left, Baldy Li, in order to prove that he was no liar, had Song Gang sit on the bed, as upright as if he were sitting in a movie theater seat. Baldy Li then placed a bench in front of Song Gang, and, lying prone on the bench, he raised his head and pointed down at the bench and explained, "Now, this is my mother."

Then he pointed at himself and said, "And I'm your dad."

After transforming the bench into Li Lan and himself into Song Fanping, he started demonstrating what lip eating was. Baldy Li pressed down tightly against the bench and hugged it to himself. He started slobbering all over the bench and wiggling against it. As he kissed and wiggled, he explained to Song Gang, "Just like this. They were just like this."

Song Gang didn't get why Baldy Li had to wiggle his body and asked, "Why do you have to move around so much?"

"That's what your dad was doing."

Song Gang giggled. "You look funny."

Baldy Li replied, "Well, your dad looked funny."

Baldy Li wiggled faster and faster on the bench. His face started turning red and his breath quickened. Song Gang became alarmed and jumped off the bed. He pushed at Baldy Li and asked, "Hey, hey, are you okay?"

Baldy Li's wiggling body slowed down. When he got up, he pointed to his crotch with a look of delight. "When you wiggle like this, your weenie gets hard and it feels good."

With great camaraderie, Baldy Li wanted Song Gang to get on the bench and try it out. Looking skeptical, Song Gang lay on the bench but saw that it was all shiny with Baldy Li's drool and snot. He sat up and shook his head. "Look, it's all your snivel."

Ashamed, Baldy Li hurriedly wiped down the bench with his sleeve and had Song Gang climb back on. Song Gang lay down but immediately got back up again, complaining, "It smells like your snot."

Baldy Li was deeply apologetic. He wanted Song Gang to share in his newfound pleasure, so he eagerly helped him lie down facing the other end of the bench. Baldy Li directed him like a coach, telling him how to wiggle and correcting his movements. When he finally felt that Song Gang's wiggling was beginning to resemble Song Fanping's, he sat down on the bed and wiped his brow, asking smugly, "Feel good? Is your weenie hard?"

Song Gang's response was a huge disappointment. He declared it to be no fun at all and added, "The bench is so hard. It just rubbed my weenie and hurt."

Baldy Li looked at Song Gang, mystified. "How could it feel bad?"

Then he helpfully placed two pillows on the bench. Still worried that it wouldn't be soft enough, he went and fetched Song Fanping and Li Lan's pillows from the inner room and also placed them on top. Smiling encouragingly, he offered Song Gang the bench. "Now it'll definitely feel good."

Song Gang didn't want to disappoint him, so he lay on the pillows and started wiggling again under Baldy Li's coaching. After a few wiggles he got up again, complaining that it still felt uncomfortable. It felt like there were little pebbles in the pillow, rubbing his weenie until it hurt.

Then, a miracle: The children discovered the remainder of the bag of White Rabbit candy, which their parents had hidden inside the pillowcase. They had turned over every cabinet in the house looking for it but could not find a single trace. They had crawled under the bed and ended up covered in dust and had burrowed under the bedspread until they were short of breath, but still hadn't managed to find the White Rabbits. It was like looking for a needle in a haystack. But just as they felt they had looked everywhere and were on the verge of giving up, the White Rabbits suddenly appeared in the pillowcase, as if by magic.

The two boys started howling like starved dogs and poured the entire bag onto the bed. Baldy Li stuffed three candies into his mouth at once, and Song Gong got in two at least. Laughing as they ate, they no longer licked or sucked but, rather, chewed with abandon, since there was plenty more. The wanted to stuff their mouths full of this exquisite sweetness and creaminess, which slid into their stomachs and spilled out through their nostrils.

The children swept through the bag like a tornado. Out of the original thirty-seven candies, there were now only four left. Song Gang suddenly got scared and burst into tears. Wiping his face, he asked what they were going to do when their parents came home and saw that they had eaten it all? Song Gang's question gave Baldy Li a start—then he proceeded to stuff the remaining four candies in his mouth without a second thought. Song Gang watched as Baldy Li ate the candy and wailed, "Why aren't you scared?"

After polishing off the candies, Baldy Li wiped his lips and said, "*Now* I'm scared!"

The two boys sat in a stupor. They looked at the thirty-seven candy wrappers scattered like fall leaves all over the bed. Song Gang could

not stop crying, worried that he and Baldy Li would be severely punished when Song Fanping and Li Lan discovered this. Song Fanping
would beat them until they were black and blue, until they looked like
he had on his wedding day. Song Gang's weeping scared Baldy Li, too.
He shuddered repeatedly, then came up with an idea. He suggested
that they find pebbles about the size of the candies and wrap them up
with the candy wrappers. Song Gang stopped crying and smiled, then
followed Baldy Li off the bed and out of the house. They looked under
the tree, by the well, in the street, even in the corner where Song Fanping usually peed until they had amassed a pile of little pebbles. Cupping them in their hands, they brought them back to the bed and
wrapped each in a candy wrapper, then put them back in the bag. Then
they put this bag of thirty-seven oddly shaped fake milk candies back
inside the pillowcase and placed the pillow back on the bed.

Once they had accomplished all this, Song Gang began to worry
again. He resumed sobbing and sniffed, "They'll still find out."

Baldy Li didn't cry. He grinned, shook his head at Song Gang, and
said to comfort him, "They don't know yet."

Even at this tender age Baldy Li was already a live-life-while-you-
can kind of guy. Once he had finished all the White Rabbit candies, his
interest in the bench returned. Amid the din of Song Gang's sobbing,
he climbed up on the bench again and started wiggling. This time he
knew exactly what he was doing. He put his weight on his weenie,
wiggling directly there. He wiggled until he was once again breathing
heavily and red in the face.

From this point on Baldy Li and Song Gang were inseparable. Baldy
Li liked having this older brother, because only after acquiring a
brother was he able to start living his life of free roaming. Before, when
Li Lan left for work at the silk factory, she would lock him in the house
and make him spend day after day there. Song Fanping, however,
would tie a key around Song Gang's neck, allowing the boys to wind
freely through the streets and alleys of Liu. Song Fanping and Li Lan
had worried that the boys would end up fighting each other every day,
never expecting that the two would end up becoming so close. They
would always be covered in scrapes and bruises from accidents but
never showed any trace of having been in a fight. Only once did they
come back with swollen lips and bloody noses, but those were a result
of fighting with some other family's kids.

After discovering the marvels of his body on the bench, Baldy Li started rubbing his weenie like an addict. He and Song Gang would be strolling down the street, and he would suddenly stop in his tracks and announce, "I need to take a few rubs."

Then he would hump a big wooden electrical pole. Listening to the buzz of the electricity, he would rub his body up and down until he was beet red and panting heavily. After he finished, he would sigh with contentment and tell Song Gang, "That feels *so* good."

Song Gang was in awe of Baldy Li's expression but was also mystified. He often asked Baldy Li, "Why can't I feel good?"

Baldy Li was mystified too and would shake his head in confusion. "Yeah, why doesn't it feel good?"

A few times as the boys were crossing the bridge, Baldy Li would suddenly be struck with his cravings. He would lie right down on the bridge and start rubbing as if he were on the bench at home. Beneath him was the town creek, and tugboats would pass underneath, whistles blowing. When the whistles blew, Baldy Li would become even more excited. One time he felt so good he started squealing with delight.

Once three middle-school students happened to walk by—the same three who had fought Song Fanping on the day of his wedding. They stood next to the bridge watching Baldy Li curiously and asked, "Hey, kid, what'cha doing?"

Baldy Li flipped himself over and answered, panting, "When I rub like this, my weenie gets hard and it feels good."

The students were dumbfounded by his response. Baldy Li proceeded to coach them, explaining that you could also hug the wooden electrical pole, but you were more likely to get tired standing up, so it was better to do it lying down. He concluded, "When you go home, you could just rub yourself on a bench."

The students started howling in amazement, "This kid has hit puberty!"

At that point Baldy Li had an epiphany: He finally understood why his rubbing felt so good while Song Gang's didn't. After the middle-school students walked off, he said to himself, *So I've hit puberty.*

Then he smugly told Song Gang, "Your father and me—we've hit puberty, but you haven't yet."

While Baldy Li and Song Gang were roaming the streets, they would often go to the west side of town, where things were busiest. The blacksmith, tailor, knife sharpener, and dentist's shops were all there, and a popsicle vendor named Wang walked up and down the street, banging on his icebox and hawking his goods.

One day as usual, the boys first stood in front of the tailor's shop and watched as Liu Town's legendary Tailor Zhang took a leather tape measure and measured a woman's neck, chest, and hips. His hands were all over the woman, but instead of getting angry, she merely giggled.

After watching Tailor Zhang for a while, the boys went over to watch the Guan father and son in the knife sharpener's shop. Old Scissors Guan was then in his forties, and Little Scissors Guan was fifteen. The two of them sat on low stools around a wooden basin filled with water. There were two whetting stones in the basin, and as the two sharpened their knives they made a scraping sound like a heavy rain.

The boys then went over to check out the shop of the town's dentist, Tooth-Yanker Yu. Yanker Yu didn't actually have a shop—he sat on the street at a table under an oilcloth umbrella. On the left side of the table was a row of tooth extractors of different sizes, and on the right were a few dozen extracted teeth, used to attract customers. Behind the table was a stool, and beside it was a rattan recliner. When a customer came by, he would lie down on the recliner, and Yanker Yu would sit on the stool. When there were no customers, Yanker Yu would lie down on the rattan chair himself. Once, as Yanker Yu was just getting comfortable he saw Baldy Li out of the corner of his eye and reflexively leapt up and started aiming for Baldy Li's mouth with an extractor. Only when Baldy Li screamed in terror did Yanker Yu realize he had mistaken the boy for a customer. He grabbed Baldy Li and tossed him out. "Damn you, with your baby teeth. Scram!"

Blacksmith Tong's shop was the kids' favorite destination. Blacksmith Tong had his own cart, which was hugely impressive—much more so than owning a truck nowadays. Every week Blacksmith Tong would go to the junkyard and bring back scrap metal. Baldy Li and Song Gang liked to watch him pound the metal, turning scrap copper into mirror frames and iron into scythes and hoes. The flying sparks made the kids squeal with excitement, and Song Gang asked Blacksmith Tong, "Are the stars in the sky also made out of metal?"

"Yup," answered Blacksmith Tong, "I pounded 'em myself."

Song Gang held Blacksmith Tong in the highest regard. He marveled to his brother that all the stars in the sky turned out to have been forged in Blacksmith Tong's shop and then launched into the sky!

Baldy Li didn't believe this and said that Blacksmith Tong was bullshitting them, that all the sparks from Blacksmith Tong's pounding ended up as ashes right outside his door.

Even though Baldy Li knew that Blacksmith Tong was full of it, he still liked to watch him work. After learning from the middle-school students the scientific explanation for his love of rubbing, he felt justified in lying down on the bench in the blacksmith's shop. Previously, he would sit there alongside Song Gang and watch Blacksmith Tong, but now he took the bench for himself and made Song Gang stand to one side. Baldy Li spread his hands and shrugged. "Sorry, I need the space. I've hit puberty."

While watching the sparks fly off the anvil, Baldy Li wiggled and panted heavily, crying out along with Song Gang, "Stars, stars, so many stars . . ."

Back then Blacksmith Tong was still a young fellow in his twenties who hadn't yet married the woman with the fat buttocks. Thickset, with tongs in his left hand and a hammer in his right, he watched Baldy Li while pounding his metal. He knew what the boy was up to and marveled that such a little bastard would be getting off. He suddenly lost his concentration and almost smashed his own hand. Spooked, he threw away the tongs and cursed as he put down his hammer, asking Baldy Li, who was panting away on the bench, "Hey, how old are you?"

Baldy Li panted, "Almost eight."

"Damn," Blacksmith Tong swore. "You little bastard, you're not even eight and you already have a sex drive."

That was how Baldy Li learned what a sex drive was. He felt that Blacksmith Tong explained things better even than the three middle-schoolers. Blacksmith Tong was, after all, far older than they. Baldy Li no longer announced that he had hit puberty but, rather, used this new term. He smugly announced to Song Gang, "You don't have a sex drive yet, but your father does, and so do I."

Baldy Li refined his technique of rubbing the wooden electrical poles. Once he had rubbed himself until he was red in the face, he would start climbing up the pole. When he reached the top, he would then slide back down again. When he reached the bottom, he would sigh with contentment and say to Song Gang, "It feels *so* good!"

One time, just as he had climbed to the top of the pole he saw the three middle-school students walking toward him and hurriedly slid down. This time he didn't bother telling Song Gang how good it felt, because he called out to the three students, correcting them, "You got it all wrong. It's not because I've hit puberty that my weenie gets all hard from the rubbing. It's that I feel my sex drive coming on."

CHAPTER 8

AFTER THEIR tempestuous honeymoon, Song Fanping and Li Lan's life became a slow stream of contentment. They left the house together to go to work, then came back together at the end of the day. The school where Song Fanping taught was close to home, so after work he would walk to the bridge and wait for three minutes until Li Lan arrived. Smiling, they would walk home shoulder to shoulder. They bought groceries together, cooked together, washed clothes together, slept together, and woke up together. There was hardly any time when they were apart.

After a year, Li Lan's migraines returned. The bliss of newlywed life had temporarily suppressed this old problem of hers, but now it was as if the pain had been accruing interest—when it struck again, it was more agonizing than before. Li Lan would no longer just whimper; instead, tears of pain would gush from her eyes. With a white cloth wound tightly around her head, she would rap her temples with her fingers all day like a monk striking his prayer counter. The knocking could be heard throughout the house.

Song Fanping became seriously sleep deprived. Often in the middle of the night he would be awakened by Li Lan's cries of pain. He would get up and bring a pail of water from the well, then soak a towel in the icy water, wring it, and place it on her forehead. This provided Li Lan with some relief. Song Fanping attended to her as though she were a patient running a high fever, getting up several times a night to bring her cool washcloths. However, he was convinced that she should enter a hospital and get treatment. He was completely dismissive of area doctors, so he sat at the dining table and wrote his elder sister in Shanghai. He would write a similar letter almost every week, urging her to help find a suitable hospital there. He peppered his letters with countless phrases like *extremely urgent* and *dire emergency*, and each time he would conclude with a string of exclamation points.

Two months later his sister finally wrote back, announcing that she had located a hospital but would need a referral from a local clinic. This news further increased Li Lan's awe of her husband's abilities.

Song Fanping requested a half day's leave from school and accompanied Li Lan to the silk factory at the end of her lunch break. He wanted to talk to her factory director and ask his permission for Li Lan to go to Shanghai to treat her migraines. Li Lan was the sort who did not even dare ask for a single day off, and therefore, after leading Song Fanping to the director's office, she told her husband that she didn't dare go in and pleaded with him to go in alone. Smiling, Song Fanping nodded and, as he walked in, told her to wait outside for the good news.

Song Fanping's earth-shattering dunk had made him a legend in Liu Town. As he introduced himself the director interrupted, saying, "No need, no need, I know who you are. You're the dunker." Then the two began chatting like old pals. They talked for more than an hour—so long that it seemed as though Song Fanping had forgotten that his wife was waiting outside. Li Lan was entranced by this conversation, and even much later, whenever she thought of her husband, she would sigh and think, *He had such a gift for gab!*

Song Fanping walked out with the director, who not only agreed to let Li Lan go to Shanghai to see a doctor but repeatedly told her, "Don't worry about anything after you get to Shanghai. Just get better. If you encounter any difficulties, let us know, and the factory will solve them for you."

Song Fanping then took his impressive gift of gab and worked the same magic at the hospital. He and a young doctor there chatted about everything from astronomy to geography, jumping from one topic to another and somehow finding agreement on everything. The two chatted until their spittle flew and their faces were flushed while Li Lan sat to one side, dumbfounded, forgetting even the pain of her migraines. She gazed upon Song Fanping with delight, having had no idea that the man she had lived with for the past year had such talents. After giving them the referral, the young doctor followed them all the way to the front door, gripping Song Fanping's hand and saying he had finally met his equal. He said they had to find time to get a jug of wine and some snacks and shoot the breeze all night long.

All the way home Li Lan was filled with joy. She would gently tug at Song Fanping's hand, and when he looked over at her, he saw that her eyes were blazing like hot furnaces. When they got home, Li Lan pulled him into the inner room and shut the door. She gripped him tightly, her head on his broad chest and tears of happiness soaking his shirt.

After her first husband had drowned in the latrine, this timid woman had become accustomed to living in shame, all alone. Now Song Fanping was giving her a happiness that she could not have dreamed of. She had someone to depend on, and what a wonderful mountain of support he was! She felt that she no longer had to walk with her head down. Song Fanping allowed her to raise her head proudly and face the world.

Song Fanping didn't understand why Li Lan had become so emotional. Laughing, he pushed her aside, asking what was the matter. Li Lan shook her head and didn't say a word. She just held on tightly, not loosening her grip until they heard Baldy Li and Song Gang hollering outside, "We're hungry! We're hungry!" Song Fanping asked her why was she crying, but she bashfully turned away and walked quickly out of their room.

Li Lan took the bus to Shanghai the next afternoon. The whole family put on clean clothes and set off at noon. Song Fanping was carrying a gray travel bag that he had bought in Shanghai during his first marriage. On one side of the bag was the word SHANGHAI in dark red. A year earlier, on the day after their wedding, Song Fanping had wanted to get a family portrait, but since his face was swollen at the time, they didn't take the photo. He had forgotten all about it, but now that Li Lan was going away to Shanghai to get treatment, he thought again of getting the portrait, so they set off for the photography studio.

When they arrived there, Song Fanping again exceeded his wife's estimation of him. He seemed to know everything, directing the photographer to adjust the lights until no shadows would be cast on any of their faces. The photographer followed his orders, shifting the lights about and nodding at his directions. After the photographer had finished setting up the lights, Song Fanping went over to the camera to take a look and then had him adjust the lights a bit more. Then he directed the boys on how to tilt their heads and how to smile. He had Baldy Li and Song Gang sit in the middle, with Li Lan next to Song Gang and himself next to Baldy Li. He told them to watch the photographer's raised hand, then even did the counting himself: "One, two, three, smile!"

The photographer clicked the shutter, and their bright smiles were preserved in a black-and-white photo. After paying, Song Fanping carefully folded the blue receipt and placed it in his wallet. He turned to the boys and told them that they would be able to see the photo in a week's time. Then he took up the gray travel bag and led his wife and children to the bus depot.

In the waiting room, they sat in a row. Song Fanping described over and over again to Li Lan what his sister looked like. He told her that his sister would be waiting by the left exit of the Shanghai bus depot and that he had asked her to be holding a copy of *Liberation Daily*. As he chattered on, a man came by hawking sugarcane, leading Baldy Li and Song Gang to look up to their parents pleadingly.

Li Lan was usually so frugal that she was loathe to spend even a cent to feed herself. But thinking that she was about to leave the boys for a while, she bought an entire sugarcane stalk for them. The children watched as the man shaved off the outer layers of the stalk and chopped it into four segments, then didn't hear a single thing their parents said after that, so absorbed were they in gnawing on the sugarcane.

When it came time to board the bus, Song Fanping's gift of gab was again displayed in all its splendor. He persuaded the ticket collector to allow the entire family to accompany Li Lan onto the bus. Once aboard, Song Fanping had Li Lan sit in her seat and then placed the gray travel bag on the luggage rack. He even asked a young man to help Li Lan get it down once they reached Shanghai. Song Fanping then got off with Baldy Li and Song Gang, and they stood together under Li Lan's window. Li Lan lingered over their three figures, nodding at everything Song Fanping said. Finally he asked her not to forget to bring the boys something when she came back. Their mouths full of sugarcane, Baldy Li and Song Gang immediately hollered out, "White Rabbit candy!"

Their parents assured the boys that there were still some White Rabbits left at home. Baldy Li and Song Gang were so terrified, they stopped chewing on the sugarcane, but fortunately just then the bus started up. As it was leaving the station, a tearful Li Lan turned to look at them once more. Song Fanping waved at her, smiling, not knowing that this would be the last time he would ever see his wife. His last impression of Li Lan was of her in profile, wiping away her tears. Baldy Li and Song Gang remembered only the billowing dust as the bus pulled away.

CHAPTER 9

AFTER LI LAN left for Shanghai, the Cultural Revolution arrived in our Liu Town. Song Fanping left the house early for school and returned late. Baldy Li and Song Gang also left early and came home late, spending the whole day wandering the streets, now filled with crowds of spectators. Every day there would be parading troops, and more and more red sashes appeared on people's arms, Mao badges on their chests, and copies of Mao's *Little Red Book* in their hands. More and more people walked along the main streets singing and barking like a pack of dogs, yelling revolutionary slogans and singing revolutionary songs. Layer upon layer of big-character posters thickened the walls, and when a breeze blew, the posters rustled like leaves on a tree. Some people started appearing with paper dunce caps on their heads or big wooden placards around their necks. There were even people who clanged on pots and pans, shouting, "Down with ourselves!" as they walked along. Baldy Li and Song Gang knew that these dunce-cap-wearing, placard-sporting, pot-clanging folk were what everyone called class enemies. Anyone could reach over and slap their faces, kick them in the stomach, throw snot at them, or piss on them. They were tormented but didn't dare say a word and were afraid to look up. Some passersby demanded that these class enemies slap their own faces and yell out slogans condemning themselves, and after they were done with themselves they should curse their ancestors. This was an unforgettable summer for Baldy Li and Song Gang. They didn't understand that the Cultural Revolution had arrived or that the world had changed around them; they only knew that now Liu Town had become as festive and rowdy as if every day were a holiday.

Baldy Li and Song Gang wandered through town like a couple of stray dogs. They followed one brigade after another, repeatedly yelling "Long live!" after one and "Take down!" after another. They shouted until their tongues were parched and their throats were raw and swollen. Meanwhile, Baldy Li seized the opportunity to violate each of the town's wooden electrical poles several times over. Whenever this barely eight-year-old boy happened upon a pole, he would pleasure himself until he was red in the face, all the while enthusiastically watching the parading crowds on the street. While his body rubbed up and down and his little fists pumped up and down, he wouldn't stop yelling, "Long live!" and "Take Down!"

When passersby happened to spot Baldy Li humping a pole, they would snicker to each other. They knew what he was up to, and though they didn't say anything aloud, they would be laughing secretly inside. There were, of course, those who didn't get it. When the woman who had started a snack shop next to the bus depot walked by and saw Baldy Li vigorously rubbing away, she asked him with surprise, "What are you doing, kid?"

Baldy Li glanced over at this woman, whom everyone called Mama Su, but didn't answer. Preoccupied with trying to hump the pole and shout slogans at the same time, he was simply too busy to respond. At that moment, the three middle-schoolers walked by. They pointed at him humping the pole, then up at the wires overhead, and exclaimed, "The kid is generating electricity."

Everyone who heard them broke out into guffaws. Song Gang, who was standing to one side, was also giggling away, though he didn't quite know why. Baldy Li was displeased, so he stopped his rubbing, wiped the sweat from his brow, and said dismissively, "You wouldn't understand."

Then he turned proudly to Mama Su and announced, "I'm feeling my sex drive."

Mama Su turned pale. She shook her head and muttered, "Bad karma, bad karma. . . ."

At that moment, the longest parade in the history of Liu Town wound its way over. All the way down the street, red flags as numerous as the hairs on a cow flapped in the wind. The large flags were as big as sheets, and the small ones were as tiny as handkerchiefs. Flagstaff clanged against flagstaff, and flag knocked against flag, whipping this way and that in the wind.

Liu Town's Blacksmith Tong raised his hammer, shouting that he wanted to be a righteous revolutionary blacksmith, smashing the beastly legs of the revolution's enemies until they were as flat as sickles, until they were reduced to scrap metal.

Liu Town's Yanker Yu raised his tooth extractor, shouting that he was going to be a judicious revolutionary dentist, pulling out all the good teeth of the revolution's enemies and all the bad ones of his class brothers and sisters.

Liu Town's Tailor Zhang hung his leather measuring tape around his neck, shouting that he wanted to be a clear-eyed revolutionary tailor, making the most beautiful clothes in the world for his class brothers and sisters and the lousiest funeral clothes for the revolution's enemies. No! He would make the lousiest corpse shrouds for the revolution's enemies.

Liu Town's Popsicle Wang hoisted his icebox onto his back, shouting that he would be a never-melting revolutionary popsicle—"Popsicles for sale! Popsicles only for class brothers and sisters and not for the revolution's enemies!" Popsicle Wang's business was red-hot, since each popsicle he sold was like a revolutionary certificate—"Come quick, come quick. All those who buy my popsicles are class brothers and sisters. Those who won't buy them are class enemies."

Liu Town's two Scissors Guan, father and son, both raised their scissors, shouting that they were going to be sharp revolutionary scissors and cut off the dicks of the class enemy. Old Scissors Guan was not yet finished, but Little Scissors Guan couldn't hold in his pee any longer and dashed out of the parade to relieve himself against the wall, shouting "Snip snip snip" and "Dick dick dick" even as he unfastened his pants.

Tall, strong Song Fanping marched at the very front of the parade. He held a giant flag with both arms stretched straight out. This red flag was as wide as a couple of bedsheets, perhaps with a few pillowcases added in. As it flapped in the wind, undulating like cascading waves, it made Song Fanping look as though he were hoisting a sheer wall of water above his shoulders. His white shirt was soaked through with sweat, his shoulder and arm muscles twitched like little squirrels, his bright red face was covered in freely flowing rivulets of sweat, and his eyes shone like bolts of lightning. Spotting Baldy Li and Song Gang, Song Fanping yelled out, "Sons, come over here!"

At that moment Baldy Li was hugging the electrical pole and curiously asking various passersby why Mama Su had cursed him as having "bad karma." When he heard Song Fanping's cry, he immediately abandoned the pole and ran over with Song Gang. They both grabbed Song Fanping's white shirt, and he lowered the flagstaff to allow them to hold on as well. In this way, Baldy Li and Song Gang held Liu Town's largest red flag and walked at the front of Liu Town's longest parade. Song Fanping strode forward with giant steps, and the two kids scurried along to keep up with him. Many little children drooling with envy and admiration ran alongside them clustered on one side of the street. The three cocky middle-schoolers also followed along, similarly crowded to the side. Baldy Li and Song Gang followed Song Fanping like two puppies keeping up with an elephant, their lungs, throats, and eyes all on fire from exertion. When they reached a bridge, Song Fanping finally paused, as did the rest of the procession.

Clumps of people crowded the streets and alleys below the bridge, with everyone looking up at Song Fanping. All the flags on the bridge, large and small, were unfurled. Song Fanping lifted the giant red flag over his head and began waving it back and forth, making it crackle like fireworks as it flapped in the wind. With their eyes Baldy Li and Song Gang tracked the path of this giant flag as it billowed left to right, flipped over, then back again. It flew over the entire bridge, and the wind from the flag blew the boys' hair back and forth. As Song Fanping waved the flag, the crowd below started to roar. Baldy Li and Song Gang saw waves of fists and heard their slogans booming like cannons.

Baldy Li started to howl, as if he were humping a pole. Flushed and hoarse, he said to Song Gang, "I feel my sex drive."

He saw that Song Gang was also flushed and hoarse and was shouting at the top of his lungs with his eyes closed. Baldy Li was delighted and, nudging Song Gang, asked, "Do you feel your sex drive, too?"

This was Song Fanping's most glorious day. After the parade, the marchers returned to their homes, but he continued walking down the main street, leading Baldy Li and Song Gang by the hand. Many people called out his name, to which he grunted in reply. Some even walked up to shake his hand. Baldy Li and Song Gang strutted with pride, feeling that everyone in town knew Song Fanping. They kept asking him enthusiastically who that man was who just called out to him and who the person was who just shook his hand. They kept on walking, farther and farther away from home. The two kids asked Song Fanping where they were going, and he replied in a ringing voice, "We're going to the restaurant for a meal."

They arrived at the People's Restaurant. The meal ticket collector, busboys, and customers all waved at them, smiling. Song Fanping waved back with his large hand, looking like Chairman Mao atop the Gate of Heavenly Peace. They sat at a table by the window as the staff encircled them and the other customers brought their dishes over and sat with them. Even the cooks in the kitchen caught wind of the news and, all covered in grease, came out to see. Everyone chattered about things ranging from the greatness of Chairman Mao and the origins of the Great Proletarian Cultural Revolution to couples' squabbles and children's illnesses. Song Fanping had waved the largest red flag in Liu Town's history and had become the most important personage in town history. He sat up straight, his giant hands spread out on the table, and each time he answered a question, he would begin with, "As Chairman Mao taught us . . ."

His responses consisted entirely of Chairman Mao's words, without a single additional word of his own. They made his listeners' heads bob up and down like woodpeckers, repeatedly saying "Ah, ah" as though they had toothaches. By this point Baldy Li and Song Gang were so hungry that their chests were flat against their backs and even their farts consisted of just fresh air, but they remained silent and gazed admiringly at Song Fanping. They felt that his voice was Chairman Mao's, and even his flying spittle was Chairman Mao's.

Baldy Li and Song Gang sat at the People's Restaurant for who knows how long. They didn't notice when the sun set or when the lights were turned on. Finally, the boys got to eat a bowl of steaming hot plain noodles. The greasy chef bowed down to them and asked, "Is the noodle broth good?"

The children answered in unison, "It's great!"

The chef grinned with pride and explained, "This is meat broth. Everyone else got only plain water, but I gave you meat broth."

After returning home that night, Song Fanping led the boys to the well to wash up. The three of them stripped down to their shorts and scrubbed their bodies with soap. Then Song Fanping drew a pail of water from the well and rinsed off the boys, then himself. Various neighbors sitting on their front stoops fanned themselves and chatted with him, discussing how magnificent the parade had been and how awe-inspiring he had looked waving the red flag. Song Fanping, exhausted from talking, gained a second wind, and his voice rang out once again. When Baldy Li and Song Gang returned to their rooms, they went to bed, but Song Fanping sat under the light and beamed as he wrote to Li Lan. Baldy Li gave Song Gang a look before falling asleep and giggled, saying that his father was red in the neck from all his writing. Song Fanping wrote for a very long time, describing all the events of the day.

When the boys woke up the next day, Song Fanping was standing at the foot of their bed. Still beaming, he stretched out his hands to the children, and they found two red Chairman Mao badges glowing in his palms. He said that these were for them and that they should wear them right over their hearts. Then he took another badge and pinned it to his own chest. Holding a copy of Chairman Mao's quotations, his face as red and bright as the badge, he stepped proudly outside. Baldy Li and Song Gang heard a neighbor ask him, "Will you be waving the red flag again today?"

Song Fanping answered, "Absolutely!"

Baldy Li and Song Gang put their ears to each other's chests in order to make sure to pin their Mao badges right over each other's beating hearts. Song Gang's badge had Mao perched atop the Gate of Heavenly Peace, while Baldy Li's Mao was standing on the surface of a giant ocean. After eating breakfast, the boys were greeted by the morning sun as they walked outside, and flags as large as sheets and as small as handkerchiefs again filled the streets.

Everyone who had been parading the previous day had happily returned, and the people who had been putting up big-character posters were again busy slapping glue onto the walls. Blacksmith Tong was again raising his hammer and shouting that he was going to smash the class enemy's beastly legs. Yanker Yu was again raising his tooth extractor and shouting that he was going to yank all the class enemy's good teeth. Popsicle Wang was again walking around with an icebox on his back, banging on it as he marched and shouting that he would sell popsicles only to class brothers and sisters. Tailor Zhang once again had his measuring tape around his neck and was shouting that he wanted to make the most tattered funeral clothes for the class enemy, then corrected himself and hastily changed it to a corpse shroud. Old Scissors Guan was again waving his scissors, snipping at the class enemy's imaginary dicks. Little Scissors Guan, who had pissed against the wall the previous day, was once again unfastening his pants. Of all the people who had previously spat, coughed, sneezed, farted, and argued, not a single one was missing this time around.

The middle-schoolers Sun Wei, Victory Zhao, and Success Liu also walked over. Looking at the Chairman Mao badges pinned to the brothers' chests, they cackled like smarmy Japanese collaborators in a World War II movie, making Baldy Li's and Song Gang's hearts skip a beat. Long-haired Sun Wei pointed to an electrical pole and asked Baldy Li, "Hey, kid, where's your sex drive?"

Baldy Li knew they were up to no good. He pulled Song Gang over for cover and shook his head. "Nope, not right now."

Sun Wei grabbed him and pushed him toward the pole, giggling: "Show us some sex drive."

Baldy Li struggled and said, "But I have no sex drive now."

Victory Zhao and Success Liu laughed, grabbed hold of Song Gang, and pushed him toward the pole as well, saying, "You show us some sex drive, too."

With an innocent expression, Song Gang explained, "I don't have any sex drive. Really, I never have."

The three middle-schoolers pushed Baldy Li and Song Gang up to the pole and pinched the boys' noses, ears, and cheeks as though they were steamed buns, until they squealed with pain. Finally, the middle-schoolers snatched off Baldy Li's and Song Gang's Chairman Mao badges and took off. Song Gang sobbed so hard that his mouth filled with tears and snot, which he swallowed then sobbed some more. He told everyone who walked by how his and Baldy Li's Mao badges had been stolen, and pointed in the direction of the students' vanishing figures. Over and over, Song Gang described the Mao badges: "Chairman Mao's face is red, a red face perched atop Tiananmen Square. The other one is a red face floating over the ocean's waves. . . ."

Baldy Li didn't cry but pointed in the direction the middle-schoolers had gone. With a look of righteous indignation, he complained to everyone who walked by, "I have no sex drive now, and they were forcing me to squeeze some out for them."

Everyone who walked by couldn't stop laughing. As Baldy Li watched Song Gang cry so hard that he shook, he became depressed as well. Wiping at his tears, he thought of how his Mao badge had been stolen by the three middle-schoolers. Song Gang pointed to his chest: "We only just put on the Mao badges this morning."

Baldy Li also pointed to his chest, saying, "My heart is still pounding inside, but there's no longer a Chairman Mao on the outside."

The boys were alone and helpless. They thought of Song Fanping, their tall, strong father, who could take down several men with a single sweep of his leg. They were convinced that Song Fanping would teach those middle-schoolers a lesson and retrieve their Mao badges, that he would grab the students by their collars and toss them into the air like little chicks, until they squawked with fear and their legs flailed about.

Song Gang said to Baldy Li, "Let's go, let's go find Papa."

By that time it was noon. The boys' stomachs were empty as they walked hand in hand down the street. Whenever someone came between them, forcing them apart, they would immediately grab each other's hands again. They went to look for the parading troops, to see if the man at the head of the line waving the red flag was Song Fanping. Then they went to the gathering place to see if the man standing in front giving a speech was Song Fanping. They walked to many, many places, asked many, many people, greeted many uncles and aunties, grandpas and grandmas, but still couldn't find Song Fanping. The boys came to the bridge where the day before Song Fanping had made the whole town holler in delight with his flag waving. Now there was no red flag, only a few people standing with their heads bowed. They were wearing tall dunce hats and big wooden placards. The boys knew that these were class enemies. They stood in front of these class enemies and spotted a few people wearing the rebels' red armbands pacing back and forth on the bridge. Song Gang asked, "Have you seen my father?"

Someone with a red armband asked, "Who is your father?"

"My father is Song Fanping," Song Gang replied. "The Song Fanping who was waving the red flag here yesterday."

Baldy Li added, "He is a very famous man. When he goes to eat noodles, they serve them to him with meat broth."

Song Fanping's voice rose from behind the two children: "Sons, I'm here."

The boys turned around and saw Song Fanping. He was wearing a tall paper hat and had a wooden placard around his neck, on which was written ~~LAND-LORD SONG FAN-PING~~. The boys couldn't read what this said, but they certainly understood the red X's scrawled across each word. Song Fanping's body blocked the sunlight like a wooden door. The two boys stood in his shade and looked up at him. His eyes were swollen from being punched, his lips bleeding from being slapped. He smiled as he looked at Baldy Li and Song Gang, though his smile appeared tight and frozen. The children couldn't understand what had happened: Yesterday he was standing on this bridge, an awesome figure, but today he had been reduced to this. Song Gang asked timidly, "Papa, why are you standing here?"

Song Fanping asked in a low voice, "Sons, are you hungry?"

Both boys nodded. Song Fanping found twenty cents in his pants pocket and gave it to them to buy something to eat. The man who was wearing the red armband yelled at him, "No talking! Lower your mutt-head."

Song Fanping obediently lowered his head, but Baldy Li and Song Gang were so startled they jumped back a few steps. The man with the red armband continued to yell, and amid the din Song Fanping snuck a peek at the boys. Seeing that he was smiling, they regained their confidence and returned to his side. They told him that their Chairman Mao badges had been taken away by those three bastard middle-schoolers. Song Gang asked him, "Could you get them back?"

Song Fanping nodded. "I could."

Baldy Li asked, "Could you beat them up?"

Song Fanping nodded again. "I could."

The boys started chuckling. The man with the red armband walked over and slapped Song Fanping twice on the face. He shouted angrily, "I told you not to speak. Why the fuck are you still talking?"

A trail of blood flowed down from Song Fanping's lips as he urged the boys, "Get out of here."

Baldy Li and Song Gang slipped away quickly. They went under the bridge, then, trembling all over, scurried away. They kept turning back to look at Song Fanping atop the bridge. His head was flopped over, as if it were merely dangling from his neck. The boys made their way to the crowded, noisy street, walked into a snack shop and bought two steamed buns, then stood outside eating them. In the distance they could see that Song Fanping was almost bent over at the waist, and it was clear that today's Song Fanping was not the one from yesterday. Song Gang lowered his head and started to weep silently, then raised his two clenched fists to his eyes like binoculars and wiped away his tears. Baldy Li didn't cry. Instead, he kept thinking about his badge with Chairman Mao atop the ocean, fearing that he would never get it back. While Song Gang wept, Baldy Li walked over to an electrical pole and humped it perfunctorily a few times. Then he returned to Song Gang and dejectedly told him, "I've lost my sex drive."

It was dark by the time Song Fanping returned home. His footsteps were as heavy as if he were dragging along two prosthetic limbs. Without a word he walked into the inner room and lay on the bed for two hours without moving; in the outer room Baldy Li and Song Gang couldn't hear a sound. The cold moonlight shone in through the window. The children became alarmed and went into the inner room. First Song Gang crawled onto the bed, then Baldy Li joined him, and together they sat at Song Fanping's feet. After a long time had passed, Song Fanping suddenly sat up and said, "Oh, I fell asleep."

Then the light came on and laughter began. Song Fanping heated up the stove and started to make dinner with Song Gang and Baldy Li at his side, learning how to cook. Song Fanping taught them how to rinse the rice and vegetables, light the coal, and cook the rice. As he stir-fried the vegetables, Song Fanping told Baldy Li to add oil and Song Gang to sprinkle in some salt. He also held their hands as they took turns stir-frying. Each of them took three turns, and after nine rounds, the greens were finally ready. The three of them sat around the table and ate. Though it was just a plate of greens, they all worked up a sweat eating. After Song Fanping finished dinner, he told the boys that though he had not taken them to the ocean since their mother had left for Shanghai, if it wasn't stormy the next day, he would take them to see the waves, to see the sky above the waves, as well as the seagulls flying between the sky and the sea.

Baldy Li and Song Gang shrieked with excitement, which startled Song Fanping so much that he covered their mouths with his hands. The look of terror on his face also frightened them. When he saw their alarm, Song Fanping immediately lowered his hands and laughed as he pointed up to the ceiling. "Your screams almost blew the roof off!"

Baldy Li and Song Gang thought that was a hoot. This time they covered their own mouths as they laughed nonstop.

CHAPTER 10

THE NEXT DAY, as they were about to set off for the seaside, a dozen or so people from Song Fanping's school sauntered in, all wearing red armbands. Baldy Li and Song Gang didn't realize that they were here to search the house, thinking instead that Song Fanping's pals had come to check on him. The boys found themselves stirred by the sight of so many red-armbanders, all full of bravado, filling up their house. Exhilarated, they wove back and forth through the crowds as if navigating a forest. Then a loud *boom!* made them shudder with terror, and they watched in horror as their dressers and bureaus were upended, their clothes and things strewn all over the ground. The red-armbanders picked through the family's possessions like scavengers, rummaging through everything looking for Song Fanping's land deeds. Song Fanping was born into the landowning class, so these people were convinced that he must be hiding land deeds, merely waiting for a regime change to take them out again. The red-armbanders flipped over the bed planks and pried up the floorboards while Baldy Li and Song Gang hid behind Song Fanping. They saw that Song Fanping still had a smile on his face, but couldn't understand why he would be pleased. These people turned Song Fanping's home into a scrap heap without finding any land deeds. They eventually filed out of the house one by one as Song Fanping, still with a smile on his face, followed them out as if seeing off guests. At one point he even asked them, "Won't you have a cup of tea before setting off?"

One of them responded, "No need."

Song Fanping stood, smiling, at the door, and only when they had left the alley did he turn to go back into the house. As soon as he got inside and sat down, his smile immediately vanished, like a light switching off. Song Fanping sat there, his face the color of iron, and for the longest time he didn't move a muscle. The two boys walked over and timidly asked him, "Are we going to the seaside?"

Song Fanping started as if woken from a deep sleep and bellowed, "Let's go!"

He looked at the sun shining outside and said, "With such good weather, of course we're going."

Song Fanping righted the armoire, repositioned the bed planks, and nailed down the displaced floorboards. Baldy Li and Song Gang followed behind him, placing the clothes back into the bureau and the knickknacks back into the drawers. It was as if the light had been turned back on, and Song Fanping was once again smiling. As he tidied the house he talked and chuckled nonstop with the kids. By noon they were finally done cleaning up, leaving the house even tidier than before. They used towels to wipe the sweat off their faces and handkerchiefs to dust off their clothes. Then they combed their hair in front of the mirror and were finally ready to leave for the seaside.

When they opened their door, they found seven or eight red-armband-wearing middle-school students standing outside, including the three who had stolen Baldy Li's and Song Gang's Mao badges. When Baldy Li and Song Gang saw the three of them, they started clamoring excitedly, and Song Gang said to his father, "Papa, they're the ones who took away our Mao badges. Go teach them a lesson."

Baldy Li shouted at the middle-schoolers, "Give them back! Give us our badges back!"

The three middle-schoolers pushed the children away, chuckling. The one with the long hair, Sun Wei, said to Song Fanping, "We're Red Guards, and we're here to search your home!"

Smiling, Song Fanping welcomed them in. "Come in, come in."

Baldy Li and Song Gang were baffled by Song Fanping's obsequious manner. The Red Guards swarmed in and again threw the house into tumult. The bureau that had just been righted was upended once again, the just-tidied bed plank was again flipped over, the floorboards that just been nailed back down were pried up again, and the clothes they had just folded were once again strewn all over the floor. When the previous group, from Song Fanping's school, came, they had primarily rifled through Song Fanping's books and papers, looking for his hidden land deeds. But these Red Guards were like bulls in a china shop, shattering pots and pans on the floor, snapping chopsticks in half, and searching the house as they stuffed things into their own pockets, periodically stopping to compare what they had each pocketed.

These Red Guards shattered, snapped, and looted Song Fanping's home all afternoon. Only after they saw that there wasn't much left to shatter or to grab, and all their pockets were stuffed full, did they finally depart, whistling happily. Long-haired Sun Wei turned around and said to Song Fanping, "Hey, come out here."

On the day of Song Fanping and Li Lan's wedding, Sun Wei, Victory Zhao, Success Liu, and their fathers had been roundly beaten by Song Fanping. With his sweeping leg kick he had swatted them down. Now, a year later, these middle-schoolers wanted their revenge. They had Song Fanping stand in the empty lot in front of the house so that they could show off their own sweeping kicks. Song Fanping stood there stalwartly, like an iron tower. The three middle-schoolers started with their warm-up exercises, squatting down and sweeping their right legs out. Even after a few tries, not one of their kicks looked like the real thing. If they didn't lose their balance and end up sitting on the ground, they would drag their foot and scrape up a cloud of dust. The other two middle-schoolers would shake their heads. "Doesn't look like a sweeping leg kick to us."

"What does it look like, then?"

"I don't know, but certainly not a sweeping leg kick."

Sun Wei asked Song Fanping, who was standing there with his head bowed, "Hey, so did that look like a sweeping leg kick?"

"It did," Song Fanping replied. "But you haven't quite gotten the knack of it."

Sun Wei said to Song Fanping, "Now, spit it out. What's the secret?"

So Song Fanping became their coach, instructing them to watch carefully. He adroitly demonstrated the kick a few times, and the students whistled and exclaimed, "Now, that's a proper sweeping leg kick." Then he broke down his movements, explaining that the sweeping leg kick actually had three steps—squat, sweep, and straighten—and that the steps had to be done in one continuous motion. He explained that the body's center of gravity had to be shifted to the front, because that gave the sweep force, and that you could use your hands for support. Then Song Fanping had them practice, stopping them at various points and demonstrating the proper form. Finally, he announced that they had mastered the form but were still not swift enough. "Only when you do it swiftly will the kick not break down into its separate components. But you can't learn to be fast in a day or two. Go home and practice every day, and when others can see only one move, you've mastered it."

All afternoon Song Fanping used both explanations and demonstrations to teach the three middle-schoolers the proper execution of a sweeping leg kick. When the students finally felt they had gotten it, they ordered Song Fanping to stand still and get a taste of their newly mastered kicks. He stood with his legs slightly apart.

The first one up was Victory Zhao, who proceeded to practice the move in front of Song Fanping, earning a round of applause from the gathering crowd: "Way to go!" But when Zhao squatted down and swept his leg over, his foot caught on Song Fanping's leg. Song Fanping remained motionless, while Zhao found himself sprawled on the ground with a mouthful of dirt, eliciting a round of laughter.

Next up was Success Liu. He looked over Song Fanping and his strong figure and worried that he too would end up with a mouthful of dirt. But when he noticed that Song Fanping had his legs apart, he grinned and said he knew how to deal with him. So he told Song Fanping to stand with his legs together, saying that was how he was going to flatten him. When he squatted down, he still worried that he would end up with a mouthful of dirt, so he didn't immediately thrust his leg out. Instead he aimed his foot full-force onto Song Fanping's shin. Song Fanping shook from the pain but didn't fall down. The spectators all cheered Song Fanping: "Right on!"

Third up was long-haired Sun Wei. He went behind Song Fanping and then backed up a good forty feet, as if he were about to do a long jump. Running all the way, he aimed his foot at the back of Song Fanping's knee and then kicked. Song Fanping immediately fell to his knees, and Sun Wei cheered for himself, "Way to go!" Then he boasted to his mates, "Look at my kung-fu."

The other students disagreed. "That's not a sweeping leg kick."

"Why not?" Sun Wei kicked Song Fanping, who was kneeling on the ground. "Tell me, was that a sweeping leg kick?"

Song Fanping nodded and answered in a low voice, "Yes, it was."

Laid down by the variant sweeping leg kick, Song Fanping watched as the middle-schoolers left, whistling off-key. He waited until they were far off before standing up. He saw his son, Song Gang, head bowed and wiping away tears, and he saw Baldy Li, his adopted son, eyes wide with terror. The boys didn't know what to do: In their minds, Song Fanping had been invincible, but now he was being bullied like a little chick. Song Fanping dusted the dirt off his pants and beckoned the boys as if nothing had happened, "You two, come over here!"

Song Gang, wiping his eyes, and Baldy Li, scratching his head, walked over unsteadily. Song Fanping laughingly asked them, "Would you like to learn the sweeping leg kick?"

The children were startled by his offer. Song Fanping looked around, then knelt down next to them and confided, "You know why they couldn't sweep me down? Because I didn't tell them the final step. The final step I was saving for you two."

Baldy Li and Song Gang suddenly forgot everything that had happened and started shrieking excitedly, as they had the night before. Song Fanping nervously clamped his hands over their mouths. The boys looked up and exclaimed together, "There's no roof to raise here."

Song Fanping nervously looked around again. "It's not a question of raising the roof. We just wouldn't want other people to learn the secret of the kick."

The boys understood. Silently they learned the technique from Song Fanping. First they stood behind him and imitated his moves, then he turned and instructed them. After half an hour he announced that they had learned the move and could now start practicing. Song Fanping stood still and let Baldy Li try out his move. Baldy Li walked up to him, squatted down, and swept his leg out. With just a gentle sweep, Song Fanping ended up flat on the ground. He got up and told Song Gang to try, and with another gentle sweep he was back on the ground. Song Fanping rubbed his bottom and groaned. He marveled at the two boys. "Your kick is too lethal! It's simply unbeatable."

Then the boys enthusiastically followed Song Fanping inside to once again clean up the house. Having mastered their unbeatable kicks, they were pumped with energy. They helped Song Fanping right the armoire and reposition the bed planks, and learned to nail down the displaced floorboards. They picked up the shards of broken bowls and snapped chopsticks and threw them into the trash heap outside. They dashed in and out, covered in sweat, but then abruptly remembered they hadn't eaten anything all day. Suddenly limp with hunger, the boys climbed into bed and fell asleep the moment they shut their eyes.

After who knows how long, Song Fanping woke them up and told them that dinner was ready. The light in the room was on. Baldy Li and Song Gang sat up in bed, rubbing their eyes, and Song Fanping carried them one after the other to the dinner table. They saw that there was just a bowl of greens and three bowls of rice, these being the only four bowls that had survived the Red Guards' rampage. They took up their chipped bowls and then realized that there were no chopsticks. All the chopsticks had been snapped in two by the Red Guards. The children held their steaming bowls of rice and eyed the glistening bowl of greens, asking themselves, *How are we going to eat without chopsticks?*

Song Fanping forgot that there were no chopsticks in the house and got up to fetch some before remembering. He stood there for a while, his powerful back motionless as the dim light threw a shadow of his head as big as their washbasin onto the wall. Eventually he turned back toward the boys with an enigmatic smile and asked them mysteriously, "Have you ever seen the kind of chopsticks the ancients used?"

Baldy Li and Song Gang shook their heads and asked curiously, "What kind of chopsticks did they use?"

Song Fanping smiled as he walked to the door. "Just wait awhile, I'll show you."

Baldy Li and Song Gang saw him tiptoe outside and carefully close the door behind him, as if he were about to enter the land of the lost. After he left, the boys looked at each other. They had no idea how Song Fanping was going to retrieve chopsticks from the ancients, but they nevertheless felt that their father was truly amazing. After a while the door opened and Song Fanping returned, smiling, his hands behind his back.

The children asked him, "So you managed to get the ancients' chopsticks?"

Song Fanping nodded. He walked over to the table and sat down, then thrust out his hands and gave Baldy Li and Song Gang each a pair of chopsticks. The boys took up the chopsticks of the ancients and examined them. They were about the same length as regular chopsticks, though they were of different thicknesses, were slightly curved, and had some knots on them. Baldy Li was the first to exclaim, "But these are twigs!"

Song Gang asked Song Fanping, "Why are the ancients' chopsticks like twigs?"

"The ancients' chopsticks *were* twigs," Song Fanping explained. "Because in ancient times there were no chopsticks, so the ancients used twigs."

The boys finally understood: In ancient times people used twigs to scoop up rice. Baldy Li and Song Gang started to dig into their meal with the freshly cut twigs, and when they ate, there was a bitter green taste to their food. Using their ancients' chopsticks, they ate ravenously, until their faces were covered in sweat. Only after they had eaten their fill and belched loudly did they notice that it was dark outside, and only then did they remember they had been planning to go to the seaside. There hadn't been any strong winds or rainstorms, and the sun had been so bright you couldn't even open your eyes, but they couldn't go. The boys immediately fell into a funk. Song Fanping asked if they liked their ancients' chopsticks, and they nodded.

Song Gang then explained mournfully, "We won't make it to the seaside today."

Song Fanping smiled. "Who said we won't?"

Baldy Li said, "The sun has already gone down."

Song Fanping replied, "The sun's gone, but there's still the moon."

They had been ready to go to the seaside when the sun was high in the sky, but they didn't set off on their way until the moon was shining brightly. The children grasped Song Fanping's hands, one on each side, and walked for a very long time along the moonlit road. When they arrived at the seaside, it was high tide. They walked along the beach, where there wasn't a soul in sight, just the cool wind and the roar of the waves. The waves rushed in, creating a long line of white froth along the endless sea. At times this whiteness would turn to gray, and sometimes it would be even darker. From a distance they could glimpse both light and dark, and the moon would appear and disappear behind the clouds. This was the first time the boys had seen the ocean in the moonlight, mysterious and protean. They started screaming ecstatically, but this time Song Fanping didn't cover their mouths. Instead, his large hands caressed the tops of their heads as he let them shout to their hearts' content. He himself seemed lost in thought, staring out at the dark sea.

After they sat down on the shore, the children started feeling terrified by the night sea. There was only the sound of the wind and waves; the moonlight appeared and disappeared; and the darkness of the sea seemed to expand and contract. Baldy Li and Song Gang held Song Fanping tightly, and he hugged them close. They sat at the sea for a long, long time, until the boys fell asleep. With one on his shoulders and the other in his arms, Song Fanping made his way home.

CHAPTER 11

STRUGGLE SESSIONS became increasingly common in our Liu Town, and the middle-school yard bustled like a temple festival from daybreak to nightfall. Song Fanping had to carry that placard with him when he left home every morning and hang it from his neck once he reached the school gate. He stood at the gate, head bowed, and only after all the people coming to the struggle sessions had entered did he remove the placard and start sweeping the street in front of the school. When each struggle session ended, he would walk back to the entrance, put on his placard, and stand there with his head bowed. People poured out, kicking, abusing, and spitting at him, and though he was jostled from side to side he didn't utter a word. Then another struggle session would begin. Song Fanping had to wait until darkness fell—and make certain that there was no one left in the schoolyard—before he could take his placard and broom and head home.

Baldy Li and Song Gang would hear the sound of his heavy steps as Song Fanping walked into the house, his face lined with fatigue. He would always sit silently on his stool for a while, then he would get up, splash his face with well water, and use a rag to wipe down the dust, footprints, and children's spittle off his placard. Throughout all this, Baldy Li and Song Gang didn't dare say a word. They waited patiently, knowing that once Song Fanping washed his face and wiped the placard clean, he would become cheerful again and talk to them about many cheerful things.

Baldy Li and Song Gang didn't recognize the characters on the placard, ~~LAND·LORD SONG FAN·PING~~, but they knew these were the words that had brought Song Fanping all his misfortune. Before they appeared, Song Fanping was exultantly waving a red flag atop the bridge; but after they appeared, even little children spat and pissed on him. One day the boys finally had to ask him, "What do these characters mean?"

Song Fanping had just finished wiping clean his placard. Taken aback, he paused for a while. Then he smiled and said to them, "Next fall you'll start school, so I'll teach you how to read, starting with these characters."

This was Baldy Li and Song Gang's first lesson. Song Fanping taught them to sit with their backs straight and their hands in front of them. Then he hung the placard on the wall and brought over one of the chopsticks of the ancients. He prepared for almost half an hour before beginning the lesson, filling them with anxious anticipation.

Finally he stood in front of the big wooden placard and coughed solemnly to clear his throat. "Now we'll begin our lesson. First let me announce two rules. First, no squirming about. Second, raise your hand if you wish to speak."

He raised an ancient's chopstick and pointed at the first character on the placard. "This character is pronounced *di*. Think, what does *di* mean? Which of you wants to guess?"

Song Fanping first pointed at the ground, then stomped his foot, all the while winking at th e boys. Baldy Li beat Song Gang to it, pointing downward and shouting, "I know!"

"Hold on," Song Fanping interrupted. "If you wish to speak, you must raise your hand."

With his hand raised, Baldy Li blurted, "*Di* means 'land,' which is what is below us, what we're standing on."

"That's correct," Song Fanping said. "You're very clever."

Then Song Fanping pointed at the second character in *landlord*. He said, "This character is even harder. It's pronounced 'zhu.' Think: Where have you heard this word before?"

Baldy Li shot his hand up before Song Gang again. This time Song Fanping didn't let him answer. He said, "You answered last time; now it's Song Gang's turn. Song Gang, think, where have you heard this character *zhu* used before?"

Song Gang timidly responded, "Is it the same *zhu* that appears at the beginning of *chairman,* as in 'Chairman Mao?'"

"Correct!" Song Fanping said. "You're very clever."

At this Baldy Li exclaimed, "He didn't raise his hand."

Song Fanping said to Song Gang. "He's right, you didn't raise your hand, but you can raise it now."

Song Gang quickly raised his hand. He asked anxiously, "Is it too late to raise my hand?"

Song Fanping laughed. "Of course not."

On this day the boys learned five characters. They first learned *land,* then the *zhu* character in "Chairman Mao." They finally understood what the placard said: It was that *Song Fanping* was the *chairman* of the *land*.

Song Fanping and his placard had to travel together every day. He took the placard with him in the morning and came back with it in the evening, just like those women who brought their grocery bags to work and back. Baldy Li and Song Gang still roamed freely, exploring the entire town. They had been absolutely everywhere, even visiting places where only ducks, chickens, cats, and dogs went. The streets were still overgrown with red flags and dotted with people as numerous as the hairs on a cow, who dispersed at the end of every day like an audience at the end of a movie. Gradually, more and more people appeared wearing dunce hats and bearing wooden placards. Initially, Song Fanping had been the only one sweeping the streets in front of the middle school, but he was joined a few days later by two other teachers. They stood next to Song Fanping, all three in a row, wearing placards around their necks. One of the two teachers was a bespectacled, scrawny old man, whose placard bore the word LAND-LORD, just like Song Fanping's. This made Baldy Li and Song Gang very excited. They said to him, "So you're also a Chairman Mao of the land."

The children's words caused the teacher to tremble. His face turned as white as a corpse, and he said to them, "I'm a landlord, I'm a bad man. Please hit me, please yell at me, please criticize me."

Baldy Li and Song Gang often spotted Sun Wei, Victory Zhao, and Success Liu practicing their sweeping leg kicks. The three middle-schoolers spent just about every day under a wutong tree by the side of the road, hugging the tree while practicing their kicks around its trunk. Sun Wei could actually circle the entire tree while kicking continuously. His movements resembled a theater troupe performer's as his long hair blew in the breeze. Victory Zhao and Success Liu could kick only about halfway around the tree before landing on their butts or dropping their raised legs midkick. Therefore, Sun Wei became their coach. Running his fingers through his hair, he would repeat what Song Fanping had taught them: "Quicker, quicker. Only when your moves are swift can you perform the three moves as one."

Baldy Li and Song Gang strutted past. They knew that these three were still missing a move, since only *they* knew the *real* sweeping leg kick. Song Fanping hadn't taught the others the real deal, having saved the most important part for the two of them. So they would walk back and forth hand in hand, watching the middle-schoolers and giggling.

The students were so absorbed in their kicks that they didn't notice that the two snot-faced little boys were secretly laughing at them. The long-haired Sun Wei started to practice circling the tree twice without stopping. Once he was going so fast he lost control, and his entire body went flying.

Baldy Li and Song Gang couldn't contain their laughter. The middle-schoolers stalked over to them, glaring. Sun Wei, covered with dust and dirt, got up, walked over to them, and spat out, "What the fuck are you laughing at?"

Baldy Li and Song Gang weren't at all scared of him. Song Gang raised his head. "We're laughing at your sweeping leg kick."

"Heh." Long-haired Sun Wei looked back at his mates oddly, saying, "How dare he laugh at my kick?"

Song Gang scoffed to Baldy Li, "*His* sweeping leg kick?"

Baldy Li chuckled and also scoffed, "*His* sweeping leg kick?"

Baldy Li's and Song Gang's cocky attitude astonished the older boys, who exclaimed, "Fuck!"

Song Gang said evenly, "Let me tell you guys. There's a move my father didn't teach you, but he taught it to us."

"Fuck!" the students retorted. Sun Wei added, "So you're saying that you also know the sweeping leg kick?"

Song Gang pointed at Baldy Li. "We both know it."

The three middle-schoolers burst out laughing. They looked over Baldy Li and Song Gang. "You know the sweeping leg kick? You're still as short as our dicks."

Long-haired Sun Wei said to Song Gang, "So sweep for me."

Song Gang said, "You stand steady first."

Sun Wei looked even more astonished. He turned to Victory Zhao and Success Liu. "He wants me to stand steady? Fuck, he thinks he can sweep me off my feet?"

Amid their snorts and laughter, Sun Wei stood in front of Song Gang. First he stood with his legs apart, then he brought them together again, and finally he ended up perched on one leg. He asked Song Gang, "So how do you want me to stand?"

Song Gang pointed to the ground. "Stand on both legs."

Sun Wei grinned and lowered his leg. Song Gang turned to Baldy Li. "You want to kick first? Or shall I?"

Baldy Li wasn't so sure of himself, so he said to Song Gang, "You go first."

Song Gang backed up a few steps and made a running start to sweep-kick Sun Wei's leg like a bunny rabbit kicking a dog. Long-haired Sun Wei just stood there smirking while Song Gang bounced to the ground like a rubber ball. Song Gang got up again, unable to understand what had happened, and looked over uncertainly at Baldy Li. At this point Baldy Li realized the truth about his and Song Gang's sweeping leg kicks, but Song Gang was still completely in the dark. The three middle-schoolers roared, and their laughter caused Baldy Li's insides to tremble. With a smile, Sun Wei swept out his leg and flipped Song Gang over. He said to Baldy Li, "See, now *that's* a sweeping leg kick."

The revolutionary crowds in Liu Town saw the three middle-schoolers kicking the two little preschoolers and scolded them furiously, saying that they were oppressing the weak, just like the military in the old society. Victory Zhao and Success Liu didn't dare reply, but long-haired Sun Wei argued, "They are landlord Song Fanping's sons. They are little landlords."

The revolutionary masses were silenced. They watched as Baldy Li and Song Gang again and again fell to the ground until both of them simply lay there, unable to get up. Sun Wei, Victory Zhao, and Success Liu were drenched in sweat and breathing heavily, but they gathered around Baldy Li and Song Gang, laughing and shouting at them to stand up again. The brothers had nothing left in them. They couldn't stand up, so they lay on the ground, saying, "We're just fine lying here."

Once they said this, they immediately realized how to escape the middle-schoolers' sweeping leg kicks, which was simply to stay lying on the ground. No matter how the older boys kicked them, cursed them, and threatened them, they steadfastly refused to get up. Finally the three middle-schoolers resorted to trickery, saying, "If you get up, we won't kick you anymore."

Baldy Li and Song Gang didn't fall for this and continued lying in the street. Sun Wei pointed at an electrical pole, trying to lure Baldy Li up. "Hey, kid, go over to the pole and vent some of your sex drive."

Baldy Li shook his head. "I don't have any sex drive now."

Victory Zhao and Success Liu also encouraged him. "If you go and rub a few times, you'll get your sex drive."

Baldy Li continued shaking his head. "No rubbing for me today. You go and get some sex drive for yourselves."

"Fuck," said the middle-schoolers. "These two little fucking cowards."

Long-haired Sun Wei commanded, "Pull those two little cowards up, then kick them down again."

Just as Victory Zhao and Success Liu were about to pull the boys up, the stout-hearted revolutionary Blacksmith Tong arrived and roared, "Stop!"

Blacksmith Tong's roar made the three middle-schoolers tremble. Sun Wei mumbled, "They're little landlords."

"What little landlords?" Blacksmith Tong pointed at Baldy Li and Song Gang. "They are the blossoms of our nation."

Sun Wei looked over Blacksmith Tong's thick arms and torso and didn't say anything more. Tong pointed at the three middle-schoolers and said, "You are also the blossoms of our nation."

The middle-schoolers peered at one another and began to cackle. They continued cackling as they walked off. Blacksmith Tong looked first at them, then at Baldy Li and Song Gang on the ground, and sauntered away, proclaiming, "You are all the blossoms of our nation."

Baldy Li and Song Gang struggled to their feet. Bruised and battered, they looked at each other. Song Gang simply couldn't understand why he wasn't able to sweep long-haired Sun Wei to the ground. He asked Baldy Li what had gone wrong. Didn't he use the crucial move? Baldy Li huffed, "That move doesn't exist. Your father was bullshitting us."

Song Gang shook his swollen face. "He's our father. Fathers don't lie to sons."

Baldy Li hollered, "He's your dad, not mine."

The two of them stood there, shouting at each other. Finally Song Gang wiped the tears from his face and blew his nose. He said, "Let's go ask Papa."

Baldy Li and Song Gang came to the front entrance of the middle school. A struggle session was getting out. Song Fanping stood with his placard hanging from his neck, along with two others, as a group of students who had just walked out surrounded them and shouted slogans condemning them. A few people wearing red armbands were also saying something. The two boys didn't know that these people, after getting out of the big struggle session inside, were holding another small rally here. The boys squeezed through the crowd and went right up to Song Fanping. Song Gang tugged at his father's sleeve, asking, "Papa, you taught us the most important move in the sweeping leg kick, didn't you?"

Song Fanping stood bowed and motionless. Song Gang started crying pitifully. He pushed at his father. "Papa, tell Baldy Li you taught us. . . ."

Song Fanping remained silent. Baldy Li started yelling, "You lied to us. You didn't teach us how to do the sweeping leg kick. You lied to us about the characters on the wooden placard. They mean 'landlord,' but you told us they meant 'Chairman Mao of the land.'"

At that moment Baldy Li had no way of knowing what a terrible fate his words would bring down on Song Fanping, and he was stunned by what followed. When the people heard Baldy Li's words, they were initially flabbergasted, then they proceeded to strike, kick, and pummel Song Fanping until he was barely breathing. They roared as they stomped and kicked him on the ground, demanding that he confess how he had wickedly attacked "our great leader, our great teacher, our great general, our great helmsman—Chairman Mao."

Baldy Li had never seen anyone pummeled like this before. Song Fanping's face was completely covered in blood, and even his hair was soaked red. He lay there as countless adults and children stomped on him, his body like a platform as countless people stepped over him. His face didn't flinch, but his eyes did—twitching to the side so that he could glimpse Baldy Li and Song Gang. When he looked at Baldy Li, it was as if he was saying something with his gaze, a gaze that terrified Baldy Li. After a while Baldy Li was squeezed out of the circle and could no longer see Song Fanping's eyes. He only saw Song Gang wailing as he tried to force his way back into the circle. There were more and more spectators, and Song Gang was pushed farther and farther away. Finally he opened his mouth, but no sound came out. He walked next to Baldy Li, his face full of tears and snot, his mouth opening and closing as if he was yelling at Baldy Li, but Baldy Li couldn't hear a thing. After Song Gang yelled silently for a while, he punched Baldy Li and Baldy Li punched him right back. The two boys took turns punching each other, as if taking turns dealing out a deck of cards. Altogether, they punched each more than thirty-six times.

CHAPTER 12

AFTER SONG FANPING had been beaten to a pulp, he was taken away and locked up in a room in a large warehouse. The following week, Song Gang and Baldy Li stopped speaking to each other. Song Gang, in any event, couldn't speak at all; he had yelled so hard that day and his throat had become so red and swollen that now, when he tried to speak, no sound came out. Baldy Li knew that it was his revelation that had sent Song Fanping to that prisonlike warehouse, and when he lay down to sleep at night, all he could think about was Song Fanping being kicked and stomped as Song Fanping's eyes anxiously sought out his and Song Gang's. Baldy Li trembled but refused to cede an inch. He mocked Song Gang for having a mouth that was good only for farting.

Baldy Li was now on his own. He roamed the streets alone, sat under trees alone, squatted by the river and drank alone, talked to himself as he stood on the street looking, waiting, hoping for another child his age to wander over. Covered in sweat and scorched by the sun, he saw around him only parading people and parading flags. Children his age were all led by their mothers' hands as they were pulled past him one after another. No one spoke to him or even deigned to look at him. Only when some passerby accidentally bumped into him or spat on his foot, only then might someone realize he was there. Only the three middle-schoolers showed any interest in him, and each time they saw him they would wave eagerly and call out, "Hey, kid, come show us some of your sex drive."

They waved at him as they enthusiastically walked over. He knew that what they really wanted was to practice their sweeping leg kicks. They wanted to kick him until he shat in his pants and his face swelled up. Baldy Li therefore ran for his life, and the three middle-schoolers ran after him, laughing and saying, "Hey, kid, don't run. We won't kick you."

That summer, in order to get away from the middle-schoolers' kicks, Baldy Li often ran until he collapsed. His eight-year-old legs sore and shaking, his eight-year-old lungs burning for oxygen, his eight-year-old heart pounding wildly, his eight-year-old self ran until he almost died. Finally, Baldy Li limped into the alley where Blacksmith Tong, Tailor Zhang, Scissors Guan, and Yanker Yu resided.

Now, of course, they were known as Revolutionary Blacksmith, Revolutionary Tailor, Revolutionary Scissors, and Revolutionary Tooth-Yanker. When a customer brought a bolt of fabric to Tailor Zhang's shop, Zhang would first grill him, asking him about his class background. If he was a poor peasant, Tailor Zhang would greet him with a smile; if he was a middle peasant, Zhang would reluctantly take the fabric; and if he was a landlord, Zhang would immediately raise his fist and shout revolutionary slogans until his ashen-faced landlord customer ran out of the shop with his fabric. Even as he disappeared down the alley, Tailor Zhang would stand at his shop door, declaiming to his departing landlord client, "I will make you the shabbiest funeral garb, no, just a sheet for wrapping your corpse."

The two Scissors Guan were even more revolutionarily enlightened than Tailor Zhang. They didn't take any money from their peasant customers, they took extra from the middle-peasant ones, while the landlord customers had no choice but to scamper away. As the landlords fled, the two Scissors Guan would raise their loudly snapping scissors and stand outside their shop yelling that they were going to snip off their landlord dicks. Scissors Guan yelled, "We're going to snip you into a cockless landlady."

Yanker Yu, meanwhile, was a revolutionary opportunist. He would ask about class background when a patient came to see him but just as often would wait until he had first opened the customer's mouth to get a clear look at his cavities. He worried that if he found he had a landlord on his hands, he would lose both the customer and the money; but if he didn't interrogate his prospective patients, he couldn't be considered a revolutionary dentist. He wanted both money and revolution, and therefore often only when he had his extractor firmly around a client's rotten tooth would he seize the moment to demand in a ringing voice, "Tell me! What's your class background?"

The customer, mouth stuffed with dental implements, would mumble unintelligibly. Yanker Yu would make a big show of bending over to listen, then loudly proclaim, "A poor peasant? Good! I will pull out your rotten tooth."

By the time he finished this declaration, Yu would be done extracting the tooth. He would then immediately thrust a cotton wad into his patient's mouth and tell him to clamp down tightly to stanch the bleeding. With his jaw clamped and his mouth stuffed, the customer, even if he had admitted to being a landlord, would be forcefully remade into a poor peasant. With a flourish, Yanker Yu would show his customer the rotten tooth. "See that? This is a poor peasant's rotten tooth. If you had been a landlord, then it would have been a perfectly healthy tooth that I would have extracted."

Then Yanker Yu would display a firm stance of clear separation of boundaries between revolution and profit, saying, "Chairman Mao teaches us that a revolution is not a dinner party. Since I extracted one revolutionary tooth, I must therefore collect ten cents of revolutionary money."

Revolutionary Blacksmith Tong never inquired about his customers' class backgrounds, convinced that he was so ideologically righteous that a class enemy would never dare to enter his shop. Tong thumped his chest and proclaimed, "Only hardworking, poor peasants would come to my shop to buy sickles and hammers; lazy landlords only know how to exploit others and wouldn't know the first thing about hammers and sickles."

The tides of revolution came roaring through town, and soon Blacksmith Tong, Tailor Zhang, and the two Scissors Guan engaged heartily and solely in revolutionary activity. With a revolutionary red armband around his bare arm, Blacksmith Tong no longer hammered out sickles and hoes but, rather, spearheads for red-tasseled spears. As soon as he finished hammering out a spearhead he would send it to the blade-sharpening shop across from his own. The two Scissors Guan now also wore revolutionary armbands on their bare arms, and they were no longer sharpening scissors but sat at their low stools sharpening spearheads, their legs apart and rivulets of sweat running down their backs. Once the two Scissors Guan sharpened the spearhead, they would send it to Tailor Zhang's store next door. Tailor Zhang was wearing an undershirt, but his arms were bare, and he too wore a revolutionary armband. He no longer made clothes; instead he now only made red flags, red armbands, and the silk tassels that hung from the spears. The Cultural Revolution was remaking Liu Town into a revolutionary battlefield, another Jing Gang Mountain—by now the town was already transformed into a scene from Chairman Mao's verse: "flags waving at the bottom of the mountain, with drums ringing from above."

Yanker Yu's arm was also adorned with a red revolutionary armband, which Tailor Zhang had given him. Yanker Yu watched Tong, Guan, and Zhang working as if in a single production line, producing red-tasseled spears, while Yu was left out in the cold. Red-tasseled spears had no teeth, so he couldn't pull or fill them, and certainly couldn't fit them with dentures. All Yanker Yu could do was lie back in his rattan recliner and wait for the call of the revolution.

In Baldy Li's wanderings, he would watch Tong, Guan, and Zhang busy producing red-tasseled spears as if they were a munitions factory. When he tired of watching, he would wander over to Yanker Yu's oil-cloth umbrella. Now that he no longer had Song Gang constantly by his side, Baldy Li was often lonely and bored. Wherever he went, he brought his yawns with him, and when Yanker Yu saw him, he would be infected by these yawns.

Alongside the row of extracted rotten teeth that Yanker Yu used to display on his table, he now very progressively displayed a dozen or so perfectly good teeth to demonstrate his class stand to everyone. He even wanted to demonstrate it to the eight-year-old Baldy Li, so he raised himself up from his rattan recliner and, pointing to the teeth, explained, "These are the healthy teeth that I've extracted from class enemies." He then pointed to the several dozen rotten teeth on the table and explained, "These are the rotten teeth that I've extracted from the mouths of my class brothers and sisters."

Baldy Li nodded without enthusiasm. He looked over the healthy teeth of class enemies and the rotten teeth of class brothers and sisters and didn't find any of them very interesting. He then sat down on Yanker Yu's stool next to the recliner and continued yawning. Yanker Yu had passed a listless morning on his recliner, and now that he finally had Baldy Li visiting, they matched each other yawn for yawn.

Yanker Yu sat up. Looking over at the electrical pole across the street, he patted Baldy Li's head and asked, "Aren't you going to go hump that pole?"

"I already did," Baldy Li replied.

"Go hump it again," Yanker Yu encouraged him.

"Nah," explained Baldy Li. "I've humped every pole in this town at least several times."

"Oh, my mother!" Yanker Yu exclaimed. "If this were ancient times, you'd be the emperor with your own harem, but now you're a serial rapist about to be jailed and executed."

When Baldy Li, who was midyawn, heard the phrase "jailed and executed," he was so startled that he swallowed the rest of the yawn and opened his eyes wide. "I'll be jailed and executed for humping electrical poles?"

"Of course." Yanker Yu pointed to the pole and asked Baldy Li, "Do you regard them as class enemies or as class sisters?"

Still wide-eyed, Baldy Li didn't understand. Yanker Yu enthusiastically continued, "If you think of the poles as class enemies, then humping them would be like criticizing them. But if you treat the poles as class sisters, you would need to register for a marriage license. If you don't register and get married, you're a rapist. Now that you've humped every pole in the town, it's as if you've molested every class sister in town. So why wouldn't they jail and execute you?"

After hearing Yanker Yu's explanation, Baldy Li was relieved of his worries over execution and imprisonment, and his wide-open eyes relaxed to narrow slits. Yanker Yu patted Baldy Li on the head and asked, "Now do you get it? Now do you understand what having a class stand is?"

"Yup." Baldy Li nodded.

"So tell me," Yanker Yu continued, "do you think of them as class enemies? Or class sisters?"

Baldy Li blinked a few times. "What if I think of them as class electrical poles?"

Yanker Yu was stunned into silence. Then he burst out laughing. "You little bastard."

After Baldy Li spent half an hour at Yanker Yu's, Yu was amused but Baldy Li was still bored, so he got up and went back to Blacksmith Tong's shop. Baldy Li sat on Tong's long bench with his back against the wall and his head half cocked, watching Blacksmith Tong energetically hammering out a red-tasseled spear. The blacksmith held the spear with his tongs in his left hand and wielded his iron hammer with his right as sparks flew all over the shop. The red revolutionary armband on Blacksmith Tong's left arm kept slipping down, and he would raise his tongs-wielding left hand to slide the armband back up, waving the spearhead in his tongs through the air. As he hammered away Blacksmith Tong looked over at Baldy Li, remembering how the little fellow used to climb onto the long bench and rub back and forth but now would just lean against it dejectedly like a diseased chicken squatting in a corner. Blacksmith Tong couldn't help but ask him, "Hey, you're not going to have sexual relations with the bench?"

"*Sexual relations?*" Baldy Li cackled a few times, thinking that it was a funny phrase. But he shook his head and laughed bitterly. "I've lost my sex drive."

Now it was Blacksmith Tong's turn to cackle. He said, "This little bastard is impotent."

Baldy Li laughed along. He asked Blacksmith Tong, "What does *impotent* mean?"

Tong laid down his hammer and wiped his face with the towel draped around his neck. "Loosen your pants and look at your weenie," he said.

Baldy Li loosened his pants and took a look. Blacksmith Tong asked, "So is it soft?"

Baldy Li nodded. "It's as soft as dough."

"That's called impotence." Blacksmith Tong hung the towel back around his neck and, squinting, explained: "When your weenie is hard like a little cannon about to fire, that means you have a sex drive. But when it's soft as dough, then you're impotent."

Baldy Li let out an "oh." As if discovering a new continent, he exclaimed, "So I'm impotent."

By this time Baldy Li was already notorious. In Liu, there were quite a few loafers loitering in the streets who would sometimes raise their fists, shout a few slogans, and follow behind some parading troupe, or sometimes they would lean idly against the wutong trees, yawning nonstop. These loafers were all acquainted with Baldy Li, and whenever they saw him, they would get excited and start chuckling, calling out to one another, "That pole-humping fellow is here."

But Baldy Li was no longer his old self. Song Fanping had been locked in the warehouse, and Song Gang, who had lost his voice, was no longer speaking to him. Alone and constantly hungry, Baldy Li walked dejectedly along the main streets, having lost all interest in the wooden poles lining the streets. The loafers, however, remained very interested in him. Keeping an eye on the parade making its way down the street, they blocked his path and pointed at the wooden poles along the street, whispering, "Hey, kid, haven't seen you hump the poles for a while."

Baldy Li shook his head and answered in a ringing voice, "I no longer have sexual relations with them."

These loafers shook with laughter and surrounded Baldy Li to prevent him from getting away. They waited until the crowds had passed, then asked him again, "So why don't you have sexual relations anymore?"

With a practiced air Baldy Li unfastened his pants and instructed them to look at his penis. He said, "See that? See my weenie?"

Knocking their heads together, they looked down Baldy Li's pants, and when they nodded, their heads knocked together again. Holding their heads, they answered that they'd seen it, and Baldy Li continued, "So is it as hard as a little cannon? Or is it as soft as dough?"

These people didn't know what Baldy Li was getting at, so they nodded, "Soft, definitely soft, like dough."

"So that's why I no longer engage in sexual relations," explained Baldy Li.

Then he waved his hands like a famous knight errant bidding farewell to his fighting days, and parted the crowd. After a few steps he turned back. Sounding as if he had seen the sorrow of the ages, he said with a sigh, "I'm impotent."

Buoyed by the crowd's laughter, Baldy Li regained his spirit. He raised his head and strutted off. And when he walked past a wooden electrical pole, he gave it a kick, as if proclaiming that he had fully ended his relationship with all such poles.

CHAPTER 13

BALDY LI didn't have a cent to his name as he roamed the streets. When he was thirsty, he drank from the river. When he was hungry, he could only swallow his saliva and head home. By that point his home was like a shattered vase. The armoire had been pushed over, but he and Song Gang didn't have the strength to lift it back up; the floor was strewn with clothes, but the children were too lazy to pick them up. Since Song Fanping had been taken away and locked up in that warehouse, crowds came to search their house twice more. Each time Baldy Li immediately ducked out, leaving Song Gang to deal with them on his own. He was sure that when Song Gang rasped to them, they would lose their tempers and smack him on the head.

During those days, Song Gang never left the house and instead started cooking like a chef. Song Fanping had once taught the boys how to cook, and while Baldy Li had completely forgotten everything, Song Gang remembered his lessons. When Baldy Li returned home dejected, his stomach growling, he'd find that Song Gang had prepared dinner, had set out their rice bowls and those two pairs of chopsticks of the ancients, and was sitting at the table waiting for him. When he saw Baldy Li walk in swallowing his saliva, Song Gang would start his rasping. Baldy Li knew that he was saying, "You're finally home." The moment Baldy Li stepped inside, he would grab his rice bowl and gulp everything down.

Baldy Li had no idea how Song Gang passed his days—how every day he would stand at the stove and light a match in order to ignite the strip of cotton, and how each day he'd have to pull the cotton out a little farther as it burned shorter and shorter. He worked himself up into a huge sweat, his hands coated in charcoal and his fingernails black, only to serve Baldy Li a pot of half-cooked rice. Baldy Li ate the rice as if he were chewing on kernels, crunching and gnawing until his stomach hurt. The vegetables that Song Gang stir-fried tasted extraordinarily foul. When Song Fanping made them, they were glistening and green, but Song Gang's always came out yellow and wilted, like pickled cabbage. Moreover, the greens would be speckled with black, charcoal-like specks and would always be either too salty or too bland. Baldy Li had stopped speaking to Song Gang, but he would lose his temper at mealtimes, complaining bitterly, "The rice is still raw, and the greens are wilted. You are a landlord's son."

Song Gang would turn beet red and rasp a string of unintelligible words. Baldy Li said, "Stop rasping, you sound like a mosquito farting or a dung beetle crapping."

By the time Song Gang regained his voice, he had learned how to cook the rice evenly. The children had long finished the last of the greens that Song Fanping had left behind for them and had almost emptied the rice barrel. Song Gang put the well-cooked rice in a bowl and placed a bottle of soy sauce next to it. When he saw Baldy Li come in, he exclaimed with surprise, "This time it's fully cooked!"

Song Gang had indeed succeeded in cooking the rice so that each grain was round and glistening. This was the best bowl of rice Baldy Li could remember ever having eaten, and though later in life he would have many far better bowls of rice, he always felt that they could not equal the one Song Gang made on this occasion. Baldy Li thought this was a case of blind luck on Song Gang's part, sheer accident that he had produced such a perfect pot of rice. After several days of half-cooked rice, they finally sat down to enjoy the real thing. They didn't have any greens, but they did have soy sauce. The boys poured the soy sauce on top of the steaming hot rice and stirred it in. The rice glistened as if lacquered with red and black paint, and the fragrance of soy sauce mingled with the steaming hot rice, filling the entire room.

By this point it was dark. The children ate their fill of this delicious, oily concoction. Moonlight shone through the window, and a breeze slid past the rooftop. Song Gang started speaking in his raspy voice, his mouth full of soy-sauce rice: "When do you think Papa will come home?"

Tears began to stream down his face even before he finished speaking. He put down his bowl and bent over, sobbing, as he continued swallowing bites of rice. Then he wiped his eyes and began wailing, his raspy voice sounding like a weak siren, a long wail followed by a short one, until his entire body shook.

Baldy Li also lowered his head, feeling terrible. He wanted to say something to Song Gang, but in the end he kept silent, merely telling himself, *He is a landlord's son.*

After fixing such an extraordinary pot of rice, the next day Song

Gang once again prepared a half-cooked one. The moment Baldy Li saw the dull specks of grain in the bowl, he knew it was over, that they had to eat raw rice again. Song Gang had been seated at the table, engaged in a science experiment. He had carefully sprinkled some salt in one bowl of rice, then carefully poured a bit of soy sauce in the other. He had then tasted each bowl, one after the other. By the time Baldy Li got home, Song Gang had obtained his results. He happily announced to Baldy Li that rice sprinkled with salt was much tastier than the raw rice mixed with soy sauce, and that the salt should be sprinkled on after each bite. By the time the salt dissolved into the rice, it would have lost some of its flavor.

Baldy Li shouted furiously at Song Gang, "I want cooked rice, I don't want raw rice."

Song Gang looked up and told him the bad news: "We're out of charcoal. The fire went out halfway through."

Baldy Li's anger faded as he had no choice but to sit down and eat the half-raw rice. No charcoal meant no fire. Baldy Li thought to himself that it would be great if only Song Gang could piss out some coal or fart out some flames. Song Gang instructed Baldy Li to sprinkle some salt on the rice and then immediately gulp it down. Baldy Li tried this, and his eyes lit up. Chewing the salt crystals and the rice kernels together produced a nice, crisp taste, and each time Baldy Li bit down on a salt crystal, a burst of flavor would fill his mouth. Baldy Li understood why Song Gang told him to eat the raw rice before the salt melted; it was like rubbing sticks together to make a fire, as the saltiness burst forth at the instant of crunching. Once the salt dissolved, the savoriness disappeared and only a stale taste of salt remained. For the first time Baldy Li found that half-raw rice wasn't half bad. But then Song Gang told him the other bad news: "Now we're out of rice, too."

Come evening, the two boys were still eating the half-cooked rice sprinkled with salt left over from lunch. The next morning they got up after the sun woke them shining on their bare bottoms. After getting out of bed, they ran to a corner outside and took a piss, then fetched a pail of well water and washed their faces. Only then did they remember that they didn't even have a fart left to eat. Baldy Li sat on the front step for a while. He wanted to see how Song Gang was going to figure out how to get something to eat. Song Gang rummaged first through the toppled armoire and then through the clothes on the floor, but he couldn't come up with a single thing to eat. Song Gang could only swallow his saliva and consider it breakfast.

There wasn't much for Baldy Li to do but to swallow his own saliva and continue roaming the streets and alleyways like a stray dog. At first he still had some spring in his step, but by noon he was like a deflated balloon. Eventually the hungry eight-year-old Baldy Li was transformed into a decrepit eighty-year-old. Even if he ignored his faintness and dizziness or the weakness of his limbs, there were the endless hiccups coming from his completely empty stomach. Baldy Li sat under a wutong tree beside the street for a very long time, tilting his head and watching the people walk past. He saw someone walk by him eating a meat bun, saw the meat juice on that person's lips, and even saw with his own eyes that person licking away the juice with his tongue. Then there was the woman who walked by eating watermelon seeds and spitting the shells right into his hair. But what infuriated Baldy Li the most was a stray dog, since even it was carrying a bone in its mouth.

Baldy Li had no idea how he made it home that evening. He only knew that he was starving. He didn't expect to find any food at home and only wanted to lie down in bed. But when he reached the front door, he suddenly spotted Song Gang sitting at the table, eating. At that moment Baldy Li was ecstatic, and though he was faint with hunger he propelled himself forward.

It was in vain. When he approached, Baldy Li realized that Song Gang had in front of him only a bowl of clear water; putting a bit of salt on his tongue, he let it slowly melt, then chased it with a sip of water, followed by a sip of soy sauce. He puffed his cheeks as if he were savoring this, and only after the taste of soy sauce had fully marinated his tongue did he take another sip of water.

Song Gang used his last bit of energy to eat his salt and soy sauce and drink his water. He was so hungry he had no desire to say anything to Baldy Li, merely pointed at the other bowl of water on the table. Baldy Li knew that this bowl had been prepared for him, and he sat down at the table. Though he was greatly disappointed, he followed Song Gang's lead. A dab of salt and soy sauce and a sip of water was better than nothing at all. Though in truth this lunch consisted of nothing, it made Baldy Li feel that at least he had eaten something. He felt a little better and lay down on the bed, muttering to himself that he wanted to see what there was to eat in his dreams. With a lick of his lips he fell asleep.

Sure enough, the moment he started dreaming he dove headfirst into a giant steamer. Hot steam poured from its sides, and several cooks dressed in white grunted "Hey-ho, hey-ho" as they labored to lift off the giant steamer's lid. Baldy Li could see that there were as many steamed meat buns inside as there were people at the struggle sessions in the schoolyard, and each of the buns was oozing meat juices. The cooks put the steamer lid back on, saying that the buns weren't done yet. Baldy Li argued that they were definitely done, the juices were already oozing out of the buns, but the cooks ignored him. He could only stand to one side and wait and wait, until the meat juices were already seeping out of the steamer, whereupon the cooks finally exclaimed, "They're done!" With another series of "Hey-ho, hey-hos" they lifted the lid and said, "Have one!" Baldy Li felt like a diver as he thrust his head into the steamer and scooped up a whole armful of meat buns. And just as he was about to bite into a juice-seeping bun, he woke up.

Song Gang, who had shaken him awake, pushed Baldy Li and cried out hoarsely, "I found it! I found it!"

The meat bun vanished without a trace after Song Gang's poking and prodding, and Baldy Li was so upset he started wailing. Wiping his tears, he kicked Song Gang while yelling, "Buns, buns, buns!" But Baldy Li immediately broke into a smile when he saw that Song Gang was waving grain ration tickets and money, of which Baldy Li could make out two five-yuan bills.

Song Gang chattered excitedly about how he came to find the money and ration tickets that Song Fanping had left them. Baldy Li couldn't understand a single word, his head being already stuffed to the brim with the thought of succulent meat buns. Suddenly getting a second wind, Baldy Li leapt off the bed and said to Song Gang, "Let's go! Let's go buy some buns!"

Song Gang shook his head. "I should first go ask Papa. If he says yes, then we can go buy them."

Baldy Li replied, "By the time we find your father, we'll have starved to death!"

Song Gang shook his head again and said, "We won't starve to death. We'll find him real soon."

They had money and grain rations, and they almost had buns—but now this idiot Song Gang wanted to go ask his goddamn father's permission! Baldy Li was so impatient he started stomping his feet. He eyed the money and tickets in Song Gang's hand and was about to make a leap for them when Song Gang, realizing that Baldy Li was about to snatch them, quickly stuffed everything into his pocket. The two ended up in a tangle and fell to the ground. Song Gang tightly covered his pockets with both hands, and Baldy Li tried to unlock his fingers to get to the pocket. Neither child had eaten anything all day, and both were weak with hunger. They fought for a while and then stopped to catch their breath, their mouths open as they huffed and panted. Then they resumed their grappling and panting. Finally, Song Gang got up off the floor and was about to dash out, but Baldy Li crawled up and blocked the door. Both boys were so tired they couldn't even stand straight. With Baldy Li at the door, they faced each other and panted, taking the opportunity to rest for a while. Then Song Gang turned to go into the kitchen, and Baldy Li heard him gulping down a ladleful of water from the cistern. A sated Song Gang walked up to Baldy Li, hoarsely yelling at him, "I'm all set to go again!"

Song Gang shoved Baldy Li aside and ran out the door, going to look for their landlord father. Baldy Li lay on the floor like a dead pig, then crawled and sat at the entrance like a sick dog. His hunger made him let out a few wails, but crying made him feel even hungrier, so he immediately stopped. Baldy Li could hear the sound of the wind blowing through the tree branches and could see the sunlight shining on his toes. He thought to himself, *If I could munch the rays of sunlight like stir-fried pork and drink the wind like a bowl of meat broth, then I'd be set.* Baldy Li sat leaning against the door frame for a while, then he got up to go to the kitchen and gulped his fill of water from the cistern. He now felt he had a bit of strength back, so he shut the door and walked into the street.

That afternoon Baldy Li paced the streets with his last remaining shreds of energy. He didn't find anything to eat, but he did run into the three middle-school students. Baldy Li was leaning against a wutong tree when he heard a few titters and someone calling out to him, "Hey, kid."

By the time Baldy Li lifted his head, they had already surrounded him. One look at their gleeful faces and Baldy Li knew that they were planning to practice their sweeping kicks again. This time he was simply unable to run away and told them, "I haven't eaten all day."

Long-haired Sun Wei said, "Let's feed you a few kicks, then."

Baldy Li pleaded with them, "No more sweeping kicks today. I'll eat them tomorrow."

"Nope," all three replied. "You have to eat them today *and* tomorrow."

Baldy Li pointed at the electrical pole not far off in the distance and continued to beg. "Don't feed me any more kicks. Why don't you let me go have sexual relations with that pole?"

The three middle-schoolers burst out laughing, and Sun Wei replied, "First you have some kicks, and when you've gotten your fill, go have relations with that pole."

Baldy Li wiped his tears. The three middle-schoolers politely deferred to one another, generously wanting to offer up the opportunity to make the first kick.

At this point Song Gang appeared. He ran from the opposite side of the street, buns in his hands, and plopped himself down right beside Baldy Li, dragging him to the ground. When both kids were seated on the ground, Song Gang, his head covered in sweat, handed Baldy Li a steaming hot meat bun. Baldy Li took it and stuffed it into his mouth. With his first bite the meat juices oozed out of the corner of his lips. Baldy Li choked before he could even finish the first bite, and he sat there motionless, his neck extended. Song Gang patted him on the back while smugly saying to the three middle-schoolers, "We're already sitting on the ground. How are you going to sweep us down?"

"Fuck." The middle-schoolers looked at one another, then repeated, "Fuck."

The three had no idea how to sweep-kick Baldy Li and Song Gang when they were already on the ground. They discussed dragging the two kids to their feet, but Song Gang warned them, "We'll scream for help. People from the street will all come over."

"Fuck that." Long-haired Sun Wei said, "If you had guts, you'd stand up."

Song Gang replied, "If you had guts, you'd sweep-kick us up."

The students eyed Baldy Li and Song Gang helplessly. Cursing, they looked at one another and watched Baldy Li eat his meat bun. After wolfing down the bun, Baldy Li regained some of his energy, and he seconded Song Gang, adding, "We're very comfortable sitting down here, even more comfortable than we would be in our own beds."

The three middle-schoolers each muttered "Motherfucker," and then Sun Wei changed his tactics. He grinned at them warmly and said to Baldy Li, "Hey, kid, why don't you get up? We promise not to sweep-kick you. Go ahead and have sexual relations with that electrical pole."

Baldy Li giggled and licked the remaining meat juice from his lips. He licked until he was lolling his head about and replied, "I no longer have sexual relations with electrical poles. You want to do it, go ahead. I'm impotent now, don't you know?"

The three middle-schoolers didn't know what *impotent* meant. They looked at one another curiously. Victory Zhao couldn't help but ask Baldy Li, "What's *impotent*?"

Baldy Li smugly explained, "Just unfasten your trousers and look at your . . ."

Victory Zhao touched his crotch and looked at Baldy Li with alarm. Baldy Li asked, "So take a look. Is your dick hard like a little metal cannon? Or is it soft and mushy like dough?"

Victory Zhao felt his dick through his pants. He retorted, "Do I need to look? Of course it's soft and mushy like dough right now."

Upon hearing that, Baldy Li exclaimed with delight, "So you're impotent, too!"

The three middle-schoolers now understood what *impotent* meant. Sun Wei and Success Liu broke out in guffaws, and Sun Wei said to Victory Zhao, "You're such an idiot. You didn't even know what *impotent* meant."

Victory Zhao felt that he had lost face, so he kicked Baldy Li. "You little bastard, you're the one who's impotent. When I get up in the morning I'm harder than an iron cannon."

Baldy Li eagerly provided Victory Zhao with guidance: "So you're not impotent in the morning, just in the afternoon."

"Bullshit," Victory Zhao replied. "All year around, twenty-four hours a day—I'm never impotent."

"Bullshit." Baldy Li pointed at the nearby wooden pole. "Go prove it with that electrical pole over there."

"Electrical pole?" Victory Zhao snorted. He said, "Only a little bastard like you would hump a wooden pole. If I'm going to have sexual relations, I'll do it with your mother."

Baldy Li dismissed him. "My mother wouldn't let you guys get near her."

Then he pointed to Song Gang standing next to him and boasted, "My mom only does it with his dad."

Sun Wei and Success Liu doubled over with laughter. Victory Zhao let out a string of curses, but the three middle-schoolers knew that the two little bastards wouldn't stand up until hell froze over. The three discussed how they were going to teach the little bastards a lesson and how maybe they should first lift them up, then sweep them back down. Baldy Li remembered how Blacksmith Tong had saved them last time, so he smilingly announced, "Blacksmith Tong is here."

The middle-schoolers turned to look down the street but saw no sign of Blacksmith Tong. So the three of them kicked Baldy Li and Song Gang each three times, making them cry out in pain, and then walked off, feeling they had finally got the advantage of things.

Baldy Li had managed to escape being sweep-kicked and even had had a meat bun. The sad thing was that he couldn't recall the taste of the bun at all. He remembered only that he had choked four times and that Song Gang had slapped him on the back. Song Gang said later that when Baldy Li was choking, his neck was stretched as long as a goose's.

Baldy Li and Song Gang were pals again. The brothers faced each other and grinned and laughed for about a minute, then they walked hand in hand down the main street. Song Gang said he had found his father, who was living in a warehouse. A bunch of people were locked up in that warehouse, some crying and others shouting. Baldy Li asked why they were crying and shouting. Song Gang replied that it seemed like people were fighting inside.

That afternoon Song Gang held Baldy Li's hand and walked down three streets, over two bridges, and through a small alley, until they finally reached the warehouse holding landlords and capitalists, modern-day and old-time counterrevolutionaries, together with all other class enemies. Baldy Li spotted long-haired Sun Wei's father—he was wearing a red armband and standing in front of the warehouse smoking. When he saw Song Gang, he asked, "How come you're here again?"

Song Gang pointed at Baldy Li. "This is my brother, Baldy Li. He wants to see our father."

Sun Wei's father looked Baldy Li over, and asked, "Where's your mother?"

Baldy Li replied, "She's in Shanghai seeing a doctor."

Sun Wei's father tossed his cigarette butt onto the ground and stomped it out. He pushed open the warehouse door and shouted inside, "Song Fanping! Song Fanping, get out here!"

When the door opened, Baldy Li spied a man inside who was on the ground, cradling his head in his hands while another man whipped him with a belt. The man on the ground was completely silent, but the man whipping him was wailing, as if he were the one being whipped. This sight gave Baldy Li the shivers, and Song Gang turned pale. They were both so shocked they didn't notice Song Fanping, who had walked out the front door. Song Fanping walked up to the boys and asked, "So you've had your meat buns?"

Baldy Li looked up to see Song Fanping's tall figure before him. His shirt was covered in bloodstains, and his face was swollen and bruised, and Baldy Li could tell that this was the result of his having been beaten half to death. Song Fanping squatted down to take a look at Baldy Li, reaching out to caress his head. "Baldy Li, you still have meat juice on your lips."

Baldy Li bowed his head and let out a few sorrowful tears. He regretted his own revelation. He thought, *If I hadn't said those things in front of the school gate, Song Fanping wouldn't be here getting tortured.* When he thought about how kind Song Fanping had been to him, Baldy Li started sobbing. "I was wrong."

Song Fanping wiped away Baldy Li's tears with his thumb and teased him, "You haven't sucked the snot into your eyes, have you?"

Baldy Li broke out into a chuckle. The crying and shouting and cursing in the warehouse became louder and louder, rumbling ceaselessly from the door's cracks. There were also sounds of moaning, almost like frogs' croaking. Baldy Li became alarmed. He and Song Gang stood by Song Fanping and shivered. Song Fanping acted as if he hadn't heard anything and chatted happily with the boys, though his left arm dangled awkwardly by his side. Baldy Li and Song Gang didn't know that his arm had been beaten until it was dislocated. They thought that it looked odd, as if he had a prosthetic limb. They asked him what was wrong, and he explained, "It's tired, so I'm letting it rest for a few days."

Song Fanping always filled Baldy Li and Song Gang with wonder. They felt that he had all sorts of mysterious powers and hidden talents, that he could even let his arm dangle and rest for a few days.

To satisfy Baldy Li and Song Gang's curiosity, Song Fanping became their coach right in front of this giant warehouse filled with wails and screams, teaching them how to let their forearms rest for a bit. He told the boys to first lower one shoulder until it was sloping down, and then to let their arm relax and hang down. He told them they couldn't use any force on the sloping arm; they had to pretend that it wasn't there. He pointed to his solar plexus, saying, 'Don't think about this arm anymore." Once he felt that Baldy Li and Song Gang had gotten the gist of it, he told them to line up and march back and forth in front of the warehouse with their sloped shoulders and dangling arms while he chanted, "One-two, one-two." Baldy Li and Song Gang noticed that with every step they took, their dangling arm would swing back and forth. The boys were delighted, pointing excitedly to each other's arm.

Song Fanping asked them, "So are your arms dangling?"

Baldy Li and Song Gang answered in unison, "They are!"

Long-haired Sun Wei's father watched them, laughing uncontrollably. First he chuckled, then he guffawed, and finally he laughed until he was squatting and clutching his stomach. He eventually stood up, clutching his belly, and said to Song Fanping, "Okay, you should go back in."

Song Fanping walked back to the warehouse, but before entering, he turned and told the boys, "Now go home and practice."

That afternoon Baldy Li and Song Gang completely forgot about the horrible sounds coming from inside the warehouse, as well as Song Fanping's bruised, swollen face. They only remembered Song Fanping instructing them to continue practicing. All the way home they enthusiastically practiced sloping their shoulders and dangling their arms. Once they got home, they lay in bed and draped their arms over the side. They discovered that it was much easier dangling their arms over the side of the bed than walking with a sloped shoulder, the only drawback being that after a while their arms would go to sleep.

CHAPTER 14

BALDY LI and Song Gang continued their parentless existence, and got by quite well. They would go together to the rice store, where they would fit their rice sack over the rubber chute and watch the rice cascade down. Then they would bang the chute opening with loud, crisp slaps until the store clerks yelled at them and a hand reached out from behind the counter to knock them on the head.

With their basket in hand, they went together to buy groceries. While selecting the greens, they would stealthily rip off the outer leaves until only the tenderest inner leaves were left, causing the old lady selling vegetables to tear up with annoyance. She cursed them over and over, calling them turtles' eggs, little bastards who would come to a bad end; saying that they would choke on a breath and get water stuck in their teeth, and end up without an asshole to crap with or a penis to piss out of.

Baldy Li and Song Gang scrimped and saved and, like monks, ate only vegetables. After a while they began to really crave meat, so they went to the river to catch shrimp. By the time they reached the river, they realized that they had no idea how to cook them. At that point they hadn't caught sight of even a shadow of a shrimp, but already they were licking their lips and discussing how they were going to cook them. Would they panfry them? Stir-fry them? Or boil them? In the end, they made a detour to the warehouse to consult with Song Fanping. When they reached the warehouse gate, they slanted their shoulders and let their elbows dangle. Song Fanping came outside to tell them that stir-frying, panfrying, and boiling would all be fine, but just to make sure that the shrimp had turned pink before eating them. Song Fanping explained, "They're done when they're as pink as the tip of your tongue."

Song Fanping told the boys that the shrimp would be swimming in the shallows. He told them to roll their pants legs up to their knees, warning, "Once the water reaches your pants, then you shouldn't go any farther. There are no shrimp in the depths, only snakes."

Baldy Li and Song Gang shuddered. They didn't realize that Song Fanping, worried that they would drown if they ventured into the deep water, was deliberately scaring them. The boys nodded and promised that they would stay in the places where the river water remained below their knees. As they set off, shoulders slanted and elbows dangling, Song Fanping called out to them again, telling them to go home and get a bamboo basket. They asked, "What for?" Song Fanping replied, "What do you net fish with?"

The boys stopped and pondered this. Song Gang replied, "A fishing rod."

"That's for rod fishing," Song Fanping explained. "For netting fish you need a fishnet, and you need a bamboo basket to catch shrimp."

With his left elbow dangling, Song Fanping cocked his right elbow as if he were holding a bamboo basket, and bending down right in front of the warehouse, he started teaching them how to use a basket to net shrimp. He said that while standing in the river they should be as alert as sentries, placing the basket in the water at an angle, and once shrimp swam in of their own accord, the boys should immediately lift the basket. He stood up, concluding, "So this is how you catch shrimp."

Song Fanping asked them whether they got it. Baldy Li and Song Gang glanced at each other and nodded. Song Fanping said that he would teach them one more time, but when he bent down again, they immediately pointed out his error. Baldy Li said, "You haven't rolled up your pants legs."

Song Fanping chuckled. He bent down again and rolled up both pants legs, then once again demonstrated how to catch shrimp. This time both boys answered in unison, "We got it."

Baldy Li and Song Gang arrived at the river, rolled up their pants, and waded in. The water rushed by below their knees. They placed the basket in the water at an angle, just as Song Fanping had done in front of the warehouse, and waited for the shrimp to swim in. They waited in the river under the summer sun for an entire afternoon, until they were covered in sweat. They were startled to discover that the shrimp in the river skipped as they swam, unlike the fish with their tails wagging. The shrimp skipped, hopped, and swam into the boys' basket, up to five swimming in at once. The boys were so delighted they started yelping but then immediately covered their mouths when they noticed that they had scared away the little river shrimp, making it necessary for them to change location. Only when the boys sat on the grass by the riverbank counting the shrimp under the glow of the setting sun did they realize they had netted sixty-seven of the little guys.

On this particular evening, the boys' expressions, their intonation, and their gait—all were the spitting image of those red-armbanders parading around Liu Town. Baldy Li and Song Gang strutted through town with their bamboo basket and their sixty-seven shrimp. Someone spotted the shrimp in their basket and couldn't help harrumphing, saying that these two little bastards really had something going. When Baldy Li heard this, he felt smug, this being the first time he liked being called a bastard. He said to Song Gang, "These little bastards have something going."

After they got home, Baldy Li told Song Gang, "Let's boil those sixty-seven little bastard shrimp."

As the water in the pot started to boil, Baldy Li excitedly pointed out to Song Gang, "Hear that? Do you hear those sixty-seven little bastard shrimp bouncing around in there?"

When there were no more sounds coming from the pot, the boys lifted the lid and saw that the shrimp inside had all turned pink. Remembering what Song Fanping had told them about when the shrimp were done, Song Gang stuck out his tongue for Baldy Li and asked if the shrimp were as pink as his tongue. Baldy Li replied, "They're even pinker."

Baldy Li also stuck out his tongue to show Song Gang. Song Gang said, "They're pinker than your tongue, too."

Together they cried, "Let's eat! Let's eat these little bastard shrimp."

This was the first time they had eaten shrimp that they themselves had caught and cooked. They had forgotten to put salt in the pot, and after taking in a few bland bites, they decided that the taste was somewhat off. Song Gang then had a flash of culinary inspiration and proceeded to pour some soy sauce into a bowl, then dipped the shrimp into the soy sauce before eating them. Baldy Li grinned from ear to ear as he ate, proclaiming that the meat on these little bastard shrimp was dozens of times tastier than those little bastard meat buns. At that moment the boys had no awareness of anything other than the shrimp they were eating. After they finished, they sat there savoring the dish, not having fully emerged from their gustatory ecstasy. Only when Song Gang let out a belch, followed by Baldy Li, did they realize that they had finished off all sixty-seven little river shrimp. The boys wiped their mouths and agreed dreamily, "Let's eat shrimp tomorrow."

In the days that followed, Baldy Li and Song Gang lost all interest in wandering the main streets. They now loved the creek with a passion. They left at dawn every day with their basket to catch shrimp, walking a long, long way down the riverbank and then back again. Their legs were as pale as corpses and swollen from all the soaking, while their faces glowed red like overfed capitalists. Completely on their own, they learned to boil, panfry, and stir-fry the shrimp. They discovered that stir-frying shrimp required soy sauce, but that salt worked better with deep-frying. When good fortune came rushing in, there was no damming it. Once the boys netted more than a hundred shrimp. They fried and fried the shrimp until they had turned black, but when they ate them, they were delighted to discover that the blackened shells were crisp and delicious, with a taste completely distinct from that of the shrimp meat. When they were halfway through and still had more than forty shrimp left, Song Gang suddenly stopped eating and suggested, "Let's take these to Papa."

Baldy Li agreed, "Yes!"

They gathered the remaining fried shrimp into a bowl, and as they were walking out the door Song Gang said that they should get Papa two ounces of yellow rice wine. Song Gang imagined that Song Fanping would be so delighted to be drinking wine and eating shrimp that he would laugh with delight. Song Gang opened his mouth and cackled, demonstrating how his father would laugh. Baldy Li said Song Gang hadn't gotten it right and sounded like he was screaming for help. Then Baldy Li showed how he thought Song Fanping would sound— his mouth would be so crammed with shrimp and wine that he would barely be able to get a sound out and instead would just emit a few gurgles of laughter. Song Gang replied that Baldy Li's version wasn't right either, that it sounded more like a yawn.

They brought an empty bowl and went to the store to buy two ounces of wine. The wine vendor caught sight of the shrimp in their other bowl and took a few greedy sniffs. He said that the shrimp smelled so good he could only imagine how tasty they would be. Baldy Li and Song Gang chuckled and confirmed—"Yup, they were even tastier than they smelled." As they turned to leave they could hear the wine vendor swallowing his saliva.

It was dusk, and with Song Gang holding the bowl of wine and Baldy Li carrying the bowl of fried shrimp, the two boys carefully made their way to Song Fanping's warehouse. There they once again ran into the three sweep-kicking middle-schoolers, who walked toward them hollering, "Hey kids!"

Oh no, they thought. If it weren't for the wine and shrimp, they would have already taken off. But now, their hands full with bowls, they could only plop themselves on the ground. Three pairs of sweep-kicking legs encircled them. Baldy Li and Song Gang, still cupping their bowls, looked up at the three middle-schoolers. Song Gang said, not without satisfaction, "We're already sitting on the ground."

Baldy Li thought that they would respond, "Stand up if you have balls." So he jumped the gun and added, "Sweep-kick us up if you have the balls." But the three middle-schoolers hadn't said a word, instead focusing all their attention on the contents of Baldy Li's bowl. Sun Wei, Victory Zhao, and Success Liu all squatted down next to Baldy Li, and Sun Wei took a deep sniff and said, "Smells real good, even better than shrimp from the restaurant."

Victory Zhao added, "Damn. They even have wine to go with it."

Baldy Li's hands started trembling as he realized that they were going to grab his fried shrimp. Sure enough, they said, "Hey, kid. Give us a taste."

Three pairs of hands simultaneously dipped into Baldy Li's bowl. Baldy Li ducked and protected his bowl, hurriedly reminding them, "Blacksmith Tong's already told you, we are the young blossoms of our homeland."

When they heard Blacksmith Tong's name, the middle-schoolers yanked back their hands. After looking around and making sure that Blacksmith Tong was nowhere to be seen and that no one else was paying them any heed, they reached over again. Baldy Li opened his mouth and prepared to bite down on any invading digits when Song Gang suddenly shouted, "Shrimp for sale! Shrimp for sale!"

As he yelled out Song Gang nudged Baldy Li with his elbow. When Baldy Li saw that Song Gang's hawking had attracted some passersby, he too began shouting, "Shrimp for sale! Fragrant fried shrimp!"

A crowd instantly gathered and stared curiously at Baldy Li and Song Gang. The three middle-schoolers were squeezed off to the sides and stood there cursing Song Gang's dad, Baldy Li's mom, as well as all of their ancestors, before finally wiping their lips and going away.

Someone asked Baldy Li and Song Gang, "How much for the shrimp?"

Song Gang replied, "One yuan a shrimp."

"What?" the man exclaimed. "Do you think you are selling gold?"

"Just smell." Song Gang let Baldy Li hold up the bowl. "These are fried shrimp."

Baldy Li raised the bowl over his head. The crowd all caught a whiff of the shrimp and someone said, "They *do* smell good. But it should really be two shrimp for a cent."

Someone else added, "With one yuan you could buy a golden shrimp. These two little bastards are real profiteers."

Song Gang stood up, retorting, "You can't eat a golden shrimp."

Baldy Li also stood up and said, "Plus, golden shrimp aren't tasty."

Seeing that the three middle-schoolers were no longer around, Baldy Li and Song Gang breathed a sigh of relief and extricated themselves from the crowd of people. Holding their bowls, the boys swaggered away and proceeded down the street and over the bridge until they reached the front gate of the warehouse. The warehouse was still being guarded by the father of long-haired Sun Wei—who had just missed an opportunity to eat Baldy Li's shrimp. Sun Wei's father saw the two boys walking toward him and chuckled, "Hey, you're not dangling your elbows anymore?"

The two boys answered, "Can't dangle 'em. We're carrying bowls."

Sun Wei's father caught a whiff of the shrimp. He walked over to peer down at the bowls, then grabbed a shrimp and started munching on it. He asked, "Who cooked these?"

Baldy Li answered, "We did."

Astonished, he said, "You little bastards, you're top chefs."

As he said this he reached into the shrimp bowl again, but Baldy Li quickly dodged. So Sun Wei's father simply thrust out both hands, demanding both the shrimp and the wine. The children backed away, dodging his grasp. After cursing "Fuck that!" he walked back to the warehouse door and kicked it open, bellowing, "Song Fanping! Get out here. Your sons brought you stuff to eat and drink!"

He lingered on the words *stuff to eat and drink,* and soon five or six people wearing red armbands rushed out. Looking all about as they hurried over, they asked, "What's there to eat? What's there to drink?"

Their nostrils flared as they sniffed, and they said, "How fragrant, even more fragrant than lard." They had been eating carrots and greens day in and day out, and tasted pork at most once a month. Now that they caught sight of the fried shrimp in Baldy Li's hands, they felt so ravenous that claws seemed to emerge from their mouths. They surrounded the two children like a high wall encircling two saplings. A din of "Lemme try it!" filled the air, and a stream of saliva rained down on Baldy Li and Song Gang's faces. Frightened, the boys cradled their bowls and yelled, "Help! Help!"

Song Fanping walked out with his dangling arm. The boys spotted their savior and cried out, "Papa, come quickly!"

Song Fanping walked over to the boys, and Baldy Li and Song Gang hid behind him. Relieved, they raised their bowls of shrimp and wine and offered them to him. Song Gang said, "Papa, we made you fried shrimp, and we got you two ounces of rice wine to go with it."

Song Fanping's left hand dangled there uselessly, so he accepted Baldy Li's bowl of shrimp with his right. He didn't eat any, however, but instead politely passed it along to those red-armbanded people. He then accepted Song Gang's wine and also extended it to them. They were all still busy munching on the shrimp, so he waited politely with the bowl of wine. There were as many hands on the shrimp as branches on a tree, and in the blink of an eye they were all gone. The red-armbanders then noticed Song Fanping standing to the side waiting politely with the bowl of wine, and so took the wine and passed it around, each one of them downing a big gulp and finishing it off in no time.

Baldy Li and Song Gang wiped at their tears. Their shrimp and wine had been for Song Fanping, but he didn't get a taste of either. Song Gang said, "We were imagining how you would laugh while enjoying our shrimp and wine."

Song Fanping knelt down and, without a word, wiped away their tears. When he smiled, the boys noticed that he too had tears streaming from his eyes.

After finishing the shrimp and wine, the red-armbanders kicked at Song Fanping and bellowed, "Get up, scram! Get back in the warehouse!"

Song Fanping wiped away his tears and patted first Baldy Li's face, then Song Gang's, and said gently, "Now go on home."

Song Fanping stood up, no longer crying. He smiled contentedly at the red-armbanders, then walked heroically toward the front gate.

When he reached the gate he turned around and, his dislocated left elbow still dangling at his side, waved to Baldy Li and Song Gang with his right hand. With that wave he looked so confident and magnanimous, like Chairman Mao waving at the parading masses from atop Tiananmen Square.

CHAPTER 15

YEARS LATER, whenever Baldy Li spoke of his stepfather, he only had one thing to say. Raising his thumb, he would sigh and say, "What a real man."

In that warehouse that was in fact a prison, Song Fanping suffered every torment and abuse imaginable. Yet he never uttered a word of complaint, even as his dislocated left arm became increasingly swollen. He also never stopped writing Li Lan. He had written his first letter on the day of his flag-waving atop the bridge. This was the most glorious moment of his life, so his letter was filled with passion and energy. This was the first time Li Lan, sitting in a hospital bed in Shanghai, had ever received a letter from a man, and what a letter it was! Reading it made her feel as though she had been given a shot of adrenaline. Baldy Li's biological father, who had drowned in the public latrine, had never written her, and for him the height of romance consisted of knocking on her window in the middle of the night, hoping to lure her out to the fields for a romp. So when she received her first letter from Song Fanping, she blushed bright red. And as Song Fanping's letters continued coming one after another, her pulse would race each time she received a new one.

By this point, Song Fanping had been thoroughly beaten down, but in order for Li Lan to feel at ease while receiving her treatment in Shanghai, he continued filling his letters with passion and energy. He didn't tell her what had actually happened but instead described how things were getting better and better, so she believed that he was riding the crest of the red waves of the Cultural Revolution. Even after Song Fanping had his left elbow dislocated, he nevertheless continued, using his right hand to embroider his glorious exploits for her, and Baldy Li and Song Gang would mail the letters off for him. The boys would come to the front gate of the warehouse, and long-haired Sun Wei's father would hand them the letters, which they would then take to the post office. When Song Fanping mailed his own letters, he always pasted the stamp in the top right corner of the envelope. But when Baldy Li and Song Gang mailed them, they didn't know where to

put the stamp. Once they saw someone else place it on the back of the
envelope, so Baldy Li did the same. The next time, when it was Song
Gang's turn, he saw that someone had pasted it over the opening, and
did the same.

By that point Li Lan was no longer able to continue her treatment in
peace. There were struggle sessions every day at the hospital, and one
after another every doctor she knew was brought down. Anxious and
worried, she was desperate to get home. But Song Fanping tried to dis-
suade her, urging her to stay in Shanghai to treat her migraines. Each
day Li Lan spent in Shanghai seemed like an eternity, and she had read
Song Fanping's letters over so many times she knew them by heart—
they were her only source of solace during this period.

She also examined the envelopes many times and noticed that from
a certain day onward, the placement of the stamps kept shifting. One
time it would be on the back of the envelope, and the next it would be
over the opening. And every time she received a letter with a stamp on
the back, she told herself that on the next letter the stamp would be
over the opening.

Baldy Li and Song Gang took turns placing the stamp on the
envelopes and putting the letters in the mailbox. They never went out
of turn. This was the source of Li Lan's uneasiness, and this uneasiness
increased daily. She started to imagine all sorts of scenarios and to suffer from insomnia, and her migraines became more severe. Li Lan,
who typically listened to Song Fanping in all things, for the first time
wrote him a firm letter. She told him that because of the Cultural Revolution there were no longer any doctors around, and therefore she
had resolved to return home.

When Li Lan had taken the bus to Shanghai to get treatment, Song
Fanping had told her that after she was cured, he would come in
person to pick her up. To assuage her uneasiness, Li Lan decided to
test the waters by asking Song Fanping whether he could come meet
her now.

This time Li Lan had to wait more than half a month for a response.
Song Fanping had just been whipped with a belt for more than an
hour, but even in his imprisonment this good man was determined to
keep his word, so without hesitation he promised his wife that he
would go to Shanghai to pick her up. He even set a date and asked her
to wait for him at noon at the front gate of the hospital.

This was the last letter Song Fanping wrote to his wife. It allowed Li Lan to weep tears of relief. And once it was dark, she was able to fall into a deep slumber.

That night Song Fanping escaped from the warehouse. He waited until Sun Wei's father was in the toilet, then quietly slipped out the front gate. By the time he reached home, it was about one in the morning, and Baldy Li and Song Gang had long since fallen asleep. They felt a hand caressing them and a light shining on them. Song Gang woke up first and rubbed his eyes. When he saw Song Fanping sitting by the bed, he let out a cry of delight. Then Baldy Li also woke up, rubbing his eyes. Song Fanping told the boys, "Li Lan is coming home." His wife, their mother, was coming home. Song Fanping said that he was going to catch the first bus to Shanghai to pick her up, and then they would take the afternoon bus back. Song Fanping pointed at the pitch-black darkness outside, saying, "By the time the sun sets tomorrow, we'll be home."

Baldy Li and Song Gang bounced on the bed like two overjoyed monkeys. With a wave, Song Fanping told them to quiet down, pointing in the direction of the neighbors on either side and reminding the boys not to wake them up. Baldy Li and Song Gang immediately covered their mouths and crept down from their bed. Song Fanping looked around at the overturned armoire and the clothes strewn all over the floor. Frowning, he said to the boys, "What if your mother comes home and finds the place looking like a dump and decides to return to Shanghai?"

Baldy Li and Song Gang thought it over and exclaimed, "Cleanup time!"

"Right!" agreed Song Fanping.

Song Fanping walked over to the overturned armoire, squatted down, and raised it with his right arm, then transferred the weight on his shoulder. When he stood up, the armoire was righted. Baldy Li and Song Fanping watched in astonishment. Song Fanping raised up such a huge armoire with just one arm—he hadn't even needed his left arm, which was still dangling there. The boys followed behind Song Fanping or, rather, they followed behind his right arm and tidied up the rest of the house. They helped his right arm pick up all the clothes on the ground; when his right arm swept, they held the dustpan; when his right arm mopped the floor, they took up some rags and wiped down the dust from the tables and chairs. By the time they finished tidying up the house, they heard the cock's crow and saw that the sky had turned as pale as a fish's belly. The boys then sat on the front stoop, watching Song Fanping raise a bucket of well water to bathe himself. As Song Fanping walked back into the house they watched him change into a clean set of clothes using just his right arm. He put on a red sleeveless shirt that had a row of characters across the chest. They couldn't read what it said, but Song Fanping explained that this was his old college basketball uniform. He also put on a pair of beige plastic sandals. These were a present from Li Lan, and he had worn them only once before, on his wedding day.

The boys noticed that Song Fanping's left elbow had thickened, and his left hand was puffy, as if he were wearing a cotton glove. They didn't understand that it was swollen, so they asked him why his left hand was now fatter than his right. Song Fanping replied that it was because his left hand had been resting all this time. "It's just been eating and lazing about, so it's gotten chubby."

Baldy Li and Song Gang now felt that their father was really a deity. He could do all his chores with one arm and let the other one rest to the point that it even grew fat. They asked him, "When will you let your right arm grow fat?"

Song Fanping chuckled. "Oh, it will."

As the sun rose Song Fanping, who had spent a sleepless night, let out a few yawns. He told the boys to get to bed, but they shook their heads and remained seated on the stoop. So Song Fanping simply stepped over them. He was off to catch the early bus in order to meet his wife in Shanghai. As his tall figure passed over the boys' heads they noticed that the morning sun had bathed the room in a red glow. The house was gleaming in its cleanliness, like a newly polished mirror, leading the boys to exclaim, "It's so clean!"

Song Gang turned around and hailed his departing father, "Papa! Come back!"

Song Fanping walked back, his footsteps ringing. Song Gang asked him, "What will Mama say when she sees the place so clean?"

Song Fanping replied, "She'll say, 'I'm not going back to Shanghai.'"

Baldy Li and Song Gang both giggled, and Song Fanping also let out a loud chuckle. He walked toward the morning sun, his feet hitting the ground like hammers paving a road. Once he was a dozen yards away,

Baldy Li and Song Gang saw him pause, reach for his dangling left
hand, and place it into his pants pocket. He then continued walking
forward, his left arm no longer dangling. With one hand in his pocket
and the other swinging freely, he looked like a dashing movie star walking into the rising sun.

CHAPTER 16

WHEN SONG FANPING arrived at the bus depot on the east side of town, he saw a man with a red armband and a wooden bat standing on the platform. When the man saw Song Fanping coming down the bridge, he immediately turned and shouted into the depot waiting room, and five armband-wearing men instantly swarmed out. Song Fanping knew they were there to seize him, but after a moment's hesitation, he walked right up to them. At first he wanted to show them Li Lan's letter, but then he decided to forget it. The armband-wearing men stood on the platform, each holding a wooden bat. Song Fanping removed his left hand from his pocket and walked up to the platform, about to explain that he wasn't running away but, rather, was going to Shanghai to pick up his wife. Several bats rained down on him, and he instinctively raised his right arm to shield himself. A bat smashed down on his right elbow, and he felt a bone-shattering pain. Yet he still waved his right arm to block the bats beating down on him. He walked into the waiting room and up to the ticket window. His right elbow, which he had used to block the wooden bats, felt as if it were about to explode in pain. His shoulders had also suffered countless blows, and one of his ears had been half ripped off. Despite the bats raining down on him and trailing him like a cloud of dust, he finally made it to the ticket counter, where he saw that the eyes of the female ticket seller were bugged out in fear. Miraculously, his dislocated left elbow now rose to block the bats as he thrust his right hand into his pocket and found his bus fare, which he then pushed through the ticket window, telling the ticket seller, "One ticket to Shanghai."

The ticket seller toppled over, passing out in fright. This new development suddenly flummoxed Song Fanping, and his dislocated left arm also dropped. He forgot that his arm had been shielding him from the blows, and in an instant a flurry of bats smashed down on his head. Bleeding and broken, Song Fanping collapsed against the wall as six wooden bats crazily smashed down on him, until one after another they shattered. They were then followed by the red-armbanders' twelve feet, which stomped and kicked him for more than ten minutes, until finally he lay there motionless. Only then did the six men, all out of breath from their exertions, pause to rub their arms and legs and wipe the sweat from their faces. They walked over to the bench under the ceiling fan, completely wiped out. Cocking their heads, they looked at Song Fanping slumped over by the wall and cursed, "Fuck."

It was around daybreak that these red-armbanders from the warehouse that was actually a prison had noticed that Song Fanping was missing. They had immediately split into two groups, with one guarding the bus depot and the other assigned to the docks. The red-armbanders' savage beating of Song Fanping that day terrified everyone, and those who had been in the waiting room all ran outside to the platform. Children wailed and women stood with their mouths hanging open in terror. Everyone stood outside the waiting room door peering in, no one daring to go back inside. Only when the tickets for the Shanghai bus were being collected did people carefully reenter, looking with trepidation at the six red-armbanders resting under the ceiling fan.

Barely conscious, Song Fanping seemed to make out the call to board. Miraculously he managed to rouse himself, standing up by leaning against the wall. He wiped at the blood on his face and hobbled toward the ticket collection window. The row of waiting passengers all gasped. When the six red-armbanders who had been resting under the ceiling fan saw that Song Fanping had gotten up and was making his way to the gate, they looked at each other in astonishment, letting out snorts of disbelief. One of them yelled, "Don't let him get away!"

They took up their splintered bats and rushed up to him, swinging with abandon. This time Song Fanping began to resist. He struck back with his right fist as he made his way to the gate. Terrified, the ticket counter slammed the metal gate shut and ran away. Song Fanping found that he had nowhere to go, so he had no choice but to strike back. By this point he was barely conscious, and the red-armbanders encircled him and pummeled him until he was covered in blood. They chased him from the waiting room to the steps outside. He resisted with all his might, but when he reached the steps, he collapsed. The red-armbanders stood in a circle around him, kicking wildly, and even bayoneting him with their splintered wooden bats. One of the wooden spikes pierced his abdomen, and his entire body convulsed. As the red-armbander pulled the spike out, Song Fanping's body tensed up as blood gushed from his gut, staining the ground red. Then he fell still.

The six red-armbanders were also drained. First they panted heavily as they squatted there, but when they realized they were under the blazing sun, they walked over to the spot under the tree and leaned against the trunk as they wiped their sweat with their shirts. They were convinced that this time Song Fanping wouldn't be able to get up again. But when the long-distance bus started pulling out of the station, he somehow managed to rouse himself and stand up, taking a few unsteady steps. He waved at the departing bus, mumbling, "I . . . haven't . . . boarded . . . yet."

The men rushed up to him again and struck him to the ground. Song Fanping no longer resisted but, rather, began to beg. At this moment, Song Fanping, who never admitted defeat, wanted so badly to live. He mustered up what remained of his strength and knelt. Spitting blood while holding back the blood gushing from his abdomen, he wept as he begged them to spare him. Even his tears flowed red. He took out Li Lan's letter from his pocket and managed to use his disabled left hand to open it, trying to prove that he wasn't running away. Not a single hand reached out to take the letter. He only received more and more kicks, and two more bat fragments pierced his body. As the spikes were yanked out blood gushed from his body as though it were a perforated wineskin.

There were some in Liu Town who personally witnessed this savage assault. Mama Su, whose snack shop was right next to the bus depot, wept a river of tears while she watched. Sounds came from her mouth, though it was hard to make out whether they were sobs or sighs.

Song Fanping was barely breathing. The six red-armbanders discovered they were hungry, so they temporarily left him aside and walked toward Mama Su's snack shop. The men felt as drained as if they had spent a day working on the docks, and when they sat down in the shop, they couldn't muster up the energy to speak. With her head lowered, Mama Su returned to her shop and sat behind the counter, silently watching these six red-armbanders, who were worse than beasts. Once they caught their breath, they asked her for soy milk, buns, and fritters, which they then ate with savage delight.

By then the five red-armbanders who had been guarding the docks arrived. When they learned that Song Fanping had been caught at the depot, they ran over enthusiastically, all drenched in sweat. They aimed their wooden bats at the motionless Song Fanping and beat him wildly until all their bats were broken as well. Then they kicked, trampled, and pummeled him. When the initial six red-armbanders finished their meal and went out of the store, these next five came in to have their breakfast. In all, eleven armband-wearing men took turns tormenting Song Fanping, who by now was no longer moving. Still they kicked at him. At last Mama Su could bear it no longer and said, "He's probably already dead."

Only then did the red-armbanders stop kicking. Wiping at their sweat, they made their victorious exit. All eleven of them had injured themselves from the kicking, so they hobbled as they left. Mama Su watched them limp away, thinking, *They are not human!* She said to herself, *How can people be this vicious?*

CHAPTER 17

MEANWHILE, BALDY LI and Song Gang were home asleep, dreaming of Li Lan's return. When they woke up, they were ecstatic to find that it was almost noon. Although Song Fanping had said that he wouldn't be home until the sun set behind the mountain, the boys couldn't wait a moment longer. At noon they headed toward the bus depot, wanting to be there when the bus carrying Song Fanping and Li Lan pulled into the station. The two boys stepped outside, their left hands thrust in their pockets and their right arms dangling at their sides, in imitation of Song Fanping's cocky gait. Trying hard to look like movie heroes, they walked with a deliberate swagger but came off looking more like simpering villains or Japanese toadies.

Baldy Li and Song Gang spotted Song Fanping the moment they stepped off the bridge. A bloody, mangled body lay across the empty lot in front of the bus depot. A few people stopped as they walked past, peering down and muttering to one another. The two children walked by him as well, not realizing who it was. He lay sprawled on the ground, one arm folded under his body and the other twisted on top; one of his legs stuck straight out and the other was curled up beneath him. Flies buzzed and swarmed all around him. His face, his limbs, his hands and feet—every bloodied bit of flesh was covered in flies. The two children were repulsed and terrified by the sight. Song Gang asked someone wearing a straw hat, "Who is this? Is he dead?"

The man shook his head, saying that he didn't know, and then walked over to a shady tree nearby and began to fan himself with his straw hat. Baldy Li and Song Gang walked up the steps of the station and into the main hall. Though they had stood outside for only a brief while, they felt that they had been parched dry by the fierce summer sun. Two large fans, whirling loudly, hung from the ceiling of the main hall, and everyone inside was gathered under them buzzing in conversation like so many flies. Baldy Li and Song Gang tried hovering at the edges of each group of people, but the breeze from the ceiling fans dissipated before reaching them. It turned out that every spot where a breeze could be felt had been occupied. So they walked up to the ticket window and stood on their tiptoes to peer in. They saw a ticket seller sitting inside, struck dumb and still reeling from the horrors of the morning. Jolted back suddenly by the sound of the boys' conversation, she focused her eyes on them and screeched, "What are you looking at?"

Baldy Li and Song Gang quickly ducked down and crept away. They walked up to the ticket checker's counter. The metal gate of the ticket counter was ajar, so the boys looked inside. Not a single bus was there, only a ticket checker holding his jar of tea. Rushing toward them, he also roared, "What do you want?"

Baldy Li and Song Gang ran away from the ticket counter and listlessly circled the main hall a few times. At this point Popsicle Wang appeared at the main entrance, carrying a small stool in one hand and an icebox full of popsicles on his back. He set his stool down at the station's entranceway, sat down, and started to bang his icebox with a block of wood, shouting, "Popsicles! Popsicles! Popsicles for our working-class brothers and sisters. . . ."

The two boys went up to him and stood there watching him and gulping down their saliva. He kept banging his wood block while keeping a wary eye on the boys. Baldy Li and Song Gang once again caught sight of the body outside, still lying in the same position. Song Gang pointed at him and asked Popsicle Wang, "Who is that?"

Popsicle Wang glanced sideways at the boys but didn't respond. Song Gang persisted, "Is he dead?"

Popsicle Wang snarled at them, "If you don't have any money, then scram. Stop standing here trying to swallow your saliva."

Startled, Baldy Li and Song Gang gripped each other's arms and ran down the station steps until they once again found themselves outside under the fierce summer sun. As they walked past Song Fanping's fly-covered body again, Song Gang suddenly stopped in his tracks and pointed at Song Fanping's beige-colored sandals. "He's wearing Papa's sandals."

Song Gang then noticed Song Fanping's red shirt. "He's wearing Papa's shirt."

The boys stood there, looking at each other. After a while Baldy Li spoke, suggesting that this wasn't Papa's shirt, because his had a row of yellow characters on it. Song Gang nodded, then shook his head, saying that the yellow characters were on the front. The children squatted down, waving away flies and tugging at Song Fanping's shirt. A few yellow characters emerged from their tugging. Song Gang stood up and burst into tears. Sobbing, he asked Baldy Li, "Is this Papa?"

Baldy Li couldn't help sobbing, too. "I don't know."

The two children stood there, weeping and looking about. No one came over. They squatted down again, shooing away the swarms of flies from Song Fanping's face, wanting to take a closer look. Was this Song Fanping? His face was smeared with blood and dirt, so they couldn't really tell. They felt that it looked a little bit like Song Fanping, but they couldn't be sure. Was it him? They got up from the ground and decided that they should ask someone.

First they walked to the spot under the tree where two men were smoking. They pointed at Song Fanping, asking, "Is that our father?"

The two men smoking under the tree froze, then shook their heads. "Don't you know your own father?"

The children walked up the station steps to Popsicle Wang. Wiping away his tears, Song Gang asked him, "Is that our father on the ground over there?"

Popsicle Wang slapped the wood block against his icebox, staring. "Scram!"

Baldy Li complained, "But we're not drooling anymore."

Popsicle Wang replied, "Scram anyway!"

Weeping, Baldy Li and Song Gang walked hand in hand into the main hall and asked the people clustered under the two ceiling fans, "Do any of you know? Is that our father lying on the ground outside?"

Their pathetic questions elicited a roar of laughter. People commented that they couldn't believe there could be such fools as these two, who didn't even know their own father and had to ask others. Grinning, one of the people waved the children over. "Hey, kids, come over here."

The boys walked up to the man, who looked down at them and asked, "Do you know who my father is?"

The children shook their heads, and the man asked again, "Then who *would* know who my father is?"

The children thought this over and replied, "You would."

"Go away, then." The man dismissed them with a wave of his hand. "Go identify your own father."

Weeping and still grasping each other's hands, the children walked out of the station and down the steps and approached Song Fanping's prone body. Song Gang sobbed, "We do know our own father. But this man's face is covered in blood, so we really can't make it out."

The boys went into the snack shop next to the station. Inside there was only Mama Su, wiping the tables. They were a little fearful and stood at the door, hesitating. Song Gang whispered, "We'd like to ask you something but don't want you to get angry."

Mama Su saw two weeping boys standing at her door, took a look at Baldy Li and Song Gang's clothes, and asked, "You're not beggars, are you?"

"No." Song Gang pointed at Song Fanping lying on the ground outside. "We'd just like to ask you, is that our father?"

Mama Su put down the rag she was holding. She now recognized Baldy Li. This was the little hoodlum who had been going around rubbing himself on all the wooden electrical poles, exclaiming that he was in heat. Mama Su gave Baldy Li a look and then asked Song Gang, "What is your father's name?"

Song Gang replied, "His name is Song Fanping."

The children then heard her gasp and wail, saying something like "Oh God," "Dear mother," or "My ancestors!" When she paused to catch her breath, she panted to Song Gang, "He's been lying there for more than half a day. I thought that everyone in his family was dead."

The two children didn't know what she was talking about. Song Gang persisted, "Is he our father?"

Mama Su wiped at the sweat on her forehead. "His name was Song Fanping."

Song Gang immediately started howling, turning to Baldy Li. "I just *knew* he was Papa. That's why I started crying the moment I saw him."

Baldy Li also burst into tears. "That's why I started crying, too."

The children began to screech and wail in the summer heat. They once again approached Song Fanping's body, their sharp wails scaring off even the swarms of flies. Song Gang knelt down to the ground, as did Baldy Li. They leaned in close to take a good look at Song Fanping. The sun had dried up the blood on his face. Song Gang peeled off the caked-up blood and finally saw his own father clearly. He turned and clutched Baldy Li's hand. "This is Papa."

Nodding, Baldy Li wailed, "This is Papa. . . ."

The two children knelt on the ground in front of the bus depot and wept loudly. Their mouths agape, they sobbed toward the sky, their wails ascending into the heavens. But like broken wings their cries would suddenly plummet to earth as the children wept open-mouthed, soundless, tears and snivel having closed up their throats. With great effort they swallowed all of it down, and again their wailing exploded. They tugged at Song Fanping's body and wept, "Papa, Papa, Papa . . ."

Song Fanping gave no response, and the children were at a loss as to what to do. Baldy Li wailed to Song Gang, "He was still fine this morning. Why is he deaf and dumb now?"

Song Gang looked toward the crowds that had gathered around them and cried, "Save my father!"

Snot and tears flowed down the children's faces. Song Gang wiped some from his face and hurled it away, accidentally hitting the pants leg of one of the spectators, who immediately grabbed Song Gang by the collar and started swearing at him. Baldy Li wiped the mucus from his face and splashed the man's sandals. The man then grabbed Baldy Li by the hair and, with one boy in each hand, thrust both of them to the ground, demanding that they use their shirts to clean up the mess they had made. Still weeping, Baldy Li and Song Gang began to use their hands to wipe up the man's pants and sandals but ended up smearing him with even more tears and snot. The man, initially furious, became merely annoyed, and said, "Quit it! Damn. Just stop wiping."

But Baldy Li and Song Gang held on to the man's legs, as if they had finally found a savior and were clinging to him for dear life. As the man backed away the boys hung on, crawling forward on their knees. They begged him, "Save our father! Please, save our father!"

The man pushed them away and raised his foot to kick them off of him, but they still clung on. After dragging the children a dozen yards, he found them still clutching him, beseeching. The man, now out of breath, stood there wiping away his sweat. He complained to the crowd, "Look at this! My pants, my sandals, my socks. What the fuck is this?"

Mama Su from the snack shop walked over and stood in front of the gathered crowd. The wailing of the children had reddened her eyes. "They're just kids."

Furious, the man responded, "What do you mean *kids*? They're two little fucking demons."

"Then do a good deed," Mama Su responded, "and help these two little demons collect their father's body."

"What?" the man roared. "You want me to carry that filthy, stinking corpse?"

Wiping her eyes, Mama Su replied, "I didn't say you needed to carry the body yourself. I have a cart here that I can lend you."

Mama Su went back to her snack shop and returned with a cart. On behalf of the two children, she begged the bystanders to help lift Song Fanping onto the cart. The crowd started dispersing, and Mama Su, losing her temper, singled out a few of them for the task: "You, you, you, and you."

Mama Su pointed at Song Fanping lying on the ground. "No matter whether this was a good man or not, now that he's dead, we have to bury him. We can't just leave him lying here."

Finally four people walked out of the crowd and squatted down, grabbing hold of Song Fanping's arms and legs. Shouting "One, two, three," they hoisted him up. All four were red in the face from the exertion, remarking that the dead man was as heavy and cumbersome as an elephant. They placed Song Fanping next to the cart, and, with another "One, two, three," they heaved him onto it, as it creaked under the weight of his large frame. The men dusted off their hands. One of them raised his to his nose, sniffed, and told Mama Su, "We want to go wash our hands in your shop."

"Then go." She nodded. She turned to the man who was still being grasped by Baldy Li and Song Gang. "Do some good, and take their father home for them."

Looking down at Baldy Li and Song Gang, he grimaced. "Looks like I've got to haul the dead man away."

He yelled at Baldy Li and Song Gang, "Let the fuck go of me!"

Only then did Baldy Li and Song Gang finally loosen their grips. They got up from the ground and followed the man to the front of the cart. Hoisting the end of the cart, the man barked at them, "Quick! Where's home?"

Song Gang furiously shook his head. He pleaded, "Take him to the hospital."

"Fuck." The man threw down the cart. "He's already dead. What fucking hospital would we go to?"

Song Gang didn't believe him and turned to Mama Su. "Is my father dead?"

Mama Su nodded. "He's dead. Go home, child."

This time Song Gang no longer wailed but, rather, bowed his head and quietly wept. Baldy Li also bowed his head and wept as they heard Mama Su tell the man pulling the cart, "You will be rewarded in the next life."

The man took up the cart and walked on ahead, snarling, "Fucking reward, yeah. Eighteen generations of my descendants are now going to be cursed along with me, is more like it."

So that was the afternoon Baldy Li and Song Gang held each other's hands and walked home, weeping, with a bloodied and battered Song Fanping lying on the cart behind them. The children wept until their hearts broke. They stumbled along, weeping and sobbing, until they choked up, but after a while their wails exploded again like grenades. Their wailing overpowered the revolutionary singing and slogan-shouting on the streets. Like the flies that had earlier swarmed around Song Fanping, the parading crowds and assorted idlers all came swarming up to them, crowding around the cart as it trudged forward. The man pulling the cart scolded Baldy Li and Song Gang, "Quit your crying! You've brought the whole damn town over. Now everyone is watching me pull this corpse."

A good number of people came over to ask who it was lying there dead on the cart. At least forty or fifty people approached the man pulling the cart, putting him in an even fouler mood. At first he responded that the dead man was named Song Fanping and was a teacher at the middle school. But as more and more spectators continued to inquire, he got tired of explaining and instead told them to use their eyes and figure it out for themselves: Whoever is crying nonstop must be the relatives of the deceased. After a while he felt that even saying this much was too exhausting, so when another person asked him, he simply said, "Don't know."

The man was drenched in sweat from pulling the cart under the fierce sun. Plus, he was pulling a cart with a dead man, and on top of that his lips were parched from answering so many questions. He was, therefore, seething when an acquaintance came up and asked him, "Hey, which of your relatives has died?"

The man pulling the cart exploded: "You're the one with the dead relative!"

The acquaintance was stunned. "What?"

He yelled again, "You're the one with the dead relative!"

Now the acquaintance's face turned black. Without a word he stripped off his shirt, revealing all his muscles, and raised his right hand to point at the man pulling the cart. "What the fuck did you say? Say it again and I'll have you lying on the cart, too."

He added, quite pleased with himself, "I'll turn this flatbed into a double bed."

The man pulling the cart threw it down and retorted, "Well, it'd be a double bed for your bedroom!"

He walked right up to the other man and screamed in his face, "You fucking listen well this time—I said every last person in your family is lying there dead!"

The other man threw a fist right into the cart puller's mouth. The cart puller staggered back a few steps, and just as he managed to steady himself, the other man followed with a kick that landed him onto the ground. He then leapt on top of the cart puller and started punching him in the face.

Baldy Li and Song Gang were still wailing as they trudged along, but when they turned around, they saw that the cart puller was crushed under another man and getting pummeled. Song Gang immediately pounced on the two men, followed by Baldy Li. The boys attacked like two wild dogs, biting the other man's legs and shoulders. The man started howling, kicking his legs and flailing his arms to throw off the two boys. When he got up, the boys pounced on him again. Song Gang had the man's elbow between his teeth, Baldy Li bit down on his waist, and together they ripped his clothes and tore his flesh. The man grabbed the boys by their hair and punched their faces, but they clung on like death itself and refused to let go. They landed wild bites all over his body, reducing this man, who was as big and strong as Song Fanping had been, to a squealing mess, like a pig at slaughter. The mêlée ended when the cart puller got up and went over to pull Baldy Li and Song Gang back, saying, "That's enough."

Only then did Baldy Li and Song Gang loosen their jaws. The other man, soaked in blood, was petrified by the boys' attack, and he stood there, staring like an idiot, as they went on their way.

They continued their journey, the boys covered in wounds and the man's face drenched in blood. People kept approaching them, though the two boys didn't dare cry anymore and the cart puller no longer said a word. As they walked the two children kept turning back to take careful looks at the man pulling the cart. When they saw that blood was mingling with the sweat dripping down his face, Song Gang pulled his shirt off over his head and passed it to him, saying, "Uncle, please wipe your sweat."

The cart puller shook his head. "No need."

Song Gang walked alongside him for a bit, holding his shirt in his hands. Then he asked, "Uncle, are you thirsty?"

The cart puller continued in silence, with his head down. Song Gang asked, "Uncle, I have money. I'll go buy you a popsicle."

The cart puller shook his head again, saying, "No need. When I'm thirsty, I just swallow my saliva."

Wordlessly the three of them headed home. For some time now Baldy Li and Song Gang had held back their tears. Song Gang would continually turn back solicitously to ask after the cart puller, but every time he did so, he would see his dead father and start weeping again. Baldy Li too was infected by his tears, though neither child dared sob out loud for fear of being scolded by the cart puller. Therefore they muffled their cries by covering their mouths, and no sound came from the cart puller behind them either. When they were almost home, they heard him speak again, his voice suddenly kind: "Stop crying, you're making my eyes red."

A dozen or so people had followed them all the way to their front door. They all stood by, but when the cart puller looked at them and asked if they could help lift Song Fanping, they remained silent. The cart puller didn't speak to them again and let Baldy Li and Song Gang help him. He told the boys to hold down the handles of the cart so that it would not tilt up on one end. Then he reached under Song Fanping's armpits and dragged the body off the cart, into the house, and onto the bed in the inner room. The cart puller was half a head shorter than Song Fanping, and dragging him was like dragging an overgrown tree. The cart puller's head drooped from exhaustion, and he wheezed like an accordion. After he had dragged Song Fanping onto the bed, the man walked out and sat down on a bench for a very long time, head bent and breathing hard. Baldy Li and Song Gang stood to one side, not daring to say a word. After he caught his breath, the man looked about him and saw people still standing outside the door. He asked Baldy Li and Song Gang, "Who else do you have?"

The children replied that they still had a mother, who was about to return from Shanghai. The man nodded and said that he felt better knowing that. He waved the boys over right in front of him, patted them on the shoulders, and asked, "You've heard of Red Flag Alley?"

The children nodded and said that they had. He continued, "I live at the front of the alley. My surname's Tao, and my full name is Tao Qing. If you need anything, come over to Red Flag Alley to look for me."

He stood up and walked to the door. The spectators outside immediately stepped aside, afraid of brushing against the man who had just embraced a dead man. Song Gang and Baldy Li followed him outside. When Tao lifted the cart, Song Gang said in imitation of Mama Su, "You will be rewarded in the next life."

The man nodded and left. Baldy Li and Song Gang saw him lift his hand to wipe his eyes.

That afternoon Baldy Li and Song Gang stayed at the dead Song Fanping's side. Song Fanping's flesh was shredded and streaked with dried blood, and the children were terrified by his appearance. His body was motionless, his gaping mouth was motionless, his eyes were wide open, and the pupils within were two dull little pebbles without a hint of light. Baldy Li and Song Gang had wept, wailed, and even bit, and now they started to tremble.

The brothers could see the heads and bodies of people hovering outside their window and hear the buzz of their conversation. Those people were discussing what kind of man Song Fanping was and how he had died. When someone mentioned how pitiful these two kids were, Song Gang let out a few sobs, followed by Baldy Li, and then both boys continued to gaze out fearfully. They also heard the buzz of the countless flies that had descended onto Song Fanping's corpse. The flies multiplied, swarming around the room like flurries of black snowflakes, to the point that their buzzing even drowned out the talk outside. Flies began to bite Baldy Li and Song Gang, as well as the people outside peering in—the children could hear the slapping of hands on limbs, faces, and chests. The spectators cursed as they left, having been driven away by the flies.

The light in the room began to glow red. The two children walked outside their house, and seeing that the sun was going down, they remembered that Song Fanping had promised he and Li Lan would be home by sunset. Baldy Li and Song Gang held each other's hand and headed once again for the bus depot. When they passed the snack shop next to the station, they saw Mama Su seated inside. Song Gang explained to her, "We're here to wait for our mother. She's returning from Shanghai."

The two children walked to the part of the station where the buses pulled in. They stood on tiptoe and craned their necks in the direction of the highway. At the far edge of the horizon, beyond the fields, a cloud of dust was rolling in. They could make out that it was a bus headed their way and could hear the blare of the bus's horn. Song Gang turned to Baldy Li and said, "Mama's back."

Song Gang's face was drenched in tears, while Baldy Li's had flowed down his neck. The bus moved toward them in a cloud of dust that enveloped and blinded them. Once the dust had dispersed, they saw passengers carrying bags and suitcases emerging from the depot. First a handful of people, then an entire line filed past the two boys, but Baldy Li and Song Gang did not see Li Lan. They waited until the last person emerged from the depot, but they still did not see their mother walk out the door.

Song Gang timidly approached the last passenger. "Is this the bus from Shanghai?"

The man nodded. He looked at the boys' tear-streaked faces and asked, "Whose children are you? Why are you standing here?"

His questions brought forth a torrent of tears from both Baldy Li and Song Gang. Startled, he grabbed his luggage and hurried away, repeatedly glancing back curiously at the two children. The boys cried after him, "We are Song Fanping's kids. Song Fanping is dead. Now we're waiting for Li Lan to come home. Li Lan is our mother. . . ."

Without waiting for the children to finish, the man had already walked far away. Baldy Li and Song Gang continued to wait at the entrance to the station, thinking that perhaps Li Lan would be on the next bus. They stood there for a long time, until the big wooden door of the main hall was shuttered and the heavy metal gate of the bus depot was locked up. They still stood there, waiting for their mother to come home from Shanghai.

Night fell, and Mama Su from the snack shop walked over to them. She stuffed two meat buns in their hands, saying, "Eat them while they're hot."

The boys ate the buns and heard Mama Su tell them, "There are no more buses coming in today, and the door of the station has already been shut. Run home now; you can come back tomorrow."

The children trusted Mama Su. They nodded, eating their buns and wiping away their tears, and then went home. As they were leaving they heard Mama Su say with a sigh, "Poor children. . . ."

Song Gang stopped, turned to Mama Su, and said, "You will be rewarded in the next life."

CHAPTER 18

AT THE CRACK of dawn, Li Lan was waiting at the front gate of the hospital. Though in his letter Song Fanping had said that he would not reach Shanghai until noon, after two months' absence the fierce wave of longing that Li Lan felt for him led her to wake up before dawn and sit on her bed, waiting for daybreak. A roommate, who had awakened in the middle of the night from postoperative pain, was so startled by the sight of the motionless, ghostlike Li Lan that she let out a scream that almost ripped open her new stitches. When she realized that it was Li Lan sitting on the bed, the patient resumed her moans of pain. Li Lan felt deeply sorry. After gently muttering a string of apologies, she picked up her travel bag, walked out of the room, and made her way to the hospital's front gate. The street was dark and empty, and the solitary Li Lan stood there with her solitary travel bag—two silent, dark shadows cast on the hospital gate. This time it was the guard's turn to be startled. The old guard with the enlarged prostate gland had awakened needing to pee and walked outside. When he saw the two dark shadows, he shuddered and wet himself, hollering, "Who's there?"

Li Lan told him who she was, what her room number was, that she was leaving today, and that her husband was coming to pick her up. Still unnerved, the old guard pointed at the other dark shadow and demanded, "Who's that?"

Li Lan lifted her bag. "It's a travel bag."

Only then did the old man relax. He circled behind the shack and pissed out the remaining urine, all the while complaining, "Scared me to death, made me fucking wet my pants. . . ."

When Li Lan heard his complaints, she remorsefully lifted her travel bag and walked through the gate and down the street to the corner. She stood next to a big wooden electrical pole and listened to the humming of the current while gazing back at the darkened gate. At this moment Li Lan suddenly felt at peace. While sitting on her bed in the room, she had felt she was waiting for daybreak; but now as she stood at the street corner she felt she was waiting for Song Fanping. In her imagination she could already see his tall, strong figure walking over, filled with passion.

Li Lan—standing there the whole time, her small, frail figure motionless in the dark—was a frightful sight. A few men walking down the street didn't notice her until they were only a few yards away. Seeing her, they jumped in surprise and immediately crossed to the other side of the street, all the while casting backward glances at her. Another man bumped into her as he was rounding the corner and was so startled he trembled all over, but then he feigned calm as he walked around her. As he walked away his shoulders were still ashudder, leading Li Lan to let out a soft chuckle. It was this eerie sound, emanating as if from a female ghost, that thoroughly undid the man, who then took off in a wild sprint.

Only when rays of sunlight illuminated the entire street did Li Lan stop resembling a ghost. She still stood at the street corner, but now she was becoming human. As the street grew busier Li Lan took up her bag and walked back to the hospital's front gate. Now her waiting had officially begun.

The entire morning, Li Lan's face was red with emotion. Along the street in front of her there was a sea of red flags and a din of slogans and chants. The parading crowds seemed interminable, heating up the already scorching summer day. The front-gate guard now recognized Li Lan and spent all the morning curiously observing this woman who had frightened him into wetting his pants. He saw that she sought out each member of the parading crowds—which is to say, every person who walked by—with a look of great anticipation. Li Lan's excitement was like a little stream flowing into the river, her eyes anxiously searching for Song Fanping amid the crowds. The guard watched her as she stood there for a long, long time, examining the crowds and wondering why no one had come to pick her up yet. So he walked over to her and asked, "When is your husband coming?"

Li Lan turned to answer. "At noon."

When the guard heard this, he returned to his post in disbelief. Glancing up at the clock on his wall, he saw that it was not yet 10 A.M. He thought to himself, *There really are all sorts of people in this world! This woman's been standing here waiting since before dawn for a man who is supposed to arrive at noon.* The guard regarded Li Lan again curiously, thinking, *So, how long has this woman gone without a man?* He couldn't resist going up to her and asking, "How long have you been parted from your husband?" Li Lan told him that it had been more than two months. The guard chuckled to himself: *So just two months and she's champing at the bit like this. She might look all frail and shriveled, but obviously in her bones she is quite the wanton hussy.*

By this time Li Lan had been waiting there for more than six hours. She had not had a drop to drink nor a bite to eat, but her face was still beaming with emotion. As noon approached, her excitement reached a fever pitch, her gaze like a nail piercing the bodies of each of the men walking by. Several times when she saw someone with a figure similar to Song Fanping's, she stood on her toes and waved as her eyes filled with tears. Though the joy was always short-lived, she remained undaunted.

Noon came and went, and Song Fanping never appeared. But Song Fanping's sister hurried over. Drenched in sweat, she emerged from a crowded bus and rushed to the hospital's front gate. When she spotted Li Lan, she excitedly shouted, "Aiya, you're still here."

Song Fanping's sister mopped her brow and prattled on. She said that all the way there she had been so worried she wouldn't make it in time that she had almost taken a bus directly to the depot, but it was a good thing she hadn't. As she spoke she handed Li Lan a bag of White Rabbit milk candies, saying that they were for the kids. Li Lan took the candy and placed it in her bag. She didn't say a single word, only smiled and nodded, all the while glancing out at the streams of people. Song Fanping's sister started watching the men on the street along with her but felt perplexed by her brother's absence and, pointing at her watch, said, "He should be here, it's almost one P.M."

The two women stood at the front gate of the hospital for about half an hour. Song Fanping's sister said that she couldn't wait any longer and had to rush back to work. Before leaving, she comforted Li Lan, speculating that Song Fanping must have gotten stuck in traffic. She noted that it took three transfers from the bus depot to the hospital, and since the streets were filled with demonstrators, traffic was a mess. As a result, it was hard for a person to squeeze through, let alone an entire bus. Song Fanping's sister hurried away but immediately rushed back to tell Li Lan, "If you don't make the afternoon bus, just come stay at my place."

Li Lan continued waiting at the hospital gate. She believed what Song Fanping's sister said, that Song Fanping was probably stuck in traffic, and she continued to watch the men on the street with passion and anticipation. She became increasingly fatigued. Faint with hunger, she sat down on the steps of the guardroom, her body leaning against the door frame; but her head was still held high, and her eyes were still watching intently. The old man in the guardroom glanced at the clock on the wall and said, "You've been here since before dawn, and now it's already past two. I haven't seen you eat or drink anything all day. Won't you go get yourself something?"

Li Lan smiled. "I'm fine."

The old man continued, "Go buy something to eat. There's a snack shop about twenty yards from here, just down to the right."

Li Lan shook her head. "What if he comes while I'm gone?"

The old man said, "I'll keep an eye out for him. Tell me, what does he look like?"

Li Lan thought for a bit, then shook her head. "I'd better stay here and wait for him myself."

The two of them fell silent. The old man returned to his post, where there was always someone at the window asking about something or other. Li Lan continued to sit on the steps, watching everyone who passed by. Finally, the old man got up and walked over to Li Lan, saying, "Let me get you something to eat."

Li Lan started. The old man repeated himself and extended Li Lan his hand. She now understood and hurriedly reached into her pockets for money and grain coupons. The old man asked her, "What would you like? Steamed buns? With meat or bean filling? How about a bowl of wonton soup?"

Li Lan handed over her money and grain coupons. "Two plain buns would be fine."

The old man took the money. "You're so frugal."

He walked away from the gate, then turned around. "Don't let anyone into the guardroom. Everything inside belongs to the nation."

Li Lan nodded. "I know."

At about half past three in the afternoon, Li Lan finally had something to eat. She slowly ripped off chunk after chunk of bun and placed them in her mouth, methodically chewing and swallowing. She hadn't had any water all day, so eating was difficult, like gulping down bitter medicine. When the old man saw this, he handed her his teacup. Li Lan raised the tea-stained cup and slowly sipped from it. She finished one bun, then wrapped up the other one and placed it in her travel bag. After having the bun, Li Lan felt herself regaining some of her strength. She stood up and said to the old man in the guardroom, "The bus he was taking would have arrived in Shanghai by eleven A.M. Even if he were walking, he should have been here by now."

The old man agreed. "Even if he were crawling, he still should have gotten here by now."

Li Lan surmised that Song Fanping must have taken the afternoon bus. She wondered if some important matter had delayed him. She felt that she should go to the bus depot herself, since the afternoon bus got into Shanghai at 5 P.M. Li Lan gave the old man a careful description of Song Fanping, adding that if Song did arrive, to please tell him that she had gone to the bus depot. The old man told her not to worry, that he would ask every tall man who came by whether he was Song Fanping.

Li Lan took up her travel bag and walked out the hospital gate. She stood for a while at the bus stop, but then returned to the guard window. When the old man saw her, he asked, "How come you're back?"

Li Lan replied, "I forgot to mention something."

The old man asked, "What?"

Li Lan looked into his eyes and said solemnly, "Thank you, you are a good man."

Small and frail, Li Lan carried her heavy travel bag and squeezed onto the bus. She swayed along with the crowd inside and was dizzied by the foul stench of armpits and feet and mouths. Then she squeezed off the bus, only to squeeze onto another one, finally arriving at the depot after three bus transfers. By then it was almost five. She stood at the station's exit, rays of sunset bathing her in a reddish glow as she watched bus after bus pull into the station and group after group of travelers emerge from the platform. Her face was once again red with excitement and her spirits were high, because she knew that when one of the passengers emerged a head taller than the rest, that man would be Song Fanping. So she set her gaze at the tops of the travelers' heads, still firmly believing that Song Fanping would walk out through the exit. The very possibility of an accident had not even crossed her mind.

At this moment Baldy Li and Song Gang were waiting for her at the bus depot back in Liu Town. As the gates of the Liu Town bus depot were closing, the gates of the Shanghai depot were also shut. As Baldy Li and Song Gang made their way home, eating the buns that Mama Su had given them, Li Lan was still waiting by the exit at the Shanghai bus depot. The sky began to darken, but Li Lan still did not see Song Fanping's tall figure. When the heavy metal gates of the bus depot were shut, she felt as if her brain had been drained of all content, and she just stood there, barely conscious.

Li Lan passed the night outside the door of the waiting room. She considered going to stay with Song Fanping's sister, but Song Fanping's sister hadn't given her the address, since neither of them expected that Song Fanping would fail to arrive in Shanghai. The sister assumed that as long as Song Fanping himself knew the address, that would be enough. Therefore Li Lan slept on the ground like a homeless beggar. Mosquitoes stung her throughout this summer night, but she did not notice as she drifted fitfully in and out of sleep.

In the latter half of the night a crazy woman came to keep Li Lan company. First the woman sat by her side, carefully examining her, cackling all the while. Li Lan, wakened by her eerie laugh, let out a gasp when she made out the filthy face and figure of the crazy woman by the glow of the streetlight. In response, the crazy woman let out a shriller, louder cry, as if Li Lan had frightened her. Then she sat down as if nothing had happened and continued gazing at Li Lan, cackling.

Li Lan was still recovering from her initial fright when the crazy woman started to hum a tune. As she hummed she also muttered, her voice popping like a machine gun. Li Lan was no longer scared. Though she could not make out what the crazy woman was saying, the continual din of a human voice actually put her at ease. With a faint smile, Li Lan fell back to sleep.

After some time had passed, Li Lan in her dreams heard the sounds of palms slapping. She raised her sleep-heavy lids to see the crazy woman, sitting by her side, flapping her arms to shoo away the mosquitoes, and sometimes slapping at them. The crazy woman repeatedly slapped her hands together, then carefully scraped the mosquitoes from her palms and put them in her mouth, chuckling as she gulped them down. Her actions reminded Li Lan of the steamed bun in her bag, so she sat up, took out the bun, and broke off half for the crazy woman.

Li Lan extended the bun almost directly to the woman's face, but she ignored it. She cackled as she slapped at the mosquitoes and placed them into her mouth. Her raised arm tiring, Li Lan was about to put it down when the woman suddenly snatched away the half bun. Then the woman immediately stood up and walked down the waiting room's steps, moaning and muttering and acting as if she was looking for something. She took a few steps south, then a few steps north, and finally raised the bun in her hand and proceeded east. As the crazy woman walked farther away, Li Lan was finally able to make out what she was saying: "Brother, brother . . ."

Li Lan was now alone again under the dim streetlight. She sat and slowly ate her bun, feeling hollow inside. As she finished, the streetlight suddenly went out, and when she looked up, she saw the first rays of daybreak. It was at that moment that her tears finally gushed forth.

Li Lan boarded the early bus. As the bus pulled out of the station she turned around, still scanning the streets outside in hopes of catching sight of Song Fanping. Only when the bus left Shanghai and the landscape outside her window had turned into fields did Li Lan close her eyes. She rested her head on the window frame and dozed off despite the bumpiness of the drive. During that three-hour journey, Li Lan repeatedly drifted in and out of sleep, and images of those envelopes floated into her mind. Why were the stamps always placed in different spots? Her earlier suspicions resurfaced and grew stronger and stronger. She knew that Song Fanping was a man of his word, and if he said that he would come pick her up in Shanghai, then he would do so at all costs. If he hadn't come, then something must have happened. This train of thought caused her heart to shudder. As the bus neared Liu Town and the landscape outside her window grew increasingly familiar, Li Lan's uneasy premonitions grew stronger and stronger. By now she was convinced that something terrible must have happened. Her whole body shook as she buried her face in her hands, and she didn't dare think more concretely. She felt that she was falling apart as tears streamed from her eyes.

When the bus pulled into the Liu Town depot, Li Lan, carrying her gray travel bag with SHANGHAI printed on the side, was the last to emerge. She followed behind the crowds, her limbs feeling as heavy as lead. Every step took her closer to bad news. When she dragged herself outside of the station, only to be greeted by two wailing boys who were as filthy as if they had been fished from a garbage dump, Li Lan knew that her terrible premonitions had proven true. Her eyes grew dark, and she dropped the travel bag to the ground. The two filthy boys were Baldy Li and Song Gang, and they were wailing, "Papa's dead!"

CHAPTER 19

LI LAN stood motionless as Baldy Li and Song Gang wailed over and over again, "Papa's dead!" She stood planted on the spot, as if her soul had left her body. In this moment of brilliant noon sunshine, she could see only darkness. It was as if she suddenly became both blind and deaf. Li Lan stood there, rigid and corpselike, for more than ten minutes before everything finally came back into focus and she could again make out the two boys crying and wailing in front of her. She could now clearly see the bus depot, the men and women walking by, and Baldy Li and Song Gang. The boys' faces were covered in snot and tears, and they tugged at her clothes, crying, "Papa's dead."

Li Lan nodded her head lightly. "I know."

She looked down at her travel bag. When she bent to pick it up, she suddenly keeled over, bringing down with her Baldy Li and Song Gang. She helped the boys up and got up herself by leaning on the bag, but when she bent down once again to pick it up, her legs again gave out from under her and she knelt down on the ground, trembling all over. Baldy Li and Song Gang watched her, terrified, and reached down to nudge her, calling out over and over again, "Mama, Mama . . ."

Li Lan got up by leaning on the boys' shoulders. She let out a long sigh, then picked up her travel bag and stumbled forward. The noon sun was making her dizzy, making her wobble unsteadily. The empty lot in front of the bus depot was still streaked with Song Fanping's blood, and a few dozen dead flies dotted the blood-darkened earth. Song Gang pointed at the blood and told Li Lan, "This is where Papa died."

The children had stopped weeping, but when Song Gang said this, he again burst into tears, and Baldy Li couldn't help but cry as well. Li Lan's travel bag again dropped to the ground. She looked down at the blood that had already turned dark, then looked around, and finally looked at the two boys, her gaze blurring as her eyes filled with tears. She knelt down, opened her bag, and took out a piece of clothing to spread on the ground. Then she carefully brushed off the flies and scooped up the dark crimson dirt into the shirt, kneeling there until she had gathered every last speck of dirt that had been stained by the blood. Even then she continued to kneel, sifting the dirt through her fingers as if she were searching for gold, still looking for the last traces of Song Fanping's blood.

She knelt there for a very long time. A large crowd gathered around, watching and discussing her. Some knew her and others did not; some of them spoke of Song Fanping, about how he had been beaten to death. The details they mentioned were ones Baldy Li and Song Gang had not known about: how the men smashed wooden bats over Song Fanping's head and kicked him in the chest, and how they stabbed his abdomen with the splintered bats. With every sentence Baldy Li and Song Gang shrieked and wept. Li Lan heard too, and her body shuddered with each new revelation. She raised her head a few times, but each time she glimpsed those who were speaking, she would lower her head again and continue gathering up Song Fanping's traces. Finally Mama Su walked over from her snack shop to scold the bystanders, saying, "Stop talking! How can you talk about these things in front of his wife and kids? And you call yourself human!"

Then she turned to Li Lan. "Why don't you take the kids home?"

Li Lan nodded. She knotted the shirt filled with dark crimson earth and placed it in her bag. It was already afternoon. Li Lan walked ahead with her heavy travel bag, and Baldy Li and Song Gang walked hand in hand behind her. The boys saw that her shoulder sloped from the weight.

All the way home Li Lan did not weep or wail but only stumbled forward. She paused to rest a few times, due to the weight of her bag, whereupon she would look back on the two boys without saying a word. They no longer wept or spoke. When an acquaintance called out her name, she would only nod her head slightly.

Li Lan walked silently back to her home. As she entered, the sight of Song Fanping's badly mutilated body on their bed caused her to keel over, but she immediately got back up. She still didn't cry but only stood shaking her head. She reached out to gently touch Song Fanping's face but then pulled her hand away in a panic, as if worried that she was hurting him. Her hand hung in the air for a moment before she started to comb a few dead flies out of his matted hair. With her right hand she slowly removed all the dead flies from Song Fanping's corpse and placed them in the palm of her left. All afternoon Li Lan stood by the bed, picking flies from the body. Several neighbors looked in from the window, and a couple of them came in to speak with her. Li Lan remained silent, only nodding or shaking her head in response to their questions. After they left, she closed the windows and door, and it wasn't until nightfall, when she was satisfied that there were no more flies on Song Fanping's body, that she finally sat down on the bed and looked out at the reflection of the sunset on their window.

Baldy Li and Song Gang had not eaten anything all day. They stood by Li Lan sobbing, but it was a very long time before Li Lan realized they were there. She turned to them and said in a low voice, "Don't cry. Don't let others hear us cry."

The boys immediately covered their mouths. Baldy Li added timidly, "We are hungry."

As if suddenly waking from a dream, Li Lan gave them money and grain coupons and told them to go buy themselves something to eat. When the boys left, they saw that she was once again sitting dully by the bed. They bought three buns, and Baldy Li and Song Gang ate theirs as they walked home. They found Li Lan still sitting on the edge of the bed, and when they handed her the third bun, she merely stared at it and asked distractedly, "What is this?"

Baldy Li and Song Gang replied, "A bun."

Li Lan nodded, appearing to understand, and then took a bite out of the bun and slowly chewed. Baldy Li and Song Gang watched her until she finished the bun. Then she said, "Let's go to sleep."

That night, as the boys lay dreaming, they sensed that someone kept walking in and out of the house, and they could also make out the sounds of pouring water. It was Li Lan, going again and again to draw water from the well. She carefully cleaned Song Fanping's corpse and changed him into clean clothes. The children did not know how the small, frail Li Lan managed to change the clothes on Song Fanping's massive body, or whether she got any sleep. The next day, after Li Lan left, Baldy Li and Song Gang discovered that Song Fanping was as neat and tidy as a groom. Even the sheets beneath him had been changed, though his scrubbed face was a mass of green and purple blotches.

Song Fanping's corpse lay on the near side of the bed. The pillow on the far side had a few strands of Li Lan's hair, and a few more were dangling from Song Fanping's neck. Li Lan must have spent the night cradled on Song Fanping's chest. This was to be the last night she spent with Song Fanping. The bloodied clothes and sheets were soaking in the wooden tub under the bed, and floating on top of the water were a few flies that had wedged themselves in the crevices of his clothing.

All night Li Lan had wept. As she wiped down Song Fanping's body, she shuddered over his bruises and wounds. Several times she almost burst out into terrible wails, but each time she managed to swallow her sobs and would bravely rouse herself, though the effort almost made her faint. Her lips bled from biting down on them. No one could imagine how she survived that night, how she reined herself in and managed not to go insane. Afterward, she lay down on the bed and placed her head on Song Fanping's chest, falling into a state that was not so much sleep as a long, pitch-black unconsciousness. Only when the sun's rays pierced the room did she rouse herself once again from the terrible pit of her pain.

Li Lan, her eyes bloodshot and puffy, left the house to go to the coffin shop, bringing with her all the money that she had in the house. She wanted to buy her husband the best coffin, but she didn't have enough money. She was only able to afford an unvarnished one made of thin wood planks, and even then only the shortest of the four. She returned shortly before noon, followed by four men carrying the thin-plank coffin on their backs. They set the coffin down next to Baldy Li and Song Gang's bed. The boys looked with fear and horror at the coffin as the four sweat-drenched men wiped themselves with their towels and fanned themselves with their straw hats. Looking about, they asked loudly, "Where is the corpse? Where is it?"

Silently, Li Lan opened the door to the inside room. The men's leader walked into the room and spotted Song Fanping on the bed. He waved for his men to follow him in. They stood by the bed quietly discussing matters for a while, then abruptly grabbed Song Fanping by the arms and legs. The leader bellowed, "Lift him up!" and the four men lifted Song Fanping, their faces as red as pig's liver. They carried Song Fanping through the door and then attempted to place him in the coffin. When Song's torso was positioned in the coffin, his feet still dangled out. The men panted noisily, trying to catch their breath. They asked Li Lan, "How much did Song Fanping weigh when he was alive?"

Li Lan was leaning against the door frame as she replied in a low voice that her husband probably weighed 180 pounds or so. All the men had looks of "Aha!" The man in charge explained, "No wonder he was so heavy. When people die, they weigh twice as much. That was probably three hundred and sixty pounds right there. No wonder I almost sprained my back!"

The men from the coffin shop then began an animated discussion about how to wedge Song Fanping's feet into the coffin. The corpse was too long, and the coffin too short. The four of them struggled for more than an hour. Song Fanping's head was already squashed and crooked, but still they could not manage to squeeze his two feet in. They discussed placing him on his side, in a fetal position, saying that then they could manage to fit all of him in.

But Li Lan balked at this. She felt that the dead should be buried faceup, since they would want to look up at the living. "You can't lay him on his side. If he's on his side, he won't be able to see us."

The man in charge retorted, "With the coffin lid and all the dirt, he wouldn't be able to see even if he were lying faceup. Hugging his knees, he'd be in the same position as he was when he was born, and furthermore it would make coming back for the next go-round easier."

Li Lan shook her head. She still wanted to say something, but the four men had already bent over and, with much grunting and huffing, rolled Song Fanping onto his side. Then they discovered that the coffin was too narrow, and Song Fanping's body was too wide and too thick. Plus his legs were too long, so even in a fetal position they couldn't fit all of him in. The men shook their heads. Lifting their shirts to wipe the sweat that had flowed from their faces down onto their chests, they complained, "What kind of fucking coffin is this? A foot-washing basin is more like it."

Li Lan lowered her head in shame. The men rested for a while, then continued discussing their options. The man in charge said to Li Lan, "There's only one way: We have to smash his knees to fold his calves over. Then he'll fit."

Li Lan turned deathly pale and shook her head over and over again. Trembling, she said, "No, no. . . ."

"Well, there's nothing else we can do."

The men got up and started collecting their levers and ropes, shrugging their shoulders and waving their hands. As they walked outside Li Lan followed them, pleading pitifully, "Is there nothing else you can do?"

They turned back, saying, "No—well, you can see for yourself."

The four men from the coffin shop carried their tools and walked into the alleyway. Li Lan trailed behind them, pleading pitifully, "Is there really no other way?"

They replied firmly, "No."

As the men walked out of the alley the man in charge paused and turned to Li Lan. "Just think. Who leaves a dead man's feet outside of the coffin? No matter what, it's still better than having his feet dangling out."

Li Lan lowered her head and said brokenheartedly, "Whatever you say."

The four men returned to the house, and Li Lan pitifully trailed in after them. Silently, she shook her head, walked up to the coffin, and gazed for a while at Song Fanping inside. She then bent down, reaching both hands into the coffin, and carefully rolled up Song Fanping's pants legs. As she did so she once again saw all the bruises on his calves. Trembling all over, she rolled Song Fanping's pants above his knees. When she looked up, her eyes met those of Baldy Li and Song Gang, and she quickly looked away. She led the boys by the hand and walked into the inner room. She shut the door behind her, sat down on the bed, and closed her eyes. Baldy Li and Song Gang sat on either side of her, her arms hugging their shoulders tight.

From the outside room the man in charge yelled, "Let's start smashing!"

Li Lan's body jerked as if she were being electrocuted, and Baldy Li and Song Gang's bodies jolted in response. By this time a crowd had gathered outside the house, including neighbors and passersby, as well as others attracted by the commotion. A mass of them crowded the door, and a few even tumbled into the house. They excitedly discussed how the men from the coffin shop were shattering Song Fanping's knees. Li Lan and the children hadn't realized how they were going to smash his knees, but now they heard them talking about bricks, which then shattered, and how they used the back of a cleaver. There was so much of a din outside that they couldn't make out clearly what everyone was saying. They could only hear people whooping and hollering, as well as the sounds of smashing, dull thuds, and occasional sharp snaps—that was the sound of bone crunching.

Baldy Li and Song Gang couldn't stop trembling. Their bodies shook until they sounded like branches being whipped in a thunderstorm. They were shocked by their own bodies—what would make them shake so hard? It was only later that they realized that it was Li Lan's arms that were shaking and her body that was vibrating like an engine.

The four men outside finally managed to shatter Song Fanping's kneecaps. The man in charge said, "Pick out those bits of brick from inside the coffin." After a while he added, "Roll down the pants legs, and stuff the calves in." Finally he knocked at their door and said to Li Lan, "Come take a last look. We're about to close the coffin."

Trembling, Li Lan stood up; trembling, she opened the door; trembling, she walked out. With unimaginable difficulty she approached the coffin, where she saw her husband's broken calves placed atop his thighs, as if they were someone else's. She teetered a few times but didn't collapse. She didn't see Song Fanping's shattered knees, since they had already placed his calves in his pants legs, but she saw the broken shards of bone and the bits of flesh that had stuck to the sides of the coffin. Li Lan grasped the coffin with both hands and looked with infinite longing at Song Fanping. Despite his contorted visage, she could still make out his former liveliness, his smile, and recall the way in which he would turn around and wave. Now he walked alone along an empty road, in a landscape devoid of mortals—the love of Li Lan's life was rushing down to the netherworld.

From where they were sitting on the bed, Baldy Li and Song Gang could hear Li Lan's voice tremble as she said, "You can close it now."

CHAPTER 20

BALDY LI and Song Gang never understood how Li Lan managed to be so strong, from the time she emerged from the long-distance bus depot and saw Baldy Li and Song Gang wailing, to when she knelt on the ground gathering up the blood-soaked earth, to witnessing Song Fanping's battered corpse, to buying a thin-planked coffin, to letting the four men from the coffin shop smash up Song Fanping's knees. Through all that she never once cried out loud. As they listened to Song Fanping's legs being smashed, several times Baldy Li and Song Gang opened their mouths and were about to cry out, but then they remembered Li Lan had told them that they shouldn't cry and promptly shut them again.

That night Li Lan prepared a tofu dinner, as was the custom of our Liu Town. She cooked a giant pot of tofu and placed it in the center of the table, along with a bowl of greens. As night fell they lit their lamp and the three of them sat at the table with Song Fanping's coffin just to the side. On top of his coffin was a small kerosene lamp, meant to illuminate Song Fanping's way to the netherworld.

Li Lan did not say a single word the entire afternoon. Baldy Li and Song Gang also didn't dare speak, so the house remained ghostly and silent. Only when Li Lan started to cook did the children hear some clattering and see the steam rising from the pot. This was the first time Li Lan had cooked at home since returning from Shanghai. Her tears streamed down as she stood in front of the kerosene stove, but not once did she raise her hand to wipe them away. As she placed the giant bowls of tofu and greens on the table Baldy Li and Song Gang saw that her tears were still gushing forth, and she continued weeping as she filled their bowls with rice. Then she turned to get the chopsticks with a dreamlike expression on her face. Weeping, she sat on the bench and stared down in confusion at the sticks in her hands. Song Gang whispered, "Those are the chopsticks of the ancients."

Through her tears she looked at the boys, and they told her the story of the chopsticks. At last she raised her hand, wiped the tears from her face, and then handed Baldy Li and Song Gang the chopsticks of the ancients. Softly she said, "These chopsticks of the ancients are wonderful."

When she said this, she turned and smiled slightly at the coffin. Her smile was as warm and familiar as if Song Fanping had been sitting right there watching her. Then she took up her rice bowl and her tears flowed anew. Sobbing, she ate soundlessly. Baldy Li saw that Song Gang's tears were also flowing into his rice bowl, and so he couldn't help crying, too. The three of them wept and ate in silence.

The morning after their tofu dinner, Li Lan solemnly washed her face and combed her hair. After she had tidied herself up, she took Baldy Li and Song Gang's hands and walked proudly outside. She led the two children through the streets awash in Cultural Revolution flags and slogans, walking as though they were alone on the street. She ignored all the people pointing at her. First she went to the fabric store, and while everyone else was buying red cloth to make flags and arm-bands, Li Lan instead purchased some black sash and white cloth. The clerks regarded her with curiosity. Someone recognized her as Song Fanping's wife and walked up to her, fists raised, shouting, "Down with counterrevolutionaries!" With equanimity she paid with her last bit of cash, rolled up the sash and cloth, and walked out of the store hugging the fabric close to her chest.

Grasping on to Li Lan's shirt, Baldy Li and Song Gang followed her into the photography studio. As she received the photograph her hands would not stop trembling; she hugged the photograph close to her chest, along with the black sash and white cloth, and continued her proud journey down the main street. At that moment she had forgotten that Baldy Li and Song Gang were following. Her head was filled with images of Song Fanping, instructing the photographer on how to position the lights and when to press the shutter, and all four of them happily walking out of the studio toward the bus depot. It was at the depot that she last waved goodbye to Song Fanping, and this was the final image she had of him. By the time she had returned from Shanghai, Song Fanping was no longer.

Li Lan pressed on, resisting the urge to take the family portrait out of the envelope she held in her trembling hands. She forced herself to walk proudly until she reached the bridge, where the parading masses blocked her way. She, of course, didn't know that Song Fanping had once stood here, gloriously waving a giant red flag, but once she stopped, she could not control herself any longer and removed the photograph. The first thing she noticed was Song Fanping's open smile, and before she could make out the other three smiling faces, she had collapsed. For three days she had borne this horrible tragedy with dignity and reserve, but now Song Fanping's smile in the photograph completely undid her.

Baldy Li and Song Gang were still holding on to her shirttails when suddenly she disappeared. Standing before them was a man with an astonished expression. The boys then noticed that Li Lan had fallen to the ground, and they cried as they squatted, nudging her. She, however, merely lay there with her eyes closed, unresponsive. Baldy Li and Song Gang burst out in terrified wails as more and more people gathered around. The two boys knelt beside Li Lan, believing that they were now all alone in this world. Weeping, they begged the bystanders to save their mother, not realizing that she had merely fainted. They sobbed as they asked, "Why has Mama fallen down?"

Everyone was talking at the same time, then one suggested, "Flip up her eyelids. Are her pupils dilated?"

Baldy Li and Song Gang rushed to flip open her eyelids. They looked at her eyes but didn't know exactly which were her pupils. Looking up, they answered, "They're very large."

This man said, "If her pupils are dilated, she's probably dead."

When the boys heard this, they clutched each other and cried even louder. Another man bent down, saying, "Stop crying, stop crying. You kids don't even know what pupils are. Feel for her pulse. If you can feel her pulse, then you know she isn't dead."

Baldy Li and Song Gang immediately stopped crying and asked anxiously, "Where do we find her pulse?"

The man extended his left hand and used his right to point it out, "Right here, on the wrist."

Baldy Li and Song Gang each grabbed one of Li Lan's hands and started feeling her wrists. The man asked them, "Do you feel anything?"

Baldy Li shook his head. "Nothing."

Baldy Li looked nervously at Song Gang, who also shook his head. "Nothing."

The man stood back up, concluding, "Then she probably is dead."

Baldy Li and Song Gang now felt that they had lost all hope. They opened their mouths and wailed. After a while they paused, then burst out again. Song Gang sobbed, "Papa's dead. Now Mama's dead, too."

At that point, Blacksmith Tong appeared on the scene. He squeezed in through the crowd and squatted down, shaking the two boys and telling them to stop their crying. He said, "What dilated pupils or beating pulse? That's for the doctor to decide. You kids don't know a thing. Listen to me: Put your ear against her chest—do you hear thumping inside?"

Song Gang wiped away his snot and placed his head against Li Lan's chest. After listening for a while, he raised his head and nervously said to Baldy Li, "I think I hear thumping."

Baldy Li also hurriedly wiped away his tears and snot and listened for a while. He also heard her heart beating. He nodded to Song Gang, "I hear it, too."

Blacksmith Tong stood up and scolded the two men who had spoken earlier, "You two don't know crap. You only know how to frighten children."

Then Blacksmith Tong told Baldy Li and Song Gang, "She's not dead. She just fainted. Why don't you let her lie there for a while? She'll come to eventually."

Baldy Li and Song Gang immediately broke into wide grins. Wiping at his tears, Song Gang raised his face to Blacksmith Tong and said, "Blacksmith Tong, you will be rewarded in the next life."

Blacksmith Tong was very pleased with Song Gang's words. He smiled. "Now, that's true."

Baldy Li and Song Gang sat quietly by Li Lan's side. Song Gang picked up the photograph that had fallen to the ground, took a look for himself, and then showed it to Baldy Li before carefully placing it back into the envelope. More and more people gathered on the bridge, and many of them squeezed over to take a look at the boys. After inquiring about them from others, they then squeezed out of the crowd again. The two boys sat there patiently. From time to time they stole a look at each other and smiled. After a very long time had passed, Li Lan finally got up. The boys were so happy they shouted to the bystanders, "Mama's woken up!"

Li Lan had no idea what had just happened, only that she was crawling up from the ground. Embarrassed, she carefully dusted herself off and once again gathered the photograph and the black sash and white cloth to her chest. She didn't say a word the entire way home. Baldy Li and Song Gang didn't dare to say anything either, but they were bursting with emotion. They held on tightly to Li Lan's clothes—having regained their mother after believing that they had lost her, they were filled with happiness. From time to time they would crane their necks to look at Li Lan's front, at her back, and exchange tiny smiles.

and Song Gang didn't dare to say anything either, but they were laying with emotion. The two boys rubbed Li Lan's clothes—laying regained their mother after believing that they had lost her; they were filled with happiness. From time to time they would raise their heads to look at Li Lan's front, at her back, and exchange tiny smiles.

CHAPTER 21

T HE FOURTH DAY AFTER Song Fanping's death, an elderly peasant pulling an old, battered cart arrived at Li Lan's front door. Standing outside the door, his shirt and pants covered in patches, the old man didn't say a word, and merely wept as he looked in at the coffin. He was Song Fanping's father, Song Gang's grandfather. He had once owned a few hundred *mu* of farmland, but after Liberation it had all been redistributed to the other peasants in the village. This old landlord—who was now poorer than the poorest "poor peasant" and no longer owned anything other than his landlord status—had come to take his landlord son home.

The previous night Li Lan had packed up Song Gang's things. Baldy Li and Song Gang sat on the bed and silently watched her remove her own belongings from the gray travel bag with the SHANGHAI logo, including the wrapped bundle of bloodstained earth and a bag of White Rabbit candies. She then placed Song Gang's clothes into the travel bag and also stuffed in the entire bag of milk candies. When she turned around to see Baldy Li's eyes filled with anticipation, she took out the bag of candy and grabbed a handful for him. She also handed a few to Song Gang and stuffed the remainder back into the travel bag. Baldy Li and Song Gang sucked on their candies, not knowing what the next day would bring. Even when Song Gang's landlord grandfather appeared at their door the following morning, they still didn't understand that they were about to be separated.

On this morning, their arms were wrapped in black sash and their waists belted with white cloth. Song Fanping's coffin was loaded onto the battered pullcart, and his travel bag was placed next to it. The old landlord lowered his gray head and pulled the cart. Li Lan followed behind, holding Baldy Li and Song Gang by the hand.

For as long as Baldy Li could remember, he had never seen Li Lan look so proud. Baldy Li's birth father had brought her nothing but hate and shame, but Song Fanping had given her love and respect. Her head held high, Li Lan set forth as though she were a member of the Red Detachment of Women. The old landlord pulling the cart, meanwhile, was bent over as though he were in the middle of a struggle session. As he pulled he repeatedly raised his hand to wipe at his tears. They came face-to-face with two parading troupes. The revolutionary crowds ceased their slogans, lowered their small red flags, and discussed among themselves as they watched these four people with their cart and coffin. A man wearing a red armband walked up to ask Li Lan, "Who's in the coffin?"

Li Lan answered proudly and calmly, "My husband."

"Who's your husband?"

"Song Fanping. He was a teacher at the Liu Town Middle School."

"How did he die?"

"He was beaten to death."

"Why?"

"He was a landlord."

When Li Lan said that, Baldy Li and Song Gang both trembled, and the old landlord was so frightened he did not dare to wipe his tears. She had proclaimed it with such clarity that the parading revolutionaries all stopped in their tracks. They were shocked that such a frail little woman would dare talk like this. The man wearing the red armband pointed at Li Lan. "Your husband was a landlord. So you're a landlord's wife?"

Li Lan nodded firmly. "Yes."

The man turned back to the revolutionary crowds. "See that! Such shamelessness . . ."

As he finished speaking he turned back and slapped Li Lan across the face. Her head wobbled and blood trickled from her lips, but she smiled proudly and continued to look the man in the eye. The armband-wearing man gave her another slap. Her head wobbled again, but she still smiled proudly as she gazed at him, asking, "Had enough?"

Li Lan's words stunned him for a moment. With the oddest of expressions he looked at her, then back at the crowd. She said, "If you've had enough, then I'll be leaving."

"Fuck," the armband-wearing man cursed. He slapped her twice more, then spat. "Beat it!"

Blood trickling from her lips, Li Lan smiled as she grasped Baldy Li and Song Gang's hands and continued walking. The revolutionary crowd on the street regarded her with astonishment. Smiling, she walked forward, telling them, "Today is the day of my husband's burial."

Tears gushed from her eyes as she spoke. Baldy Li and Song Gang also began to sob, as did the old landlord up ahead. Li Lan scolded Baldy Li and Song Gang, "Don't cry."

In a ringing voice she admonished them, "Don't cry in front of other people."

The two boys covered their mouths. They stopped their sobbing but not their tears. Li Lan had forbidden them to cry, but her own face was covered with tears. She smiled through them and continued walking.

They walked out the south gate, over a creaky wooden bridge, and could make out the chirping of cicadas. They realized that they had already reached the dirt road leading to the countryside. By then it was noon, and as far as the eye could reach there were fields, interspersed with the occasional curl of rising smoke. The summer fields were empty and bare. It was as if they were the only four people on earth, aside from Song Fanping, who was lying in the coffin. His elderly father finally let himself sob out loud, his back bent like an old ox plowing the earth as he dragged along his dead son. He shook all over as he walked; even his sobs shook. His weeping ignited Song Gang and Baldy Li's wails, and the boys started sobbing loudly through their fingers. They had covered their mouths with their hands, but their sobs now burst from their noses; they used their hands to hold their noses, but then the sobs would burst from their lips. The two boys timidly looked up at Li Lan, who said, "Go ahead and cry."

After she spoke, Li Lan was the first to break out crying. This was the first time that Baldy Li and Song Gang heard her piercing wails. She wept without restraint, as if she wanted to rip out her throat with her sobs. Song Gang dropped his hands and also began to sob out loud, and Baldy Li immediately followed suit. The four of them sobbed loudly as they walked, no longer worrying about being seen. Amid the vast fields and under the distant sky they wept together, as a family. As if she were gazing into the sky, Li Lan raised her face and sobbed; Song Fanping's elderly father bent over and wept, soaking the earth with his tears. Baldy Li and Song Gang repeatedly wiped away their tears, splashing them onto Song Fanping's coffin. They cried wholeheartedly, their howls sounding like a series of land mines, startling the sparrows from the trees lining the sides of the road.

The four walked and wept for a very long time, until Song Fanping's elderly father could walk no farther. He put the cart down and knelt on the ground. He had wept until his back hurt, and he could no longer move. They stopped, and gradually their crying abated. Li Lan wiped away her tears and said that she would pull the cart. Song Fanping's father refused, saying that he would accompany his son on his last journey.

Afterward they no longer wept but walked on silently. There was only the sound of the cart's creaking wheels. They arrived at the village where Song Fanping was born. A few shabbily clad relatives stood at the village gate. They had already dug the grave under an elm tree at the edge of the village and stood there with their shovels. As Song Fanping's coffin was lowered into the grave and a few relatives covered it with dirt, his father knelt nearby, picking out the rocks. Li Lan knelt down and did the same. After the grave was filled and covered with a mound of earth, the two of them slowly stood up.

They all then made their way to the father's thatched hut. Inside there was a single bed, a battered armoire, and a worn table. The relatives sat around the table and ate, and Baldy Li and Song Gang joined in the meal of pickled vegetables and rice. Song Fanping's aged father sat on a low stool in a corner of the room and wiped at his tears, not eating a single bite. Li Lan didn't eat either. She removed Song Gang's clothes from the travel bag, folded them neatly, and placed them inside the old battered armoire. Baldy Li saw that she also placed the bag of White Rabbit candies inside the armoire. After she was done, she didn't know what else to do, so she stood by the armoire and watched the two boys.

This was an afternoon of silence. After the relatives finished eating and left, the four of them sat wordlessly inside the hut. Baldy Li caught sight of the trees and pond outside the house. He also spied sparrows singing in the trees and swallows flying from the beams. Song Gang saw these things, too. The boys very much wanted to go outside to look around, but they didn't dare to; instead they sat on the bench stealing glances at the sad figures of Li Lan and Song Fanping's father. Finally Li Lan spoke. She said that they ought to be going if they hoped to make it back to town before dark. Rising with difficulty, Song Fanping's father made his way to the battered armoire and took out a small can. He grabbed a handful of fava nuts and stuffed them into Baldy Li's pocket.

Once again they returned to the edge of the village. A few leaves had fallen on the mound that was Song Fanping's grave. Li Lan went over and picked them off, throwing them to one side. She did not cry, and the boys heard her softly say to the grave, "Once the boys grow up, I'll come keep you company."

Li Lan turned, walked up to Song Gang, and squatted down to caress his face as he caressed hers. Li Lan hugged him tight and couldn't help bursting into tears. "Son, take good care of Grandpa. Grandpa is old now, so he wants you to stay by his side. Mama will come to see you often. . . ."

Song Gang didn't understand what Li Lan was talking about. He nodded, then looked over at Baldy Li. Li Lan wept with Song Gang in her arms, then wiped her tears and stood up. Looking over at Song Fanping's father, her lips moved as if to say something but no sounds came out. Finally she took Baldy Li's hand.

Li Lan led Baldy Li down the dirt road. She didn't look back. Her steps were as heavy as two mops dragging across the floor. Even at this moment Baldy Li still didn't realize that he was about to be parted from Song Gang. As Li Lan led him down the road he turned to look back at Song Gang, wondering why he wasn't coming with them. Song Gang's grandfather held Song Gang's hand as Song Gang stood in front of his father's grave, watching in confusion as Baldy Li and Li Lan slowly walked away. He also didn't understand why he had been left behind. As Li Lan and Baldy Li walked farther away he saw that Grandpa was waving farewell to them. Hesitantly he also lifted his hand and waved. Baldy Li kept turning back to look at Song Gang, and when he saw that Song Gang was waving at him, he also started waving.

CHAPTER 22

FROM THAT POINT, Baldy Li was on his own. In those days Li Lan left early and returned late. The silk factory where she used to work had stopped production in order to carry out revolutionary activities, but since Song Fanping had left her with a landlady designation, every day she had to go to the factory to receive criticism. Without Song Gang, Baldy Li no longer had a pal. All day, every day, he wandered the streets, as adrift and aimless as a leaf floating down the river and as pitiful as a scrap of paper blowing in the wind. He didn't know what to do, knowing only to walk about, sit when he was tired, drink from a faucet when he was thirsty, and go home to eat leftovers when he was hungry.

Baldy Li didn't know what was happening in the world as more and more people were forced to parade through the streets wearing dunce caps and wooden placards in the name of the Great Proletarian Cultural Revolution. Mama Su from the snack shop had also been dragged out to be struggled against. They accused her of being a prostitute, on the ground that she had a daughter and no husband. One day Baldy Li glimpsed a red-haired woman standing on a bench on the street. He had never seen someone with red hair, so his curiosity led him over. When he got closer, he saw that her hair was actually stained red with blood. She stood, head lowered, on the bench, a placard hanging around her neck. The woman's daughter—a girl named Missy Su, who was only a few years older than Baldy Li—stood by her mother's side. Only when Baldy Li had walked directly under Mama Su and looked up at her lowered face did he recognize her as the owner of the snack shop.

There was another bench next to Mama Su's, and on it stood long-haired Sun Wei's father. Even this man—who had once brawled with Song Fanping and had stood guard in front of the warehouse wearing his red armband—was now wearing a dunce cap and a wooden placard. Sun Wei's grandfather had owned a rice shop in Liu Town before Liberation. The shop had gone bankrupt during the war, but as the Cultural Revolution struggles delved deeper and deeper, Sun Wei's father was now also dug out as capitalist, and the placard hanging around his neck now was even bigger than the one Song Fanping had worn.

Sun Wei was now as alone as Baldy Li. Once his father was labeled a class enemy, his erstwhile buddies, Victory Zhao and Success Liu, immediately distanced themselves from him. Whenever they ran into Baldy Li, they would leer at him. Baldy Li knew that they wanted to practice their sweep-kicks on him, so he would dash away, or if he couldn't, he would plop himself on the ground, saying, "I'm already down."

Victory Zhao and Success Liu couldn't do much with that, so they gave him a kick, cursing, "That fucking kid. . . ."

They used to call him just "kid," but now they called him "fucking kid." Baldy Li often caught sight of Sun Wei. He frequently wandered the streets by himself, his head cocked, and sometimes he leaned against the bridge railing. No one hailed him, no one patted him on the shoulder, and when Victory Zhao and Success Liu saw him, they would pretend that they didn't recognize him. Only Baldy Li still acted the same as always, and would either run away or plop himself on the ground.

Baldy Li eventually grew tired of running away. Every time he would run until he was out of breath, his lungs burning. He decided that he'd rather just plop himself on the ground, which would not only be more relaxing but would afford him a view of the street. Now whenever he ran into long-haired Sun Wei, he'd sit right down as if he were trying to snatch a good seat. Cocking his head up at Sun Wei, he'd say, "I'm already down. The most you can do is give me a kick."

Sun Wei—who still called Baldy Li "kid" and not "fucking kid"— chuckled and nudged the boy's bottom with his foot. "Hey, kid, why do you plop down whenever you see me?"

Baldy Li answered craftily, "I'm terrified of your sweep-kick."

Long-haired Sun Wei chuckled some more. "Get up, kid, I won't kick you."

Baldy Li shook his head. "I'll get up after you leave."

"Fuck," he said. "I really won't kick you anymore. Get up."

Baldy Li didn't believe him. "I'm quite comfortable sitting right here."

"Fuck," Sun Wei spat out and stalked off. As he walked away he recited a line from Chairman Mao: "*I ask, in this boundless land, who is master of his destiny?*"

These two lonely fellows would often run into each other on the streets. At first Baldy Li would either keep a safe distance from Sun Wei or he would immediately plant himself on the ground, and each time Sun Wei would chuckle. Baldy Li always guardedly watched Sun Wei's legs to make sure that they wouldn't sneak in a kick. One day at noon Baldy Li finally let down his guard. At this time most people in town were locking up their faucets; in a great thirst, Baldy Li tried faucet after faucet until, on the eighth try, he found one that hadn't been locked up. He turned it on and filled his belly with water and also stuck his head underneath to cool himself off. Just as he finished twisting the faucet shut, someone came from behind him, turned it on again, and drank for a good long time, his mouth sucking on it as if it were a sugarcane. As this person drank he stuck his backside in the air and let out a string of farts, making Baldy Li giggle. When the person finished, he turned to Baldy Li and said, "Hey, kid, what are you laughing at?"

Baldy Li now saw that it was Sun Wei, but he was so busy giggling, momentarily he forgot to sit down. He said to Sun Wei, "Your farts sound like snores."

Sun Wei chuckled as he turned the stream of water down to a trickle. He dabbed some water on his fingers to comb his hair and asked Baldy Li, "Where's that other kid?"

Baldy Li knew he was referring to Song Gang and replied, "He went back to the countryside."

Sun Wei nodded. He turned off the faucet and shook out his long hair, then waved for Baldy Li to follow him. Baldy Li walked a few steps before he suddenly remembered the sweep-kick, whereupon he immediately planted himself on the ground. Sun Wei walked a bit farther before noticing that Baldy Li wasn't following, and when he turned around, he saw that Baldy Li was again seated on the ground. Curious, he asked, "Hey, kid, what are you doing?"

Baldy Li pointed at Sun Wei's legs. "You have sweep-kicking legs."

Sun Wei burst into laughter. "If I had wanted to kick you, I would have already done so."

This struck Baldy Li as logical, but he still didn't fully believe Sun Wei. Cautiously, he suggested, "You just forgot to kick me earlier."

Sun Wei waved his hand, saying, "Nah. Get up, I won't kick you anymore. We're friends now."

The words "We're friends now" thrilled and surprised Baldy Li, and he almost leapt up. Sun Wei indeed didn't sweep-kick him; rather, he placed his hand on Baldy Li's shoulder, and they walked down the street as if they were old pals. With a toss of his long locks, Sun Wei intoned, "*I ask, in this boundless land, who is master of his destiny?*"

Baldy Li beamed with excitement. Sun Wei, who was seven years older than he, was his friend. Now that Song Fanping had passed away, Baldy Li's new friend was certainly the Number One Sweep-kicker in town. Sun Wei's hair, which usually covered his ears, blew in the breeze, and he recited the Chairman's verses as he ambled along, sometimes adding an "*Alas!*" at the end of the line for emphasis. Sun Wei's improvements on the originals impressed Baldy Li. He also felt that walking alongside Sun Wei brought him great clout. He was no longer intimidated by anyone, not even the armband-wearing men.

As they ascended the bridge they ran into Victory Zhao and Success Liu, both of whom looked upon Sun Wei walking with the young Baldy Li with great curiosity. Ignoring them, Sun Wei continued with his recitation of Chairman's Mao verse, "*I ask, in this boundless land . . .*"

Baldy Li rather overeagerly rushed to complete the couplet: "*. . . who is master of his destiny?*"

Victory Zhao and Success Liu whispered to each other, laughing. Sun Wei knew that they were making fun of him, so in a low voice he scolded Baldy Li, "Hey, kid, stop walking next to me. Follow behind."

Baldy Li's swagger instantly dissipated. He no longer had the right to walk shoulder to shoulder with Sun Wei and could only follow behind him like a little lackey, his shoulders slumped and his head drooped. Trailing behind Sun Wei, Baldy Li now understood that the only reason Sun Wei had recruited him as a friend was because he had none left. All the same, he still followed closely behind Sun Wei, since trailing him was better than being on his own.

What Baldy Li didn't expect was that the next day long-haired Sun Wei would come knocking on his door. Baldy Li was just finishing breakfast when he heard Sun Wei reciting Chairman Mao's verse outside the door: "*I ask, in this boundless land, who is master of his destiny?*"

Overjoyed, Baldy Li opened the door. Sun Wei beckoned him like an old friend. "C'mon, let's go."

The two of them walked for a bit. Baldy Li cautiously followed alongside Sun Wei, relieved not to see any reaction from him. When they reached the end of the alley, Sun Wei suddenly stopped and asked Baldy Li, "Take a look for me. Do I have a rip in my pants?"

Baldy Li crouched down and peered at the seat of Sun Wei's pants but didn't spot anything. He replied, "No rips."

Sun Wei said, "Look more closely."

By this point Baldy Li's nose was almost touching Sun Wei's butt, but he still didn't spot anything. Suddenly Sun Wei let out a loud fart, blasting Baldy Li's face like a gust of wind. Sun Wei guffawed and, walking off, chanted loudly, "*I ask, in this boundless land . . .*"

Baldy Li quickly chimed in, "*. . . who is master of his destiny?*"

Baldy Li knew that Sun Wei was taunting him, but he didn't care. He only cared that Sun Wei let him walk alongside him, rather than making him trail behind.

For the rest of the summer, Baldy Li and Sun Wei spent all their time together. They loafed about in the streets past sunset, sometimes staying out long after the moon had come up. Sun Wei didn't like deserted areas, preferring the crowded main streets. Like a fly hovering over a pile of dung, Baldy Li trailed him everywhere; and the two wandered the streets, not knowing what else to do. Sun Wei was enamored with his own long hair, and at least twice a day he would walk down the steps to the riverbank and, squatting down, take up some water to style the locks framing his face. He would then admire his blurry image in the river and blow a few smug whistles. Baldy Li eventually figured out why Sun Wei liked to amble up and down the main streets: What he liked were the large glass windows of the stores. Whenever he stopped in front of one and started whistling, Baldy Li knew even without looking that Sun Wei was once again tossing his hair about.

They often ran into Sun Wei's father on the street. On those occasions, Sun Wei would look down and hurry away as if he were worried about being recognized. Sun Wei's father wore a tall dunce cap and swept the streets as Song Fanping had once been made to do. Each morning he would start at one end of the street and sweep his way to the other end, and each afternoon he would sweep his way back. People often lectured him, saying, "Hey there, have you confessed all your mistakes?"

He stuttered in reply, "Yes, yes."

"Did you leave anything out? Think more carefully."

He nodded obsequiously. "Yes, I will."

Sometimes it would be children who would lecture him: "Raise your fist and shout, 'Down with myself.'"

And he would raise his fist and shout, "Down with myself!"

On those occasions Baldy Li would itch with the desire to yell at him too, but with Sun Wei by his side, he couldn't bring himself to do so. One time Baldy Li really couldn't help himself, and when Sun Wei's father had finished shouting "Down with myself!" Baldy Li said, "Shout it twice."

Sun Wei's father raised his fist twice, shouting, "Down with myself!" Sun Wei stomped on Baldy Li's foot, cursing, "If you're going to fucking kick a dog, you should first see who it belongs to."

But when Sun Wei ran across other dunce-cap-wearing people being struggled against, he would happily throw in a kick himself as he walked past. Baldy Li would follow suit, and the two would be pleased with themselves as if they had just had a bowl of house-special noodles. Sun Wei said to Baldy Li, "Kicking bad guys is as natural as wiping yourself after taking a shit."

Sun Wei's mother had once been a woman with a vicious tongue. On Li Lan and Song Fanping's wedding day, she had been the one who let loose with a string of the foulest curses over a wayward hen. But now that her husband was wearing a dunce cap and a wooden placard, it was as if she had become a different person and was now soft-spoken and obsequious. Baldy Li often appeared at her front door in the morning, and she knew that he was her son's only friend; so whenever she ran into him, she was as affectionate as if she were his mom. If she noticed that Baldy Li's face was dirty, she would fetch a towel to wipe it, and if Baldy Li had a button missing on his shirt, she would have him take it off, then she would sew it back on right then and there. When no one was listening, she would ask after Li Lan. Baldy Li always shook his head and said that he didn't know, whereupon she would sigh and turn away before he could see her cry.

Baldy Li and Sun Wei's friendship didn't last very long. Now in addition to the parading masses, the streets were also full of people wielding scissors and razor blades. Whenever they spotted someone with tailored pants, they would drag him out and shred his pants legs until they were like the ends of a mop; when they saw a long-haired man, they would wrestle him to the ground and chop at his hair until it looked like a roughly weeded patch of grass. Men wearing tailored pants and sporting long hair were obviously bourgeois, and Sun Wei's long hair could not escape this fate. One morning, just as he and Baldy Li reached the main street and spotted Sun Wei's father sweeping at a distance with his head bent, a few men wielding scissors and razors ran toward them. At that moment Sun Wei was still busy reciting, "*I ask, in this boundless land, who is master of his destiny?*"

Baldy Li heard the clatter of footsteps behind him, and he turned around to see a few red-armbanders rushing at them with scissors and razors in their hands. Baldy Li didn't know what was going on. But when he turned back to look at Sun Wei, he saw that he had already dashed off frantically toward his father, with the red-armbanders close behind.

Usually, when Baldy Li's middle-schooler friend ran into his father on the street, he would walk past, eyes averted. But this time, in order to protect his beloved head of long hair, he ran toward his father, screaming, "Papa, save me!"

Another red-armbander suddenly jumped in front of Sun Wei and kicked him to the ground. When Sun Wei got up to continue running, the group of men tackled him. By this time Baldy Li had caught up and saw that Sun Wei's father was also rushing over. A gust of wind blew the father's dunce cap to the ground, so he ran back to place it on his head and then continued running toward his son.

Several of the stronger red-armbanders pinned Sun Wei to the ground and started pushing the razor across his gorgeous long hair. Sun Wei resisted with all his might; even after his arms were pinned down, he still kicked his feet as if he were swimming. Two red-armbanders sat on him, holding down his legs. Though his body was immobilized, Sun Wei strained to lift his head up, screaming, "Papa, Papa . . ."

The razor blade in the red-armbander's hand was slashing through Sun Wei's hair and neck like a machete. Between the red-armbander's downward thrusts and Sun Wei's struggles, the razor blade slashed deeply into Sun Wei's neck. Blood gushed all over the blade, but the red-armbander still slashed, ultimately slicing through the jugular vein.

Baldy Li witnessed the horrific scene as blood spurted in a two-yard-long arc like a fountain. The faces of the red-armbanders were sprayed with blood; shocked, they all leapt back like springs. When Sun Wei's father rushed over and saw that his son's neck was spurting blood, he pleaded with the group to spare his boy. As he knelt on the blood-drenched ground his cap fell off, but this time he didn't retrieve it.

Instead he cradled his son in his arms as Sun Wei's head flopped over like a doll's. He screamed his son's name, but there was no response. With a look of terror he asked the crowd, "Is my son dead?"

No one answered. The red-armbanders responsible for Sun Wei's death were all mopping the blood from their faces and looking about in a panic, struck dumb by what had just happened. Sun Wei's father bellowed at them, "You! You killed my son!"

As he shouted he rushed at them. They backed away in terror, and he, with his fist clenched, didn't know who to pursue. At this moment four other red-armbanders walked over. When they spotted Sun Wei's father, they scolded him, ordering him back to his sweeping. Sun Wei's father's crazed fists crashed down on them, and the four beat him brutally in return. They rolled around like a pack of wild animals as the crowds hovered, rushing back and forth. Sun Wei's father used his fists, feet, and head, roaring like a crazed beast, and even the four red-armbanders together couldn't manage to take him down. He had once fought Song Fanping, and back then he had been no match for Song; but at this moment Baldy Li was certain that it would be Song Fanping who was no match for Sun Wei's father.

More and more red-armbanders congregated in the street. There were now more than twenty of them, and they encircled Sun Wei's father, taking turns beating him down until he was flat on the ground. Still, they continued to shower him with punches and kicks, and only when he was completely motionless did the red-armbanders pause to catch their breath. When he came to again, they bellowed at him, "Get up. Get going."

Sun Wei's father by now had resumed his former air of diffidence. Wiping at the blood on his lips, he dragged his bruised body up, but not before retrieving his dunce cap, stained with his son's blood. He solemnly placed it back on his head and, as he followed them with his head hung low, he caught sight of Baldy Li. He wept and said, "Go tell my wife our son is dead."

Shaking all over, Baldy Li arrived at Sun Wei's house. It was still morning, so when Sun Wei's mother saw Baldy Li standing by himself at her door, she assumed he had come looking for her son. Curious, she asked, "Didn't you two go out together just now?"

Baldy Li nodded his head. He was trembling so hard he couldn't say a word. When Sun Wei's mother saw the blood on Baldy Li's face, she gasped and asked, "Did you get into a fight?"

Baldy Li swiped his hand across his face. When he saw the blood on his hand, he realized that it was Sun Wei's. Shaking and sobbing, he said, "Sun Wei is dead."

Baldy Li saw the horror creep over Sun Wei's mother's face as she stared at him. He repeated himself and, feeling that she was not registering what he was saying, he added, "On the main street."

Sun Wei's mother stumbled out of her house and to the end of the alley until she reached the main street. Baldy Li followed behind her, stammeringly describing how her son had died and how her husband had battled the red-armbanders. Sun Wei's mother quickened her pace until she was no longer reeling with shock; speed gave her balance, and when she reached the main street, she broke into a run. Baldy Li ran behind for a few steps but then paused as she ran to where her son was lying. Baldy Li saw her fall to the ground, then heard a shattering series of wails, each sob wrenched from her chest as if with a dagger.

From that point on, Sun Wei's mother never stopped weeping. Even after her eyes became red and as puffy as two lightbulbs, her weeping continued unabated. In the days that followed, each morning she would support herself against the walls of the alley and walk to the end, then support herself along the walls of the main street and walk to the spot where her son had died. She would stand there, gazing down at the traces of his blood, and weep unceasingly. Only after the sun had set would she support herself against the walls and stumble home. The next day she would be there once again, sobbing. When acquaintances went over to comfort her, she would turn away, bowing her head deeply.

Her gaze grew unfocused, her clothes shabby, and her hair and face increasingly filthy. Her gait became odder and odder: As she stepped out with her right foot she would swing her right arm forward, and as she stepped out with her left foot she would swing her left arm forward. As they say in Liu Town, she was walking lopsided. She would walk to the spot where her son had died and sit there, her entire body slack as if she was barely conscious, her weeping sounding like the buzz of mosquitoes. Most people thought that she had lost her mind, but when she would accidentally catch someone's eye, she would turn away and stealthily wipe away her tears. Eventually, in order not to let others see her cry, she started sitting with her face against a wutong tree and her back to the street.

There was much talk among the people of Liu. Some concluded that she had gone mad; others noted that she was still capable of feeling shame, so obviously she hadn't gone completely insane. However, even they admitted that, judging by her odd behavior, she at the very least had fallen into a deep depression. One day her shoe fell off, and from that point on she never again wore shoes. Various pieces of clothing also fell by the wayside, and she never replaced them, until finally one day she sat there stark naked. By that time, the traces of her son's blood had been completely washed away by the rain, yet she still stared at the ground, weeping inconsolably. When she noticed someone looking at her, she would turn away and lean into the tree trunk, stealthily wiping her tears. Now the people of Liu Town were all in agreement that she had, indeed, gone completely mad.

This pitiful woman no longer knew where home was. At nightfall she stood up and wandered the streets and alleys of Liu Town, looking for her home. Like a ghost she silently paced the streets, often giving the town's residents a good scare. Later she even forgot where her son had died. All day she rushed about frantically like someone trying to catch a train, running from one end of the street to the other calling out her son's name, as if she were calling him home for dinner: "Sun Wei! Sun Wei!"

Then one day she vanished from Liu Town altogether. She was gone for almost half a month before people realized they hadn't seen her for a long time. They asked one another, "How did Sun Wei's mother suddenly disappear?" Sun Wei's former buddies, Victory Zhao and Success Liu, however, knew where she had gone. They stood amid the crowds and pointed north, explaining, "She's gone. She's long gone."

"Gone?" the crowds asked. "Where did she go?"

"She's gone to the countryside."

Victory Zhao and Success Liu were perhaps the last people to see her leave. That afternoon they were pissing on the wooden bridge outside the southern gate when they caught sight of Sun Wei's mother. She had once again been clothed, Mama Su having quietly dressed her in a shirt and slacks one night, but as she walked out the gate she had lost her pants again and was menstruating. The sight of blood trickling down her legs as she walked over the wooden bridge had shocked Victory Zhao and Success Liu into silence.

On the day that his son died, Sun Wei's father was locked into the warehouse that was really a prison cell. He once had guarded Song

Fanping here, but now it was his turn; it was said that he slept on what was once Song Fanping's bed. His son's ghastly death had made him temporarily lose his mind and caused him to beat up some armband-wearing rebels. From the first night the red-armbanders locked him inside the warehouse, they started to torture him. They bound his arms and legs and then placed a feral cat down his pants. The pants were fastened tight on either end, so that the cat tried to scratch and bite its way out, causing him to cry out all night in unbearable pain. Everyone else locked in the warehouse shuddered at the sound, and a few of the more cowardly ones even wet their pants.

The next day these red-armbanders switched to a new form of punishment: They had him lie facedown on the ground while they rubbed the soles of his feet with a metal brush. Pained and tickled, he started to thrash his arms and legs as if he were swimming. The red-armbanders watching him broke out into guffaws, asking, "Do you know what this is called?"

Though his entire body was in spasms, Sun Wei's father still had to answer. Through his tears he stammered, "I-I-I don't know. . . ."

A red-armbander smiled. "You know how to swim, don't you?"

Sun Wei's father was now completely out of breath, but still he had to answer. "I do, I do. . . ."

"This is called 'a duck paddling in water.'" The red-armbanders were laughing so hard they bent over. "Now you're a duck paddling in water."

The third day the red-armbanders had more in store for Sun Wei's father. They lit a cigarette, inserted it upright in the dirt, and commanded him to take his pants off. Even the act of removing his pants made Sun Wei's father grimace in pain, and his teeth knocked together as loudly as Blacksmith Tong's hammer and anvil. The feral cat had shredded the skin on both his legs, and the pants legs had stuck to the bloody wounds. When he took off his pants, he felt as though he were skinning himself as pus and blood trickled down his legs. The red-armbanders then ordered him to sit down on the cigarette, and he tearfully complied. One of them crouched down on the ground to have a closer look; he directed the father's butt this way and that until the lit end of the cigarette was aimed straight at his asshole. Then the man commanded, "Sit down!"

Sun Wei's father sat down on the lit end of the cigarette. He could feel it burning his anus, and he heard a crackling sound. By this point he no longer felt any pain. He only smelled the odor of burning flesh. That red-armbander still commanded, "Sit down! Sit down!"

His bottom reached the ground, and the cigarette was crushed inside his anus. He lay on the ground as if dead while the red-armbanders guffawed, asking him, "Do you know what this is called?"

Completely spent, he shook his head. "I don't know."

"This is called 'smoking through your asshole.'" The red-armbander threw him a kick for emphasis. "Will you remember that?"

His head lowered, he responded, "I will remember 'smoking through your asshole.'"

Sun Wei's father was tortured continuously. His legs became swollen, continued to ooze pus, and began to smell increasingly foul. Every time he defecated he was in unbearable agony. He didn't dare wipe himself, since each wipe brought on searing pain. As his feces stuck to his burnt flesh, his anus started to rot. The man was rotting all over, and he was in pain when he stood, when he sat, when he lay down, when he moved, even when he remained motionless.

He was in a state worse than death, and each day brought new tortures. Only deep in the night did he have a moment of peace. As he lay in bed, racked with pain, the only part of him that didn't hurt was his thoughts. He thought over and over again of his son and wife and kept wondering where his son had been buried. He imagined over and over a beautiful landscape of green hills and lakes, and he imagined his son buried somewhere amid this landscape. At times he felt that this beautiful place seemed very familiar; at other times he didn't recognize it at all. Then he would dwell obsessively on how his wife was doing. He imagined her heartbreak at losing their son, thinking of how she would have lost a lot of weight and would be staying at home all day, waiting for his return.

Every day he thought of suicide, and only by thinking constantly of his son and his helpless wife did he manage to survive each new day's torture. He imagined his wife walking to the front gate of the warehouse every day, hoping to see him; so whenever he heard the warehouse gate open, he would anxiously glance outside. Finally he couldn't bear it any longer and knelt down, kowtowing and begging a red-armbander to let his wife see him if she came by. That was when he learned that his wife had gone mad and had been wandering the streets without a stitch of clothing.

The red-armbander cackled and called over a few others. They told him that his wife had long since lost her mind. They stood in front of him, taunting him with a description of his wife's body, saying that she had huge tits but too bad they were droopy, and that she had a thick bush but too bad it was so filthy, with pieces of hay sticking to it. . . .

Sun Wei's father fell to the ground motionless, so heartbroken that he could no longer cry. When night fell and he lay on his bed, racked with pain, he realized that now it even hurt to think. It was as if there were a meat grinder inside his head, grinding his brain into bits. Around two o'clock that morning he had a moment of clarity. This is when he made up his mind to take his life, and the decision instantly cleared the pain in his head, making him completely lucid. He recalled that there was a long iron nail under the bed. About a month earlier he had his first thought of suicide when he discovered this nail, and now his final thought of suicide returned to it. Getting out of bed, he knelt on the ground and searched for a long time until he found it again. Using his shoulders to lift the bed frame, he pulled out one of the bricks propping up the bed and then sat down by the wall. At this moment he no longer felt any of his pains and bruises, as if he had already left them behind. Breathing in deeply twice, he held the nail with his left hand and pointed it down on his skull. With his right hand he raised the brick and thought of his dead son. Smiling, he said softly, "I'm coming."

As his right hand smashed the brick down on the nail, it seemed as if the nail drilled into his skull, but he could still think clearly. He raised his right hand to smash it down a second time. He thought of his wife, who had gone mad, and the thought of how she was now going to be all alone made him weep. Softly he said, "I'm sorry."

The second time he smashed down, the nail drilled farther and seemed to reach his brain. His mind was still active, and his last thought was of the vicious armband-wearing bullies. Suddenly he was filled with hatred and anger, and his eyes bulged as he conjured up those red-armbanders in the dark of the night. Crazily he bellowed, "I'm going to kill you all!"

With all the life that was left in him, he smashed the big metal nail straight into his brain. This time it went in completely, and the brick smashed into smithereens.

Sun Wei's father's final angry roar frightened everyone in the warehouse out of their sleep. Even the red-armbanders were terrified. When they turned on the light, they saw Sun Wei's father slumped against the wall, his eyes staring straight and motionless, and the ground covered with broken shards of brick. At first no one realized that he had killed himself. They didn't know why he was sitting there, and a red-armbander even began to scold him, "Fuck! Get up! Fuck— look how he's staring."

When the red-armbander walked over to kick him, Sun Wei's father's body slid down the wall. Startled, the red-armbander jumped back a few steps and told two other prisoners to go take a look. The two men walked over and squatted near the body. They looked him over and saw all his bruises and wounds but couldn't figure out how he had died. The two men then righted him, and when they lifted him up, they saw that the top of his head was covered in fresh blood. They examined it more closely, feeling around until they finally figured it out: "There's an iron nail here. He drove a nail into his skull."

The unimaginable manner in which Sun Wei's father killed himself rapidly spread throughout Liu Town. When the news reached Li Lan, she was at home—she heard the neighbors talking about it, standing outside her window. Everyone expressed amazement and incredulity: How was it possible to smash a two-inch-long nail into your own skull? They talked about how the nail had been thoroughly embedded in his skull, as if he were making a cabinet, to the point that you couldn't even feel the end of the nail on his scalp. They asked with shuddering voices, "How could he do it? It would be nearly impossible to smash such a nail into someone else's skull, let alone your own." Li Lan listened at the window, and after they walked off, she turned back into the room and smiled sadly to herself. "If a person is determined to die, he'll find a way."

CHAPTER 23

THE STREETS of our Liu Town descended into chaos. Almost every day there were beatings among the revolutionary masses. Baldy Li didn't understand why these men, who all wore the same red armbands and waved the same red flags, were beating one another up with fists, flagpoles, and wooden bats, tearing at one another like wild beasts. One time Baldy Li saw them wielding kitchen cleavers and axes, until the electrical poles, the wutong trees, the walls, and the streets were all splattered with their blood.

Li Lan no longer let Baldy Li leave the house, even sealing the window shut so that he wouldn't be able to sneak out. When she left for the silk factory in the morning she would lock him in the house, and the door would remain shut until she returned home in the evening. Thus began Baldy Li's truly solitary childhood. From daybreak to nightfall, his world consisted of two rooms, and so he began his all-out war against the ants and the cockroaches. He would often crouch under the bed with a bowl in his hand and wait for the ants to emerge; when they did, he would first splash them with water and then smush them to death one by one. Once a fat mouse scurried right past his face, and that terrified him so much that he no longer crawled under the bed. Later he began to attack the cockroaches in the armoire, locking himself inside with them in order to trap them. By the light seeping in through a crack in the door, he would chase them and crush them with his shoe. Once he fell asleep inside the armoire and was still dreaming happily when Li Lan got home. Poor Li Lan was so panicked that she hollered for him all over the house and even dashed outside to look down the alley. When he finally emerged, she collapsed to the floor, her face pale and one hand clutching her chest, unable to speak a word.

Just when Baldy Li was at his loneliest, Song Gang made the long journey to come see him. Bringing along five White Rabbits, Song Gang set off in the morning from the village without telling his grandfather. Asking for directions along the way, he arrived at Baldy Li's house around noon and knocked on the window, shouting, "Baldy Li! Baldy Li! Are you in there? It's Song Gang."

Baldy Li was dozing off out of boredom when he heard Song Gang's shouts. Jumping up to the window, he knocked on the glass, shouting, "Song Gang! Song Gang! I'm in here."

Song Gang responded, "Baldy Li, open the door!"

Baldy Li said, "The door's locked from the outside."

"Open the window."

"The window's been sealed shut."

The two brothers banged on the window and hollered at each other for a long while. The lower panes of the window had been covered over with newspaper, so they couldn't see each other and could only communicate by shouting. Baldy Li then moved a stool over to the window so that he could perch there and look down through the only pane on top that hadn't been papered over. In this way, he finally caught sight of Song Gang, and Song Gang finally caught sight of him. Song Gang was wearing the same set of clothes he had worn to Song Fanping's burial. He looked up and said, "Baldy Li, I've missed you."

Song Gang smiled, a little embarrassed. Baldy Li banged the window with both hands, crying, "Song Gang, I've missed you, too."

Song Gang took out the five White Rabbits from his pocket and lifted them up to show Baldy Li. "See these? I brought them for you."

Baldy Li joyfully shouted, "Song Gang, I see them! Song Gang, you're so good to me."

Baldy Li started drooling immediately, but the window separated him from the candies in Song Gang's hand. He shouted to Song Gang, "Figure out a way to get the candy in here."

Song Gang thought for a moment. "Maybe I can stuff it in through a crack in the door."

Baldy Li hurried down from his perch and went to the door. He saw the candy wrapper pushing through the widest crack on the door but unable to make it in. Song Gang reported, "It won't fit."

Baldy Li anxiously scratched his head. "Think of something else."

Baldy Li heard Song Gang's labored breathing on the other side of the door. After a while he said, "I really can't get it in. Here, take a sniff first."

Song Gang thrust the candy close to the crack in the door. Baldy Li glued his nose to the crack and inhaled as deeply as he could. Finally he caught a whiff of the candy and burst into tears. Song Gang asked from outside, "Baldy Li, why are you crying?"

Through his tears Baldy Li replied, "I can smell the White Rabbits."

Song Gang started giggling. When Baldy Li heard him, he also started giggling, alternating his sobs with his giggles. The two boys then sat on the ground, one inside the house and the other outside, and chatted for a long time. Song Gang told Baldy Li about the countryside: how he had learned to fish, climb trees, plant sprouts, thresh wheat, and pick cotton. Baldy Li told Song Gang about all the things that had happened in town: how long-haired Sun Wei was dead, and how even Mama Su from the snack shop was now wearing a wooden placard. When he described how Sun Wei had died, Song Gang started weeping. "That poor guy."

The boys spoke through the door as if nothing separated them. They chatted all afternoon, but when Song Gang saw that the sun was setting on the alley, he hurriedly stood up and told Baldy Li that he had to get going. It was a long way home, so he had to get on his way. Baldy Li knocked from inside, pleading with Song Gang to stay for a while longer. "It's not dark yet. . . ."

Song Gang rapped back. "But once it's dark, I won't be able to find my way."

Before Song Gang left, he hid the White Rabbits under the front stoop, explaining that if he put them on the window ledge someone else might take them. But he came back after taking a few steps, explaining that he was worried that worms under the stoop might eat the candy, so he plucked two wutong leaves, carefully wrapped the candy inside, then put them back under the stoop. He peered through the crack in the wall, took another look at Baldy Li, and said, "Goodbye, Baldy Li."

Sadly Baldy Li asked, "When will you start missing me again?"

Song Gang shook his head. "I don't know."

Baldy Li listened as Song Gang walked off, his nine-year-old footsteps as light as a chick's. Baldy Li kept his eyes glued to the crack in the wall, guarding his milk candies like a hawk. Whenever anyone walked by, Baldy Li's heart would beat wildly, afraid they would flip over the stone stoop. He hoped that dusk would come quickly so that Li Lan would come home and open the door, allowing him to finally get his hands on the White Rabbits.

Song Gang quietly walked to the end of the alley and onto the main street. He looked all about him as he walked, seeing familiar houses and trees, and people fighting, crying, and laughing. Some of the people seemed to know him, and so he smiled at them, but no one paid him any heed. A bit disappointed, he walked down the two main streets, over the wooden bridge, and out the town's southern gate. He lost his way at the first fork in the road after leaving the main gate and merely stood there, not knowing which way to turn. He could see that on one side were fields and houses, while the other side stretched out to the horizon. Song Gang stood at the intersection for a long time until he saw a man walking down the road. He cried out, "Uncle, uncle," and asked the man how to get to his grandfather's village. The man shook his head, saying that he didn't know, and then walked off. Song Gang stood amid the fields under the endless expanse of sky, becoming increasingly terrified. After letting out a few sobs, he wiped his tears and walked back through the southern gate into Liu Town.

Even after Song Gang left, Baldy Li's eyes remained glued to the crack in the door. His eyes were tired and blurry when he suddenly saw Song Gang walking back toward him. Baldy Li thought that Song Gang had started missing him again already and had walked back to see him. He pounded the door happily, shouting, "Song Gang, did you start missing me again?"

Song Gang shook his head. "I'm lost. I don't know the way home and don't know what to do."

Baldy Li chuckled and rapped on the door, comforting Song Gang. "Don't worry. Just wait till Mama gets home. She knows how to get to your house, so she could take you back."

Song Gang decided that Baldy Li had a point, so he nodded and peered at Baldy Li before settling himself back down on the ground. Baldy Li also sat down. The two boys resumed their chatting, their backs against each other, separated by the door. This time it was Song Gang who told Baldy Li all the things that were going on in town, all the people he had seen on the street who were fighting and crying and laughing. As Song Gang spoke he suddenly remembered the White Rabbits, so he hurriedly lifted the stone stoop and retrieved them. He said, "That was close"—the worms had just eaten through the leaf wrappers but fortunately hadn't gotten to the candy. He carefully put the five pieces of candy into his pocket and then placed his hand protectively over it. After a while Song Gang said softly, "Baldy Li, I'm really hungry. I didn't have lunch. Could I have the candies?"

Baldy Li hesitated, unwilling to spare them. Outside Song Gang continued, "I'm starving. Just let me have one."

Baldy Li nodded and said, "Why don't you have four of them. Just save me one."

Song Gang shook his head. "I'll just have one."

Song Gang took one of the candies out of his pocket, examined it, then brought it up to his face and sniffed for a while. Baldy Li didn't hear any chewing, only sniffing, so he asked, "Why does your chewing sound like sniffing?"

Song Gang giggled. "I'm not eating. I'm just sniffing."

Baldy Li asked, "Why aren't you're eating?"

Song Gang swallowed his drool, saying, "I'm not going to eat it. They're all for you. I'll just take a few sniffs."

Right then Li Lan came home. From inside Baldy Li first heard his mother's shout of surprise and delight, then her rapid footsteps; then he heard Song Gang cry out, "Mama!" Li Lan ran up to the house and scooped Song Gang up in her arms, all the while chattering non-stop like a machine gun. Baldy Li, meanwhile, was still locked inside. He banged at the door with all his might, shouting and crying, but it took a while before Li Lan registered his cries and opened the door.

Baldy Li and Song Gang finally saw each other again in person. The two boys grabbed each other's hands and bounced up and down, hooting and hollering, until they both worked up a headful of sweat and the snivel from their noses dribbled into their mouths. They jumped about for more than ten minutes before Song Gang remembered the White Rabbits in his pocket. Wiping the sweat from his forehead, he rooted around for the candies, counting out "one, two, three, four," and "five," as he placed them one by one into Baldy Li's hands. Baldy Li put four of them in his pocket but unwrapped the last one and popped it into his mouth.

Li Lan had suffered through a whole day of struggle sessions at the silk factory and was worn down and weary as she approached home. But the moment she saw Song Gang, her face lit up with excitement. This was the first time since Song Fanping's death that she had been this happy. She exclaimed that she was going to give the two boys a good meal to celebrate Song Gang's visit, and, taking them both by the hand, she set off for the People's Restaurant to get noodles. As they walked along the streets at dusk Baldy Li felt as if he had not been out-side for years. He was so joyful that he no longer walked but skipped, and Song Gang did likewise. Li Lan led them with a broad smile, and her happiness infected the boys as they skipped along even more cheerfully.

As they reached the bridge they saw Mama Su from the snack shop standing there with a wooden placard around her neck. Her daughter, Missy Su, stood by her side, clutching her shirttail. Song Gang walked up to Mama Su and asked, "Why would someone as kind as you have to wear a wooden placard?"

Mama Su, her head bowed, did not respond, but Missy Su wiped her tears upon hearing Song Gang's words. Li Lan also stood there with her head bowed, whispering to Baldy Li and giving him a gentle nudge to share a candy with Missy Su. Baldy Li gulped, fished out a White Rabbit from his pocket, and painfully surrendered it to Missy Su, who reached out a tear-dampened palm and accepted it. Mama Su then looked up and smiled at Li Lan, and Li Lan smiled back. Li Lan stood for a while, then tugged at Song Gang's hand. Song Gang knew it was time to go. He said to Mama Su, "Don't worry. You will be rewarded in the next life."

Mama Su responded in a low voice, "You're a good boy. You will also be rewarded."

Mama Su then looked at Baldy Li and Li Lan and added, "You will all be rewarded."

Li Lan led Baldy Li and Song Gang to the People's Restaurant. The boys had not been there for a long time, the last time having been with Song Fanping, right after his flag-waving atop the bridge, when all of them were in heightened spirits. That time, everyone in the restaurant had gathered around as they ate their noodles, and the cook had even served them a special meat broth. Now the restaurant was nearly deserted. Li Lan ordered two bowls of plain noodles for the boys but didn't get anything for herself, explaining that she still had leftovers at home. As Baldy Li and Song Gang slurped down their bowls of steaming hot noodles, their noses were almost dripping into their soup. The noodle soup seemed to be as delicious as before. When the cook who had served them the last time saw that no one was paying attention, he came over and whispered, "I gave you the meat broth."

Li Lan led the two boys by the hand and walked along the street for a very long time. They passed by the basketball court that had once been all lit up. The three of them sat on stones next to the court and gazed out at the vast, empty ball court under the moonlight. Li Lan remembered how this space had once been brilliantly illuminated and how Song Fanping had outshone everyone in that fierce game. She particularly remembered that awesome dunk of his, how the crowds momentarily fell silent, then exploded in gasps and cheers. Li Lan smiled to herself and told the boys, "Now that your father has passed away, there's no one in the world who can dunk a basketball like he could."

Song Gang stayed for two days at Baldy Li's place, but on the third morning his grandfather came, carrying a pumpkin on his back. He declined to come inside, preferring to stand outside, head bowed. Li Lan greeted him warmly, calling him Father and leading him inside by the sleeve. The old landlord blushed and shook his head. There was nothing Li Lan could do to persuade him, so she brought a stool outside and invited him to sit down. The old landlord declined and instead continued to wait patiently for Song Gang to finish his breakfast, moving only to place the pumpkin beside the door. When Song Gang emerged, his grandfather took him by the hand and, bowing slightly to Li Lan, led him away.

Baldy Li ran to the door and sadly watched Song Gang depart. As he walked Song Gang kept looking back sadly at Baldy Li, then he raised his arm above his his head and waved, and Baldy Li waved back.

After this, Song Gang came to town about once a month. He no longer came alone but, rather, accompanied his grandfather when he came to peddle vegetables. The two of them would set out for town before it was light, while Baldy Li was still sound asleep. As they entered through the southern gate Song Gang would run along the dark streets to Baldy Li's house, carrying with him two heads of fresh greens. Quietly leaving the greens at the door, he would run back to the market and sit by his grandfather's side, calling out, "Fresh vegetables!"

Song Gang and his grandfather would often finish with their peddling just as the sun was coming up. His grandfather, with empty baskets, would lead Song Gang by the hand and circle back to Baldy Li's house, where the two of them would stand quietly outside the door, listening for any stirring inside and wondering if mother and son had woken up yet. Li Lan and Baldy Li would invariably still be asleep, the two heads of greens still waiting by the door. So Song Gang and his grandfather would silently take their leave.

During that first year, every time Song Gang came to town he would bring Baldy Li a few White Rabbits, wrapping them in wutong leaves and leaving them under the stone stoop in front of the door. Baldy Li had no idea how many White Rabbits Li Lan had given Song Gang, but during that first year Baldy Li almost always had White Rabbits to look forward to.

After rising and opening the door, Li Lan would spot the dew-misted vegetables waiting outside and call out to Baldy Li, "Song Gang's been here!"

Baldy Li's first action would always be to flip over the stone and retrieve the candy, and then he would dash out into the street. Li Lan knew that Baldy Li wanted to see Song Gang, and therefore she wouldn't try to stop him. After finding no trace of Song Gang at the market, Baldy Li would immediately turn around and run toward the southern gate. A few times the brothers actually caught sight of each other there. Baldy Li would spy Song Gang in the distance, walking behind his grandfather and his baskets, and Baldy Li would shout at the top of his lungs, "Song Gang! Song Gang!"

Hearing him, Song Gang would turn around and shout, "Baldy Li! Baldy Li!"

Baldy Li would stand there, continuing to call out Song Gang's name. As he walked Song Gang would repeatedly look back at Baldy Li, waving and calling out his name. Baldy Li called out until he lost sight of Song Gang, and even then he continued calling out, "Song Gang! Song Gang!"

With every shout, he would hear echoes in the distance: "Gang . . . Gang . . . Gang . . ."

CHAPTER 24

TIME DRIFTED silently and unnoticed past our Liu Town, and before anyone realized it seven years had gone by. In Liu Town, a widow was not supposed to wash her hair for a month after her husband's death, and sometimes the custom would be extended to half a year. Li Lan stopped washing her hair altogether following Song Fanping's death. For seven years she didn't wash it, instead slicking it down with oil. She would neatly comb her black, greasy hair and proudly walk down the main street with the kids of Liu Town trailing behind, taunting, "Landlord's wife, Landlord's wife . . ."

Li Lan never shed her proud smile. Though she and Song Fanping had spent only fourteen months together as husband and wife, for Li Lan it meant more than if it had been a lifetime. Seven years of not washing her hair, combined with the layers upon layers of oil she applied, resulted in a foul odor emanating from her head that grew increasingly noxious. At first it was just the house, which would smell like worn socks the moment she returned home; then the odor grew so strong that everyone would smell it as she walked down the street. Everyone in Liu Town now ran away from her. Even the kids who used to call her "Landlord's wife" would cover their noses and run away, yelling, "That stinks, stinks . . ."

Li Lan's hair became her badge of honor. She wanted everyone to think of her always as Song Fanping's wife. After Baldy Li entered school, each time he had to fill out his father's name, she always made him write "Song Fanping," after which he had to write "landlord" in the Family Class Background box. As a result, Baldy Li was maligned and abused at school, and his classmates all took to calling him Little Landlord. Aside from Li Lan and Song Gang, who would occasionally visit him from the countryside, no one else seemed to know his name was Baldy Li, and in the end even the teachers used his class designation to address him, as in "Little Landlord, stand up and read that passage."

When Baldy Li turned ten, he remembered that he had a birth father—the one who had drowned in the latrine while ogling women's bottoms. Baldy Li resolved to use his birth father's name so he could escape the bad luck of being called a landlord. When he once again had to fill out a name for the blank under Father, he decided to resist and asked his mother, "What should I write?"

Li Lan, who was in the middle of cooking, was taken aback by Baldy Li's question. She looked at her son in confusion, then answered, "Song Fanping."

Baldy Li lowered his head. "I mean my other dad. . . ."

Li Lan gave him a withering look and replied firmly, "You have no other dad."

Li Lan lived her identity as a landlord's wife with pride—it kept Song Fanping alive in her heart. Her pride lasted seven years, until the year Baldy Li turned fourteen. That was the year Baldy Li was caught spying on women in the toilet. Li Lan immediately fell apart, and later, when once again Baldy Li had to fill out a form, she erased Song Fanping's name and substituted a name that was entirely foreign to Baldy Li—Liu Shanfeng—and also changed the Family Class Background box from "landlord" to "poor peasant." After Li Lan handed the revised form to Baldy Li, she noticed he again erased "Liu Shanfeng" and "poor peasant" and replaced them with "Song Fanping" and "landlord." Fourteen-year-old Baldy Li no longer cared that he was a little landlord. Grumbling as he erased his birth father's name, he said, "Song Fanping's my dad."

Li Lan stared at her son as if he were a stranger. His words shocked her. When he raised his head to look at her, she immediately looked down, mumbling, "Your birth father's name was Liu Shanfeng."

"What Liu Shanfeng?" Baldy Li tossed out the words with contempt. "If he were my dad, then Song Gang wouldn't be my brother."

Ever since Baldy Li had become notorious for peeping in the women's toilet, he was no longer called Little Landlord and became known instead as Little Buttpeeper. His birth father, who had long been forgotten, together with his own notorious deed, was now ubiquitous again, like an excavated relic, and referred to by Baldy Li's classmates as Old Buttpeeper. Even the teachers adopted Baldy Li's new nickname, saying, for instance, "Hey, Little Buttpeeper, go clean the toilets."

Li Lan was once again trapped in her shame, just as she had been when her first husband had drowned in the public latrine. All the pride that Song Fanping had granted her suddenly dissipated. She no longer walked down the street with her head held high but instead became as fearful and timid as she had been fourteen years earlier. Now every time she went out she walked with her head bowed and turned toward the wall, feeling as though all eyes were upon her. She no longer wanted to go outside; even when she was home, she locked herself in, sitting on her bed like a bump on a log. Her migraines also returned, and her teeth once again chattered from dawn until dusk.

Baldy Li by this time was busy peddling the secrets of Lin Hong's bottom, and his face glowed with health from having downed countless bowls of house-special noodles, along with an occasional bowl of plain noodles.

Baldy Li strutted down the street like a celebrity, not minding at all being called Little Buttpeeper. The folks who called him that didn't know a thing. As for those who were in the know—folks like Victory Zhao, Success Liu, Little Scissors Guan, and others, basically everyone who had done business with him over the secrets of Lin Hong's bottom—they all called him King of Butts. By this time Victory Zhao was Poet Zhao and Success Liu was Writer Liu, and it was these two Men of Talent who had come up with Baldy Li's new nickname. He was quite satisfied with King of Butts. *Gotta tell it like it is*, he thought.

The teenage Baldy Li and the two young men Poet Zhao and Writer Liu were best pals for a few months. What they had in common was the study and discussion of Lin Hong's beautiful backside. Liu Town's two Men of Talent racked their brains to come up with myriad literary phrases—graphic, lyrical, descriptive, metaphorical, clinical, and analytical—and they laid them all at Baldy Li's feet for him to choose the ones that most accurately captured the wonders of what he had seen. But once they had exhausted all possible ways of discussing the matter, their friendship with Baldy Li came to a natural conclusion. Several times in the dark of night, the two Men of Talent went to pilfer books from a room that was filled with tomes confiscated during the Cultural Revolution while Baldy Li served as their lookout. Many of the wondrous and poetic phrases that they came up with to describe Lin Hong's bottom were discovered in these stolen books.

Blacksmith Tong was the only one among those in the know who did not refer to Baldy Li as King of Butts. He had wanted to use a cheap bowl of plain noodles to obtain Baldy Li's secrets, but the boy had not fallen for it. Therefore, Blacksmith Tong, out a bowl of noodles and with nothing to show for it, would curse Baldy Li every time he saw him: "Little Bastard Buttpeeper."

Baldy Li took absolutely no offense, instead reasoning with him, "You might as well call me King of Butts like everyone else."

Sometimes Baldy Li would run into Lin Hong on the street. She was eighteen then, and at the height of her beauty. All the men stared slack-jawed as she walked by, but only Baldy Li had the guts to greet her enthusiastically, as if she were an old flame of his. "Lin Hong, it's been a long time! What have you been up to?"

Lin Hong blushed in fury and shame. She couldn't believe that this little fifteen-year-old Peeping Tom of a hoodlum was actually sidling up to her. Completely ignoring the shocked and mocking glances of the passersby, Baldy Li continued warmly, "How is everyone in your family?"

Lin Hong said through gritted teeth, "Just go away!"

Hearing this, Baldy Li looked behind him and waved off the people around them as if she had been speaking to someone else. Then he volunteered his protective services to Lin Hong, who by this point was furious to the point of tears. He asked, "Where are you headed? I'll escort you."

Lin Hong couldn't bear another moment of this and screamed loudly, "Go away! Jerk!"

Baldy Li again looked behind him, whereupon Lin Hong pointed directly at him. "I'm telling *you* to go away!"

Amid the laughter of the crowds, Baldy Li watched as Lin Hong walked off. Smacking his lips regretfully, he told the onlookers, "She's still mad at me."

Then he shook his head and sighed ruefully. "I shouldn't have taken that wrong turn in life."

Reports of Baldy Li's various misdeeds trickled down to Li Lan's ears, causing her to bow her head even farther. She had borne her first husband's scandal, and now she had to bear her son's notoriety. She, whose face had once been bathed in tears daily, now had no more left to shed. But she didn't say a word to Baldy Li about his doings, because she knew that she had no control over him. Often she would be awakened in the middle of the night by her migraines and would lie there, wondering what was to become of Baldy Li. She spent one sleepless night after another asking in distress, "Dear God, why did I have to give birth to such a demon?"

As Li Lan's spirit collapsed, her health also faltered. Her migraines became more and more severe, and then her kidneys started failing. While Baldy Li was enjoying his meals of house-special noodles and fattening himself up, Li Lan was no longer going to work, having taken a long sick leave to rest at home. Her complexion had become waxy and sallow, and when she went for her daily shots at the clinic, the doctors and nurses could smell the sour, foul odor emanating from her even through their surgical masks. They turned their heads away as they spoke with her or gave her shots. Her illness eventually worsened to the point where she tried to check into the hospital. They told her, "Go wash your hair before checking in."

Li Lan hung her head in shame the entire way home and spent the next couple of days holed up in misery. During that time she thought of nothing but Song Fanping, his smile and his words; she felt that washing her hair would be a betrayal of him, the love of her life. Ultimately she concluded that she did not have much longer to live and would soon be going to the netherworld to be reunited with Song Fanping, and perhaps even he might be bothered by the foulness of her hair. So one Sunday afternoon she placed a set of clean clothes in a basket and pulled Baldy Li aside just as he was leaving the house. After hesitating for a moment, she said, "I don't think I will be getting better, so I'd like to clean myself before dying."

This was the first time since his Peeping Tom incident that Li Lan asked Baldy Li to accompany her in public. Though her son had shamed her as much as her first husband had, and though she could never forgive her first husband even after he had lost his life, her son was different. After all, they were of the same flesh.

As Li Lan and Baldy Li walked down the street toward the bathhouse, she suddenly noticed that he was taller than she, which brought a smile to her face and she held his arm a little more tightly. By then, even the act of walking left her exhausted, and every twenty or so yards she had to find a tree to lean against. As they walked Baldy Li waved and greeted all those who knew him, then explained to her who they were. Li Lan was shocked to discover that this fifteen-year-old son of hers seemed to know far more people than she ever had.

It was about a third of a mile from their home to the bathhouse, but it took Li Lan more than an hour to cover the distance. Each time she rested against a tree, Baldy Li would wait patiently to one side, describing to her what was going on in town. All of this was news to Li Lan, and she suddenly regarded Baldy Li with a newfound respect. She briefly felt happy but then thought to herself, *If only Baldy Li were as upright a young man as Song Gang, then he really could make a good life for himself.* Then she reminded herself, *My son is a demon.*

After arriving at the front door of the bathhouse, Li Lan leaned against the wall and rested a bit more. She took Baldy Li's hand and asked him not to leave but to wait for her outside. Baldy Li nodded as he watched his mother walk in. She walked as if she were an old lady, but her hair, which had not been washed for seven years, was black and shiny.

Baldy Li stood outside the bathhouse for what seemed like an eternity. First his legs ached, then even his toes. He saw a stream of people exiting the bathhouse, their cheeks ruddy and their hair wet. Some of them remembered to taunt him as Little Buttpeeper, while others addressed him as King of Butts. Baldy Li didn't even deign to look the former in the eye but greeted the latter with warm smiles, since these were noodle clients, and Baldy Li believed that customers always came first.

Blacksmith Tong also emerged from the bathhouse. When he saw Baldy Li standing there, he cursed him, "Little Bastard Buttpeeper." He also pointed at the bathhouse, saying, "Why don't you go peep in there? There are so many butts you wouldn't know where to begin."

Baldy Li sniffed. "What would you know? When there are so many butts, how could you concentrate? You don't even know where to focus."

He held up five fingers and, with an authoritative air, lectured Blacksmith Tong: "You can't look at more than five butts at once, and at a bare minimum you need at least two. This is because with any more than five you would get confused, but with only one you wouldn't have anything to compare it to."

Hearing this, Blacksmith Tong seemed to have an epiphany. With a worshipful tone he said to Baldy Li, "You Little Bastard Buttpeeper— you've really got talent. I'll have to treat you to house-special noodles sometime."

Baldy Li put up his hand modestly and corrected Blacksmith Tong, "Please call me King of Butts."

This time Blacksmith Tong went along with the correction and affirmed, "You really are the King of Butts."

So Liu Town's King of Butts, Baldy Li, waited outside the bathhouse for his mother for more than three hours. He alternated between wild impatience and anxious concern, wondering, *Did she pass out in there?* After three hours had passed, a woman with a head full of gray hair walked out slowly behind a group of young women. Baldy Li was so busy checking out the wet-haired young women that he didn't even notice the elderly woman coming toward him. The gray-haired woman paused in front of him and said, "Baldy Li."

Baldy Li was stunned and simply couldn't believe that this woman was his mother. When Li Lan went in, her hair was still black, but now she stood before him with it completely gray. In memory of Song Fanping, she had not washed her hair for seven years, and with this washing she had washed all the black right out.

For the first time Baldy Li realized that his mother had aged and now looked like a granny. She gripped his arm and laboriously made her way home. When acquaintances along the way caught sight of Li Lan, they would invariably be stunned, examining her up close and gasping, "Li Lan? Are you Li Lan?"

Li Lan nodded. Exhausted, she answered, "Yes, it's me."

CHAPTER 25

UPON RETURNING HOME, Li Lan examined herself carefully in the mirror. She too was shocked by the suddenness of her aging and was struck by a sense of foreboding, a feeling that, after checking into the hospital, she would never return home. Though she had washed all the foulness from her hair, she didn't immediately go to the hospital but instead stayed home for a few more days. During that time, she would either lie in bed or sit at the table, gazing at Baldy Li with concern and sighing, saying, "What will become of you?"

Li Lan began to deal with her personal effects, but what worried her most was Baldy Li—what would happen to him after she died? She worried that he would not come to a good end. If at fourteen he was already peeping at women's bottoms in the toilet, who knew what horrible things he would be into by the time he turned eighteen? She worried that he would end up in jail one day.

Li Lan decided to arrange everything as best she could for him before entering the hospital. Clutching their family registry to her chest, she had Baldy Li take her to the local Civil Affairs Bureau. As she entered she keenly felt herself marked as both a landlord's wife and a hoodlum's mother. She hung her head in shame as she tiptoed nervously into the office, asking, "Who's in charge of orphans?"

Baldy Li helped Li Lan into a room, where they saw a man in his thirties reading a newspaper at his desk. Baldy Li recognized him right away—this was the man who had helped lug Song Fanping's body back from the bus depot seven years earlier. Baldy Li pointed at him excitedly, exclaiming, "It's you! You're Tao Qing."

Li Lan yanked Baldy Li's sleeve, trying to curb her son's rudeness. She bowed deeply, inquiring obsequiously, "Would you happen to be Comrade Tao?"

Tao Qing nodded and put down his paper. He took a careful look at Baldy Li and seemed to remember him. Li Lan was standing at the door, not daring to step inside, and said with a trembling voice, "Comrade Tao, I have something to inquire."

Tao Qing smiled. "Please come inside."

Li Lan shifted uneasily. "My class background is not good."

Tao Qing continued smiling. "Come inside."

As he spoke he pulled a chair over and invited Li Lan to sit down. Li Lan fearfully stepped in but didn't dare to sit down. Tao Qing gestured at the chair. "Please sit down first."

Hesitantly Li Lan sat down. She respectfully handed Tao Qing her family registry. Pointing to Baldy Li, she explained, "This is my son. His name is in the registry."

Tao Qing flipped through the booklet. "I see that. How can I help you?"

Li Lan smiled bitterly and proceeded. "I have uremia, and my days are numbered. When I'm gone, my son will be left orphaned. Will he be able to receive any aid?"

Tao Qing stared at Li Lan in astonishment. He looked at Baldy Li and nodded. "Yes, he would. He'd qualify for eight yuan a month, plus twenty *jin*'s worth of grain, oil, and cloth ration coupons every season. And he'd receive aid until he starts work."

Li Lan explained uneasily, "My class background is bad. I'm a landlord's wife. . . ."

Tao Qing smiled and handed the registry back to Li Lan. "I understand your situation. Don't worry, just leave things to me. Your son can come look me up."

Li Lan finally let out a sigh of relief. Her happiness brought a bit of color to her cheeks. Tao Qing chuckled as he continued to look at Baldy Li, saying, "So you're Baldy Li. You're quite famous. What's the other one's name?"

Baldy Li knew that he was asking about Song Gang and was just about to answer when Li Lan stood up uneasily. She knew that when Tao Qing said Baldy Li was famous, he was referring to the Peeping Tom incident in the toilet, so she uttered a few quick words of thanks and immediately asked Baldy Li to help her out. Only after they had left the room and the Civil Affairs building did Li Lan feel she could pause and rest. Taking labored breaths, she sighed and said, "That Comrade Tao is a good man."

That was when Baldy Li told her that Tao Qing was the man who had brought Song Fanping's body back from the bus depot. When Li Lan heard this she immediately flushed bright red and, no longer needing Baldy Li's assistance, hurried back to Tao Qing's office, saying, "You are our savior. Let me kowtow to you."

Li Lan threw her body to the ground to kowtow, slamming her fore-head to the ground and breaking into heartrending sobs. Startled, Tao Qing stood up and only gradually understood through Li Lan's barely coherent words why she was kneeling in front of him. He quickly reached out to raise her up, but Li Lan knelt down again to kowtow twice more. Tao Qing had to cajole her for a long time like a child before she would allow herself to be helped up. He helped her all the way to the front of the Civil Affairs building, and as they parted Tao Qing gave her a thumbs-up sign and said quietly, "Song Fanping—what a man."

Li Lan was so overcome she started trembling all over. After Tao Qing walked off, Li Lan was still wiping her tears and joyfully repeating to Baldy Li, "Did you hear that? Did you hear what Comrade Tao just said?"

After leaving the Civil Affairs Bureau, Li Lan proceeded to the cof-fin store. Her forehead still bleeding, she had to pause every few steps, and every time she stopped she couldn't help repeating Tao Qing's words, "Song Fanping—what a man."

With great pride she gestured in front of her and told Baldy Li, "Everyone in Liu Town thinks that about him. They just don't dare to say it out loud."

They slowly made their way to the coffin store. When they finally arrived, Li Lan sat on the front stoop, panting and wiping at the blood on her forehead. She smiled and announced to the people inside, "I'm here."

Everyone in the coffin store recognized her and asked, "Who are you buying a coffin for this time?"

Embarrassed, Li Lan replied, "For myself."

Initially startled, they all broke out laughing and said, "We've never had a living person buying a coffin for himself before."

Li Lan also smiled. "Yes, I've never heard of it either."

Pointing to Baldy Li, she continued, "My son is still young and wouldn't know what kind of coffin to get, so I thought that I'd reserve one and he can come pick it up later."

Everyone in the coffin store knew of the notorious Baldy Li. Cack-ling, they looked at him as he stood diffidently by the door, then remarked to Li Lan, "Well, he's not *that* young."

Li Lan lowered her head. She knew why they were cackling. Li Lan selected the cheapest coffin, one that cost only eight yuan. It was the same kind of unvarnished, thin-planked coffin that she had bought Song Fanping. Her hands trembling, she fished out her money wrapped in a handkerchief and paid them four yuan, with the remainder to be paid when the coffin was picked up.

After going to the Civil Affairs Bureau to take care of Baldy Li's orphan aid and then purchasing a coffin at the coffin store, Li Lan felt that the two biggest burdens she had been shouldering were now taken care of. She could check into the hospital the following day, but by her reckoning it was only six days until the Qingming holiday, when they would pay their respects to the dead. She shook her head, telling herself that on Qingming she wanted to go visit Song Fanping's grave in the countryside, and then she would check into the hospital.

Li Lan slowly dragged her body, which felt increasingly like a deadweight, to Liu Town's bookstore. At the stationery counter she purchased a packet of white paper, then she slowly made her way home, resting repeatedly along the way. Sitting at the table, she started to make paper ingots and coins. On every Qingming festival since Song Fanping passed away, Li Lan had cut out a basketful of paper ingots and coins and then would set off on the long journey to the countryside to burn them at his grave.

By this point Li Lan was so ill she barely had any strength left. After each ingot, she had to rest for a while. Her hand trembled as she struggled to draw lines on the coins or write out the characters GOLD and SILVER on the ingots. It took her four whole days to finish what she ordinarily would have completed in an afternoon. She then placed the paper ingots in the basket and carefully rested the paper coins strung together with white thread on top of them. Smiling, she let out a long sigh, followed by some tears, sensing that this was probably the last time she would be able to visit Song Fanping's grave.

That night she called Baldy Li to her bedside and examined him carefully. She was comforted to see that her son looked nothing like that man named Liu Shanfeng. Her breathing labored, she told him, "The day after tomorrow is Qingming. I'd like to go visit the grave, but I don't have the energy to make it that far."

"Ma, don't you worry," Baldy Li replied. "I'll carry you."

Li Lan smiled and shook her head, then mentioned her other son. "Why don't you go to the countryside tomorrow and bring Song Gang back? The two of you can take turns carrying me."

"No need to fetch Song Gang." Baldy Li firmly shook his head. "I can carry you by myself."

"No," Li Lan said. "The road is too long; you would exhaust yourself trying to carry me alone."

"If we get tired, we'll rest under a tree." Baldy Li waved dismissively. "We'll just sit and rest."

Li Lan still shook her head. "Go fetch Song Gang."

"No need," Baldy Li replied. "I'll think of something."

Baldy Li yawned and said he was going to the outer room to go to bed. At the door he turned to Li Lan and said, "Ma, don't you worry. I guarantee that I'll get you comfortably to the countryside, and then bring you comfortably back to town."

Baldy Li, who by now was fifteen, lay down in his bed. Within five minutes he had come up with a plan, and so he closed his eyes and immediately started snoring.

It wasn't until afternoon the next day that Baldy Li leisurely made his way out of the house. First he went to the hospital, where he paced the halls as if he were a visitor coming to see a relative; the moment he noticed that no one was at the nurse's station, he ducked right in. Once inside, he took his time, selecting from among a dozen or more used IV bottles, raising each of them to see which had the most glucose left. Once he had made his selection, he swiftly hid it under his shirt, ducked back out of the nurse's station, and left the hospital.

Baldy Li paraded down the street with his swiped bottle. From time to time he dangled it in front of his eyes, trying to figure out exactly how much glucose was left inside. He guessed that there was probably half an ounce, but in order to be sure, he walked into a soy sauce store and asked the vendor how much liquid he thought there was inside. The soy sauce vendor was of course an old hand at this sort of thing. He gave the bottle a couple of twirls and announced that between half an ounce and an ounce was left. Pleased with this estimate, Baldy Li took back the bottle and said, "This is pure nutrition."

Baldy Li walked smugly with his glucose into Blacksmith Tong's shop. Baldy Li knew that Blacksmith Tong had his own pullcart, and he was hoping to borrow it for a day to take Li Lan to the countryside. Baldy Li stood at the door of the shop and watched Blacksmith Tong raining down sweat while working a piece of metal. After a while Baldy Li waved at him benevolently, as if on an inspection visit, and said, "Take a rest, take a rest."

Blacksmith Tong put down his hammer and wiped his sweat-drenched face with a towel. He watched as Baldy Li sauntered into his shop and comfortably took a seat on the long bench he used to sexually exploit. Blacksmith Tong growled, "You little bastard. What do you want?"

Baldy Li chuckled. "I'm here to collect my debts."

"Fuck," spat Blacksmith Tong, as he whipped his towel in the air. "And what debt would that be, you little bastard?"

Baldy Li continued chuckling. He reminded Blacksmith Tong, "Remember what you said to me two weeks ago in front of the bathhouse."

"What did I say?" Blacksmith Tong honestly couldn't remember.

Baldy Li pointed to himself. "You said that I, Baldy Li, was truly something, and that someday you were going to treat me to a bowl of house-special noodles."

Blacksmith Tong remembered now. He hung his towel back around his neck and growled, "Yeah, so I did say that. What are you going to do about it?"

Baldy Li decided to shift to flattery. He said, "Who doesn't know your stature in this town? When you, Blacksmith Tong, say 'Jump,' everyone asks, 'How high?' You would never go back on your word, would you?"

"You really are a little bastard," Blacksmith Tong said, laughing. He couldn't maintain his bullying tone any longer, but he did find a loop-hole. Smugly, he said, "It's true I said I'd treat you to a bowl of house-special noodles someday. But someday—that could be any day. I certainly don't know when."

"You got me!" Baldy Li showed his admiration by giving him a thumbs-up but then immediately cut to the chase. "How about this: I won't have you treat me to a bowl of house-special noodles, but if you lend me your cart for a day, we'll call it even."

Blacksmith Tong had no idea where Baldy Li was going with this. He asked, "So why do you want to borrow my pullcart?"

"Aiya!" sighed Baldy Li. He explained to Blacksmith Tong, "My mother wants to go sweep my father's grave in the countryside. You know how sick she is. She certainly couldn't make it by walking, so that's why I want to borrow your pullcart."

As he spoke he put the IV drip bottle down on the bench. Blacksmith Tong pointed at it and asked, "What's that for?"

"This is a military canteen," proclaimed Baldy Li. He explained, "The road to the country is long and the sun will be strong, so what happens when my mother gets thirsty? I'm going to fill this bottle with water and nurse her along the way with it. That's what this military canteen is for."

Blacksmith Tong said, "Oh," and added, "I would have never pegged you, little bastard, for a filial son."

Baldy Li smiled modestly. He gave the drip bottle a few swirls and observed, "There's somewhere between half an ounce and an ounce of glucose nutrition in there."

Blacksmith Tong said generously, "Well, seeing that you're being such a filial son, I'll lend you the cart."

Baldy Li thanked him repeatedly. He then patted the long bench and waved Blacksmith Tong to sit down next to him. Baldy Li said mysteriously, "I won't just borrow your pullcart with nothing in return. Good deeds are to be repaid in kind, as they say."

Blacksmith Tong didn't understand. "What do you mean, repaid in kind?"

Baldy Li whispered, "Lin Hong's butt. . . ."

"Oh!" Now everything became clear.

Intrigued, Blacksmith Tong sat next to Baldy Li as the latter began to divulge the secrets of Lin Hong's butt with the most florid of descriptions. Just as he was getting to the most exciting part, Baldy Li's lips ceased moving. Blacksmith Tong waited patiently for him to start up again, but when he did he no longer spoke of Lin Hong's bottom but, rather, of how Poet Zhao nabbed him at that critical moment. Blacksmith Tong was crushed. He stood up, rubbing his hands and pacing about back and forth, then broke out in curses: "That bastard Poet Zhao. . . ."

Though he had gained only the faintest glimpse of Lin Hong's bottom, Blacksmith Tong was still filled with goodwill toward Baldy Li. When he lent Baldy Li his pullcart, he told him, "Whenever you need the cart, just give me a holler and take it away."

Baldy Li stashed his pilfered glucose drip in his pocket and pulled Blacksmith Tong's cart up to Yanker Yu's stand. He now had his eyes on Yanker Yu's rattan recliner. He planned to tie the recliner onto Blacksmith Tong's cart so that Li Lan could ride lying down all the way to the countryside.

When Baldy Li walked up, Yanker Yu was himself stretched out on the chair, napping. Baldy Li set the pullcart down with a resounding thump. Yanker Yu woke up with a start, but when he opened his eyes and saw it was merely Baldy Li with a pullcart and that neither of them was a customer, he promptly shut his eyes again. Baldy Li inspected everything with the air of a visiting officer. Hands clasped behind his back, he examined the dental tools and teeth displayed on the table.

It was already the tail end of the Cultural Revolution, and the revolution was no longer a roaring tide but more like a trickling stream. Yanker Yu no longer had to display his class loyalty with an exhibit of mistakenly extracted healthy teeth; on the contrary, they now threatened to hurt his reputation as a dentist. Tacking to the political winds, Yanker Yu had hidden away his healthy-teeth display behind his cash. He figured that after flowing west for a while the river might begin flowing east again, and the revolutionary stream could again turn into a tide, so he might as well save the healthy-teeth display for another cycle.

Baldy Li examined the table for a while but didn't spot any healthy teeth. He rapped the table and loudly asked, "What about the healthy teeth? Where are the healthy teeth?"

"What healthy teeth?" Yanker Yu opened his eyes in annoyance.

"Those healthy teeth you pulled." Baldy Li pointed at the table, "They used to be sitting right here."

"Shut your trap," Yanker Yu said angrily. Sitting up, he insisted, "I've never pulled a single healthy tooth. I only pull them out when they're rotten."

Baldy Li hadn't expected Yanker Yu to get so riled up, so he immediately smiled ingratiatingly, changing course as smoothly as Yanker Yu had. Baldy Li slapped his forehead, saying, "Yes, yes, you have certainly never extracted a good tooth. I must have remembered wrong."

As he spoke Baldy Li pulled up a stool next to the recliner and started to flatter Yanker Yu just as he had done with Blacksmith Tong, saying, "You, Yanker Yu, are the premier tooth extractor within a hundred miles. You could pull a rotten tooth out with your eyes closed."

Yanker Yu's fury transformed into satisfaction, and he smiled. "Now, that's the truth."

Feeling that Yanker Yu was now ripe for the plucking, Baldy Li began, "So you have been here for some twenty years. You must have seen all the young ladies in Liu Town, right?"

"Young ladies?" Yanker Yu bragged, "I've seen them all—even the not-so-young ones. Throughout Liu Town, I know right away whenever a young lady gets married or an old lady gets buried."

"So, in your opinion," prodded Baldy Li, "who is the prettiest young lady in Liu Town?"

"Lin Hong," Yanker Yu replied without hesitation. "Without question, it would be Lin Hong."

"So"—Baldy Li chuckled—"who among all the men in Liu Town has seen Lin Hong's bare butt?"

"You, of course." Yanker Yu pointed at Baldy Li and laughed heartily. "You little bastard."

Baldy Li nodded and then leaned in closer and whispered, "So would you like to hear about it?"

Yanker Yu's laughing face immediately became solemn. He sat up from his recliner and peered about the alley. When he saw that no one was around, he whispered to Baldy Li, "Tell me!"

Yanker Yu's eyes glittered, and his mouth hung wide open as if he were waiting for a dumpling to drop down from heaven. But Baldy Li, a master of calculation, chose this very moment to fall silent. What the men in Liu Town said about him was true: This fifteen-year-old little bastard played a better game than a career card shark in his fifties. Yanker Yu saw Baldy Li's lips sealed tightly shut and anxiously prodded, "Well, go on!"

Very deliberately, Baldy Li ran his hand over Yanker Yu's rattan recliner. The corners of his mouth turned up slightly as he said, "Loan me this chair for a day, and I'll map out every millimeter of Lin Hong's bottom for you."

When Yanker Yu heard that Baldy Li wanted to borrow the recliner, he immediately shook his head. "I can't do that. How can I pull teeth without this recliner for customers to lie down on?"

Baldy Li reasoned with him patiently, "You'd still have your stool. Given your world-renowned skills, they could be standing up and you'd still manage."

Yanker Yu cackled a couple times as he did a quick mental calculation of the pros and cons of the arrangement. Perhaps losing the recliner for a day in exchange for the secrets of the beautiful Lin Hong's bottom would not be such a bad deal at all. He nodded in agreement, then raised a finger, saying, "Okay, but just for one day."

Baldy Li already had his lips up to Yanker Yu's ear as he launched into a vivid narration. Having worked through fifty-six bowls of house-special noodles, and with the literary embellishments from Poet Zhao and Writer Liu, Baldy Li by now had a story burnished to a high sheen. Lin Hong's bottom could not have been made more bewitchingly captivating. Yanker Yu listened, rapt with emotion. He tensed up as if listening to the thrilling climax of a ghost story, then Baldy Li's lips suddenly stopped moving. He gazed over at Yanker Yu's oilcloth umbrella, and Yu became so anxious he cried out, "Go on!"

Baldy Li smacked his lips and pointed at the umbrella. "I want to borrow the umbrella for a day, too."

"You're asking for too much," replied Yanker Yu angrily. "First you borrow my recliner and now my umbrella—all I'll have left is this table. My stand will look as bare as a newly plucked chicken."

Baldy Li shook his head. "Perhaps you'd be bare tomorrow, but you'd have your feathers back the very next day."

Yanker Yu burned with anxious curiosity. He felt as if he had been reading a serialized novel and had just reached a cliff-hanger, so he couldn't do anything but agree to loan out his umbrella as well. Baldy Li went on for a few more sentences on Lin Hong's bottom, but what Yanker Yu heard next was all about Poet Zhao's hand. Dumbfounded, he took a little while to recover enough to ask, "What happened? How did Lin Hong's bottom turn into Poet Zhao's hand?"

"I can't help it." Baldy Li sighed. "That bastard Poet Zhao ruined my moment, and yours, too."

Now Yanker Yu fell into a blind rage, all of it directed toward Poet Zhao. Gritting his teeth, he snarled, "That bastard Zhao, I swear I'm going to pull out one of his good teeth."

With Blacksmith Tong's pullcart and Yanker Yu's recliner and umbrella in tow, Baldy Li then stopped by the warehouse of the town's department store. There he sweet-talked and peddled the secrets of Lin Hong's bottom yet again and managed to borrow a pile of rope. Now his mission was accomplished and, whistling a revolutionary tune and pulling the cart noisily behind him down the main street, he returned home victorious.

By this point it was dark and Li Lan had already gone to bed. In anticipation of the long road ahead the next day, she had eaten and retired early. Ever since Baldy Li had become notorious all over Liu Town, Li Lan had felt that she had completely lost control of this son of hers. He often returned home late at night, and she could do nothing but sigh.

When Baldy Li arrived home, he saw that the lights were out, so he knew his mother had gone to bed. He set the cart down lightly and crept into the house, where he turned on the light and sat at the table to wolf down the dinner his mother had set out for him. Then he got to work. By the light of the room's lamp and the moon outside, he first placed the recliner on top of the pullcart, securing it tightly with the rope. There was an opening for a cup in the chair's armrest, so Baldy Li stuck the umbrella handle through it and then used the rope to fasten it securely in place.

By that point it was well past midnight, but Baldy Li did another careful inspection of the rig, reinforcing various parts with rope. When he was finally done, he circled the cart twice more, his hands behind his back. He couldn't stop grinning. He felt that the cart, chair, and umbrella were as firmly bound together as arms and legs on a torso. Satisfied, he let out a huge yawn and went in to go to bed. Once he was lying down, though, Baldy Li discovered that he couldn't fall asleep, so worried was he that someone would steal his masterpiece. So he grabbed his blanket and went outside. He crawled up onto Blacksmith Tong's cart and lay down on Yanker Yu's recliner. Now feeling secure, he started snoring the moment he shut his eyes.

Li Lan woke up at daybreak to find Baldy Li's bed empty and his blanket missing. Unable to figure out what had happened, she shook her head and opened the front door, then gasped when she saw the odd contraption sitting outside with her son sleeping on top.

Li Lan's gasp woke Baldy Li from his dreams. Seeing his mother's astonished expression, he rubbed his eyes, climbed down from the cart, and proudly explained that the pullcart belonged to Blacksmith Tong, the recliner and the oilcloth umbrella were Yanker Yu's, and the hemp rope binding it all together was borrowed from the department store's warehouse. Baldy Li exclaimed, "Ma, now you can travel in comfort!"

Li Lan regarded her demon of a son and wondered, *How in the world could a fifteen-year-old pull off a feat like this?* She felt that she really didn't know him at all, this son who seemed to be able to whip something out of his bag of tricks every other day.

Mother and son had breakfast, and Baldy Li then lifted their hot-water thermos and carefully poured water into the glucose bottle. "There's somewhere between half an ounce and an ounce of nutritious glucose in here," he told Li Lan, adding that it was in case she got thirsty on the road.

Baldy Li thoughtfully placed his neatly folded blanket over the chair, explaining that it was going to be a bumpy ride but the padding should do the trick. With his left foot holding down one of the pullcart's handles, he gently helped Li Lan climb onto the cart and lie down on the chair. She cradled the basket with the paper ingots and coins and looked up at the oilcloth umbrella over her head, realizing that it was to keep the sun and rain off her. Baldy Li then handed her the bottle with the hot water and glucose mixture. As Li Lan accepted the bottle tears rushed down her face. Baldy Li saw that she was weeping and asked, astonished, "Ma, what's wrong?"

"Nothing at all." Li Lan dabbed at her eyes, then smiled. "Son, let's get going."

That morning Li Lan took a ride on the most luxurious pullcart Liu Town had ever seen. The cart wound its way down the main street with Baldy Li at the fore. The crowds stared, mouths open in astonishment. They simply couldn't believe their eyes; never in their wildest dreams having imagined such a contraption. Someone called out to Baldy Li, asking him how he had managed to put this thing together.

"This thing?" Baldy Li smugly replied. "This thing is my mom's exclusive-use cart."

Everyone was befuddled. "What's an exclusive-use cart?"

"You've never heard of an exclusive-use cart?" Baldy Li asked, then continued proudly: "The jet that Chairman Mao flies in is his exclusive-use jet, the train compartment that Chairman Mao travels in is his exclusive-use compartment, and the car that Chairman Mao rides in is his exclusive-use sedan. Why? Because no one else can use them. My mom's cart is her exclusive-use cart. Why? Because no one else can ride in it."

Everyone broke out into knowing laughter, and even Li Lan couldn't help but laugh out loud. With myriad emotions Li Lan watched as her son proudly pulled her exclusive-use cart through the streets. This son, who had once shamed her as deeply as her first husband, Liu Shanfeng, now filled her with a pride akin to what she had felt with Song Fanping.

The women in Liu Town thought that Li Lan's cart resembled a wedding sedan. Giggling nonstop, they called out to Li Lan, "Are you getting married off today?"

"No, no," Li Lan replied, blushing. "I'm going down to the countryside to sweep my husband's grave."

Baldy Li pulled Li Lan's exclusive-use cart out the southern gate. When she heard the creaking of the wheels, Li Lan guessed that they had just gone over the wooden bridge and were now bumping along down the dirt road. She could smell the country air as a fresh spring breeze wafted past her; she raised herself, holding on to the umbrella pole, and looked out to a field of golden greens glistening in the sun. She watched the winding paths that framed each paddy, the various details of houses and trees at a distance, the ducks flying over the nearby pond and their reflection in the water, together with the sparrows flying by the road. This was the last trip that Li Lan would take along this dirt road; despite its bumpiness, she fully enjoyed the beautiful spring day while riding along on the cart.

Li Lan looked down at her son pulling the cart with all his strength. Baldy Li was now bent over and constantly wiping the sweat from his brows. Feeling sorry for him, she urged him to take a rest, but Baldy Li shook his head and replied that he wasn't tired. Li Lan tried to get him to pause and drink from the drip bottle, but he again shook his head. "That glucose water is nutrition for you."

When she saw how good her son was to her, Li Lan wept tears of joy. Sobbing, she said, "Good son, please, I'm begging you, take a rest and have some water."

Just then Baldy Li caught sight of Song Gang in the distance, standing at the entrance to the village. He saw that Song Gang's grandfather was seated on the ground and leaning against the tree. Every year at Qingming, Song Gang and his grandfather would wait at the village entrance for their arrival. Song Gang spotted a very odd cart coming toward him, but he didn't dream that it would be Baldy Li pulling Li Lan. When Baldy Li saw Song Gang, his bent-over body straightened out a bit and he broke into a run, jostling Li Lan back and forth. Baldy Li yelled out at the top of his lungs, "Song Gang! Song Gang!"

When Song Gang heard Baldy Li's cries, he ran toward them, arms waving, and shouting, "Baldy Li! Baldy Li!"

CHAPTER 26

U PON RETURNING from her trip to Song Fanping's grave, Li Lan lay down on her bed to think things over. She felt that she had completed all the necessary preparations, and so the next day she could check into the hospital without worries. As she had expected, her illness became much graver once she arrived in the hospital, and it became clear that she would never check out again. Within two months, she was reduced to voiding her bladder through a catheter, ran an unabated high fever, and spent most of her days asleep.

As Li Lan's condition deteriorated Baldy Li stopped going to school and instead began spending every day at her bedside. Deep into the night, each time Li Lan woke from her stupor she would see her son asleep next to her, head leaning against the bed railing. Weeping, she would muster the energy to urge him to go home and rest.

When Li Lan felt that the end was approaching, she began to desperately miss her other son. She asked Baldy Li to lean over, and, with a voice as weak and soft as a mosquito's buzz, she asked him again and again to bring Song Gang back from the countryside.

The road to the countryside was long, and it would take at least half a day to get there and back. Baldy Li set off to fetch Song Gang but, worried about his mother in the hospital needing his care, paused at the wooden bridge outside the southern gate. He waited on the bridge for two hours, and whenever he spotted a peasant leaving through the gate, he would ask him what village he was from. He asked more than a dozen people but didn't find anyone from Song Gang's village. Finally an old man with a hog approached. By that point Baldy Li had pretty much given up hope and was preparing to run like a marathoner all the way to the countryside. When the old man replied that he was from Song Gang's village, Baldy Li leapt down from the bridge railing and almost gave the man a hug. Shouting, he asked the man to send word to Song Gang urging him to rush to town. "It's an emergency. Tell him to come find Baldy Li."

It was dawn by the time Song Gang arrived. Baldy Li had spent another night at the hospital and had just gotten home and fallen asleep when Song Gang knocked on the door. Drowsily, Baldy Li opened the door, and Song Gang, who by this time was a head taller than he, nervously asked, "What's going on?"

Baldy Li rubbed his eyes. "Mama doesn't have much longer and wants to see you. Quick, go to the hospital."

Song Gang burst into tears, and Baldy Li said, "Don't cry now, just get going. I'll sleep a bit more and then come join you."

Song Gang turned around and rushed off to the hospital. Baldy Li shut the door behind him and went back to sleep. He had planned to nap only for a short while, but his accumulated exhaustion got the better of him and he slept until noon. By the time he arrived at the hospital, he was astonished by the sight that greeted his eyes: Li Lan was actually sitting up, and her voice sounded much stronger than it had been the day before. Song Gang was sitting on the edge of the bed, telling her about events in the village. Baldy Li wondered whether it was the sight of Song Gang that made her instantly better. He didn't realize that she was temporarily in remission, enjoying a sudden burst of energy at the end of her life's journey. She even smiled when she spotted Baldy Li entering the room, saying, "You've lost so much weight."

Li Lan told them that she missed her own home very much. She explained to the doctor that she was feeling much better today, and since both her sons were now with her, she would like to go home and take a look. The doctor, aware that she was nearing the end, agreed that she might as well go home but warned Baldy Li and Song Gang that she shouldn't stay out for more than a couple of hours.

Song Gang carried Li Lan on his back and walked out of the hospital. As they walked down the street Li Lan looked about at the people and houses with the astonishment of a newborn. A few acquaintances even called out to her, asking whether she was feeling better. Li Lan seemed extremely happy as she answered, "Yes, much better." When they walked past the basketball court, Li Lan thought again of Song Fanping. With her hands clasped around Song Gang's shoulders, she was the picture of contentment. She said, "Song Gang, you look more and more like your father every day."

Once they reached home, Li Lan gazed fondly at the table, the chairs, and the armoire; at the walls, the windows, the cobweb in the corner of the room, and the layer of dust on the desk—her eyes soaking up everything as if they were sponges. As she sat down on one of the chairs, with Song Gang supporting her from behind, she asked Baldy

Li to bring her a rag. She started to carefully wipe the dust off the table, saying, "It's so nice to be home."

Then, feeling tired, she asked Baldy Li and Song Gang to help her lie down on the bed. She closed her eyes as if asleep, but after a while she opened them again and had Baldy Li and Song Gang sit together at her bedside. In a frail voice she then told them, "I'm about to die."

Song Gang started sobbing, and Baldy Li also lowered his head and wiped at his eyes. Li Lan said, "Don't cry, don't cry, my sons. . . ."

Song Gang nodded obediently and stopped his sobbing. Baldy Li also raised his head. Li Lan continued, "I've already reserved a coffin. Please bury me next to your papa. I promised him that I was going to wait till you were grown up to go find him, but I'm afraid I can't hold on any longer."

Song Gang burst out into loud sobs, and the sound of his weeping brought Baldy Li's head down again. Li Lan repeated, "Don't cry, don't cry."

Song Gang wiped his eyes and muffled his sobs, but Baldy Li still had his head buried in his chest. Li Lan smiled, saying, "I've cleansed myself already, so no need to bathe me after I'm gone. Just put me in a clean set of clothes. Don't give me a sweater, though, because the knots in the yarn would trip me on my way to the netherworld. Dress me in cotton instead."

Exhausted, she closed her eyes and rested. A dozen minutes passed before she opened her eyes again and told her sons, "I just heard your father call out to me."

Li Lan smiled contentedly. She asked Song Gang to pull out a wooden chest from under the bed and remove the bundle inside. Baldy Li and Song Gang unwrapped the bundle and saw that it contained the bag of soil stained with Song Fanping's blood, a handkerchief wrapped around the three pairs of ancients' chopsticks, and three copies of their family portrait. Li Lan said that two of the copies were for Baldy Li and Song Gang; since they would marry and start their own families, she wanted to make sure that each had his own copy. The third she wanted to take with her to the netherworld to show Song Fanping, noting, "He never had a chance to see the portrait."

She also wanted to take with her the pairs of ancients' chopsticks, as well as the dirt stained with Song Fanping's blood. She instructed, "Once I'm set in the coffin, spread the bloody dirt all over my body."

As she spoke she asked her sons to help her up so that she could reach her hand into the soil. Seven years had passed, and the blood-stained dirt had turned completely black. She felt around, saying, "It feels very cozy inside."

Li Lan smiled contentedly. "I'm about to see your father, so I'm very happy. Seven years—he's been waiting for me for seven years. I have so many stories to tell him, stories about Song Gang and about Baldy Li—it would take me days and days just to get through them all."

When she looked again at Baldy Li and Song Gang, she wept. "But what will become of you? You are fifteen and sixteen years old—I really can't bear to part with you. My sons, you really have to take good care of yourselves. You are brothers and must look after each other."

As Li Lan finished speaking she closed her eyes and seemed to doze off for a bit. When she opened her eyes again, she asked Baldy Li to go and buy a few buns. Having diverted Baldy Li, she then held Song Gang's hand and told him her final wishes: "Song Gang, Baldy Li is your little brother. You must take care of him all your life. I'm not worried about you, but I am worried about him. If he takes the straight path, he will make something of himself; but if he goes the other way, I'm worried that he will end up in jail. You have to watch out for him and not let him go the wrong way. Song Gang, promise me that, no matter what Baldy Li might do, you will take care of him."

Song Gang nodded as he wiped at his tears. "Mama, don't you worry. I'll take care of Baldy Li for as long as I live. Even if I have one bowl of rice left, I'll let him have it, and if I have just one shirt left, I'll give it to him."

Weeping, Li Lan shook her head. "If there is one bowl of rice left, the two of you should split it; and if there's one shirt left, you should take turns wearing it."

This was the last day of Li Lan's life. She slept on the family bed until dusk, and when she woke up she heard Baldy Li and Song Gang whispering to each other. Rays from the setting sun shone into the room, warming it with reds and oranges. The sound of Baldy Li and Song Gang talking to each other convinced Li Lan of their intimacy. She smiled, then softly said that it was time to return to the hospital.

Song Gang carried Li Lan out the front door. As Baldy Li followed them out, she remarked, "It's good to be home."

Baldy Li and Song Gang remained with Li Lan at the hospital. Her spirits seemed to revive somewhat. She would doze for a while, then stay awake for a while. Every time she woke up and spotted her sons sitting at her bedside whispering away, she would urge them once again to return home and get some sleep.

Baldy Li and Song Gang stayed in the hospital until one in the morning and then walked home along the deserted streets. Baldy Li knew that Song Gang had become very interested in reading, so he told him about a room in Red Flag Alley that contained all the items confiscated during the early days of the Cultural Revolution. They had everything there: books, paintings, toys, stuff that you couldn't even imagine. Baldy Li told Song Gang that Victory Zhao and Success Liu had raided the place a few times, and every time they made off with lots of good books. Baldy Li explained, "Do you know how Victory Zhao became Poet Zhao, and Success Liu, Writer Liu? It's because they stole these books and read them that now they can write books themselves."

Baldy Li and Song Gang crept up to the room. They had planned on breaking the windows and climbing in, but when they got there, they saw that the window had no panes left. After they crept in, they realized that someone had long ago cleaned the place out, leaving only a few empty cabinets. They searched every corner of the room, every nook of every cabinet, but managed to find only a single red high-heeled shoe. Thinking they had found something special, they stashed it under their clothing, crept out through the window, and ran. When they reached a completely deserted streetlamp, Baldy Li and Song Gang stopped and studied the item for a good long while. They had never seen a high-heeled shoe before, nor even a red shoe, and asked each other, "What is this thing?"

The brothers went back and forth on whether it was indeed a shoe. They wondered if it might be a toy boat. In the end they concluded that it was a toy—not a toy boat but a toy shoe. Baldy Li and Song Gang happily carried the red high-heeled shoe back with them to their home, then sat on the bed examining it for a bit longer. They still agreed that the high-heel was a toy but of a sort that they had never seen before. Then they hid it under the bed.

By the time Baldy Li and Song Gang woke up the next day, the sun was shining on their bottoms. They rushed to the hospital, but Li Lan's bed was empty. As they were standing there in a panic, looking all about them and not knowing what to do, a nurse walked in and informed them that Li Lan was dead and laid out in the morgue.

Song Gang immediately burst into loud wails. Sobbing, he walked down the hospital's aisles toward the morgue. Baldy Li initially didn't cry as he followed Song Gang in a daze, but when he saw his mother lying stiffly on a concrete cot in the morgue, he burst out into wails too, crying even louder than Song Gang.

Li Lan's eyes were still open. She had wanted so badly to see her sons before dying, but the last glimmer of light disappeared from her gaze without her getting a final glimpse of her beloved sons.

Song Gang knelt on the floor in front of the concrete cot and wept until he shook all over, while Baldy Li, standing at the foot of the bed, wept and trembled like a sapling in the wind. Together they wept, calling out for their mama. It was not until this moment that Baldy Li truly understood that he was now an orphan and that he and Song Gang were all they each had left in this world.

Song Gang then hoisted Li Lan's body onto his back. With Baldy Li following behind, the three of them went home. Song Gang wept continuously as he carried Li Lan down the street while Baldy Li also repeatedly wiped his eyes. The two of them no longer howled, instead sobbed silently. As they reached the basketball court Song Gang cried out loud again, saying to Baldy Li, "Yesterday when we reached here, Mama was still talking to me."

Song Gang wept so hard he could not take another step. Baldy Li urged him to let him carry their mother, but Song Gang shook his head, explaining, "You're my younger brother. I have to take care of you."

Sobbing, the two youths made their way with the corpse down the streets of Liu Town. The body kept sliding down Song Gang's back, so Baldy Li propped it up from behind. Song Gang repeatedly stopped to bend down so that Baldy Li could gently hoist the body back up. Eventually Song Gang was doubled over with the effort, with Baldy Li trotting alongside helping to support the body. The two young men carefully tended to Li Lan's corpse as if she were merely asleep and they were afraid of hurting her. When people saw them, they were all heartbroken. When Mama Su and Missy Su saw them, tears trickled down Mama Su's face as she said to her daughter, "Li Lan was such a good woman. It's such a pity that she's now gone and left her good sons behind."

Two days later the two youths reappeared in the streets, this time pulling Blacksmith Tong's cart. Atop the cart was Li Lan in the coffin that she had selected herself. Inside the coffin was a portrait of their family, three pairs of ancients' chopsticks, and dirt that had once been soaked through with Song Fanping's blood. Song Gang walked in front, pulling the cart, while Baldy Li followed, guiding it from behind. The two worried that the coffin might slip off the cart, so they both squatted down in order to roll the cart horizontally. Song Gang's body was bent over like a bow, as was Baldy Li's. Heads bowed, they walked in silence as the wheels creaked along the stone slabs on the street.

Seven years earlier another pullcart holding another coffin had passed down this same street, and the body lying inside had been Song Fanping's. At that time, it had been the old landlord pulling in front and Li Lan and the two children pushing from behind. This time the two boys were young men, and it was Li Lan who was lying in the coffin.

They walked out the southern gate and onto the dirt road leading into the country. Seven years earlier, this was the spot where Li Lan had said, "Go ahead and cry," and where all four of them had erupted in sobs, their wailing startling even the sparrows in the trees. Now the boys were again pulling a cart carrying a thin-planked coffin, and the fields were just as wide, the skies just as vast, but this time there were only two of them, and they had no tears left. With their backs bent, one in front and one in back, one pulling and one pushing, they were positioned lower than the coffin on the cart. From a distance they didn't resemble two people so much as an oversize cart.

The two young men escorted their mother to the village where Song Fanping was born and raised. Song Fanping had been waiting in his grave by the village entrance for seven years, and now his wife was finally here to keep him company. The old landlord waited at his son's grave, his entire weight resting on a tree branch serving as a cane; he looked frail and weak, as if he were also taking his last breaths and would have collapsed to the ground without the branch. The old landlord was so poor he couldn't even afford a cane, so Song Gang had fashioned this one by whittling down a tree branch. There was a grave already dug next to Song Fanping's, thanks once again to the poor relatives who stood there leaning on their shovels, wearing clothes just as tattered as they had been seven years earlier.

Once Li Lan's coffin was lowered into the grave, the old landlord, his face covered in tears, could no longer hold himself up. Song Gang helped lift him to a seated position. The old landlord leaned against a tree and watched as dirt was shoveled into the grave, sobbing over and over, "It was my son's good fortune to marry such a good woman. It was my son's good fortune to marry such a good woman. It was my son's good fortune . . ."

Li Lan's mound was now piled as high as Song Fanping's grave. The old landlord wept as he spoke of what a good daughter-in-law he had had: He said that Li Lan came every Qingming festival to sweep the grave, and every New Year's she came to pay her respects to him. Song Gang asked Baldy Li to help his grandfather up and carry him back home. Baldy Li walked off with the old landlord on his back, and the poor relatives followed behind, carrying their shovels. Song Gang watched them walk away. Once he was alone, he knelt in front of Li Lan's grave and promised her, "Mama, don't you worry. Even if I only have one bowl of rice left, I'll give it to Baldy Li to eat, and even if I have only a single piece of clothing, I'll give it to Baldy Li to wear."

PART TWO

PART TWO

CHAPTER 27

THE DEAD had departed; the living remained. Li Lan headed into the netherworld, walking along a penumbral path in search of Song Fanping's spirit amid a sea of ghosts. She was no longer aware of her sons' wanderings in the mortal world.

Song Gang's grandfather, the old landlord, was himself in his twilight years and confined to his bed. Every few days he would have only a single mouthful of rice and a few sips of water; as a result, he had been reduced to little more than skin and bones. Recognizing that he was about to expire, the old landlord would pull Song Gang toward him and hold him tight while staring out the door. Song Gang understood what his grandfather was trying to communicate with his gaze. Therefore, on clear, cloudless evenings, he would carry his grandfather on his back, and together they would walk past each house in the village as the old landlord gazed upon each familiar face as if he were bidding farewell. Upon arriving at the village entrance, Song Gang would pause under the elm tree, his grandfather still on his back, and the two of them would silently watch the sun set while standing next to Song Fanping and Li Lan's graves.

The grandfather was now as light as a bundle of kindling on Song Gang's back. Every night after returning home from the village, Song Gang would lay his grandfather down and find him as still as death. The next day, however, the old man's eyes would open again at the crack of dawn, the life inside still flickering. Day after day, he looked as if he were already dead when in fact he was still holding on, though he no longer had the energy to speak or even to smile. One evening as Song Gang and his grandfather were standing under the elm tree next to Song Fanping and Li Lan's graves, the old man's appointed time finally arrived. Song Gang couldn't see that his grandfather was smiling behind him but heard him whispering softly in his ear: "Ah, the end of bitter days."

With this, the old landlord's head dropped onto Song Gang's shoulder and lay there motionless, as if he were asleep. Song Gang, his grandfather still on his back, gazed at the road leading to our Liu Town as it gradually became more indistinct in the encroaching darkness, and eventually he turned and walked back into the village under the light of the moon. As he walked Song Gang felt his grandfather's head on his shoulder rocking back and forth in time with his footsteps. Upon returning home, Song Gang carefully put his grandfather to bed and tucked him in as usual. That night, the old landlord opened his eyes twice, trying to catch a glimpse of his grandson, but all he could see was silence and darkness. After that his eyes never opened again.

Song Gang got out of bed the next morning without realizing that his grandfather had passed away, nor did he realize it that entire day. It was not at all uncommon for the old landlord to lie in bed without eating or drinking or even appearing to breathe, so Song Gang didn't think twice about it. At dusk he picked up his grandfather as usual but noticed that his body had become stiff, and as he walked out the door his grandfather's head slid off Song Gang's shoulder. Song Gang quickly reached back to reposition the head and continued walking past each of the houses in the village. The whole time his grandfather's head swung in time with his footsteps, a pendulous weight on his shoulders. It slid down several more times as they approached the entrance to the village, until finally Song Gang felt the chill of his grandfather's face when he reached behind to right the head. Song Gang paused under an elm tree and placed a finger under his grandfather's nostrils but did not feel any breath; instead, he felt his own finger grow cold, and it finally sank in that his grandfather had died.

The next morning the villagers saw Song Gang hunched over, supporting his dead grandfather on his back with his left arm and carrying a straw mat and an iron shovel under his right. He stopped at one house after another, announcing bleakly, "Grandfather has died."

Several of the old landlord's poor relatives followed Song Gang to the village entrance to help him spread out the mats; they were joined by other villagers. Song Gang carefully lowered his grandfather onto the mat as if he were laying him down in bed. Several relatives helped roll up the mat, then wound three loops of heavy twine around the bundle. This would serve as the old landlord's coffin. A few men from the village helped to dig a grave, and Song Gang carried the bundle containing his grandfather over to the grave and knelt down beside it. He placed his grandfather inside, stood up and wiped the tears from his eyes, then started filling the grave. Watching the now solitary Song Gang, the women from the village couldn't help shedding tears.

The old landlord was buried next to Song Fanping and Li Lan. For fourteen days Song Gang wore a hemp shirt in mourning, and at the conclusion of his second seven-day mourning cycle, he packed his things, leaving the shack and the few pieces of furniture to his relatives. Someone happened to be going into town, so Song Gang asked him to relay a message to Baldy Li: Song Gang was coming home.

Song Gang was awake by four the next morning, and when he opened his door, he saw that the sky was still full of stars. Remembering that he was about to see Baldy Li, he hurriedly shut the door and set off for the village entrance. When he got there, he stood for a while in the moonlight, gazing back at the village where he had spent the past ten years and down at Song Fanping and Li Lan's graves as well as the old landlord's freshly dug one. Then he set out on the desolate road under the moonlight, heading toward the sleeping town of Liu. Song Gang bid farewell to his grandfather, upon whom he had depended for the preceding ten years, and left to resume his life with Baldy Li.

At dawn Song Gang entered Liu Town through the southern gate. Completely covered in dust from the road, he was finally returning home. He was carrying the same travel bag that Li Lan had taken with her to Shanghai when she sought medical treatment there; the same bag she had when, traveling back from Shanghai, she received news of Song Fanping's death; and the bag into which she had stuffed the bundle containing the soil soaked with Song Fanping's blood. And when Song Gang went to the countryside to live with his grandfather, this was the bag that Li Lan used to pack Song Gang's clothing and the White Rabbit candies. Now Song Gang was carrying the bag back again, though all that it now held was a few pieces of old clothing. This constituted the extent of Song Gang's possessions.

Having left Liu Town as a child, Song Gang was returning home a handsome young man. But when he arrived, Baldy Li was not home, because, knowing that Song Gang was returning that day, he had also woken up at four and set off before dawn to have the locksmith make Song Gang a new key. He naturally hadn't expected that Song Gang would set off in the middle of the night and be waiting at their doorstep by dawn. Song Gang stood there with his travel bag for more than two hours while Baldy Li stood on the main street waiting for the locksmith to open his shop. Song Gang was now as tall as his father had been, though not as well built. Instead, he was pale and lean, with a shirt too short and sleeves and pants legs lengthened with patches from different colored fabrics. Song Gang stood patiently in front of the door to their house, waiting for Baldy Li to return home. He passed the travel bag back and forth from one hand to the other, careful not to place it on the ground so that it wouldn't get dirty.

On his way back to the house, Baldy Li spotted Song Gang from far away: this tall brother of his, holding a travel bag and standing blankly at the front door. Baldy Li snuck up on Song Gang from behind and kicked him in the rear. Song Gang staggered for a moment and then heard Baldy Li's laughter. The two brothers proceeded to chase each other around in front of the house for a full half hour, raising a huge cloud of dust in the process. Baldy Li alternated between kicking his feet and swinging his leg as Song Gang hopped and jumped out of the way—all the while holding onto his travel bag. They continued scuffling, Baldy Li attacking like a spear and Song Gang defending himself like a shield. Eventually the brothers collapsed into a hysterical heap, laughing until tears flowed from their eyes and snot from their noses, then both of them doubled up coughing. Finally Baldy Li, gasping for breath, took out the new key and handed it to Song Gang, saying, "Open the door."

Baldy Li and Song Gang were like weeds that, despite having been trampled underfoot, had continued to grow vigorously. Not a single factory was willing to hire the infamous Baldy Li upon his graduation from middle school. However, by that time the Cultural Revolution had concluded; Deng Xiaoping's Reform and Opening Up Campaign had just begun; and their old benefactor, Tao Qing, was now the deputy director of the county's Civil Affairs Bureau. Tao Qing—recalling Song Fanping's abject death in front of the railway station and how Li Lan, in her gratitude for his help, had kowtowed with such force that her forehead was reduced to a bloody pulp—decided to give Baldy Li a hand up in life. He arranged to have him assigned to the Good Works Factory, which employed only charity cases and which happened to be administered by the Civil Affairs Bureau. Besides Baldy Li, the Good Works Factory had fourteen other employees: two cripples, three idiots, four blind men, and five deaf men. Song Gang's legal place of residence was still Liu Town, so upon his return he was assigned to work in the metal factory, where Success Liu–cum–Writer Liu was now section chief for supplies and marketing.

The two brothers collected their first month's wages on the same day. Song Gang got home first, since the metal factory was closer. Firmly grasping the eighteen yuan in his pocket, he stood in the doorway waiting. When Baldy Li arrived, his wages grasped tightly in his sweat-covered palms, Song Gang asked excitedly, "Did you receive yours?"

Baldy Li nodded. He saw Song Gang's delighted expression and asked, "How about you?"

Song Gang also nodded. The two walked into the room and quickly shut the door and pulled the curtains, as if afraid of thieves. Then they both began to laugh hysterically as they laid out their wages on the bed: thirty-six yuan in all, each of the bills damp with sweat from their palms. The two sat on the bed and counted the thirty-six yuan over and over again. Baldy Li's eyes lit up while Song Gang's crinkled into narrow slits. Song Gang by this point was very nearsighted and had to bring the money right up to his nose to see it. Baldy Li suggested that they pool their earnings and that Song Gang be in charge of them. Song Gang felt that since he was the elder, it was indeed appropriate that he should assume that responsibility. Therefore, he collected the bills on the bed one at a time, arranged them in a neat pile, and let Baldy Li count them one last time. Then Song Gang also counted the pile of bills a final time before sighing contentedly. "I've never seen so much money before."

While speaking, Song Gang stood up on the bed and bumped his head on the ceiling. He then bent over and unbuttoned his pants, revealing underwear stitched together from old scraps. There was a small pocket sewn on the inside of his underwear, and it was in this pocket that Song Gang carefully stashed their combined earnings. Baldy Li complimented Song Gang on the pocket and asked who had made it for him. Song Gang replied that he had stitched it himself, adding that he had also cut the pattern and sewn the underwear. Baldy Li expressed his admiration and asked, "Are you a man or a woman?"

Song Gang laughed. "I also know how to knit a sweater."

After the brothers received their first month's wages, the first thing they did was go to the People's Restaurant for a steaming bowl of plain noodles in broth. At first Baldy Li wanted to order the house-special noodles, but Song Gang argued that they should wait until they were living more comfortably before pampering themselves like that. Baldy

Li acknowledged that Song Gang had a point, and since this time the money was coming out of his own pocket rather than that of someone trying to buy the secrets to Lin Hong's bottom, he readily agreed to have just the plain noodles. Song Gang walked up to the cashier, unfastened his pants, and, as the woman at the register watched, proceeded to fumble around inside. Baldy Li immediately burst into peals of laughter while the middle-aged clerk, who seemed altogether too familiar with this sort of scene, waited impassively for Song Gang to fish out the money. He finally succeeded in extracting a one-yuan bill from his underwear pocket and handed it over to the clerk, then stood there patiently holding up his pants while waiting for her to give him change. Two bowls of plain noodles cost eighteen cents, and after he received his eighty-two cents in change, Song Gang meticulously folded up the money, starting with the larger bills and proceeding to the smaller ones, and then placed everything, including the two pennies, back in the secret pocket in his underwear. Then he tied his pants back on and accompanied Baldy Li to an empty table.

After the brothers finished their plain noodles, they left the People's Restaurant while wiping the sweat from their foreheads and proceeded to the Red Flag fabric shop to pick out some dark blue khaki cloth. This time it was a young woman who was working at the counter, and she watched in horror as Song Gang once again undid his pants and started fumbling around inside. The young woman blushed crimson as Baldy Li leered at her, and she abruptly turned away to speak to one of her workmates. Song Gang fumbled around in his pants for a long time, all the while counting out loud. When he finally pulled out the money, it was precisely the amount he needed to pay for the fabric. As the redfaced young woman accepted the money, Baldy Li asked Song Gang in surprise, "Where did you learn that trick?"

Song Gang squinted at the red-faced clerk, but his nearsightedness rendered him oblivious to her embarrassment. Smiling, he fastened his pants and explained to Baldy Li, "Since I fold the bills in order from the smallest to the largest, I always know which bills are in front."

With their bundles of khaki fabric in hand, they proceeded to Tailor Zhang's shop and asked him to make each of them a Mao suit. For the third time Song Gang stuck his hand down his pants and started fishing inside. Tailor Zhang draped his tape measure around his neck and, seeing Song Gang with his hand inside his pants, laughed and said, "What a great place to hide your money."

Song Gang pulled out the money and handed it to Tailor Zhang, who then held it up to his nose and sniffed, saying, "It smells of dick."

Though he couldn't see clearly, Song Gang gathered that Tailor Zhang had sniffed his cash. As they left the shop Song Gang, squinting, asked Baldy Li for confirmation: "Was he sniffing our bills?"

Realizing then that Song Gang was extremely nearsighted, Baldy Li insisted that they go to the optician to buy him a pair of glasses. Song Gang shook his head, saying that they should wait until they were living more comfortably. Baldy Li had compromised earlier in not ordering the house-special noodles, but now he held his ground. He stopped in the middle of the street and shouted at Song Gang, "By the time things are more comfortable, you may very well have already gone blind!"

Song Gang was flabbergasted by Baldy Li's outburst, and through his squinting he could see that a good number of people had stopped to watch them. He asked Baldy Li to lower his voice, but Baldy Li spat back that if Song Gang didn't go get glasses today, they might as well split up. In a ringing voice he commanded, "Let's go! Let's go get you some glasses."

As Baldy Li said this he began to strut toward the optician's shop, with a reluctant Song Gang following behind. They were no longer striding side by side, as they had been a moment earlier, but instead walked in single file. The two looked as though they had just been in a fight, with Baldy Li parading ahead as the victor and Song Gang trailing dispiritedly behind.

By the following month the brothers had their dark blue Mao suits and Song Gang was wearing a pair of black-rimmed glasses. Baldy Li had insisted on the most expensive frames in the shop, thereby reducing Song Gang to tears. On the one hand, Song Gang begrudged spending so much money; on the other hand, he was moved by his brother's generosity, deciding that Baldy Li was really quite all right after all. After putting on his new glasses and walking out of the optician's shop, Song Gang gestured excitedly to Baldy Li and exclaimed, "Everything is so clear now!"

He told Baldy Li that, with the new glasses, the world became as clear as if it had just been freshly scrubbed. Baldy Li laughed and said that now that Song Gang had an extra pair of eyes, he should alert Baldy Li when he spotted a pretty woman. Song Gang nodded and laughed as well and started scanning the street for a pretty woman for Baldy Li. Wearing brand-new khaki Mao suits, the two brothers walked down the main street of Liu. A few elders playing chess by the side of the road looked up in surprise and remarked that, the night before, these two had been dressed like beggars but today they looked like county cadres. Sighing, the elders said, "It's certainly true that *clothes make the man.*"

Song Gang was tall and slim, had a handsome face, and now looked quite scholarly with his dark-rimmed glasses. Baldy Li, on the other hand, was short and squat and, even in his Mao suit, still looked like a bandit. The brothers were inseparable as they strolled down the streets of Liu. The town elders gestured to them, saying that one looked like a civil official and the other a military official. The young women of Liu, meanwhile, were not so polite, instead comparing them to the Buddhist monk Tripitaka in the folktale *Journey to the West* and his companion Pigsy.

CHAPTER 28

SONG GANG had secretly fallen in love with literature and was very respectful of the metal factory's section chief for supplies and marketing, Writer Liu. There was a tall pile of literary journals on Writer Liu's desk, and every time he opened his mouth he uttered a string of fanciful ruminations. Writer Liu loved to expound on literature, and when he buttonholed someone at the factory, he could go on for hours. Unfortunately, the workers at the metal factory couldn't understand a word he said. They would stare at him blankly with stupid grins on their faces, secretly asking each other whether Liu was even speaking Chinese or perhaps another language altogether. Why couldn't they understand a single word he said? These remarks reached Writer Liu, and he thought to himself, *These vulgar masses!*

With the arrival of the literature aficionado Song Gang, Writer Liu felt as if he had received a precious treasure. Song Gang not only understood Liu's literary ruminations but seemed completely devoted, nodding and laughing at the appropriate moments. Writer Liu was delighted, feeling that having such a friend was invaluable, and every time he encountered Song Gang he would ramble on endlessly. Once they were in the restroom together, and, after peeing, Writer Liu grabbed Song Gang and spoke to him for more than two hours right there next to the urinal—paying no heed to the stench or to the people squatting and grunting as they shat. After Writer Liu acquired this new student, he felt that he had become a literary advisor. The vulgar masses didn't make him feel this way; even after he had talked his lips raw, they would still just stare at him with stupid grins on their faces. Writer Liu began lending Song Gang some of the literary journals in his office. One day he took a copy of *Harvest*, carefully wiped the dust off the cover with his sleeve, and proceeded to inspect it page by page in front of Song Gang, demonstrating that it was pristine and not dirty or damaged in any way. He told Song Gang that when he returned the magazine, Writer Liu would again inspect it page by page. "If it is damaged in the least, you will have to pay a fine."

Song Gang took Writer Liu's literary journal home with him and began reading ravenously, then found himself inspired to start secretly writing a story. He worked on his story for half a year, writing on scrap paper for the first three months and correcting it for another three months. Then he carefully copied the manuscript onto lined paper. Song Gang's first reader was, of course, Baldy Li, who cried out in surprise when he received the work, "It's so thick!"

Baldy Li counted the pages and discovered that the story was thirteen pages long. Baldy Li looked at Song Gang with newfound respect and said, "You are really amazing, writing thirteen whole pages."

When Baldy Li started reading it, he cried out again in surprise, "This is actually really well written!" He diligently finished the story and didn't cry out again but, rather, became contemplative. Song Gang watched him nervously, not knowing whether his first story had been successful. Nervously he asked Baldy Li, "Is it any good?"

Baldy Li didn't reply but remained contemplative. Song Gang asked again, "Did I write it very messily?"

Baldy Li remained pensive, and Song Gang felt a wave of disappointment wash over him. He became convinced that he had written the story in a completely disordered fashion, and therefore Baldy Li couldn't understand it at all.

All of a sudden Baldy Li finally uttered a single word, "Good!" He then added, "Really well written." He earnestly told Song Gang that this was a good story, and even though it was not at the level of stories by literary giants like Lu Xun and Ba Jin, it was better than anything Writer Liu or Poet Zhao could have written. Baldy Li waved excitedly and added, "Now that we have you, Writer Liu and Poet Zhao will be left permanently in the dust."

Song Gang was surprised and pleased, and that night he was so excited he couldn't sleep. With Baldy Li snoring beside him, Song Gang looked back over his story five more times. He became increasingly convinced that it did not merit Baldy Li's effusive praise and that Baldy Li had complimented it only because they were brothers. However, Song Gang ultimately concluded that Baldy Li's praise was not entirely unfounded. For instance, when he went back and reread the specific passages Baldy Li had singled out, he found that they were actually not bad at all. Song Gang then mustered up the courage to take the draft to Writer Liu for critique. If Writer Liu also said that it was well written, then it must be true.

The following day Song Gang nervously showed his story to Writer Liu. Liu was initially startled, never having expected that this disciple of his would turn around and write a story of his own. At that moment Writer Liu was on his way to take a shit, with a roll of toilet paper in his hand. Therefore, he grabbed Song Gang's thirteen-page story along with the toilet paper and read it as he headed to the restroom. He continued reading the story as he did his business, finishing both tasks more or less at the same time. He emerged from the restroom with half a sheet of unused toilet paper resting on top of Song Gang's manuscript, and, brows furled in consternation, he walked back to the supplies and marketing office. Writer Liu then spent the entire afternoon in the office correcting Song Gang's story, using a red pen to mark up every page and even filling the blank space on the last page with three hundred more words of critique. When he got off work, Song Gang nervously appeared at the door of the supply and marketing office. Writer Liu solemnly gestured him in and gave him the thirteen-page document, declaring with utmost seriousness, "All of my comments are written here."

As he accepted the manuscript, Song Gang's heart skipped a beat. The pages were so smothered in Writer Liu's red markings that he could barely see the original, making Song Gang feel that his story must have been very problematic. At this point Writer Liu proudly pulled a story of his own from his desk drawer and handed it to Song Gang, asking him to take it home and read it carefully. Acting as if he were handing Song Gang a masterpiece, Liu said, "See how this is written."

That night Song Gang carefully read over Liu's corrections and exhortations but found himself confused and unable to figure out what Writer Liu was trying to say. Song Gang then read Writer Liu's new work and found himself similarly unable to make heads or tails of it.

Baldy Li saw Song Gang working through the night and, curious, came over to see what he was doing. He first read Writer Liu's critiques of Song Gang's story and declared, "This is bullshit." Then he took Writer Liu's new work and counted the pages. Finding that there were only six, he fanned them disdainfully, asking why it was so short. Baldy Li began reading the story, but before he had finished, he threw it aside, pronouncing it "dull—a total bore."

Baldy Li yawned, lay down on the bed, and started snoring as soon as his head hit the pillow. Song Gang continued earnestly reading both his own corrected story and Writer Liu's new work. The corrections and critique made him feel confused and disappointed, particularly the critique in which Liu essentially undermined Song Gang's entire story, although it was true that Liu did add a few words of encouragement at the end. Song Gang believed that Writer Liu was trying to give him a sort of bitter medicine and was grateful that he had taken the time to write out his corrections and critiques. He therefore felt that he should repay the debt by writing out some comments of his own on the blank page at the end of Writer Liu's manuscript. He started diligently writing, first offering a few words of praise and then pointing out several of the work's shortcomings. Unlike Writer Liu's, Song Gang's critique was not a mess of crossed-out errors and corrections; rather, he first wrote out a draft, corrected it several times, and then carefully copied it onto the final page of Writer Liu's manuscript.

When he got off work the next day, Song Gang returned Writer Liu's new story to him. Writer Liu sat in his chair with his legs crossed, smiling as he waited to hear Song Gang sing his praises. The last thing he expected to hear, therefore, was Song Gang telling him, "All of my comments appear on the final page."

Writer Liu's expression immediately changed, and he hurriedly turned to the last page of his work, where he did indeed find Song Gang's critique. Absolutely furious, Writer Liu jumped up from his chair, pounded the table, and pointed his finger at Song Gang's nose, roaring, "You, you, you . . . How dare you break earth over the mighty?"

Writer Liu was so furious he started sputtering. But Song Gang merely stood there in dumbfounded silence, completely baffled by Writer Liu's anger. He hemmed and hawed, then asked, "Breaking what earth?"

Writer Liu took his story, turned to the last page, and asked, "This— what is this?"

Song Gang uneasily replied, "These are my comments."

Writer Liu was so furious he flung his story to the floor, but he immediately regretted it and quickly picked it up again. While caressing his manuscript, he continued shouting at Song Gang, "You, how dare you scribble on my text?"

Finally understanding why Writer Liu was so angry, Song Gang became unhappy himself. He said, "You also scribbled on mine."

Writer Liu heard this with astonishment and became even more furious, pounding his desk and shouting, "Who are you? And who am I? What is your manuscript? You should be flattered if I were to even deign to piss and crap on your manuscript, you motherfucker!"

Hearing this, Song Gang also became furious. He walked forward a few steps and pointed at Writer Liu, saying, "You leave my mother out of this, because if you curse my mother, I'll . . ."

"You'll what?" Writer Liu raised his fist, but realizing that Song Gang was half a head taller than he, he immediately lowered it again.

Song Gang hesitated, then said, "I'll beat the crap out of you!"

Writer Liu roared back, "Nonsense!"

For Song Gang, who was normally so respectful toward him, to speak of beating up Writer Liu made Liu so furious that he picked up a bottle of ink from his desk and flung it at him. The red ink splattered all over Song Gang's glasses, his face, as well as his clothes. Song Gang took off his ink-covered glasses and placed them in his pocket, then rushed at Liu with both hands extended as if about to put him in a chokehold. The rest of the people in the factory's supplies and marketing section rushed up and pulled Song Gang away. Writer Liu then took the opportunity to retreat to a corner of the room and barked out to his workers, "Arrest him!"

Several of Liu's workers pushed Song Gang back to his workshop. Song Gang, his face bright red, sat down on a long bench as rivulets of ink ran down his face and torso. The workers from Liu's office sat next to him and tried to comfort him, while the workers in Song Gang's own workshop crowded around to hear what had happened. Liu's employees recounted to Song Gang's workshop artisans the fight between Song Gang and Writer Liu. Someone asked what the source of the conflict was, whereupon the supplies and marketing people admitted confusion. Shaking their heads, they said, "We can't begin to understand the affairs of literati like them."

Song Gang sat there without saying a word, unable to understand why the normally sophisticated and urbane Writer Liu had been cursing him out like a shrew, using language even coarser than a peasant's. Song Gang burned with righteous indignation, wondering where Writer Liu got off talking to him like this. The people gathered around him had dispersed, and Song Gang walked over to the public fountain to wash the red ink off his face and glasses. After the red stain had been washed off, Song Gang's complexion became pale with fury. With this pale, furious face he returned to his workstation, and that afternoon when he got off work, it was with the same pale, furious face that he returned home.

When Baldy Li got home, he saw Song Gang sitting at the table, stewing. Noticing the red ink splattered across Song Gang's clothing like markings on a map, Baldy Li asked what had happened. Song Gang told him everything, and when he finished, Baldy Li didn't say a word but instead turned on his heels and walked out the door. He knew which alley Writer Liu lived in, and stalked off to teach the pretentious asshole a lesson.

The moment he reached the main street Baldy Li ran into Writer Liu, who was just emerging from his alley. Liu was carrying a soy sauce bottle, which he was on his way to refill at his wife's behest. Baldy Li stopped and called out to Liu, "Hey, little guy, come here."

Writer Liu felt that this voice sounded very familiar, and he turned to see Baldy Li standing there cockily, waving at him from across the street. Liu was reminded of how, when they were young, Victory Zhao would often have Sun Wei call out to Baldy Li like this whenever they wanted to give him a taste of their leg-sweeping kicks. But now it was Baldy Li who was calling out to him. Aware that Baldy Li was hailing him because of the matter with Song Gang, Writer Liu hesitated for a moment but then crossed the street with his soy sauce bottle and walked right up to him.

Baldy Li gestured angrily at him and cursed, "You son of a bitch, how dare you splatter ink all over my brother, Song Gang? You fucking bastard!"

Writer Liu sputtered. Whereas earlier he had backed away from a fight with Song Gang on account of the fact that Song Gang was half a head taller than he, Baldy Li was half a head shorter, so Writer Liu felt he had nothing to worry about. He wanted to curse out Baldy Li instead but saw that a group of onlookers had gathered and therefore decided it would be better to preserve his dignity. He coldly replied, "Please watch your mouth."

Baldy Li snorted. With his left hand he grabbed Liu by the collar, and curling his right into a fist, he snarled, "I do indeed have a foul mouth, and I plan to foul up your clean face."

Baldy Li's bluster made Writer Liu quake a little. Liu realized that although Baldy Li was half a head shorter, he nevertheless looked extraordinarily strong. He struggled to free himself from Baldy Li's grip, attempting to maintain his writerly dignity in front of the assembled crowd. While weakly swatting at the hand with which Baldy Li was holding him by the collar, hoping that he would let go of his own accord, Writer Liu said primly, "I am an intellectual, and I won't get entangled with the likes of you."

"Well, I especially like beating up intellectuals."

Writer Liu had not even finished speaking when Baldy Li started punching him one, two, three, four times with his right fist, punching him so hard that Writer Liu's head snapped back and forth. Baldy Li followed up his advantage with punches five, six, seven, eight until Writer Liu's entire body swayed as he fell to his knees. Baldy Li pulled Liu back to his feet and then pounded him four times in the face. The soy sauce bottle in Liu's hand fell to the ground and shattered. Liu seemed to have passed out, but Baldy Li held him up while continuing to pound his face like a punching bag. Writer Liu's eyes swelled to narrow slits, and his nose began spurting blood. In all, Baldy Li punched Writer Liu twenty-eight times, leaving him looking as if he had barely survived a car wreck. Finally Baldy Li's left hand, with which he was holding Liu up, began to tire, and when he released his grip, Writer Liu collapsed like a sack of sand. Baldy Li quickly grabbed Liu's clothing from behind and, as Writer Liu fell to his knees, Baldy Li continued to hold his collar, not letting him topple over. Baldy Li laughed as he announced to the assembled crowd, "And this is what is known as an intellectual."

Then Baldy Li proceeded to use his right fist to pound Writer Liu's back and quickly punched him eleven times in succession while Liu grunted in pain. Baldy Li noticed that Liu's voice had changed from his earlier shrill screams to a series of dull moans. With a surprised expression, Baldy Li told the assembled crowd, "Do you hear? This intellectual is chanting a laborer's work song."

Then, as if he were performing a science experiment, Baldy Li punched Writer Liu in the back again and heard Liu grunt, "Heaveho." Baldy Li pounded him five more times, and Writer Liu responded with five more "heave-ho" grunts, sounding as if the two of them had previously rehearsed their call-and-answer routine. Baldy Li excitedly continued to beat Liu as he told the crowd, "I am helping to bring out his true laborer colors!"

By this time Baldy Li was covered in sweat. When he released his left hand, Writer Liu's body crumpled to the ground and lay motionless like a slaughtered pig. Baldy Li wiped the sweat from his brow and said with satisfaction, as if he were concluding a lesson, "We'll stop here for today."

In reality, Baldy Li was just getting started. He remembered that Writer Liu had another intellectual comrade, Poet Zhao, and therefore announced to the assembled crowd, "Poet Zhao is also an intellectual. Please tell him that within the next six months I'll plan to help bring out his true laborer colors, too."

Baldy Li swaggered off, leaving Writer Liu crumpled beneath a wutong tree, completely covered in blood. Passersby crowded around him for a while, pointing and offering their opinions. Baldy Li had aimed his twenty-eight punches at Writer Liu's five facial orifices, leaving him lying motionless on the street and barely able to discern the world around him. Finally some workers from the metal factory passed by on their way to work and, seeing their section chief lying there covered in blood, they rolled their eyes, grinned, then quickly carried him to the hospital.

As Writer Liu lay in the emergency-room bed, he insisted that the person who had beaten him was not Baldy Li but, rather, Li Kui. The factory workers didn't know what to make of this and asked him, "Which Li Kui?"

Writer Liu coughed up some blood as he answered, "The one who appears in Water Margin, who is also known as the Black Whirlwind."

The workers were flabbergasted, saying that that Li Kui was not from Liu Town but, rather, was a character in a novel. Writer Liu nodded, saying that Li Kui had emerged from the novel to smack him around. Several workers burst out laughing, asking him why in the world Li Kui would want to do that. Writer Liu took the opportunity to curse Li Kui a few times, saying that he was all brawn and no brain, his muscles having crowded out his wits. He said that Li Kui received mistaken information, went to the wrong place, and beat up the wrong person. After explaining this, Writer Liu continued coughing up blood and asked in a dull voice, "How could Baldy Li be a match for me?"

Several workers thought to themselves that this was the end and pulled over a doctor to ask whether their section chief had been beaten senseless. The doctor shook his head and replied that Liu's condition was not that serious, that he was merely suffering from a case of delusional memory. He added, "If he sleeps it off, he'll be fine."

Baldy Li had threatened that his next victim would be Poet Zhao. When word of this threat finally made its way to Poet Zhao himself, he turned pale with fury. He snorted five or six times in succession, and then Zhao, who rarely cursed, pronounced, "That little bastard."

Poet Zhao told the Liu Town crowds that formerly, which is to say eleven or twelve years earlier, he had repeatedly given Baldy Li the taste of his heel, whereupon Baldy Li had wailed and stumbled about, sometimes halfway across the street. Poet Zhao declared that Baldy Li was human scum. He told how at fourteen Baldy Li had peeked at women's bottoms in the public toilet, and how after he, Poet Zhao, had nabbed him, Baldy Li had secretly nursed a grievance against him, waiting for a chance to exact revenge. As Poet Zhao recalled that day of glory when he paraded Baldy Li down the street, his face began to warm and his voice became loud and clear. When some in the crowd repeated that Baldy Li was planning to beat Zhao until the poet became a laborer, Poet Zhao's complexion turned pale again. So angry that his voice quavered, he said, "I'll beat him up first, you just watch. I'll first take this laborer and beat him into an intellectual, beat him until he never curses again, until he treats people politely, until he respects the elderly and loves the young, until he is refined and cultivated."

Some of the townspeople laughed. "If you continue beating him like this, won't you beat him into a Poet Li?" asked one.

Poet Zhao was momentarily confounded, then muttered, "I might as well beat him into a Poet Li."

Poet Zhao had spoken boldly while out on the street, but once he got home he started to feel apprehensive. Now agitated and fearful, he calculated that if he and Baldy Li were indeed to duke it out, his height would probably give him only a slight advantage, and he couldn't even be certain of that. He worried that Baldy Li was so impulsive that he wouldn't know how to keep his beatings in moderation. Remembering how Baldy Li had struck Writer Liu in the face twenty-eight times and left him suffering from delusional paranoia, it occurred to Zhao that if Baldy Li were to strike him in the face twenty-eight times, he might end up not just filled with temporary delusions but permanently retarded. After realizing this, Poet Zhao started doing everything in his power to avoid having to leave the house. If there was something for which he absolutely had to go out, he would first carefully reconnoiter the unfamiliar terrain like a military scout; if he caught the slightest whiff of Baldy Li, he would immediately duck and cower in the nearest alley.

After his beating, Writer Liu spent two full days in the hospital and then rested at home for another month. As for Baldy Li, apart from being summoned by Tao Qing to the Civil Affairs Bureau office for a reprimand, he was off the hook. When people asked Baldy Li why he wanted to beat the intellectual Writer Liu until he turned back into the laborer Success Liu, Baldy Li would immediately answer with a grin, "*I* didn't beat him. It was Li Kui who beat him."

Song Gang was deeply troubled by the fact that Baldy Li had beaten someone to the point that he had to be hospitalized. Though everything Liu had said and done that day infuriated Song Gang, he nevertheless felt that it was not right for Baldy Li to beat him so badly. Song Gang wanted to go visit Writer Liu but was afraid that Baldy Li would disapprove. When he saw that Writer Liu had almost recovered and would soon return to work at the metal factory, Song Gang decided that he could not put the visit off any longer. Stammeringly, he suggested, "We should go pay a visit to Writer Liu."

Baldy Li waved him off. "If someone is to go, it should be you. I'm not going."

Song Gang continued to hem and haw, saying that if you beat someone up, you should take them something. Baldy Li didn't know where Song Gang was going with this, and asked, "What are you trying to say with all that muttering?"

Song Gang had no alternative but to tell Baldy Li the truth, which was that he wanted to buy a few apples to take to Writer Liu. When Baldy Li heard the word *apple*, his mouth immediately began to water, and he told Song Gang that he himself had never eaten an apple. He added, "Is this not letting that laborer off lightly?"

Song Gang did not reply but just lowered his head and sat at the table. Baldy Li recognized that Song Gang was distressed and therefore patted his shoulder and said, "Okay, go buy some apples and pay him a visit."

Song Gang smiled with gratitude, and Baldy Li shook his head, saying, "I don't care about a few apples. I'm just afraid that, after all the effort I expended in bringing out his inner laborer, a few apples might encourage his intellectual pretentiousness to return."

Song Gang bought five apples from a fruit stall. He then returned home and picked out the biggest and freshest to leave for Baldy Li, placing the remaining four apples in an old book bag. Song Gang arrived at Writer Liu's house carrying the bag. By that time Writer Liu had recuperated and was sitting in his courtyard chatting with neighbors. Hearing that Song Gang was at the door, Liu sent someone to ask what he wanted while he hurried back to bed.

Cautiously entering Writer Liu's room, where Liu was lying in bed with his eyes shut, Song Gang walked to the front of the bed. Liu opened his eyes to glance at him, then quickly shut them again. Song Gang stood in front of Liu's bed for a while and eventually softly said, "I'm sorry."

Writer Liu opened his eyes but quickly closed them again. Song Gang stood there a while longer, then opened his book bag and took out the four apples. When Liu saw the four apples on the table, he smiled and said to Song Gang, "You are truly courteous."

As Writer Liu was saying this he took an apple, wiped it on the bedsheet, then hurriedly took a bite. Liu's eyes narrowed to small slits in delight, and he crunched down melodiously, chewed melodiously, and swallowed the apple in a melodious manner. As Baldy Li had expected, after Writer Liu took a bite of the apple he immediately recovered his intellectual airs and began animatedly discussing literature with Song Gang as if nothing had transpired between them.

CHAPTER 29

HALF A YEAR passed, and not only did Baldy Li not find an opportunity to beat Poet Zhao's laborer identity back into him; he even pretty much forgot all about his promise to do so. Instead, he found himself increasingly busy, having been appointed director of Liu Town's Good Works Factory. When he first arrived, two cripples served as the factory's director and deputy director, but within half a year both of them were obediently following Baldy Li's orders.

Thus Baldy Li became Factory Director Li, even though he was still only twenty years old. Originally, when the factory had only two cripples, three idiots, four blind men, and five deaf men working for it, it would lose money hand over fist, and therefore year after year it was necessary to ask Tao Qing to bail them out. Tao Qing had built the factory for the sole purpose of providing its fourteen handicapped workers with a way of making a living. The factory, however, did not make a profit—he constantly had to make up for its losses out of his own pocket. Tao Qing hired Baldy Li because Baldy Li's mother had kowtowed to him so vigorously that she bloodied her forehead. What he didn't expect was that during Baldy Li's first year at the factory he would manage to turn the entire place around. Baldy Li not only brought in enough money to pay the salaries of the fourteen employees but also earned a profit of 57,224 yuan. The second year he was even more impressive, earning Tao Qing a profit of more than 150,000 yuan, or 10,000 yuan per employee. When the county governor saw Tao Qing, he was full of smiles, saying that Tao was the richest Civil Affairs Bureau director in all of China. He then privately asked that Tao Qing use some of the Good Works Factory's profits to plug a hole in the county's public finance deficit.

Tao Qing was therefore promoted to bureau director, and although he had not been to the Good Works Factory for the preceding several years, on that particular day he happened to wander up to the factory. Tao Qing had long known that the two crippled directors were ineffective to the point of being merely figureheads and that Baldy Li had become the de facto director. Tao Qing also knew that within half a year of Baldy Li's arrival, he had taken the two cripples, three idiots, four blind men, and five deaf men to the photography studio to pose for a group portrait, and then had taken this family photo on a long bus ride to Shanghai. Before getting on the bus, Baldy Li bought ten plain steamed buns at Mama Su's snack shop. He rushed around Shanghai for two days, visiting seven stores and eight companies and showing everyone his Good Works Factory group portrait. He would introduce each of the people in the photo to the corporate directors he met, explaining which were the cripples, the idiots, the blind and deaf men. Then he would point himself out in the photo, saying, "That only leaves this one, who is neither blind, deaf, crippled, nor an idiot."

Everywhere he went, Baldy Li tried to solicit people's sympathy. By the time he finished all ten of his steamed buns, he had received a long-term contract from a large company to put the finishing touches on paper boxes, and thus began the Good Works Factory's glorious path to brilliance.

When Tao Qing entered the factory that day, the crippled deputy factory director was just emerging from the restroom. Tao Qing asked him where the factory director was, and the deputy director replied that he was working in the workshop. Tao asked him to call the director over, and then he walked into the director's office. Tao Qing noted the group portrait hanging on the wall and remembered that the last time he came to this office there had been two desks, where the crippled directors had been playing chess, retracting illegal moves and happily cursing each other. Now there was just one desk. Tao Qing felt that something was a little fishy—perhaps the crippled factory director had kicked the crippled deputy director out of the office? As Tao Qing was sitting down in the chair behind the desk, Baldy Li ran in, shouting, "Bureau Director Tao has arrived, Bureau Director Tao has arrived!"

Tao Qing saw that Baldy Li was very happy and cheerfully said, "You're not doing bad at all. Not bad at all."

Baldy Li shook his head modestly. "I've only just begun and still need to work harder."

Tao Qing nodded approvingly and asked Baldy Li whether he was satisfied with his job. Baldy Li nodded repeatedly, saying that he was indeed. Tao Qing chatted with Baldy Li for a while, then glanced out

234 * YU HUA

the door and wondered why the crippled director hadn't arrived yet. The workshop was right next door, and although it was true that the crippled director walked slowly, he should still have arrived by now. Tao Qing asked Baldy Li, "Why hasn't your factory director arrived yet?"

Baldy Li was momentarily speechless, but he recovered in an instant, pointing to himself and saying, "*I'm* here. I'm the director."

"You're the director?" Now it was Tao Qing's turn to be taken aback. "Why was I not informed?"

Baldy Li laughed. "You are so busy, I was reluctant to take up your time, so I simply neglected to tell you."

Tao Qing's face fell. He asked, "What happened to the original two directors?"

Baldy Li shook his head. "They are not directors anymore."

Tao Qing understood now why there was just one desk in the office. He asked Baldy Li, "Is this your desk?"

Baldy Li nodded. "Yes."

Tao Qing declared sternly, "The appointment and removal of the factory director should be approved by committee, discussed first with the head of the Civil Affairs Bureau, and then approved by the county government."

Baldy Li nodded repeatedly. "Yes, that's right, you can officially remove the former factory director, and then officially hire me for the same position."

Tao Qing became serious. "I don't have that authority."

"Director Tao, you are too modest." Baldy Li laughed as he pointed to Tao Qing. "When it comes to who serves as the director of the Good Works Factory, doesn't your word go?"

Tao Qing didn't know whether to laugh or cry and replied, "You simply don't follow the rules, do you?"

What came next rendered Tao Qing even more at a loss for words. Baldy Li, who seemed to have already appointed himself factory director, escorted Tao Qing on a tour of the workshop in charge of gluing cardboard boxes, where fourteen handicapped workers all greeted him by calling out, "Director Li!" Even the original two crippled factory directors respectfully called out, "Director Li." Factory Director Baldy Li stood next to Bureau Director Tao Qing and applauded vigorously, as did the fourteen handicapped workers. Baldy Li felt that the applause was not loud enough and therefore shouted to his loyal minions, "Director Tao has come to see us! Make your applause as loud as fireworks!"

His loyal minions applauded so vigorously that their entire bodies swung into motion. Baldy Li still felt that it was not enough, and gestured frantically, saying, "Shout, 'Welcome, Bureau Director Tao!'"

The two cripples and the four blind men all shouted at the top of their lungs, "Welcome, Bureau Director Tao!"

The five deaf workers opened their mouths and laughed, not knowing what the two cripples and four blind workers were shouting. Baldy Li rushed over and signaled for the deaf workers to watch his lips. His mouth opened and closed like a fish spurting out water, and finally he was able to teach the five deaf workers the correct formations. Of the five, three were also mute, and therefore only two of them were able to vocalize at all. The sound of the "Welcome, Bureau Director Tao" was now deafening, which pleased Baldy Li immensely, and he gave everyone a thumbs-up sign. Then Baldy Li discovered a new problem, which was that the three idiots couldn't pronounce the words "Bureau Director Tao" and instead were calling out, "Welcome, Factory Director Li." This embarrassed Baldy Li, and he immediately rushed over to the three idiots and taught them to shout "Welcome, Bureau Director Tao" as if he were teaching them to sing a song. Baldy Li's two arms danced up and down, his voice grew hoarse from shouting, but the three idiots still called out, "Welcome, Factory Director Li." Tao Qing couldn't help laughing, and Baldy Li said with embarrassment, "Director Tao, give me a little time. The next time you come, I guarantee that they'll all call out 'Director Tao.'"

"No need." Tao Qing shook his head. "They are shouting 'Director Li' very capably."

When Tao Qing walked out of the workshop, he turned around, looked at the two crippled factory directors, and said to Baldy Li, "I originally thought that the two factory directors were mere figureheads, but now I realize that they can't even be considered ornaments."

Two months later, Baldy Li received his official appointment as the director of the Good Works Factory. Baldy Li was summoned to Tao Qing's office, where Tao read the county-approved promotion letter out loud. Baldy Li blushed with excitement and told Tao Qing that the three idiots at the Good Works Factory could now shout "Bureau Director Tao" quite fluently. Tao Qing laughed and confessed that there was considerable resistance to officially appointing Baldy Li as factory director, due to his spotty past. Tao Qing chuckled, but then confided quite seriously that everyone saw Baldy Li as his surrogate, and therefore he hoped Baldy Li would take better care of his public image and in particular curb his hoodlum behavior. Finally, he gave Baldy Li his profit target, sticking out two fingers and saying, "This year you must bring in two hundred thousand yuan in profit."

Baldy Li held up three fingers. "I will raise three hundred thousand yuan, and if I don't, I will resign."

Tao Qing nodded with satisfaction. Baldy Li rolled up the appointment letter approved by the county government and was about to stick it in his pocket when Tao Qing pointed to the document and said, "What are you doing with that?"

Baldy Li said, "I'm taking it home."

Tao Qing shook his head. "You really don't understand how things are done. This document must be taken to the Organization Bureau for filing; you are now a national cadre."

"I'm a national cadre?" Baldy Li registered a look of pleasurable shock, adding, "Then it is all the more important that I take this home to show Song Gang."

Tao Qing recalled the Song Gang he knew from twenty years earlier—a pitiful but adorable little boy. Tao hesitated a moment, then he agreed to let Baldy Li take the appointment letter home to show Song Gang, but on the condition that he return it the very next afternoon. As Baldy Li was leaving he bowed to Tao Qing and said earnestly, "Thank you, Director Tao, for appointing me factory director."

Tao Qing patted his shoulder and said, "What are you thanking me for? It was you who carried out the execution first and sought a permit for it later."

The expression *to carry out the execution first and seek a permit for it later* gave Baldy Li a good chuckle. After walking out of the courtyard of the Civil Affairs Bureau, he repeated the phrase to himself yet again, but this time he found that it had somehow soured on his lips.

Carrying the appointment letter in his hands, Baldy Li walked home and showed the letter to everyone he met, telling them proudly that he was now Director Li. When he encountered Blacksmith Tong on the bridge, he pulled Tong over to sit next to him on the railing and proudly told him he was now director of the Good Works Factory. He added that, actually, he had long been running the factory but, extending the letter with trembling hands, he added, "This piece of paper makes it official."

"That's right," Blacksmith Tong agreed. "It's just like a marriage certificate—who waits until the day of their marriage before sleeping together? The marriage certificate simply grants them an official identity. This is called *legitimization*."

"Yes, *legitimization*—that's what it's called," Baldy Li exclaimed, adding, "It's as if I knocked a girl up and left her no choice but to marry me. Or, as Director Tao put it, I carried out the execution first and sought a permit for it later."

When Baldy Li returned home, Song Gang had prepared lunch, had set the table, and was sitting there waiting for him. Baldy Li, flushed with success, sat down at the table, glanced disdainfully at the food, and muttered, "The formidable Factory Director Li has to eat this cheap food every day."

Song Gang did not realize that Baldy Li had been officially appointed factory director and thought that he was still bragging about his de facto directorship. He grinned, then picked up his rice bowl and began to eat, whereupon Baldy Li opened up his director's-appointment letter and extended it for Song Gang to read. Song Gang read it while chewing his rice, then excitedly jumped up from his seat and started crying out. Since his mouth was still full of food, however, he was totally incomprehensible. He spat the food into his hand and shouted, "Baldy Li, you really are—"

Baldy Li calmly corrected Song Gang, "I'm Director Li."

"Director Li, you really are Director Li!"

Song Gong excitedly cried out as he jumped around the house, shouting "Director Li" over and over again, pounding Baldy Li in the chest three times with his fist full of food, splattering the food all over Baldy Li's face. Baldy Li wiped Song Gang's chewed-up food from his face and began laughing uncontrollably. But Song Gang was still pounding his chest with his fist, so Baldy Li sprang out of the way. It was like the time when Song Gang returned from the countryside, travel bag in hand: The two of them ran around the room laughing hysterically, with Song Gang chasing Baldy Li and Baldy Li trying to stay out of the way of Song Gang's fist. They upended all the chairs and stools in the room and jostled the table so hard that the bowls of rice and food went flying. Song Gang finally lowered his fist and, realizing that he was still clutching the food he had spit out of his mouth, wiped his hand with a rag. He tidied up the spilled food on the table and straightened up the chairs that had been knocked over. Then, making a *please* gesture to Baldy Li, who was still laughing hysterically, he bowed and said, "Director Li, please eat."

Baldy Li exhaled and shook his head. "I, Director Li, want to have a bowl of house-special noodles."

Song Gang's eyes lit up, and he waved his hand. "Yes, let's eat house-special noodles. Let's celebrate."

Song Gang looked disdainfully at the food on the table, patted Baldy Li on the shoulder, then walked out of the room with him and locked the door. He proceeded a few steps, paused, and asked Baldy Li how much a bowl of house-special noodles cost. Baldy Li replied thirty-five cents a bowl. Song Gang nodded and walked back to the door, then leaned against it as he unfastened his pants and reached into his underwear. After fumbling about for a while, he pulled out seventy cents and placed it in his pocket, then spiritedly continued forward. As they walked Song Gang explained to Baldy Li, "You are now a factory director, making me a factory director's brother. I can't continue reaching into my pants for money in public, making you lose face."

The two brothers paraded like heroes down the main street in Liu Town. Baldy Li continued to grasp the promotion letter in his hand, and Song Gang stopped twice and asked to see the letter again. Song Gang stood in the middle of the street reading the letter aloud as if he were reciting poetry, and when he finished he turned to Baldy Li and said sincerely, "I am truly happy."

The two brothers walked into the People's Restaurant, and as soon as Song Gang stepped in the door, he shouted to the woman at the counter, "Two bowls of house-special noodles!"

Song Gang then walked up to the cashier and pulled exactly seventy cents out of his pocket. Slapping the money down on the counter, he startled the female cashier, who muttered, "Only seventy cents—you'd think it was ten yuan, with all that ruckus."

The two brothers finished their house-special noodles and returned home with their faces covered in sweat. On the way home, Baldy Li opened up his appointment letter three more times to read it to various acquaintances, and Song Gong stopped twice more to recite it. Once they returned home, Song Gang offered to keep the letter, afraid that Baldy Li would lose it. Upon hearing Song Gang's suggestion, Baldy Li

mimicked Bureau Director Tao, explaining, "You really don't understand how things are done. This appointment letter must be taken to
the Organization Bureau to be put on file, because now I am a national
cadre."

Baldy Li's comment made Song Gang even more elated, and he felt
that this little brother of his was truly extraordinary. Song Gang then
grasped the appointment letter in his hand and read it one more time,
as if he were trying to devour every word. It occurred to him that he
would never see this appointment letter again, and the thought filled
him with regret. But then he had an inspiration. He immediately
fetched a sheet of paper and used black ink to neatly copy the letter,
then used red ink to carefully draw the seal mark that appeared on top.
Baldy Li expressed his approval, saying that Song Gang's seal was even
more realistic than the original. After drawing it, Song Gang laughed,
as if a heavy burden had been lifted from his shoulders, and handed the
letter back to Baldy Li. Taking up his own copy, he said proudly, "In the
future, we can look at this one."

Song Gang kept track of both of their salaries, and every time he
wanted to spend money, he made a point of consulting with Baldy Li
and securing his permission. After Baldy Li formally assumed his position as factory director, Song Gang offered to go buy him a pair of black
leather shoes, arguing that as factory director he couldn't keep wearing
his tattered old sneakers. Baldy Li was very pleased to see his new
shoes, and counting on his fingers all the important people in the
county—from the county's party secretary, governor, and bureau chief
on down to the various factory directors—he concluded that all of
them wore black leather shoes. He added, "Now I'm an important person, too."

Baldy Li's sweater was also in tatters. Furthermore, it had been knitted from various different colored spools of yarn, patched together
long ago by Li Lan from the remains of several other sweaters. Song
Gang bought a pound and a half of beige yarn, and after work he
started knitting Baldy Li a new sweater, periodically holding it up to
Baldy Li's body to size it. A month later the sweater was finished, and it
fit perfectly. On Baldy Li's chest there was the embroidered outline of a
wave, on top of which was a boat, its sails unfurled. Song Gang
explained that the sailboat symbolized Baldy Li's bright future. Baldy
Li happily exclaimed, "Song Gang, you are truly extraordinary. You can
even do women's work."

Since he had begun wearing the black leather shoes, Baldy Li had only left the house wearing his dark blue Mao suit, buttoned all the way up. But once he started wearing the beige sweater Song Gang knitted for him, Baldy Li let his Mao tunic hang open as he walked around in order to give people a clear view of the waves and the sailboat on his chest. With his hands in his pockets, the flaps of his tunic tucked behind his elbows, he stuck out his chest as he walked, grinning to everyone he encountered.

The women in Liu Town had never seen a sweater with a sailboat embroidered on the front, and therefore when they saw Baldy Li's they immediately crowded around him to examine how it had been made. They crowed their approval, exclaiming, "There is even a sail on top!"

Baldy Li lifted his head and allowed them to appreciate his sweater, listening as they complimented the sailboat. They asked him whose extraordinary skill had produced it. Baldy Li responded proudly, "Song Gang. Aside from bearing children, Song Gang can do anything."

After the women of Liu finished admiring the handiwork on the boat and the sail, they turned their attention to what kind of boat it was. They asked Baldy Li, "Is this a fishing boat?"

"A fishing boat?" Baldy Li replied. "This is called a Great Prospects Ship."

Their rude and ignorant questions infuriated Baldy Li. He pushed away their hands, feeling that allowing them to admire his tall mast sailing into the future was like serenading cows with violins. As he stalked off he turned and angrily spat out his parting words: "What are you women good for besides having children?"

CHAPTER 30

AUH UA

AFTER BALDY LI was appointed factory director, he would often attend meetings with the county's other factory directors, all of whom similarly wore Mao suits and black leather shoes. Baldy Li would smile and shake their hands, and within a few months he was accepted as one of their "brothers." From that point on, Baldy Li became a bona fide member of Liu Town's high society, whereupon he assumed a haughty demeanor, always holding his head high when speaking.

One day he unexpectedly ran into Lin Hong on the bridge and was immediately struck dumb. While the Lin Hong that Baldy Li had peeped at was a very pretty seventeen-year-old, she was now twenty-three and the embodiment of womanly charm. Lin Hong walked across the bridge staring straight ahead, but when she passed Baldy Li someone happened to call out her name. She spun around, and her long braid barely missed hitting him in the face. Baldy Li watched her in a state of infatuation, repeating dreamily, "Beautiful, so beautiful . . ."

Baldy Li hadn't seen Lin Hong in a long time, not since being appointed factory director, and he had almost forgotten all about Liu Town's resident beauty. Upon encountering her on the bridge that day, however, he became so excited he developed a nosebleed, with two streams of blood gushing from his nose into his mouth. As a result, Baldy Li enjoyed another brief moment of fame, almost as great as that time several years earlier when he was caught being a Peeping Tom. Everyone in our Liu Town laughed heartily over this incident, remarking that nothing since Baldy Li was caught spying on women's bottoms had provided them with comparable entertainment. Liu Town, they said, was becoming duller by the year, its residents increasingly dispirited, and therefore it was a good thing that Baldy Li had decided to make a public spectacle of himself again, and wouldn't you know it, it was once again all about Lin Hong.

Baldy Li ignored their laughter, saying that the blood was merely an "offering" and asking, "Who else in the world could claim to have offered up his lifeblood for love?" Patting his chest, he declared, "The glory belongs solely to me."

The elders of Liu were more tactful and remarked, "It is true that famous people do famous things."

When this reached Baldy Li's ears, he nodded with satisfaction. "Well, the rich and famous always live larger than ordinary folks."

Baldy Li, who had previously beaten Writer Liu to the point that he developed a case of delusional memory, seemed to have contracted a similar delusional syndrome. He racked his brain trying to explain why Lin Hong had leaned so close to him when she passed, so close that her long braid almost caressed his nose. Combining illusions of love with delusions of grandeur, he concluded that she must be in love with him; and even if she hadn't fallen in love with him yet, there was no question that she was about to. Baldy Li decided that there had been altogether too many people on the bridge and in the street, and if their encounter had taken place in the middle of the night with no one around, Lin Hong would certainly have stopped to gaze longingly at him, committing to memory every wrinkle and blood vessel in his face. Upon reaching that conclusion, he grinned stupidly as he informed Song Gang, "Lin Hong fancies me."

Song Gang knew about Lin Hong and knew that this Liu Town beauty was the object of all the townsmen's fantasies. Song Gang himself felt that she was as unattainable as the moon and the stars, and therefore Baldy Li's assertion that she was interested in him left Song Gang speechless. Was it possible that Lin Hong would fancy the same Baldy Li who had peeped at her in the public toilet more than six years earlier? Song Gang wasn't so sure. He asked Baldy Li, "And why do you think Lin Hong fancies you?"

"Because I'm Factory Director Li, of course!" Baldy Li patted his chest and added, "Just think, among the twenty-odd factory directors in and about Liu Town, aren't I the only bachelor?"

"You're right!" Song Gang replied, nodding vigorously. "In the old days they used to speak of a fine match being that of a talented man and a beautiful woman. That describes you and Lin Hong perfectly!"

"Of course!" Baldy Li excitedly punched Song Gang. His eyes lighting up, he said, "That's precisely what I'm talking about."

Song Gang's comment helped Baldy Li pinpoint the theoretical foundation for his and Lin Hong's romance, after which he began to pursue Lin Hong in earnest. Many of the young men of Liu had pursued or were in the midst of pursuing Lin Hong, but ultimately these men of weak will and weaker courage would throw up their hands. Only the remarkable Baldy Li refused to admit defeat.

Baldy Li pursued Lin Hong with a vengeance and anointed Song Gang as his military advisor. Song Gang had read his share of tattered old books on the art of war and said that in olden times, before engaging in battle, it was customary to send a messenger with a declaration of war. "What I don't know is whether in a *combat d'amour* it is also necessary to first send a messenger."

"Of course we should," Baldy Li said. "Let Lin Hong prepare herself, because otherwise it may all be too sudden for her. What will we do if she simply faints from the excitement?"

Baldy Li selected five six-year-old boys he ran across on his way to work at the Good Works Factory to serve as his messengers. These boys had been playing in the street when they started pointing at Baldy Li and arguing. One boy said that this baldy was none other than the one who was said to have peeped at Lin Hong's bottom and who was rumored to have developed a nosebleed upon seeing her again. Another boy said that this must be someone else, because that person was called Baldy Li. When Baldy Li heard them, he thought that if even these little ruffians knew of the rumors, he must already have become a legendary figure in Liu Town. He paused and waved them over. The snot-nosed boys came and looked up at the infamous Baldy Li, who pointed at himself and said, "This old man is Baldy Li."

Several of the boys stared at Baldy Li in happy astonishment. Baldy Li gestured for them to wipe their noses and then asked, "You also know Lin Hong?"

The boys all nodded and replied, "The Lin Hong who works at the knitting factory."

Baldy Li snorted in amusement and said that he wanted to give them a glorious assignment: "Run over to the knitting factory and wait at the door for Lin Hong to get off work, like a midnight cat waiting at a mouse hole for a midnight mouse. When she does comes out, I want you to call out to her . . ." Baldy Li then shouted out in a boy's voice, "'Baldy Li wants to court you!'"

The boys giggled and hollered in unison, "Baldy Li wants to court you!"

"That's right," Baldy Li said approvingly and patted them on their heads. "There is one more sentence: 'Are you ready?'"

The boys cried out, "Are you ready?"

Baldy Li was very satisfied and complimented the boys on having learned so quickly. He counted them and found that there were five boys. He retrieved a nickel from his pocket, bought ten pieces of hard candy from a street stall, and then gave one to each boy, placing the five remaining pieces back into his own pocket. Baldy Li told the boys that when they finished their task, they could come for the rest of their reward. Then Baldy Li, like a general on a battlefield directing his soldiers to advance, gestured in the direction of the knitting factory and shouted, "Forward, march!"

The boys immediately unwrapped their candies and stuffed them into their mouths, then stood there without moving, happily sucking on their candy. Baldy Li gestured again, but they still didn't budge. Finally, he said, "Damn it, hurry up and go!"

After looking at one another, they asked Baldy Li, "What does *to court* mean?"

"*To court?*" Baldy Li pondered hard and then said, "*To court* means to marry someone, to sleep together at night."

The boys giggled, and Baldy Li once again pointed to the knitting factory with his short, stubby finger. They walked forward while crying out, "Baldy Li wants to court you! Get married! Sleep with you! Are you ready?"

"Fuck. Get back here!" Baldy Li called out urgently. "Don't mention anything about marriage or sleeping together. Just focus on the courtship part."

That afternoon Baldy Li's five emissaries of love walked toward the knitting factory, shouting all the way. The people of Liu stared in amazement upon seeing them go by, never in their wildest dreams having imagined that Baldy Li would resort to such a tactic as having a bunch of snot-nosed and split-pants-wearing boys court Lin Hong on his behalf. Everyone laughed and shook their heads, saying that Baldy Li must have shit and piss for brains to come up with such an idiotic plan. They concluded that he, having spent all his time with two cripples, three idiots, four blind men, and five deaf men, had allowed his own brain to become handicapped.

Poet Zhao was also there and agreed with everyone's assessment. Noting that he had known Baldy Li for a long time, Poet Zhao said that although in the past Baldy Li had not been very clever, neither had he been stupid, but since he had gone to work at the Good Works Factory—and especially since becoming the director of the cripples, idiots, and blind and deaf men—he had become dumber and dumber. Poet Zhao summed up the situation with an old expression: "This is a case of *those close to ink become black, and those close to cinnabar become vermilion.*"

The boys sucked in their snot and hollered as if they were singing a song, first shouting "to court" for the length of one entire street, and then switching to "get married" for the second. By the time they reached the third street, they were calling out "go to bed." It was only then that they remembered Baldy Li's instructions that they not mention going to bed, so they backtracked and again sang about getting married but then remembered that he had instructed them not to speak of getting married either. When they tried to backtrack even further, they couldn't for the life of them remember the phrase *to court*. They stopped in the middle of the street and looked around, wiping their noses with their hands and then wiping the snot on their bottoms, making their pants look as shiny as if a slug had crawled all over them.

Poet Zhao happened to be wandering down the third street and overheard the boys' argument. Reminded of how Baldy Li had bragged that he was going to beat him until his true laborer colors showed, Zhao laughed bitterly, then waved the boys over and told them quietly, "The word is *intercourse*."

The five boys looked at one another and felt that this sort of sounded like the phrase they had forgotten, yet it didn't seem quite right. Poet Zhao quickly added, "It is definitely *intercourse*."

The boys nodded and happily proceeded to the knitting factory. At the entrance they started calling out, and when they saw the gatekeeper, they shouted in unison in the direction of the closed iron gate, "Baldy Li wants to have intercourse with you!"

The old man initially leaned over curiously, and only after they had shouted it three times did he finally understand. Furiously, he grabbed the broom behind the door and rushed at them, making the boys scurry away in terror. The gatekeeper waved the broom and cursed, "Fuck your mother, and your grandmother, too!"

The boys apprehensively regrouped and embarrassedly told the old man, "Baldy Li told us to say that."

"Fuck Baldy Li's mother." The old man threw the broomstick down and yelled, "Does he dare come have intercourse with me? I'll rip him a new one."

The boys' heads shook their heads vigorously, explaining to the old man, "Not with you, with Lin Hong."

"It doesn't matter who it's with, it's still not okay," the old man said sternly. "Even if it were with his own mother, it still wouldn't be okay."

The five boys didn't dare approach the factory gate again; instead they hid behind a nearby tree, staring intently at the old man. As soon as he came out they immediately ran away, and when he went back inside, they cautiously walked back to the tree and peeked out. Following Baldy Li's instructions, the boys waited, like a midnight cat waiting at a mouse hole for a midnight mouse, until the closing bell rang, signalling the end of the workday. Then they saw Lin Hong walking over with a crowd of female workmates. Two boys who recognized Lin Hong started waving energetically at her while the other three kept an eye out for the old man in the entranceway. The two boys called out softly, "Lin Hong, Lin Hong."

As Lin Hong was walking, chatting with the other women, she heard the mysterious call and stopped curiously to see the five boys hiding behind the tree. Her companions also stopped and joked that Lin Hong's beauty had spread so far and wide that even little boys wearing split pants came looking for her. At that moment, the boys shouted in unison, "Baldy Li wants to have intercourse with you!"

One boy then specified, "That is the same Baldy Li who peeked at your bottom in the public toilet."

Lin Hong immediately turned deathly pale. Initially stunned, the other women then covered their mouths and stared giggling. The boys continued shouting, "Baldy Li wants to have intercourse with you."

Lin Hong became so furious that her eyes welled up with tears. She bit her lip and rushed forward. Her workmates behind her couldn't stop laughing. The boys then remembered that there was another phrase that they hadn't yet uttered, and so they pursued her like a bunch of rabbits and shouted after her, "Are you ready?"

Now that they had completed the glorious task that Baldy Li had assigned them, they proceeded to traipse, flushed with excitement, around the group of factory workers. The young women caressed the boys' heads and faces adoringly and asked them to describe everything from beginning to end. They did so, and the women doubled over in peals of laughter, laughing so hard that they couldn't get back up.

The boys ran back to the Good Works Factory, which by this point had also closed. Then they asked for directions and ran, hollering, to

Baldy Li's house. As Baldy Li and Song Gang walked out the five children met them at the door with their right hands extended. Baldy Li knew that they had come to collect their reward, so he removed the five pieces of candy from his pocket and placed them one by one in their palms. The children immediately ripped off the wrappers and popped the candies into their mouths. Baldy Li asked them hopefully, "Did she smile?" He mimed a shy smile for them and asked, "Did she smile like this?"

The children shook their heads and replied, "No, she cried."

Baldy Li looked at Song Gang in surprise and said, "She must have been very moved."

He again asked the children hopefully, "She must have blushed?"

The children again shook their heads and replied, "No, she turned pale."

He looked at Song Gang in befuddlement. "That can't be—she should have blushed."

"No, she definitely turned pale," the children replied.

Baldy Li started to look at the children suspiciously and said, "Did you by any chance shout the wrong thing?"

"Of course not," they replied. "We shouted, 'Baldy Li wants to have intercourse with you.' We even added, 'Are you ready?'"

Baldy Li roared like a crazed beast, "Who told you to say *intercourse*? Who the fuck told you to say *intercourse*?"

The children started trembling from head to toe and stammered as they tried to explain. However, they didn't know Poet Zhao, and therefore they couldn't clearly identify who it was who had given them the wrong word. They slowly backed away as they spoke, then turned and fled. Baldy Li was so furious that his face turned ashen, even whiter than Lin Hong's had been. He waved his fist and roared, "That son-of-a-bitch class enemy, whoever he is, I swear I'll ferret him out, and will definitely carry out a proletarian revolution against him!"

Baldy Li was so furious that his chest heaved in and out like an accordion. Song Gang patted his shoulder and told him that there was no point in getting angry. Instead, Song Gang suggested, Baldy Li should immediately go find Lin Hong and apologize. So the following afternoon, when it was time for Lin Hong to get off work, Baldy Li and Song Gang were waiting outside the main door of the knitting factory. When the bell rang signaling the end of the workday and the women workers started filing out, Baldy Li began to feel a little nervous. He said it was time to go out to face the firing squad. He asked Song Gang to keep a close eye out, and if things started to look bad, Song Gang should immediately tug at his clothes.

From far away Lin Hong spotted Baldy Li standing at the factory gate. She heard the other women gasp in astonishment as she walked toward the gate with a pale face. When she saw Song Gang standing next to Baldy Li, she couldn't help staring at him—this being the first time she had noticed the tall and dashing Song Gang.

When Baldy Li saw Lin Hong walk through the gate, he called out sorrowfully, "Lin Hong, it was all a misunderstanding! Yesterday, those little bastards said the wrong thing. I didn't tell them to say *intercourse* but, rather, *to court*. I, Baldy Li, want *to court* you."

When the women leaving the factory heard Baldy Li's sorrowful cries and saw his sorrowful expression, they again erupted into waves of laughter. Lin Hong was already numb with fury, and she walked past Baldy Li in complete silence. He followed closely behind her, raising his fist, beating his chest like a drum, and shouting, "I swear by all that is sacred and holy in the world!"

Baldy Li paid no attention to the tittering of the female factory workers, and instead continued to proclaim sorrowfully, "Those little bastards really did shout the wrong thing. There was a class enemy who messed things up."

Eventually Baldy Li began to calm down. He stopped pounding his chest and instead started knocking his own head. "That class enemy is destroying our proletariat revolutionary spirit, deliberately getting those little bastards to shout out *intercourse*. Lin Hong, don't worry, no matter how deeply hidden this class enemy is, I will make sure to ferret him out and conduct proletarian revolution against him."

Then Baldy Li said in all sincerity, "Lin Hong, whatever you do, don't forget class struggle!"

Finally Lin Hong couldn't stand it anymore. She turned around to face Baldy Li, who was still hollering behind her. Gritting her teeth, she uttered the foulest words she had ever uttered: "I hope you die!"

This made Baldy Li stop dead in his tracks, as if he didn't know what had hit him. It was not until the other factory workers walked past and their hysterical laughter died away that he finally recovered from the shock. He wanted to chase after her, but Song Gang restrained him. Pausing, Baldy Li gazed longingly at Lin Hong's departing shadow.

The brothers headed home. Baldy Li did not feel at all that he had failed and maintained his proud stride. Song Gang, by contrast, trailed listlessly at his side. He ventured nervously, "I don't think Lin Hong is interested in you."

"That's absurd," Baldy Li responded, adding confidently, "It's simply inconceivable that she would not be interested."

Song Gang shook his head and said, "If she really fancied you, she would not have said such an ugly thing."

"What do you know?" Baldy Li lectured Song Gang like an old hand. "Women are like that. The more they like you, the more they act like they hate you. When they do want you, they pretend that they don't."

Song Gang felt that what Baldy Li said sounded plausible. He regarded Baldy Li with surprise. "How do you know all this?"

"Worldly experience," Baldy Li replied proudly. "Just think, I often attend meetings with the other factory directors, all of whom are worldly, clever people, and they say this is how things are."

Song Gang nodded his head in admiration and conceded that the people Baldy Li hung out with were indeed a cut above the rest, and indeed it seemed that their worldliness had broadened Baldy Li's perspective, too. Just then Baldy Li abruptly cried out, "There's an aphorism that captures this idea." Baldy Li slapped his head and said regretfully, "Fuck, why can't I think of it?"

The entire walk back, Baldy Li struggled to remember the aphorism. He spit out seventeen more "fucks" but couldn't think of it. Song Gang tried to help, but by the time they got home they still hadn't made any progress. Song Gang then immediately went to look up the phrase in his middle-school dictionary of aphorisms, leafing through it on his bed for the longest time. Eventually he asked Baldy Li, "Is it *playing cat and mouse?*"

"Yes, that's it!" Baldy Li cried out. "She's playing cat and mouse with me."

That night Baldy Li and Song Gang burned the midnight oil discussing how to break through Lin Hong's game of cat and mouse. When it came time to discuss battle tactics, Song Gang suddenly appeared full of wisdom. He closed his eyes and tried to recollect what he could from the half of a tattered volume of Sunzi's *The Art of War* he'd read. He then opened his eyes, analyzed Lin Hong's oppositional tactics again, and said approvingly, "The cat and mouse strategy is fantastic. She can advance to make gains, and then retreat to secure her position."

After that, Song Gang took the dictionary of aphorisms and continued leafing through it. Upon finding five more apt aphorisms, he proudly held up five fingers, telling Baldy Li, "If you use these five stratagems, you will be assured of breaking through Lin Hong's game of cat and mouse."

"What are they?" Baldy Li asked excitedly.

Song Gang counted out on his fingers: "*Beating around the bush. Coming straight to the point. Laying siege at the outskirts of the city. Penetrating behind enemy lines. Beating to a pulp.*"

Song Gang explained to Baldy Li that he had already deployed the first two strategies. Yesterday, when he had the boys go and call out for him, this was *beating around the bush*. Today when he personally went to confront her, this was *coming straight to the point*. Why is the third strategy called *laying siege at the outskirts of the city*? Because one shouldn't go in alone again; rather, Baldy Li should have all his Good Works Factory workers go in on his behalf, to give Lin Hong a taste of the strength of his numbers. As for the fourth strategy, *penetrating behind enemy lines*, Song Gang said that this was the most crucial one and the key to his success.

Baldy Li's eyes glittered as he asked, "How do I penetrate behind enemy lines?"

"Go to her house," Song Gang said. "*Penetrating behind enemy lines* means to go into her home and conquer her parents—this is referred to as *catching the thieves by first capturing their chief.*"

Baldy Li nodded his head vigorously, asking, "And what is *beating to a pulp*?"

"Pursue her every day without giving up, until she finally gives you her hand in marriage," Song Gang said.

Baldy Li pounded the table fiercely and shouted, "Song Gang, you certainly live up to the title of being my military advisor."

Baldy Li immediately sprung into action, and the very next afternoon he started laying siege at the outskirts of the city. He took his fourteen crippled, idiot, blind, and deaf loyal minions and swaggered through the streets of Liu. Many of the townspeople saw this scene and laughed so hard their bellies ached and their throats became raw. Baldy Li was afraid the two cripples would lag behind everyone else, so he had them walk at the very front of the procession. When the rest of the courtship brigade tried to advance, however, they found their progress blocked by the cripples, leaving everyone in complete disarray. One of the cripples at the front listed to the left and the other listed to the right, and as they proceeded they gradually ended up on opposite sides of the road. This left the three idiots behind them completely confused. At first they took several steps to the left, then doubled back and took several steps to the right. The three idiots swerving left and right as they walked together hand in hand made the four cane-carrying blind men knock themselves silly. After they had fallen down and gotten back up, there was only one blind man who was still marching in the right direction—two were going backward, and the fourth found his way obstructed by a wutong tree. He kept tapping the tree with his cane and calling out, "Director Li, Director Li, where am I?"

Baldy Li was soon bathed in sweat from his exertions. As soon as he had reorientated the first two blind men, the blind man who was originally walking in the correct direction had been knocked over by the three idiots, while the fourth blind man under the wutong tree was still calling out for help. Thankfully, there were the five deaf men. Baldy Li energetically directed them to stand in line and then sent one of them to retrieve the blind man under the wutong tree, two to look after the three idiots, and the remaining two to go help the blind man who had fallen over. Baldy Li seemed to be performing a dance, hopping all over the place as he directed the five deaf men while simultaneously pointing to his own ear as he explained to the onlookers, "These five are deaf."

As Baldy Li tried to rein in his courtship brigade, he discovered that the crux of the problem lay with the two cripples. Therefore, he sprinted to the front of the procession and directed them to switch positions, so that the one who listed right was now on the left-hand side and vice versa. This way they no longer drifted apart but, rather, hobbled together. Every few steps they would bump into each other, and after separating they would walk a few more steps and bump into each other again. Baldy Li continued his street dance, wildly gesticulating at the five deaf men, who finally understood what to do. Two of them walked to the left of the brigade, and the other three walked to the right, like gendarmes maintaining the order of the procession.

This courtship brigade finally found its footing. Baldy Li wiped the sweat from his brow and faced the crowd laughing on the side of the street, like a leader waving a greeting. The onlookers chattered to each other, wondering where this brigade was headed. Baldy Li announced that he was bringing along all of the Good Works Factory's workers to lay siege at the outskirts of the knitting factory, in order to declare his undying love to Lin Hong: "I want Lin Hong to know that my love for her is taller than a mountain and deeper than the sea."

This was an unheard-of event in Liu Town, and everyone rushed toward the knitting factory. A number of sales clerks took time off from work, and even more people slipped out from the factories to come and watch the spectacle, completely packing the streets with spectators. Everyone crowded around Baldy Li's courtship brigade like waves around a whirlpool, and together they surged toward the knitting factory.

The old gatekeeper at the factory was very excited to see such a sea of people, and he noted that not since the end of the Cultural Revolution had he seen so many people in the same place at once. Then, with a turn of humor, he added, "For a second I thought that Chairman Mao himself had arrived."

The crowds, however, replied humorlessly, "Chairman Mao has been dead for several years now."

"I know that," the gatekeeper snapped. "Who doesn't know that our beloved Chairman Mao has passed away?"

Baldy Li's courtship procession stood at the factory gate, and he instructed his fourteen loyal minions to form two divisions, with the two cripples, four blind men, and two of the deaf men standing in the vanguard, and the three idiots and the remaining three deaf men taking up the rear. Baldy Li had spent the entire morning back at the factory rehearsing this formation: the eight crippled, blind, and deaf men in the vanguard shouting out in unison and the three deaf-mutes in the rear clapping vigorously. As for the three idiots, Baldy Li had learned well the bitter lesson from the last time Tao Qing came to observe them—that three feet of ice cannot be produced by a single day's frost. Baldy Li knew that when the time came for them to call out Lin Hong's name, they would call out "Director Li" instead, and therefore he had spent the entire morning teaching them how to lift their hands and cover their mouths. Baldy Li was most worried about these three idiots, and now that they were waiting at the factory gate, he had them practice covering their mouths three more times. When he lifted his hands to his mouth, the three idiots did the same. Baldy Li inspected each of them and then announced with satisfaction, "You have covered them so well that not even water could seep through."

By this point the crowd's roar was deafening, and Baldy Li turned toward them, lifted his arms, and then thrust them back down again. In a manner reminiscent of the famous conductor Herbert van Karajan, Baldy Li lifted his arms seven times and thrust them back seven more times, and finally the crowd's roar began to subside. Baldy Li lifted his index finger and spun around as he began to *shhhh* everyone. He repeatedly pivoted his body a full 180 degrees, almost making himself dizzy, until the crowd eventually grew silent. Baldy Li then cried out, "Everyone cooperate, *okay?*"

"Okay!" they shouted.

Baldy Li nodded with satisfaction, but the crowd started buzzing again. Baldy Li immediately lifted his finger and *shhhh*ed them again while pivoting his body back and forth.

The bell announcing the end of the workday had not rung yet, but the knitting factory's Director Liu was an infamous chain-smoker. The thirty something director smoked three packs a day, puffing nonstop from morning to night. Smoking a cigarette, he was accompanied by several people to the entranceway, where he learned that Baldy Li was laying siege to his factory and furthermore had brought virtually the town's entire population with him. As he strode toward the gate he jumped back in surprise when he saw the enormous crowd massed oppressively outside like a dark cloud and thought to himself that this Baldy Li really was an utter and complete bastard. Director Liu and Baldy Li often attended meetings together and therefore knew each other quite well. Director Liu greeted Baldy Li from far away and said warmly, "Director Li, Director Li . . ."

As he arrived at Baldy Li's side Director Liu forgot that his cigarette was about to burn down to his finger and complained softly, "Director Li, what are you doing here? Just look at how you have completely blocked the entranceway. What will the workers do when they get off work?"

Baldy Li laughed and said, "Director Liu, I just need you to let Lin Hong come out for a second. We will have a couple of things to tell her, after which I will immediately withdraw my troops and return home."

Director Liu recognized that this was the only solution. Furiously throwing away the cigarette that had already started to burn his fingers, he nodded. He pulled out another cigarette and lit it, and after taking a deep drag, he turned around and asked one of his companions to go and fetch Lin Hong.

Ten minutes later, Lin Hong appeared, her hands clasped together, head bowed, and her gait as stiff as that of Baldy Li's cripples. Lin Hong's appearance made the crowd roar with anticipation. Baldy Li turned around anxiously to face them and once again lifted and lowered his arms like von Karajan. The crowd's roars gradually leveled off, and Baldy Li turned and saw that Lin Hong had arrived. He quickly waved to his fourteen loyal minions and, with his left hand covering his mouth, he pointed majestically at the sky with his right. The three idiots in the rear responded the fastest and immediately covered their mouths with their hands, after which the two deaf-mutes started clapping. Then the eight crippled, blind, and deaf men in the vanguard started shouting out in unison, "Lin Hong! Lin Hong! Lin Hong!"

The crowd also began to chant, "Lin Hong! Lin Hong! Lin Hong!"

The crippled, blind, and deaf men then shouted, "Please come and be the Good Works Factory's First Lady. Please come and be the Good Works Factory's First Lady. . . ."

The crowd buzzed with confusion. But after the eight crippled, blind, and deaf men had recited the message four times, the crowd finally understood what they were saying and began to roar like the sea, stripping the message down to its essence and making it into a chant: "First Lady! First Lady! First Lady!"

Tears welled up in Baldy Li's eyes and he exclaimed, "The roar of the masses is so powerful."

Lin Hong, approaching with her head bowed, stopped in her tracks, petrified with fear, and looked up at the crowd. Then she turned around and started walking back inside. As soon as Lin Hong turned to leave, one of the three idiots, who up to that point had been obediently covering his mouth, unexpectedly caught a glimpse of her beauty as she lifted her head. He immediately lost control of himself, pushed the idiot standing in front of him aside, and ran in pursuit of Lin Hong with both arms extended. Drooling madly, he kept repeating, "Missy, hug me, please hug me. . . ."

The crowd murmured in surprise, then exploded into a boom of laughter like an airplane taking off. Baldy Li had not expected that he would have to deal with a love-crazed idiot. Cursing to himself, he rushed forward and grabbed the idiot, roaring under his breath, "Get the fuck back here, you crazy idiot."

The love-crazed idiot struggled to free himself from Baldy Li's grasp and continued to pursue Lin Hong, still shouting, "Missy, a hug . . ."

Baldy Li rushed forward and grabbed him again, then quietly reasoned with him: "Lin Hong can't hug you because she wants to hug me. If she hugs me, she will be a first lady, but if she hugs you, she will be an idiot lady."

With Baldy Li grabbing him, the love-crazed idiot found himself unable to continue pursuing Lin Hong. He became very angry and proceeded to punch Baldy Li in his left eye so hard that he cried out in pain. Baldy Li seized the idiot's clothing from behind and gestured to his thirteen other minions, commanding, "Quick, take him away."

The idiot couldn't understand why he was now suddenly unable to pursue Lin Hong. He began to flail his arms madly like a drowning man. The thirteen loyal minions all rushed forward, the five deaf men in front, the remaining three idiots following confusedly behind, and the two cripples hobbling after them; even the four blind men realized that something had happened and were approaching slowly, tapping their canes. Baldy Li's five deaf and two crippled loyal minions helped wrestle the love-crazed idiot to the ground. The two noninfatuated idiot minions stood to the side laughing idiotically, and the four blind loyal minions stood in a row like four workers on a picket line, rhythmically tapping their canes on the ground. When the infatuated idiot found himself on the ground, he screamed like a pig at the slaughterhouse, "Missy, a hug . . ."

Baldy Li's attempt to court Lin Hong by the stratagem of laying siege at the outskirts of the city therefore had to conclude in a hurry. Covering his left eye with one hand, Baldy Li gestured for his thirteen loyal minions to drag the infatuated idiot back to the Good Works Factory. As before, the two cripples led the way, followed by the five deaf men and two idiots dragging their love-crazed counterpart, with the four blind men following closely behind. Even as he was being dragged away, the infatuated idiot continued to cry out "Missy" and "hug me." The five deaf men had to continuously wipe his spittle from their faces, as did the other two idiots. The two idiots, not entirely clear where the spittle was coming from, lifted their heads and looked curiously at the sky, unable to understand why their faces were so wet.

The people of Liu all discussed these events avidly and agreed that the most interesting part of this afternoon's proceedings was not Baldy Li and Lin Hong but, rather, Baldy Li and that infatuated idiot, especially when the idiot punched Baldy Li, leaving him with a black eye the size of an apple. Everyone laughed uproariously at this and chattered nonstop about how they hadn't expected the idiots under Baldy Li's command to turn around and strike their own team, leaving Baldy Li with only one usable eye. As the old saying goes, *For a friend one will take two daggers in the chest, but for a woman one will stab a friend twice*—an irrefutable logic that applied perfectly to the situation. The crowd started speculating about how Baldy Li might have to wear an eye patch over his black eye and said, "Baldy Li is going to be a European pirate."

Two days after laying siege at the outskirts of the city, Baldy Li, his left eye still very swollen, went to Lin Hong's house to execute the stratagem of penetrating behind enemy lines. This time he asked his brother to accompany him, arguing that he might need to call on Song Gang's advice at any moment. If he once again ran into unexpected difficulties, Song Gang should immediately come up with other clever stratagems to help him out. Baldy Li held up three fingers and asked that Song Gang contribute at least three stratagems for him to pick from. Then the two of them—one tall and the other short, one resembling a civil official and the other a military official—set off down the streets of Liu.

Baldy Li couldn't stop chuckling the entire way. He felt that Song Gang's suggestion that he penetrate behind enemy lines and conquer Lin Hong's parents was a stroke of genius. All along the way Baldy Li kept giving Song Gang the thumbs-up sign, saying, "Your suggestion that in order to capture the thieves one must first capture their chief is truly wicked."

With a literary journal under his arm, Song Gang walked anxiously at Baldy Li's side. Baldy Li's look of confidence and determination actually exacerbated Song Gong's doubts about their latest plan. Of the five stratagems he had suggested for Baldy Li, the first three had failed miserably, and he feared that this fourth one would not fare much better. When they arrived at the door to Lin Hong's home, Song Gang paused apprehensively and told Baldy Li that he would wait for him outside. Baldy Li protested, saying that since he had come all this way, how could he not go in? He tried to drag Song Gang in with him, but Song Gang resisted and said that he was simply too embarrassed.

"What's there to be embarrassed about?" Baldy Li yelled on Lin Hong's doorstep. "It's not you who is courting her; all you need to do is stand by and observe."

Song Gang blushed and said quietly, "Don't shout. It would make me embarrassed just to stand by and watch you court her."

"You good-for-nothing." Baldy Li shook his head impatiently. "All you are good for is living vicariously as my advisor."

Then Baldy Li proudly walked into Lin Hong's courtyard. Though several families shared this courtyard, no one was around. Crying out happily, "Uncle, Auntie, how are you?" Baldy Li picked at random one of the three doors that had been left open and found a young couple sitting at a table and staring at him in astonishment. He quickly waved and said with a laugh, "Wrong door!"

He then went into another open door and found that this was indeed the correct one. Lin Hong's parents were both inside, but they didn't know Baldy Li, so when they caught sight of a short and swarthy young man calling them Uncle and Auntie, they simply stared at each other in astonishment, at a loss as to who this could possibly be. Baldy Li stood in the middle of the room looking around and asked with a laugh, "Has Lin Hong gone out?"

Lin Hong's parents nodded, and her mother said, "She went shopping."

Baldy Li nodded back, and with both hands stuffed in his pockets, he walked toward Lin Hong's kitchen and looked around. Lin Hong's parents wondered who this could be as they followed Baldy Li into the kitchen. He walked up to the coal stove, leaned over, opened the cardboard box in which the coal was stored, and saw that it was full. Baldy Li then stood up and asked Lin Hong's father, "Uncle, did you buy this coal yesterday?"

Lin Hong's father, still in a bit of a daze, nodded, but then shook his head and said, "No, I bought it the day before yesterday."

Baldy Li nodded, then walked over to the rice jar, lifted the wooden lid, and saw that it was full of rice. He then turned around and asked, "Uncle, did you buy this rice yesterday?"

This time Lin Hong's father initially shook his head, but then nodded. "I bought the rice yesterday."

Baldy Li then pulled his hand out of his pocket, rubbed his bald head, and informed Lin Hong's parents, "In the future, I'll take responsibility for buying all your coal and rice for you. You two needn't trouble yourselves with these tasks."

Lin Hong's mother couldn't stand the suspense any longer. She asked Baldy Li, "Who *are* you?"

"You don't know me?" Baldy Li asked in surprise. "I am the director of the Good Works Factory. My name is Li Guang, and my nickname is Baldy Li."

Baldy Li had barely finished speaking before Lin Hong's parents faces darkened. Realizing that this was the Peeping Tom who, years earlier, had spied on their daughter's bottom in the public toilet, and who more recently had repeatedly reduced her to tears, they were aghast that Liu Town's most infamous hooligan would dare come to their door. They roared with anger, "Out, out! Get out!"

Lin Hong's father grabbed a broom from behind the door, his wife took the feather duster from the table, and together they began to strike Baldy Li's bald head. Shielding his head with his hand, Baldy Li sprinted out the door. When he emerged, all the other families were standing in the courtyard watching. Lin Hong's parents were shaking with fury while Baldy Li looked baffled, raising his hands as if in surrender and repeatedly explaining, "It was a misunderstanding, a complete misunderstanding. I taught those children to say *to court,* but there was a class enemy who messed things up. . . ."

Lin Hong's parents cried, "Get out, get out!"

"It was really a misunderstanding," Baldy Li continued. "That infatuated idiot shot out from the middle of the road; there was nothing I could do. . . ."

As Baldy Li was saying this he turned to Lin Hong's neighbors and explained to some of the onlookers, "It is said that *it is difficult for a hero to resist the wiles of a beautiful woman.* Turns out it's true for idiots, too."

Lin Hong's parents were still shouting, "Get out!"

Lin Hong's father struck Baldy Li on the shoulder with the broomstick, and his wife repeatedly batted her feather duster at his nose. Baldy Li was dismayed. Ducking their blows, he pleaded with Lin Hong's mother, "Please don't be like this. After all, we're all going to be family. You will be my father-in-law and mother-in-law, and I will be your son-in-law. If you are like this now, how will we be able to get along when we become family?"

"Bullshit!" Lin Hong's father roared as he beat Baldy Li's shoulders with the broom.

"Stinky bullshit!" Lin Hong's mother cried as she pounded Baldy Li's head with the feather duster.

Baldy Li quickly fled to the street, sprinting a dozen yards in a single bound. When he looked back and saw Lin Hong's parents still standing in the doorway, he stopped and was about to offer more explanations. At that point Lin Hong's father turned to the crowd in the streets and gestured at Baldy Li with his broomstick, saying, "You're the proverbial ugly toad who thinks he can have the swan."

"I tell you"—Lin Hong's mother pointed at him with her feather duster as she shouted—"my flower of a daughter will never be planted in a pile of cow dung like yourself."

Baldy Li looked at the people who had come to enjoy the spectacle; looked at Lin Hong's parents, who were beside themselves with fury; and then looked at Song Gang, standing there uneasily. Baldy Li waved Song Gang over, and the two of them walked together down the streets of Liu. Baldy Li had always felt that he was an important personage, and even if he couldn't be considered one in a million, he was at the very least one in a hundred. He had never expected that Lin Hong's parents would regard him as an ugly toad or a pile of cow dung. He felt a great sense of loss and cursed incessantly: "Motherfucker!" he said to Song Gang. "Heroes too can suffer setbacks."

The ugly-toad-and-cow-dung humiliation that Baldy Li had suffered at the hands of Lin Hong's parents left him annoyed for an entire week. But after a week had passed, his determination to court Lin Hong revived, and he once again began to pursue her with great enthusiasm. He decided to employ Song Gang's final stratagem of beating his opponent to a pulp. Therefore, he began to pursue Lin Hong through the streets, always asking Song Gang to accompany him whenever he went out. Wherever Lin Hong was in public, Baldy Li would assume the role of both lover and bodyguard, escorting her around. When she shed tears of humiliation and bit her lips in anger, Baldy Li would chatter warmly with her. He would even play the role of a fiancé and introduce Song Gang to her, saying, "This is my brother, Song Gang, and when we get married, Song Gang will be my best man."

If Baldy Li, acting as both lover and bodyguard, so much as glimpsed another man taking a look at Lin Hong, he would shake his fist and say fiercely, "What are you looking at? If you look again, I'll punch your lights out."

CHAPTER 31

EACH TIME Lin Hong returned home after being trailed around town by Baldy Li, she would lie in bed, hug her pillow, and weep. Ten times she did this, but then she decided it was time to wipe her tears. She realized it did no good for her to hide out and cry— she must instead figure out a way to deal with that shameless Baldy Li. His *beating to a pulp* stratagem encouraged Lin Hong to hurry up and find a boyfriend. This was a common solution sought by many young women back then, and Lin Hong was no exception. She felt that as long as she had a boyfriend, she would be able to extricate herself from Baldy Li's attentions. She went through each of the Liu Town bachelors in her head and came up with several potential candidates. Then she put on makeup, wrapped a beige silk scarf around her neck, and went out.

Lin Hong, who previously very rarely went out, now became our Liu Town's street angel, on whom all the men would feast their eyes. Sometimes she would walk with her mother and sometimes with the other women workers at her factory. Almost every day at dusk she would stroll around in the evening light, and after sunset she would continue walking in the moonlight. She was aware that her reputation as a beauty had already spread far and wide, and she also knew that many of the men of Liu had crushes on her—but what she didn't know was where she would find the man she would love. In the past she had counted on her parents to make decisions for her, but her parents were too easily satisfied, immediately falling for any man who came knocking who was the slightest bit acceptable and saying that at least he was better than that Baldy Li. However, these young men all failed to make an impression on Lin Hong, much less find their way into her heart. As a result, she had no choice but to take the matter into her own hands and pick out a satisfactory husband for herself. She walked back and forth with a pretty smile on her pretty face. Every now and then she would encounter a handsome young man and gaze at him intently. Then she would walk away five paces, turn around, and shoot him another glance, at which point she would invariably see an infatuated face staring back at her.

Altogether there were twenty young men at whom Lin Hong looked more than once, nineteen of whom were infatuated with her. The only one who didn't respond at all was Song Gang. The nineteen who were infatuated with her felt that she clearly meant something when she looked at them. That backward glance, as she was walking away— a glance as rich as a garden overflowing with sensory delights—made their hearts flutter and kept them up at night.

Of those nineteen, eight were married, and they would sigh in disappointment, complaining bitterly that they had made their momentous decision too early in life without having taken the opportunity to sow their wild oats. Of those eight, there were two whose wives were quite ugly, and these two were even more frustrated, waking in the middle of the night completely furious and unable to resist pinching their wives in anger. When their wives woke up from the pain, the husbands would start snoring deeply, pretending to be asleep. One of these men always pinched his wife's thighs, the other her bottom. Both wives were in such pain that they didn't know what to do. When they examined their bruises, they concluded that their husbands must be suffering from a sort of narco-sadism, never suspecting the truth. The women complained incessantly all day, and at night steadfastly refused to sleep in the same bed with their spouses, explaining that it gave them the creeps.

Of the twenty men Lin Hong looked at twice, nine already had girlfriends, and these nine would also sigh incessantly, regretting their own impatience to get a free taste of cow's milk and lamenting that drinking early was not nearly as important as drinking well. They started considering the idea of dumping their girlfriends and running off in pursuit of Lin Hong. Of those nine, eight were swayed by considerations of profits and losses and decided that, although it was true that their girlfriends were not as beautiful and captivating as Lin Hong, they had gone to considerable trouble to court them, seduce them, and bed them. No matter how good Lin Hong might be, she had merely glanced at them twice, unlike their girlfriends, who were safely in hand. These men were of the opinion that a bird in the hand was better than two in the bush. Therefore, even though they were entranced by Lin Hong, they didn't make any concrete advances. Of the nine, these eight were methodical pursuers of love—only the ninth was an opportunistic pursuer. He began by tentatively placing bets on both horses. One night he slept happily with his current girlfriend and felt emotions as deep as the sea; the following night he secretly bought two movie tickets, hiding one in his inner breast pocket and asking an acquaintance to give the other to Lin Hong on his behalf.

By that point, Lin Hong had become the town's resident Sherlock Holmes and had investigated the personal backgrounds of all twenty of the town's handsome young men. Therefore, she knew that this opportunist who sent her a movie ticket was already living with a girlfriend. Lin Hong didn't reveal any emotion when she accepted the ticket, but her heart skipped a beat as she thought that this was someone who was about to get married yet still dared to make a pass at her. People at that time were still very conservative, and as soon as a couple slept together they were perceived as having lost value. When a new house or new car becomes old, one can only go to a secondhand market to exchange them. Lin Hong knew that the girlfriend of this opportunist was a cashier at the Red Flag fabric store; therefore she went to the store and, while admiring the multicolored fabrics on display, spoke with the girlfriend. Lin Hong took out the movie ticket and handed it to her; then, noting the woman's confusion, explained that the ticket was given to her by the woman's boyfriend. After Lin Hong told this confused and anxious young woman the full truth, she warned her, "Your boyfriend fancies himself Liu Town's resident Don Juan."

This opportunistic lover, it turns out, was none other than Poet Zhao, who was initially quite well respected but later became hopeless and despondent. That evening, unaware of what Lin Hong had done, he went expectantly to the theater. Some even say that he was whistling. Poet Zhao wandered around outside for half an hour, and only when the film had started did he sneak in like a thief. Zhao was going from a bright area to a dark area, so he had to find his seat by feel. He couldn't clearly see the face of the person sitting next to him but thought that it was Lin Hong. He confidently whispered her name a few times, then added that he had known all along that she would come.

Poet Zhao then leaned over and poured out his heart to his companion, still assuming she was Lin Hong. He had not yet finished speaking when he abruptly heard an ear-piercing screech and was rewarded with a few hard slaps to the face. Finding himself suddenly under attack, he had no idea what was happening, and even less how to protect himself. Dumbfounded, he craned his neck and turned toward his attacker, thereby exposing his entire face to the oncoming slaps. As his girlfriend shrieked in fury she didn't sound like herself, so Poet Zhao didn't recognize her voice and continued to believe that it was Lin Hong who was slapping him. He therefore became very indignant, wondering, *Who in the world flirts like this?* He quietly urged, "Lin Hong, Lin Hong, be careful of your image. . . ."

At this point Poet Zhao's girlfriend screamed, "I'll fucking kill you, philanderer!"

Poet Zhao was finally able to make out his girlfriend's face and fearfully hugged his head as he allowed her to beat the stuffing out of him. The movie that was showing was *The Shaolin Temple*. Later audience members would say that they enjoyed double screenings of *The Shaolin Temple* that night—one starring Jet Li and the other with Poet Zhao. Furthermore, everyone agreed that Poet Zhao's version was more impressive, that his girlfriend was even better than the Wulin master, and that the martial arts she used in cursing and beating Poet Zhao were even more deadly than Jet Li's. From that day on Poet Zhao became notorious, his reputation for wickedness exceeding even Baldy Li's after he was caught peeping at Lin Hong's bottom. Zhao's girlfriend immediately kicked him out and married someone else, and went on to bear her new husband a cherubic son. Though he was deeply regretful, from that point on Zhao never managed to have another girlfriend, let alone a wife. After learning this painful lesson, Poet Zhao waxed lyrical to Writer Liu with a sigh, "They speak of going for wool only to end up shorn. 'Tis I, 'tis I."

Writer Liu laughed appreciatively but thought to himself that since he also had designs on Lin Hong, it was really but for the grace of God that he had avoided losing his current wife and ending up like Poet Zhao. Writer Liu patted Poet Zhao's shoulder, then—though it was unclear whether he was congratulating himself or consoling Poet Zhao—he concluded, "It is a wise man who knows his own limitations."

Of the nineteen infatuated men, only two were bona fide bachelors, and these two initiated courtship procedures, both declaring that they had neither a marital history nor even a girlfriend history. One even showed Lin Hong's parents his medical records, which stated that he had no history of mental illness or any other chronic illness. The other, when he learned of this, immediately presented his parents' medical histories. Spreading them out as if he were unfurling a pair of scroll paintings, he showed Lin Hong's parents that his own parents had no history of mental illness or chronic illness either. As for himself, he patted his chest and said that he had no medical history at all. He claimed that he had never been sick in his life and in fact didn't even know what it meant to be sick. He said he was so healthy that he had never even sneezed, and that as a child he found it very curious when someone sneezed, thinking that their nose was farting. As soon as he said this, his own nose started to itch and his mouth opened of its own accord. Realizing that he was about to sneeze, he made dramatic gestures as he swallowed the sneeze, looking as if he were gulping down poison. He feigned a yawn and said with embarrassment, "I didn't sleep well last night."

These two bona fide bachelors both paid several visits to Lin Hong's house. Though they saw with their own eyes her tepid response, the polite smiles from Lin Hong's parents inflated their hopes. Already imagining themselves as prospective sons-in-law, these two bachelors started calling Lin Hong's parents Mom and Dad. Covered in goose bumps from embarrassment, the parents demurred, "Don't call us that, don't call us that."

One of the bachelors was comparatively tactful and switched back to calling them Uncle and Auntie. The other, however, was even more obtuse than Baldy Li and continued calling them Mom and Dad, explaining that since he would be calling them that sooner or later, he might as well start now. Lin Hong's parents snapped back, "And who is your dad? Who is your mom?"

Lin Hong despised these two handsome misers, who kept coming to her house empty-handed just before dinner and dawdling in order to get a free meal. It's true that once one of them did give Lin Hong some melon seeds to snack on. He kept reaching into his pocket while they were chatting but waited until her parents retreated to the kitchen to hand her the seeds, looking as if he were giving her some South African diamonds. Lin Hong saw that the seeds were already soaked with the sweat from his palm and mixed with lint from his pocket. Revolted, she turned away, pretending she hadn't seen them, and thought to herself that this oaf was even worse than Baldy Li, if that were possible.

Initially Lin Hong's parents, upon seeing a suitor lingering about when they were ready to eat, would courteously invite him to stay for dinner. After each of these bachelors had had dinner once at Lin Hong's home, he immediately bragged to everyone that he and Lin Hong were officially an item. They would even spice things up a bit, one boasting that Lin Hong's mother had served him personally, the other claiming that Lin Hong had fed him with her own spoon. The bachelors even asked their friends to help spread the stories of their romantic adventures with Lin Hong. Their friends, however, suspected that none of this was true; and while it would have been easy to simply repeat the stories, they would lose face if Lin Hong disavowed them. The two bachelors, however, saw things differently, and upon hearing each other making up preposterous stories, they felt the need to make even more outlandish claims so as not to fall behind. Even if they fell short in the end, they nevertheless felt that to have courted Lin Hong in the first place was definitely something to be proud of and would certainly raise their personal worth—which would come in handy in courting other girls.

These two sensationalizers finally encountered each other on the street. As one of them was proudly recounting stories of his romantic adventures with Lin Hong, the other, walking by, couldn't stand it anymore and shouted, "Bullshit!"

The two then stood there in the middle of the street and proceeded to curse each other, spittle flying everywhere. Everyone watched as they simultaneously rolled up their left sleeves, then their right. The onlookers retreated to give them room, fearing that a fierce battle was about to erupt. The two suitors then squatted down and rolled up their pants legs, exciting the onlookers even more. Everyone was certain that they were about to put up a ferocious fight, a fight for the ages. After the two had rolled their pants legs up above their knees, they noticed that they now had nothing left to roll up, but they still didn't come to blows; rather, they continued cursing each other as before, the only difference being that now they wiped the spittle from their mouths with more intensity.

As everyone was waiting with anticipation Baldy Li appeared on the scene. Having just given Tao Qing his work report over at the Civil Affairs Bureau, he was on his way to the Good Works Factory when he saw a huge crowd of people. He pulled one of the onlookers aside and asked what was going on. With a certain degree of exaggeration the person exclaimed, "World War Three is upon us!"

Baldy Li's eyes glittered, and he shoved his way through the crowd. When the people of Liu Town caught sight of him, they became even more excited, saying that now there was sure to be a great show, that what had already been a competition between two heroes had now become, with the arrival of Baldy Li, a *Romance of Three Kingdoms*. Hearing the two men—fingers pointed at each other's chests and spittle flying everywhere—each claiming Lin Hong as his own, Baldy Li immediately erupted in a fury and launched himself between them. Grabbing each by the collar, he roared, "Lin Hong is *my* girlfriend!"

The two suitors hadn't expected Baldy Li to appear and immediately stopped in shock. Baldy Li roared again as he released the one on his right and swung his fist at the one on his left, giving him a black eye. Then he proceeded to give the one on his right a black eye as well. That morning Baldy Li ended up beating both men so badly that they were left moaning in anguish. The onlookers were now so giddy that they repeatedly stomped their feet, sensing that this was even better than returning to the Three Kingdoms period and watching Cao Cao beat up Liu Bei and Sun Quan. Several onlookers became so frenzied that they imagined themselves to be the famous *Three Kingdoms* strategist Zhuge Liang and urged the two suitors to join forces and attack Baldy Li together. One onlooker pointed at one of the suitors and shouted battlefield strategies at him as though he were Liu Bei: "Join forces with the Kingdom of Wu to defeat the Kingdom of Wei! Join with Wu to defeat Wei!"

After Baldy Li beat the two so badly that their heads started spinning, the crowd's calls became increasingly muffled, though Baldy Li's shouts could still be clearly made out. He continued to pound them mercilessly while at the same time submitting them to a policelike interrogation: "Tell me, quick, whose girlfriend is Lin Hong?"

Both responded with their last breath, saying, "Yours, yours."

The onlookers shook their heads in disappointment, saying, "They are both hopeless."

Baldy Li shoved the two aside and glared at the onlookers. Those who had just been pretending to be Zhuge Liang were so terrified that they tucked their heads in and retreated, not daring to say another word. Baldy Li waved at the onlookers, warning them, "If anyone dares to claim that Lin Hong is his girlfriend, I will beat him so badly he won't even be reincarnated."

Baldy Li then turned and left. Many in the crowd heard him smugly saying to himself, "Chairman Mao put it well when he said that power comes from the muzzle of a gun."

Baldy Li beat the two romantic sensationalizers so badly that they would never forget it, and never again did they dare pursue Lin Hong.

Having completely lost face, whenever they encountered her in the street, they would lower their heads and scurry by in embarrassment. Lin Hong couldn't help but laugh, thinking that that hooligan Baldy Li had finally done something right.

When she cast her eye over all of Liu Town, she saw that, though the town's bachelors might be as common as weeds, there was not a single towering oak among them. She was increasingly desolate, feeling completely on her own with no hope for the future. Despite everything, one person began to stand out more clearly in her mind—a pale, handsome man wearing glasses, who was beginning to occupy her thoughts. Although this person was not a towering oak, from Lin Hong's perspective he was at least a tender sapling and, at any rate, was better than all those weeds. As long as he was a tree, there was the possibility that he could one day scrape the sky, while the weeds would never do more than spread along the ground. This person was Song Gang.

CHAPTER 32

AT THE TIME, Song Gang was a model youth. He was always carrying a book or magazine under his arm, he was polite and refined, and if he noticed a young woman looking at him, he would invariably blush. During the period when Baldy Li was pursuing Lin Hong, Song Gang was always at his side, and because he was Baldy Li's constant companion, Lin Hong glimpsed him far more often than she did any of the other young men of Liu. Baldy Li pursued Lin Hong so single-mindedly that there was no other thought in his head, and consequently he remained oblivious to the fact that Lin Hong had taken a liking to the quiet Song Gang.

Baldy Li stood stupidly in the middle of the street serving as Lin Hong's personal bodyguard, adamantly refusing to let other men so much as glance at her. Song Gang always lowered his head and quietly walked beside him. Lin Hong grew accustomed to Baldy Li's pestering and learned to ignore it and walk without exhibiting any expression. Sometimes when she was turning a corner she would sneak a peek at Song Gang, and on several occasions she managed to catch his eye, though each time he would immediately avert his gaze. Lin Hong couldn't help but smile at this. When Baldy Li said infuriating things, she couldn't resist peeking at Song Gang and would always see his melancholic expression. From this she understood that Song Gang felt sorry for her, and that gave her a feeling of contentment. Baldy Li came to pester her pretty much every day, so Lin Hong would see Song Gang virtually every day. Every time she glimpsed Song Gang's confused or melancholic expression, her heart would pound like water burbling from a fountain. She wasn't even annoyed by Baldy Li anymore, since he made it possible for her to see Song Gang every day. When Lin Hong went to sleep at night, the unforgettable image of Song Gang with his head bowed would silently enter her dreams.

Lin Hong hoped that one day Song Gang would suddenly appear in her doorway and walk in like those other suitors. She felt that he was not like the others. She imagined how he would stand, embarrassed, outside the door, and after coming in would stammer incoherently. She decided that she liked precisely this kind of man, and when she imagined Song Gang's embarrassed expression, she could feel herself blush.

One evening Sang Gang really did arrive and stand uncertainly in Lin Hong's doorway. With a quivering voice he asked Lin Hong's mother, "Auntie, is Lin Hong home?"

Lin Hong was in her room, and her mother came to tell her that the young fellow who was always hanging out with Baldy Li had come to see her. Suddenly flustered, Lin Hong was about to go out when she changed her mind. Instead she softly said to her mother, "Ask him to come in."

Lin Hong's mother chuckled to herself. She went back out and, in a friendly voice, told Song Gang that Lin Hong was in her room and wished for him to go in. Song Gang walked hesitantly into Lin Hong's room. He hadn't come on his own behalf: rather, Baldy Li had forced him to. Having followed the *beating to a pulp* stratagem for five months now without any success, Baldy Li had concluded that it was useless and therefore he should perhaps revert to the stratagem of *penetrating behind enemy lines*. Remembering the ugly-toad-and-cowdung humiliation he had suffered at Lin Hong's home, however, Baldy Li felt that it was not advisable for him to return in person and instead entrusted his military advisor, Song Gang, to serve as his intermediary. Song Gang was not at all willing but, after Baldy Li threw a tantrum, had no choice but to tough it out and go.

When he entered Lin Hong's room, she was standing with her back to him, braiding her hair in front of the window. As she stood under the rays of the setting sun the shadow of her delicate figure flickered everywhere. The evening breeze blew in gently lifting her white dress and wafting a mysterious fragrance past Song Gang, leaving him weak-kneed. At that moment he felt that Lin Hong was like an immortal atop a cloud. Half of her long hair was spread over her right shoulder; the other half lay across her left shoulder in a three-strand braid, trembling slightly in her hand. At that moment, the evening clouds were bathed in the red light of the sunset, and Lin Hong's slender, pale neck appeared to glow under Song Gang's gaze, making him stare as stupidly as had the infatuated idiot who worked for Baldy Li.

Lin Hong heard Song Gang's rapid breathing behind her but calmly continued to braid her hair. When she finished her left braid, she lightly shook her head and lifted her hand, causing the long hair on her right side to fall over her shoulder and land softly on her chest. She began making a second braid, at which point her slender, pale neck shimmered into view, and Song Gang's breathing sounded like it had been smothered. Lin Hong laughed softly and, with her back still toward Song Gang, said, "Say something, why don't you?"

Song Gang jumped in surprise, and only then did he finally remember his mission. He stammered, "I have come on behalf of Baldy Li."

Song Gang was so nervous that he forgot what he was supposed to say, but when Lin Hong heard that he had come on behalf of Baldy Li, her heart sank. She bit her lip and, after a moment's hesitation, decided to spell things out for him: "If you have come on behalf of Baldy Li, then you should leave now. If you have come on your own behalf, you may have a seat."

Lin Hong blushed at her own boldness. She heard Song Gang bump into a chair and thought that he was about to sit down, but then heard him stumble out. He had heard the first half of what she said but didn't catch the second half, and by the time she turned around he had already left.

After Song Gang departed that evening, Lin Hong cried in frustration and swore that she wouldn't give this idiot any more chances. But as she lay in bed that night, her heart softened. She thought of all those shameless suitors who had pursued her and then remembered Song Gang's graceful bearing. She was confident that he was someone she could rely on, and furthermore he was more handsome than all the other suitors put together.

Lin Hong continued to hope against hope that Song Gang would come and court her of his own accord. But after several months passed and she had not heard anything more from him, she found herself liking him more and more. Virtually every night she would long for him, remembering the image of him with his head lowered, his sorrowful eyes, and his occasional smile.

As time passed she felt that she couldn't continue to wait for Song Gang to come court her and instead needed to be more assertive. But every time she saw him, he always had that hooligan at his side. Twice she happened to run into him alone on the street, but when she shot him a longing glance, he scurried away with his head down, like a criminal fleeing the police. Lin Hong was heartbroken. She gritted her teeth at the mere thought of him while at the same time continuing to love him passionately. The third time she encountered him alone, Lin Hong realized that this was not an opportunity to be wasted. Therefore, she came to a full halt on the bridge and, blushing furiously, called out his name.

When Song Gang, who was just about to scurry away again, heard Lin Hong's voice, he shuddered from head to toe. He turned and looked about him in every direction, as if there might be someone else named Song Gang with him on the bridge. There were a few other people out walking, and they were all watching Lin Hong curiously after hearing her call out Song Gang's name. Although she was still blushing beet red, she asked him in front of everyone, "Come over here."

When Song Gang walked over, looking like a child about to be punished, Lin Hong said loudly, "Tell that Li fellow not to harass me anymore."

Song Gang heard this and nodded and was about to walk off when Lin Hong whispered, "Don't go."

Thinking that he must have misheard her, Song Gang stared at Lin Hong, not knowing what to do. At that point they happened to be alone on the bridge, and an unprecedented tenderness suddenly appeared on Lin Hong's face as she softly asked Song Gang, "Do you like me?"

Song Gang went pale with shock, and Lin Hong blushingly added, "I like you."

Song Gang stared at her blankly. Lin Hong saw that some people were walking onto the bridge and whispered her final line: "Tomorrow night at eight o'clock, wait for me in the little grove behind the movie theater."

This time Song Gang understood perfectly what Lin Hong was saying, and it left him in a delirium for the entire day. He sat in a corner of the workshop asking himself whether everything that had transpired on the bridge was real. He mentally reviewed again and again all the details of the encounter, which caused him all at once to blush and turn pale, feel distressed and grin idiotically, all at the same time. Song Gang's workmates giggled as they discussed him, but he didn't even notice. Only when they called out his name did he stare at them as if waking from a dream. His confused expression made his workmates laugh even harder, and they asked him, "Song Gang, what are you day-dreaming about?"

Song Gang lifted his head and grunted in reply, then lowered it again and continued his reverie. One workmate teased him: "Song Gang, you should go take a piss!"

After his grunt, Song Gang did in fact stand up and walk out, intending to go to the bathroom. While his workmates laughed uproariously, he walked to the door of the workshop and paused, as if he had just remembered something. He then walked back to the same corner of the factory and sat back down again. His workmates laughed hysterically and asked him, "Why did you come back?"

Song Gang responded absentmindedly, "I don't have to pee."

By evening, the events on the bridge had become increasingly real in Song Gang's memory. His thoughts were focused on Lin Hong's blushing face and her trembling voice, as well as her nervously skittering eyes. Especially her whispered "I like you" made his heart skip a beat every time he remembered it.

At that point, Song Gang was sitting at home, having already had dinner. Baldy Li, sitting at the table with him, studied him suspiciously, since Song Gang was grinning idiotically as though he had swallowed the wrong medication. Baldy Li softly called out his name, "Song Gang, Song Gang . . ."

Song Gang didn't respond, and Baldy Li suddenly pounded the table, shouting, "Song Gang, what's wrong?"

Song Gang finally recovered his demeanor, and in a normal tone of voice asked Baldy Li, "What did you say?"

Baldy Li looked at Song Gang and said, "Why, when you laugh, do you sound like one of the idiots who work for me at the Good Works Factory?"

Song Gang was disconcerted by Baldy Li's confused look. He avoided Baldy Li's gaze, bowed his head, and hesitated for a moment. Then he lifted his head and stammered, "What would you do if it turned out Lin Hong likes someone else?"

"I'd slaughter them," Baldy Li replied without hesitation.

Song Gang paused and then continued, "Who would you slaughter, that man or Lin Hong?"

"Of course I'd slaughter the man." Baldy Li waved his hand and then wiped his mouth. "Lin Hong I would spare; I want to keep her around as my wife."

Song Gang was deeply shaken but continued, asking, "And if I happened to be the one whom Lin Hong liked, what would you do?"

Baldy Li laughed out loud and struck the table with both hands, saying firmly, "That's inconceivable."

Seeing Baldy Li's confident expression, Song Gang's heart sank. Facing this brother of his, with whom he shared everything, Song Gang felt that he could not hide the truth any longer. He drew a deep breath, as if he had fallen into a distant memory, and then related with great difficulty the entire encounter on the bridge. When he concluded, Baldy Li stared at him with eyes as wide as saucers as he gradually calmed down. When Song Gang finally finished his tortured confession, he sighed and began watching Baldy Li nervously. Song Gang was waiting for Baldy Li to roar with fury.

What Song Gang didn't expect, however, was that Baldy Li would look at him calmly, blink his eyes, and then narrow them to thin slits. Baldy Li looked at Song Gang suspiciously. "What exactly did Lin Hong tell you?"

Song Gang replied, "She said she likes me."

"Inconceivable." Baldy Li stood up and told Song Gang, "Lin Hong can't possibly like you."

Song Gang blushed and said, "Why is that not possible?"

Baldy Li sat on the table and peered imperiously down at Song Gang. "With so many men in Liu Town pursuing her, and each of them being far better than you, how could Lin Hong possibly have fallen for you? You are an orphan, with no mother or father."

Song Gang rebutted, "You are also an orphan."

"I might be an orphan"—Baldy Li nodded, then patted his chest— "but I am also a factory director."

Song Gang continued to argue, "But maybe Lin Hong doesn't care about all that."

"How could she not care?" Baldy Li shook his head and said to Song Gang, "Lin Hong is better than a celestial immortal, while you are just a poor lad. The two of you . . . it's simply inconceivable."

Song Gang recalled a beautiful legend, observing, "The seventh celestial maiden fell for the common mortal Dong Yong."

"That's just a legend; it isn't real." Baldy Li suddenly noticed something and gazed carefully at Song Gang, asking, "Do you like Lin Hong?"

Song Gang blushed again. Baldy Li bounded down from the table, stood in front of Song Gang, and said, "I'm telling you, you *can't* like Lin Hong."

Song Gang replied unhappily, "Why can't I like Lin Hong?"

"Fuck!" Baldy Li suddenly cried out, his eyes growing wide, then shouted at Song Gang, "Lin Hong is mine. How can you like her? You are my brother, and while others can compete with me for her, you can't."

Song Gang didn't know what to say and stared at Baldy Li in confusion. Suddenly Baldy Li said warmly, "Song Gang, we are brothers who have always depended on each other. You know that I like Lin Hong, so why do you want to like her as well? That would be incest!"

Song Gang lowered his head and didn't say anything else. Baldy Li felt that Song Gang was ashamed, so he patted Song Gang's shoulder reassuringly and said, "Song Gang, I trust you and know that you wouldn't do anything to betray me."

Baldy Li, still convinced that Lin Hong was secretly infatuated with him, looked at Song Gang and reasoned out loud, "Why didn't Lin Hong say that to someone else? Why did she have to say it to you, of all people? Perhaps she is using you as a way of communicating with me?"

That night Song Gang couldn't sleep and kept tossing and turning, distracted by Baldy Li's contented snores and soft giggles. Lin Hong's beautiful figure and expression would flicker in and out of view in the darkness, making Song Gang long for her even more. At one point he forgot Baldy Li and, as a result, was able to enjoy a modicum of happiness. Song Gang's imagination soared in the darkness, and he pictured himself and Lin Hong strolling hand in hand through the streets of Liu, then owning a home together and loving each other like a married couple. However, this imaginary contentment immediately evaporated. Song Gang remembered Song Fanping's death in front of the bus depot, his and Baldy Li's tears, and his grandfather dragging the coffin home in a pullcart. He remembered the entire family walking down the muddy country road sobbing, and how frightened he had been when the sparrows by the road had abruptly flown away. He remembered how he and Baldy Li had dragged Li Lan's body back to the village like two sworn brothers. Finally, Song Gang remembered Li Lan grasping his hand before her death, making him promise to look after Baldy Li. By this point, Song Gang's tears were pouring down his face and soaking his pillow. Heartbroken, he realized he would never be able to betray Baldy Li. Eventually the sun came out and Song Gang finally fell asleep.

Around noon he left the metal factory early and walked briskly to the main gate of the knitting factory. There he waited for Lin Hong to get off work and come out. He wanted to tell her that he wouldn't be able to meet her in the grove behind the theater, and he felt that that single phrase would communicate his resolve.

Song Gang waited under the same wutong tree where Baldy Li's five emissaries of love had stood and shouted "intercourse." When the bell rang announcing the end of the workday, he suddenly felt an unprecedented sense of anguish, as if he were on the verge of death. He needed to say the one thing that he least wanted to say in his life; but he knew if he managed to get it out, he would no longer have to struggle with himself over Baldy Li.

Lin Hong walked out of the factory as usual, accompanied by the usual crowd of workmates. She noticed Song Gang standing surreptitiously under the tree and called him an idiot under her breath. She had expected to see him that night at eight o'clock, not here at noon. When her workmates saw Song Gang, they started tittering, because they knew that he was Baldy Li's brother. They covered their mouths and whispered to each other that they couldn't imagine what bizarre stratagem Baldy Li had dreamed up this time. Because Lin Hong was with her workmates, she didn't give Song Gang a second look as she passed, instead just glancing at him out of the corner of her eye. It seemed to her that he didn't move at all, rooted to the spot like a small tree next to a larger one. Again she tenderly cursed him under her breath, "You idiot."

Song Gang really did look like an idiot standing there, and when Lin Hong walked by him, his mouth moved a bit but he didn't utter a sound. It was only after she and her workmates had walked away that he realized she hadn't even glanced at him. He suddenly felt that Baldy Li had been right in saying Lin Hong couldn't possibly like him. The cold expression with which she had passed him certainly proved that point. This realization immediately made him feel that he had been relieved of a heavy burden, and he headed home feeling as light as a sparrow. He smiled a crooked smile, as though he were waking up from a dream and recalling its various lovely moments. The fantasy was better than the reality, he felt, since the dream version was so much less anxiety-producing.

That night Song Gang was still relaxed and happy, humming a tune as he cooked Baldy Li's dinner, and he continued humming as they ate. Baldy Li watched Song Gang suspiciously and noticed that although it was almost eight o'clock, Song Gang didn't seem to have the slightest inclination to leave. Baldy Li, meanwhile, was himself thinking about that little grove behind the theater. He sat at the table, looking out the window at the moon, and tapping the table with his finger. Then, with a peculiar expression, he asked, "Why don't you go out?"

Song Gang knew what he was referring to and shook his head in embarrassment, saying, "You were right, Lin Hong can't possibly like me."

Baldy Li didn't understand why Song Gang was saying this, so Song Gang told him about his attempt to meet Lin Hong at the knitting factory, explaining that when she saw him she acted as if she didn't even recognize him. When Baldy Li heard this, he nodded knowingly and then pounded the table and shouted, "That's how it should be!"

Song Gang jumped in surprise, and Baldy Li stood up and said, "Everything Lin Hong said must have been directed to me."

Baldy Li confidently walked out the door and rushed toward the grove behind the theater. While running past the theater, he suddenly remembered that he was now a factory director and therefore couldn't rush around like a young hothead. He switched to a more leisurely pace, but by the time he reached the grove, he once again looked like someone arriving for a date.

Lin Hong was waiting there. She had intentionally arrived fifteen minutes late, thinking that Song Gang would be waiting for her. Not finding him there, she was about to get annoyed when she heard soft footsteps behind her, footsteps that sounded like someone arriving for a secret rendezvous. Lin Hong couldn't help but smile, surprised that the usually upright Song Gang should be capable of such stealth. But then she heard Baldy Li's coarse laughter.

She jumped in surprise, then turned and saw that it wasn't Song Gang at all, but instead Baldy Li was standing there laughing in the moonlight, boasting, "I knew that you were waiting here for me, and knew that what you said to Song Gang was actually meant for me."

Lin Hong stared at him in shock, at a loss as to how to respond. Baldy Li tenderly complained, "Lin Hong, I know that you like me. Why don't you just come out and say it?"

As Baldy Li said this he attempted to grasp her hand, causing Lin Hong to call out in alarm, "Get away, get away from me!"

Lin Hong screamed and ran out of the grove, with Baldy Li hot on her heels, repeatedly calling out her name. Then she suddenly stopped, turned around and, pointing at him, said, "Stop right there."

Baldy Li stopped and asked unhappily, "Lin Hong, what are you doing? What kind of flirting is this?"

"Who is flirting with you?" Lin Hong was so angry that her entire body started shaking. "You ugly toad."

As she was saying this she quickly walked away. Baldy Li, having been called an ugly toad, stood there staring resentfully at Lin Hong as she disappeared. He began to walk away himself but then remembered how her parents had also called him an ugly toad and a pile of cow dung, and he cursed, "Your dad is an ugly toad, and your mom is a pile of cow dung. Fuck!"

Baldy Li returned home looking like a defeated rooster in a cock-fight. Disconsolate, he sat down, then furiously pounded the table while wiping the sweat from his brow. Song Gang sat on the bed holding a book, watching Baldy Li nervously. Baldy Li's appearance suggested to Song Gang what had happened, so he carefully asked, "Did Lin Hong go to the grove?"

"Yes," Baldy Li said angrily. "She fucking called me an ugly toad."

Song Gang watched Baldy Li distractedly as memories of his own encounters with Lin Hong rushed back to him: every word she said to him on the bridge, as well as while braiding her hair in her bedroom— these scenes were as clear as if they were playing right in front of his eyes. And now, in a moment of clarity, Song Gang finally became convinced that he was indeed the one whom Lin Hong liked. At that point, Baldy Li began to study the distracted Song Gang intently and said, as if he had suddenly made an unexpected discovery, "Maybe Lin Hong really fucking does like you."

Song Gang shook his head sadly, and Baldy Li asked him suspiciously, "Do you like Lin Hong?"

Song Gang nodded, and Baldy Li pounded the table and cried out imperiously, "Song Gang, Lin Hong is mine, and you can't fucking like her. If you like her, we can no longer be brothers but instead will become enemies, and more specifically class enemies."

Song Gang listened to Baldy Li's cries with his head lowered, and after Baldy Li had gone through all the curse words he could think of, Song Gang finally lifted his head and laughed miserably. "Relax, I won't get together with Lin Hong. I don't want to lose my brother."

"Really?" Baldy Li began to laugh.

Song Gang nodded earnestly, whereupon tears began to roll down his cheeks. After wiping his tears, he pointed to the bed on which he was sitting and said, "Do you remember? Before she died, Mother made me carry her home, and then she lay in this bed. . . ."

"I remember." Baldy Li nodded.

"And do you remember how then you went out to buy some stuffed buns?"

Baldy Li nodded again, and Song Gang continued: "After you left, Mother took my hand and made me promise to look after you. I told her not to worry and said that I would give you my last piece of clothing and my last bowl of rice."

After he said this, tears ran down Song Gang's cheeks, and Baldy Li also began to cry, saying, "Did you really say that?"

Song Gang nodded, and Baldy Li wiped his tears and said, "Song Gang, you are really a good brother."

CHAPTER 33

BALDY LI continued to pursue his *beating to a pulp* courtship stratagem, but never again did he ask Song Gang to accompany him. Baldy Li said that he would feel very uneasy if Song Gang and Lin Hong were so much as to catch sight of each other. Therefore, he asked that Song Gang avoid Lin Hong at all costs, and if he were to run into her in the street, he should avoid her as if she were a leper. Baldy Li then began to model himself after Song Gang, reasoning that if Lin Hong liked Song Gang, it must be because Song Gang was so refined and never cursed and was always studiously carrying a book around with him. Baldy Li therefore completely transformed himself, and whenever he was near Lin Hong he too would make sure to have a book with him. He also stopped bullying the other men of Liu; instead he smiled effusively like a politician on the stump, and every time he encountered someone he knew, he would greet them with a warm handshake. When the people of Liu saw this new Baldy Li, they all said that it was as if the sun had suddenly risen in the west. They always saw Baldy Li leafing through his book and muttering to himself like a Confucian scholar whenever he was at Lin Hong's side. Everyone muffled their laughter with their hands and whispered that Lin Hong had rid herself of a love-crazy hooligan but had gained a love-crazy monk. When Baldy Li noticed that the onlookers were very curious about his incessant reading, he proclaimed loudly, "Reading is good, and going a day without reading is even more uncomfortable than going a month without taking a shit."

Baldy Li said this for Lin Hong's benefit, but as soon as the words were out of his mouth he immediately regretted them, feeling that his comparison was perhaps too crass. After he returned home, he asked Song Gang for advice and subsequently changed his line to "Reading is good. You can go a month without eating, but you can't go a day without reading."

The people of Liu disagreed, pointing out that if you don't read for a day, you can still survive, whereas if you go a month without eating, you will surely die. Baldy Li dismissed the naysayers as a bunch of cowards and said valiantly, "If you go a month without eating, you would in fact starve to death, but if you go a day without reading, it would result in a life worse than death."

Lin Hong continued walking expressionlessly. She heard this back-and-forth between Baldy Li and the onlookers and noticed the onlookers' laughter and Baldy Li's excitement, but she herself maintained a studious indifference to it all.

After Baldy Li adopted the identity of a Confucian scholar, he became very bookish and would frequently spout pearls of wisdom, only occasionally straying into obscenity. When Lin Hong heard Baldy Li's obscenities, she thought to herself, *You can't teach a dog not to eat shit.*

Lin Hong knew what kind of scum Baldy Li was and didn't feel at all as though the sun were now rising in the west. Instead, she was convinced that he was up to his old tricks, and at the end of the day he was merely the same ugly toad and pile of cow dung, just as, at the end of the day, the Monkey King in *Journey to the West* was still, despite his seventy-two incarnations, merely a monkey.

On the night of the rendezvous in the grove, Lin Hong had been furious when Baldy Li, rather than Song Gang, appeared. She then attempted to excise Song Gang from her heart. When she glimpsed him on the street a few days later, she laughed coldly and thought to herself that this guy was a perfect idiot who wouldn't get another chance. She lifted her head high and walked toward him, telling herself that she wouldn't give him a second glance. The last thing she expected, however, was for Song Gang to run away as soon as he saw her coming. The next several days, every time Song Gang caught sight of her, he would run away as though she were a leper—exactly as Baldy Li had instructed. This ritual gradually ate away at her pride and left her feeling completely bereft.

In this way, Song Gang unintentionally made his way back into Lin Hong's heart. She noticed her heart's peculiar transformation: The more Song Gang avoided her, the more she liked him. Every night, rain or clear, Lin Hong would find herself remembering his handsome figure as she was trying to fall asleep—his smile, his bowed head and pensive appearance, his soulful look every time he saw her. She found everything about Song Gang as sweet as could be. After a while, her memories of him became an intense yearning, as if he were her lover from whom she was separated by a vast distance.

Lin Hong was convinced that Song Gang was secretly in love with her and that he was avoiding her on Baldy Li's account. The mere thought of Baldy Li turned her pale with fury. His fearsome appearance made all the other young men of Liu too terrified to court her— though, truth be told, in her eyes they were all worthless wretches. Song Gang was different, and Lin Hong would often fantasize that he was courting her. Each time after her daydream she would shake her head and sigh, knowing that he would never come visit her on his own accord. Deciding that it was time for her to take the initiative again, she resolved to write him a note—seven lines and eighty-three characters long, together with thirteen punctuation marks, to be exact. Of those eighty-three characters, she devoted fifty-one to cursing Baldy Li and the remaining thirty-two to urging Song Gang to come meet her at eight o'clock that evening under the bridge. Lin Hong folded the note into the shape of a butterfly and hid it inside a brand-new handkerchief, then waited in the street for Song Gang to get off work. The last sentence in the note asked that Song Gang return the handkerchief to her when he came to meet her. She felt that, by adding this line, she was guaranteeing that he would not stand her up.

It was a drizzly autumn evening. As Lin Hong stood under a wutong tree drops of water fell from the leaves onto her umbrella, making a pattering sound as they landed. She looked out on to the misty street and saw several umbrellas go back and forth, as well as several youngsters without umbrellas. She then saw Song Gang rushing straight toward her from across the street. He wasn't wearing his coat but, rather, was holding it over his head to deflect the rain, and as he rushed forward the coat looked like a flag flapping in the wind. Lin Hong hurried down to the street and used her umbrella to gesture for him to stop. He hydroplaned past her like a car, almost slamming into her umbrella. When she moved the umbrella out of the way, she saw his startled expression, whereupon she stuffed her handkerchief into his hand and immediately turned and walked away. After she had walked ten yards, she turned to look back at Song Gang and saw him staring at her dumbfounded, holding the handkerchief in both hands. His coat fell to the ground, and several pairs of feet trampled over it. Lin Hong turned back around and, grasping her umbrella, walked away smiling, having no idea what would happen next.

Song Gang spent that drizzly evening in a daze. Eventually he managed to get home, and then, with a pounding heart, he opened up the handkerchief and found the note folded into the shape of a butter-fly. With trembling hands he began to unfold the note, but Lin Hong had folded it in a very complicated way, and he was afraid he would open it incorrectly. Therefore, it took him forever to unfold it. When he finally succeeded, he read, with bated breath, Lin Hong's eighty-three-character message over and over again. Several times the sound of his neighbors' footsteps startled him so badly that he hurriedly stuffed the note into his pocket, thinking that it was Baldy Li returning home. Only when he heard the neighbors unlocking their front doors did he breathe a sigh of relief and take the note back out and begin reading it again. Afterward, he lifted his head and distractedly watched the raindrops roll down the windowpane as the fire of love, which had virtually been extinguished from his heart, was ignited once again.

Song Gang was desperate to go see Lin Hong and several times even walked to the door, but each time the thought of Baldy Li stopped him in his tracks. He stared, bewildered, at the drizzle outside, then closed the door again. In the end, it was the final line of Lin Hong's note, where she asked that he return the handkerchief, that gave Song Gang the courage to go meet her.

Baldy Li would normally have returned home from work by that point, but on that particular day he happened to have been delayed at the factory, thus giving Song Gang his opportunity. After leaving the house he rushed to the bridge, knowing that if he were to run into Baldy Li, all it would take would be for Baldy Li to call out to him, and Song Gang would lose his courage. He walked down the stairs at the river's edge, and when he arrived under the bridge, it was six in the evening, two hours before his scheduled meeting with Lin Hong.

Song Gang stood there, his entire body trembling. He could hear countless footsteps on the bridge over his head, as if crowds of people were walking on the roof of his house. He watched the river gradu-ally grow dark as rain pelted the waves, making the river look as though it too was trembling. He felt very anxious waiting there, alter-nating between excitement and depression, determination and despair. After more than an hour, the sky turned completely dark, and Song Gang finally began to calm down. In his mind's eye he saw the sorrow-ful gaze Li Lan had given him before she passed away, and therefore he again rejected happiness and swore to himself that he wouldn't betray Baldy Li. He told himself that he had not come here for a date with Lin Hong but only to return her handkerchief. In the dark he lifted the handkerchief to look at it, as if he were bidding it farewell, and then resolutely placed it in his pocket. He exhaled and felt much more relaxed.

Lin Hong appeared at eight thirty, walking down the steps with an umbrella. She gazed for a while in the direction of the area under the bridge and eventually made out a tall shadow silently standing there. Having determined that this was indeed Song Gang and not the short and stocky Baldy Li, Lin Hong smiled with relief and approached.

When she reached Song Gang's side, she closed her umbrella and shook it a few times. Then she looked up at Song Gang, but in the dark she couldn't make out his expression. She heard his nervous breathing and sensed him lift his right hand. She then looked down, and her heart missed a beat when she noticed that he was holding her handkerchief. She didn't accept it, because she knew that as soon as she did, this date would be over. Therefore, she turned her head away and saw lights from the streetlamps overhead flickering on the river's surface. She heard Song Gang's increasingly hurried breathing and couldn't help laughing as she said, "Say something. I didn't come here to listen to you breathe."

Song Gang shook his right hand and with a shaky voice said, "This is your handkerchief."

Lin Hong replied angrily, "You came here just to give me this?"

Song Gang nodded. "Yes."

Lin Hong shook her head and laughed bitterly, then looked up at Song Gang in despair and asked, "Song Gang, do you not like me?"

Even in the dark, Song Gang still did not dare look directly at her, so he turned his face away and with a heartbroken voice said, "Baldy Li is my brother."

"Don't bring Baldy Li into this," Lin Hong interrupted him and promptly added, "Even if you and I don't get together, I would never end up with him."

After hearing this, Song Gang again lowered his head and didn't know what to say. When Lin Hong saw his pained expression, she bit her lip and said tenderly, "Song Gang, this is the last time, so please think about it carefully, because there won't be another opportunity."

Lin Hong became increasingly grief-stricken as she added, "Soon I will be someone else's girlfriend." After saying this, she stood there in the dark watching Song Gang expectantly, but all he did was softly repeat the same line, "Baldy Li is my brother."

Distraught, Lin Hong turned away and once again looked at the lights on the river. Song Gang lifted his right hand holding the handkerchief, but she remained silent, as did he. After a while, she asked sorrowfully, "Song Gang, can you swim?"

Song Gang, not knowing what else to say, nodded. "I can."

"I can't," Lin Hong said. She turned her face to look at Song Gang and added, "If I jump into the river, will I drown?"

Song Gang couldn't understand why she was asking this and stared at her, speechless. Lin Hong extended her hand in the darkness and stroked Song Gang's face, and he jumped as if he had received an electric shock. She pointed to the river water and, sounding as if she were taking an oath, asked Song Gang, "I'm asking you for the last time: Do you like me?"

Song Gang opened his mouth, but no sound came out. Lin Hong's finger was still pointing at the river water as she said, "If you say you don't like me, I'll jump in."

Song Gang was stunned, and Lin Hong added urgently, "Answer me!"

Song Gang said in a beseeching tone, "Baldy Li is my brother."

Lin Hong was devastated. She could not believe that Song Gang would stick to repeating that same phrase. She spat out, "I hate you!"

She then proceeded to jump into the river, shattering the lights reflected on the surface. Song Gang watched as her body fell, and the droplets of water struck his face like hailstones. He watched as her body disappeared and then struggled to break back through the water's surface. He immediately jumped into the bone-piercingly cold river after her. He felt that the weight of his body was forcing hers back down even while she was struggling to make her way up. Lin Hong grabbed on to his shirt; Song Gang kicked with his feet and, holding her tightly with both hands, pulled her to the surface. When she emerged, water spurted from her mouth, all over Song Gang's face. He hugged her body to him and, paddling with his feet, swam over to the bank with Lin Hong hugging his neck with both arms.

He lifted her onto the steps and then knelt down and softly called out her name. He saw her open her eyes, and it was only then that he realized he was holding her. In alarm, he released her and stood up. Her body lay sprawled on the steps, and she continued to cough and spit up water. Then she struggled to sit up, lowered her head, and hugged her knees. Completely soaked and shivering in the cold wind, she sat there waiting for Song Gang to come over and embrace her, as he had when they were in the water. However, the similarly soaked Song Gang merely stood there, aware only of his own shivering. Heartbroken, Lin Hong stood and slowly walked up the steps, her body swaying precariously. Song Gang didn't think to follow her and offer his support. Hugging herself and still shivering, Lin Hong continued up the stairs. She sensed that Song Gang was following her, but she didn't turn around and instead kept going until she reached the street. At that point, she could no longer hear his footsteps, yet she still didn't turn around. Her tears mixing with the rain on her face, she walked on.

After Song Gang climbed up to the street he just stood there, feeling as though his heart had been pierced by a knife. He watched Lin Hong walk down the wet street, head bowed and hugging her shoulders. The rain glittered under the streetlamps like snowflakes, and the street itself seemed asleep. Song Gang watched Lin Hong's figure as she gradually disappeared in the distance; then, after lifting his hand to wipe the tears and rain from his face, he set off in the opposite direction.

Baldy Li was in bed when he heard Song Gang walk in the door. He turned on the light and stuck his head out from under the covers, calling out, "Where did you run off to? I waited forever for you."

Baldy Li sat up with his covers wrapped around him and saw the soaking-wet Song Gang sitting on the bench. Not noticing Song Gang's grief-stricken expression, he continued, "You didn't make us dinner. I, Director Li, worked hard all day, only to come home and find nothing to eat, not even leftovers. I waited forever for you, but eventually had no choice but go out and buy some stuffed buns."

After his exclamation, Baldy Li asked Song Gang, "Have you eaten?"

Song Gang stared at Baldy Li in confusion, almost as if he didn't recognize him. Baldy Li roared, "Have you fucking eaten or not?"

Song Gang trembled from head to toe. Finally understanding what Baldy Li was asking him, he shook his head. "No, I haven't."

"I figured you hadn't." Baldy Li proudly pulled a bowl out from under the covers, with two steamed buns inside. Handing the bowl to Song Gang, he said, "Eat them quickly while they're still warm."

With a sigh, Song Gang reached out to accept the bowl and place it on the table, then continued gazing at Baldy Li. Baldy Li pointed at the bun and shouted, "Eat!"

Song Gang sighed again, shook his head, and said, "I don't want to."

"These are meat buns!" Baldy Li said.

Baldy Li then noticed that a large pool of water had accumulated on the floor underneath Song Gang's bench and was flowing in all directions, with several rivulets almost reaching the bed. The water kept dripping from Song Gang's soaked clothes, and only then did Baldy Li notice that Song Gang was not simply soaked from the rain but, rather, looked as if he had been pulled out of the river. He asked in surprise, "How is it that you are as wet as a dog?"

Then Baldy Li noticed that Song Gang was still grasping a handkerchief in his right hand, and the handkerchief was also dripping water. Baldy Li pointed to the handkerchief and asked, "What is that?"

Song Gang looked down at the handkerchief in his right hand and jumped in surprise. He remembered that he was holding the handkerchief when he jumped into the river to rescue Lin Hong, but he hadn't realized that he still had it in his hand. Baldy Li climbed out of bed and stared at Song Gang suspiciously, asking, "Whose handkerchief is this?"

Song Gang placed the handkerchief on the table, wiped the water from his face, and said gloomily, "I went to see Lin Hong."

"Fuck."

Baldy Li saw Song Gang sneeze three times in a row; therefore, he cut his curses short and instead told him to quickly go change his clothes and get under the covers. As he was saying this he himself started to sneeze and immediately returned to bed. Song Gang nodded, stood up from the bench, and took off his soaking-wet pants. When Song Gang climbed under the covers, he suddenly remembered something. He climbed back out of bed and retrieved Lin Hong's note from his pants pocket, though by now it was merely a crumpled wad of paper. Song Gang handed the soaked mass to Baldy Li, who accepted it with a suspicious look, asking, "What is this?"

Song Gang answered with a sneeze, "Lin Hong's letter."

When Baldy Li heard this, he half got out of bed and very carefully unrolled the ball of paper. The ink had bled, creating an indistinct landscape painting. Baldy Li immediately jumped out of bed, stood on the table, and placed the unfolded note under the bright lightbulb. Even after the bulb had dried it, Baldy Li still couldn't make out what it said and so he had no choice but to ask Song Gang, "What did Lin Hong write?"

Already in bed, with his eyes closed, Song Gang said, "Turn off the light."

Baldy Li quickly did, then lay down in his own bed. With the two brothers each in their respective beds, Song Gong, amid spasms of coughing and sneezing, narrated in fits and starts the events of that evening. Baldy Li listened silently, and after Song Gang was finished he whispered, "Song Gang."

Song Gang replied with a "Huh?" and Baldy Li carefully asked, "You didn't escort Lin Hong home?"

Song Gang wheezed, "No."

Baldy Li smiled silently in the darkness and again said softly, "Song Gang." Song Gang once again replied with a "Huh?" Then Baldy Li said earnestly, "You really are a good brother."

Song Gang didn't respond, and Baldy Li called out his name several times until Song Gang finally replied, "I want to go to sleep."

Song Gang spent the entire rainy night coughing and sleeping fitfully. While sleeping, he felt befuddled, as if he were still under water. While awake, he felt that he couldn't breathe, as if there were a heavy stone resting on his chest. When the morning light finally streamed in his window, he opened his eyes and realized that he had actually fallen asleep. Song Gang saw that it was a clear morning after a night full of rain. The eaves were still dripping, and rivulets were running down the outside of the window, but the room was bathed in bright sunlight. Outside, sparrows were singing and the neighbors chatted loudly with each other. Song Gang sighed, having made it through the difficult night. This beautiful morning made him happy and at ease. He sat up in bed and saw that Baldy Li was still sleeping soundly, so he called out, as was their custom, "Baldy Li, Baldy Li! Time to get up!"

Baldy Li's head poked out from under the covers, and Song Gang laughed. Baldy Li rubbed his eyes, not sure what Song Gang found so funny. Song Gang explained that Baldy Li looked like a turtle sticking its head out. He then acted out the motions, covering himself with blankets and then, with a muffled voice, asking Baldy Li if he looked like a turtle. Then he suddenly poked his head out and held it there. Baldy Li rubbed his eyes and laughed, saying, "You do! You really do look like a turtle."

Later Baldy Li remembered the events of the previous night and looked at Song Gang with surprise. Song Gang, acting as if nothing had happened, jumped out of bed and got a clean set of clothes from the closet. He then put some toothpaste on his toothbrush, picked up his cup and basin, threw his hand towel over his shoulder, and walked to the well to wash his face and brush his teeth. Baldy Li heard Song Gang chatting with several neighbors over by the well, occasionally emitting bursts of laughter. Baldy Li scratched his head suspiciously and cursed, "Fuck."

Song Gang had a peaceful day, occasionally remembering the previous night's incidents under the bridge and in the river, as well as the image of the soaked Lin Hong walking up the road. These memories left him momentarily shaken, but he immediately recovered his equilibrium and did not dwell on them. After his difficult night, Song Gang had finally achieved some peace. The life-or-death experience with Lin Hong the previous night was like the conclusion of a story, and this story, which had taken his breath away, was now over, and a new story could begin. As the sun follows rain, Song Gang's mood brightened.

After work that afternoon, Baldy Li brought home some big red apples. Song Gang had already prepared dinner, and Baldy Li, with a grin, placed the apples on the bench, then laughed mischievously throughout dinner. Baldy Li's laugh disquieted Song Gang, because he didn't know what Baldy Li was plotting. After dinner, Baldy Li suddenly announced that he had gone to the knitting factory to investigate and discovered that Lin Hong had not shown up at work because she was sick with a fever, having spent the entire day in bed. Baldy Li tapped the table with his finger and said, "You should go to her house immediately."

Astonished, Song Gang looked suspiciously at Baldy Li and then at the apples, thinking that Baldy Li wanted him to take the apples to Lin Hong. Song Gang shook his head and said, "I can't go, and even less can I take these apples."

"Who said anything about you taking the apples? The apples are for me to take." Baldy Li pounded the table and stood up. He handed Song Gang the handkerchief, which was now dry, and said, "This is what you should take with you, to return it to her."

Song Gang continued to watch Baldy Li suspiciously, still not knowing what he had up his sleeve. Baldy Li enthusiastically explained his plan. First Song Gang would take the handkerchief into Lin Hong's room while Baldy Li waited outside with his apples. When Song Gang walked up to Lin Hong's bed, he would stand there without saying a word, and when she awoke and saw him, he would say coldly, "This time you should give up all hope." He would throw the handkerchief

onto Lin Hong's bed and immediately turn and leave. After Song Gang
emerged, it would be Baldy Li's turn to go in with the apples to console
her. After Baldy Li finished explaining his plan, he wiped his spittle and
said proudly, "This way Lin Hong's feelings for you will finally be extinguished and she will begin feeling true affection for me instead."

Song Gang bowed his head. Baldy Li was completely intoxicated by
his master plan and excitedly asked Song Gang, "Is this not a truly diabolical plot?"

Seeing Song Gang sitting silently and with a bowed head, Baldy Li
waved and said, "Okay, you should go."

Song Gang shook his head sadly, unwilling to go. He said, "I can't say
what you're asking me to say."

Baldy Li was unhappy. Counting on his fingers, he said, "Just think
of the five stratagems you suggested for me: *beating around the bush,
coming straight to the point, laying siege at the outskirts of the city,
penetrating behind enemy lines,* and *beating to a pulp.* Of those, not a
single one was helpful. You have been completely useless as my military advisor. Therefore, it is now up to me to come up with a new diabolical plot."

Having said this, Baldy Li lifted his thumb and pointed out the door.
"Go, quick."

Song Gang still shook his head. Biting his lip, he said, "I really can't
say what you want me to say."

"Fuck!" Baldy Li exclaimed. "Song Gang, we are brothers. Can't you
help me this once? I swear that this will be the last time. I'll never again
ask for your help."

As he was saying this Baldy Li pulled Song Gang from his seat and
pushed him out the door. He stuffed the handkerchief into Song
Gang's hand and himself picked up the apples. Then the brothers
headed to Lin Hong's house. At this point it was dusk, and the street
was bathed in a damp mist. Baldy Li walked happily in front with the
apples in his hand, and Song Gang followed with the handkerchief and
a heavy heart. The entire way, Baldy Li tirelessly gave Song Gang
words of encouragement, offering him one blank check after another.
He promised that after he and Lin Hong became a couple, the first
thing he would do would be to help Song Gang find a girlfriend even
prettier than Lin Hong. If such a woman couldn't be found in Liu, he
would search the surrounding towns, and if she couldn't be found
there, he would go to the city to look for her. If she couldn't be found in

the city, he would search the entire province, and if she couldn't be found in the province, he would search the entire country. If she couldn't be found in China, he would search the entire world for her. Baldy Li laughed. "Perhaps I might end up finding you a blond, blue-eyed girlfriend. That way you could live in a Western house, eat Western food, sleep in a Western bed, hug a Western girl's waist, kiss a Western girl's lips, and give birth to a pair of mixed-race twins."

As Baldy Li was animatedly describing Song Gang's Western future, Song Gang walked with a bowed head along the thoroughly rustic street. He didn't hear a word of what Baldy Li was saying but simply followed mechanically behind him. When Baldy Li paused to chat with other passersby, Song Gang would also pause and stare confusedly at the setting sun. When Baldy Li set off again, Song Gang would again lower his head and follow him. When the people of Liu saw Baldy Li carrying the apples, they asked, "Are you going to visit a friend or a relative?"

"Why does it have to be either a friend or a relative?" Baldy Li retorted happily.

When they arrived at the entrance to Lin Hong's house, Baldy Li came to a halt and patted Song Gang's shoulder. "It's up to you! I'll wait here for news of your success."

Then Baldy Li added affectionately, in what amounted to his trump card, "Remember, we are brothers."

Song Gang watched Baldy Li's flushed face in the evening light, shook his head and laughed bitterly, then turned and walked into Lin Hong's home. When Song Gang abruptly showed up, Lin Hong's parents were in the middle of dinner. They were somewhat surprised to see him and obviously knew what had happened the previous evening. Song Gang felt that he should make a bit of conversation, but his mind was a complete blank. He merely stood there without saying anything, unable to step through the doorway, until finally Lin Hong's mother stood up and called out to him, "Come on in."

Song Gang finally stepped through the doorway, but after he walked to the center of the room, he didn't know what he should do next. Lin Hong's mother smiled as she opened the door to Lin Hong's bedroom, quietly telling Song Gang, "She might already be asleep."

Song Gang nodded expressionlessly and then walked into the bedroom, which was bathed in evening light. He saw Lin Hong asleep on the bed as peaceful as a kitten. He walked forward uncertainly a couple of steps, until he was standing in front of her bed. The covers had fallen off, revealing the tender outline of her body, and her hair covering her pretty face. Song Gang felt the blood rush to his head and his pulse start racing. Sensing someone moving in front of her bed, Lin Hong half opened her eyes and smiled in pleasant surprise when she realized it was Song Gang. She closed her eyes again and grinned for a while, then opened them and extended her hand to him.

At this point Song Gang finally remembered what he was supposed to say to her. He took a deep breath and stuttered, "This time you should give up all hope."

Lin Hong shuddered as if she had been shot and stared at Song Gang with wide eyes. At that instant he saw the terror in her eyes, after which she closed them painfully, with tears running down her cheeks. His entire body shuddering, Song Gang placed the handkerchief on her covers, then rushed out of her room as if he were fleeing for his life. When he reached the door to the house, he seemed to hear Lin Hong's parents saying something, but after a moment's hesitation he rushed out.

When Baldy Li saw Song Gang rush out as if he had seen a ghost, he delightedly asked him, "Did you succeed?"

Song Gang unhappily nodded his head, tears streaming down his face, then hurried away, determined never to look back. Baldy Li watched him leave and muttered, "What's he crying about?"

Then Baldy Li sauntered into Lin Hong's house, stroking his bald head as if he were combing his hair, and weighing the apples in his hand.

While Lin Hong's parents were trying to figure out what had just happened, Baldy Li sauntered in and greeted them as Auntie and Uncle, then continued on into Lin Hong's room. He turned around and closed her door, and as he did so he winked mysteriously at her parents. Both parents scratched their heads and stood there staring at each other.

Baldy Li smiled as he walked toward Lin Hong's bed and said, "Lin Hong, I heard that you were sick, so I bought you some apples."

Lin Hong, who had not yet recovered from the preceding shock, stared at Baldy Li with a look of utter incomprehension. He was secretly pleased that she was not kicking him out, and so he sat down on her bed and took the apples one after another, placing them next to her pillow, and bragged, "These are the reddest and biggest apples

Liu Town has ever seen. I went to three separate fruit stalls to find them."

Lin Hong was still staring speechlessly at Baldy Li, and Baldy Li felt as though he were on the verge of success. He tenderly grasped her right hand, caressing it and lifting it to his face. At this point she finally came to her senses, immediately pulled back her hand, and let out a bloodcurdling scream.

Lin Hong's parents heard the scream and rushed into her room. There they saw Lin Hong, huddled in the corner of the bed, pointing at Baldy Li and shouting, "Out! Get out of here!"

Without even having a chance to explain himself, Baldy Li again fled from Lin Hong's house. This time her parents didn't use broomsticks and feather dusters to kick him out but, rather, their own hands and fists. In front of all the assembled onlookers, they cursed Baldy Li again and again, using not only the "ugly toad" and "cow dung" curses from before but also adding "hooligan," "bum," and "bastard" to the mix.

Amid their curses, Lin Hong's parents finally remembered their daughter and rushed back into the house to see her. Baldy Li stood there resentfully; his own belly was full of curses, but at that moment he couldn't think of a single one. The onlookers laughed as they watched him, and one after another they asked him what had happened.

"Nothing." Baldy Li shook his head as though nothing were wrong, and said simply, "It is merely a lovers' quarrel."

With this, Baldy Li prepared to turn around and was about to leave when Lin Hong's parents reemerged, carrying the apples. They called out to him and hurled the apples like hand grenades at his head. Baldy Li ducked and dodged, and after Lin Hong's parents had finished throwing the apples and headed back inside, he turned to the onlookers and innocently shook his head. He squatted down and picked up all the apples, saying, "These are my apples."

Baldy Li walked home with his smashed apples. The townspeople watched him rub one against his shirt, lift it to his mouth, and take a bite, mumbling, "This tastes good." While he was walking away chewing his apple, the onlookers heard him recite a verse of Chairman Mao's poetry: "This is the start of a Long March, a Long March. . . ."

CHAPTER 34

AFTER SONG GANG left Lin Hong's home that evening, tears streaming down his face, he wandered the streets of Liu, heartbroken and hopeless. Lin Hong's terrified gaze repeatedly appeared before him, again making him feel as though a dagger had been driven through his heart. Every time he crossed a bridge, he wanted to throw himself into the river below; and whenever he passed an electrical pole, he wanted to hurl himself into it headfirst. Someone passed by pushing a cart containing two folded wicker baskets and a pile of rope. Song Gang immediately grabbed the rope and scurried away. The person put down his cart and chased Song Gang down, grabbing him and asking, "Hey, what're you doing?"

Song Gang froze and stared fiercely. "Committing suicide, can't you see?"

The cart pusher did a double take. Song Gang tied the rope around his neck and yanked it upward with his hand, sticking out his tongue for good measure. He laughed fiercely and said, "I'm hanging myself, can't you see?"

The cart pusher did another double take and stared, speechless, as Song Gang walked away. He then cursed as he returned to his cart, complaining that he was fucking unfortunate—that it wasn't even nightfall yet and already he'd had to deal with a nut job. Not only had the nut job startled him twice, but furthermore he had stolen his rope. He cursed incessantly as he pushed his cart, and after walking the length of the longest street in Liu, he arrived at the front door of Lin Hong's house. Baldy Li had just finished picking up his apples and was eating one of them as he walked over. The cart pusher cried out aggrievedly to Baldy Li, "I've had such fucking bad luck, running into a nut job. . . ."

"*You're* the fucking nut job," Baldy Li answered scornfully and walked off.

After Song Gang tied the rope around his neck, he simply left it on, as if it were a scarf made of twine. He walked briskly, looking as though he were rushing to his death. The rustling of his clothes and his rapid pace made him feel as though he were walking on air. It seemed to him that he covered the length of the street in a flash, and in no time he turned into the alleyway and arrived at his own doorstep.

Song Gang took out his key and opened the front door, and after entering the dark room it was a while before it occurred to him to turn on the lights. He then looked up and inspected the ceiling beams, telling himself that these would do just fine. He placed a bench under one of the beams and stood on it. Only then did he notice that he no longer had the rope in his hand. He looked around suspiciously, not remembering where he had left the rope and thinking that maybe he had left it in the road. He jumped down from the bench and headed toward the door. When a burst of wind blew in his face, he heard a rustling sound. He then laughed as he realized that the rope was tied around his neck.

Song Gang stood again on the bench, removed the rope from his neck, carefully tied it around the beam, and then made a noose. He yanked it firmly, placed his head into the noose, and tightened it. He then exhaled deeply and closed his eyes. A gust of wind reminded him that he had left the door ajar. He opened his eyes and saw that the door was swinging open and shut. Therefore, he removed his head from the noose, jumped off the bench, and went to close the door. Then he once again stood on the bench and placed his head in the noose. Closing his eyes, he inhaled one last time, exhaled, then kicked the bench out from under himself. He immediately felt as though his body had been stretched out and his breathing cut off. It was at this point that he got the vague impression that Baldy Li had returned.

When Baldy Li pushed the door open and walked in, he immediately saw Song Gang's body flailing about in midair. He cried out in horror and rushed forward to grab Song Gang's legs, struggling to support his body. Quickly realizing that this wasn't working, he started rushing around the room like a caged beast. When he saw a vegetable knife, he suddenly had an idea. He picked up the knife, righted the bench, stood on it, and proceeded to jump, using the knife to slice through the rope. When Song Gang's body dropped, Baldy Li also fell to the ground. He turned over and knelt there, hugging Song Gang's shoulders and rocking back and forth. He wept as he cried out, "Song Gang, Song Gang . . ."

Baldy Li bawled, tears and snot running down his face. At that point, Song Gang's body moved, and he started to cough. When Baldy Li realized that Song Gang was still alive, he wiped his tears and snot and started to laugh, then started crying again. Sobbing, he exclaimed, "Song Gang, what did you think you were doing?"

Song Gang coughed as he leaned against the wall to sit up. He stared blankly at Baldy Li and heard him repeatedly calling his name. Song Gang opened his mouth, but no sound came out. He opened his mouth again, and this time said softly, "I no longer want to live."

Baldy Li reached out his hand to stroke the red welt on Song Gang's neck, and through his tears he cursed his brother, "If you had fucking died, what the fuck would I have done? You are my only fucking relative, and if you had fucking died, I would have become a fucking orphan."

Song Gang pushed Baldy Li's hand away and, shaking his head, said, "I like Lin Hong, even more than you do. You not only don't want me to be with her but furthermore keep demanding that I hurt her."

Baldy Li wiped his tears and said angrily, "Is it really worth it to kill yourself over a woman?"

Song Gang rushed at Baldy Li, saying, "If it were you, what would you do?"

"If it were me," Baldy Li shouted back, "I would slaughter you!"

Song Gang looked at Baldy Li in surprise and, pointing at himself, said, "But I'm your brother!"

"Even as a brother, I would still slaughter you," Baldy Li immediately retorted.

Song Gang stared in astonishment and eventually began to laugh. He looked carefully at Baldy Li, this brother of his, with whom he shared everything. Baldy Li's comment gave Song Gang instant release, and he felt that now he had complete freedom to devote himself to Lin Hong. Song Gang laughed out loud and told Baldy Li sincerely, "That was truly well said."

Song Gang, who just moments earlier had been crying "I don't want to live," now started laughing happily. Baldy Li was deeply disconcerted by this and watched Song Gang leap up as if he were competing in the high jump and proceed quickly to the door. Not knowing what Song Gang was planning, Baldy Li struggled up and cried out, "What are you going to do?"

Song Gang turned around and said calmly, "I'm going to go see Lin Hong. I want to tell her that I like her."

"You can't do that!" Baldy Li cried. "You can't fucking do that. Lin Hong is mine."

"No." Song Gang shook his head firmly. "Lin Hong doesn't like you. She likes me."

Baldy Li at this point once again drew on his trump card, exclaiming passionately, "Song Gang, we are brothers."

Song Gang replied happily, "Brothers can also slaughter."

As Song Gang was saying this he stepped out the door and walked away. In his fury Baldy Li punched a wall but then immediately grimaced in pain. As he rubbed and blew on his injured hand, his howls of fury turned into yelps of pain. After his pain had subsided, he looked out into the empty night and shouted to Song Gang, who was already out of sight, "Get out of here! You fucking value women over friends, and even over your own brother."

As Song Gang walked along the moonlit street, the autumn leaves drifting by, he couldn't stop laughing. He had kept things bottled up for a long time and only now could finally express his happiness. He drank in the cool breeze as he strolled toward Lin Hong's house. On his way, he felt that the Liu Town evening was so beautiful, with the sky full of stars, the autumn breeze blowing, and the tree shadows waving back and forth. The lights from the streetlamps and the moon were intertwined, like Lin Hong's braids. A few pedestrians appeared in the peaceful street, and as they walked beneath the streetlamps it looked as though they were glowing, making Song Gang stare in surprise. When he walked over the bridge, he was even more astounded, seeing the river full of stars and moonlight.

CHAPTER 35

ALL NIGHT Lin Hong's parents felt as if they were riding an emotional roller coaster. First Song Gang walked into Lin Hong's room and broke her heart. Then Baldy Li came and made her scream in horror. Lin Hong's parents spent the entire evening sobbing and sighing, and they had just gone to bed when they heard someone knocking at the door again. They looked at each other, unable to imagine who might be visiting at that hour. They got dressed and were headed for the door when the knocking abruptly stopped, making them suspect that perhaps they'd been hearing things. They were about to head back to bed when the knocking started up again. Lin Hong's mother leaned toward the door and asked, "Who is it?"

"It's me," Song Gang replied from outside.

"Who are you?" Lin Hong's father asked.

"I am Song Gang."

When Lin Hong's parents heard that it was Song Gang, they grew angry. After exchanging glances, they opened the door and were about to start reprimanding him when he happily announced, "I've returned."

"You've *returned*?" Lin Hong's mother said. "But this isn't your home."

"Bizarre," Lin Hong's father muttered.

The happiness instantly vanished from Song Gang's face. He looked at them uneasily, sensing that they had a point. Lin Hong's mother was about to launch into a scolding but changed her mind. Instead she coldly told him, "We've already gone to bed." Then she closed the door. As the parents returned to bed, Lin Hong's father became enraged as he recalled all that had happened to his daughter. He cursed Song Gang: "What a cretin."

"A complete cretin," spat his wife.

It seemed to Lin Hong's mother that Song Gang had a bloody welt on his neck, and she asked her husband if he had noticed it. He thought for a moment and nodded. Then they turned out the light and went to sleep.

Song Gang stood at the door to Lin Hong's house for a long time, completely at a loss. The night was so quiet that you could hear a pin drop. Two cats climbed onto the roof of the house, meowing as they chased each other around, and their shrill cries caused Song Gang's heart to shudder. Only then did he realized that it was the dead of night. He started to regret that he had come knocking on Lin Hong's door so late, and therefore he left her courtyard and went back out to the street.

After walking around for a while, Song Gang gradually began to cheer up. He experimented with having his heel strike the ground first, as if he were training for a speed-walking race, and in this way he walked back and forth down the main street of Liu Town. After he had made five round-trips, he felt that he still had pent-up energy. Shortly before dawn he approached the gate to Lin Hong's house for the seventh time that night. He decided to halt his march and set up camp in front of the house, waiting there for the sun to come up.

Song Gang squatted against a buzzing electrical pole and laughed quietly. He didn't realize, however, how the sound of his laughter would resonate in the still night. One of Lin Hong's neighbors happened to be heading home from a night shift and, hearing the sound of laughter emanating from the electrical pole, wondered in alarm if this cackling electrical pole was perhaps a sign of an impending earthquake. Upon closer inspection, however, he realized that the laughter was coming from a dark form at the base of the pole. He had no idea what kind of animal this could be and was so spooked that he threw open the door to his house and rushed in.

Lin Hong's mother got up at the crack of dawn. While she was taking out the chamber pot, she saw Song Gang standing there, covered in dew. She jumped in surprise and looked up at the sun that had just risen. She thought to herself that it hadn't rained, then realized that he must have gotten covered in dew from standing there all night. He smiled broadly at her, like a big wet dog. She felt that he was smiling rather strangely and therefore put down the chamber pot, went back inside, and told her husband that Song Gang looked as if he had been standing outside all night long. She speculated, "Perhaps he has gone insane?"

Lin Hong's father's jaw dropped in surprise, and he hurried outside as if to glimpse a rare panda. When he saw Song Gang standing there grinning, he asked him curiously, "Have you been standing here all night?"

Song Gang nodded happily, and Lin Hong's father asked himself how someone could be so happy after having stood outside all night. He walked back into the house and told Lin Hong's mother, "I agree that he doesn't seem quite right."

When Lin Hong woke up that morning, she found that her fever had gone down and she felt somewhat better. When she sat up, however, she realized she was still quite weak, so she lay back down. It was at this point that she learned that Song Gang had been standing outside all night. She first reacted with surprise; then, remembering the previous night's events, she bit her lip, and tears of shame flooded her eyes. She covered her head with her blanket and sobbed. After she had cried for a while, she wiped her tears with the handkerchief Song Gang had returned to her and then told her father, "Make him go away. I don't want to see him."

Lin Hong's father walked out and said to Song Gang, who was still standing there grinning, "You should go. My daughter won't see you."

Song Gang wiped the smile from his face and stared at Lin Hong's father, at a loss as to what to do. When the father saw that Song Gang was making no move to leave, he began shooing him away as one would a flock of ducks. After he had shooed Song Gang a dozen yards away, Lin Hong's father paused and pointed at him, saying, "Move along. I don't want to see you here again."

Lin Hong's father walked back into the house and reported that he had shooed the idiot away. He reported that it had been quite difficult, because after every step that idiot would turn back around and stand there without moving as if he were a pile of dirt. The father concluded by citing Chairman Mao's aphorism that *if one doesn't make use of a broom, dirt won't disappear on its own,* then he spat out seven "idiots" in succession. When Lin Hong heard the seventh "idiot," she began to feel uneasy. She muttered to herself, "He isn't an idiot. He is just loyal."

Lin Hong's father winked at his wife and laughed to himself as he headed back into the courtyard. Another neighbor coming home after having bought some fried dough sticks for breakfast then remarked to Lin Hong's father, "The fellow you shooed away is still standing there."

"Really?" Lin Hong's father replied. He went back inside and walked up to the window. He rolled up the blinds and peeked out, and sure enough he saw Song Gang. Smiling, he told Lin Hong's mother to take a look as well, and she too saw Song Gang standing there with his head bowed, looking utterly despondent. She couldn't help but laugh and told her daughter, "Song Gang has returned."

Lin Hong saw her parents' knowing smiles and realized what they were thinking. She turned and faced the wall so they wouldn't be able to see her face. She recalled the events of the previous night, and again grew angry, saying, "Ignore him."

Lin Hong's mother said, "If you ignore him, he will continue standing there."

"Then make him go away," she pleaded.

This time it was Lin Hong's mother who went out. She walked over to Song Gang, who was standing there uneasily, and asked gently, "Why don't you leave now and come back in a few days?"

Song Gang stared at her in confusion, not understanding what she meant by this. Lin Hong's mother was able to see the bloody welt on Song Gang's neck clearly and asked him, "What's wrong with your neck?"

"I tried to kill myself," he replied uneasily.

"Kill yourself?"

"I tried to hang myself," said Song Gang, then added, embarrassed, "I didn't succeed."

Concerned, Lin Hong's mother walked back into the house and proceeded to her daughter's bed. She said that Song Gang had tried to hang himself, explaining that the previous evening she had noticed the bloody welt on his neck and this morning when she saw it again the welt appeared even deeper and thicker than before. She sighed and prodded Lin Hong, who was still lying there facing the wall, "You should go out and see him."

"I won't go." Lin Hong twisted her body around. "Let him die."

As Lin Hong said this she felt a stab of pain in her heart. She felt increasingly uneasy as she lay there thinking of Song Gang standing outside. The thought of the bloody welt on his neck made her even more distressed. Feeling an urge to go out and see him, she sat up and looked at her mother, who tactfully retired to the outer room. Lin Hong slowly got out of bed, washed her face and brushed her teeth, then sat in front of the mirror and began carefully combing her long hair, parting it into two braids. Then she stood up and announced to her parents, "I'm going to go buy some fried dough sticks."

When Song Gang saw Lin Hong emerge, he was so overcome he almost burst into tears. He hugged his shoulders as if he were cold and kept opening his mouth, but no sound came out. Lin Hong glanced at him with no discernible expression, then walked past him to the fried dough shop. Song Gang, his body still damp with dew, followed closely behind, and when he finally succeeded in speaking, he said hoarsely, "Tonight at eight o'clock I'll wait for you under the bridge."

"I won't go," Lin Hong replied quietly.

She walked into the shop as Song Gang waited dejectedly outside. After she bought the fried dough sticks and came back out, she saw clearly the welt on Song Gang's neck, and her heart skipped a beat. At this point he cautiously suggested a different rendezvous site. "Should I wait for you in the grove behind the theater?"

Lin Hong hesitated a moment, then nodded. Song Gang was overjoyed but at a loss as to what to do next. He followed Lin Hong as she returned to the gate to her house. As she walked in she turned around and quietly gave him a sign to leave. He nodded and, after she had gone inside, finally turned around and left.

Song Gang spent the entire day in a daze. He fell asleep thirteen times at the factory—five times in a corner of the workshop, twice while eating lunch, three times while playing cards with his workmates, twice while leaning against the machinery, and once while peeing in the bathroom with his head resting against the wall. Then, as dusk approached, he excitedly proceeded to the grove behind the movie theater, pacing furtively back and forth like a fugitive along the path out front. Several acquaintances walked by and called out to him, asking what he was doing, but he only mumbled something incoherent. They laughed and asked if he had lost his wallet. He nodded, and they then asked if he had lost his wits, too. He nodded again, whereupon they laughed loudly and walked away.

That night Lin Hong was an hour late. Her beautiful figure slowly proceeded down the moonlit path, and Song Gang waved excitedly when he saw her. However, people were still walking about not too far from them, so she said quietly, "Don't wave, just follow me."

She walked toward the grove, with Song Gang following closely behind, and again said softly, "Don't follow so close."

Song Gang stopped, but, not sure precisely how far from her he should be, he merely stood there without moving. Lin Hong continued for a while before she noticed that he was still standing there, so she called out softly, "Come on."

Then he rushed forward again. Lin Hong walked into the grove, with Song Gang close behind. She then proceeded to the center, looked around, and after confirming that they were alone, she finally stopped. She heard Song Gang's footsteps approach and then stop, leaving only the sound of his shallow breathing. Lin Hong knew that Song Gang was standing directly behind her. She stood there without moving, and Song Gang did the same. Lin Hong wondered why this idiot didn't come around in front of her. She waited for a while, but he still stood there, breathing shallowly. Finally she had no choice but to turn around and saw him trembling in the moonlight. Looking closely at his neck, she could vaguely make out the red welt and asked, "What happened to your neck?"

Song Gang launched into a long, complicated explanation. Stammering and semi-incoherent, he explained how Baldy Li had forced him to say that phrase to her. After he had uttered it, he returned home and tried to hang himself—only Baldy Li happened to return and rescued him. Lin Hong's eyes kept tearing up as Song Gang told his story, and when he was finished, he stammered as he retold everything from the beginning. Lin Hong reached out and covered his mouth, telling him to say no more. When her hand touched his lips, his entire body started to tremble. She pulled away her hand, lowered her head, and wiped away her tears. Then she lifted her head and ordered, "Take off your glasses."

He quickly removed his glasses but didn't know what to do next. Lin Hong again commanded him, "Put them in your pocket."

Song Gang placed his glasses in his pocket but still didn't know what to do next. Lin Hong laughed affectionately, came forward, and caressed his neck. She pressed her lips against the welt on his neck and said protectively, "I love you, Song Gang. I love you."

Trembling, he embraced her and started to cry tears of joy—crying so hard that he couldn't catch his breath.

CHAPTER 36

SONG GANG decided to move out of Baldy Li's home and live on his own. Afraid of encountering his brother, he snuck home during the day, packed all his clothing into that old travel bag, and divided their money into two equal portions. Taking one portion for himself, Song Gang left the other on the table for Baldy Li, together with all of the leftover change, and then added the house key Baldy Li had made him. Finally he shut the door and left the house that he and Baldy Li had called home and moved into the dormitory at the metal factory.

After maintaining a secret love affair for a month, Song Gang and Lin Hong finally decided to make their love public. This, of course, was Lin Hong's decision. For the location, she selected the movie theater, and that night the people of Liu were surprised to see the two of them walk in together, she nibbling on some melon seeds as he chatted away. After they found their seats, they sat down together, and Lin Hong continued nibbling her melon seeds and chatting with Song Gang as though no one were around. It was Song Gang who amiably nodded and greeted each of their acquaintances. The men of Liu experienced a gamut of conflicting emotions, and after the film began, all of them, regardless of whether they were still bachelors or already married, spent half their time watching the movie and the other half spying on Lin Hong and Song Gang. Those seated beside them turned their heads, those in front looked back, while those behind craned their necks to peer down at them. Later that night, countless lustful men tossed and turned, unable to sleep and overcome with jealousy.

After that outing, Lin Hong and Song Gang were often seen in public together. She appeared even more beautiful than before, and always had an easygoing smile. The town's elders all agreed that this was obviously a girl who was soaking in honey. When Song Gang walked at her side, he was so happy he didn't know what to do. Even after several months, he maintained his look of awed contentment. The elders opined that he didn't at all look like a lover and that even the truculent Baldy Li fit the role better—Baldy Li at the very least was an overzealous bodyguard, whereas Song Gang looked more like a lackey.

In his delirious happiness, Song Gang spent virtually all his savings on a shiny new Eternity bicycle. What was this Eternity bicycle? It was the equivalent of a Mercedes or BMW today. Only three Eternity bicycles were issued to Liu Town every year, so even if you had money to spare, you still might not be able to buy yourself one. Lin Hong's uncle, however, happened to be the manager of the metal-goods company, and it was completely at his discretion to whom those three Eternity bicycles would be sold. He cut an impressive figure, and most people, when they saw him, couldn't help bowing down. In order to allow Song Gang to truly stand out from the hoi polloi of Liu Town, Lin Hong repeatedly entreated her uncle to help her beloved obtain an Eternity bicycle. Lin Hong's father also pressured this younger brother of his, and her mother almost started cursing him out. In the end, the uncle had no alternative but to grit his teeth and take the bicycle that he was originally going to issue to the head of the county's Department of Armed Forces and assign it to Song Gang instead.

Song Gang seemed buoyed by the winds of good fortune as he sailed through Liu Town's streets and alleys on his brand-new bicycle. The shiny bicycle dazzled everyone's eyes, and the clear ring of its bell made their mouths salivate. After dismounting, he would take out a large ball of cotton that he kept stuffed under the seat and carefully wipe the dust off the bicycle, making sure that this Eternity bicycle remained eternally clean. His bicycle was always spotless, despite wind, rain, or even snow. In fact, it was cleaner than his person, since he would bathe only four times a month but would wipe down his bike every day.

Those days, Lin Hong felt like a princess. Every morning when she heard the clear sound of the bell ringing outside her door, she knew that her exclusive-use vehicle, that shiny new Eternity bicycle, had arrived. She would emerge with a smile on her face and would sit facing sideways on the back of the bicycle. All the way to the knitting factory she would soak in the envious gazes of passersby. Every day when she got off work and walked out the factory's front gate, the handsome Song Gang would be waiting there. She would then sit on the shiny new bicycle with that handsome man in front of her. As soon as she mounted she would remind him, "Ring the bell. Quick, ring the bell."

Song Gang would immediately ring the bell several times in a row. Turning around and looking back at her workmates, Lin Hong would feel a surge of pride that they had to pedal themselves home after working all day, while she could be chauffeured back on her own exclusive-use vehicle.

Whenever she was astride the bike, the Eternity bell rang continuously. When they passed acquaintances on the street, she would remind Song Gang to ring the bell, and he would always do his best to make the ring last as long as possible.

It was at that point that the town's elders decided that Song Gang had finally acquired a lover's airs. They remarked that he rode his bicycle like a general on horseback, and when he rang his bell, it was as if he were flicking his whip.

Song Gang rode his bright and shiny Eternity bicycle with Lin Hong sitting behind him, ringing his bell whenever they passed anyone. The only exception was when he encountered Baldy Li. Baldy Li was still furious with him and would stare straight ahead whenever they passed. Song Gang, meanwhile, would turn away guiltily, as though he had done something wrong. Lin Hong, for her part, would urge that he ring the bell whenever they passed Baldy Li, but on those occasions Song Gang wouldn't be able to produce his distinctive ring; instead the bell would sound scattered and intermittent. Understanding the reason for this, Lin Hong would reach forward and hug his waist, pressing her face against his back as she stared at Baldy Li with a look of pride and contentment. Seeing him pretend to be calm, she would laugh. "Song Gang, look whose wet dog this is!"

When Baldy Li heard this, he would let out a long string of "fuck you's" that went on even longer than Song Gang's bicycle bell. Then his face would drop, and at the thought of his woman and his brother running off together, he would proceed to curse up a storm. Watching as the Eternity bicycle disappeared into the distance, Baldy Li would recover his confidence and say to himself, *Life is long, and at the end of the day, who's to say who'll be the wet dog?*

He'd then vow, *I will get myself an extra-large Eternity bicycle, with the classic beauties Xi Shi sitting in front, Diao Chan behind me, Wang Zhaojun in my lap, and Yang Guifei perched on my back. With these four beauties I will ride for fucking forty-nine days, riding from the present into the past and back again. If I feel like it, I might even decide to ride into the future. . . .*

Once Lin Hong and Song Gang's affair was finally made public, the town's biggest romantic cliff-hanger was finally resolved, thereby breaking the hearts of all the remaining bachelors. Each of them went in search of other single women, and as a result, the amorous activity in Liu Town abruptly blossomed like spring bamboo after a shower, sweetening the streets and alleys of Liu and making it so the elders couldn't even take it all in. They counted on their fingers and said, "It looks like everyone has a woman . . . everyone except Baldy Li. Hasn't he landed anyone yet?"

The townspeople rarely saw Baldy Li out in the street, but when they did, he seemed to have lost a lot of weight, as if he had been gravely ill.

The night after his unsuccessful suicide, Song Gang had seized his happiness and walked out the door. Baldy Li cursed him furiously for an hour, then snored furiously for eight hours. When he woke up the next morning and saw that Song Gang's bed was still empty, he searched the room inside and out but couldn't find any evidence that Song Gang had returned. He tsk-tsked Song Gang, not realizing that his brother had spent the entire night standing guard in front of Lin Hong's house. Believing that Song Gang was merely trying to avoid him, he snorted, "You may be able to avoid me for a night, but you can't avoid me your entire life."

The next day Song Gang still had not returned home. That night Baldy Li sat at the table dreaming up one plot after another to enact against his brother but had to discard them all because they didn't strike him as sufficiently diabolical. He finally came up with a tear-jerking scheme that would consist of grabbing Song Gang's arm and then, in a rain of tears and snot, recalling their childhood together. As youngsters he and Song Gang had been as thick as thieves, given that they were both orphans and needed to rely on each other for survival. Baldy Li was confident that if he did this, Song Gang would surely bow his head in humiliation and return Lin Hong to him. Baldy Li was very proud of this plot and was convinced that it was truly diabolical. He waited up half the night, until he couldn't stop yawning and his eyelids were battling each other, but when Song Gang still hadn't returned, Baldy Li finally had no choice but to go to bed, cursing nonstop. Before retiring, he looked around and thought to himself that what they said was true: *You can take the monk out of the temple, but you can't take the temple out of the monk*—so sooner or later this monk would have to come home again, whereupon Baldy Li could try out his tear-jerking scheme.

When Baldy Li got home from work two days later and saw the

money and the key on the table, he understood that something momentous had occurred and that the monk would not be returning to the temple after all. He was so furious that he stalked in circles around the house, trying out every single curse word in the Chinese language. He didn't stop there but went on to use all the Japanese curse words he had learned from movies about the War of Resistance. He wanted to use some American curse words too, but since he didn't know a single one, he had no choice but to sit mutely on the side of his bed and stare into space. He felt that he had underestimated his brother. Song Gang had studied that tattered half copy of Sunzi's *Art of War*, and before Baldy Li had a chance to try out his scheme, Song Gang had already employed what Sunzi himself had called the last and best of the thirty-six stratagems: *leaving*.

That night, Baldy Li suffered from insomnia for the first time in his life, and for the next month he found himself constantly tired and without appetite. He lost weight and the urge to speak, though out in the streets he still appeared majestic and commanding. He ran into Song Gang several times, but Song Gang always scurried out of the way before he approached. He also encountered Lin Hong, but she was always with Song Gang, affectionately grasping his hand. Soon after, Song Gang started riding around on his Eternity bicycle with Lin Hong sitting in back. By this point, Baldy Li no longer felt sad but, rather, that he had thoroughly lost face.

The people of Liu Town were blessed with good memories, and they all remembered exactly what Baldy Li had proclaimed when he beat up those two amorous impostors. Baldy Li had boasted that he would beat anyone who dared claim to be Lin Hong's boyfriend so badly that he would never make it back for another incarnation. Therefore, some young rascals, whenever they encountered Baldy Li in the street, would taunt him, "Wasn't Lin Hong your girlfriend? How is it that, in the blink of an eye, she suddenly became Song Gang's?"

Upon hearing this, Baldy Li would respond furiously, "If he weren't Song Gang, I would have slaughtered him long ago! I would have carried his head on a pole and gone off to roam the rivers and seas! But who is Song Gang? Song Gang is my brother, to whom I have sworn my life. So I have no choice but to grit my teeth and swallow my anger."

The welt on Song Gang's neck from his suicide attempt took more than a month to heal, and whenever Lin Hong thought about it, her eyes would immediately well up with tears. She told her parents the

308 • YU HUA

true circumstances behind his suicide attempt and couldn't resist telling some of her closest friends at the factory as well. Lin Hong's parents and those friends at the factory then told other friends, and soon tens, hundreds, and even thousands of people knew about it as the story of Song Gang's suicide attempt spread around town like a virus. The women of Liu were extremely envious of Lin Hong, and all of them went to ask their current or future husbands, "Would you commit suicide for me?"

The men of Liu were utterly miserable. Not only did they have to feign sincerity and swear, "I would, I would, I would," but they also had to put on a good show of being heroes who would face death without fear. The women of Liu repeatedly asked the same question, and their men would give the same answer a hundred times over, or at the very least five or six. A few of the men came under such pressure that they had no alternative but to tie a noose around their own necks or place a knife to their wrists, solemnly vowing, "Just give the command, and I will kill myself."

Meanwhile Poet Zhao was still unencumbered by love. With his former girlfriend off cavorting with another, and his future girlfriends still with their current boyfriends, he found himself in a loveless period of his life. He therefore gloated over the misfortune of the other townsmen, secretly convinced that it was their own fault. He bragged that he would never find a girlfriend who would make him want to commit suicide but, rather, would find one willing to commit suicide for him. He announced proudly, "Consider famous beauties such as Lady Meng Jiang and Zhu Yingtai. In all the great love stories, it's always the woman who dies for her lover."

Poet Zhao therefore felt that he and Baldy Li could definitely commiserate, insofar as they had both been kicked onto their asses by Lin Hong. From the time of Writer Liu's beating, Poet Zhao had avoided Baldy Li, though the past few times they had run into each other on the street, Baldy Li had nodded to him. Poet Zhao felt that he was safe now, and he started trying to get closer to Baldy Li. Seeing him approaching on the street, poet Zhao would greet Baldy Li loudly: "Director Li, how have you been recently?"

"Awful," Baldy Li replied irritably.

Poet Zhao laughed and patted Baldy Li's shoulder. In front of the passersby, he started talking nonstop about how Baldy Li should not have rescued Song Gang when he hanged himself; how Song Gang, the moment he was rescued, proceeded to steal Baldy Li's Lin Hong from him; and if Song Gang hadn't been rescued . . . "Perhaps the pendulum of love would have swung back again toward you?"

Baldy Li was very displeased by Poet Zhao's remarks and wondered how this turtle spawn dared to wish that Song Gang had died. Completely oblivious to Baldy Li's growing fury, Poet Zhao prattled on, pleased with his own cleverness. "This is like the story of the farmer and the snake. When the farmer saw a frozen snake in the road, he picked it up and placed it against his chest. After the snake thawed out, it bit the farmer and killed him."

In the end, Poet Zhao completely forgot himself and pointed at Baldy Li, saying, "You are that farmer, and Song Gang is that snake."

Baldy Li exploded, grabbing Poet Zhao by the collar and screaming, "*You* are that fucking farmer, and you're also that fucking snake!"

Poet Zhao's face went ashen with surprise, and he watched as Baldy Li raised the fist with which he had terrorized Liu Town. Poet Zhao immediately grasped Baldy Li's fist with both hands and pleaded, "Don't be angry, Director Li. Please don't be angry. I meant well. I was looking out for you."

Baldy Li hesitated a moment, then decided that Poet Zhao did seem as if he meant well. Therefore, he lowered his fist, let go of Poet Zhao's collar, and warned him, "You fucking listen. Song Gang is my brother, and even if it were the end of the world, he would still be my brother. If you fucking dare say another bad word about him, I swear I'll . . ."

Baldy Li paused for a moment, hesitating over whether to use *beat* or *slaughter*, and ultimately came firmly down on the side of *slaughter:* "I'll slaughter you."

Poet Zhao nodded as if in agreement, then turned and left. He was thinking that he must put some distance between himself and this heathen. After scurrying away ten paces, he noticed that everyone in the street was laughing at him. Therefore, he immediately slowed down, trying to make it look as if he was completely unhurried. He sighed, then said to the onlookers, "You can never win, can you?"

As Baldy Li watched Poet Zhao walk away he suddenly remembered the vow he had made while beating Writer Liu. Immediately he waved Poet Zhao back, saying, "Come back! Get the fuck back here!"

Poet Zhao's heart froze, but he was too embarrassed simply to run away in front of so many people. He therefore paused, and in order to maintain an appearance of unconcern, he slowly turned around. Baldy

Li continued to beckon him, and warmly said, "Quick, come back. I still haven't helped you regain your true laborer colors."

Sensing the crowd's anticipation and recognizing that he was in a bad way, Poet Zhao began to feel his heart pounding wildly. In a burst of inspiration, he waved his hand and demurred, "Some other time, perhaps."

As he said this Poet Zhao pointed at his head and explained, "I just had an idea for a poem and want to hurry home to write it down. Otherwise, it'll be gone forever."

When he heard about Poet Zhao's inspiration, Baldy Li waved him away. The crowds were disappointed and complained to Baldy Li, "How could you let him go?"

Baldy Li watched Poet Zhao walk away, then remarked calmly to the onlookers, "Poet Zhao has it hard, as it is even more difficult for his brain to conceive an idea than it would be for his belly to conceive a child."

As he said this Baldy Li walked away with a magnanimous expression. When he passed the fabric store, Lin Hong was inside, happily chatting with the clerk while picking out fabric to make clothes for herself and Song Gang. But Baldy Li didn't notice her, nor did he realize that she and Song Gang were preparing for their wedding.

CHAPTER 37

FOR THEIR wedding day, Lin Hong reserved seven tables at the People's Restaurant and planned to invite friends and relatives from both the bride's and the groom's sides to join them for their wedding banquet. She wrote her guests' names down on a sheet of paper and gave Song Gang another sheet and asked him to do the same. He raised the pen as if he were lifting a heavy weight, and after what seemed like an eternity he had still not managed to write down a single name. Finally he stammered that he only had one relative in the world, and that was Baldy Li. When Lin Hong heard this, she was very displeased. "Aren't I your relative?"

Song Gang shook his head, saying that was not what he meant. He lovingly reassured her, "You are my closest relative."

Lin Hong laughed happily and said, "And you are mine."

He took up his pen again but found himself still unable to set down a single name. He carefully asked Lin Hong if he could invite Baldy Li to attend the wedding banquet, explaining that although they hadn't seen each other recently, they were still brothers. He repeatedly insisted that if she didn't agree, he would definitely not invite Baldy Li. In the end, Lin Hong finally said, "Go ahead and invite him."

Lin Hong saw the look of delight on Song Gang's face and laughed. "Write it down."

After Song Gang wrote Baldy Li's name down on the blank sheet of paper, he quickly added the names of all his fellow factory workers. After a moment's hesitation, he also wrote down Writer Liu's name. Afterward, Song Gang filled out the red invitation cards based on the names they had agreed upon. Lin Hong leaned her head on his shoulder, watching the beautifully written characters flow from the tip of his pen, and sighed. "Beautiful. Your handwriting is just beautiful."

That afternoon Song Gang took the invitations, rode his shiny Eternity bicycle to the fork in the road, and waited there for Baldy Li to get off work. Song Gang sat on his bike and rested one leg on a wutong tree to maintain his balance. When Baldy Li approached, Song Gang did not try to ride away as usual but instead began calling out enthusiastically. Song Gang's warmth confused his brother, who turned around and looked behind him, thinking that Song Gang was speaking to someone else. When Baldy Li approached, he heard Song Gang calling out his name. "Baldy Li!"

Baldy Li pointed to himself and asked, "Are you talking to me?"

Song Gang nodded. Baldy Li looked up at the sky and feigned puzzlement, remarking sarcastically, "But pigs aren't flying yet."

Song Gang laughed in embarrassment. Baldy Li watched him as he sat on his Eternity bicycle, his right foot resting against the wutong tree, looking very cocky. Baldy Li became more and more envious, saying, "Fuck, you look just like a celestial immortal."

Song Gang jumped off the bike, held the handlebars, and invited Baldy Li to climb on and be a celestial immortal for a while. Baldy Li had never ridden a bicycle before, and had never even sat on the back of someone else's. Nevertheless, he looked like an old hand as he threw his leg over the crossbar, though after he sat down he didn't know what to do next. His body first leaned to the right and then to the left. His hands, as stiff as two sticks, grasped the handles as if they were a rope that had been thrown to rescue him. Song Gang grasped the bicycle's back wheel between his legs and urged Baldy Li to relax and hold the handlebar straight. Then he began pushing from behind. At first Baldy Li's body rocked back and forth, and Song Gang had to reach out to steady him and keep him from falling over. Gradually Baldy Li started to get a feel for the bike and was able to maintain his balance. With Song Gang pushing faster and faster, Baldy Li didn't even have to pedal. Song Gang began to run, making Baldy Li feel as though he were flying over the streets of Liu. Baldy Li cried out excitedly, "What a strong wind! What a strong wind!"

Song Gang was sprinting and soon was covered in sweat and struggling to catch his breath. He ran so hard his eyes glazed over and he began frothing at the mouth. The wind blew past Baldy Li's ears, through his clothes, and flowed smoothly over his bald head. He gestured to Song Gang, saying, "Faster, faster. Run faster!"

Song Gang pushed the bike down the street until he felt he couldn't run another step. He gradually slowed to a stop and once again grasped the back tire between his legs, supporting Baldy Li as he climbed down. Then Song Gang squatted down and panted for about half an hour. Baldy Li, however, was eager for more. He caressed Song Gang's Eternity bicycle with both hands and recalled the sweet feeling of wind rushing past him. He then looked down at Song Gang, panting help-lessly, and it was only then that he realized that Song Gang had been pushing him the entire way. He squatted down as if he were trying to help Song Gang catch his breath and gently patted his back. Baldy Li said to him, "Song Gang, you are extraordinary. You are truly an igni-tion engine incarnate." Then Baldy Li added regretfully, "It's too bad that you are not a real engine. If you were, then I could bike all the way to Shanghai."

Song Gang smiled as he panted. Holding his belly, he stood up and said, "Baldy Li, in the future you too will have a bicycle of your own, and at that point we can bike to Shanghai together."

Baldy Li's eyes were as bright and shiny as Song Gang's Eternity bicycle. He patted his bald head and said, "That's right, I will eventu-ally have a bicycle of my own, and then we can bike to Shanghai together."

After a brief hesitation, Song Gang announced uncertainly, "Baldy Li, Lin Hong and I are getting married."

As he was saying this Song Gang handed Baldy Li the invitation and asked him to come to their wedding banquet. Baldy Li's exultant expression immediately turned dark. Refusing the invitation, he slowly turned and walked away. As he left he said sadly, "The rice is already cooked. What is there to celebrate?"

Song Gang stared after him as Baldy Li walked away, and the frater-nal affection that they had momentarily regained dissipated like a wisp of smoke. Song Gang pushed his bicycle down the street with a heavy heart, forgetting even to ride it. He returned to Lin Hong's home, took out the invitation, and placed it on the table. When Lin Hong saw that he had brought Baldy Li's invitation back with him, she remarked, "So Baldy Li won't be coming?"

Song Gang nodded and said uneasily, "It seems as if he still hasn't given up hope."

Lin Hong snorted. "The rice is already cooked. What kind of hope is he holding on to?"

Song Gang heard this with surprise, wondering how it was that she and Baldy Li had used the same expression.

Of the seven banquet tables Lin Hong and Song Gang reserved at the People's Restaurant, Lin Hong's guests occupied six and Song Gang's just one. Baldy Li didn't attend. Neither did Writer Liu. While Liu suggested that he was disdainful of attending Song Gang's wedding banquet, the real reason was that he was simply too cheap—if he had come, he would have had to give the newlyweds a red envelope full of money. Liu stuck out his pinkie and said that Song Gang was an inconsequential person and he made it a practice never to impose on the hospitality of inconsequential people. However, he suggested he would condescend to visit Song Gang's new matrimonial quarters and take a look around, and he would offer his congratulations during the traditional festivities to be held there. All of Song Gang's workmates from the factory attended, and they happened to fill up precisely one table. The wedding banquet began at six that evening. Every table had ten dishes, including chicken, duck, fish, and pork. The guests drank fourteen bottles of *baijiu* liquor and twenty-eight bottles of rice wine. Eleven of the guests got slightly tipsy, seven of them got half drunk, and three got completely wasted. The three who got wasted each crawled under a separate table and started vomiting, inducing the seven guests who were only half drunk to start vomiting as well. The eleven tipsy guests also got into the mood, opening their mouths and letting out eleven different flavors of belches. As a result, Liu Town's most distinguished banquet hall in the People's Restaurant was left in complete disarray, smelling like a fertilizer factory. In the end, the air was so full of foul odors that it became impossible to catch a trace of the fragrant banquet dishes themselves.

That night Baldy Li also got drunk. He sat at home alone drinking *baijiu*, altogether drinking an entire *jin* of it. This was the first time he had ever gotten drunk, and afterward he cried himself to sleep. When he woke up the next morning, he was still whimpering. The neighbors heard him crying over his lost love and remarked that Baldy Li's crying ran the gamut of emotions: At different times he meowed like a cat in heat, screeched like a pig being slaughtered, lowed like a cow grazing grass, or crowed like a rooster greeting the dawn. The neighbors were very annoyed, saying that he made such a ruckus that they barely slept all night; even if they did manage to fall asleep, they had continuous nightmares.

After bawling for an entire night, the next day Baldy Li went to the hospital to have a vasectomy or, more specifically, a vasoligation. First he went to the Good Works Factory to obtain a certificate from his work unit. In this case, Baldy Li was not only the person requesting the operation but also the work unit supervisor in charge of approving the request. Therefore, he approved his own request and quite properly affixed a seal to the certificate. With this in hand, Baldy Li walked into the hospital clinic's surgical unit with a martyred air, slapped the certificate onto the doctor's desk, and announced loudly, "I have come to heed the call of China's birth control policy."

The doctor, of course, recognized that the person walking up to him demanding a vasectomy was the famous Baldy Li. He watched as Baldy Li stabbed at his abdomen with his hands as if they were knives, and wondered how there could be a man like this. He then looked at Baldy Li's work unit certificate and, noticing that Baldy Li was both the applicant and the supervisor approving the application wondered how there could be a certificate like this. He couldn't help but laugh, saying, "You've never been married and don't have any children. Why do you want a vasectomy?"

Baldy Li said heroically, "If I get a vasectomy without even having been married, won't that fulfill the population control policy that much better?"

The doctor wondered how in the world there could be a logic like this. He lowered his head and started laughing. Baldy Li impatiently pulled him up from his seat, as if *he* were the one planning on giving the doctor a vasectomy. He then wrestled the doctor into the operating room, where he unfastened his own belt, pulled down his pants, unbuttoned his shirt, lay down on the operating table, and ordered, "Ligate me!"

The operation was finished in less than an hour, after which an exuberant Baldy Li walked out the front door of the hospital. In his left hand he carried the medical certificate, and with his right hand he cupped his stitched-up groin. He stopped to rest every few steps until he arrived at Lin Hong and Song Gang's nuptial home.

Lin Hong's twenty workmates from the knitting factory had come to attend the traditional celebration of the matrimonial quarters. Writer Liu had also come and was sitting there happily with the twenty female factory workers, a blissful expression on his face. The girls hung a string from the ceiling and tied an apple to it, then urged the newlyweds to try to bite it at the same time. When Baldy Li walked in, the girls cried in alarm, since they all knew the history of his relationship with Lin Hong and Song Gang—a relationship that was somewhat of a love triangle, yet not quite, and that no one could figure out. Everyone assumed that Baldy Li had come to pick a fight. Lin Hong also tensed up when she saw him marching in with dead-set eyes, certain that he was up to no good. Song Gang was the only one who didn't notice anything wrong; simply overjoyed to see that his brother had come, Song Gang greeted him with a cigarette and said happily, "Baldy Li, you finally made it."

Baldy Li shoved Song Gang's hand aside and said, "I don't smoke."

The girls all fell silent, petrified with fear. Baldy Li calmly handed Lin Hong the vasectomy certificate. Lin Hong, not knowing what this was, made no move to accept it but, rather, looked over at her new husband. Song Gang reached for it, but Baldy Li pushed his hand away, instead handing the certificate to one of the girls and asking her to pass it to Lin Hong. Lin Hong took this medical record but didn't understand its significance. Baldy Li instructed, "Open it and look inside. What does it say?"

Lin Hong opened it and saw the word *vasoligation*. She still didn't understand and whispered to one of the girls standing next to her, "What does *vasoligation* mean?"

While several girls were crowding forward to look at the case history, Baldy Li said to Lin Hong, "What does *vasoligation* mean? It means *castration*. I just went to the hospital to have myself castrated."

The girls cried out in surprise, and Lin Hong went pale. During that period it was common in Liu to have newly purchased roosters caponized, then cook and eat them once they were full grown. That way, they would be especially tender, and wouldn't have that distinctive rooster taste. People usually called these caponized roosters *fresh* roosters. Upon hearing that Baldy Li had gone to the hospital to have himself castrated, one of the girls asked in surprise, "Are you now a *fresh* man?"

At this point Writer Liu decided to make his presence known. He slowly stood up and took the medical record from Lin Hong. He read over it and with a scholarly tone corrected the girl, saying, "No, castration and vasoligation are two entirely different things. After castration you become a eunuch, while after vasoligation you can still . . . ."

Writer Liu glanced at the girls in the room and didn't finish his sentence. The girl persisted: "Can still what?"

Baldy Li impatiently specified, "Can still sleep with you."

The girl blushed with fury and replied through gritted teeth, "No one would want to sleep with you."

Writer Liu nodded in agreement with Baldy Li and added, "It just means that he can't have children."

Baldy Li nodded enthusiastically at Writer Liu's clarification. He took back his medical record and said to Lin Hong, "Given that I can't have children with you, I won't have any with anyone." Having said this, the unswervingly faithful Baldy Li turned and walked out of Lin Hong's new home. Once outside he paused, then turned to her and said, "Remember: Baldy Li will always get right back up from where he fell."

Then he spun around like a Spanish toreador and left. For the first seven steps he heard no sound from the newlywed house. As he took his eighth step, however, the entire house behind him burst into laughter. He hesitated a second, then shook his head in disappointment. Song Gang came running after Baldy Li, who was by now limping away. He grabbed Baldy Li by the arm and said, as if wanting to say a whole lot more, "Baldy Li . . ."

Baldy Li paid Song Gang no heed. Instead, grasping his groin, he continued limping down the street with a martyred air, with Song Gang following close behind. After a while, Baldy Li turned and said quietly, "Go on back."

Song Gang shook his head. He opened his mouth, but the only thing that came out were the words "Baldy Li . . ."

Baldy Li saw Song Gang standing there without moving and quietly urged him, "Damn it, today you are the groom. Go on back inside."

Song Gang finally found the words to say what was on his mind: "Why would you want to cut off all hope of having descendants?"

"Why?" Baldy Li repeated miserably. "Because I have become disillusioned with the mortal world."

Song Gang shook his head sadly. He watched Baldy Li walking slowly down the road. After about ten paces, Baldy Li turned around and told Song Gang sincerely, "Take good care of yourself."

Song Gang felt a stab of sorrow. He knew that from this point on the two brothers would go their separate ways. As he watched Baldy Li limp away he suddenly remembered the first time they had parted. His grandfather had held his hand at the village gate, watching as Li Lan led Baldy Li by the hand down the country road.

Liu Town's toreador walked away without turning back. On the street he encountered Little Scissors Guan. Little Guan saw that Baldy Li was limping and grasping his abdomen with his left hand, so he called out to him curiously. He asked if he had a bellyache. Baldy Li had not yet had a chance to respond when Little Guan peremptorily suggested, "Roundworms. I'm sure it's roundworms chewing up your intestines."

At that point Baldy Li was still reveling in the martyrdom of his vasectomy. With the air of one who had made a heroic sacrifice, he grasped Little Guan, held up his medical record, and asked scornfully, "What are roundworms?"

Then he opened his medical record and showed it to Little Guan, specifically pointing out the word *vasoligation* on the front. Little Guan carefully read through the record, constantly complaining about how poor the doctor's handwriting was. After he finished, he still didn't know what *vasoligation* meant, so he asked Baldy Li to explain.

Baldy Li perked up and announced proudly, "*Vasoligation*? That means *castration*."

Little Guan asked in astonishment, "You cut off your dick?"

"What do you mean by *cut off*?" Baldy Li was not pleased by Little Scissors Guan's choice of words and corrected him. "It was not cut off, it was ligated."

"That is to say," Little Guan asked, "you still have your dick?"

"Of course I do." Baldy Li stroked his crotch with his right hand and added, "It is still completely intact."

Then Baldy Li heroically said, "I originally wanted to cut it off, but then when I thought about having to squat down to pee like a woman, I felt that would be rather unbecoming and therefore decided to have it ligated instead."

Baldy Li patted Little Guan's shoulder, grasped his abdomen, and, waving his vasectomy certificate, slowly limped away. Little Guan stood there laughing uncontrollably. Then, pointing at Baldy Li, he told everyone that Baldy Li had gotten himself ligated, which is to say castrated—although, he then noted for the sake of precision, Baldy Li's dick was still intact. As Baldy Li walked farther and farther into the distance, the crowd around Little Guan kept growing. They excitedly discussed Baldy Li, agreeing that this had been a most entertaining day. What the crowd did not anticipate, however, was that a decade later Baldy Li would single-handedly account for the GDP of the entire county.

CHAPTER 38

BALDY LI'S road to GDP-dom began in Liu Town's Good
Works Factory. How could he have known that his early romantic setback was a blessing in disguise? After he had his heart broken by
Lin Hong, he went back to the factory and proceeded to produce one
profit miracle after another. This was the era when Deng Xiaoping's
reforms had just begun to affect the general economy. The more Baldy
Li thought about it, the more convinced he became that he was an
entrepreneurial genius. If he was able to strike it rich leading a motley
crew of two cripples, three idiots, four blind men, and five deaf men,
then if he were able to command fifty college graduates, forty M.A.'s,
thirty Ph.D.'s, and twenty postdoctorate fellows, wouldn't he become
as rich as an oil tanker?

As soon as Baldy Li reached this earth-shattering conclusion, he
immediately ordered his fourteen loyal minions to put down whatever
they were working on and attend the most urgent emergency meeting
in the factory's history. A moment earlier he had been on the phone
negotiating a new contract for his factory, but as soon as he hung up he
decided to resign. He proceeded to deliver an hourlong impassioned
speech in which he spent fifty-nine minutes praising his own achievements and the final minute reapproving the two cripples as the factory's director and deputy director. He concluded by sadly declaring
that they, the Good Works Factory's workers, had unanimously
accepted Director Baldy Li's letter of resignation. Baldy Li tearfully
concluded, "Thank you!"

After Baldy Li gave his thanks, he sprinted away. His fourteen loyal
minions sat there without moving. The three idiots hadn't understood a
word of what he had said, and so after Baldy Li left they remained
cheerfully oblivious. The five deaf men had just watched Baldy Li's
thick lips move up and down, and upon seeing him stop moving his lips
and abruptly leave, their first thought was that he had gone to the restroom. Therefore, they sat and waited patiently for him to return and
resume moving his lips. The two cripples looked at each other, not
knowing what was going on. Five years earlier, Baldy Li had held a sim-

ilar meeting with all of the employees, at which he abruptly dismissed the crippled director and deputy director and appointed himself factory director. This time he was dismissing himself instead and reinstating the two cripples in their former positions. The four blind men stared ahead blankly with their dark eyes. Their minds were much clearer than those of the remaining cripples, idiots, and deaf men, and therefore they were the first to fully realize that Baldy Li would not be returning. One of the blind men laughed, then the other three started laughing as well. The three idiots were jolly to begin with, but upon seeing the four blind men also getting jolly, the idiots, not willing to fall behind, broke out into loud guffaws. The five deaf men couldn't hear, but they could *see* everyone laughing and thought that Baldy Li must have made a joke as he was rushing off in search of a restroom. Therefore, the five of them also broke into guffaws—the three deaf-mutes simply miming. Finally it had dawned on the two cripples who had just been reinstated as factory director and deputy that Baldy Li had quit, but they couldn't understand why everyone was so tickled. The crippled factory director remarked that Baldy Li had always treated them very generously, and therefore he suggested that perhaps it was a bit unseemly for everyone to be so happy at his resignation. The deputy director nodded repeatedly, saying that the director was exactly right and had expressed exactly his thoughts. The four blind men chuckled and asked whether anyone was curious about why Baldy Li would want to quit when things were going so well. Obviously it was because he had been promoted to the Civil Affairs Bureau. The blind man concluded blindly, "Factory Director Li has gone on to become Bureau Director Li."

"You have a point," the two cripples responded.

Bureau Director Tao Qing and the Civil Affairs Bureau didn't learn about Baldy Li's resignation until a month later, by which point the fourteen cripples, idiots, and blind and deaf men had completed all of the work contracts Baldy Li had obtained for them. The two cripples had moved back into the director's office, dug up their old chessboard, and once again spent the entire day playing chess and cursing each other. The remaining twelve workers sat in the workshop with nothing to do. The three idiots remained jolly and oblivious, and the four blind men and five deaf men engaged in yawning competitions.

Everyone started to miss Director Li, and at the proposal of the four blind men and with the permission of the two cripples, the factory's fourteen loyal minions haphazardly made their way to the courtyard of the Civil Affairs Bureau. Once there they called out, "Bureau Director Li, we have come to see you!"

Tao Qing, who was in the middle of hosting a meeting, leaned out his window and saw the motley band standing in the courtyard, hollering. He was in the process of reading aloud an official directive issued from the Communist Party's central command, and all the commotion outside infuriated him. He threw the document down and said angrily, "This time Baldy Li has gone too far, thinking that he could move his Good Works Factory here to the Civil Affairs Bureau."

Tao Qing then waved at a section chief sitting next to him, telling him to go outside and get rid of them. The section chief became even angrier than the bureau director and furiously upbraided the crowd, "What do you think you're doing? We're in here studying a directive sent down by the Party's central command."

The two cripples—who, having been factory directors, naturally understood the importance of studying Central Party directives—were startled into silence. The four blind men couldn't see a thing, and therefore had never granted much importance to Central Party documents. When they heard the section chief's rebuke, they replied insolently, "Who are you? How dare you speak to us like this? Even Bureau Director Li would never speak to us like this."

When the section chief saw the four blind men leaning rakishly on their canes, he became even angrier, screaming, "Get out! All of you, get out of here!"

"Go in! You go back inside!" the blind men screamed back. "Go in and tell Bureau Director Li that all of the factory employees miss him and have come to see him."

"What do you mean by Bureau Director Li?" the section chief asked, perplexed. "There is no Bureau Director Li here. The bureau director's name is Tao."

"You are lying," the blind man responded.

The section chief didn't know whether to laugh or cry at this, deciding that this was truly a case of blind men speaking blindly. At this point Tao Qing emerged, his face contorted with fury. He didn't catch sight of Baldy Li but roared into the motley crowd anyway, "Baldy Li, get over here."

The four blind men didn't know who it was who had just come out, and therefore continued asking impetuously, "Who are you? How dare you address Bureau Director Li like that?"

"What do you mean, Bureau Director Li?" Tao Qing was also baffled.

"Oh, you don't even know who the bureau director is," the blind men said haughtily. "It is none other than our own former Factory Director Li, who has come to assume directorship of the Civil Affairs Bureau."

Tao Qing looked at the section chief but couldn't understand what the blind men were talking about. The section chief immediately admonished them, saying, "That's ridiculous. If Baldy Li had been appointed bureau director, then what would our Bureau Director Tao do?"

The four blind men were speechless as they suddenly remembered that the Civil Affairs Bureau already had a director. One of the blind men, however, remained unconvinced, and suggested, "Perhaps Bureau Director Tao has been promoted to county governor?"

"That's right," the other blind men happily agreed.

Tao Qing was initially furious, but upon hearing the blind men promote him to county governor, he couldn't help but break into laughter like the three idiots. Only then did it dawn on him that Baldy Li was not in the crowd. Spotting the two cripples hiding behind the five deaf men, he pointed at them and said, "You two, come over here."

The two cripples realized that things were not looking good and that the whole business about Baldy Li having been promoted to bureau director must have been a fanciful fabrication on the part of the blind men. They hesitantly came out from behind the five deaf men, one limping in one direction and the other limping in the other, until they finally found themselves standing in front of Tao Qing.

It was then that Tao Qing finally got to the bottom of things, learning that Baldy Li had abruptly resigned a month earlier and that there had been no news from him since. Baldy Li had not discussed the situation at all with his workers but, rather, had simply announced that everyone accepted his letter of resignation. Upon learning this, Tao Qing turned pale and his lips started trembling with fury. He sputtered, "Baldy Li has no respect for organization, for discipline, for authority, or for the masses." Tao Qing was so worked up that, for the first time in more than a decade, he started cursing, "That son of a bitch turtle spawn!"

Tao Qing ordered the two cripples to take the workers back to the Good Works Factory. Upon returning to the meeting room, Tao no longer had any interest in studying the Central Party document and instead turned the discussion to Baldy Li's serious mistakes. He suggested that Baldy Li be permanently expelled from the People's Government system. The People's Ministry unanimously agreed with Bureau Director Tao's suggestion, and thereupon printed out an official document to notify the county government of their decision. After affixing his seal, Tao Qing read through it one last time, and said, "In dealing with an obstinately insubordinate person like Baldy Li, we can't allow him to get away with a *resignation*. He can only be *fired*."

CHAPTER 39

JUST AS Baldy Li was being fired by Tao Qing, he himself was seated at Mama Su's snack shop next to the bus depot. Holding a ticket to Shanghai in one hand and a meat bun in the other, Baldy Li sat there cheerfully. As he bit into the steaming hot bun, squinting his eyes with pleasure, he proudly boasted to Mama Su that, from this point on, he would make his own fortune. Baldy Li glanced down at the ticket in his hand and saw that in about an hour he would be jumping onto the bus to Shanghai. Keeping time by the clock hanging on the snack shop wall, he solemnly counted down the seconds as if he were a rocket about to launch. He waved at Mama Su and said, "In an hour I will spread my wings like a great roc and soar away!"

Immediately after Baldy Li had sprung his resignation like a guerrilla attack, he had retreated to his home and shut his door. Then he spent half a day and half a night mapping out the trajectory Li the Great Roc would take. On the basis of his success at the Good Works Factory, he felt that his new undertaking must begin from a processing business; after he had accumulated some capital he could begin manufacturing his own products. The question was, what kind of products should he process? At first, Baldy Li wanted to enter the same cardboard box business he had pioneered at the Good Works Factory, since it was something he already knew well. After much consideration, however, he reluctantly decided that he had to give up his old business. There were his fourteen loyal minions at the factory to consider, and Baldy Li felt that he couldn't rob them of their rice bowls. Ultimately, he decided to go into the clothing business, and as long as he could secure some orders from some big Shanghai companies, his business would rise like the morning sun.

And like the morning sun, Baldy Li took a world map and strode into Blacksmith Tong's shop. At that point, Blacksmith Tong was the chairman of Liu Town's Private Entrepreneurs' Business Association. Baldy Li needed investment capital and knew that he would not be able to secure a single cent from the State, so his thoughts turned to Blacksmith Tong. During Deng Xiaoping's Reform and Opening Up Campaign, private entrepreneurs like Blacksmith Tong had become rich. Baldy Li cheerfully strode into Blacksmith Tong's shop and immediately disarmed him by greeting him as Chairman Tong. Tong set down his hammer, wiped away his sweat, and said, "Director Li, please don't call me Chairman Tong, call me Blacksmith Tong—it sounds much more vigorous."

Baldy Li laughed out loud and replied, "Well, then, don't call me Director Li, call me Baldy Li—it sounds more vigorous, too."

Baldy Li then informed Tong that he was no longer a factory director, since he had quit. He stood next to Blacksmith Tong's furnace and, with spittle flying everywhere, enthusiastically told him about his business plan. He repeatedly reminded Tong that with only fourteen handicapped workers he had been able to earn tens of thousands of yuan a year. Therefore, were he able to have 140 or even 1,400 healthy workers, as well as a handful of college grads, M.A.'s, and Ph.D.'s and even some postdoctorate fellows, who could say how much money he'd be able to make? Baldy Li counted on his fingers, calculating out loud, but after half an hour he still hadn't come up with an answer. His head covered in sweat, Blacksmith Tong waited patiently and finally asked, "How much *would* you be able to make?"

"I really can't figure it out," said Baldy Li, shaking his head. He opened his eyes wide and said dreamily, "What I see before me is not dollar bills but, rather, an open expanse of ocean."

After this romantic rhapsody, Baldy Li immediately became pragmatic again and added, "At any rate, I wouldn't have to worry about food or clothing or having money in my wallet."

Then he reached out to Blacksmith Tong like a highway bandit and said, "Hand over your money, and I'll give you one share for each one hundred yuan. For each share you buy, I'll give you one portion of the eventual profits."

Blacksmith Tong flushed as red as his furnace, his enthusiasm stoked by Baldy Li's promises. After wiping his hand on the front of his shirt, he held up three fingers and said, "I'll take thirty shares."

"Thirty shares will cost three thousand yuan!" Baldy exclaimed in surprise, then added enviously, "You really are rich!"

Blacksmith Tong laughed and said casually, "I can afford three thousand yuan."

Baldy Li then opened up his world map and told Blacksmith Tong that he would begin by adding the final processing for a Shanghai clothing company; then, when the time was right, he would start his clothing line. It would be called Baldy Brand, and he planned to make it the global leader. Baldy Li pointed at the world map and said, "Each of the dots on the map corresponds to a specialty store that will sell Baldy Brand clothing."

Noticing a problem, Blacksmith Tong asked anxiously, "They are all Baldy Brand? There won't be any other brands?"

"No," Baldy Li replied bluntly. "What would I want with other brands?"

Blacksmith Tong said unhappily, "If I am going to invest three thousand yuan, I should at least get my own brand."

"You have a point," Baldy Li conceded. "We'll also give you your own Blacksmith Brand."

Baldy Li then pointed to his khaki Mao tunic and said, "This jacket is one of my Baldy Brands, and I would never let it go. I will embroider the Baldy Brand logo on the lapel. You, however, can select from among the pants, shirt, undershirt, or underwear."

Blacksmith Tong felt that Baldy Li's request was reasonable and therefore agreed to pick from the remaining articles of clothing. He didn't give the undershirt or underwear a second glance but hesitated between the pants and the shirt. He liked the shirt, and particularly the thought of his logo embroidered on the front; but then it occurred to him that the shirt would be worn under a jacket, so the only thing showing would be part of the collar. Worried that with the shirt he would not have enough exposure, he instead chose the pants for his signature Blacksmith Brand. Blacksmith Tong pointed to the world map and asked, "Everywhere there are dots, there will also be Blacksmith Brand clothes?"

"Of course." Baldy Li patted his chest. "Everywhere my Baldy Brand is sold, there will also be your Blacksmith Brand."

Blacksmith Tong happily lifted his index finger and said, "I will add another ten shares, or one thousand yuan, for my Blacksmith Brand."

Baldy Li had not expected that Blacksmith Tong would plop down four thousand yuan and therefore was laughing heartily as he left Tong's shop. Blacksmith Tong was one of the leaders within Liu's independent business community, and the strength of his example was incalculable. When word spread that Blacksmith Tong had invested four thousand yuan, combined with Baldy Li's impressive achievements at the Good Works Factory, many other business owners were soon lining up in front of Baldy Li's world map to purchase shares.

After leaving Blacksmith Tong's shop, Baldy Li next visited Tailor Zhang, and within ten minutes they too had reached an agreement. Baldy Li agreed to give Zhang, who was completely entranced by all the dots on the world map, the brand rights to the shirts. Zhang immediately took a needle and started pointing out all of the dots in Europe, not omitting even those in the tiniest countries. When he thought of his Tailor Brand shirts becoming world famous, he became so excited that he raised his index finger and said, "I'll take ten shares."

Baldy Li grandly awarded Tailor Zhang an extra ten shares, therefore giving him twenty shares for the price of ten. Baldy Li explained that the extra ten shares were in recognition of Zhang's technical skills. Tailor Zhang would be the technical supervisor of the clothing company and would both train the workers and oversee quality control.

Having now five thousand yuan in start-up capital, Baldy Li then proceeded on to Little Scissors Guan in his blade-sharpening shop and to Yanker Yu under his oilcloth umbrella. Old Scissors Guan had been ill for the past few years and had not worked for quite a while. Little Guan, therefore, had begun to take over the blade-sharpening shop, becoming, as he put it, its commander without troops. Baldy Li gave Little Guan rights to the undershirts, and Little Guan was very satisfied with his Scissors Brand undershirts, saying that its two straps did in fact look like a pair of scissors. Little Guan took ten shares for one thousand yuan.

Baldy Li next went to Yanker Yu's territory. Yanker Yu was the same as before, with an enormous oilcloth umbrella stretched open at the end of the street, under which he had arranged a table with a row of dental tools and an array of dozens of extracted teeth. When he had patients, he would sit on the stool, but when he didn't, he would lie back in his rattan recliner. He had already repaired this recliner more than a dozen times, and the different shades of rattan patches made it look like a map of Liu Town. Yanker Yu had watched as the Revolution faded from a surge to a trickle, and now couldn't even tell where the trickle was headed. He knew that the Revolution, like everything else, was old and retired, and he was convinced that it would never return during his lifetime. He felt that those dozen or so good teeth he had extracted by mistake were no longer revolutionary treasures and instead might even become a dozen stains on his career. Therefore, one dark and stormy night, he snuck out of the house and furtively tossed them into the sewer.

Yanker Yu was now more than fifty years old, and upon hearing Baldy Li's plans, he sat up excitedly from his recliner, took the world map Baldy Li was holding, and studied it intently. Then he pronounced, "I, Yanker Yu, despite having already lived out more than half my life, have never yet crossed the county line. Instead of exotic scenery, all I have seen is the insides of people's mouths. Therefore, I'm counting on you to succeed, and once I become rich along with you, I'll be damned if I continue pulling teeth, or even so much as look into another open mouth. I want to travel to scenic sights around the world and visit all the locations marked on the map with these dots."

"This is truly a soaring ambition!" said Baldy Li, giving Yanker Yu an enthusiastic thumbs-up.

Yu, however, was not finished. Looking disparagingly at the dentistry implements on the table, he announced, "I'm going to throw these all away."

"Don't do that," Baldy Li said. "You should take them with you when you travel to see the scenery at these points on the map. That way, if you get the urge, you can extract a few white people's and black people's teeth while you are there. Having already pulled so many Chinese teeth, once you become rich, you can switch to pulling foreigners' teeth."

"You have a point," Yanker Yu conceded, eyes sparkling. "I've been pulling teeth for thirty years now, but all of those have belonged to our compatriots. I haven't even had a chance to pull a single Shanghainese tooth, much less a foreign one. I want to pull teeth from people from every point on this map."

"Yes!" Baldy Li shouted in agreement. "While other people aspire to read ten thousand books and walk ten thousand *li*, you aspire to walk ten thousand *li* and pull ten thousand teeth."

Next they had to address the question of Yu's brand. Yu was very dissatisfied with the prospect of having brand-name underwear, which was the only kind of clothing left. He cursed Baldy Li to his face: "Fuck you, you gave the pants, shirt, and undershirt away to others, and now you want to give me the underwear. This just shows that you have no respect for me."

"I swear," Baldy Li said passionately, "I have the greatest respect for you. I simply followed this road to your place, and how can I help it if you happen to live at the end of the street? If your shop had been at the head of the street, you would have had your pick."

Yanker Yu wouldn't let Baldy Li off the hook so easily and said, "I have been squatting here at the end of this street for longer than you have been alive. Even when you were a little ragamuffin, you would come by several times a day. But now your wings have grown, so you don't come by anymore. Why didn't you come find me earlier? Your fucking teeth don't hurt, so . . ."

"You're right about that," Baldy Li admitted. "This is what is known as remembering the well-diggers when you want to drink water, and remembering Yanker Yu when you have a toothache. If my tooth were to hurt, you'd definitely be the first person I'd come see."

After Yanker Yu expressed his dissatisfaction with the underwear, he also complained about the notion of a Yanker Brand, saying that it "sounded bad."

"In that case, how about if we call it Tooth Brand Underwear?" Baldy Li suggested.

"That also sounds bad," Yanker Yu said.

"How about Ivories Brand?" Baldy Li asked.

Yanker Yu considered for a moment and agreed. "Ivories Brand would do. I'll take ten shares for one thousand yuan. If you also give me the undershirt brand to go with it, I'll buy twenty shares."

Baldy Li raised his victory flag. After having spent the morning wagging his jaw, he had succeeded in raising seven thousand yuan in start-up capital. He didn't realize, however, that Popsicle Wang had been following him closely all along. Popsicle Wang, who during the Cultural Revolution had announced his intention of inventing a revolutionary popsicle that would never melt, was also now in his fifties. When Baldy Li unfurled his world map at the blacksmith shop, Popsicle Wang happened to be walking by and overheard Baldy Li's extravagant claims. Popsicle Wang was flabbergasted to see Blacksmith Tong hand over four thousand yuan. Wang then continued to tail Baldy Li and observed as Tailor Zhang, Little Scissors Guan, and Yanker Yu together invested another three thousand yuan. Seeing all this, Popsicle Wang became as restless as an ant on a hot frying pan and decided that this was an opportunity he simply couldn't afford to pass up. As Baldy Li was strolling contentedly down the street, Wang grabbed him from behind, held up five fingers, and said, "I'll take five shares."

Baldy Li had never imagined that Popsicle Wang would be able to pull together five hundred yuan. Even he himself, the famous Factory Director Li, could not have come up with five hundred yuan even if he pooled all of his assets. He looked at Popsicle Wang, grinning there in his tattered clothing, and cursed, "Fuck! You private entrepreneurs have all the money, and we cadres are left with nothing."

Popsicle Wang nodded and bowed. "Now you are also a private entrepreneur. You will soon be as rich as an oil geyser."

"Not an oil geyser," Baldy Li corrected him. "I'll be as rich as a ten-thousand-ton oil tanker."

"Yes, yes," Popsicle Wang said in a flattering tone. "Therefore, I will follow closely behind you."

Baldy Li looked at Popsicle Wang holding up his five fingers and shook his head sadly. "I'm sorry, I don't have any brands left to give you. I gave Yanker Yu the last brand, for the underwear."

"I don't want my own brand." Popsicle Wang waved his five fingers back and forth. "All I want is shares."

"That won't do." Baldy Li shook his head emphatically. "I have always done things in a fair and just manner, and it wouldn't be acceptable if Blacksmith Tong, Tailor Zhang, Scissors Guan, and Yanker Yu all had their own brands and you didn't."

Baldy Li lifted his head, stuck out his chest, and walked away. Already having seven thousand yuan in venture capital, he wasn't interested in Popsicle Wang's additional five hundred yuan. Wang trailed pathetically behind him, still holding up his five fingers as if his hand were a prosthetic. He continued beseeching Baldy Li, suggesting that in his oil tanker there could be some of Popsicle Wang's oil as well. Wang lamented his own troubles, explaining that, selling popsicles, he could earn money only during the summer, and therefore during the remaining three seasons he had to rely on odd jobs. Now that he was getting older, it had become harder for him to find these jobs. When he started speaking about the future, Wang's eyes welled up with tears. His entire life savings amounted to only five hundred yuan, and he wanted to invest it all in Baldy Li's glorious new enterprise, thereby earning himself a comfortable future.

At this point Baldy Li suddenly thought of something. He paused, slapped his bald head, and shouted, "There are also socks."

Popsicle Wang at first didn't respond. Baldy Li pointed at the fingers Wang was holding up and said, "Put those fingers away. I have decided to accept your five hundred yuan. I'll give you the brand for the socks, which we'll call Popsicle Brand."

Popsicle Wang was delighted. He wiped his hand repeatedly on his chest, saying, "Thank you, thank you. . . ."

"Don't thank me," Baldy Li said. "Thank your forebears."

"Who were my forebears?" Popsicle Wang had no idea what Baldy Li was referring to.

"You don't know about your forebears? You truly are a confused bastard." Baldy Li tapped Popsicle Wang's shoulder with his map. "Your forebears are whoever the people were who invented socks. Just think, if no one had invented socks, there would be no Popsicle Brand socks, I wouldn't be able to accept your money, and consequently there would be none of your oil in my tanker."

"Oh." Popsicle Wang finally understood. Holding his hands together, he intoned, "Many thanks to my forebears."

Once Baldy Li had raised his 7,500 yuan in start-up capital, he began canvassing all the empty buildings in Liu, ultimately selecting a former warehouse to serve as his factory. This was the same warehouse where Song Fanping had been locked up, and where the long-haired middle-school student's father had driven a nail into his own skull. The warehouse had been empty for many years. After renting it, Baldy Li immediately brought in thirty sewing machines. He then proceeded to hire thirty country girls and asked Tailor Zhang to provide them with technical training. Tailor Zhang said that the warehouse was far too big—that it could hold up to two hundred sewing machines. Baldy Li held up three fingers and said, "Within three months I will have brought over so much clothing from Shanghai for finishing that even two hundred sewing machines working twenty-four hours a day won't be able to keep up."

Baldy Li spent a month making all the arrangements. He decided to go to Shanghai; everything was now ready, and all he needed was the actual products. After purchasing the sewing machines, he handed over the remaining start-up capital to Tailor Zhang and told him to use it to pay the rent for the warehouse and the salaries of the thirty country girls. Most important, he asked Zhang to train the country girls in a single week, explaining that within a week the first shipment of clothing would arrive from Shanghai. Baldy Li further explained that he wouldn't return for a while, because he would be running around

Shanghai like a mad dog, his goal being to bring all of Shanghai's clothing business back to Liu. He asked Tailor Zhang to watch for telegrams, saying that every time he secured new business, he would notify Zhang by telegram. Finally, he firmly gripped Zhang's hand and said, "I will now hand everything over to you while I go to Shanghai to secure the final ingredient."

Thus, Baldy Li ended up at Mama Su's snack shop waiting for the bus. He had no idea that Tao Qing had already expelled him from the People's Government system. He had his entire savings of four hundred yuan in his shirt pocket, and this would have to suffice for room, board, and other expenses for his trip to Shanghai. Nevertheless, he was confident that before he had a chance to spend the four hundred yuan, all of Liu would be humming with the sound of his sewing machines. The first time Baldy Li had gone to Shanghai on behalf of the Good Works Factory, he had also sat at Mama Su's snack shop while waiting for the bus. That time he was carrying with him the group portrait of the Good Works Factory workers; this time all he had was his world map. While eating his meat bun, he showed Mama Su the map, and now it was her turn to be startled by the dots that had previously sent Blacksmith Tong and the others into such paroxysms of excitement.

Mama Su had heard about Baldy Li's grand ambitions and knew that Blacksmith Tong, Tailor Zhang, Scissors Guan, Yanker Yu, and Popsicle Wang had all joined his dreams of world conquest. She initially felt that she would believe it when she saw it, but after hearing Baldy Li bragging extravagantly while eating his meat bun, she became even more excited than Popsicle Wang and couldn't wait to join in as well. Baldy Li shook his head and wouldn't allow her to invest. "There are no brands left," he said. "The jacket is my own Baldy Brand, the pants are Blacksmith Brand, the shirt is Tailor Brand, the undershirt is Scissors Brand, the underwear is Ivories Brand, and I almost forgot about the socks, which have now become Popsicle Brand."

Mama Su said that she didn't want a brand, but Baldy Li insisted that it wouldn't do for her not to have one. The two argued back and forth until finally Baldy Li noticed her ample chest and exclaimed, "How could I forget that you are a woman? There is also a bra."

Baldy Li looked down at his half-eaten bun and added, "Your brand can be called Meat Bun Bra. If you purchase fifteen shares, then, together with the ten shares I gave Tailor Zhang for his expertise, we will have precisely one hundred shares."

Mama Su was so pleased that she didn't care that Meat Bun Bra sounded a bit vulgar. She said delightedly, "I just went to the temple a couple of days ago to burn incense, and it was thanks to that that today I had the good fortune of running into Baldy Li."

As soon as she said this Mama Su became very impatient to return home to get her savings. Baldy Li said there wasn't enough time, because he was about to get on the bus, so he would just make a mental note of her fifteen shares. Mama Su, however, was worried that by the time Baldy Li returned triumphant from Shanghai, he would no longer recognize her shares. Therefore, she insisted, "It is not enough to make a mental note. We should record this in writing."

Mama Su immediately walked out the door, asking Baldy Li to wait until she returned with the money. Baldy Li hollered for her to come back, then said, "I could wait for you, but the bus won't wait for me."

Seeing that it was almost time, he picked up his bag, rolled up his map, and walked out of Mama Su's shop. Mama Su followed him all the way to the door of the depot waiting room. Seeing him standing in line to have his ticket checked, she yelled, "Baldy Li, when you return, you can't forget your promise. I watched you grow up."

Baldy Li suddenly remembered his childhood, including how Song Fanping was beaten to death right in front of the station, how he and Song Gang had cried abjectly, how it was Mama Su who lent them her cart, and how it was she who asked for Tao Qing to haul Song Fanping's corpse home. Baldy Li looked at her and said, "I remember all that happened when I was young. Song Gang and I waited here for our mother to return from Shanghai. Nobody even noticed us, but you gave us some stuffed buns to eat and arranged for us to go home."

Baldy Li's eyes grew red. He wiped them as he walked to the ticket counter, then turned around and said, "I won't forget my promise, don't you worry."

CHAPTER 40

BALDY LI spread his wings and soared to Shanghai, and Black-smith Tong, Tailor Zhang, Scissors Guan, Yanker Yu, and Popsicle Wang all craned their necks to watch him go. Each night when the five of them went to bed, all they could see when they shut their eyes was those dots on the world map, shimmering like stars in the night sky. Popsicle Wang also dreamed of that ten-thousand-ton oil tanker riding the ocean waves. For Mama Su, the dots were a compulsory course that she would review in her head before going to bed. However, she still felt somewhat ill at ease, given that her fifteen shares had not been formally recorded in the ledger. After Baldy Li left, she took the buns she had just removed from the steamer and proceeded to visit Tong, Zhang, Guan, Yu, and Wang, telling them each in detail about her fifteen shares. As the saying goes, the best way to win people's hearts is through their stomachs, and so Tong, Zhang, Guan, Yu, and Wang all nodded complacently to her story as they sat there eating her steamed buns. Mama Su finally felt slightly more at ease, thinking that even if Baldy Li were to go back on his word, these five men who had wiped the juice from her meat buns off their lips could serve as her witnesses.

After Baldy Li left, Blacksmith Tong's shop served as the partners' regular meeting place, and as soon as night fell Zhang, Guan, Yu, and Wang congregated there. Mama Su's snack shop was way over at the bus depot, so she was always the last to arrive, usually not until the moon was high in the night sky. The six of them would sit together laughing, praising Baldy Li profusely and recounting his successes at the Good Works Factory. The stories became increasingly exaggerated, and the partners' expectations for their new business also grew exponentially. Blacksmith Tong observed that the business world was currently dominated by Cantonese, and regardless of whether one was Cantonese, it was still necessary to speak the dialect. He added, "I'm sure that by the time Baldy Li returns, he will be speaking with a strong Cantonese accent, like a Hong Kong businessman."

Then they heard Tailor Zhang's work report. In order to train the thirty country girls, Zhang had temporarily closed his tailor shop. He said that the girls had all brought their own bedding, and fortunately it was now March and the warehouse was quite big, so they could bunk down on the floor. They slept in three rows, like female soldiers. Tailor Zhang said that, of the thirty girls, some were clever and others were slow. The clever ones could master the sewing techniques in only three days, while the slower ones needed from ten days to two weeks. Blacksmith Tong said that ten to fifteen days was much too slow, because Baldy Li would be bringing them a lot of business in less than a week. What would they do if, when the time came, they were not able to handle things?

Tong, Zhang, Guan, Yu, Wang, and Su discussed matters, and meanwhile one week after another passed with no news from Baldy Li. Gradually the partners grew more reserved in their comments and began to reaccess the situation. Popsicle Wang was the first to speculate, "Could Baldy Li have run away?"

"That's crazy," Tailor Zhang immediately retorted. "When he departed, he left me all of his money. What would he run away with?"

Blacksmith Tong nodded and said, "In business, some things proceed quickly and others take more time."

"That's right," Yanker Yu added. "Sometimes I can extract ten teeth in a single day, while other times I might go several days without extracting a single tooth."

"Sharpening scissors is the same way," Little Scissors Guan said. "Sometimes I am unbelievably busy, and other times I have so much time on my hands I could die of boredom."

Two more weeks went by, yet there still wasn't any news from Baldy Li. The six partners continued meeting every evening in the blacksmith's shop, though now the last one to arrive was no longer Mama Su but Tailor Zhang. Every afternoon he would go to the post office, full of hope, and ask if Baldy Li had sent any telegrams from Shanghai. The clerk in charge of receiving telegrams would always see Tailor Zhang poking his head in with an ingratiating smile on his face half an hour before he was scheduled to get off work. The clerk would wave, and before he even had a chance to say a word, Tailor Zhang's face would immediately grow dark as he realized that there was no telegram. By the time the clerk had opened his mouth, Zhang would already be halfway out the door. A depressed Tailor Zhang would still linger outside the post office as one by one the workers got off work, and would ask the person locking up to please send any telegram arriving that night from Baldy Li to Blacksmith Tong's shop. Zhang would then hurry home, catatonically eat his dinner, and gloomily proceed to Tong's shop.

The six partners would then sit gazing at the stars and waiting for Baldy Li's telegram to arrive. They continued waiting like this for a month and five days. The partners had been left like a pitch-black night sky, without a single star or a glimmer of moonlight—completely in the dark and with no idea of what to do next. They sat in the blacksmith shop watching each other. At first they were very talkative, but eventually they simply sat there silently, each thinking about his own affairs. Little Guan couldn't help but complain. "Shanghai seems to have swallowed Baldy Li up like a dog swallowing a meat bun, eh?"

At their last gathering, when Popsicle Wang had wondered out loud whether Baldy Li had run off, his speculation had roused the ire of the others. But this time everyone seemed to be in accord with Little Guan's complaints. Yanker Yu was the first to agree with Little Guan: "That's right. After I extract a tooth, regardless of whether it is good or bad, it always bleeds. Baldy Li went to Shanghai, and regardless of whether he found any business there or not, at the very least we should have had some news by now."

"As I said from the very beginning," Popsicle Wang added, "is it not possible that Baldy Li simply ran away?"

"It just doesn't make sense for him to have run away," Tailor Zhang said, sighing. "But I really can't explain how it is that there has been absolutely no news from him."

Mama Su suddenly thought of another possibility and speculated nervously, "What if he had an accident?"

"What sort of accident?" Little Guan asked.

Mama Su looked at her five partners, hesitated a moment, and said, "I don't know whether I should say it out loud or not."

"Say it!" Yanker Yu said anxiously. "What is it that you shouldn't say?"

Mama Su stammered, "Shanghai is a big place, packed with cars. Perhaps Baldy Li was run over? Maybe he is stuck in the hospital?"

The other partners abruptly fell silent and became quite concerned by Mama Su's scenario, realizing that they couldn't rule out the possibility that Baldy Li might have been run over by a car. They all prayed for him to be protected by the gods and not be run over; or, even if he were hit by a car, that it be just a scrape, and please not to let him be severely injured, and especially not to let him be hit so hard that he'd become permanently crippled, idiotic, blind, or deaf.

Finally Tailor Zhang spoke up. He reported that this month's rent had been paid, and the thirty country girls had been given their wages. Combined with the money spent on the thirty sewing machines, there was only four thousand yuan left over. Tailor Zhang summed up anxiously, "This money represents our own sweat and blood."

Zhang's comment made everyone's heart tremble. Mama Su also became very nervous, but when she remembered that she had not yet added her money to the pot, she felt a little better. Everyone then looked to Blacksmith Tong—the chairman of the Private Entrepreneurs' Business Association, and also the largest investor in their venture—and waited for him to suggest what their next step should be. Tong hadn't said a word all evening, but with everyone looking to him, he had no choice. He sighed and said, "Let's wait a few more days."

A telegram from Baldy Li finally arrived two days later. He didn't send the telegram to Tailor Zhang but, rather, to Mama Su. The telegram consisted of only two sentences, stating that Baldy Li had decided that Mama Su's Meat Bun Brand bras didn't sound very sophisticated, and therefore he wanted to change them to Dim Sum Brand bras.

With Baldy Li's telegram in hand, Mama Su jogged the entire way to Blacksmith Tong's shop. The shop, which had been quiet for a long time, suddenly erupted in excitement. The partners immediately recovered their initial optimism and began excitedly discussing their new prospects. They speculated that it must have taken Baldy Li so long to write them because he had found so much business in Shanghai that he couldn't even find the time to write. They alternated between complimenting and cursing Baldy Li, between saying that he was a complete asshole and insisting that he was intentionally scaring them to death.

Then Popsicle Wang noticed a problem with the telegram, and his flushed face went pale. Waving the telegram around, he said, "This doesn't say anything about business."

"That's true." Little Guan also went pale. "It doesn't mention anything about business."

The other four quickly took the telegram and read through it again, then looked at one another. Tailor Zhang was the first to say something on Baldy Li's behalf: "If he is suggesting that Mama Su change the name of her brand, he must already have scored a few business deals."

"Tailor Zhang is right." Blacksmith Tong pointed at the bench on which they were sitting. "I know Baldy Li. When he was a little runt, he would come here every day and engage in sexual relations with this long bench. That little asshole is not like other people, and everything he does he wants to do to excess—"

"Blacksmith Tong is right," said Yanker Yu, interrupting him. "This little asshole has a bigger appetite than anyone I know. That time he came to borrow my recliner, he also wanted to borrow my oilcloth umbrella and almost borrowed my table as well. As a result, in a single day he transformed my magnificent dental stall into a naked sparrow."

"Yanker Yu is correct," added Little Guan, recalling incidents involving Baldy Li. "This little bastard could do business from an early age, using Lin Hong's bottom to cheat me out of a bowl of house-special noodles. As he ate happily I was left drooling."

"You are right," Popsicle Wang chimed in. "That little bastard's ambitions are sky-high. Other people are content with becoming as rich as an oil well, while he wants to be as rich as a ten-thousand-ton oil tanker."

Seeing the five of them so confident, Mama Su began to worry anew about her fifteen shares, saying, "When Baldy Li brings a whole bunch of business back here, what will I do if he doesn't recognize my shares? You all have to serve as my witnesses!"

"Don't worry." Blacksmith Tong pointed to the telegram in Tailor Zhang's hands. "This telegram is your evidence, and as such is much more compelling than anything the five of us could say."

Mama Su immediately grabbed the telegram from Tailor Zhang and, cradling it to her chest like an infant, said happily, "Fortunately, I went to the temple to burn some incense, whereupon Baldy Li sent this telegram. Now he won't be able to ignore my fifteen shares. Burning incense is truly effective!"

After Baldy Li sent his enigmatic telegram, this document became like the Communist sun rising in the East, instantly liberating his six partners from the shackles of darkness and despair. Their excitement sustained them for another half a month, but there was no more news from Baldy Li. The partners yearned through the day, yearned through the night, yearned every hour, every minute, and, in the end, every second. But still there was no trace of Baldy Li. He had vanished in Shanghai like a stone in the ocean. From that point on, no more of his telegrams arrived in Liu.

Their hopes dashed once again, the six partners returned to passing their days and nights in extreme anxiety. Two months had now gone by. Tailor Zhang paid the second month's rent for the warehouse and gave the country girls their second month's salary. Then, with a trembling voice, he said, "Only two thousand yuan remains of our sweat-and-blood money."

Everyone shuddered, Mama Su with them, until she again remembered that she hadn't contributed any money to the pot, and once again she felt at ease. At this point, the partners experienced a definite crisis of confidence in Baldy Li. It was Yanker Yu who first expressed his dissatisfaction: "Who does this bastard think he is? Are we doing business together? Or are we playing hide-and-seek?"

"You're right," Tailor Zhang agreed. "Even if a pin falls to the ground, it still makes a sound. It's not right for Baldy Li to disappear like this without giving us any notice."

"Don't even mention a pin," Little Guan added angrily. "Even a fart will make a sound."

Popsicle Wang added, "That little bastard is not worth a fart."

Blacksmith Tong was pale with fury but still didn't say anything. Everyone else looked at him reproachfully. Tong understood what they were thinking as if they had said it aloud: *If he hadn't invested those first four thousand yuan, our own money would have stayed in our pockets.* Blacksmith Tong, however, was stewing indignantly: *They say that the power of example is infinite, but being the one to set an example just makes you the scapegoat.*

The six partners fell silent, then Tailor Zhang continued in a quavering voice, "In another month, there won't be enough money to pay the rental fees and salaries." His voice was cold and flat, and after he finished speaking, he gazed at Tong in a cold and flat manner. Blacksmith Tong felt that the others were also staring him in the eye— except Yanker Yu, who was staring straight at his mouth, as if counting the good teeth.

Blacksmith Tong sighed deeply and said, "How about this: Let's first let the thirty country girls go. When we need them, we can always call them back."

The other partners didn't answer but, rather, continued staring coldly at Blacksmith Tong. He knew that they were thinking about the rental fees for the warehouse, and that none of them was willing to continue throwing his remaining money into it. Blacksmith Tong shook his head, then nodded and said, "How about this: Let's first cancel the rental on the warehouse, and if Baldy Li does return with new business, we can always rent it again."

Some of the partners began nodding, and Tailor Zhang raised a question: "What about the thirty sewing machines?"

Blacksmith Tong pondered for a moment, then suggested, "Let's divide the sewing machines based on how much each of us contributed and take them home."

Tailor Zhang personally sent the thirty country girls home, personally canceled the warehouse rental, and personally divided up the thirty sewing machines based on the amount each partner had invested. Mama Su hadn't contributed any money, so she of course didn't receive a sewing machine. With all of these funereal affairs now taken care of, the partners continued meeting every evening in Blacksmith Tong's shop, only now they sat as mute as six ghosts, and by nightfall the shop was as silent as a grave.

Another month went by, and still there was no news from Baldy Li. Mama Su was the first to stop attending the nightly meetings, and Tailor Zhang, Little Guan, and Yanker Yu soon followed her. In the end it was only Popsicle Wang, who had invested the least amount of money, who still duly reported at the blacksmith's shop every evening. He would sit there in front of the downcast Blacksmith Tong, sighing, wiping away his tears, and pathetically asking, "Has our sweat-and-blood money been lost like this?"

"There's nothing we can do," Blacksmith Tong replied with a hollow look in his eyes. "When it comes time to sever one's flesh, one has no alternative but to slice it off."

CHAPTER 41

JUST WHEN the partners had all but lost hope, Baldy Li reappeared, completely covered in dust from his travels. By this point, he had been gone from our Liu Town for three months and eleven days. He walked into Liu Town's bus depot one evening, still wearing the same clothes and still carrying his bag in one hand and the world map in the other. He walked right into Mama Su's snack shop and sat down. She initially didn't recognize him, because when he left he had a shiny bald head but now he had long hair and a full beard. He pounded the table and shouted, "Mama Su, I'm back!"

Mama Su jumped in surprise. Pointing at Baldy Li's long hair, she asked, "What in the world is this?"

"I've been unbelievably busy," Baldy Li replied, shaking his head. "I was so busy in Shanghai that I didn't even have time to shave my head."

Mama Su clasped both hands to her chest and looked over at her daughter, who was standing there with an astonished look. Carefully, she inquired, "And how did that go?"

"I'm starving," Baldy Li barked at Mama Su. "Quick, fix me five steamed meat buns."

Mama Su quickly told her daughter to bring Baldy Li some buns. He grabbed one and stuffed it into his mouth, saying, "Go tell Blacksmith Tong and the others to meet at the warehouse. I'll be there as soon as I finish my buns."

Baldy Li's demeanor convinced Mama Su that he had secured a lot of business. Therefore, she nodded, and left. After she had walked twenty yards or so, she suddenly remembered that that they had canceled the rental of the warehouse, so she hurried back and, standing in the doorway, said uncertainly, "Do you mean hold a meeting at Blacksmith Tong's place?"

Since Baldy Li's mouth was stuffed at that moment, he had no choice but to nod affirmatively. Mama Su then dashed off toward the town's western alley as if she had received an imperial mandate. When she reached Tailor Zhang's shop entrance, she shouted, "Baldy Li has returned!"

Mama Su called out for Zhang, Guan, and Yu to come over. When Blacksmith Tong heard her, he also came running out. Tong, Zhang, Guan, and Yu then stood in the doorway of the blacksmith's shop, listening as Mama Su breathlessly told them about how Baldy Li had suddenly walked through the door of her snack shop, how he had pounded the table and shouted. When they finished hearing her account, Blacksmith Tong was silent for a moment, then said with a smile, "Mission accomplished."

"Just think," Blacksmith Tong added. "If Baldy Li hadn't been successful, would he be so bold as to have summoned us to a meeting? No, he would have hidden his face."

Tailor Zhang, Little Scissors Guan, and Yanker Yu nodded enthusiastically and happily cursed him, "That little bastard, that little bastard, that little bastard. . . ."

Blacksmith Tong asked Mama Su with a smile, "Does that little bastard now speak with a strong Cantonese accent, like a Hong Kong businessman?"

Mama Su thought carefully, then shook her head. "He still speaks with a distinct Liu Town accent."

Blacksmith Tong was skeptical. He prompted, "At the very least he must speak a few words of Shanghainese?"

"No Shanghainese either," Mama Su said.

"That little bastard certainly doesn't forget his roots," praised Blacksmith Tong.

Mama Su nodded and said, "His hair is very long now, like a rock star."

"I get it," Blacksmith Tong exclaimed, rather pleased with his powers of deduction. "That little bastard certainly has high aspirations. He has no interest in being merely a Hong Kong businessman but, rather, is modeling himself on a foreign businessman. Just think, Marx and Engels were both foreigners, and they both had long hair and full beards."

"That's right," Mama Su agreed. "He does have a full beard now."

Mama Su had shifted into high gear by this point. She wiped the sweat from her brow and said that she had to go notify Popsicle Wang. Little Scissors Guan said that he had just seen Wang walk out of the western alley carrying a soy sauce bottle. Mama Su immediately set off toward the western alley, in the direction of the town's soy sauce store.

Blacksmith Tong, Tailor Zhang, Little Guan, and Yanker Yu, their faces flushed bright red, sat down in the blacksmith shop and started laughing hysterically like four lunatics. They danced around crazily, bumping into walls. Blacksmith Tong was the first to calm down, then he gestured for Zhang, Guan, and Yu to sit on the bench. He told them that Baldy Li didn't yet know that they had stopped paying rent on the warehouse, that they had divided up the thirty sewing machines, or that they had sent the thirty country girls home. He said that when Baldy Li learned this, he might very well explode and curse them. "When Baldy Li curses people, his mouth is like a machine gun. Whatever you do, be sure to remain calm and don't lose your temper. Let him curse and then wait for his anger to subside. Then we'll explain our predicament to him."

"Blacksmith Tong is right." Tailor Zhang said to Little Scissors Guan and Yanker Yu, "You two be sure to remain calm."

"Don't worry," Little Guan said. "Even if he curses the shit out of my father, I still won't get angry."

"Yes," Yanker Yu agreed. "As long as Baldy Li brings us a lot of business, I won't object if he curses my family back eighteen generations."

Blacksmith Tong was reassured by their promises. He looked around his shop and remarked on how he didn't have a proper chair in the entire place. With Baldy Li returning victorious, they should at least find him a good chair to sit in. Yanker Yu immediately got up and brought over his rattan recliner. Tailor Zhang and Little Guan shook their heads at this tattered thing and declared that it was simply too shabby for words. Blacksmith Tong shook his head as well. Yanker Yu was irked by their reaction and defended his precious chair: "It may look shabby, but it is actually very comfortable."

At that moment Mama Su and Popsicle Wang hurried in, and Mama Su reported that she had seen Baldy Li strutting over in this direction. Blacksmith Tong quickly lay down on Yanker Yu's recliner to see how it felt and agreed with Yu: "It'll do."

When Baldy Li, now long-haired and bearded like a foreign businessman, sauntered into the blacksmith shop and saw his six partners standing there respectfully with pleased expressions, he laughed out loud. "Long time no see!"

When Blacksmith Tong saw the dust-covered Baldy Li, he invited him to sit in the recliner, saying, "You have finally returned. You must be very tired."

The others echoed, "You must be very tired."

"Not at all," Baldy Li said with a wave. "You can't complain when you're doing business."

Blacksmith Tong and the others chuckled and nodded enthusiastically. Baldy Li didn't take the chair but, rather, parked himself on the long bench, then placed his bag and the map on the bench beside him. Tong and the others insisted that Baldy Li sit on Yanker Yu's recliner, but Baldy Li shook his head. He winked at Blacksmith Tong and said, "I'll sit right here. It's a long story, but this bench and I go way back."

Blacksmith Tong laughed and said to the others, "As I was saying, Baldy Li is not one to forget his roots."

Seeing that his six partners were still standing, Baldy Li gestured for them to sit down. They all shook their heads, insisting that they were perfectly happy as they were. Baldy Li nodded and allowed them to continue standing. He crossed his legs, leaned against the wall, and, looking as if he were settling in to receive a work report, said, "I've been gone for more than three months. What kind of progress have you made over here while I was away?"

The six partners stared at each other, speechless, then everyone turned to Blacksmith Tong. Tong hesitated a moment, then stepped forward as if he were about to scale a mountain of swords. He coughed a couple of times, cleared his throat, and slowly began to speak. He described in detail everything that had transpired since Baldy Li left and concluded by saying, "There really was nothing else we could have done. We hope you'll understand."

After he finished listening to Tong's account, Baldy Li lowered his head. The partners watched him nervously, quite certain that as soon as he raised his head again he would begin cursing them. When he did finally look up, however, he surprised them all by saying graciously, "While there is life, there is hope."

The six partners let out six deep sighs of relief, after which they started to laugh. Blacksmith Tong promised Baldy Li, "It would only take us a day to rent the warehouse again and move the sewing machines back in. In two more days, we could call the thirty country girls back."

Baldy Li nodded and then said, "No hurry."

What did he mean by "No hurry"? The partners stared at him dumbfounded as Baldy Li sat there comfortably on the bench with his legs crossed. At this crucial moment, Zhang, Guan, Yu, Wang, and Su once again looked, out of habit, at Blacksmith Tong, waiting for him to speak. Tong again stepped forward and inquired delicately, "You have been gone for more than three months. So what kind of progress did you make over in Shanghai?"

"Shanghai is a big place." Baldy Li immediately became very excited upon hearing the word *Shanghai.* "Opportunities to earn money are as plentiful as the hairs on a pig, and even saliva can be exchanged for gold."

Tailor Zhang cautiously corrected him, suggesting, "Don't you mean as plentiful as the hairs on a cow?"

"Somewhat less than the hairs on a cow," Baldy Li replied, trying to be as precise as possible. "But a pig has about the right number of hairs."

Seeing Baldy Li suddenly so animated, the six partners glanced at one another and flashed reassured grins. Baldy Li continued passionately, "Shanghai is a huge place, and if you walk a few steps in any direction, you will find a bank with a long line of customers depositing or withdrawing money, the ATM whirring away. The department stores are all several stories high, and climbing up and down in them is like scaling a mountain. Inside, everyone is packed in like at a movie theater, and we won't even mention how crowded the streets are. All day long, they are so crowded that people don't seem like people anymore, more like damn ants moving in anthills."

Baldy Li went on and on about what a big place Shanghai was, his spittle flying everywhere, including all over Blacksmith Tong's face. Tong wiped his face and noticed that the other partners were laughing along, not realizing that Baldy Li had completely digressed from the question at hand. Tong had no choice but to interrupt and carefully remind him, "You were going to tell us how your discussions with Shanghai's clothing companies went—"

"I had lots of discussions," Baldy Li interrupted, not waiting for Blacksmith Tong to finish his question. He proudly counted on his fingers: "I spoke with twenty clothing companies, of which three were foreign companies."

Little Guan exclaimed in surprise, "So that's why you look like Marx and Engels."

"What about Marx and Engels?" Baldy Li had no idea what Guan was talking about.

Tailor Zhang explained, "With your long hair and beard, we figured you must have been speaking with foreign businessmen and therefore had begun to look like a foreigner."

"What do you mean, 'look like a foreigner'?" Baldy Li still didn't understand.

Blacksmith Tong saw that he was about to digress again, and immediately jumped in: "We were discussing your business negotiations. How did they go?"

"They went well," Baldy Li answered. "And not just business. I also reached an agreement with them on the question of the brand names—"

Mama Su shouted, "And that's why you sent me that telegram, saying that you wanted to change Meat Bun Brand to Dim Sum Brand?"

Baldy Li racked his brains as if trying to remember. Suddenly, eyes gleaming, he said, "Yes, yes, that's right."

Mama Su shot the others a triumphant glance, and they nodded. Blacksmith Tong realized that Baldy Li was about to digress again and quickly prompted, "Of the twenty companies you spoke to, how many did you reach an agreement with?"

Baldy Li sighed, and the sound of that sigh was like a bucket of cold water dumped over the heads of his partners. Their newfound excitement fell from their faces. Baldy Li gazed at each of them in turn, held up five fingers, and said, "Five years ago I went to Shanghai to drum up business for the Good Works Factory, and all I had to do was take out the family portraits of the handicapped workers, combined with my earnest attitude, and I could move every employee of every company, thereby raising an enormous amount of business for the factory. Five years later I took my world map and again went to Shanghai to drum up business, only this time for myself. This time I was even more sincere, even more earnest, and even more mature than before, but . . ." Baldy Li retracted his five fingers and mimed the act of counting cash. "Now we live in a different era. Society has changed, and it is necessary to offer large bribes in order to get business. I had never expected that these evil winds would have swept over the country so quickly." Baldy Li's fingers stopped counting his imaginary money. Instead he held up his fingers again and sighed. "In just five years' time, those winds have blown over our entire country."

His six partners stared at him in shock. Blacksmith Tong nervously followed up, "So did you offer bribes?"

"No." Baldy Li shook his head. "By the time I finally figured out this principle of offering bribes, I only had enough money in my pocket to buy a one-way bus ticket back to Liu."

"So that means," Blacksmith Tong deduced with a quavering voice, "that you didn't secure a single business deal?"

Baldy Li answered definitively: "Nope. Not a one."

As if struck by lightning, the six partners reeled from the impact of Baldy Li's answer. They stood staring at one another in stunned silence. Tailor Zhang was the first to recover and, trembling all over, he asked Baldy Li, "So our blood-and-sweat money has been lost, just like that?"

Blacksmith Tong was also shaken to the core. He glanced over at Tailor Zhang but couldn't make out whether he was nodding or shaking his head.

Popsicle Wang began to sob. "That was the money that was going to save my life!"

Mama Su also began to sob, but when she remembered that she hadn't contributed any money in the first place, she immediately stopped. Little Guan and Yanker Yu were completely bathed in cold sweat as they stared at Baldy Li in alarm, stammering, "You, you, how could you have lost our money?"

"You can't say that the money was lost," Baldy Li answered. Looking at their stricken faces, he said resolutely, *"Failure is the mother of success,* and if you can help me raise money for another hundred shares, I'll go back to Shanghai and give everyone bribes and promise that I'll bring you back a lot of business."

Popsicle Wang was still sobbing. He rubbed his eyes and said to Blacksmith Tong, "Well, I don't have a single cent left."

Blacksmith Tong looked at the disconsolate Yanker Yu and Scissors Guan, then at Tailor Zhang, who was trembling from head to toe. Finally, he shook his head, let out a deep sigh, and said, "How do you expect us to have any more money?"

"You don't have any more money?" Baldy Li looked very disappointed. He waved his hand, saying, "Then there is nothing I can do. We must accept this loss, and my own four hundred yuan is also lost."

When Baldy Li was finished, he couldn't help but giggle at the look of shock and distress on the faces of his business partners. Popsicle Wang pointed at him and asked Blacksmith Tong, "How dare he laugh at a time like this?"

"In life you'll win some and lose some, and you've got to take it like a man," Baldy Li lectured his partners. "The six of you are sitting there so depressed, like war captives. Can't you even handle this sort of minor setback?"

"Fuck you!" Blacksmith Tong roared. "You're the one who is like a war captive."

Blacksmith Tong raised his right hand and pounded Baldy Li's face as if he were hammering iron. With one blow he knocked Baldy Li off the bench, then roared, "I put up four thousand yuan!"

Baldy Li jumped up, holding his face, and said angrily, "What do you think you're doing?"

He sat back down on the bench and again crossed his legs, looking as if he was prepared to talk things over with Blacksmith Tong. Tailor Zhang, Scissors Guan, and Yanker Yu all cried out, "A thousand yuan!" and immediately launched themselves on Baldy Li, kicking him until he jumped onto the bench. He squatted there and shouted, "What do you think you're doing?" Zhang, Guan, and Yu had also accidentally kicked one another and were now crying out in pain. Popsicle Wang was the last to join in and, with the air of a martyr, launched himself toward Baldy Li as if he had been fired from the muzzle of a gun. Crying out "Five hundred yuan!" and swooping in like a kamikaze pilot making his last dive, he grabbed Baldy Li's shoulders and bit down hard, as if he were trying to bite off a five-hundred-yuan hunk of flesh. Screaming like a slaughtered pig, Baldy Li jumped down off the bench and shook himself violently until he was finally able to dislodge Popsicle Wang from his back. Seeing that things were not going well, Baldy Li took his travel bag and world map and ran out of the blacksmith shop. Standing outside the door, where he felt that he was now safely distanced from peril, he pointed angrily at people inside and shouted, "What are you doing? What are you doing? Even if business doesn't go well, we still have our principles. We should sit down and discuss things rationally."

Baldy Li had planned to continue arguing with them, but seeing Blacksmith Tong come out waving his hammer, he changed his mind and hastily added, "But let's not discuss this anymore today."

Recognizing that this was probably a good time to retreat, Baldy Li turned and sprinted away. Blacksmith Tong chased him with his hammer all the way to the end of the alley before finally stopping. He then hollered after Baldy Li as he scurried away, "You fucking listen to me.

The next time I see you, I'll beat you up, and every descendant of mine will beat up every one of yours!"

After uttering this heroic threat and heading back, Blacksmith Tong remembered his lost four thousand yuan and wilted like crops hit by a sudden frost. With a drooping head he returned to his shop. At the thought of how their money had been squandered, tears began to well up in the other partners' eyes. Spotting Blacksmith Tong walking back with his hammer, Popsicle Wang began to wail and Tailor Zhang sobbed, "So all of our blood-and-sweat money has been lost, just like that?"

Upon hearing this, Little Guan and Yanker Yu also burst into tears. Blacksmith Tong threw his hammer down next to the stove and sat down on Yanker Yu's recliner, pounding his head with his fist. Pretending that his head was actually Baldy Li's, he pummeled himself with all his strength. "I'm a son of a bitch!" Blacksmith Tong cursed himself. "How could I have trusted that son of a bitch, Baldy Li?"

Little Guan and Yanker Yu also started pounding their own heads and cursing themselves, "We sons of bitches . . ."

Mama Su was the only one who hadn't lost money, and seeing her former partners beating and cursing themselves, she started to cry. She wiped away her tears as she murmured, "Fortunately, I went to the temple to burn incense. . . ."

After Blacksmith Tong had nearly beat himself unconscious, he gritted his teeth and swore, "If I don't beat that bastard Baldy Li until he is completely incapacitated, then I don't deserve to be considered a man."

Upon hearing Blacksmith Tong's oath, Popsicle Wang wiped away his tears. With a look of steely determination, as if he were a heroic martyr off to assassinate the tyrant king, he raised his fist and swore, "I will make sure to beat him until he can't even move."

Little Guan and Yanker Yu also took oaths. Little Scissors Guan swore that he would snip off Baldy Li's dick, his nose and ears, and his fingers and toes. Yanker Yu swore that he would yank out every tooth in Baldy Li's mouth and extract every bone in his body. Still, they all remained choked with fury, so they continued to swear, and to slice and extract, until in their imagination Baldy Li was nothing but a human stump.

Tailor Zhang was more cultured than the others, but even he started swearing like a drunken sailor, vowing that he would cut off Baldy Li's

head. In order to prove that this wasn't an idle boast, he revealed that
he had a Japanese sword hidden under his bed, and although it was a
bit rusty, he would need just a couple of hours with Little Guan's whet-
stone and he could have it like new—sharp enough to lop off Baldy Li's
head with a single stroke.

Mama Su heard their oaths and blanched with fear. Upon hearing
that Tailor Zhang planned to slice off Baldy Li's head, she took him at
his word. But glancing at his thin and refined arm, she couldn't help
but worry. "Baldy Li's neck is as thick as an ordinary person's thigh. Are
you sure that you can slice through it?"

Tailor Zhang stared at her in surprise. Upon further reflection he
decided that he wasn't sure that he could and replied, "I wouldn't necessarily cut off his head."

"If you don't cut off his head," Little Guan yelled, "you should at
least slice off his balls."

Tailor Zhang, however, shook his head, saying, "I'm not capable of
such a dirty trick."

CHAPTER 42

TONG, ZHANG, GUAN, YU, AND WANG were all true to their word, and from that point on, every time they ran into Baldy Li in the street, they would pummel him mercilessly. Just as a writer is known by his distinctive turns of phrase, a boxer is defined by the turn of his fist. Each of them, therefore, pounded Baldy Li in his own distinctive way. Blacksmith Tong, for instance, would raise his hammerlike fist and slam it into Baldy Li's face with such force that Baldy Li would stagger backward. Tong would then swagger away, staring straight ahead, never hitting Baldy Li a second time. Thus Blacksmith Tong could be said to have a single-strike style. Meanwhile, whenever Tailor Zhang encountered Baldy Li, he would scream at him in a disappointed tone, "You, you, you!"—but by the time his fist reached Baldy Li's face, it had become merely a finger poking at it like a sewing machine needle. Thus Tailor Zhang could be said to have finger-poking style.

Yanker Yu, though, approached the task like a professional. He would always aim his tooth-yanking hand straight at Baldy Li's teeth, pounding them until Baldy Li's mouth was full of blood and Yu's fingers were covered with teeth marks. Yanker Yu would hold his hand as though he had just burned it, yelping fiercely but thinking that at least he had left Baldy Li rummaging on the ground for his missing teeth. The next time he saw Baldy Li, though, he would still have the same mouthful of pearly white teeth. Crying out in amazement, Yanker Yu would make Baldy Li open his mouth wide and would then stick his hand inside and count carefully, confirming that, in fact, there was not a single tooth missing. Therefore, every time Yanker Yu pummeled Baldy Li, he would cry out, "What excellent teeth!"

Little Scissors Guan, meanwhile, had a down-and-dirty street-fighting style. The first time they ran into each other, he kicked Baldy Li's feet with such force that Baldy Li doubled over, thereby exposing his crotch, whereupon Little Guan then kicked him hard in the balls. Baldy Li collapsed in pain, grasping his groin with both hands and rolling on the ground in agony. Afterward, whenever they met, Baldy

Li would immediately hold his legs together and protect his crotch with both hands. Little Guan repeatedly kicked Baldy Li's shins and then his thighs until he himself was covered in sweat, but still he couldn't get the man to open his legs. Little Guan would become increasingly frantic and, while kicking Baldy Li, would cry out, "Spread 'em, damn it. Spread 'em!"

Baldy Li would shake his head and, pointing at his precious treasures, say, "They have already been ligated. Why don't you have pity on them and let them be?"

Popsicle Wang's style was along the lines of using a blunt knife to saw flesh. Every time he encountered Baldy Li, he would burst into tears as if his parents had just died. He would then grab Baldy Li by the collar and pummel him again and again until Baldy Li knelt to the ground holding his head in his hands. Popsicle Wang then would place his left hand on Baldy Li's shoulder to support himself and pummel him with his other fist. He would continue in this manner for more than an hour, including a twenty-minute break in between to catch his breath. While resting, Popsicle Wang would wipe away his tears and say plaintively to the crowd, "Five hundred yuan!"

The five creditors beat Baldy Li from early spring straight through midsummer, until he looked like a wounded soldier returning from battle. Every time he appeared on the streets of Liu, Baldy Li would either have a swollen face or else be limping and cradling an injured arm. By this point Baldy Li's clothes were completely in tatters, his hair longer than Marx's, and he had a beard shaggier than Engels's. No one knew what had happened to the awe-inspiring Baldy Li of the past or why he had been replaced by this beggarlike figure. After his hair had grown down to his shoulders, the town's two Men of Talent gave him foreign rock-star nicknames. Writer Liu called him Beatle Li, and Poet Zhao called him Michael Jackson Li. The people of Liu, however, didn't get the point of these names. Having heard only of the Chinese pop star Teresa Teng, they had no idea who the hell the Beatles and Michael Jackson were. When they tried to find out from Writer Liu and Poet Zhao, the Men of Talent haughtily turned and walked away. Liu and Zhao were displeased with the general ignorance of the townspeople, and in walking away, they sought to rise unsullied from the muck. The townspeople therefore had no alternative but to ask Baldy Li himself. Although he had no idea who these rock stars were either, he enthusiastically responded to the crowd's questions with a shake of his head: "Dunno—they're foreigners."

Of the five boxing styles adopted by his five creditors, Baldy Li was most terrified of Little Scissors Guan's down-and-dirty style. Although Blacksmith Tong's punch was solid, accurate, and fierce, it was still a one-shot affair. And once Yanker Yu discovered how strongly rooted Baldy Li's teeth were, he began to punch with less and less force. Baldy Li grew most accustomed to Tailor Zhang's elegant and refined poking, with Popsicle Wang's blunt-knife style running a close second. Although Popsicle Wang would rain punches down on him nonstop, he was not very strong, and therefore the thick-skinned Baldy Li was not afraid of him. So the last thing he expected was that, as spring turned to summer, the most fearsome of the five would turn out to be Popsicle Wang. When summer came, Wang started hauling around his popsicle case on his back and holding a wooden cane in his hand. As he walked the streets hawking his popsicles, he would strike the case with his cane, and upon seeing Baldy Li, he would proceed to strike him with the cane as well. This traditional weapon caused Baldy Li unspeakable pain, and when it came down on his long-haired head, he would almost pass out. Once Baldy Li had been reduced to squatting with his head in his hands, Wang would simply sit on his popsicle case and continue pounding Baldy Li's head with his cane, all the while sighing repeatedly over the five hundred yuan he had lost and continuing to hawk his popsicles. In order to protect his head, Baldy Li had no choice but to sacrifice his hands. As a result, they became red and swollen, having been pounded by Popsicle Wang's stick until they looked like braised pig's feet. He would nevertheless continue protecting his head, reasoning that it was more valuable, since he would still have to rely on it to do business.

As Mama Su watched Popsicle Wang pounding Baldy Li with his stick, she finally couldn't take it any longer. She went up and grabbed Wang's hand, admonishing him, "If you act like this, you will eventually get your retribution."

Popsicle Wang stopped but cried pathetically, "My five hundred yuan!"

Mama Su said, "Regardless of how much money it was, you won't get it back by beating him."

When Wang walked off with his popsicle case on his back, Mama Su looked down at Baldy Li, who was kneeling on the ground cradling his head in his hands. She couldn't help but nag him a little, "You know that they will beat you, so why do you keep walking around through the streets every day? Couldn't you just hide out at home?"

Baldy Li first looked up to ascertain that Popsicle Wang had left, then slowly lowered his hands from his head. He stood up and replied, "I get bored to death if I hide out at home." With this, he shook his long hair and walked away as though nothing had happened.

Mama Su shook her head and, sighing, said, "It's a good thing I went to the temple to burn incense and as a result didn't lose any money. Otherwise, I too would want to beat you."

Mama Su let out another sigh and, as Baldy Li walked away, exclaimed, "Burning incense is certainly effective!"

Poet Zhao watched Baldy Li repeatedly get beat up and noticed that he never fought back. At first Zhao was not sure what to make of this, but as he watched the five creditors beat Baldy Li to a pulp from spring straight through to summer, and how even the weakling Popsicle Wang could beat him to his heart's content for an hour, he felt a surge of courage. Remembering how Baldy Li had boasted that he would beat him until his true laborer's colors showed and completely discredit him in front of the entire town, Zhao thought to himself, *If I don't avenge that humiliation, how can I even consider myself a man?* He decided the time was right to avenge his loss of face.

That day, when Popsicle Wang finished beating Baldy Li and was walking away with his popsicle chest on his back, Poet Zhao happened to walk up. He aimed a few tentative kicks at Baldy Li, who was still lying on the ground holding his head. Noticing several onlookers walking back and forth, Zhao said loudly, "I thought this day would never come! Baldy Li has become Michael Jackson Li and has been beaten so badly that he doesn't even dare fight back."

Baldy Li lifted his head and shot Poet Zhao a look, as if he couldn't trouble himself to respond. Zhao took this to mean that Baldy Li was scared of him and therefore kicked him again and pronounced arrogantly, "Didn't you say that you wanted to beat me up? Why haven't I seen you do anything yet?"

Baldy Li slowly stood up, and Poet Zhao, now daring to go even further, gave him a shove. Zhao looked out at the passersby and crowed to Baldy Li, "Just try to move!"

Poet Zhao had just turned back from glancing at the passersby when he found himself face-to-face with Baldy Li's fists. Baldy Li used his swollen left hand to lift Poet Zhao by the collar and his swollen right hand to pound Zhao's face. Before Poet Zhao even knew what was happening, Baldy Li had pounded his face to a pulp. Poet Zhao groaned, realizing that Baldy Li was still as ferocious as ever. He immediately knelt to the ground, but Baldy Li continued to rain punches down on him, intoning, "They beat me, but I don't fight back because I was the one who lost their money. However, I didn't lose your money, and therefore I'd be happy to beat you to death."

Although Poet Zhao was being beaten senseless, he heard Baldy Li's speech clearly and finally understood why he had not fought back before. Realizing that he was in serious trouble, he immediately let out his loud laborer grunts and moans, but Baldy Li continued beating him. Therefore, Poet Zhao had no choice but to say, between grunts and moans,

"They're out, they're out."

"What's out?"

Poet Zhao saw that Baldy Li had paused and therefore quickly grunted twice more, then grasped Baldy Li's hand and pleaded, "You hear my laborer grunts and moans? You've beaten them out of me."

Baldy Li laughed and said, "I hear them, but that's still not enough."

He lifted his right fist, scaring Poet Zhao so much that he sputtered out a few more grunts and moans and then added pathetically, "Congratulations, congratulations. . . ."

Baldy Li asked, "Congratulations for what?"

"Congratulations for beating my laborer identity back to the surface."

With Poet Zhao speaking this abjectly, Baldy Li couldn't bring himself to strike him again. He lowered his fist and loosened his grip on Zhao's collar. Then he laughed as he patted Poet Zhao's shoulder and said, "Don't mention it."

With that, Baldy Li—after having been beaten to a pulp by his former partners for three straight months—finally reemerged on Liu's streets with his former swagger. The townspeople grinned as they watched Poet Zhao slink away, then noticed that Writer Liu was also standing in the crowd. Squinting, the onlookers watched Liu with one eye, and Baldy Li resting and panting on the ground with the other. Everyone remembered how Baldy Li had once beaten up Writer Liu, and the nostalgically minded among them hoped history would repeat itself. Everyone watched Writer Liu intently as they discussed Baldy Li: He had lost weight and been beaten black and blue by his five creditors, so no one had expected that he would be able to beat up the healthy Poet Zhao as easily as an eagle grabbing a chick. Everyone looked at Writer Liu and concluded, "It is certainly true that *a starving camel is still bigger than a well-fed horse.*"

Liu understood the implication of what they were saying and recognized that they desired nothing more than to see him follow in Poet Zhao's footsteps. Flushing bright red, he considered turning around and leaving, but he knew that if he did, he would become fodder for everyone's after-dinner jokes. Determined to save face, Writer Liu had no choice but to stand there resolutely. The onlookers tried to egg Baldy Li on, but he merely sat with his back against a wutong tree, his stomach growling in hunger. He was in the process of swallowing his own saliva to assuage his hunger and seemed deaf to everyone's taunts. The onlookers then attempted to rile him, asking how Men of Letters could be so cowardly. They said that Poet Zhao's earlier obsequious expression made him worse than a traitor, and that he had not only lost face but had even caused his parents to lose face.

"He not only caused his parents to lose face," one of the onlookers added. "He even lost face on behalf of Writer Liu."

"That's right," the onlookers agreed.

Writer Liu's face became mottled with fury. He knew that these little bastards were simply trying to incite a fight, and cautioned himself that he must not, under any circumstances, act rashly and open himself up for another beating from Baldy Li. But with everyone staring at him, he felt it was necessary to come forward and say a few words. Therefore, he rose to the occasion, stepping forward and loudly agreeing with everyone, "Yes, Poet Zhao has lost face on behalf of all the Men of Letters in the world."

With this declaration, Writer Liu lived up to the title of one of Liu Town's Men of Talent. In a single sentence he evoked all writers and poets from the past and present, in China and abroad, to serve as his human shields. Seeing everyone standing there dumbfounded, Liu realized that with one stroke he had succeeded in turning the tables in his favor. Now that he'd gotten started, he was so proud that he couldn't stop: "Even Lu Xun has lost face with this, as well Li Bai and Du Fu, not to mention Qu Yuan. Mr. Qu drowned himself on account of his love for his country, but still Poet Zhao caused him to lose face by association. There are also foreign writers, such as Tolstoy and Shakespeare, and even Dante and Homer, who have now lost face on account of Poet Zhao!"

The onlookers burst into laughter, and even Baldy Li joined in. He appreciated Writer Liu's comments and said happily, "I didn't realize that I had made so many famous people lose face."

At this point Song Gang rode by on his shiny Eternity bicycle. He saw that the crowds had completely blocked off the street, so he repeatedly rang his bell. Song Gang was in a hurry to get to the knitting factory to pick up Lin Hong. When Baldy Li heard the sound of the bicycle bell, he knew that it was Song Gang. Supporting himself with the wutong tree, he stood up and called out, "Song Gang, Song Gang, I haven't eaten anything all day."

CHAPTER 43

IT HAD BEEN more than a year since Song Gang and Lin Hong's wedding, and their Eternity bicycle had been flashing through the streets of Liu for two years. Song Gang carefully wiped his bicycle down every day until it gleamed like the morning after a cleansing rain. Every day Lin Hong rode behind him, hugging his waist with both arms and pressing her cheek into his back, looking as serene as if she were pressing her head into a soft pillow. Their Eternity bicycle would not stop for wind or rain, and as the clear sound of the bell rang through the town, the town elders all remarked that the couple was indeed a match made in heaven.

Lin Hong was delighted to hear of Baldy Li's misfortunes. Before, whenever she heard his name, she would immediately become mortified, but now she would simply laugh and say, "I always knew that he would eventually come to this. That kind of person . . ." Lin Hong wouldn't continue—Baldy Li was a well-known hooligan, and if she said too much she might invite his fury to rain down on her.

One time Lin Hong turned around and asked Song Gang, "Don't you agree?"

Song Gang was silent. He was so troubled by Baldy Li's misfortunes that he lost all desire to eat or sleep. Displeased by Song Gang's silence, Lin Hong nudged him, "Say something!"

Song Gang had no choice but to nod but muttered, "When he was still a factory director, he was doing okay."

"Factory director?" Lin Hong said disparagingly. "How can you be considered a factory director if all you direct is something like the Good Works Factory?"

Song Gang looked at his beautiful wife and smiled gratefully at his own happiness. Lin Hong asked, "Why are you smiling?"

Song Gang replied, "I'm smiling at my own good fortune."

Though Song Gang was basking in connubial bliss, the thought of Baldy Li continued to haunt him like a shadow, and Song Gang felt as though a heavy stone were weighing down his heart. He secretly blamed Baldy Li for giving up his perfectly good job as factory director in order to try to start a business of his own, as a result of which he had lost every cent, now owed a fortune to his creditors, and furthermore had been beaten to a pulp.

One night Song Gang dreamed of Li Lan. At first, he dreamed of her holding his and Baldy Li's hands as they walked along the streets of Liu; then he dreamed of the scene immediately preceding her death, when she grasped his hand and made him promise to take good care of Baldy Li. In his dream, Song Gang began to cry miserably, and that woke up Lin Hong. She roused him and asked anxiously what was wrong. Song Gang shook his head. He pondered his dream, then told her that he had dreamed of Li Lan. Song Gang hesitated a moment, then told Lin Hong about the heartrending conclusion of the dream, when Li Lan grasped his hand and asked him to take good care of Baldy Li. Song Gang had promised her that even if he had just a single bowl of rice left he would give it to Baldy Li, and if he had just one last piece of clothing, he would also give it to Baldy Li. Lin Hong yawned and interrupted him, saying, "She wasn't even your mother."

Taken aback, Song Gang was about to respond when he heard her steady breathing and realized that she had fallen back to sleep; he therefore swallowed his retort. Lin Hong did not know much about Song Gang and Baldy Li's childhood and didn't appreciate how much their shared history meant to Song Gang. She simply knew that Song Gang was her husband and that he would embrace her every night when they went to bed, allowing her to rest peacefully.

Once they were married, Lin Hong took charge of the household finances. She felt that Song Gang, being so tall, probably got hungry faster than other people; therefore, she put twenty cents and two grain coupons in his pocket, saying that this was money to nourish his body, and if he was hungry he should go to an eatery and buy something. Lin Hong would conscientiously inspect his pocket every evening, and if had spent the money and grain coupons, she would replace them. For a long time, however, every time Lin Hong checked his pocket, she would find the same money and grain coupons. One day she finally became angry and asked him why he didn't spend the money.

"I wasn't hungry," Song Gang replied with a smile. "Ever since we got married, I haven't been hungry."

Lin Hong also smiled, but that night when she lay in bed, she tenderly stroked his chest and asked him to tell her honestly why he didn't spend the money. Song Gang hugged her and offered a variety of explanations. He said that Lin Hong was always so economical and could never bear to spend two cents when one cent would suffice. Nevertheless, she always gave Song Gang the best morsels of food, and whenever she went to the store, she would always think of what Song Gang needed and never buy anything for herself. To tell the truth, Song Gang couldn't help adding, he often felt hungry, but he could never bring himself to spend the money or grain coupons in his pocket.

Lin Hong said that since Song Gang's body belonged to her, he should take good care of himself for her sake. She therefore made him promise that when he was hungry, he would buy himself something to eat. Song Gang was dumbstruck by this, and all he could do was nod in response. Then Lin Hong fell asleep, as peaceful as an infant, with her breath gently blowing on his neck. For a long time Song Gang was unable to sleep and lay there embracing Lin Hong with his left arm and stroking her body with his right. Lin Hong's body was warm and smooth, like a flame.

Lin Hong continued checking Song Gang's pockets every day to see if he had spent his money or grain coupons, and she continued to shake her head and ask reproachfully why he still hadn't spent the money. Song Gang no longer tried to claim he wasn't hungry but, rather, replied honestly, "I couldn't bring myself to."

Periodically Lin Hong would remind him, "You promised."

Song Gang, however, would always stubbornly reply, "I just couldn't."

Once when he said this, he happened to be taking Lin Hong to work on his bicycle. She was sitting behind him with her arms around his waist and her cheek pressed against his back. She said, "Why don't you just consider it money spent on me, okay?"

Song Gang still insisted, "I couldn't," and rang his bell. As it turned out, Song Gang actually didn't have any money in his pocket at that point. The last time he dropped Lin Hong off at the knitting factory and was on his way to the metal factory, he had run into a famished Baldy Li, who was gnawing on some sugarcane stalks he had picked up from the ground. During that period Baldy Li was so poor that he never knew where his next meal would come from, and though he was often limping and his elbows were out of joint, he still sauntered about as if he owned the town. He savored the discarded sugarcane stalks as though he were eating the best banquet food. When he saw Song Gang riding his way, he turned away, pretending he didn't recognize him. Song Gang's heart ached when he caught sight of Baldy Li's bedraggled state. He stopped in front of Baldy Li, took the money and the grain coupons out of his pocket, and called out, "Baldy Li!"

Baldy Li turned around while still chewing on the sugarcane. He looked about and asked, "Who's calling me?"

"It's me," Song Gang replied, handing Baldy Li the money and coupons. "Go buy yourself a steamed bun."

Baldy Li originally intended to keep up his act, but when he saw Song Gang hand him the money and the grain coupons, he immediately grinned and took them, saying warmly, "Song Gang, I knew that you wouldn't abandon me. Do you know why?" Baldy Li then answered his own question. "It's because we are brothers. Even if it were the end of the world, we would still be brothers."

After this, every time Baldy Li saw Song Gang ride by on his bike, he would call him over and accept the money and grain coupons Song Gang was carrying in his pocket. He did so with such an air of entitlement that it seemed as if it were actually his own money and was merely stored in Song Gang's pocket for safekeeping.

CHAPTER 44

THE DAY Baldy Li beat up Poet Zhao and also scared the stuffing out of Writer Liu, he rested under a wutong tree listening to everyone discuss what had just happened. As he gulped down his saliva to quell the rumblings in his stomach, he heard the ringing of the Eternity bicycle bell. Baldy Li knew that Song Gang was on his way over, so he immediately stood up and called out, "Song Gang, Song Gang. I haven't eaten anything all day."

When Song Gang heard Baldy Li's cries, he immediately stopped ringing his bell and pedaled over. Weaving through the crowd, he came up to Baldy Li and shook his head at his bedraggled appearance. He started to get down off his bike, but Baldy Li stopped him and said, "No need to get down, just give me some money."

Song Gang remained on his bike and pulled out two ten-cent bills from his pocket. Baldy Li cockily took them, as if Song Gang owed him the money. Song Gang then reached into his pocket to get the grain coupons, but Baldy Li, knowing Song Gang was on his way to pick up Lin Hong, waved him away as if he were brushing away a gnat and said, "Go on, leave."

Song Gang retrieved the grain coupons from his pocket and handed them to Baldy Li. Baldy Li, however, shook his head, took one look at them, and said, "I don't need these."

Song Gang asked Baldy Li, "Do you have grain coupons?"

Baldy Li replied impatiently, "Go quickly. Lin Hong is waiting for you."

Song Gang nodded and put the grain coupons back in his pocket, then rode his bicycle through an opening in the crowd. As he was leaving he turned around and said, "Baldy Li, I'm off."

Baldy Li nodded and watched Song Gang speed away. He then turned to the crowd and said, "This brother of mine is as garrulous as an old woman, isn't he?"

With Song Gang's two ten-cent bills in hand, Baldy Li walked away, his long hair flying in the wind. The crowd watched as he walked toward the People's Restaurant, thinking that he would have a couple of bowls of noodles. To their surprise, however, he walked right past the restaurant and into a barbershop next door. They all gasped— *Wasn't Baldy Li absolutely famished? Did he consider a haircut as equivalent to a bowl of noodles?* Someone remarked, "Hair and noodles do have some things in common—namely, they are both long and thin."

Someone else added, "Women's hair is like noodles, while men's hair is too short and doesn't resemble noodles as much as it resembles whiskers."

Everyone laughed out loud at the thought of Baldy Li eating women's hair as though it were noodles. Writer Liu decided that the crowd was imbecilic, so he corrected them in a loud voice, saying that even if Baldy Li were starving to death, he wouldn't eat hair. He further explained that Baldy Li had gone to shave his head bald again and suggested that Baldy Li was as hungry as a character in some story by Lu Xun (he couldn't remember which one) who, rather than thinking of how to fill his belly, was instead concerned with his shining bald pate. Writer Liu couldn't resist adding, "Baldy Li is fucking incorrigible."

Just as Writer Liu had predicted, when Baldy Li emerged from the barbershop, he was once again bald. At noon the next day, the people of Liu saw the bald-headed Baldy Li strolling down the street. His head was shiny, and even his swollen face seemed to give off a rosy glow, as though he had just eaten a whole fish and a bowlful of meat. Although the famished Baldy Li still limped like an injured soldier, he nevertheless cheerfully greeted all his acquaintances. Burping with hunger and rubbing his stomach, he walked along the road as though he had eaten an entire tableful of food. Everyone asked him, "What delicacies did you eat, to keep you burping like this?"

"I didn't eat anything," Baldy Li answered, rubbing his empty belly. "I am burping air."

Baldy Li then walked to the Good Works Factory. He hadn't been there for more than seven months, and as soon as he walked into the factory yard he heard the two cripples in the director's office cursing each other and knew that they were back to playing chess. He walked into the director's office, burping loudly, and when the cripples spun around and saw him, they flung down their chess pieces and rushed forward, calling out, "Director Li, Director Li!"

The two crippled factory directors led Baldy Li to the workshop next door, where the three idiots, four blind men, and five deaf men were all snoozing or staring off into space. The cripples shouted at them, "Director Li is here!"

After having been beaten mercilessly by his former partners for three straight months, Baldy Li had returned to his former factory and the site of his former glories. His fourteen loyal minions crowded around and curiously examined the bruises on his face and his braised-pork-feet–like hands. The fourteen loyal minions continued calling out "Director Li" for ten minutes, and after their shouts started to die down, Baldy Li again began to burp. He burped three times in a row, and the two cripples looked at him enviously, saying, "Director Li, what delicious food did you have for lunch?"

"I am just burping empty air. And why is that? It is because I haven't eaten anything all day. And not only today—actually I haven't had a full meal for three months, and as a result, I have been burping empty air for three straight months."

First the two cripples gasped in astonishment, followed by the four blind men. The five deaf men couldn't hear what Baldy Li was saying, but upon seeing everyone else's surprised expressions they also gasped in surprise. The three idiots just kept cackling away. Baldy Li took advantage of the situation and extended his open hands, saying, "Dig into your pockets, and take out all of your money and grain coupons. Help your Director Li get a good meal."

The two cripples understood what he was saying and immediately dug into their pockets. The four blind men heard Baldy Li and did the same. The five deaf men couldn't hear what was being said, but they could see, and they realized they were expected to donate their money and grain coupons as well, so they also dug into their pockets. The three idiots, however, just stood there cackling; therefore, the two cripples went to empty the three idiots' pockets, but when they didn't find any money or grain coupons, they began to curse: "Damn it."

These loyal minions were able to come up with only a few coins and some wrinkled grain coupons, but they handed it over to Baldy Li, who lowered his head and carefully counted the pile. The grain coupons added up to precisely a pound of grain, and the coins totaled forty-eight cents. Swallowing his saliva, Baldy Li said regretfully, "If only I had twenty-six more cents, I could have two bowls of house-special noodles."

The two cripples turned their pockets inside out to show that they had handed over everything they had. They told the four blind men to turn their pockets inside out as well, then told the three idiots and five deaf men to do the same. In the end, they had no choice but to shake their heads and inform Baldy Li regretfully, "There's no more."

Baldy Li gestured magnanimously. "Even if I can't have two bowls of house-special noodles, at least I can have five bowls of plain noodles."

Then Baldy Li, surrounded by his fourteen loyal minions, left the factory and headed toward the People's Restaurant. His minions' pockets were all turned inside out, as though they had been robbed. The expressions on their faces, however, were as proud as if they had just received their paychecks. The two cripples still walked in front, followed by the three idiots holding hands, with the four blind men picking up the rear. Baldy Li and the five deaf men then divided into two groups of three and walked on either side of the procession to maintain order. Having learned from their experience when they marched on the knitting factory to help Baldy Li declare his love for Lin Hong, this time they marched in an orderly fashion, functioning as an honor guard phalanx.

They marched grandly into the People's Restaurant, where Baldy Li threw his fistful of coins onto the meal ticket counter. He had just added the wrinkled bills on top when the crippled factory director said, "Five bowls of plain noodles!"

"Nonsense," Baldy Li corrected him. "I don't want five bowls of *plain* noodles. I want one bowl of house-special noodles and one bowl of plain noodles."

The cripple asked Baldy Li, "Didn't you burp empty air for three straight months?"

Baldy Li, his bald head shining, said, "Even if I had burped empty air for three fucking years, I still wouldn't be able to eat five bowls of noodles in one sitting. The most I can eat is two; and if I am only going to have two bowls, naturally one will be house-special noodles."

The cripple understood, and in a loud voice told the waitress at the counter, "One plain and one special—two bowls altogether."

Baldy Li was very pleased with the cripple's summation of his order and complimented him, "Well put!"

Then he sat down at a round table with his fourteen loyal minions. The two cripples sat on either side of him, to show their status, and the three idiots and five deaf men took the remaining seats. They all looked around at the restaurant's decorations and then at the passersby out-side. The four blind men sitting across from Baldy Li were the calmest of all, merely holding their canes and grinning.

The waiter brought over the two bowls of noodles, but when he saw fifteen people sitting around the table, he didn't know where to place them. Baldy Li waved at him, saying, "Both are for me."

The two steaming bowls of noodles were placed in front of Baldy Li, who then pointed at them with his chopsticks and asked with a smile, "Which will I eat first? The advantage of starting with the house special is that I would eat the best one first, but then I wouldn't be able to appreciate the plain one. This strategy would be one of seeking quick profits. On the other hand, if I start with the plain one followed by the house special, I would be able to appreciate the flavor of each, and fur-thermore they would get increasingly flavorful through the meal. This latter strategy is one of long-range ambition."

Baldy Li hadn't even finished his speech when he heard his fourteen loyal minions all swallow eagerly. He could see the idiots drooling and realized that if he didn't stop talking, they were likely to pounce on his noodles, so he said loudly, "I'll fucking eat the house special one first!"

Protecting the bowl of plain noodles with his left hand, Baldy Li grabbed his chopsticks with his right. He then buried his face in the bowl of house-special noodles, sucking and slurping with great satisfac-tion. He finished the entire bowl in one gulp, and only then did he lift his head and wipe the grease from his lips and the sweat from his brow. Hearing his loyal minions all still swallowing eagerly, he promised them, "In the future, when I have money, I'll treat you to bowls of house-special noodles every day."

The fourteen loyal minions stared at Baldy Li's bowls intently, watching as he drank down every last drop of broth. Eventually, he stood up and said emotionally to his minions, "With heaven above me, the earth below, and all of you in between, I, Baldy Li, swear to heaven, earth, and to all of you: I have decided to return and continue being your Factory Director Li!"

The fourteen loyal minions stared in surprise. The four blind men were the first to respond, and began to applaud. The two cripples immediately joined them, followed by the five deaf men, although they actually had no idea what Baldy Li had just said. The three idiots, still drooling everywhere, were the last to join in. The applause continued for a full five minutes, during which time Baldy Li stood there with his head raised and his chest out, smiling happily. Then, surrounded by his loyal minions, he left the restaurant and headed straight for Tao Qing's Civil Affairs Bureau. Retaining the configuration they had when they had set off, they marched through the streets of Liu. Baldy Li rubbed his belly and burped loudly, walking contentedly next to the crippled factory director. The cripple heard Baldy Li's burp and asked with a laugh, "This time it wasn't an empty burp?"

"Not at all!" Baldy Li replied emphatically, and his tongue curled in his mouth, tasting his most recent burp. He told the crippled factory director, "It is flavored—a three-flavored, house-special burp."

Baldy Li burped the entire way there. When they were about to arrive, the taste of the burps in Baldy Li's mouth began to change. Curling up his tongue several times, he told the cripple disappointedly, "Damn it—the house-special noodles that I ate first have now disappeared."

"So soon?" the cripple asked in surprise. He turned around and looked at Baldy Li. "Are you still burping?"

"Now they are plain burps!" Baldy wiped his mouth and added, "I am beginning to digest the plain noodles I ate last."

At that point Tao Qing was in the process of chairing a meeting and was reading an official document aloud, like a monk intoning scriptures. When he heard the commotion outside, he looked out the window and saw the courtyard packed with handicapped workers from the Good Works Factory. Tao put down the document he was holding and, frowning, walked out of the conference room and toward the grinning Baldy Li. Baldy Li burped up some more plain noodles and then warmly grasped Tao Qing's hand, announcing, "Bureau Director Tao, I have returned!"

Tao Qing looked at Baldy Li's swollen face and perfunctorily shook his braised-pork–like hand, asking solemnly, "Who has returned?"

"I have." Baldy Li pointed to himself. "I have returned to be factory director!"

As soon as Baldy Li said this, the four blind men started applauding, followed by the three idiots and then the five deaf men. Only the two cripples didn't applaud; they had lifted their hands to applaud as well, but when they noticed Tao Qing's expression, they put them down and didn't dare continue.

With a stern face, Tao ordered, "Don't applaud."

The four blind men's applause immediately died down, but the three idiots were enjoying themselves so much that they didn't notice what Tao Qing had said. Seeing the blind men suddenly hesitate, two of the deaf men stopped applauding while the other three continued. Sensing that all was not well, Baldy Li turned around and raised and lowered his arms as if he were conducting a symphony, and immediately the applause stopped. Pleased, he turned to Tao Qing and said, "They have stopped applauding."

Tao Qing nodded solemnly and told Baldy Li that it had been very wrong of him to walk away from his position, and as a result the Civil Affairs Bureau had fired him. Therefore, it was not possible for him to return to his job at the factory. Looking at the fourteen handicapped factory workers all standing in an orderly fashion in the courtyard, he added, "Although the Good Works Factory is a—"

Tao Qing stopped himself and didn't utter the word *handicapped*. Instead he merely said, "The Good Works Factory is a government work unit and is not your home. It is not up to you to decide when you want to come and go."

"Well put," said Baldy Li, nodding. He then added, "The Good Works Factory is a government work unit and is not my home. However, I regard the factory as my home, and that is why I have returned!"

"That won't be possible," Tao Qing retorted. "You have not shown respect for our organizations or leaders—"

Tao hadn't yet finished speaking when one of the blind men laughed and said, "Director Li left without saying anything—that showed a lack of respect for leaders. However, Bureau Director Tao's inability to understand our needs demonstrates a lack of respect for the masses."

Baldy Li chuckled when he heard this, but noticing that Tao Qing was furious, he stopped. Tao was about to start cursing but swallowed his anger when he looked at the handicapped workers. He wanted the cripples to take everyone away, but they were hiding at the back of the crowd. Tao Qing realized he couldn't count on them, so instead he told Baldy Li, "Take everyone away."

Baldy Li immediately instructed the handicapped workers, "Let's go!"

He and his fourteen loyal minions left the courtyard of the Civil Affairs Bureau as Baldy Li explained that it was not yet the end of the workday and therefore everyone should go back to the factory. Seeing his loyal minions obediently walking away, he suddenly felt bad. He consoled them by proclaiming loudly, "My words are like flowing water and, once out, cannot be gathered back. You can be assured that I will definitely return to serve as your factory director."

When the four blind men heard Baldy Li's promise, they stopped, held their canes between their legs, and started applauding. The two cripples, three idiots, and five deaf men stopped and applauded as well. Baldy Li watched them turn around as if they were about to walk back toward him once again and thought, *These folks are even more sentimental than Song Gang.* He quickly waved at them and strode away without looking back.

Over the next several days, Baldy Li paid visits to the county's party secretary, the director of the county's Organization Bureau, as well as various other county officials—fifteen people in all—and earnestly declared his determination to return as director of the Good Works Factory. The party secretary and the county Organization Bureau director had him thrown out without even giving him a chance to finish. Then Baldy Li adopted a different tack: He latched on to the thirteen other officials and pathetically went on and on. When they heard him, they all immediately doused his hopes with an abrupt "No way," saying that the nation has its own structure, and once people leave, they can't be permitted to return. *What fucking structure?* Baldy Li asked himself. *These bastards from the county government all drink congratulatory drinks but refuse to drink forfeit shots.* He grew increasingly angry and vowed to make them all drink forfeit shots; therefore, he decided to stage a sit-in. Each morning Baldy Li planted himself in the entranceway to the county government building and remained there until everyone got off work at the end of the day, whereupon he would walk home with the county government officials.

While Baldy Li was sitting cross-legged in the middle of the entranceway, he had the expression of a solitary guard heroically trying to prevent thousands of enemies from getting through. At first none of the townspeople could figure out what he was up to, so he explained, "I am staging a sit-in."

Everyone laughed and said that he, sitting there impressively, didn't look as if he were staging a sit-in but, rather, as if he were a knight-errant in a martial arts movie, trying to avenge some wrong. Some of the townspeople suggested that he should look pitiful for his sit-in, so it would be better if he were to break an arm or a leg. If he were able to secure the sympathy of both party and people, he would surely be permitted to resume his position as the Good Works Factory director.

When Baldy Li heard their suggestions, he shook his head and said, "It wouldn't be of any use."

He gestured at the county government building behind him and said that he had already whipped out his most pathos-ridden speech for the fifteen—one more than the fourteen handicapped workers at the Good Works Factory, mind you—bastards working inside those offices. He had scraped and begged, he had flattered and repented, and in the end it didn't count for squat. So there was nothing left for him to do but to hold his sit-down strike, and he would continue sitting here until the end of time if that was what it took. When the crowds heard his bold proclamation, they shouted their support and asked him what it would take for him to end his sit-in. He held up two fingers and said that there were only two options: "One, that I be allowed to return as the director of the Good Works Factory, or two, I die sitting here."

Baldy Li, still in his tattered clothing, didn't have anything to eat or drink, and therefore he would pick up whatever odds and ends he could find, including canned goods, bottles of mineral water, newspapers, and cardboard boxes, which he then piled up in the entrance-way. The government employees on their way to work knew that Baldy Li collected scrap, so they all brought him their old newspapers, boxes, et cetera Baldy Li then made the space next to the entranceway into a recycling center. Therefore, whenever he saw someone walking by with a newspaper, he would call out and ask if he could have it when they were done. Similarly, when people walked by with drinks, he would ask for their empty bottles. Sometimes he would see people wearing old clothes and would suggest, "It is really quite a loss of face for someone of your position to be wearing such tattered clothing. How about if you take it off and give it to me?"

Baldy Li had wanted to return to the Good Works Factory but didn't succeed and instead went into the scrap business. The townspeople started calling him Scrap Collector Li. At first he collected scrap in order to feed himself, never imagining that this would make him famous; he was soon known far and wide as the Scrap King of Liu, equaling his childhood reputation as Liu's King of Butts. Whenever the townspeople had something to throw out, they would ask him to come retrieve it. While he was still staging his sit-in, about which he was exceedingly conscientious, he would tell them that he couldn't go retrieve it at that moment, but he would commit their address to memory, and he'd promise, "I'll come for it when I get off work."

CHAPTER 45

LIN HONG was completely immersed in her happiness. Her handsome husband would take her to the knitting factory every morning on his shiny and fashionable Eternity bicycle. Walking into the factory, she would repeatedly turn and see Song Gang standing next to his bicycle waving at her. When she walked out each evening, he would be waiting there for her, smiling broadly. Lin Hong didn't know that he was helping Baldy Li behind her back, and by the time she discovered it, this had been going on for a month.

The first time Lin Hong noticed that the money and grain coupons were missing from Song Gang's pocket, she smiled and, without saying anything, replaced them with another twenty cents and two more grain coupons. Standing nearby, Song Gang also didn't say anything, though her heartfelt smile made him feel very uneasy.

Lin Hong didn't realize that Baldy Li made off every day with Song Gang's money and grain coupons. Every day without fail she would refill Song Gang's pockets. At first she was delighted that he seemed to be taking better care of himself and had finally recognized that, when he was hungry, he should buy himself something to eat. Gradually, however, she began to find it strange that he had gone from not being willing to spend anything at all to always spending everything he had with him, never even coming back with any change. She figured that, no matter what he was buying himself to eat, at least there should be some change left over. She looked at him suspiciously, but he avoided her gaze. Finally she asked him directly, "What do you eat every day?"

Song Gang opened his mouth, but no words came out. Lin Hong asked him again, but he merely shook his head and said that he hadn't eaten anything. She stared in astonishment, but he again avoided her gaze then reluctantly confessed, "I give it all to Baldy Li."

Lin Hong stood speechless in the middle of the room. Only then did she remember that Baldy Li had become a beggar, because up to that point she had completely forgotten about his existence. In her world there was only Song Gang; now that bastard Baldy Li had once again shoved his way in. When Lin Hong estimated that, over the course of the past month, Baldy Li had taken about six yuan from them, she couldn't help crying. Repeating "Six yuan" over and over to herself, she noted that, if they economized, that would have been enough for the two of them to live for an entire month.

Song Gang bowed his head and sat down on the edge of the bed, unable to bring himself to look at her. It wasn't until she burst into tears and asked him how he could have done something like this that he finally raised his head, looked her in the eye, and said, "He is my brother."

"But he isn't even your biological brother," Lin Hong responded. "And even if he were, he should still support himself."

"He is my brother," Song Gang repeated. "Eventually he will be able to support himself, but before our mother died, she asked me to look after him—"

"Don't bring up that stepmother of yours," Lin Hong interrupted.

Song Gang was hurt by Lin Hong's remark and shouted back, "She was my mother!"

Lin Hong stared at Song Gang in astonishment—this being the first time since their marriage that Song Gang had raised his voice to her. She shook her head silently. Realizing that Song Gang had yelled at her after she said "stepmother," she knew that she had misspoken. She didn't dare say another word, and the room fell silent.

Song Gang sat with his head bowed, a blizzard of memories swirling back to him. It was as if he and Baldy Li had forged a path through a blizzard, a path that had gradually extended to the present day but had then suddenly disappeared. He was lost in thought and at a loss as to what to do. It was as if the white snow blanketed all possible paths. It wasn't until he caught sight of Lin Hong's feet as she stood there in the middle of the room that he finally came to his senses. He noticed that her shoes and pants were both threadbare and knew that her shirt was old, too. When he thought of how she economized every day, he became distraught and felt that it had been truly wrong of him to give Baldy Li money behind her back.

After a long time passed, Lin Hong realized that Song Gang had no intention of speaking. Feeling herself getting angry again, she snapped, "Say something."

Song Gang lifted his head and earnestly said, "I was wrong."

Her heart immediately softened. She looked at Song Gang's earnest eyes and couldn't help but sigh. Then she started trying to console him, saying that six yuan was not very much money, that they could pretend it had been simply stolen. She suggested that sometimes an unexpected loss might help avert a future adversity. Lin Hong insisted, however, that Song Gang have nothing more to do with Baldy Li. She took another twenty cents and two grain coupons from her purse and placed them in Song Gang's pocket. He was moved by her gesture but said, "I don't need any more money."

"You do need it." Lin Hong looked at him. "But you should definitely spend it on yourself."

After they went to bed that evening, they engaged in their usual pillow talk. Song Gang tenderly embraced Lin Hong, and Lin Hong, with a sweet smile, basked in his inexhaustible love for her. Even after she fell asleep, a smile remained on her face.

When he got off work the next day, Song Gang rode his bike to the knitting factory to pick Lin Hong up. When Baldy Li, who was still staging his sit-in, spotted him, he immediately jumped up and called out. Song Gang's heart skipped a beat when he heard Baldy Li. He brought the bike to a halt and stood there, and as he heard Baldy Li walking over, Song Gang was afraid he would ask him again for money. Baldy Li did, in fact, extend his hand and say shamelessly, "Song Gang, I haven't eaten or drunk anything all day."

His pulse pounding, Song Gang reflexively reached into his pocket and grabbed the money and grain coupons he had there. Then, however, he blushed and shook his head. "I don't have anything today."

Baldy Li was tremendously disappointed and reluctantly pulled back his hand. He swallowed his saliva and, with a downcast expression, said, "I have been swallowing my saliva all day, and now I have to swallow my own fucking saliva all night as well."

At this point, Song Gang, as if possessed, took the money and grain coupons out of his pocket and handed them to the downcast Baldy Li. Baldy Li laughed in surprise and cursed as he accepted the money, "Damn it, you've also learned duplicity!"

Song Gang laughed sadly as he rode away. That night the moment Song Gang had been dreading most took place after dinner, when Lin Hong checked his pocket and discovered that his money and grain coupons were gone. This time she had been expecting to find them there, and when she found that they were gone, she became very alarmed. She looked at Song Gang fearfully, hoping that he would tell her that this time he had spent the money on himself. When she put her hand in his pocket, Song Gang closed his eyes in agony, and when he reopened them and saw her frightened face, he said with a trembling voice, "I was wrong."

Lin Hong realized that it was Baldy Li who had taken the money and grain coupons. She looked disappointedly at him and then began screaming in fury, "Why did you have to do that?"

Song Gang was mortified. He wanted to explain, but the only words that came out were "I was wrong."

Lin Hong wept tears of fury. Biting her lip, she said, "I just gave you this money yesterday, and today you immediately went and gave it to Baldy Li. Couldn't you at least have waited a few days? Couldn't you have just let me be happy for a few days?"

Song Gang hated himself. He gritted his teeth as if he wanted to castigate himself, but what came out were those same three words: "I was wrong."

"Don't say that again!" Lin Hong cried. "That's all you can say, and I'm tired of hearing it."

Song Gang didn't dare say anything else. Instead, he bowed his head and stood in a corner, as his father, Song Fanping, had done when he was being struggled against during the Cultural Revolution. Lin Hong cried as she spoke, and Song Gang stood there without showing any reaction. Lin Hong felt angry and hurt and wanted to give Song Gang the cold shoulder, so she lay down on the bed and muffled herself with the covers. He stood silently for a while and then began to move around the room. Lin Hong heard the sounds of pots and dishes and knew that he was fixing dinner. The room gradually grew dark as he finished dinner, took it to the table, and then prepared the bowls and chopsticks. Lin Hong thought that he should come over and say something, but he merely sat down at the table. The room fell once again into deathly quiet. Lin Hong fumed as the room became pitch-dark but still he just sat there without moving, as if he were waiting for her to wake up and have dinner with him.

Lin Hong knew that Song Gang was capable of sitting like that forever; if she remained in bed until the sun came up, he would sit there until morning. Even his breathing was almost imperceptible, as if he were afraid of waking her up. Lin Hong began to feel sorry for Song Gang, thinking of all his good qualities, his love for her, his honesty and loyalty, as well as his good looks. . . . Upon thinking of his good looks, she grinned and couldn't resist calling out to him, "Song Gang."

He stood up, but she didn't say anything more. He hesitated a moment, unwilling to sit back down. When Lin Hong saw his hesitation, she once again couldn't help grinning and said softly, "Song Gang, come over here."

He walked to the bedside and leaned over. Lin Hong continued with a quiet voice, "Song Gang, sit down."

He carefully sat on the edge of the bed. She took his hand and said, "Come closer."

He sat closer, and Lin Hong held his hand to her breast, saying, "Song Gang, you are too softhearted. In the future, I won't be able to give you any more money."

Song Gang nodded in the dark. Lin Hong placed his hand on her face and asked, "You aren't angry, are you?"

Song Gang shook his head. "No."

Lin Hong sat up, pulled over his other hand, and told him tenderly, "I don't want to say anything bad about Baldy Li. And even if he were a good person, the problem is that we still wouldn't be able to support him. How much do we earn each month? In the future, we might have children and will have a responsibility to raise them, and therefore we can't afford the added burden of having to support him. Now that Baldy Li is unemployed, if he can't get by, he will become completely dependent on you. Song Gang, it's not the present I'm worried about; it's the future. Please, for the sake of our future children, you need to cut off relations with Baldy Li."

Song Gang nodded again in the dark, but Lin Hong couldn't see him clearly and asked, "Song Gang, did you nod?"

Song Gang nodded again and said, "Yes, I nodded."

Lin Hong paused, then asked, "Am I right?"

Song Gang nodded. "You are right."

After the storm that evening, everything returned to a state of calm, and in the days that followed Song Gang began to avoid Baldy Li. When Song Gang got off work and went to the knitting factory to pick up Lin Hong, he had to go past the gate to the county government building where Baldy Li was holding his sit-down protest. In order to avoid him, Song Gang took the long way around, thereby making Lin Hong wait a long time at the factory. It used to be that he would be waiting there as soon as she walked out the door, but now she would sit there waiting, craning her neck this way and that, and it was not until long after her workmates had already gone home that he hurriedly biked over. One day she finally lost her temper and sat gloomily on the back of his bike, not saying a single word the entire ride. When they got home, she started to upbraid Song Gang, saying that she was very anxious waiting there at the gate, worried that something might have happened to him and thinking that perhaps he had crashed into an electrical pole and cracked his skull open. Song Gang hemmed and hawed as he tried to explain that he was late because he had taken the long way around in order to avoid Baldy Li. Hearing this, Lin Hong responded loudly, "What are you afraid of?"

Lin Hong said that the more people were afraid of someone like Baldy Li, the more he would bully them. She told Song Gang that, in the future, he would go right past the door to the county government.

"You shouldn't go see him. Just act as if he isn't there."

Song Gang asked her, "And if he calls out to me?"

"Act as if you didn't hear him," Lin Hong answered. "Act as if he doesn't exist."

CHAPTER 46

BY THIS POINT, Baldy Li had accumulated a small mountain of scrap in front of the entranceway to the government building. He had also adjusted the style of his sit-in, sitting cross-legged in the center of the courtyard only during peak periods, when people were coming to and from work. The rest of the time, Baldy Li could be found bent over, tirelessly sorting through the scrap, his butt lifted up above his head. He painstakingly made his way through it several times and then back again, as though he were panning for gold. But when he heard the bell announcing the end of the workday, he dashed back to the entranceway and, with a heroic air, once again assumed his solitary post. Spotting him as they filed out, the government workers chuckled and said that Baldy Li sitting there looked even more self-important than the county governor when presenting a report at a countywide meeting. Baldy Li was quite satisfied with this assessment and lauded the workers as they passed, "Well said!"

He hadn't seen Song Gang in more than a month. When Song Gang once again rode his Eternity bicycle past the entranceway, Baldy Li ignored the fact that he was in the middle of a sit-in and sprang up and waved both hands, shouting, "Song Gang, Song Gang!"

Song Gang pretended he hadn't heard him, but it seemed as if each of Baldy Li's cries was a hand tugging him back, preventing him from pedaling away. After a brief hesitation, he turned around and slowly rode toward Baldy Li. Song Gang was very nervous and didn't know whether he should tell Baldy Li that he didn't have a single cent in his pocket. Baldy Li excitedly greeted him, pulled Song Gang down from his bicycle, and announced mysteriously, "Song Gang, I've struck it rich!"

Baldy Li took an old watch from his pocket, and with his other hand he tapped Song Gang on the head, asking him to inspect the watch carefully. Baldy Li said excitedly, "Do you see the foreign words on the front? This is a foreign watch, and the time it keeps is not Beijing time but, rather, Greenwich Mean Time. I found it among these scraps."

Song Gang couldn't see the watch hands and asked, "Why doesn't it have any hands?"

"I'll attach three pieces of wire to serve as hands," Baldy Li said. "I just need to spend a little bit of money repairing it, and then the Greenwich Mean Time will run smoothly!"

Then Baldy Li placed the foreign watch in Song Gang's pocket, saying magnanimously, "It's for you."

Song Gang hadn't expected that Baldy Li would give him something that he, Baldy Li, prized so much. He embarrassedly took the watch out and handed it back, saying, "You keep it."

"No, you take it," Baldy Li insisted. "I found this watch ten days ago and have been waiting for you to come by ever since so I could give it to you. Where did you disappear to this past month?"

Song Gang blushed bright red and didn't know how to respond. Thinking that he was still worried about accepting the watch, Baldy Li placed it directly into Song Gang's pocket and said, "Since you take Lin Hong to and from work every day, you need a watch. I don't need one. When the sun rises in the morning, I come here to do my sit-in, and when it sets, I return home to sleep."

With this, Baldy Li lifted his head and looked around for the setting sun, ultimately pointing at it through the tree leaves, and proclaimed, "*That* is my watch." Noticing Song Gang's confusion, he added, "Not the tree, the *sun*."

Song Gang laughed, and Baldy Li said, "Don't laugh. Go quickly, Lin Hong is waiting for you."

Song Gang mounted the bicycle, and, with his feet still on the ground, he turned and asked Baldy Li, "Have you been all right this past month?"

"Great!" Baldy Li urged Song Gang forward. "Go quickly."

Song Gang asked again, "Have you been eating well?"

"What have I eaten?" Baldy Li squinted his eyes as he pondered. Then he shook his head and said, "I can't remember. At any rate, I didn't starve to death."

Song Gang wanted to say more, but Baldy Li impatiently shooed him on his way. "Song Gang, you are simply too much like an old lady."

Saying this, he began to push Song Gang from behind, pushing him five or six yards until Song Gang finally began pedaling on his own accord. Baldy Li watched as Song Gang rode away, then walked back to the middle of the gate. Just as he was sitting down, however, he remembered that all the county government workers had already gone home. Somewhat at a loss, Baldy Li cursed, "Damn it."

After Song Gang picked up Lin Hong and took her home, he hesitated a long time, but in the end he decided not to take out the watch Baldy Li had given him, preferring to tell her about it later. He didn't have money or grain coupons in his pocket, but he still had his lunch. He and Lin Hong would always make a little extra at dinnertime and put the leftovers in a couple of containers to serve as their lunch the next day. During the period Song Gang was avoiding Baldy Li, he would only occasionally wonder how Baldy Li was doing. But once he saw Baldy Li again, he couldn't help thinking of his brother all the time. Song Gang was quite moved at the thought of Baldy Li treasuring this handless foreign watch and holding on to it ten full days just to give it to him. At lunchtime the next day, Song Gang remembered Baldy Li and therefore biked over to the government building with his lunch box. Baldy Li was in the process of rummaging through the scrap heap and consequently didn't notice when Song Gang rode up behind him. Song Gang rang his bicycle bell, causing Baldy Li to jump with surprise and turn around. When he saw the lunch box Song Gang was holding in his hand, Baldy Li smiled and said, "Song Gang, you knew I was hungry!"

Baldy Li took the lunch box Song Gang was handing him and hurriedly opened it, and he saw that the food inside hadn't even been touched. He paused and asked, "Song Gang, you haven't eaten any?"

Song Gang smiled. "You go ahead. I'm not hungry."

"No." Baldy Li handed the lunch box back to Song Gang. "Let's eat together."

Baldy Li got a pile of old newspapers from the scrap heap and spread them out for Song Gang to sit on while he plopped himself down directly on the ground. The brothers sat side by side in front of the scrap heap. Baldy Li once again took the lunch box Song Gang was holding and used a chopstick to draw a trench down the middle, telling Song Gang, "This line is the thirty-eighth parallel: To the north is North Korea, and to the south is South Korea."

He stuffed the lunch box into Song Gang's hands, saying, "You go first."

Song Gang pushed it back, replying, "No, you go first."

"If I ask you to go first, you should go first," Baldy Li said, annoyed.

Song Gang didn't push the lunch box back again but, rather, started to eat. Baldy Li leaned over and peered into the box, saying, "You are eating your way into South Korean territory."

Song Gang chuckled. He was a slow and meticulous eater, and Baldy Li started to salivate waiting for him to finish. Hearing Baldy Li swallowing his saliva, Song Gang stopped and handed the box to Baldy Li. "You eat now."

"You go ahead and finish," said Baldy Li, pushing the box back. "But could you hurry it up? You even eat like an old woman."

Song Gang hurriedly stuffed the rest of the food into his mouth, Baldy Li then took the lunch box and inhaled his half of the food. He was finished before Song Gang had a chance to gulp down the food still in his mouth. Baldy Li affectionately patted him on the back, helping him to swallow. When he was finally done, Song Gang wiped his mouth and then wiped the tears from his eyes, suddenly remembering his conversation with Li Lan right before she died.

When he noticed Song Gang crying, Baldy Li was startled and asked, "Song Gang, what's wrong?"

Song Gang said, "I just remembered Mother. . . ."

Baldy Li froze as Song Gang continued, "She was concerned about you and asked that I look after you. I promised her that, even if I had only a single bowl of rice left, I would give it to you. She shook her head and said if there was only one bowl of rice left, we should share it."

Song Gang pointed to the empty bowl on the ground and said, "And that's what we're doing."

The brothers both returned to that earlier, painful period. Sitting in front of the mountain of scraps, they wiped away their tears and recalled how, as children, they had walked hand in hand down from the bridge in front of the bus depot, where they found Song Fanping lying dead on that hot summer day; and how they had stood hand in hand in the exit of the bus depot until nightfall, waiting for Li Lan to return from Shanghai. The final scene was of the two brothers pulling a cart with Li Lan's coffin to the countryside, returning their mother to their father.

Then Baldy Li wiped away his tears and told Song Gang, "Our childhood was simply too bitter."

Song Gang also wiped away his tears, nodded, and said, "We were bullied by everyone."

"Now things are better." Baldy Li laughed. "Now no one dares bully us."

"No, they're still not better," Song Gang replied.

"How are things not better?" Baldy Li asked, turning around to look at Song Gang. "You are married to Lin Hong, isn't that good? You can't recognize good fortune because you are living in it."

"I was speaking of you," Song Gang said.

"What about me?" Baldy Li looked back at his mountain of scraps. "I'm not doing badly."

"Not badly? You don't even have a job."

"Who says I don't have a job? Sitting here in protest *is* my job."

Song Gang shook his head and asked anxiously, "What will you do afterward?"

"Don't worry," Baldy Li replied. "Things will naturally work themselves out."

Song Gang still shook his head. "I'm worried sick about you."

"What are you worried about? I'm the one doing the pissing, and I'm not worried. Why should you worry if you are only the one carrying the chamber pot?"

Song Gang sighed and didn't say anything more. Baldy Li excitedly asked him about the foreign watch, whether Song Gang had gotten it fixed yet or not. Song Gang abruptly picked up the lunch box from the ground, stood up, and announced that he had to go back to the factory. He then mounted his bicycle and rode away, holding his lunch box in one hand. Baldy Li watched him ride away, shouting out, "Song Gang, you can even ride a bicycle with one hand?"

Song Gang glanced back and laughed. "What's so great about that? I can ride with no hands."

He extended his arms, as if he were soaring through the air. Astounded, Baldy Li ran after him, shouting, "Song Gang, you're really amazing!"

For the next month, every day at noon Song Gang would take his lunch box to Baldy Li and the two of them would sit in front of the pile of scraps, chatting and laughing as they divided and ate the food. Song Gang didn't dare let Lin Hong know about these rendezvous, so though he was famished every night, he was always careful not to rouse her suspicions by eating more than usual, even to the point of eating less than he normally would. Lin Hong noticed that Song Gang seemed to have lost his appetite and asked anxiously whether he had been feeling all right. He stammered that it was true he had lost his appetite, but that he hadn't lost his vigor. He reassured her that he was perfectly fine.

In a small town there are no secrets, and about a month later Lin Hong finally learned what was going on. It was a coworker at the knitting factory who told her. The previous day the coworker had taken the day off and around noon happened to pass in front of the front gate of the government building, where she saw Song Gang and Baldy Li sitting together on the ground and sharing the food in Song Gang's lunch box. The next day the coworker giggled as she told Lin Hong about how those two brothers, eating there together, looked even more affectionate than a married couple. At that point Lin Hong was sitting in the workshop doorway eating her lunch. Hearing her coworker's description, she immediately put down her lunch box and stormed out of the factory.

By the time she arrived at the government building, the brothers had finished eating and were sitting there chatting and laughing, with Baldy Li loudly recounting some story or other. Her face ashen, Lin Hong walked up to them. When Baldy Li spotted her, he scrambled up and warmly called out, "Lin Hong, you've come."

Song Gang, meanwhile, had turned pale, and Lin Hong looked at him coldly, then turned and walked away. Baldy Li had just retrieved a pile of newspapers from the scrap heap and was about to invite Lin Hong to sit down when he noticed that she had already left. He said disappointedly, "You came all the way over here. Why don't you at least sit down and join us for a while?"

Song Gang stood there, not knowing what to do. He watched Lin Hong walk away until finally it occurred to him to run after her. He therefore jumped onto his bicycle and sped after her. Lin Hong was walking forward in a dignified manner, and when she heard Song Gang ride up beside her, suggesting quietly that she sit behind him, she pretended not to have heard him and acted as though no one were there. She walked away with her head held high, staring straight ahead. Song Gang didn't dare say anything else; instead he jumped off his bicycle and followed silently behind her. They acted like two complete strangers, walking silently down the main street of Liu. Many townspeople saw them and stopped to watch curiously, recognizing that something had happened between them. Someone called out Lin

Hong's name, but she made no response. Someone else called out to Song Gang, who also didn't answer, though he did nod and smile. His smile, however, was forced, and Poet Zhao, who happened to be on the street and was the kind of person who could always make a mountain out of a molehill, pointed to him and told everyone, "Do you see that? That is a bitter smile."

Song Gang pushed his bicycle as he followed Lin Hong all the way to the entrance of the knitting factory. She didn't glance back at him the entire way, and even when she walked into the factory, she didn't turn to look at him. Sensing that Song Gang was still standing there, she slowed down a little, and suddenly her heart softened. Though she wanted to turn and look at him, she restrained herself and continued forward into the factory workshop.

Song Gang stood rooted outside the gate and remained there as Lin Hong disappeared in the distance. After the bell sounded announcing the end of the lunch break, the gate area emptied out, as did his heart. Song Gang stood there for a long time, then finally turned around and pushed his bike away. He forgot to ride his shiny Eternity bicycle, and instead pushed it all the way back to the metal factory.

Song Gang was in torment all afternoon, spending most of his time in the workshop staring into a corner. He alternated between being at a loss and concentrating intently, but after concentrating his mind would inevitably revert to being a complete blank again. It was not until the bell rang announcing the end of the workday that he finally came to his senses. He ran out of the workshop, jumped on his bike, and shot out of the factory. He pedaled furiously down the street, and when he arrived at the door to the knitting factory, the workers were still filing out. Song Gang stood there holding his bicycle and saw Lin Hong emerge, chatting with a few of her workmates. He cheered up when he saw her but then became somber again, uncertain whether or not she would be willing to ride back with him.

To his surprise, she simply walked up to him as though nothing had happened, waved goodbye to her workmates, and climbed on the back of his bicycle. Song Gang was momentarily stunned but then breathed a sigh of relief. With a flushed face, he mounted the bicycle and, ringing his bell, rode off down the street. Happy again, Song Gang felt reenergized and pedaled furiously, with Lin Hong first holding on to his seat and then, as their speed increased, eventually grabbing on to his clothing.

Song Gang's happiness did not last very long. Once Lin Hong returned home and closed the door, she again became as frigid as she had been that afternoon in the street. She went over to the window and, after pulling the shades, stood silently staring at the window shade as though she were looking at the scenery outside. Song Gang stood in the middle of the room and after a while muttered, "Lin Hong, I was wrong."

Lin Hong merely snorted and continued standing there, eventually turning around and asking, "Wrong about what?"

Song Gang bowed his head and told her truthfully about how he had been sharing his lunch with Baldy Li for the past month. Lin Hong shook her head and wept as she listened, distressed at the thought that Song Gang would starve himself in order to feed that bastard Baldy Li. When Song Gang saw that she was crying from anger, he shut his mouth and stood uncertainly to one side. After a while she wiped away her tears. Then Song Gang finally took out the foreign watch and, stammering, told her that he had broken off relations with Baldy Li, but that day when he rode by in front of the government building, Baldy Li called out to him and gave him this watch, reminding him of their former brotherly love. As Song Gang stammered out this explanation Lin Hong looked carefully at the watch and suddenly exclaimed in surprise, "But it doesn't have any hands—you call this a watch?"

With this, she finally exploded and tearfully cursed Baldy Li. Starting with his having peeked at her bottom in the public toilet, she cursed him for all of the embarrassment he had caused her, right up to his having brought his Good Works Factory workers to the knitting factory to harass her in front of everyone. Lin Hong listed all of Baldy Li's transgressions, and in the end she became so depressed, she simply wept. Even after she had tried to commit suicide by jumping in the river, Baldy Li still wouldn't let her be and forced Song Gang to come and tell her, "It is time you gave up hope," pushing Song Gang to the point that he himself almost committed suicide.

Lin Hong wept until she could barely speak. After she finished cursing Baldy Li, she started in on Song Gang. She said that she had been scrimping and saving ever since they married so that she could buy him a Diamond brand watch, and she simply couldn't believe that Baldy Li won him over so easily with a broken watch someone had thrown away. She then abruptly stopped crying, wiped away her tears, and muttered sadly, as if to herself, "Well, he didn't have to win you over—you and he are family. I'm the one who inserted myself and split the two of you up."

Finished with her crying and cursing, Lin Hong wiped her tears and fell into a long silence. Then she let out a long sigh, looked at Song Gang sorrowfully, and with a measured voice said, "Song Gang, I've reached a decision. You should go back to living with Baldy Li, and we should get divorced."

Terrified, Song Gang shook his head. He opened his mouth several times, but no words came out. Lin Hong watched his reaction and couldn't help feeling sorry for him. She once again started crying and shook her head, saying, "Song Gang, you know I love you, but I can't continue living like this."

Lin Hong walked to the cabinet, took out several pieces of clothing, and put them in a travel bag. She proceeded to the door, then turned around to look at Song Gang, who was standing there trembling with terror. She hesitated a second but still opened the front door. Song Gang suddenly knelt down and begged her tearfully, "Lin Hong, please don't go."

Her first impulse was to rush over and hug him, but she restrained herself and said in a gentle voice, "I'm going back to my parents' house for a few days. You should stay here and think things over and decide whether you want to be with me or with Baldy Li."

"I don't need to think about it," Song Gang replied with tears running down his face. "I want to be with you."

Lin Hong held her face and cried, asking, "And what about Baldy Li?"

Song Gang stood up and said resolutely, "I will go tell him that I want to sever our relationship. I'll go right now."

Lin Hong couldn't resist running over to him. The two embraced tightly in the doorway, then Lin Hong leaned close to him and asked quietly, "Do you want me to go with you?"

Song Gang nodded emphatically. "Let's go together."

With rekindled love, they wiped each other's tears, then left the house together. Out of habit, Lin Hong walked over to their bicycle, but Song Gang shook his head and said he didn't want to ride, because he wanted to think carefully as he walked about what he would tell Baldy Li. Lin Hong looked at him in surprise, but he merely held up his hand and walked on. She obediently followed, and the two of them proceeded out the alley and toward the main road. Lin Hong walked arm in arm with Song Gang, repeatedly looking up at him and seeing an unprecedented look of determination on his face. She suddenly felt that her husband was immensely strong, and this was the first time since their marriage that she'd had this feeling. In the past Song Gang had always acceded to her wishes, but she felt that from now on she would always listen to him.

Under the final rays of the setting sun, they arrived at the gate to the government building, where they saw Baldy Li rummaging through his scrap. Lin Hong tugged Song Gang's arm and asked, "Have you decided what you are going to say to him?"

"Yes." Song Gang nodded. "I want to return that comment to him."

Lin Hong didn't understand. "Which comment?"

Song Gang didn't answer but, rather, brushed off Lin Hong's hand and walked straight toward Baldy Li. Lin Hong paused and watched his tall and impressive figure as he approached the short and squat Baldy Li, then heard Song Gang say with a deep voice, "Baldy Li, I have something to say to you."

From Song Gang's tone, Baldy Li sensed that something was wrong, combined with the fact that Lin Hong was standing behind him. He looked suspiciously at Song Gang and then at Lin Hong. Song Gang took the handless watch out of his pocket and handed it back to Baldy Li. Realizing that Song Gang's intentions were not good, Baldy Li accepted the watch, wiped it carefully, and put it on his own wrist, then asked, "What do you want to say to me?"

Song Gang softened his tone and earnestly told his brother, "Baldy Li, now that my father and your mother are gone, we are no longer brothers—"

Baldy Li nodded and interrupted him. "You are right. Because your father was not my birth father and my mother was not your birth mother, we therefore are not biological brothers—"

"Therefore," Song Gang interrupted Baldy Li in turn, "I won't come asking you for anything, and I ask that you not come asking me for anything. From now on, we will go our separate ways—"

"What you are saying," Baldy Li interrupted again, "is that we should completely sever our relationship?"

"That's right." Song Gang nodded emphatically, then threw down his trump card: "It is time that you gave up all hope."

Lin Hong opened both arms to embrace Song Gang as he walked back to her. He also hugged her, and the two of them walked away arm in arm. Baldy Li scratched his head as he watched them depart, not understanding what Song Gang meant by "It is time that you gave up all hope." He muttered to himself, "I should fucking give up hope of what?"

Song Gang and Lin Hong remained arm in arm as they walked down the street and into their little alley. When they got home, Song Gang suddenly grew silent and sat without saying a word. Lin Hong saw his somber expression and knew that he was feeling anguished. Given the amount of history he and Baldy Li shared, it was inevitable that they would remain in each other's thoughts. She therefore didn't scold him, thinking to herself that he would be better in a few days. Lin Hong was confident that the longer she and Song Gang lived together, the more his and Baldy Li's shared history would recede into the distance.

After he went to bed that night, Song Gang remained depressed and kept sighing. Lin Hong gently patted him and lifted her head slightly, whereupon Song Gang, out of habit, reached around and hugged her. She snuggled up to him, telling him not to worry and to go to sleep. Lin Hong herself then drifted off, though Song Gang remained awake for a long time. That night he dreamed he was crying, and his tears rolled down onto Lin Hong's face. She woke in surprise and turned on the light, waking Song Gang as well. Lin Hong saw that his face was covered in tears and speculated that perhaps he had dreamed of his stepmother. She then turned off the light and patted him comfortingly, asking, "Were you dreaming about your mother again?" This time she deliberately didn't say *stepmother*.

Song Gang shook his head in the dark and carefully recalled his dream. Then he wiped the tears from his face and said, "I dreamed that we got divorced."

CHAPTER 47

BALDY LI continued his sit-in in front of the county government building, but as his scrap accumulated into a small mountain he no longer had time for sitting. Instead he spent all his time scurrying back and forth, sorting his scraps into different categories, then using a variety of market channels to sell them throughout the country. He did spend two hours sitting cross-legged on the ground, working on the foreign watch, painstakingly adding three pieces of wire of different lengths, then proudly putting it on his left wrist. Before, he would always use his right hand to point and gesture, but now that he had his new foreign watch he began using his left hand instead. Whenever anyone walked by, his left hand would start waving warmly of its own accord. Soon many of the townspeople had seen his watch, and several of them crowded around to inspect it, asking curiously, "Why do the hands look like wires?"

Baldy Li replied irritably, "All watch hands look like wires."

The townspeople then spotted another flaw. "The watch has the wrong time."

"Of course the time is wrong," Baldy Li replied proudly. "This watch keeps Greenwich Mean Time, while you keep Beijing time. That is the difference."

Baldy Li happily wore his Greenwich Mean Time foreign watch for about half a year, whereupon one day he suddenly switched to a new, domestic Diamond brand watch. When everyone saw this, they exclaimed, "You've switched watches?"

"Yes, I switched back to Beijing time." Baldy Li shook his shiny new watch as he added, "Greenwich Mean Time has its advantages, but in the end it is not appropriate for Chinese sensibilities, and therefore I switched back to Beijing time."

Everyone asked enviously where he had salvaged this shiny new Diamond watch. Baldy Li grew angry and pulled a receipt from his pocket and showed them. "I bought it myself."

The townspeople were astounded. How was it possible for a mere scrap collector to buy himself a Diamond watch? Baldy Li opened his tattered coat in front of everyone and pulled out the wallet tied to his waist. He then unzipped it, revealing a thick wad of bills, and said, "Look at this, look at this neat pile of bills."

Everyone stared slack-jawed with astonishment. After a while, someone remembered Baldy Li's foreign watch and asked ingratiatingly, "What did you do with that Greenwich Mean Time foreign watch?"

"I gave it away," Baldy Li said. "I gave it to the infatuated idiot who used to work for me."

Wearing his new Beijing-time watch, Baldy Li continued to exert himself. He obtained some bamboo poles and reeds and began erecting a thatched shed right there in front of the government building. Thirteen of his former Good Works Factory workers (the exception being the infatuated idiot) came over to help. The four blind men stood in a row and passed the reeds to one another. The two idiots were responsible for supporting the bamboo poles, while the two cripples, who both had strong hands, were responsible for binding the bamboo together. The five deaf men, meanwhile, provided the hard manual labor; three of them stayed on the ground and used some of the reeds to construct a wall, and the two others climbed up and used the rest of the reeds for the roof. All the while Baldy Li barked directions, as if he were overseeing a construction site. Shouting and hollering and bathed in sweat, they all worked tirelessly for three straight days, until finally the thatched shed was complete. Only then did Baldy Li remember the infatuated idiot and ask the crippled factory director about him. The cripple replied that the idiot had never been late going to or from work but that ever since he started wearing the foreign watch, he hadn't been seen again at the factory. He then asked Baldy Li, "Do you think he's become confused by the Greenwich Mean Time?"

"Definitely." Baldy Li laughed. "That's what they call jet lag."

The lot of them brought over the table and chairs from Baldy Li's house, as well sheets, clothes, toiletries, coal, oil, a stove, dishes, chopsticks, glasses, and many other things. Baldy Li proudly moved into his shed and pitched camp right there outside the government building gate. Not long afterward, the people of Liu noticed that workers from the Ministry of Post and Telecommunications had connected a telephone line to the shed—the first private telephone in Liu Town. The crowds discussed this tirelessly, exclaiming, "Who could have imagined this day!" Baldy Li's phone rang continuously from dawn to dusk and late into the night. The county government workers remarked that Baldy Li's phone rang more often than that of the county governor.

In the process of setting up his scrap business, Baldy Li stopped simply collecting everyone's unwanted scraps and instead started purchasing them. The pile of scrap outside the government building grew into a huge mountain, and his shed was also full of it. According to Baldy Li, the scraps inside the hut were of the highest quality. People walking by would often see him sitting happily in the middle of these high-quality scraps, looking as if he were sitting amid a pile of jewels. They also saw trucks come by every week to cart away the sorted scrap. Baldy Li stood in front of his shed and watched the trucks drive away, licking his fingers as he counted his wad of bills.

Baldy Li was still shabbily dressed, but he had now switched to a bigger wallet; even so the amount of cash inside made it bulge out as if it were pumped full of air. In his breast pocket he carried a little notebook; in the front he recorded his scrap-business transactions, while in the back he recorded the debts he had incurred in the attempt to set up his clothing business.

His five former business partners had resigned themselves to their bad fortune and given up hope of having their loans repaid. They never imagined that after Baldy Li started earning money through his scrap business, he would come back and repay them.

One afternoon Popsicle Wang walked past Baldy Li's shed, and Baldy Li, wearing only a pair of shorts and naked from the waist up, rushed out of his shed and excitedly called out to him. Wang, his ice chest still on his back, turned around slowly and saw Baldy Li waving at him, saying, "Come, come over here."

Popsicle Wang stood there without moving, uncertain what Baldy Li wanted from him. When Baldy Li said he wanted to return his money, Wang thought that he had misunderstood and even turned around to see if Baldy Li was speaking to someone else. Baldy Li pointed impatiently at him and said, "I'm talking to you, about the debt that I owe you."

Popsicle Wang walked over, hardly able to believe his ears, and sat down with Baldy Li inside the shed, in the middle of a huge pile of scrap. Baldy Li flipped through his little notebook, calculating the original loan and the accrued interest. Meanwhile, Popsicle Wang curiously looked around at Baldy Li's shed, seeing that it had everything one might need to eat and drink, as well as an electric fan blowing directly on Baldy Li. Wang said enviously, "You even have an electric fan!"

Baldy Li grunted in response and reached over to press the swivel button. The fan now swiveled to include Popsicle Wang, who exclaimed, "What a cool breeze. . . ."

Baldy Li calculated Popsicle Wang's loan and interest and said with embarrassment, "I don't have much money at the moment, and therefore I'll have to repay you in installments. I'll pay you a portion every month, and within a year I will have paid it all back."

Baldy Li opened his wallet, took out some money, and counted it carefully. He returned the majority of the bills to his wallet and stuffed the remainder into Wang's hand. Popsicle Wang's hand trembled as he accepted the money, and his lips trembled as he registered his surprise. He said that he never thought Baldy Li would have recorded the loan and claimed that he himself had forgotten about it. As he spoke Wang's eyes grew red, and he said that never in his wildest dreams did he imagine he would ever recover his five hundred yuan. Then, referring to the interest, he added, "And now I find that the money has even given birth to a new son."

Popsicle Wang carefully placed the money in his pocket, then leaned over to remove a popsicle from his ice chest. Explaining that he didn't have anything else to give, he handed Baldy Li the popsicle. Baldy Li, however, shook his head and said, "I won't take a single needle or thread from the masses."

Popsicle Wang responded that this wasn't a needle and thread from the masses but, rather, simply a token of his appreciation. Baldy Li responded that, then, he should definitely not eat it, given that it was a token of appreciation. He asked Wang to put the popsicle away, adding, "Could you instead please do something for me? Please notify Blacksmith Tong, Tailor Zhang, Little Scissors Guan, and Yanker Yu that I will begin repaying my debt to each of them as well."

That evening, Tong, Zhang, Guan, and Yu, as well as Popsicle Wang himself, dropped by Baldy Li's shed to pay him a visit. They stood in front of the shed and called out affectionately, "Director Li, Director Li . . ."

Baldy Li walked over, shirtless, and waved at them, saying, "I'm not Director Li anymore. Now, I'm Scraps Li."

The former partners burst out laughing. Blacksmith Tong glanced at the others, and they glanced back, and he realized that it was again incumbent on him to speak first. Therefore, still chuckling, he said, "I hear that you plan to return our money?"

"It's not a question of returning your money but of repaying my debt," Baldy Li corrected him.

"Isn't that the same thing?" Blacksmith Tong continued, nodding vigorously. "I also hear something about there being interest?"

"Of course there will be interest," Baldy Li said. "I am like a People's Bank, and you are my depositors."

The five of them nodded in agreement. Baldy Li then turned and looked at his shed, remarking that it was too small to accommodate six people and therefore they would have to settle their accounts outside. Baldy Li plopped down on the ground and opened his little notebook, muttering to himself as he made the requisite calculations. His shorts were dirtier than a rag. Four of the former partners hesitated, not certain whether they were expected to sit down with him. Each had made a point of bathing and putting on clean clothes before coming to visit. Therefore, they all watched Blacksmith Tong to see what he would do. Tong decided that, for the sake of money, he was not only willing to sit on the ground but would even sit in cow dung if necessary. After Blacksmith Tong plopped himself down, the other four quickly followed suit. Then, with all six of them sitting in a circle, Baldy Li made calculations and gave each of them money. Blacksmith Tong then apologized solemnly to Baldy Li on their collective behalf, saying that they shouldn't have tried to press the money out of him so hard that he was left with a swollen face and a black eye. Baldy Li listened attentively and then pedantically corrected him: "My swollen face and black eye were not the result of your pressing me for money but, rather, were the result of your beating me."

The five former partners laughed in embarrassment, and Blacksmith Tong, again speaking on behalf of everyone, said, "From now on, whenever you want to beat us, you are welcome to do so, and we promise we won't fight back. This promise is good for a year."

The other four repeated, "It's good for a year."

Irritated, Baldy Li retorted, "You are using your own mean ways to judge a gentleman's heart."

The news that Baldy Li had begun repaying his debts quickly spread throughout town, generating great excitement and discussion. Everyone agreed that Baldy Li was simply extraordinary and remarked that if he was able to make himself rich simply by collecting scrap, imagine how rich he could become if he were trading gold. When Baldy Li heard this, he demurred: "The masses are speaking too highly of me. What I'm running here is a nickel-and-dime business—just earning a few bucks to feed myself."

After this expression of modesty, Baldy Li couldn't help going on to reflect upon all the ironic reversals of the recent past. When he quit his job at the factory and soared away to try to start a clothing factory, he pretty much lost everything but the shirt on his back. When he decided to return to the Good Works Factory, he was turned away, leaving him no choice but to stage a sit-in protest. When he started collecting scrap simply to feed himself, who knew that it would turn into his stock-in-trade? He then summarized what he had learned, telling the people of Liu, "In business, if you deliberately plant a flower, it might not bloom, but sometimes when you accidentally seed a willow, it ends up providing you with shade."

CHAPTER 48

BROTHERS · 393

BALDY LI'S business grew rapidly until finally the county's political leaders found themselves at their wits' end. With his pile of scrap looming like a mountain over the government building, the leaders reckoned that he had been squatting there for almost four years and had been running his scrap and recycling business for three. At first he had piled his scrap next to the entranceway, but now he had four mountains of it on either side and had even hired ten part-timers, who worked the same hours as the government office itself. At first people would see trucks come in only to haul the scrap away, but eventually they also started seeing trucks hauling scrap in—Baldy Li had become a scrap wholesaler with a national network. Everyone stared in astonishment, asking whether Baldy Li was vying for the position of chief of a national Beggars' Gang. Baldy Li shook his head and said bluntly that he was a businessman and had absolutely no interest in power. He had already helped our Liu Town develop into one of the most important scrap and recycling centers in East China, and he explained, "This is only the first step in a Long March. The next step will be all of China, and then the entire world. The day is not far off when Liu Town will become the scrap center of the world. Just think, Liu Town is just what Chairman Mao described when he said, 'All the beautiful scenery is concentrated here.'"

The county's political leaders had all been poor and therefore did not mind filth or the smell of scrap wafting into their offices. They were worried that higher leaders would come down to observe them and would blanch at the sight of four enormous piles of scrap right outside the government building. The higher leaders would be very angry and say that this didn't at all resemble a government institution but, rather, a trash center. There was nothing the county leaders feared more than not being promoted. If the higher leaders were displeased, it could have a very significant effect on the county leaders' career paths. Several county leaders were so anxious that they held an emergency meeting to discuss the problem, hoping to preemptively deal with the situation before Baldy Li turned Liu Town into a global trash center. Otherwise, things would become that much more difficult to resolve.

The county leaders agreed to treat cleaning up the mountains of trash as one of the county's public-image projects. They considered two plans. The first was to mobilize the military and civil police to forcibly clean up Baldy Li's mountains. This approach was quickly rejected. As soon as Baldy Li had started earning money from his scrap business, the first thing he had done was to start repaying his debts, thereby increasing his prestige among the masses to the point that it already exceeded that of the county governor himself. The county leaders were afraid that the masses would take advantage of the situation to stir up trouble and vent their pent-up anger. Recognizing that it was dangerous to incur the wrath of the masses, the leaders decided that it was not so hard to deal with a single Baldy Li. Therefore, they turned to their second approach, which was to grant his request to return to the Good Works Factory as director. In this way, they not only would redeem a comrade but furthermore would rid themselves of the those mountains of junk.

Tao Qing, the director of the Civil Affairs Bureau, received the secretary county governor's instructions and went to speak to Baldy Li. Tao Qing had fired Baldy Li four years earlier but now found himself trying to hire him back, a turn of events that greatly vexed Tao Qing. He told himself that he knew what Baldy Li was made of—if you gave him an inch, he'd take a mile. Therefore, Tao decided that it would be important to put Baldy Li firmly in his place before offering him his old job back.

Tao Qing walked over to the foot of the four mountains of scrap, where Baldy Li was busy directing his ten part-time workers. Tao stood behind Baldy Li for a while without his noticing, until finally Tao Qing had no choice but to clear his throat to get Baldy Li's attention. Baldy Li turned and saw his former leader and immediately cried out warmly, "Bureau Director Tao, you've come to visit me!"

With the proper tone of majestic condescension befitting his position, Tao Qing waved and said, "I happened to be in the area and thought I'd drop by."

"Dropping by to see someone still counts as coming to see them," Baldy Li replied happily. Then he called out to the ten part-time workers, "My former leader and superior, Bureau Director Tao, has come to see us. Everyone please give him a warm welcome."

396 • YU HUA

The ten part-time workers put down what they were working on and started up a scattered round of applause. Tao Qing frowned and nodded briefly to them. Baldy Li was dissatisfied and urged under his breath, "Director Tao, won't you say something to them, like 'Comrades, you are working hard'?"

Tao Qing shook his head and said, "No, I won't say anything."

"Okay, then." Baldy Li nodded, then said to the workers, "You can get back to work. I'm going to take Director Tao to my office."

Baldy Li solicitously invited Tao Qing into his shed, asking him to sit in the only chair while he himself sat on the bed. Surrounded by trash, Tao looked around and saw that the shed had everything anyone might need. As the saying goes, despite its tiny size, a sparrow still has all five organs. Tao Qing also noticed the electric fan and remarked, "You even use an electric fan!"

"I've used it for two summers now," Baldy Li replied proudly. "Next year I won't need it anymore, since I plan to install central air."

Tao Qing felt that Baldy Li was deliberately taunting him and therefore, gesturing to the shed, replied evenly, "An air conditioner wouldn't work well here, would it?"

"Why not?" Baldy Li asked.

"This shed is too drafty," Tao Qing explained. "An air conditioner would waste too much electricity."

"Then I'll just pay a slightly higher electric bill," Baldy Li replied. "With air-conditioning, in summer this shed will become an elite hotel."

Cursing Baldy Li under his breath, Tao Qing stood up and walked out. Baldy Li hurried after him and asked solicitously, "Director Tao, won't you sit a little longer?"

"No, thanks." Tao Qing shook his head. "I have a meeting to attend."

Baldy Li quickly turned to his ten part-time workers and prompted, "Director Tao is leaving. Everyone please applaud."

The workers let out another scattered round of applause, and Tao Qing again simply nodded in acknowledgment. Baldy Li said ingratiatingly, "Director Li, I'll walk you out."

Tao Qing waved him away. He took a few steps and then, pretending he had just remembered something, abruptly stopped and said to Baldy Li, "Come over here."

Baldy Li ran over, and Tao Qing patted his shoulder and said, "You should write a self-criticism."

"What do you mean, a self-criticism? Why should I write a self-criticism?"

"Regarding what happened four years ago," Tao Qing said. "Write a self-criticism, acknowledge your mistake, and I can arrange for you to return to your position as director of the Good Works Factory."

Baldy Li finally understood. He chuckled disdainfully. "I lost interest in that factory director position long ago."

Cursing Baldy Li again under his breath, Tao Qing said seriously, "Please consider it. This is a good opportunity."

"A good opportunity?" Baldy Li pointed to his four mountains of trash and said grandly, "*These* are my opportunities."

His face dark, Tao Qing continued, "I urge you to reconsider."

"I don't need to reconsider," Baldy Li replied firmly. "Why would I want to give up all this business in order to be a director of some charity factory? That's like telling me to trade in my watermelon for a sesame seed. . . ."

The county governor was very angry that Tao Qing had failed to convince Baldy Li to return to the factory. He said Tao Qing should never have fired Baldy Li in the first place: "Firing him was like releasing a tiger into the wilds—and now you have brought disaster to the entire county."

Tao Qing subserviently endured the governor's reprimands, then returned to the Civil Affairs Bureau to find two section chiefs to chew out. The two section chiefs were bewildered at why they were being reprimanded, having no idea what they had done wrong. His anger vented, Tao Qing vowed to pay no more attention to Baldy Li's scrap business. Another month passed and Baldy Li not only had not left but, furthermore, had redoubled his efforts and started on a fifth mountain of scrap. The governor knew that he couldn't count on Tao Qing to resolve the problem, so instead he sent his own right-hand man, the county government office manager, to deal with Baldy Li.

Baldy Li owed Tao Qing a debt of gratitude from way back, so naturally he was respectful to Tao when he came. As for that office manager, Baldy Li owed him nothing. When the office manager arrived, Baldy Li was in the process of sorting his scrap. With a warm smile and warm voice, the office manager stood behind him and spoke as he trailed Baldy Li back and forth, but Baldy Li only occasionally tossed off a curt reply while continuing to work on his scrap. The office manager, noticing that the hour was ticking by but that Baldy Li was not warming up to him, decided that he had no alternative but to play his final card. He told Baldy Li, "The governor asks that you go see him in his office."

Baldy Li shook his head and said, "I don't have time right now."

The office manager patted Baldy Li on the shoulder and shared with him the good news that the county's party secretary and deputy party secretary had both looked into the matter and agreed to allow him to resume his position as the director of the Good Works Factory. The office manager therefore urged him to see the governor without delay. "Go quickly. This is an opportunity you shouldn't pass up."

Baldy Li was not at all impressed, and without even bothering to look up he retorted, "Haven't you noticed that I am sorting through thousands of opportunities every day?"

The office manager returned dejectedly and repeated to the county governor what Baldy Li had said. The governor, now extremely irked, threw down the document he was holding and said, "What does he mean by saying he has thousands of opportunities every day? I'm the only one with thousands of opportunities every day."

After his tantrum, the county governor determined to go see Baldy Li himself. A few days later the deputy provincial governor was coming to visit, and the five mountains of scrap had to be cleaned up before he arrived. Although the county governor was furious, he was all smiles when he greeted Baldy Li: "Baldy Li, are you still sorting through your thousands of opportunities every day?"

Seeing that the governor himself had come, Baldy Li set aside what he was working on and straightened up to speak with him. He was much more humble than he had been with the office manager, saying, "What is this about my having thousands of opportunities every day? You are the only one with thousands of opportunities every day."

The governor didn't want to stand in front of Baldy Li's mountain of trash for too long—he feared that it would give the masses the wrong impression if he were seen—so he went straight to the point and told Baldy Li that the county had accepted his petition to return as director of the Good Works Factory. The only condition was that he had to clean up these five mountains of scrap within the next forty-eight hours. After hearing the governor's proposal, Baldy Li didn't respond but instead lowered his head and continued sorting his scrap. The governor stood to one side waiting for Baldy Li to answer, growing increasingly angry and resentful that Baldy Li wouldn't even acknowledge what a great kindness had been bestowed upon him. After sorting scrap for a while, Baldy Li found a mineral water bottle with some water left in it, so he unscrewed the cap and took a swig. Then, wiping his mouth, he asked the governor what his monthly salary would be if he returned to the factory.

The governor said that he wasn't certain, but that the State determined the salaries of cadres. Baldy Li then asked how much the governor himself made each month, and he replied vaguely that he earned several hundred yuan. Baldy Li laughed, pointed to his ten sweaty part-time workers, and said, "Even they make more than you do." He then added good-naturedly, "Governor, why don't you come work for me? I'll pay you one thousand yuan a month, and if you perform well, I will even give you a bonus."

The governor left absolutely livid, and when he returned to his office, he threw an even bigger tantrum. He called the office manager again and said that he was handing Baldy Li over to him. Regardless of what it might cost, it was essential that he have the mountains of scrap cleared away before the deputy provincial governor arrived. The office manager dejectedly returned to the gate, and when he saw Baldy Li, he cut straight to the chase. "Tell me, what would it take to get you to move?"

When Baldy Li heard this, he knew that his plan had come to fruition. He declared that he would never return to the Good Works Factory. Standing there in his tattered clothes, he said that the salary at the factory wasn't high enough for him, then spiritedly added, "And furthermore, *a good horse never grazes in the same spot twice.*"

Then, just as the office manager was at his wits' end, Baldy Li changed his tune. He said that his salvage and recycling company was not merely a business; it was a way of promoting socialism and of serving the people, and therefore it needed the support of the State. He said that he had been planning for some time to move these piles of scraps away from the entrance because he didn't want to cause the county leaders and residents to lose face. The only problem was that he didn't have anywhere to move to, and therefore he continued eking out a living here.

Baldy Li said this quite earnestly, and the office manager nodded emphatically. Taking advantage of the situation, Baldy Li suggested that the county's Real Estate Bureau owned several unused shops along the main street, as well as that empty warehouse that he had previously rented for his garment factory. The warehouse was quite out of the way and had a large empty lot in front that would be perfect for laying out his scrap. Those street-front shops, meanwhile, he could use as scrap retail stores and recycling centers. This way, they could make use of shops and a warehouse that were sitting empty while getting rid of the mountains of trash in front of the government building. "This is a solution that would please everyone."

The county office manager nodded and said he would look into it. A little more than an hour later, he and the Real Estate Bureau director returned together and told Baldy Li that the county had agreed to rent him three empty street-front stores at a low price and would permit him to use that empty warehouse for three years. The only condition was that he had to have the five mountains of scrap cleaned up within forty-eight hours.

"Two days?" Baldy Li shook his head. "Two days is too long. As Chairman Mao said, *We must seize every minute between dawn and dusk.* I will have this cleaned up within a day."

Baldy Li was true to his word. He hired 140 peasants and, combined with his 10 part-time workers and himself, the 151 of them worked twenty-four hours straight, and the five mountains of scrap vanished as if by magic. Not only did they sweep everything clean; they even placed two neat rows of potted lilies where the scrap heaps had been. When the county governor and the party secretary came to work the next morning, they stared in astonishment, thinking that they had come to the wrong place. Even the governor couldn't help but exclaim, "In all fairness, it must be admitted that Baldy Li has his good qualities."

The people of Liu had gotten used to Baldy Li's mountains of scrap. When they suddenly vanished, everyone ran around excitedly with the news, as if a new continent had been discovered. One after another they came to the entranceway of the government building to marvel at the sight and remarked that only now did they notice that the scenery around the entranceway was as beautiful as a painting.

One week later, Li's Salvage and Recycling Company held its grand opening. Two days earlier Blacksmith Tong had called a meeting with Tailor Zhang, Little Scissors Guan, Yanker Yu, and Popsicle Wang, whereupon they had reached two decisions. First, everyone would pool their money and buy a pile of firecrackers; and second, they would invite all their friends and relatives to attend. The day of the opening, about a hundred people came to offer their congratulations, as well as two hundred more spectators who crowded around to ogle at the hour-long fireworks display. The scene was as lively as a temple fair at New Year's. A beaming Baldy Li was still dressed in his usual ragged clothes, though for the occasion he sported a giant red corsage pinned to the front of his shirt. He stood on a table and spoke to the well-wishers, stammering and overcome with emotion. "Thank you . . . thank you . . . thank you . . . thank you. . . ."

After he had stammered out a whole string of thank-yous, he finally said relatively fluently, "Even if someone in the family had gotten married, we still wouldn't have had this many guests. Even if we had had a death in the family, we still wouldn't have seen this many people at the funeral. . . ."

The guests erupted in thunderous applause, and Baldy Li, who had just regained his composure, once again was overcome. Wiping his eyes and sniffling, he opened his mouth to speak but found himself completely choked up. He let out a few sniffles before finally being able to speak again. Sobbing, he said, "There's an old song you have all probably heard:

Neither the earth nor heaven is as vast as the kindness of the Party.
Neither mother nor father is as close as Chairman Mao.
A thousand or ten thousand goodnesses can't compare to the goodness of socialism.
And neither the river nor the sea is as deep as class love.

Baldy Li wiped his eyes and said, "I want to change the words to this song, and sing the new version for you." He then began to sing through his tears:

Neither the earth nor heaven is as big as the kindness of the Party and your kindness.
Neither mother nor father is as close as Chairman Mao and all of you.
A thousand or ten thousand goodnesses can't compare to the goodness of socialism and all of your goodness.
And neither the river nor the sea is a deep as your class love.

CHAPTER 49

BALDY LI'S scrap business boomed. A year later he obtained a passport with a Japanese visa so that he could travel to Japan to drum up some business. Before leaving, he paid a visit to his five former partners, asking them if they were interested in investing again. Baldy Li was now not lacking in money, but seeing that he was about to become as rich as an oil tanker, he immediately thought of his five former partners and felt that he should give them another opportunity, allowing them to follow him on the road to wealth.

Still in his tattered clothing, Baldy Li went to see Blacksmith Tong. The last time he arrived with his world map; this time he came with his passport in hand. He shouted at a sweat-covered Blacksmith Tong, "I'll bet that you've never seen a passport, have you?"

Blacksmith Tong had certainly heard about passports, but he had never seen one. Wiping both hands on his apron, he took the passport and examined it. He leafed through it enviously and cried out, "What is this foreign paper pasted inside?"

"This is a Japanese visa."

Baldy Li proudly put his passport away, carefully placing it in the pocket of his tattered shirt. He then sat down on the long bench with which he had had sexual relations as a boy, hiked up one leg, and grandiosely discussed his plans for his scrap business. He said that China could no longer satisfy his business needs, but perhaps the world could. He would first go to Japan to make some purchases. Blacksmith Tong asked, "Purchase what?"

"Purchase scrap," Baldy Li said. "I will start an international trade in scrap."

Then Baldy Li asked Blacksmith Tong whether he was interested in investing again. He said that he was now in a much better position than he had been four years earlier. If Blacksmith Tong was interested in investing now, he wouldn't charge him one hundred yuan for a share but one thousand. Even at one thousand yuan a share, Blacksmith Tong would still be getting a good deal. After Baldy Li finished, he threw Blacksmith Tong a nonchalant, take-it-or-leave-it glance.

Blacksmith Tong remembered the painful lesson he had learned the last time he invested, and a feeling of uneasiness welled up as he looked over at Baldy Li, standing there in his tattered clothing. He reasoned: *When this little bastard stayed put in Liu Town, he actually managed to get quite a few things done. But once he crosses the town line, who knows what kind of trouble he'll get into?* Blacksmith Tong shook his head and said that he wouldn't invest, explaining, "I'm content with what little I have and don't aspire to make a fortune."

Baldy Li laughed as he stood up, and with a magnanimous expression he walked to the door and once again pulled out his passport. Waving it at Blacksmith Tong he said, "I am now an international warrior."

Baldy Li left the blacksmith shop and then proceeded to visit Tailor Zhang and Little Scissors Guan. After hearing his plans to develop an international scrap business, they both hesitated, asking him if Blacksmith Tong had agreed to invest. Baldy Li shook his head, saying that Tong was content with what he had and lacked greater ambitions. Zhang and Guan said that they too were content with what they had and didn't have greater ambitions. Baldy Li looked at them pityingly and nodded as he said to himself, *In order to be an international warrior, one must have courage.*

As soon as Baldy Li left, Tailor Zhang and Little Scissors Guan rushed into Blacksmith Tong's shop and asked about investing in Baldy Li's new venture. Blacksmith Tong frowned. "All Baldy Li has to do is leave Liu Town and I go into a frenzy. Furthermore, scrap is not exactly an up-and-up kind of business."

"That's right," agreed Tailor Zhang and Scissors Guan, nodding.

Blacksmith Tong spat on the ground and continued: "Four years ago he was asking for one hundred yuan a share, but now it has risen to one thousand yuan a share, and he even has the gall to say that we're getting it cheap. This bastard's prices are rising much too fast."

"That's right." Tailor Zhang and Little Scissors Guan both nodded again.

"Even during the Sino-Japanese War, prices didn't rise this quickly," Blacksmith Tong said angrily. "It's peacetime now, and this bastard is still into war profiteering."

"Yes, that's right," Tailor Zhang and Scissors Guan agreed. "That bastard."

Baldy Li ran into Popsicle Wang in the street, and because of his former partners' earlier lack of enthusiasm, by the time he offered Wang the possibility of investing in his business, he was really just going through the motions. When Baldy Li concluded his pitch, Popsicle Wang fell into deep thought. He also remembered the painful lesson from last time around. Unlike Blacksmith Tong, Wang didn't stop there but went on to recall how Baldy Li had repaid his loans and how he had managed to make an opportunity where none seemed possible. Then Wang considered his own miserable situation: He had saved up one thousand yuan, but that was certainly not enough for him to retire on. Therefore, he figured he might as well gamble again, and if he lost, at least he had already lived the better part of his life. Baldy Li stood there waiting as Popsicle Wang—silent, his head bowed—seemed lost in thought. Finally Baldy Li lost his patience: "Are you in or out?"

Popsicle Wang looked up and asked, "So for five hundred yuan I would only get half a share?"

"That's a bargain, even at half a share," Baldy Li said.

"I'm in," Popsicle Wang said, gritting his teeth. "I'll put in one thousand yuan."

Baldy Li looked at him with surprise. "I never would have expected that you would be the one with grand aspirations. So it's true when they say that you can't judge a book by its cover."

Finally, Baldy Li went over to Yanker Yu's. Yu was in the midst of a career crisis. The county's Hygiene Bureau had announced that "free-lance" doctors like himself now had to take an exam: Those who passed would be given a formal medical license, while those who didn't would be stripped of their right to practice. As Baldy Li walked over, Yanker Yu had a thick *Human Anatomy* textbook in his lap and was reciting with his eyes closed. However, every time he got through the first half of a sentence, he would find that he had forgotten the second half; and after he opened his eyes to check on the second half of the sentence, he would find that he had already forgotten the first half. Yanker Yu kept opening and closing his eyes, as if he were exercising his eyelids.

Baldy Li plopped himself down on Yanker Yu's rattan recliner. Yu initially thought he had a customer, but when he opened his eyes, he found that it was only Baldy Li. Yanker Yu slammed his *Human Anatomy* textbook shut and asked angrily, "What is the most immoral thing in the world?"

"What *is* the most immoral thing in the world?" Baldy Li had no idea.

"The human body is the most immoral thing." Yanker Yu slapped the cover of the *Human Anatomy* volume. "A healthy human body not only contains many organs but has even more muscles, blood vessels, and nerves. I am no longer young—how can I ever learn them all? Don't you agree that this is immoral?"

Baldy Li nodded his agreement. "It is indeed fucking immoral."

As if a dam had burst open, Yanker Yu let loose a torrent of grievances. He said that in the thirty-odd years he had worked as a freelance dentist, he had extracted countless teeth and everyone loved him, calling him the best tooth-yanker within one hundred *li*. Now the fucking county Hygiene Bureau wanted everyone to take an exam, and this is where his career would fucking come to its bitter end. Yanker Yu's eyes grew red. He had enjoyed a spotless reputation his entire career, and now it was all going down the drain because this damn *Human Anatomy* textbook was proving to be his stumbling block. Yanker Yu watched the crowds strolling up and down the street and said heartbrokenly, "The crowds are just going to stand by as the leading tooth-yanker within one hundred *li* disappears."

Baldy Li couldn't help laughing. He reached out and patted the back of Yanker Yu's hand, asking if he was willing to invest again. Yanker Yu squinted his eyes, and like the other partners immediately embarked on a series of mental calculations. When he thought of Baldy Li's previous failure, he became panicky, but when he looked at the *Human Anatomy* textbook in his hands, he became even more panicky. After considering the issue from every conceivable angle, he asked whether his former partners had decided to reinvest or not. Baldy Li responded that Tong, Zhang, and Guan had chosen not to, but that Popsicle Wang would. Yanker Yu was astonished to hear that Popsicle Wang, having lost his investment once, would be willing to try a second time. He mumbled to himself, "Where did Popsicle Wang find the guts to do this?"

"He has soaring ambitions," Baldy Li said approvingly and added, "Just think, he doesn't have anyone he can count on, so naturally he counts on me."

Yanker Yu looked at the *Human Anatomy* volume he was holding in his hand, and it occurred to him that he didn't have anyone to count on either. He immediately grew bold and held up two fingers, saying, "I also have soaring ambitions. I'll put in two thousand yuan, for two shares."

When he finished, Yanker Yu threw his textbook to the ground and stomped on it. Grasping Baldy Li's hand, he exclaimed passionately, "I will follow you to the ends of the earth, Baldy Li. You have had such success with junk—who knows what you would have been capable of with nonjunk. Perhaps you could even have founded a nation—"

"I'm not at all interested in politics," said Baldy Li, cutting him off.

Yanker Yu, however, was not through. "What about your world map? Are all those dots still there? After you and I strike it rich, we should definitely visit all those sites."

The second time Baldy Li soared away from Liu Town, he again stopped at Mama Su's snack shop before leaving. As he ate his steamed bun he pulled his passport out of his ragged clothes and showed it to her, to expand her horizons. She took the passport with surprise, inspected it, then compared the photo with Baldy Li himself, saying, "The person in the photo looks a lot like you."

"What on earth do you mean, he looks like me?" Baldy Li protested. "That *is* me."

Mama Su continued to study the passport intently and asked in surprise, "With this you can go abroad to Japan?"

"Of course," Baldy Li said, retrieving his passport from Mama Su. "Your hands are covered with grease."

Embarrassed, Mama Su wiped her hands on her apron while Baldy Li used the sleeve of his shirt to wipe the grease off his passport. Noticing his tattered clothing, she asked, "You're going to wear this to go to Japan?"

"Don't worry, I won't make our nation lose face," Baldy Li said as he patted the dust on his clothing. "When I reach Shanghai, I'll buy a decent outfit."

When Baldy Li had filled his belly and was ready to walk out of Mama Su's shop, he remembered how four years earlier she had almost invested in his earlier venture, and he felt that he should give her a chance as well. Baldy Li briefly told her about the possibility of investing again. Mama Su's heart lurched, and she remembered the loss they had suffered the previous time, and how the reason she didn't lose her investment then was because she happened to have gone to the temple to burn incense. Recently business at her snack shop had been good, and she had been so busy that she hadn't been to the temple for three weeks. She warned herself that without having burned some incense, she shouldn't risk anything. Therefore, she shook her head and said that this time she wouldn't invest. Baldy Li nodded in disappointment for her and turned to leave, setting off valiantly toward the Liu Town bus depot. Thus for a second time he spread his wings and soared away.

CHAPTER 50

BALDY LI spread his wings and soared to Tokyo, Osaka, and Kobe, not skipping over Hokkaido and Okinawa either. He loitered in Japan for more than two months, during which time he amassed 3,567 tons of discarded "junk suits." These so-called junk suits looked brand-new, had impeccable tailoring, and fit just as well as the Italian-made Armani suits Baldy Li would later wear. The Japanese sold these old suits to Baldy Li for next to nothing, and Baldy Li in turn hired a Chinese freighter to ship them back to Shanghai. He wasn't willing to hire a Japanese freighter because, he explained, the Japanese charged far too much. In fact, merely hiring workers on the Japanese docks to load the suits onto the ferry would end up costing more than the 3,567 tons of suits themselves.

He sold the suits soon after he got to Shanghai. Within a few days so many scrap kings had come from all over the country that they were said to have completely filled a four-star hotel on Nanjing Road. The scrap kings hauled their cash around in large hemp sacks—dragging these sacks behind them as they trudged into the lobby of the hotel to register, dragging them onto the elevators, and continuing to drag them into their respective rooms. In the end, however, all the money in their sacks ended up in Baldy Li's hands. Li's junk suits were thereby distributed throughout the entire country via railways, highways, and waterways. As a result, throughout China people were removing their old wrinkled Mao suits and donning instead Baldy Li's Japanese junk suits.

Baldy Li of course never forgot those of us back in Liu, and he specifically set aside five thousand junk suits to bring back. By this point, Western suits had become quite fashionable in Liu, and when the town's young men needed new suits for their weddings, they would always ask Tailor Zhang to make them. After twenty years making Mao suits, now that Western-style suits had become fashionable Zhang switched to making them instead. The way he saw it, it was quite simple: Both kinds of suits had the same shoulder padding, so all you had to do was add a collar and lapels to a Mao suit and you would have a Western one. Invariably, though, after a couple of months, the young men of Liu found that Zhang's knock-off Western suits would begin to lose their shape. So when Baldy Li brought his suits back from Japan, the town found itself in a consuming frenzy, with huge crowds jostling toward the warehouse, diving into Baldy Li's pile of suits as if they were diving into a river. While searching feverishly for their size, everyone remarked on how the suits, even though they looked brand-new, were cheaper than secondhand ones sold elsewhere. Within a month Baldy Li had sold his entire stock of five thousand suits.

Li's Salvage and Recycling Company was livelier than a teahouse. Upon returning to Liu, Baldy Li had immediately changed back into his tattered old clothes and cheerfully sat there as people crowded around him every day, listening attentively to tales of his adventures in Japan. Every time he got to the part about how expensive things were in Japan, he would grit his teeth in mock anguish. He described how, for the price you would pay for a breakfast of fritters and soy milk in Japan, in Liu you could buy an entire pig. Plus, he added, a bowl of soy milk there was absurdly small, "not like the huge bowls we have here in Liu. The bowls they use in Japan are even smaller than our teacups, and their fritters are thinner than chopsticks." Everyone listened intently and agreed that it would be impossible to live in Japan. Indeed, were the gluttonous Pigsy from *Journey to the West* to spend time there, even he would become thinner than the White-Boned Demon.

"That's right, you simply can't live there," said Baldy Li. "Japan has money but no culture."

"Japan has no culture?" everyone repeated in surprise.

Baldy Li jumped up, and everyone opened a path for him. He walked over to the blackboard for recording sales, took up a piece of chalk, and wrote the number 8. Then he turned around and asked, "How do you pronounce this number?"

Everyone shouted, *"Ba."*

"Correct." Baldy Li nodded with satisfaction. "This is an Arabic numeral."

Baldy Li threw down his chalk, sat back down in his seat, and announced, "The Japanese don't understand Arabic numerals."

"Really?" Everyone's jaws dropped in astonishment.

Baldy Li crossed his legs and said proudly, "While I was in Japan, I wanted to spend some of the money I was earning, so where do you think I went? Naturally, I wanted to go to the poshest place I could find: a bar. But would I know where to find such a bar? I didn't even know the Japanese word for 'bar.' If I used the Chinese word for 'bar,' the Japanese wouldn't know what I was talking about. What could I do?"

Baldy Li paused dramatically. He licked his lips and gazed out at the crowd, savoring for a moment the crowd's impatient anticipation before continuing. "I, Baldy Li, had an inspiration. It occurred to me that even if the Japanese don't understand Chinese, shouldn't they at the very least understand Arabic numerals?"

The crowd nodded, and Baldy Li continued: "Therefore, I wrote the number 8 on my palm, which, read out loud, sounds like the word for 'bar,' right?"

"That's right," the crowd shouted back.

"I, Baldy Li, therefore was completely flabbergasted to find that, when I showed seventeen different Japanese people the number on my palm, not a single one of them had any idea what I was talking about. Is it therefore not true that the Japanese have no culture?"

"They indeed have no culture," the crowd cried out.

"But," Baldy Li concluded, "they do have money."

CHAPTER 51

NYONE IN LIU with any pride and self-respect whatsoever wore one of Baldy Li's junk suits. As for those without any pride and self-respect, they also wore his suits. After the men put on their handsome suits, they beamed with pride and bragged that they looked just like foreign heads of state. When Baldy Li heard this, he burst into peals of laughter, declaring that he was doing the town a great service by populating it with thousands upon thousands of foreign heads of state. The women, meanwhile, all continued to wear the same old hickish clothing they'd always had, leading the men to mock them as "local specialties." After mocking the women in this way, the men would then stand in front of the shop windows admiring themselves in their Western suits, remarking that if they had known that they would come to look like foreign heads of state, would they have married such local specialties in the first place? Of all the men in town, Baldy Li was the only one who didn't wear a Western suit. In Baldy Li's mind, even the best Western suit was ultimately still someone else's "junk suit," and no matter how tattered his own clothing was, it was nevertheless still his own. He didn't express these opinions out loud, and when people asked him why he kept wearing such tattered clothes, he would reply modestly, "I'm in the tattered-goods business, so of course I should wear tattered clothes."

Those Japanese junk suits each had a family surname stitched on their inner breast pocket. When the Liu men started donning the suits, they were fascinated by these surnames and would spend all day opening their jackets and looking to see which family's suits they were wearing, then bursting into fits of laughter.

At that time, Poet Zhao and Writer Liu were still wrapped up in their literary daydreams. Upon hearing that Baldy Li had brought over a shipment of Japanese suits, they immediately rushed over to his warehouse to rummage through the huge mountain of clothing. Writer Liu searched for three hours before eventually finding a Mishima suit. Poet Zhao refused to take this affront lying down and proceeded to spend four hours before finally finding himself a Kawabata suit.

As a result, Liu's two most eminent literary figures were both quite pleased with themselves, and when they ran into people, they immediately pulled open their jackets, showing off their Mishima and Kawabata labels. They informed the town's ignorant masses that these two surnames belonged to extraordinary families, and that Japan's two most accomplished authors were named Mishima and Kawabata—that is, Yukio Mishima and Yasunari Kawabata. While explaining this, their faces flushed bright red as if, in wearing Mishima and Kawabata suits, they had already become the town's own Yukio Mishima and Yasunari Kawabata. Now when Liu's two Men of Talent ran into each other in the street, they would first bow to each other before politely exchanging pleasantries.

One such time Writer Liu nodded his head and smiled as he inquired of Poet Zhao, "You have been well lately?"

Poet Zhao also smiled and nodded. "I have been well."

Writer Liu asked, "Have you penned any poems lately?"

"Lately I haven't been writing poetry," Poet Zhao replied. "Instead I have been planning out an essay. I already have a title: 'Liu Town the Beautiful and Myself.'"

Writer Liu shouted his approval: "But for two words it could be Yasunari Kawabata's famous essay 'Japan the Beautiful and Myself'!"

Poet Zhao nodded modestly and inquired of Writer Liu, "And you, sir, have you penned any short stories lately?"

"These days I haven't been writing stories," Liu answered. "Instead I have been plotting out a novel, whose title will be *Temple of the Peaceful Heaven*."

"That is a great title," Poet Zhao exclaimed loudly. "But for two words it could be Yukio Mishima's masterpiece *Temple of the Golden Pavilion*."

The town's two Men of Talent bowed to each other once more and then set off at stately paces in opposite directions. Liu's townspeople watched them with amusement, remarking that these two idiots had just been seen chatting with each other, so how was it that an hour later this had become "lately"? And what was up with this business of bowing to each other? The Liu elders who still remembered having seen Japanese soldiers during the war explained that when Japanese meet, they always bow to each other. Some of the townspeople pointed to the departing Writer Liu and Poet Zhao and said skeptically, "But those two are quite obviously Liu town idiots, not Japanese idiots."

Yanker Yu and Popsicle Wang strutted spiritedly through the streets of Liu. Baldy Li had struck it rich with his Japanese junk suits, and since these two had bought in, their boats now rose with the tide, and cash filled their pockets. Yanker Yu tossed out his thick *Human Anatomy* textbook, put away his dentistry implements, and announced his retirement. He added that from now on there wouldn't be another tooth pulled within a hundred-mile radius of Liu, and even if all the Liu townsfolk were about to die from toothaches, he would still pay them no heed. Popsicle Wang immediately followed Yu's lead, throwing away his icebox and announcing that the following summer there would be no sight of it and that even if the Liu townspeople were all dying of thirst, he would still pay them no heed.

Yanker Yu wore a Matsushita suit while Popsicle Wang wore a Sanyo one, and both strolled idly up and down the streets of Liu. When they ran into each other, they couldn't help laughing, happier than a pair of toads feasting on the succulent flesh of a swan. Then Yanker Yu would pat his pocket and ask Wang, "Do you have any money?"

Wang would pat his own pocket and answer, "Yup."

Yu, intoxicated with his sudden wealth, concluded, "This is what is called reaching heaven in a single step."

Then, out of curiosity, Yanker Yu asked Popsicle Wang which family's suit he was wearing. Wang dramatically pulled open his jacket and displayed the Sanyo name embroidered on the inside of his breast pocket. Yu exclaimed in surprise, "It's the Sanyo family, the electronics kings!"

Wang laughed with satisfaction. Yu, not to be outdone, pulled open his own suit jacket. Wang looked in and saw the name Matsushita and also remarked in surprise, "Yours belongs to the Matsushita family, owners of Panasonic!"

"Sanyo and Matsushita are both electronics kings, meaning that you and I are in the same field." Yu waved his hand and added, "We're not only in the same field; we're fierce competitors."

"That's right." Wang nodded emphatically.

At that point Song Gang, who was also wearing a Japanese junk suit, walked over. When all the men in Liu started wearing suits, Lin Hong rushed over to Baldy Li's warehouse and spent a couple of hours rummaging around for a suit for her husband. Song Gang's handsome figure in a handsome black suit was a sight to behold as he strutted through town. Everyone who saw him in his suit shouted out their approval, saying that Song Gang was even more commanding than the Warring States period poet Song Yu and even more dashing than the Western Jin Dynasty gallant Pan An. Yanker Yu and Popsicle Wang heard everyone's shouts of approval and made a show of also nodding their heads, although in reality they were a bit envious. Yu gestured for Song Gang to come over, and when he approached, Yu asked him, "Whose is yours?"

Song Gang pulled open his jacket and said, "The Fukuda family's."

Yu looked at Popsicle Wang, and Wang said, "I've never heard of them."

"I haven't heard of them either," added Yu with satisfaction. "Compared with the Matsushita and Sanyo families, the Fukuda are clearly quite insignificant. However," Yu suggested, "if you change a single character in Fukuda, then you have Toyota, which is a huge car manufacturer."

Song Gang smiled. "Well, this Fukuda suits me fine."

Yu shook his head regretfully at Wang, who did the same. Even though their physiques and appearance could not compare with Song Gang's, the lineage of their suits was obviously far superior. Yu and Wang therefore continued to strut proudly though the streets of town, then entered the little alley where they both lived and walked right up to Tailor Zhang's little stand. At that moment, Zhang, also in a junk suit, was sitting on the bench where his customers usually sat. Yu and Wang laughed as they stood in his doorway, but Zhang merely stared at them blankly, completely lost in thought. Yu asked Zhang, "Whose is yours?"

Zhang snapped out of his reverie and saw Yu and Wang standing there. He laughed bitterly. "Baldy Li is such a bastard. Now that he's brought all these imported suits here, no one wants me to make them anything."

Yanker Yu had no interest in Tailor Zhang's woes. He repeated, "Whose is yours?"

Tailor Zhang sighed and waved his hands. "No one will ask me to make them suits anymore."

Yanker Yu shouted impatiently, "I'm asking you which family's suit are you wearing?"

Finally understanding, Tailor Zhang peeked inside his jacket: "Jiushan."

Yanker Yu and Popsicle Wang looked at each other, and Wang asked

Tailor Zhang, "Is that the same Jiushan who was one of the Japanese enemies in the Cultural Revolutionary model opera *The Red Lantern*?"

Tailor Zhang nodded. "Yes, that's the one."

Somewhat disappointed to discover that Tailor Zhang wasn't wearing a no-name suit, Wang asked, "Does this also count as a famous name?"

"It is indeed a famous name," Yu replied. "But *in*famous."

Popsicle Wang nodded emphatically. "Yes, definitely infamous."

Yanker Yu and Popsicle Wang felt as if they had survived a close call at Tailor Zhang's. They smugly continued forward, finally reaching Little Scissors Guan's stand. Little Guan had found himself two junk suits, one black and the other gray, whereupon he abruptly decided he no longer wished to keep sharpening scissors. He stood in front of his stand flaunting his exquisite sense of style, wearing his black suit in the morning and his gray suit in the afternoon. Whenever he encountered anyone, he would start chattering endlessly while lightly brushing the dandruff off his shoulders—using his left hand to brush his right shoulder and his right hand to brush his left. Ever since the men of Liu started wearing these junk suits, at every occasion they would open each other's jackets and ask, "Whose is yours?" This quickly became a fad, and Little Scissors Guan finally noticed that his own suits were not name brands, which left him depressed for several days. Eventually he plucked off the no-name labels from the breast pockets of his suits and stitched the names Sony and Hitachi in their place. Little Scissors Guan was thinking that Sony and Hitachi were famous electronics brands, but what he didn't realize was that they were brand names, not surnames. When Yanker Yu and Popsicle Wang approached, Little Scissors Guan, wearing his black Sony suit, proudly leaned over and eagerly asked, "Whose are yours?"

"The Matsushita family's." Yu opened his jacked to show Little Scissors Guan and pointed to Popsicle Wang, saying, "His is a Sanyo."

"Not bad," Little Scissors Guan said, nodding approvingly. "Those families are not bad at all."

Yanker Yu laughed, saying, "Which family's is yours?"

"Also not bad." Little Guan pulled open his jacket. "Sony."

"You too are an electronics king!" Yanker Yu shouted with glee.

Little Scissors Guan pointed behind him, saying proudly, "In my closet I also have a Hitachi brand suit."

Popsicle Wang noted with surprise, "Your two suits are in the same business?"

Yanker Yu added, "You are your own competitor."

"You are correct." Little Scissors Guan was very satisfied with Yu's remark and patted him on the shoulder. "This is called challenging oneself."

Yanker Yu and Popsicle Wang tittered as they left Little Scissors Guan's shop and proceeded to Blacksmith Tong's. Tong was wearing a dark blue suit, over which he had his trademark apron. The apron was covered with little comet-shaped burn holes. Yu and Wang stared in disbelief at the sight of Tong wearing a suit to do his hammering and soldering, leading Popsicle Wang to whisper to Yanker Yu, "Can a Western suit also be used as work clothes?"

Overhearing them, Tong proclaimed, "A suit *is* work clothes." He put down his iron hammer and added, "The foreigners on television all wear suits to work."

"Yes, that's true." Yanker Yu instructed Popsicle Wang, "Suits serve as foreigners' work clothes."

Popsicle Wang looked at his own suit and said, somewhat disappointed. "So all this time we've been wearing work clothes?"

Unfazed, Yanker Yu excitedly asked Blacksmith Tong, "Whose is yours?"

Blacksmith Tong calmly removed his apron and opened his jacket. "It's the Tong family's."

Yanker Yu was startled. "They also have the Tong surname in Japan?"

"I stitched it on myself," Tong explained with unmistakable pride. "I asked my wife to remove the original Japanese name and replaced it with my own."

Yu nodded and said, "Your own surname is certainly fine, it's just that it isn't famous."

Tong snorted and, putting his apron back on, said, "You people in your foreign clothes have completely forgotten your Chinese ancestry and have lost all integrity. Why were there so many traitors during the war? One has only to look at people like you to understand why."

Saying this, Tong lifted his hammer and continued pounding the iron, whereupon Yu and Wang turned around and walked away. Yanker Yu said angrily to Wang, "Damn, if he has so much integrity, then why's he still wearing a Japanese suit?"

"That's right," Popsicle Wang said. "Isn't that like trying to hawk your wares as a whore but still competing for a chastity medal?"

Soon even the county governor started wearing a Japanese junk suit. His was embroidered with the surname Nakasone, which was the name of the Japanese prime minister at the time: Yasuhiro Nakasone. The governor had heard that Baldy Li had obtained a shipment of Japanese suits, and he noticed that the people in the provincial government were all wearing these suits. He immediately wanted one for himself and asked Tao Qing to accompany him to Baldy Li's warehouse to take a look. The governor got himself this Nakasone suit, and Tao Qing got a Takeshita one. When the governor tried his on, he found that it fit very well, almost as if it had been specifically tailored for him. He looked at himself in the mirror, thinking he never would have guessed he was so similar to Yasuhiro Nakasone. Of course, the governor could not go about town flashing his adopted family name as Yanker Yu and Popsicle Wang did. As a result, it was only when he removed his jacket to drape it over his chair that people spotted the Nakasone name, whereupon they would invariably cry out, "Governor, you are wearing a suit of the Japanese prime minister!"

The governor would be secretly pleased but feign disapproval, saying, "It's coincidental, purely coincidental."

Tao Qing, however, was quite displeased, given that he was the one who had found the Nakasone suit in the first place. He was on the verge of trying it on when he noticed the governor glaring at him. Tao Qing therefore didn't dare take the Nakasone suit, and the governor snatched it up. Tao Qing managed to squeeze out a smile and compliment the governor on how well the suit fit, and in order not to expose his own political ambitions, he then grabbed another suit, a Takeshita, for himself. After this, every morning when Tao put on his Takeshita suit, he would remember bitterly the Nakasone. Unexpectedly, half a year later, Yasuhiro Nakasone stepped down as prime minister, and his replacement's name turned out to be Noboru Takeshita. Meanwhile, the county governor was transferred away, and Tao Qing was promoted in his place. In his new capacity as county governor, Tao gazed at his reflection in the mirror in his Takeshita suit, and as a flood of emotions rushed through his mind, he muttered, "It is indeed fate."

CHAPTER 52

AFTER BALDY LI made his fortune from junk suits, his first thought was of Song Gang. Now that his plans had come to fruition, he decided to invite Song Gang to join him in creating a business empire together. Baldy Li turned the house upside down looking for the sweater Song Gang had knit him when he first became factory director. The next day he wore it, with his coat open so that the image of the Great Prospects Ship embroidered on the front of the sweater was clearly visible, and sailed majestically through the streets of Liu to Song Gang's place. He hadn't been there since the day he had shown up with his vasectomy certificate following Song Gang's wedding. Baldy Li stood there, watching Song Gang and Lin Hong through the window, and when the two of them opened the door and walked out, he excitedly pulled open his tattered coat and said warmly, "Song Gang, do you remember this sweater? Do you remember this Great Prospects Ship? Song Gang, you were right, I am now finally captain of my own Great Prospects Ship. Song Gang, why don't you come and be the ship's first mate?"

When Song Gang opened the door and saw Baldy Li standing there, he jumped with surprise, never expecting to see his brother waiting outside his house. He hadn't said a word to Baldy Li for several years, and when they would run into each other in the street, he would quickly ride past on his bike. Therefore, when Baldy Li started shouting something about a Great Prospects Ship, Song Gang looked uneasily at Lin Hong, but Lin Hong remained calm and collected. Song Gang bowed his head as he pushed his bike across the threshold and then, his head still bowed, waited for Lin Hong to climb on and sit behind him.

Baldy Li continued warmly, "Song Gang, I didn't sleep well last night since I was thinking all this through. It occurred to me that you are too honest, too easy to be taken advantage of, so I can't put you in charge of anything except the finances, but if you would come and manage my finances, it would take an enormous load off my mind."

As Song Gang started to ride away he told Baldy Li coldly, "I already told you: You should give up hope."

When Baldy Li heard this, he simply stared in astonishment. He had never imagined Song Gang could be so heartless. After staring for a while, he rushed after Song Gang, cursing, "Song Gang, you bastard. You fucking listen to me—last time it was you who severed our relationship, but this time I'm the one who is breaking things off. From now on, we are no longer brothers!"

Baldy Li was crushed, and as he rushed after Song Gang and Lin Hong, he called out, "Song Gang, you bastard. You have forgotten about our childhood!"

Song Gang heard Baldy Li's curses as he was riding away, and that final "You have forgotten about our childhood" instantly brought tears to his eyes. He rode away in silence, and Lin Hong, sitting behind him, also didn't utter a sound. Song Gang's attempts to be heartless toward Baldy Li were all for the sake of Lin Hong, but she showed no reaction whatsoever, making him uneasy. After he turned the corner, Song Gang softly called out, "Lin Hong, Lin Hong . . ."

Lin Hong grunted in response and whispered back, "Baldy Li meant well . . ."

Song Gang felt even more uneasy, and he asked her in a hoarse voice, "Did I say something wrong?"

"No, you didn't say anything wrong." Lin Hong wrapped her arms around Song Gang and pressed her cheek against his back. Song Gang finally relaxed and let out a long sigh. He heard her say, "No matter how much money he now has, it's from collecting scrap. What's so great about that? At the end of the day, we still have our state-issued jobs, and if he doesn't have one, things will be very difficult for him down the road."

After being rebuffed at Song Gang's, Baldy Li thought back to his fourteen loyal minions at the Good Works Factory. He went to the Civil Affairs Bureau to look for Director Tao Qing, who was about to become county governor, although he himself didn't know it yet. Tao Qing was in the process of agonizing over what to do with the Good Works Factory, which was bleeding money year after year, when Baldy Li walked in and announced that he wanted to purchase it. Tao Qing stared at him in astonishment, not knowing whether or not Baldy Li was for real. Baldy Li explained emotionally that, although those fourteen handicapped workers were not his relatives, they were nevertheless closer than kin. Tao Qing was secretly elated: The Good Works Factory had become the Civil Affairs Bureau's biggest burden—they couldn't even give it away—but now here was Baldy Li wanting to spend good money to buy it. The two of them immediately reached an agreement and shook on it. After buying the Good Works Factory, Baldy Li proceeded to renovate it and transform it into the Liu Town Economic Research Center, even changing the nameplate on the door. Within a few days he decided that the word *center* was too ordinary, and since he had just been to Japan, he altered the nameplate to say Liu Town Economic Research Business Corporation. He then issued each of his fourteen loyal minions a letter of appointment, appointing the crippled factory director to the position of corporation director and the deputy factory director to the position of deputy corporation director. The remaining twelve workers he appointed as senior researchers, allowing each of them to enjoy a salary equivalent to that of a university professor. When the two cripples accepted their letters of appointment, they were both extremely excited, knowing that Baldy Li would now provide for them for life. However, they tearfully asked him, "Director Li, what will we study?"

"You can study chess," Baldy Li said. "What else are you capable of studying?"

"Okay." They nodded, then asked, "And what about the twelve senior researchers?"

"The twelve senior researchers?" Baldy Li thought for a moment and then said, "The four blind men will study light and the five deaf men will study sound. But about the three idiots? Fuck, let them study evolution."

After providing for his fourteen loyal minions, Baldy Li hired two horticulturists from the province to reseed the area outside the county government building, plant some flowers, and even build a fountain. The entranceway became a scenic spot, and every evening and weekend the townspeople would bring the young and elderly, sighing at the beautiful scenery. When the senior leaders came for their inspection, they saw that in place of the mountains of scrap there were now green grass, fresh flowers, and a fountain. They couldn't resist pausing for a while in the entranceway to express their admiration. The county officials were ecstatic, and the Nakasone suit–wearing county governor personally paid a call to Baldy Li, thanking him on behalf of the county government as well as the entire province. Baldy Li not only didn't gloat or trumpet his successes; he even took the governor's hand and apologized repeatedly to the governor himself, the county government, and the people of the entire province, saying that he should never have left those mountains of scrap in the entranceway. Paying for the new landscaping, he explained, was simply his way of making amends.

Baldy Li became a favorite of the county officials, and soon he was appointed as representative to the provincial People's Congress. Half a year later, when the county governorship was handed over to the Takeshita suit–wearing Tao Qing, Baldy Li's status was elevated even higher, as he was appointed representative to the Standing Committee of the provincial People's Congress. Even after making his fortune, however, Baldy Li continued to wear his tattered clothes, even when attending the provincial People's Congress—looking like a beggar who had wandered up to the platform. County Governor Tao Qing couldn't bear it any longer and while addressing the assembly, publicly beseeched Baldy Li to take care of his appearance. As soon as Tao uttered his request, Baldy Li, who had just finished giving his comments, returned to the stage. The representatives thought he was about to announce that he wouldn't wear tattered clothes anymore, but he surprised everyone by explaining instead why he dressed this way: Back when he had no money, he had to struggle arduously, and now that he had money, he had to struggle more arduously. Pointing to his tattered clothing, he said, "This is inspired, on the one hand, by the Spring and Autumn Period story of King Gou Jian of Yue, who slept on sticks and ate bitter food; and, more recently, by how the poor and middle-class peasants during the Cultural Revolution contrasted their past misery with their present happiness."

At the end of the year, Baldy Li called Yanker Yu and Popsicle Wang to his office at Li's Salvage and Recycling Company, announcing that profits and dividends from the past year had not been bad at all. Yanker Yu had two shares for his two thousand yuan investment and Popsicle Wang had one share for his thousand yuan, meaning that Yanker Yu would receive dividends of twenty thousand yuan and Popsicle Wang ten thousand yuan. At the time there didn't yet exist one-hundred-yuan bills, the largest bill being only ten yuan. Therefore, Baldy Li pushed twenty thick piles of bills toward Yanker Yu and ten thick piles toward Popsicle Wang. The two of them looked at each other, unable to believe their good fortune. Baldy Li leaned back in his chair as if he were watching a movie, laughing at them.

Yanker Yu and Popsicle Wang counted to themselves, calculating that in less than a year their initial investment had yielded a return of 1,000 percent. Yu and Wang laughed idiotically, and Yanker Yu mumbled to himself, "Never in my wildest dreams did I imagine that a two-thousand-yuan investment would yield twenty thousand yuan in profits."

"It's not profit," Baldy Li corrected him. "These are dividend payments. You two are my shareholders, and from now on you will receive dividend payments every year."

Popsicle Wang asked as if in a dream, "I'll receive another ten thousand yuan every year?"

"Not necessarily," Baldy Li answered. "Next year you might receive fifty thousand yuan."

Popsicle Wang seemed as if he were about to have a seizure, almost falling out of his chair. Yanker Yu asked in astonishment, "And will I receive a hundred thousand yuan?"

"Of course," Baldy Li nodded. "If Popsicle Wang receives fifty thousand yuan, you will receive a hundred thousand yuan."

Yu and Wang again looked skeptical. They glanced at each other and wondered how there could ever be such a good deal. Popsicle Wang asked Yanker Yu carefully, "Is this for real?"

Yanker Yu nodded but then shook his head and said, "I don't know."

Baldy Li laughed out loud and said, "You can pinch yourselves, and if it hurts, then you'll know it's real."

They quickly pinched themselves, and then Yanker Yu asked Popsicle Wang, "Did it hurt?"

Popsicle Wang shook his head nervously. "No, it didn't."

Yanker Yu also became nervous. "I didn't feel it either."

Baldy Li laughed uproariously, shouting, "I'm laughing so hard my belly hurts. You didn't pinch yourselves hard enough. Give me your hands; I'll pinch them for you."

Yanker Yu and Popsicle Wang extended their hands to Baldy Li, who gave them both a fierce pinch, making them cry out in pain: "Ouch!"

Yanker Yu was overjoyed and said to Popsicle Wang, "It's real!"

Popsicle Wang was even more pleased. He extended his hand to Yanker Yu, saying, "Mine is even bleeding."

With their big mouths, Yanker Yu and Popsicle Wang functioned as the town's radio broadcast station. After their bumper crop, they both eagerly told everyone about how they had struck it rich. Everyone became extremely envious, and when Blacksmith Tong, Tailor Zhang, and Little Scissors Guan heard, they fell into a deep funk. Those days, Tailor Zhang and Scissors Guan met every day to complain about Blacksmith Tong, regretting that they hadn't invested in Baldy Li's new enterprise. Under their repeated retellings, the story eventually morphed into Blacksmith Tong's having prevented them from investing, and they became convinced that if it hadn't been for his interference, they would now be as impressive as Yanker Yu and Popsicle Wang, or more so. In hindsight they both became as prescient as the legendary Three Kingdoms strategist Zhuge Liang, saying that they would have sold off their possessions and invested the resulting money in Baldy Li's scrap business if it hadn't been for Blacksmith Tong.

Tong knew those two bastards were getting together every day and cursing him, but he pretended not to notice. He sat in his shop and also regretted his missed opportunity, thinking that the first time he invested when he shouldn't have and the second time he failed to invest when he should have. Blacksmith Tong sat rubbing his fists together, thinking he must have been blind, and venting his frustration on his ten fingers.

Mama Su was also regretful. The second time Baldy Li had set off from Liu Town, he had asked her if she wanted to invest; Mama Su had thought about how she hadn't been to the temple in a long time, so had shook her head and declined. Later, every time she recalled this, she would sigh, thinking that if only she had gone to the temple to burn incense, she would definitely have invested. She told everyone she encountered, "I hadn't burned incense at the temple, and that's why things didn't work out for me."

After returning from Japan, Baldy Li realized that his scrap business had reached its peak and would have nowhere to go but down. Therefore he decided to develop some new enterprises. First he opened a clothing factory, and in memory of old times he appointed Tailor Zhang to serve as his technical deputy director. Tailor Zhang was extremely grateful. With a tape measure draped around his neck, he conscientiously oversaw the quality in the workshop, being always the first to come to work in the morning and the last to leave in the evening. After the clothing factory started to enjoy some success, Baldy Li redoubled his efforts, opening two restaurants and a bathhouse and even dabbling in real estate. When it came time, at the end of the following year, to distribute dividends again, Yanker Yu and Popsicle Wang did indeed receive one hundred thousand and fifty thousand yuan, respectively. This time, however, they weren't surprised but, rather, acted as if they were expecting it. When they arrived, they each brought a travel bag and, while stuffing the bags full of bills, they appeared as relaxed as if they were filling a rice jar with rice.

Baldy Li sat in his chair watching Yanker Yu and Popsicle Wang as they calmly stuffed one pile of bills after another into their travel bags. He was very satisfied with their attitude and complimented them. "Both of you have matured."

Yanker Yu and Popsicle Wang laughed reservedly and calmly sat down. Baldy Li bowed his head as if lost in thought, then looked up and mused, "It is said that *a tradesman walks while a mogul sits*. In other words, only when your business dealings have reached the point where you can trade while staying put can they be considered as having reached their maximum potential, and only then can you be considered a major player in the business world. If you have to run around yourself, then you must be engaged in only small deals—meaning that you're a mere tradesman."

Baldy Li told Yanker Yu and Popsicle Wang that his family of businesses kept on growing: He was still pursuing his scrap business and hiring more and more workers for his clothing factory, even as his two restaurants and his bathhouse were booming, and he also had several ongoing real estate projects. As a result, he spent every day running around like a chicken with its head cut off. He said that for now he was still okay, but that in the future, when he had forty or even four hundred businesses, he couldn't possibly manage even if he bought himself an F-16 fighter plane for transportation. He had thought that he had become a major player in the business world, but now he had come to realize that he was still a salesman on the go. Baldy Li then stood up and announced that he had decided to be a sitting mogul, establishing a holding company modeled on the Qin emperor's unification of China. He would bundle his various businesses into his holding company, then simply sit in his office and trade from there, using a centralized model to do business and only occasionally going to visit his various businesses in person. When Baldy Li saw Yu and Wang nodding enthusiastically, he asked them, "Do you know why the first Qin emperor unified China?"

The two looked at each other and shook their heads. "We don't know."

"It was because," Baldy Li said proudly, "that bastard wanted to get into some serious big business. That bastard didn't want to be a mere traveling salesman any longer but instead wanted to be a seated mogul."

Yanker Yu and Popsicle Wang were stirred by Baldy Li's grand vision. They asked him, "After you become a mogul, what will become of us?"

"You will be shareholders and trustees in my holding company." Baldy Li pointed at himself and said, "I will be the chairman of the board of directors and the company president."

Yanker Yu and Popsicle Wang looked at each other and laughed, and Popsicle Wang asked Baldy Li, "Will we have trustees' business cards?"

"Of course." Baldy Li was feeling generous. "And if you want another position, we could consider also appointing you vice president."

"Yes, absolutely!" Yanker Yu cried out, and said to Popsicle Wang, "The more titles, the better."

"Of course." Popsicle Wang nodded, then asked Baldy Li, "Are there any other positions you could give us?"

"No." Baldy Li grew angry. "How could there be so many positions for you?"

Sensing Baldy Li's annoyance, Yanker Yu quickly nudged Popsicle Wang and chastised him, saying, "You shouldn't be too greedy."

After assuming their new titles, Yanker Yu and Popsicle Wang starting distributing their new business cards even faster than Baldy Li. They would stand in the middle of the street handing them out to everyone who walked by, as if they were handing out sales flyers.

Blacksmith Tong and Little Scissors Guan also received Yu's and Wang's business cards. After Tailor Zhang threw in his lot with Baldy Li, Little Guan found himself with no friends left and with no choice but to renew his friendly alliance with Blacksmith Tong. With Yanker Yu's and Popsicle Wang's name cards in hand, Little Guan remarked to Blacksmith Tong that those two bastards were really letting their petty successes go to their heads, to the extent that even the town's chickens, ducks, cats, and dogs must have received their cards by now.

The intelligent and capable Blacksmith Tong was the first person in Liu to follow Baldy Li's lead into entrepreneurial wealth. Seeing that the people of Liu were doing better than ever and that even peasants living in the countryside were becoming increasingly wealthy, he realized that there was no future in being a blacksmith. Therefore, he stopped making cleavers for the townspeople and sickles and hoes for the farmers, and suddenly one day his entire blacksmith shop was gone, having been transformed into a specialty store selling all sorts of cutlery.

Blacksmith Tong didn't smoke or drink, and he worked the counter energetically. His ironworker hands may have looked rough and clumsy, but he could count piles of cash faster than a bank teller. Rapidly licking his finger and counting the bills, he looked as if he could give a bank's automated bill counter a run for its money.

Once Blacksmith Tong opened his cutlery shop, Little Scissors Guan's customers began to dwindle. Scissors Guan became very angry. Feeling that Blacksmith Tong had destroyed his business, he vowed to break off all relations, and once again their friendly alliance was destroyed. As business at Blacksmith Tong's cutlery shop boomed, Scissors Guan lost all his remaining customers, until finally he had no alternative but to close down his shop and simply roam the streets every day. He would frequently run into Yanker Yu and Popsicle Wang, who were similarly wandering aimlessly, and the three of them would then hold meetings like in the old days. Scissors Guan would vehemently curse Blacksmith Tong for first discouraging him from investing in Baldy Li's business and then stealing his livelihood and forcing him to close the knife-sharpening stall, which had been in his family for three generations, leaving him no recourse but to roam.

Yanker Yu and Popsicle Wang sympathized with Little Guan's predicament, and Wang suggested, "Why don't we go to President Li and ask him to give Scissors Guan a job?"

"Why ask President Li?" Yanker Yu replied. "We are both vice presidents. We might not be able to offer anything else, but we should at least be able to arrange for him to serve as a doorman."

"You want me to be a doorman? Fuck that!" Little Guan was enraged when he heard Yanker Yu's suggestion. "If it had not been for a minor mistake in the beginning, I would now be a trustee and vice president like yourselves, and furthermore would have been ahead of you in line."

Little Guan left in a huff. Popsicle Wang looked at Yanker Yu in astonishment, and Yu sniffed disapprovingly, "That was a classic case of *the dog biting the hand that feeds it*."

Little Guan finally made up his mind that if he could no longer get by in Liu Town, he might as well go out into the world to seek his fortune. He remembered the first time Baldy Li traveled to Shanghai and lost their entire investment. The second time, however, he went to Japan and made a fortune. Little Guan decided that if he was going to go away, he should go as far away as possible.

The spring flowers had bloomed, and as Little Guan determinedly walked down the street to the bus depot carrying one bag and dragging another, his father hobbled pitifully behind him. Little Guan had told everyone who would listen that he was going to travel farther and see even more of the world than Baldy Li ever had and had sworn that by the time he returned he would be richer in experiences and wealthier than Baldy Li. Old Guan couldn't keep up with him and fell farther and farther behind. He beseeched his son not to leave, calling out hoarsely, "You are not fated to be rich. Others might be able to make a fortune by going out into the world, but you certainly won't."

Little Guan paid his father no heed and energetically waved good-bye to the people of Liu. Everyone assumed he was going to Europe or America, and they shouted their congratulations, asking where he was going first. Little Guan's reply, however, greatly disappointed them: "I'm first going to Hainan Island."

They replied, "But Hainan Island isn't even as far as Japan."

"It's true that it's not as far as Japan," Little Guan noted, "but it is much farther than Baldy Li went the first time he left Liu, when he went to Shanghai."

Little Guan boarded the bus and was about to depart when Old Guan finally caught up. Grasping his walking stick with both hands, he watched as the bus drove away in a cloud of dust. With tears running down his cheeks he cried out, "Son, if you are fated to have only fifteen ounces of rice in this life, then even if you go away to seek your fortune, you still won't end up with a full pound."

Baldy Li also took his leave from Liu Town. Headed for Shanghai, he was wearing his usual tattered clothing as he made his way to the bus depot. Following behind him was a young man carrying his bags like an attendant. When people saw them, they asked who the youngster was, and Baldy Li replied that it was his driver. The crowds tittered—"So Baldy Li has hired himself a driver but doesn't even have a car"—and reported that they saw Baldy Li and his driver board the long-distance bus to Shanghai.

Baldy Li returned several days later. This time he didn't take the bus but, rather, rode back in a red Santana sedan he had bought in Shanghai. The driver drove Baldy Li's car into Liu Town and stopped in front of a department store. When Baldy Li emerged from his sedan, he was wearing a black Armani suit, having thrown away his tattered clothing while in Shanghai.

No one recognized Baldy Li when he first stepped out of his sedan. Everyone had grown accustomed to seeing him in his old and tattered clothing, and for him to suddenly be sporting a fancy Armani suit threw everyone for a loop. Furthermore, in those days only party leaders had sedans, so everyone speculated avidly about which important personage he might be. They felt that his shiny bald pate looked familiar, but they couldn't quite place it. Was he a TV actor? A high-level cadre from the provincial capital? Just as they were concluding that he must be a party leader from Beijing, the infatuated idiot, still wearing his watch set to Greenwich Mean Time, wandered over and called out in a ringing voice, "Director Li."

The crowds were stunned, marveling, "So it's actually Baldy Li!"

Someone added, "This person does look like Baldy Li—in fact, they are virtually identical!"

CHAPTER 53

OUR LIU TOWN was turned upside down. The big-shot Baldy Li and County Governor Tao Qing now spoke as one and jointly announced that they were going to tear down the old Liu Town and build a new one. Everyone said that this was a classic case of collusion of business and government, with Tao Qing providing the official documents and Baldy Li providing the capital and labor. They demolished one street after another, gradually transforming the face of the entire town. For five full years, Liu Town was covered in dirt and dust from dawn to dusk. Everyone complained that they were inhaling more dust than oxygen and that the layer of dirt permanently caked on their necks was thicker than a scarf. They said that Baldy Li was like a B-52 bomber, carpet-bombing the formerly beautiful town. A few educated townspeople became more embittered than the rest; they remarked that the classic novel *Romance of Three Kingdoms* had a scene that was set in Liu, *Journey to the West* had a scene and a half, while *Water Margin* had two entire scenes—but now Baldy Li had demolished the town and its landmarks.

Baldy Li demolished the old Liu Town and built a new one. In just five years he expanded the roads and alleys and built countless new buildings, after which the townspeople stopped finding dirt on their collars and the amount of oxygen in their lungs again exceeded the dust. They still complained, however, saying that even though their old houses might have been old and decrepit, at least they had gotten them from the government. Although the new houses were big and new, it was nevertheless necessary to buy them from Baldy Li. There is a saying that *rabbits will spare the grass growing next to their burrow*. But Baldy Li was really rotten to the core and had chomped down on every last blade of grass around his home, given that all of his profit was extracted directly from his fellow townspeople. The people of Liu also complained that today's money had depreciated, that one thousand yuan today wasn't worth as much as one hundred yuan used to be. The town elders complained that now that the streets had been broadened, they were full of cars and bicycles, and the sound of horns could be heard from morning to evening. In the past, though it was true that the streets were indeed cramped and narrow, two people could nevertheless stand on either side and chat all day long without growing tired. Now, however, the streets were so broad that if two people stood on opposite sides, they wouldn't be able to hear each other, and even if they stood next to each other, they had to shout to make themselves heard over the din. There used to be only a single department store and one clothing store; but now there were at least seven or eight supermarkets, and clothing stores had begun to sprout up like mushrooms after a shower, to the point that both sides of the street were now lined with displays of garish garb for men and women.

The townspeople of Liu watched in astonishment as Baldy Li became as rich as a ten-thousand-ton oil tanker. If you ate at the most extravagant restaurant in Liu, it would be owned by Baldy Li; if you bathed at the ritziest bathhouse, it would be owned by Baldy Li; and if you went shopping at the largest shopping center, it also would be owned by Baldy Li. The ties everyone wore around their necks, the socks they wore on their feet, their undershirts and underwear, their leather jacket and leather shoes, sweaters and coats, as well as their Western suits—they were all international name brands whose China-based factories were run by Baldy Li. Baldy Li designed the houses that everyone lived in and supplied the fruits and vegetables they ate. He even bought up the crematorium and cemetery, so that the town's dead had to be handed over to him. He provided those of us in Liu Town with everything, from what we ate to what we wore, from where we lived to what we used, and from birth to death. No one knew for certain how many businesses he owned or how much he earned. He once patted his chest and boasted that the entire fucking county government was run on the fucking taxes he paid. Someone observed obsequiously that Baldy Li was responsible for virtually the entire county's GDP. When Baldy Li heard this he was very satisfied, nodding in agreement. "I am indeed the entire fucking GDP."

Yanker Yu and Popsicle Wang got filthy rich along with him. Popsicle Wang spent every day strolling down Main Street, now that he no longer had to earn a living. But he would complain anxiously that he didn't know how to spend money since he was meant to be poor. Now he had so much money he couldn't count it all, much less spend it. After Yanker Yu struck it rich, he disappeared without a trace, spending all his time off traveling and sightseeing. He covered the entire country in five years and now was traveling the world as part of a tour group. As for the fourteen handicapped workers at the Good Works Factory, in the blink of an eye they became fourteen senior researchers, and from that point on they enjoyed their high prestige and lived in comfort. Everyone agreed that they had turned into fourteen dandies.

It was during this period that the metal factory went bankrupt, and as a result Writer Liu and Song Gang became unemployed. Writer Liu ran a gamut of emotions, never having expected that the world would change so quickly or that the scrap-collecting Baldy Li would become the town's multimillionaire while he himself would lose his job and end up with nowhere to go. When Liu ran into Song Gang in the street, they commiserated with each other. Liu patted Song Gang's shoulder, then suddenly thought of something, saying, "No matter what, you are still Baldy Li's brother. . . ."

Writer Liu cursed Baldy Li passionately, asking how there could be someone like him who, after striking it rich, began looking after everyone yet completely ignored his own brother. Not only Yanker Yu and Popsicle Wang but also the fourteen handicapped workers from the Good Works Factory had become the town's nouveaux riches, while Baldy Li's own brother was so poor that he didn't have enough to eat. Baldy Li seemed to have paid no attention and pretended he didn't know what had become of Song Gang. Writer Liu seized on this issue to suggest, "Your relationship to Baldy Li reminds me of that famous line by Du Fu: *Within the vermilion gates everything reeks of wine and meat, while in the street lie frozen bones.*"

"I haven't starved to death," Song Gang replied coldly, "and Baldy Li doesn't reek of wine and meat."

The day Song Gang lost his job was like any other. That evening he rode his Eternity bicycle over to the knitting factory to pick up Lin Hong, as he had done every day, rain or shine, for more than a decade. By this point, the other women at the knitting factory had their own bicycles, all foreign brands, and many of them rode mopeds. In fact, the stores in Liu Town no longer sold Eternity bicycles. Although Lin Hong and Song Gang didn't live extravagantly, they did have a color television, a refrigerator, and a washing machine; to buy a new bicycle, therefore, would not have been a big deal for them. Lin Hong recognized that their bicycle was old and outdated, but she held off buying a new one precisely because for more than ten years Song Gang had used that Eternity bicycle to take her to and from work. While her other female workmates all rode their brand-new bicycles or mopeds, Lin Hong still hopped onto the backseat of the Eternity bicycle, hugging Song Gang's waist and smiling contentedly. Now her happiness lay not in having her own special bicycle but, rather, in the decade-long faithfulness her man and his bicycle had shown her.

Having just lost his job, Song Gang stood with his bicycle outside the knitting factory in the evening light, staring through the iron gate at the workers inside. The bell rang, marking the end of the workday, and when the gate swung open, several hundred bicycles, motorized bicycles, and mopeds poured out as if competing in a race, their bells and horns all sounding at once. After this wave of vehicles passed, Song Gang spotted Lin Hong walking down the empty road, looking like a piece of coral the tide had left behind on the beach.

The news that the metal factory had gone bankrupt quickly swept through the town. When Lin Hong heard it that afternoon, her heart sank. She wasn't concerned that Song Gang would become unemployed but, rather, worried about how he would take it. When she walked out the factory gate and over to his side, she looked up at her husband's bitter smile. His mouth twitched, and he started to tell Lin Hong that he had lost his job. Lin Hong, however, didn't let him continue, but rushed to say, "I already know."

Lin Hong saw a small leaf in his hair that she figured he got while passing under a tree on his way to pick her up. She reached out to brush it away, smiled, and said, "Let's go home."

Song Gang nodded, then turned and climbed back onto his bicycle as Lin Hong sat sidesaddle behind him. Song Gang rode his creaky old-fashioned Eternity bicycle through the streets of Liu, with Lin Hong hugging him from behind and pressing her face into his back. He felt that she was holding him tighter than usual and that her face was pressed into his back more tenderly than before. He smiled.

When they got home, Lin Hong went into the kitchen to cook dinner, and Song Gang turned his bicycle over and propped it up in front of the door. Taking out his tools, he first removed the wheels, then the pedals and the middle triangular frame. After taking the entire bicycle apart, Song Gang arranged the pieces neatly on the ground and, sitting on a stool, took a rag and started to carefully clean each one of them. Night fell and the lights came on, and after Lin Hong finished cooking dinner, she walked over to call Song Gang to come eat. Song Gang, however, shook his head and said he wasn't hungry, telling her to go ahead and eat first.

Ling Hong brought over a bowl of food and a chair and also sat down in the doorway, watching Song Gang as she ate. The sight of Song Gang expertly wiping down the bicycle pieces was quite familiar to her; she couldn't remember how many times she had remarked that he took care of his bicycle as he would his own child. Now she said it again, and Song Gang laughed. When he had put back together a piece he had wiped clean, he told Lin Hong that the next day he was going to go look for work, but he didn't know what he would be able to find. In particular, he didn't know when he would have to be at work in the morning and when he would get off in the afternoon, and therefore he might not be able to continue taking her to work and picking her up. Then he stood up, straightened his stiff back, and told her, "From now on, you should ride your own bike home."

Lin Hong nodded and said, "Okay."

Song Gang carefully reassembled the bicycle, oiled the bearings, wiped his hands with a rag, and took a few turns in front of the house. No longer hearing the creaking sound, he hopped off in satisfaction and lowered the seat. Then he pushed the bicycle over to Lin Hong and asked her to climb on and give it a try. She had finished eating but was holding the bowl of food she had prepared for Song Gang. After he took the bowl from her, she accepted the bicycle. He then sat down where Lin Hong had just been sitting and ate his dinner while watching her climb onto his bicycle under the light of the streetlamps. Lin Hong rode three loops while Song Gang watched, and she announced that it felt fine, that this ten-year-old Eternity bicycle felt just like new. Song Gang, however, noticed a problem and set his bowl and chopsticks down on the stool. After she got down from the bicycle, he lowered the seat even more, then asked her to climb on and try again. Seeing that she was now able to rest both of her feet on the ground at the same time, he nodded with satisfaction and urged her, "When you brake, keep both feet on the ground. That way you won't fall."

CHAPTER 54

MEANWHILE, Song Gang and Lin Hong's house was torn down, and they moved to the first floor of a new building across the street. Mama Su also had to move her snack shop to the building across from Lin Hong's house. Poet Zhao's house was torn down as well, forcing him to move to the second floor of Song Gang and Lin Hong's building. Poet Zhao deliberately positioned his bed directly over theirs, and in the dead of night he would lie there, hoping to hear sounds of their lovemaking. Unable to hear anything, he placed his ear directly against the concrete floor but still couldn't hear anything and wondered how in the world there could be such a deathly silent matrimonial bed. Song Gang and Lin Hong had been married for many years, but they still hadn't had any children. He felt that the problem surely lay with Song Gang and speculated that he must be impotent. He secretly told Writer Liu his theory, adding, "When they go to bed together at night, they are like two guns equipped with silencers."

After Song Gang lost his job, he found a new job as a dockworker down at the wharf, carrying parcels from the ships to the warehouse and vice versa. He was paid by the piece, and therefore the more parcels he moved, the more he was paid. He rushed frantically with the large parcels up and down the hundred-yard path from the wharf to the warehouse—and while everyone else would just carry one, he would always carry two at once. Every day the elders who sat chatting on the side of the road would hear him wheezing like an accordion as he ran back and forth. His clothes completely drenched in sweat, he looked as if he had just climbed out of the river. Even his sneakers were soaked with sweat, making swishing sounds as he hauled the parcels back and forth. The elders would shake their heads and say, "That Song Gang values money more than life itself."

Song Gang's workmates would each make three or four round-trips, then sit on the riverbank steps to rest. There they would drink some water, smoke, and chat for half an hour before finally going back to work. Song Gang, however, would never sit on the steps to rest. Instead, he would make seven or eight trips, until—his face pale and his lips trembling, feeling that he was about to collapse—he would place the last parcel on the ship. Walking down the plank back to shore, he'd see his workmates on the steps waving at him but, feeling he didn't even have the strength to cover the remaining ten yards, he'd fall to the ground as soon as he got off the plank. Therefore, his break would consist of sprawling there, with grass wedged under his collar and river water flowing past his arm, his eyes closed tightly, his chest rising and falling rapidly, and his heart pounding like a fist against his chest cavity.

By resting on the ground like this, Song Gang could recover his strength faster. Every time he lay down, his workmates sitting on the stone steps would laugh at him, calling him a crazy fool. Song Gang was so exhausted he couldn't hear what they were saying. Feeling that the ground was spinning, he'd clench his eyes until he could discern the sunlight through his closed lids and his breathing slowed back down to normal. At that point, having rested for less than ten minutes, he'd hear his workmates calling out his name. He'd slowly climb back up and see them waving to him, holding their water glasses out to him and offering him a cigarette. He'd smile and wave, then walk over to the water faucet on the dock to fill his belly, whereupon he'd take two more parcels and begin rushing back and forth again.

Working on the docks, Song Gang earned twice as much as his fellow workers and four times as much as he had made under the metal factory's iron-rice-bowl system. The first time he gave Lin Hong his salary, she jumped with surprise, astounded that he could have earned so much as a dockworker. Counting it, she said, "You are earning more in a month than you used to earn in four months at the factory."

Song Gang grinned and said, "Actually, losing one's job isn't so bad after all."

Lin Hong realized that he was literally trading his blood and sweat for these earnings and urged him not to work so hard, saying, "We can survive regardless of how much money we have."

Every evening when Song Gang returned home, he'd be so tired he could hardly hold his head up and would fall asleep immediately after dinner. Before, he used to sleep very peacefully, but now he'd sigh and snore up a storm. He'd frequently wake up Lin Hong, who would find herself unable to fall back to sleep. Listening to his irregular snoring and occasional cries, she felt extremely anxious, concerned that he remained exhausted even in his sleep.

By morning, he'd be full of life again, and Lin Hong would feel reassured. He would eat his breakfast with a broad smile on his face and, carrying his lunch box, would march off in the direction of the rising sun. Lin Hong walked by his side, pushing her antiquated Eternity bicycle. The two of them would walk together for about fifty yards, then stop at the corner, where Song Gang would watch as Lin Hong mounted her bicycle, urging her to be careful. She would nod and ride off to the west, while Song Gang headed east toward the wharf.

In the end, Song Gang worked the docks for only two months, because in the third month he sprained his back. He was carrying two large parcels and had just stepped off the plank when someone on the boat called out to him. He turned around too quickly and heard his body make a horrible cracking sound. Realizing that he was injured, Song Gang immediately dropped the parcels, but when he tried to move, he felt an excruciating pain in his back. Holding his lower back with both hands, he smiled painfully as he looked over at his two workmates, who asked in alarm what had happened. Song Gang grimaced. "I think I broke something."

The two workmates immediately threw down their own parcels and helped carry him to the stone steps beside the river, asking him what he had broken. Song Gang pointed to his lower back, explaining that he had heard a cracking sound when he turned around. One of the workmates asked him to lift his hands, and the other asked him to shake his head. Reassured to see that he could do so, they explained that the only bones in his lower back were his vertebrae, and if they were broken, his upper body would have been paralyzed. Song Gang lifted his arms and shook his head again, and then he too felt reassured. Holding his lower back with his right hand, he said, "When I heard the cracking sound, I assumed that it was a bone breaking."

"You merely sprained your back," they told him. "When you sprain something, it sometimes also makes that kind of sound."

Song Gang chuckled, and his workmates urged him to go home. He shook his head and said he would just rest on the steps for a while. In the two months he had been working the docks, this was the first time he had ever sat on the steps where the other workers rested. The steps were covered with cigarette butts, and a dozen or so white porcelain cups were arranged in a row. Each worker had written his name on his cup in red marker. Song Gang laughed, deciding that the next day he would bring his own cup, and it too would be porcelain. In the warehouse there was a bucket of red paint, and all he would need to do would be to insert a stick into the paint; he too could write his name on his cup.

Song Gang sat for more than an hour next to the rushing river, watching his workmates huffing and puffing as they hauled parcels back and forth. Finally he couldn't resist standing up, experimentally moving his waist a little, and finding that it was not as painful as before. Feeling that he was okay, he stepped onto the plank and walked into the ship's hold. Remembering how he had injured himself, Song Gang hesitated a moment and then decided to pick up only one parcel rather than two. He had just brought the parcel up to his shoulder and energetically straightened his waist when suddenly he let out a cry of pain and immediately collapsed in such a way that the large bundle pinned down his head and shoulders.

Several of Song Gang's workmates removed the bundle and helped pull him up. A searing pain made him cry out in agony, and his body doubled up into a fetal position. Two workmates carefully helped lift him onto the back of a third worker, who then carried him down off the plank as Song Gang continued crying out in pain. Realizing that his injury was very serious indeed, the workers pulled up a cart, and when they placed him on it, he screamed in agony like a pig being slaughtered. As they pulled the cart along the cobblestone streets of Liu, he continued writhing in agony, and every time the cart hit a bump he would moan in anguish. Song Gang knew that his workmates were taking him to the hospital, but when they entered the main road, he cried, "I don't want to go to the hospital. I want to go home."

His workmates looked at each other, then proceeded to pull the cart up to his door. That afternoon, Song Gang, lying in excruciating pain on the pullcart, ran into Baldy Li, riding in his red sedan. Song Gang spotted his younger brother, but Baldy Li didn't notice him. Baldy Li sat with his arm around a seductive, out-of-town woman, laughing happily. When the sedan drove in front of the pullcart, Song Gang opened his mouth, but no sound came out. In the end, he merely called out silently, "Baldy Li."

CHAPTER 55

LIN HONG was just about to get off work when she heard about Song Gang's injury and immediately rushed home on her bike, pale with anxiety. After frantically opening the front door, she saw Song Gang curled up on the bed in the dark, staring at her silently. She closed the door, walked over and sat on the bed, and tenderly stroked his face. He looked at her and said with embarrassment, "I sprained my back."

Lin Hong began to cry as she hugged him, asking softly, "What did the doctor say?"

When Lin Hong moved Song Gang's body, he squeezed his eyes in agony. This time he didn't cry out but, rather, waited for the pain to subside. Then he opened his eyes and said, "I didn't go to the hospital."

"Why not?" Lin Hong asked anxiously.

"I just sprained my back," Song Gang said. "I'll rest for a few days, and then I'll be fine."

Lin Hong shook her head and said, "That won't do. You must go to the hospital."

Song Gang smiled sadly. "I can't move now. I'll go in a few days."

Song Gang lay in bed for half a month before he was finally able to get up and walk around, though he still wasn't able to straighten his back. Hunched over at the waist and with Lin Hong's help, he hobbled to the hospital, where they applied four hot cups and five medicated plasters to his back, costing him more than ten yuan. It occurred to him that, at this rate, the money he had earned through two months of backbreaking labor at the docks wouldn't be enough to cover his medical fees. Therefore, he didn't return to the hospital, telling himself that a sprain is like a cold, and it will cure it itself even if you don't treat it.

After resting at home for two months, Song Gang was finally able to straighten his back, and again he went to look for work. Those days, he would support his waist with his hand all day, hobbling along through the streets and alleys of Liu, looking everywhere for work, but who would want to hire someone with a bad back? He would leave home every morning full of hope but return each evening with a sad smile, and Lin Hong would know from his expression that he had not had any success. She struggled to cheer herself up and reassured him that if they economized a bit, they could both live comfortably on her salary. At night when they climbed under the covers, Lin Hong gently caressed his waist, saying that as long as she was around, he didn't need to worry about the future. Song Gang exclaimed, "I've let you down."

At that point, Lin Hong was forcing herself to be optimistic. Actually, business at the knitting factory had not been very good for several years, and now they were starting to lay people off. That chain-smoking Director Liu had always had designs on her and had called her into his office several times. Closing the door, he would tell her quietly that her name had twice appeared on the list of workers to be laid off, but each time he had removed it. After telling her this, he would stare expectantly at her ample breasts. Director Liu, in his fifties, had been a chain-smoker for the past forty years, and as a result his teeth were completely stained black, as were his lips. When he leered at Lin Hong with his lecherous expression, his two drooping eye bags looked like two tumors.

Lin Hong sat facing him on pins and needles. She understood perfectly well what he was suggesting. He repulsed her, and even from across the table his entire body reeked of cigarette smoke. But she remembered that Song Gang was injured and had already lost his job, meaning that she couldn't afford to lose hers as well. Therefore she had no alternative but to sit there with a smile on her face, hoping fervently that someone would walk through the door and permit her to escape.

Director Liu waved a pen at her, saying this was the pen with which he had scratched her name from the list. Seeing her smile without answering, he leaned forward and whispered, "Won't you even say 'thank you'?"

Lin Hong smiled and said, "Thank you."

Director Liu then went further and said, "How are you going to thank me?"

Lin Hong continued smiling and said, "Thank you."

Director Liu tapped the table with his pen, listing the names of several other factory workers and describing how, in order to avoid being laid off, they had each voluntarily slept with him. Lin Hong still smiled. Director Liu looked at her lecherously and asked again, "How do you plan to thank me?"

"Thank you."

"How about this." He put down the fountain pen, stood up, and walked around the table. "Let me hug you as I would a sister."

Seeing him come around the table, Lin Hong immediately headed for the door. On her way out she smiled and said, "I'm not your sister."

As she was leaving his office she heard Director Liu cursing. Still smiling, she returned to her workshop. However, when she got out of work and rode her Eternity bicycle home, she remembered the lecherous way in which the director had stared at her and his broad hints, and she felt a wave of humiliation sweep over her.

Several times Lin Hong considered telling Song Gang about what had happened, but each time she saw his exhausted appearance and his forlorn smile, she found that she couldn't bring herself to mention it. It seemed to her that telling him about her humiliation now would merely add salt to his wounds. One day followed another, however, and Song Gang still hadn't managed to find work. Lin Hong suddenly remembered Baldy Li, who was becoming wealthier than ever and now employed more than a thousand workers. One night, after a brief hesitation, she suggested, "Why don't you go see Baldy Li?"

Song Gang bowed his head and didn't respond. He remembered how he had resolved to completely sever relations with Baldy Li, and therefore he simply couldn't go back and ask for his help now that Baldy Li was rich and successful. Seeing that Song Gang wasn't responding, Lin Hong added, "Surely he wouldn't ignore you. . . ."

Song Gang lifted his head and said stubbornly, "I have already severed my relationship with him."

At that point Lin Hong almost told him about the humiliation she had suffered in Director Liu's office, but she bit her tongue. Instead, she merely shook her head and didn't say anything more.

Song Gang knew that he was no longer able to perform heavy labor, so he instead started looking for another line of work. He told Lin Hong that as he was walking around he would often see young girls from the countryside selling white magnolia flowers strung together with wire thread. The young women of Liu wore the flowers on their chest or tied to their braids. Song Gang said shyly that the flowers were very becoming. He had learned that these flowers were purchased from the nursery, costing an average of just five cents per bundle. Lin Hong looked at Song Gang in surprise, unable to imagine a grown man like him carrying a basket selling magnolia flowers. He entreated her, "Let me give it a try."

Lin Hong agreed, and Song Gang went out bright and early the next day with a little basket, a roll of wire, and a pair of scissors, and walked for more than an hour to the nursery. There he bought the flowers, sat down in the grass, and proceeded to string them together with the needle and wire. Then he placed them in the basket and walked back toward town.

Song Gang squinted his eyes in the sun and headed toward the horizon. After about ten minutes he started to sweat and began to worry that the sun would wilt his flowers. Therefore, he walked into a field beside the road and picked several melon leaves, laying them carefully over the flowers. Still anxious, he went to a nearby pond and sprinkled some water on the flowers. Reassured, he continued forward, periodically looking down at his little flowers hiding under the melon leaves, as though he were peering down at a swaddled baby. He felt that he hadn't been this happy in a long time. Walking along the narrow path through the vast fields, he would give his flowers a little more water every time he passed a pond.

By the time Song Gang returned to Liu Town it was already noon. Not taking time for lunch, he stood in the middle of the street and started hawking his magnolia blossoms. He carefully arranged the melon leaves around the edges of the basket so that green leaves would surround the white flowers. He stood under a wutong tree holding his basket, smiling at everyone who walked past. Some people noticed the flowers he was holding but would only glance down and continue on their way. A couple of young women looked at his flowers and exclaimed appreciatively how charming these magnolia blossoms surrounded by green leaves were, but Song Gang merely smiled at them. As they walked away he felt a pang of regret, realizing that he should have cried out "For sale," since they apparently hadn't realized he was selling the flowers.

Then a peasant girl walked by, hawking the same flowers. Carrying her basket in her left hand, she held a string of flowers in her right as she walked back and forth shouting, "Magnolia blossoms for sale!" Song Gang followed the girl, similarly holding his basket in his left hand and a string of flowers in his right. Every time she cried out, "Magnolia blossoms for sale," Song Gang would add shyly, "Me, too."

Seeing a young woman walking over, the peasant girl called out, "Big sister, won't you buy a string of magnolia blossoms?"

Song Gang leaned over, hesitated, and then said, "Me, too."

He followed the peasant girl halfway down the street, saying a dozen or so "Me, toos." Displeased, she turned around and said to him, "Don't follow me."

Song Gang stood still and watched in confusion as she walked away. At that point Popsicle Wang ambled over and started bellowing with laughter. Wang had been sauntering around all day, but upon seeing Song Gang with a basket of flowers and following a little girl peddling flowers, he started laughing so hard his stomach began to hurt. He walked over and pointed to Song Gang, saying, "You can't just follow her around all day."

"Why not?" Song Gang asked.

"I used to sell popsicles for a living," Popsicle Wang said proudly. "If you always follow someone else, everyone would simply buy from the person in front, and then who would buy from you? This is like fishing—two people can't fish in the same hole; they have to separate."

Song Gang nodded and, with flowers in his right hand and the basket in his left, headed in the opposite direction from the girl. Popsicle Wang then thought of something else and called out, "When the girl sees a young woman, she calls her 'big sister.' You, however, would need to call her 'little sister.'"

Song Gang hesitated and then said, "I can't say that."

"Then don't say it," Popsicle Wang said. "But you can't go around calling young women 'big sister.' You're thirtysomething years old."

Song Gang humbly nodded and was about to walk away when Popsicle Wang called out to him again. Wang took a one-yuan bill from his pocket and said, "I'll take two strings."

Song Gang accepted the money and then passed him the two strings of blossoms, saying "thank you" over and over again.

"Remember," said Popsicle Wang as he accepted the flowers with both hands and lifted them to his nose. "I, Popsicle Wang, was the first person to buy your flowers. If, therefore, you go on to start a flower business, I want to come and invest."

Popsicle Wang shifted into his role as investment banker and proudly told Song Gang, "I successfully invested in the scrap business and could just as well invest in the flower business."

Popsicle Wang lifted the two strings of magnolia blossoms and sniffed them greedily as he walked away, looking as if, rather than sniffing flowers, he was actually sucking on two cream popsicles.

As the day wore on Song Gang learned how to hawk his magnolia blossoms, albeit in an embarrassed tone of voice. He even learned a few tricks of his own, such as how to stand at the door of a clothing store waiting for young women to pass by. He wouldn't go in and disturb the customers as they were picking out clothes but instead would wait patiently for them to come out and then hand them the flowers, saying modestly, "Please buy a string of white magnolia blossoms."

Song Gang always had a tender smile on his handsome face, and the young women of Liu liked that smile and therefore bought his lovely white flowers. Several of the young women who knew him and knew about his back injury asked in concern how he was doing. Song Gang smiled and replied that his back was healed but that he could no longer do heavy labor. He would then add, embarrassed, "That is why I am selling flowers."

With his basket in hand, Song Gang visited each of the clothing stores in Liu, standing out front for a long time. Every time he sold a string of flowers, he would break into a grateful smile. He didn't eat anything all day but still didn't feel hungry. As soon as one store would close up for the night he would immediately move on to the next. He lost all track of time, knowing only that it was quite late. He wandered around under the moon and the streetlamps, selling one string of flowers after another. When there was only one string left and the last clothing store was closing up for the night, Song Gang was about to head home when a young woman carrying an assortment of shopping bags approached. When she saw Song Gang's final string of flowers in his basket, she took out her purse and asked how much it cost.

Song Gang looked down at those final two blossoms and replied apologetically, "I can't bear to part with them."

The woman stared at him in confusion and asked, "But aren't you here selling flowers?"

"Yes," Song Gang explained. "But I'm keeping these last two for my wife."

The woman nodded, put away her purse, and walked off. Song Gang followed her and asked solicitously, "Where do you live? I could bring you one tomorrow, at no charge."

"No need," the woman replied without turning around.

By the time Song Gang got home, it was past ten o'clock. He saw that the front door was open and Lin Hong was standing there peering out. When she saw Song Gang approach, she let out a deep sigh of relief and then reprimanded him, "Where did you go? I've been worried sick."

With a huge smile, Song Gang grasped her hand and accompanied her into the house. After they closed the front door, he didn't even pause to sit down before launching into a detailed description of his day. It had been a long time since Lin Hong had seen him so excited. Still holding his basket in his hand, Song Gang pulled a handful of change out of his pocket as he spoke and continued describing how he had sold his flowers while at the same time counting his money. He happily announced that he had earned twenty-four yuan and fifty cents, then handed Lin Hong the money, saying, "I could have made it twenty-five yuan even, but I couldn't bring myself to earn those last fifty cents."

Song Gang removed the final two blossoms from his basket and placed them in Lin Hong's hand, recounting how that young woman had wanted to buy them and how he had refused. He told Lin Hong, "I was saving these for you and couldn't bring myself to sell them."

"You should have sold them," Lin Hong quickly replied. "I don't want any. . . ."

Seeing the light in Song Gang's eyes immediately dim, Lin Hong didn't continue. Instead, she took his basket and urged him to sit down and eat. It was then that Song Gang realized that he was actually quite famished, and therefore he took a bowl of food and wolfed it down. Lin Hong walked to the mirror and placed the string of blossoms in her braid, then draped the braid over her chest and sat down next to him, hoping that he would notice the flowers. Song Gang, however, paid no attention to her braid, focusing instead on her happy smile, which in turn made him more contented than ever—inspiring him to once again launch into a detailed description of his day. Finally he sighed, saying that he had never imagined that he could make as much with such light work as he had while working the docks. At this point, Lin Hong pretended to get angry, nudging him and asking, "Don't you see?"

As he noticed the blossoms in her hair Song Gang's eyes lit up. He asked, "Do you like them?"

"I do." She nodded.

That night Song Gang slept peacefully. Hearing his rhythmic breathing, Lin Hong felt that it had been a long time since he had slept so soundly. She, on the other hand, couldn't sleep. She placed the magnolia blossoms on her pillow and smelled their fragrance, sighing over Song Gang's loyalty and love for her. At that moment the humiliation she had endured from Director Liu meant nothing. Then she began to feel anxious about Song Gang's future prospects, realizing that no one could sell flowers their entire lives. Especially for a grown man like Song Gang, carrying around a basket every day was a humiliating job.

Lin Hong's fears quickly became a reality as her workmates at the knitting factory began to mock Song Gang all day long. They said that they had never seen a man selling flowers, especially not someone as big and tall as Song Gang, and remarked that when Song Gang was hawking flowers his voice became quite soft, more like a young woman's than a man's. They said these things not only behind Lin Hong's back but also to her face, making her blush with embarrassment. When she returned home, Lin Hong exploded at Song Gang, telling him not to continue humiliating himself. Song Gang, however, stubbornly refused to stop, even though his profits were steadily declining. Many of the young women in Liu knew Song Gang, and rather than pay for their flowers, they asked him to give them to them for free. Song Gang couldn't bring himself to turn them down, and as a result, they took all the flowers he had gone to such trouble to obtain and thread together. Even the workmates who mocked Song Gang to Lin Hong's face nevertheless shamelessly demanded blossoms from him and wore them in their braids draped over their chests. Then, when they saw Lin Hong, they taunted her, saying, "Your Song Gang gave these to us."

Lin Hong turned and walked away, then exploded at Song Gang when she saw him that evening. With the door closed and in a low voice, she said furiously, "I won't permit you to continue selling flowers."

For Song Gang, that night seemed to go on forever. Lin Hong was exhausted and went straight to bed after just a few bites of dinner. Song Gang also ate very little, then sat at the table for a long time, finally coming to the conclusion that selling flowers was not a viable solution. He was depressed to have to quit his new job so soon. That night he quietly lay down beside Lin Hong and, listening to her light breathing, gradually grew calmer. He didn't know about the humiliation she had endured at the factory as the result of chain-smoking Director Liu's advances.

When Song Gang woke up the next morning, he saw that Lin Hong had already gotten up and was in the bathroom brushing her teeth and washing her face. He quickly got out of bed, got dressed, and walked toward the bathroom. Lin Hong looked at him silently, her mouth full of toothpaste, and Song Gang announced, "I'm not going to sell flowers anymore."

He hesitated a moment, then headed to the door. Lin Hong came out of the bathroom and called out to him, asking him where he was going. He turned and said, "I'm going to go look for work."

Holding a towel in her hand, Lin Hong asked, "Have you eaten breakfast?"

"I'm not hungry." Song Gang shook his head and opened the door.

"Don't leave."

Lin Hong then stuffed some money into his pocket, telling him to go buy himself something to eat. Looking up and seeing Song Gang's smile, she felt a stab of sadness and bowed her head. Song Gang smiled as he patted her back, then turned around and walked out. Lin Hong walked him to the door, as if he were about to embark on a long journey. She quietly told him, "Take good care of yourself."

Song Gang nodded, then continued on. She called out to him, "Go see Baldy Li."

Song Gang paused, then shook his head firmly, saying, "I won't go see him."

Lin Hong sighed, watching her stubborn husband walk down the street under the morning sun. Song Gang began the slow process of looking for a new job, and for the next year he would head out early every morning and return late each night, searching determinedly for a way to earn money. His face quickly grew pallid, and after dragging his exhausted body home every evening, he would merely sit silently at the dinner table. Lin Hong couldn't bring herself to look him in the eye, knowing that he was once again returning empty-handed. With a shamed expression, he would silently eat his dinner and go to bed, and when the sun woke him the following morning, he would optimistically set forth again. Over the course of that year, he did succeed in finding some part-time jobs, such as occasionally filling in for the gatekeeper at the warehouse. Similarly, when the clerks at the market, movie theater and bus and ferry terminals had to take time off, Song Gang would fill in for them as well. He became Liu Town's chief sub, with up to twenty-four different jobs waiting for him to come and step in at a moment's notice. Despite that, the total number of days he worked over the course of the year added up to less than two full months.

Lin Hong grew increasingly worried, frequently sighing and sometimes even cursing. Though her sighs and curses actually weren't directed toward Song Gang—rather, they were because she was reminded of the disgusting Director Liu—Song Gang assumed that they were because of him. Therefore, every day when he returned home, he bowed his head and became increasingly silent. Even though he earned very little money, he nevertheless gave it all to Lin Hong. What made him feel worse was that when he handed her the tiny sum of money that represented the culmination of his efforts, she would always shake her head, turn away in disappointment, and say quietly, "Why don't you just keep it?" This comment pierced Song Gang's heart like a dagger.

Two years after he twisted his back, Song Gang was finally able to find a permanent job, at the concrete factory. He would be able to work year-round, and if he wanted, he could even work overtime on weekends. With this, a smile returned to his face, and he regained the confidence he used to have while riding his Eternity bicycle. After finding his new job, Song Gang didn't return home but went directly to the gate of the knitting factory, waiting there for Lin Hong to get out. As the other women rushed out on their new bicycles, motorized bicycles, and mopeds, Lin Hong fell behind, pushing the antiquated Eternity bicycle out the front gate. When she emerged, a flushed Song Gang greeted her, announcing, "I have a job!"

Seeing Song Gang's excited appearance, Lin Hong felt a twinge of sadness. She let him ride the bicycle while she sat behind him as she used to, hugging his waist with both arms and pressing her cheek into his back. That night she noticed that Song Gang had aged a lot: His forehead and eyes were now full of wrinkles, and his thick hair was now sparse. She felt bad for him, and while lying in bed, she massaged his back for a long time. That night they hugged each other tight as though it were their wedding night.

Those days Song Gang worked especially hard, afraid that he would be fired again. His job at the factory was one that no one was willing to do: pouring the cement powder into bags. Even with a face mask, he would still inhale tremendous amounts of cement dust, and within two years his lungs were completely ruined. Lin Hong wept many bitter tears over this. Once again Song Gang lost his job, but he didn't go to the hospital for treatment because he couldn't bring himself to spend the money.

Song Gang again assumed the position of Liu Town's chief sub. After his lungs were ruined, he wouldn't sleep in the matrimonial bed anymore, afraid that Lin Hong would catch his illness. He asked to sleep on the couch, but Lin Hong refused, saying that if Song Gang wasn't willing to sleep in the bed with her, then she would be the one who would sleep on the couch. As a result, Song Gang had no choice but to sleep at Lin Hong's feet. On the days that he had a job, he would leave wearing a face mask in order not to pass his lung disease on to others. Song Gang was the only person in Liu who wore a face mask all year long, even during the hot summer, and even the town's youngest children recognized him instantly when they saw him slowly walking down the street, hailing him: "The chief sub has arrived."

CHAPTER 56

BALDY LI had put Song Gang out of his mind.

He held up two fingers, saying that during the day he raked in the money, while at night he raked in the women. He said that he was insanely busy, and apart from money and women he didn't know anything about anything. Baldy Li never did get married, and slept with so many women that even he couldn't keep count. When someone asked him exactly how many women he had slept with, Baldy Li pondered for a while, calculated, and finally responded, not without regret, "Not as many as I have workers."

Baldy Li not only slept with the local women; he also slept with women from all over the country, from Hong Kong, Taiwan, and other overseas Chinese communities, including more than a dozen foreign women. He slept with all sorts of women—tall and short ones, fat and thin ones, beautiful and ugly ones, young and old ones. Everyone said that Baldy Li was very broad-minded: that as long someone was female he wouldn't reject her, and if a sow was led to his bed, he would probably sleep with it as well. Some of the women slept with him on the sly and also accepted money from him on the sly, while others would sleep with him and then take his money and brag openly. They bragged not about the fact that they had slept with him but, rather, about how fabulous and amazing he was in bed. They said that he was an animal in the sack, like a machine gun firing endless rounds, and that he would screw you until your legs went into spasms and you could barely walk the next day, leaving you amazed that you made it off the bed alive.

The salacious rumors concerning Baldy Li were more numerous than explosions on a battlefield. Some of the women he slept with had their eyes on his wealth. The first to make a move was a young woman in her twenties who had come from the countryside to find work in Liu Town. She brought her newborn baby to Baldy Li's office and asked him happily what they should name it. Baldy Li stared at her blankly but couldn't place her. He asked skeptically, "What the fuck does this have to do with me?"

The young woman started bawling, asking how a father could fail to recognize his own son. Baldy Li looked at her and pondered for a moment, but for the life of him he couldn't remember ever having been with her. He asked, "Did you really sleep with me?"

"How could you even ask that?" The woman brought the baby over for Baldy Li to take a look. Still bawling, she said, "Just look, he has your eyebrows, and your eyes, your nose, your mouth, your forehead, your chin. . . ."

Baldy Li glanced at the baby and decided that, other than looking like a baby, it really didn't look like anyone in particular. The woman then pulled down its diaper, saying, "Even his penis looks just like yours."

Baldy Li was furious that this woman would have the gall to speak of his enormous member and this baby's tiny, soybean-size penis in the same breath. As he howled in fury several of his assistants helped usher the hysterical woman out the door.

This young woman then started demonstrating outside the main gate of Baldy Li's company headquarters. Every day she would sit there, holding her baby, sobbing as she told everyone who would listen how Baldy Li's sense of compassion had been snatched by a dog, eaten by a wolf, chewed by a tiger, and shat out by a lion. Several days later, another woman arrived with a baby, claiming that it was Baldy Li's daughter. She tearfully recounted how Baldy Li had tricked her into bed and had gotten her pregnant. Crying even more tragically than the first, she sobbed that when she gave birth, Baldy Li didn't even come to see her. Then a third woman arrived, with a four- or five-year-old boy in tow. She was calmer than the previous two and didn't cry as she sternly accused Baldy Li of going back on his word—claiming that it was only after he had sworn they would marry and live happily ever after that she had agreed to go to bed with him. She pointed to her son and said that, based on his age, he would be Baldy Li's firstborn and heir. As soon as she finished, a fourth woman appeared with a seven- or eight-year-old boy and insisted that *her* son was Baldy Li's firstborn and rightful heir.

Women claiming to have slept with Baldy Li kept arriving with their children, until finally there were more than thirty of them, all crowded into the street in front of Baldy Li's company headquarters. Day in and day out, they would cry and complain about Baldy Li's philandering. They chattered noisily amongst themselves, transforming the street in front of Baldy Li's headquarters into a small marketplace. They would get into spectacular fights jockeying for position, spitting and pulling one another's hair, scratching one another's faces, and clawing at one another's clothes. From dawn till dusk, the street was full of women's curses and babies' cries.

There were so many women protesting outside that Baldy Li's employees couldn't make it in to work, and enormous traffic jams developed in the street outside his headquarters. The director of the local branch of China's Women's Federation and all her underlings appeared in full force to exhort the women to go home and trust that the government would work out an equitable solution to their disputes with Badly Li. The women, however, adamantly refused to budge and instead entreated the federation director to have the Women's Federation come and force Baldy Li to marry them. The director didn't know whether to laugh or cry at this, reminding them that the law only permitted a man to have a single wife and therefore there was no way for Baldy Li to marry them all.

The county's director of transportation called up Baldy Li and said that the county's most important street had been completely blocked for more than a month, and as a result the county's economy had taken a huge hit. County Governor Tao Qing also called him up, saying that Baldy Li was now the most influential person in the county and that if this matter was not resolved satisfactorily, not only would it be a blow to Baldy Li's image but, furthermore, the entire county's reputation would be severely impacted. Baldy Li chuckled on the other end of the line and said to just let them continue demonstrating. Tao Qing argued that already more than thirty women were demonstrating, and if they didn't act now, there soon could be even more. Baldy Li replied, "The more the better. As they say, *the more fleas you have, the less you are afraid of being bitten.*"

Among the protestors were some who had indeed slept with Baldy Li, some who knew him but hadn't slept with him, and others who had never even met him. Among the women who had slept with him were some who genuinely believed that he was the father of their children, and they were naturally bolder than the others. They discussed matters among themselves and decided that, rather than being tired, thirsty, and hungry demonstrating outside all day, they might as well take Baldy Li to court.

Once Baldy Li was named as a defendant, a vast crowd congregated inside and outside the courthouse. He appeared in court wearing a suit and patent-leather shoes, with a little red flower pinned to his lapel, since he was just coming from the opening ceremony of one of his new companies. Beaming like a groom, he made his way through the crowds into the courthouse and then proceeded to the defendant's seat as though he were about to present a report. He sat in court listening to the women testify, as attentive as a child listening to a story. When they tearfully described their beautiful experiences with him, he blushed and repeatedly asked in astonishment, "Really? Was it really like that?"

After about two hours he began to grow weary. The testimony was becoming increasingly repetitious, and the majority of the women hadn't even testified yet. Baldy Li decided that he had had enough and requested permission to speak. After the judge acknowledged him, Baldy Li reached into his breast pocket and very carefully pulled out his trump card: the hospital record of his vasectomy from more than a decade earlier.

He handed the vasectomy report to the judge, who read it and then proceeded to laugh uncontrollably for more than two full minutes. Finally regaining his composure, he announced that Baldy Li was innocent, explaining that Baldy Li had had a vasectomy more than a decade earlier and therefore could not possibly have fathered any of these children. Everyone in the courthouse fell into stunned silence, but after a few minutes they exploded into laughter as well. The thirty original plaintiffs stood there in shock, looking at one another with expressions of astonishment. When the judge informed Baldy Li that he could countersue the women for slander and fraud, a dozen or so of them turned pale, a couple fainted, four burst into tears, and three tried to sneak out but were promptly nabbed by the crowds and brought back. Meanwhile, the women who had actually slept with Baldy Li declared that they would challenge the judge's decision and would continue to press their cases on the ground that, even if Baldy Li hadn't fathered their children, he had still slept with them and destroyed their hymens, which were more valuable to them than life itself. If they didn't succeed in the city's middle court, they would appeal to the upper court. If they still didn't prevail, they would appeal all the way to the Supreme Court in Beijing. If they didn't succeed there, they would take their case all the way to the World Court in The Hague.

The crowds retorted, "If you sue Baldy Li for having slept with you, Baldy Li could also sue you for having slept with him. If you want him to compensate you for your lost hymens, he could demand that you compensate him for his lost virginity."

The courtroom became as cacophonous as a chicken farm, with the crowds siding with Baldy Li and taunting the female swindlers, asking the judge to arrest the lot of them. No matter how hard the judge pounded his gavel and how loudly he shouted for order, it was of no use. It was only after Baldy Li got up and bowed respectfully to the crowd that they finally began to calm down. He said, "Fellow townspeople, thank you, thank you. . . ."

Baldy Li emotionally dabbed at his eyes and then continued, "The fact that I have my current career is due entirely to your support. Today I want to speak to you from my heart. It is true that I, Baldy Li, have slept with a great number of women, but the truth of the matter is that I am actually quite miserable, insofar as I've never come across a single hymen in all these years."

The townspeople burst into riotous laughter, slapping their bellies and shouting, "Excellent!" Baldy Li gestured for them to quiet down, then continued: "The reason I decided to have a vasectomy was because the woman I loved decided to marry someone else. From that point on, I fell into despair and lost all scruples, or why else would I have slept with so many women? If a man chooses to sleep around, all the women he comes across will of course also be loose. Today I have reached an epiphany and realized, to put it coarsely, that not until you've slept with a woman with her hymen intact can you say that you've really slept with a woman. Or, to put it more elegantly, it is only after you have slept with a woman who genuinely loves you that you can be said to have really slept with a woman. The sad truth of the matter is that there hasn't been a single woman who has genuinely loved me. And so it doesn't matter how many women I've slept with. I might as well have been sleeping with myself."

The townspeople were now laughing so hard they couldn't catch their breath, and the sound of their delirious gasps and guffaws resonated throughout the courtroom. Displeased, Baldy Li cried out, "I'm not joking!"

After everyone had quieted down, Baldy Li patted his chest earnestly and said, "I am speaking from my heart." He dabbed at his eyes and then continued to share his heartfelt sorrows. "To tell the truth, I am no longer able to court a woman. I once tried courting a few

454 • YU HUA

young women, but it didn't work out. Why? Because I am already debauched."

He tried to explain. "In courtship, women are always likely to get emotional, and sometimes they'll throw a minor tantrum or two. Whenever that happens, I can't help cursing and shouting at them, 'Damn it, what kind of attitude is this?' After I shout out a few times, the nice ones always run away!"

Baldy Li paused, then smiled bitterly. "Why? Because I have already become used to paying for sex. Naturally, women who are sleeping with me because I have paid them have better attitudes. For me, sleeping with women is like doing business and has nothing at all to do with love. I am no longer able to respect women, and since I can't respect them, I therefore can't court them. That is my tragedy!"

Amid the laughter of the townspeople, Baldy Li concluded his speech. After wiping his eyes, he then pointed to the thirty plaintiffs and said magnanimously, "This hasn't been easy for them either—they protested in front of my company for an entire month." He turned to one of his underlings. "Tell my CFO to pay each of them one thousand yuan, and we will treat it as one month's wages."

The townspeople shouted their approval. The former plaintiffs each relaxed and put aside their anger, thinking that although they hadn't succeeded in stealing a chicken, at least they hadn't lost a fistful of rice in the process, and furthermore, they did come away with enough money to buy another fistful. Amid everyone's shouts of approval, Baldy Li walked out of the courthouse, beaming with satisfaction. Before stepping into his Santana sedan, he turned around and waved to the cheering crowd; after getting into the car, he rolled down his window and continued waving at them, even after the car had driven off.

After this incident Baldy Li viewed the medical record of his vasectomy operation as a great treasure and thought it was truly fortunate that he had decided, in a fit of anger, to have the operation. He had never imagined that it would save him so much trouble. He carefully tore the page documenting his vasectomy out of the booklet, had a framer mount it, then hung it right between his masterpieces by Qi Baishi and Zhang Daqian.

The townspeople agreed that Baldy Li's decision to have a vasectomy had been a stroke of genius. Just think, if he hadn't had the vasectomy, then who knows how many little Baldy Lis might be running around in every street and alley, including perhaps a few big-nosed, blond-haired, and blue-eyed ones?

Then everyone let their imaginations go wild as they invented a pre-history for Baldy Li's operation, transforming into something truly legendary the tale of his decision to have the vasectomy after having had his heart broken. They told how he had taken a rope and tied it around his neck and tried to hang himself from a tree branch, but how neither the rope nor the branch held, and consequently he fell to the ground and ended up with a mouthful of mud. Next they described how he tried to drown himself in the river, but after jumping in, he remembered that he actually *did* know how to swim and therefore wasn't able to drown himself. They imagined him climbing out of the river and cursing, "I can't seem to fucking kill myself!" So he returned home and removed his pants, took out his penis and placed it on the cutting board, picked up the cleaver, and was about to lop it off when he suddenly had to take a piss. When he returned from the bathroom, he discovered that he couldn't bear to part with his penis after all. Therefore, he went to look for a razor blade to slice off his balls, but he discovered that they were so terrified they had shrunken up. Baldy Li therefore felt sorry for them and couldn't bring himself to slice them off. It was only then that he went to the hospital to have the vasectomy.

Now that Baldy Li's vasectomy from a decade earlier was brought to light, the people of Liu once again started paying attention to Lin Hong. Many would point, feeling sorry for her, shaking their heads at her fate. Some of the women of Liu liked to gloat over other people's misfortunes, and they sniffed that Lin Hong might appear clever but was actually quite stupid, while others sighed that this was just another instance of *beauty being often cursed with a harsh fate*. But some of the men of Liu Town tried to defend her, saying that no one could have anticipated what would happen, and even a fortune-teller can only predict other people's futures but not his own. They said that if everyone could predict the future, the emperors of the past would never have lost their mandate of power, and Lin Hong would never have given up Baldy Li.

CHAPTER 57

WRITER LIU, one of our Liu Town's two Men of Talent, had attended the hearing at the courthouse, where he saw firsthand that hilarious scene and heard with his own ears Baldy Li's heartfelt speech. Writer Liu was so excited that night that he couldn't sleep, feeling that he had stumbled across a once-in-a-lifetime story. Therefore, he climbed out of bed, got dressed, and proceeded to spend the entire night writing a lengthy article entitled "Millionaire Crying Out for Love." In his article, Writer Liu deployed the Lofty, Expansive, and Thorough rhetorical precepts to embellish Baldy Li's story. He prettified Baldy Li's having slept with hundreds of women into his having had his heart broken by hundreds of women. He wrote that Baldy Li had fervently sought his romantic ideal in each of these encounters, but each time he found himself entangled not with a virgin but, rather, with a slut.

Writer Liu also sought to trace the source of Baldy Li's woes to his traumatic childhood—transforming the adventures of a fourteen-year-old Baldy Li peeping at bare bottoms in the public toilet into a tale of tragic victimhood. He recounted how the young Baldy Li had entered the latrine, squatted down, and grunted a couple of times; and how, before he had even started to defecate, his key accidentally slid out of his pants pocket and fell into the cesspool below. As he was leaning down to look for it, a certain Mr. Zhao came in and, ignoring Baldy Li's protests, grabbed him and accused him of being a Peeping Tom, then paraded him up and down the streets and alleys of Liu. Under Writer Liu's pen, Liu Town's other Man of Talent, Poet Zhao, was transformed into an anonymous Mr. Zhao, a hopelessly confused fellow who couldn't tell his ass from a hole in the ground. Writer Liu movingly described how a pure youth thereby became besmirched by false accusations, and how that youth unexpectedly didn't fall into depravity but, rather, from an early age simply bit his lip, endured the unjust humiliation, and grew up to exert himself for the sake of others, finally succeeding in building a vast business empire.

This article was initially published in the city's evening paper. When

Baldy Li read it, he was very satisfied, especially with the part describing how his key had fallen out of his pocket and how he had leaned over to try to fish it out of the cesspool. Baldy Li repeatedly praised the article, pounding the table with his left hand as he waved the newspaper with his right hand and shouting, "That bastard Writer Liu is truly talented. With this key, he has single-handedly redressed Liu Town's most notorious false accusation!" Grinning, Baldy Li proclaimed, "When it comes to history, the truth will always win out."

Baldy Li did have one small complaint about the title of the article. He held up five fingers and said that he had at least fifty million yuan in personal assets, so how was it that Writer Liu described him as being a mere *millionaire*? However, he didn't make a big deal about this and reasoned to one of his underlings, "For someone who has never seen much money, it's impressive that he should even be able to write the word *million*."

Within two months Writer Liu's article had been reprinted in several hundred local papers and tabloids throughout the country. With each reprinting it continued to evolve, and the title was changed to "Multimillionaire Crying Out for Love." When Baldy Li read this, from a small town hundreds of *li* away from Liu, he was even more pleased with the new title and declared, "This article was written with an attention to pursuing truth from facts."

After Writer Liu's article had circulated throughout the entire nation, it finally returned to Liu, appearing in a provincial paper, though this time the headline had been upgraded to "Billionaire Crying Out for Love." When Baldy Li read this, he laughed modestly. "That is a bit of an exaggeration."

Writer Liu had never imagined that his article would be reprinted so many times—the number of newspapers it had appeared in was almost as large as the number of women Baldy Li had slept with. After all these years Writer Liu finally became famous and was finally able to vent his long-standing frustration at having no one know who he was. With a broad smile he walked down the main street of Liu Town waving a money order and telling everyone he met, "Every day I receive a money order and have to go to the post office." Then he sighed loudly. "It's exhausting being a celebrity."

After the article made Writer Liu famous, Poet Zhao regretted that he hadn't also gone to the courthouse to observe the proceedings and that he hadn't been the one to write an article about Baldy Li. Poet

Zhao pointed to the part of the article describing the young Baldy Li in the public toilet and resentfully told the townspeople, "That was my story to tell! Writer Liu stole it from me."

Liu's two Men of Talent were bound to run into each other eventually, and they finally did at the opening ceremony of Blacksmith Tong's supermarket. By that point, Blacksmith Tong already owned three stores, but seeing newfangled stores known as supermarkets pop up all over China like bamboo shoots after a spring shower, he advanced with the times and opened a 32,000-square-foot supermarket of his own. He then set about orchestrating a truly extravagant opening ceremony. Unable to persuade County Governor Tao Qing to appear in person, he instead settled for the county governor's secretary; and similarly unable to persuade the bureau directors, he instead settled for inviting the section chiefs. Baldy Li, who was occupied with his business and interviews, was also unable to come, but he sent an enormous floral arrangement. Yanker Yu was aboard the Eurostar train en route from Milan to Paris at the time, but when he crossed the Swiss border, he sent a congratulatory telegram, asking Popsicle Wang to read it aloud at the grand opening. Wang, however, discovered that he wasn't able to read it, since two lines of text were in a foreign language, and he didn't even know whether it was Italian or French. Blacksmith Tong excitedly took the note from him and waved it to the crowd, saying, "Even foreign friends have sent congratulatory telegrams!"

Blacksmith Tong also invited Liu Town's two society notables, Writer Liu and Poet Zhao. When Zhao spotted Liu, his face turned dark, while Writer Liu was all smiles. The two stood side by side without saying a word. For a while they coexisted peaceably in this manner, but as Blacksmith Tong was introducing his honored guests, he inadvertently opened up a can of worms. Tong first gestured to Writer Liu and said, "This is the author of the famous 'Millionaire Crying Out for Love.'" The crowd erupted in applause, and Writer Liu beamed.

Blacksmith Tong then introduced Poet Zhao: "And this is Mr. Zhao, a pivotal figure in 'Millionaire Crying Out for Love.'" The crowd sat on their hands, instead greeting Zhao with a chorus of snorts and laughs.

Ever since he had been cast as "a certain Mr. Zhao" in Writer Liu's article, Poet Zhao had been absolutely furious, and now that Blacksmith Tong had introduced him in this way, Zhao found that he couldn't restrain himself any longer. Pointing at Writer Liu, he complained bitterly, "If you had any guts whatsoever, you would simply have written 'Poet Zhao,' but since you are a total coward, you hid behind the vague 'a certain Mr. Zhao.'"

Writer Liu smiled broadly and urged Poet Zhao not to get angry: "Be careful about getting so upset at your age. You might have a stroke."

Liu's thinly veiled barb made Zhao's formerly pale face flush red with fury. Poet Zhao accused Writer Liu in front of everyone, demanding, "This was clearly my story, so what right did you have to write about it?"

"What do you mean, this was your story?" Writer Liu feigned ignorance.

"Baldy Li's peeking at women's bottoms in the public toilet was clearly my story to tell." Poet Zhao pointed at the assembled crowds and added, "All of Liu's men and women of a certain age will surely remember that I was the one who caught him, and that it was I who marched him through the streets."

"You are correct." Writer Liu nodded. "Baldy Li's peeking at women's bottoms was indeed your story to tell. But I didn't write about that. I wrote about Baldy Li's search for his dropped key—and that was *my* story."

The crowds burst into laughter and agreed that Writer Liu had a point. Poet Zhao was left speechless, and his face drained of color once again. Observing the two squabbling with each other, Blacksmith Tong became anxious that they not ruin his grand opening, so he gestured for the fireworks to start. With one loud blast of the fireworks, the crowd promptly forgot Writer Liu and Poet Zhao and ran over to watch the display.

Writer Liu's article made Baldy Li famous throughout the country, and countless newspaper reporters and television personalities descended upon Liu Town. As soon as Baldy Li opened his eyes in the morning, he found himself having to give interviews; and when he lay down to sleep at night he was awakened by a distant reporter calling on his cell phone for an interview. At the height of the media frenzy there were four cameras filming him, twenty-three flashbulbs flashing, and thirty-four reporters crowding around, asking him questions.

Baldy Li was as excited as a little dog finding a pile of juicy bones.

He recognized that this was a once-in-a-century business opportunity, and therefore in answering the reporters' questions about love, he opportunistically switched the subject back to his businesses. After making a few grand pronouncements about love, he immediately changed the topic to his tragically impoverished youth. He explained that the reason he was nicknamed Baldy Li was that his mother would always tell the barber to shave him bald, because the family was too poor to afford frequent haircuts. In describing his childhood, Baldy Li would always start crying. Wiping his tears, he thanked Deng Xiaoping's Reform and Opening Up Campaign, thanked the Party and the nation, as well as all of his compatriots. After offering his thanks, he launched into the tale of how he got his start in business and how he had created the magnificent empire he had today. At this point he put up his hands and modestly explained that he by no means thought of his own business empire as *magnificent* but, rather, he was simply echoing the language the press had used in describing it.

From that point on, whenever Baldy Li appeared in the media, it was no longer as a man forsaken by love but as the very model of a business titan. He proved himself worthy of his reputation and soon had twisted all the papers in the country around to the subject of his business ventures. In this way, his corporation also became famous, and countless investment checks followed closely on the reporters' heels, followed in turn by countless business partners. Millionaires from throughout China, from Hong Kong, Macao, and Taiwan, and even from overseas Chinese communities, wanted to invest and open new factories and companies with Baldy Li. All levels of the government also enthusiastically supported him. Whereas before it would take him a year or two to get a new venture approved, now he could get permits issued within the month.

During those heady days Baldy Li would sleep only two or three hours a night. Between interviews and business dealings, he would hand out and accept dozens of business cards. In the past, many of the people who came to do business with him turned out to be swindlers, but Baldy Li could tell at a glance who genuinely wanted to collaborate with him and who merely wanted to get their hands on his money. His eyes would often narrow to a squint when he did business, to the point that people would think he had fallen asleep, though in reality he was more clearheaded than anyone else. He was willing to collaborate with anyone but on the condition that they first deposit their collaborative capital in his own corporation's bank account. Anyone imagining that Baldy Li would allow his own capital to be accessible was delusional: He wouldn't let the swindlers get close enough to smell his farts, much less touch his money.

With reporters Baldy Li was extravagantly generous, inviting them to eat, drink, and enjoy themselves and sending them on their way with large piles of gifts. By contrast, he would never spend a cent on people who came to discuss business with him. He would meet with them at his company headquarters's café, and upon concluding their business, he would insist on splitting the bill, saying, "In accordance with international business protocol, each pays his own bill."

Baldy Li's café was the most outrageous rip-off in all of China. Even at the cafés in Beijing's and Shanghai's five-star hotels, where they served coffee made from freshly ground imported coffee beans, a cup of coffee would cost you only forty yuan. At Baldy Li's, you would be charged one hundred yuan for a cup of instant Nescafé. The swindlers would quietly fret that not only did they not manage to swipe a cent from Baldy Li's coffers; they were being extorted themselves.

Liu Town's hotel, restaurant, and retail industries began to take off. Crowds of visitors blew through like blizzards, and they would stay in Liu Town's inns, dine in its restaurants, and shop in its stores. Coming from all over the country, they spoke many different dialects, but when they arrived in Liu, they communicated with one another in standard Mandarin. The townspeople, who were used to conversing only in the local dialect, now found themselves rolling their tongues all day speaking Mandarin. If they weren't paying attention, they might continue rolling their tongues upon returning home or when eating dinner— even after going to bed, couples often found themselves rolling their tongues and lapsing into Mandarin.

The people of Liu saw Baldy Li every day—when they opened their newspapers, they would see him smiling at them; when they listened to the radio, they would hear his chuckle; and when they watched television, they would see his smiling face. Not only did Baldy Li become famous, but he brought fame to the entire town. It might have had an illustrious history going back more than a thousand years, but now people hardly remembered to call Liu Town by its name. Everyone

had fallen into the habit of mentioning Baldy Li every time they
opened their mouths, and as a result they naturally began referring to
Liu Town as Baldy Li's Town. When visitors happened to drive
through, they would roll down their windows and ask, "Is this Baldy
Li's Town?"

CHAPTER 58

WHILE BALDY LI was at the peak of his good fortunes like a sun at high noon, Song Gang was still wandering around town wearing his face mask and looking for part-time work. Lin Hong continued to be called into chain-smoking Factory Directory Liu's office, and now Liu didn't stop with verbal harassment but instead began to harass her physically as well. He would position his chair next to hers and caress her hand with feigned affection. She wanted more than anything to stand up and slap him, but remembering that Song Gang was unemployed, she restrained herself and settled for merely brushing his hand off. Director Liu was someone who, if you gave him an inch, would take a mile. Therefore he started kissing her face with his black-toothed mouth, nauseating Lin Hong. She pushed him away, got up, and walked toward the door. Just as she was about to open it and walk out, he came up behind her and, with one hand grabbing her breasts and the other stuck down her pants, pulled her back toward the couch. Lin Hong desperately clutched the door handle with both hands, knowing that her only hope was to open the door. At that point someone happened to walk in, and Director Liu immediately released her. Lin Hong sprinted out the door, hearing Liu cursing behind her. She then straightened her clothes and her hair and hurriedly walked away. It was not yet time to get off work, but she nevertheless rode her bike out the main gate and, tears streaming down her face, rode home through the streets of Liu.

Song Gang had just returned and sat down on the couch. He hadn't yet taken off his face mask when he saw Lin Hong walk in crying. Song Gang, not knowing what had happened, anxiously stood up. When Lin Hong saw him, she starting crying even harder, and Song Gang urgently asked what had happened. She opened her mouth, but upon seeing Song Gang standing there pathetically with his face mask, she decided not to tell him how Director Liu had tried to take advantage of her, remembering that Song Gang was already suffering an unbearable burden. The reason she had endured Director Liu's advances for so long was precisely because Song Gang had lost his job, and she kept telling herself that if he were to get a good job, she wouldn't need to continue subjecting herself to this abuse. Therefore, she told him, "You need to go see Baldy Li."

When she saw Song Gang hesitate and then obstinately shake his head, she couldn't help crying out, tears streaming down her face, "When Baldy Li made his fortune, he thought of you, his brother, and came expressly looking for you. But you turned him down."

"You were also here with me," Song Gang muttered.

"Did we discuss it?" Lin Hong shouted back. "Such an important thing, but you didn't discuss it with me first and instead simply turned him down."

Song Gang bowed his head. When Lin Hong saw this, she shook her head angrily, saying, "That's all you can do, bow your damned head."

She kept shaking her head, unable to understand how Song Gang could be so stubborn. There are some people who don't start crying until they see the coffin, but Song Gang seemed to be the sort who wouldn't cry even after the coffin was laid out in front of him. Lin Hong therefore decided to go see Baldy Li herself. She told Song Gang about her plan, saying that even aside from their history of depending on each other for survival, the mere fact that they grew up together made it incumbent on Baldy Li to give Song Gang a job. Wiping away her tears, Lin Hong told Song Gang, "I'll just tell him you are ill and ask him if he would be willing to give you a job."

As she was saying this Lin Hong opened her dresser, wanting to find something pretty to wear to see Baldy Li. She laid her clothes out on their bed and spent about an hour trying to choose something, weeping the entire time. She noticed that all of her presentable outfits had been purchased many years earlier and had long since gone out of style. Still weeping, she put on an outfit that, though out of fashion, was nevertheless still presentable. Having gained weight since she bought it, she found that it was now as tight as a bandage wrapped around her body.

Song Gang watched her sadly, feeling that he had truly let her down. He got up from the sofa and said firmly, "I'll go."

Song Gang went outside and headed toward Baldy Li's company. The poorest person in Liu Town was going off to meet the richest one. They had formerly been brothers and were still brothers now. When Song Gang walked into Baldy Li's company, he stood in the lobby and stared for a while until he finally spotted Baldy Li in the café, holding forth with a group of reporters. He walked over and said quietly, "Baldy Li."

It had been many years since anyone had addressed Baldy Li thus—these days everyone addressed him as Boss Li. Suddenly hearing someone using his old nickname, Baldy Li wondered who this could be. He turned and saw Song Gang standing there in his face mask, his eyes smiling behind his glasses. Baldy Li stood up and told the reporters, "I must excuse myself for a second."

He pulled Song Gang into the elevator and then into his office. After closing the door, the first thing he said was "Take off your mask."

From behind the mask, Song Gang replied, "I have a lung infection."

"Fuck your lung infection." Baldy Li ripped off Song Gang's mask and said, "This kind of thing is not necessary between brothers."

Song Gang said, "I'm afraid I'll infect you."

Baldy Li said, "I'm not afraid."

Baldy Li told Song Gang to sit down on the couch, and he sat down beside him and said, "So you have finally fucking come to see me."

Song Gang looked about Baldy Li's enormous office and said in wonder, "If Mama were still alive, how delighted she would be to see you in this office."

Baldy Li felt a pang of tenderness. Placing his hand on Song Gang's shoulder, he asked, "Song Gang, what's happened to your health? I've been so busy the past few years, I haven't had a chance to look after you. After hearing that you were injured, I wanted to come and see you, but I got busy with other matters and forgot."

Song Gang smiled sadly and described to Baldy Li how he had hurt his back working on the docks and then ruined his lungs working at the concrete factory. After hearing this, Baldy Li leapt up from the couch and started cursing him, "You fucking idiot. Why do you go everywhere looking for a job when you could have just come to me? You fucking idiot, look at what you've done to yourself. Now your back and lungs are both ruined. You fucking idiot, why didn't you come to ask for my help?"

Baldy Li's curses warmed Song Gang's heart, making him feel that they were indeed still brothers. Song Gang laughed and said, "Well, now I've come."

"Now it's too late," Baldy Li said, exasperated. "You are already disabled."

Song Gang nodded and then asked with embarrassment, "Can you give me a job?"

Baldy Li sighed and nodded his head. He sat down again next to Song Gang and patted his shoulder, saying, "First you must recover your health. I'll have someone send you to the best hospital in Shanghai for treatment. We need to get you cured."

Song Gang shook his head. "I didn't come to you for medical treatment. I came because I need a job."

"Fuck," Baldy Li cursed, then said, "Okay, why don't you come take a vice president position in my office? If you want to come to work, you can, but if you prefer, you can just stay at home and rest. The important thing is for you to get well."

Song Gang shook his head and said, "I can't do that job."

"You fucking bastard," Baldy Li cursed again. "What can you do?"

"Everyone calls me Chief Sub," Song Gang replied in a self-mocking tone and then laughed. "I can only do jobs like cleaning up, sorting letters and newspapers, et cetera I am incapable of doing anything else. I don't have the ability—"

"You good-for-nothing fucking bastard. When Lin Hong married you, she must have been blind." Baldy Li shook his head. "How could I, Baldy Li, ask my brother to do those kinds of things. . . ."

After cursing for a while, Baldy Li realized that it was useless to continue reprimanding Song Gang and said, "Why don't you go on home? I still have a gaggle of reporters waiting for me. We'll discuss your situation later."

Song Gang put his face mask back on and felt content as he emerged from Baldy Li's office. Even though Baldy Li had repeatedly called him a fucking bastard, the more Baldy Li cursed him, the happier Song Gang became. When he returned home, he took off his mask, sat down on the couch, and delightedly said to Lin Hong, "Baldy Li is still the same as ever. He called me a fucking bastard over and over again, saying that I was good for nothing and that you must have been blind to have married me."

At first Lin Hong was also happy, but soon she became confused. She asked him, "Did Baldy Li give you a job?"

"He told me to get well first," Song Gang replied.

Lin Hong asked skeptically, "So he didn't give you a job?"

"He wanted to make me a vice president, but I didn't agree," Song Gang replied.

"Why not?"

"Because I'm not qualified," he explained.

Lin Hong began crying again. She wiped her tears and couldn't help saying, "You are truly hopeless."

Song Gang began to feel uneasy and said softly, "He told me to first recover my health."

"But where are we going to get the money to pay for your medical care?" Lin Hong began crying brokenheartedly.

At this point there was a knock on the door. Lin Hong wiped her tears, opened the door a crack, and saw the CFO from Baldy Li's company waiting outside. He gestured for her to come out. Lin Hong stared for a second, then wiped her eyes and followed him out. She walked about thirty yards down the street with him, whereupon he stopped and handed her a bankbook. He explained that the account was in Lin Hong's name and contained one hundred thousand yuan, which Baldy Li was giving Lin Hong and Song Gang to cover their living and medical expenses. He added that Baldy Li was worried that Song Gang wouldn't accept the money and therefore was giving it to Lin Hong instead. He asked Lin Hong to keep it a secret from Song Gang. As he was about to leave the CFO said to Lin Hong, "Boss Li says Song Gang's illness is quite serious, so you should take him to the hospital as soon as possible. Boss Li says that you need not worry about money, and that from now on he'll deposit another one hundred thousand yuan into this account every six months. And if that isn't enough, just let us know. Boss Li says that he will make sure you are taken care of."

With the bankbook in her hand, Lin Hong stood there staring blankly. How much money was one hundred thousand yuan? She had never before even thought of this number. She noticed various passersby staring at the bankbook and jumped in alarm before collecting herself. She quickly hurried home, but as she was about to go inside she abruptly changed her mind. Baldy Li's CFO had instructed her not to tell Song Gang, and therefore she turned around and went to the bank and withdrew about two thousand yuan, deciding to take Song Gang to the hospital the very next day. Then she slowly headed home, with memories of the grinning Baldy Li flooding her mind. She decided that Baldy Li was actually a very good man and that she had been wrong to have despised him.

CHAPTER 59

LESS THAN two months after Writer Liu first enjoyed his moment of fame, he noticed that he had become passé. It seemed as if no one noticed him anymore, and the royalty checks also stopped arriving. He became indignant, feeling that he had single-handedly created Baldy Li's current supercelebrity status, while he himself, by contrast, had been promptly forgotten. Without exception, all of the reporters who arrived in town wanted to talk to Baldy Li and none even deigned to glance at Writer Liu. Once he pulled aside several reporters in the street and told them that he was the one who had written the original article about Baldy Li. They grunted but then hurried on to interview Baldy Li, afraid that if they arrived late, they would miss their turn for the day.

Finding himself once again without an income or an audience, Writer Liu wandered the streets wearing a wrinkled suit, with a straggly beard, and disheveled hair. His black shoes were so coated in dust that they had become gray. Since the out-of-towners ignored him, he turned instead to the townspeople themselves. He'd pull a local aside and prattle on endlessly, describing how Baldy Li had achieved his fame as the result of his own tremendous contributions. Writer Liu's rants would always conclude with the same phrase: "I have expended all my efforts embroidering someone else's wedding gown."

Writer Liu's rantings soon spread all over town until finally they reached the ears of Baldy Li. Saying, "I want to teach him some manners," he had his underlings go and fetch Writer Liu.

When Baldy Li's underlings found Writer Liu, he was standing in the middle of the street munching on an apple. They walked over and told him that Baldy Li wanted to see him. Liu was so excited that he started to choke on his apple. He bent over, his face completely red, and then, coughing and thumping his chest, he followed Baldy Li's two underlings. He continued thumping his chest all the way to the entrance of Baldy Li's headquarters, whereupon he finally succeeded in coughing up the piece of apple that had gotten lodged in his throat. Panting and wiping his tears as if he had just returned from the dead,

Writer Liu told the underlings, "I know why Boss Li wants to see me. I've been waiting for his call. I know what kind of person Boss Li is. When Boss Li drinks water, he doesn't forget the person who brought it from the well."

When Writer Liu entered Baldy Li's thousand-square-foot office, Baldy Li was on the phone with someone discussing business. Writer Liu looked about, exclaiming and sighing, and when Baldy Li finally got off the phone, Writer Liu said with a broad smile, "I had long heard how magnificent your office was, and now I see that its reputation is well deserved. I have visited the county governor's office, and although his is big, it is a mere bathroom compared to yours."

Baldy Li's cold gaze extinguished Writer Liu's excitement. Baldy Li scowled. "I hear that you have been spreading rumors."

Writer Liu turned pale and started shaking his head and saying repeatedly, "No, no, not at all. . . ."

"Fuck." Baldy Li pounded the table. "Fuck."

As Writer Liu heard these two "fucks," his entire body started to shake. He thought this was surely the end. Baldy Li was at the height of his powers, and if he wanted to get rid of Writer Liu, he could do so as easily as squashing a fly. Baldy Li laughed coldly and asked, "What have you been saying? Is it true you said you made my wedding gown?"

Writer Liu nodded and bowed, saying, "I'm sorry, Boss Li, I'm sorry. I shouldn't have said that."

Baldy Li tugged at his suit and asked, "Is this the wedding gown you made me?"

Writer Liu shook his head repeatedly. "No, no . . ."

"Do you know what brand this is?" Baldy Li said proudly. "This is an Armani. And do you know who Armani is? He's Italian, and the world's most famous designer. Do you know how much this suit cost?"

Writer Liu started to shake his head. "Very expensive. Certainly very expensive."

Baldy Li held up two fingers: "Two million lira."

Writer Liu heard "two million" and was so astounded that his knees started to wobble. How could this bumpkin know what a *lira* was? He was just convinced that foreign money was more expensive than Chinese money. He shouted, "Two fucking million!"

Baldy Li saw Writer Liu's look of astonishment and smiled slightly, saying, "I'll give you some advice: You should watch your mouth."

Writer Liu continued nodding. "Yes, yes, I certainly will. As they say, loose lips sink ships, so I'll certainly watch mine."

After Baldy Li had shown Writer Liu some severity, his expression abruptly changed and he said amicably, "Won't you have a seat?"

For a second Writer Liu didn't know how to respond, so Baldy Li again invited him to sit down. Only then did Liu carefully sit, whereupon Baldy Li said cordially, "I read that article you wrote. You are a fucking genius. How in the world did you come up with the idea of that key?"

Writer Liu let out a sigh of relief and said happily, "That was sheer inspiration."

"Inspiration?" Baldy Li thought that was too deep for him. "Don't use such fucking abstract concepts. Speak more directly."

Writer Liu chuckled knowingly and, turning his head toward Baldy Li, confided, "I also used to peek at women's bottoms in the public toilet, so I have some experience in these matters."

"Really? You've done it, too?" Baldy Li asked excitedly. "What kind of experience?"

"I used a mirror." Writer Liu stood up and started to demonstrate. "I would position it so that I could look at their bottoms in the mirror. That way I wouldn't fall into the cesspool and also could watch and make sure no one else came in."

"Fuck." Baldy Li hit his forehead. "Why didn't I think of using a mirror?"

"But at least you were able to see Lin Hong's bottom," Writer Liu said fawningly. "The only one I was able to see was that of Blacksmith Tong's wife."

"Fuck," Baldy Li said again, his eyes glimmering. "You are truly a fucking genius. I have three loves in life: money, genius, and women. You bastard, therefore, exemplify my second love. My company has now grown large, and large companies need a media spokesman. I think that you, bastard, are a perfect candidate for this position."

With that, Writer Liu became Baldy Li's official PR person. When the townspeople of Liu saw him again a few days later, he was no longer a country bumpkin but was now decked out in a stylish suit, polished shoes, a white shirt with a red tie, and neatly combed hair. Whenever Baldy Li got out of his Santana, Writer Liu, who was now known as PR Liu, would be right at his heels. PR Liu took to heart Baldy Li's advice that he watch his mouth, and from that point on the people of

Liu found that getting any dirt out of him was tougher than pulling teeth. PR Liu privately told friends, "I can't speak as freely as I used to, because I am now Boss Li's mouthpiece."

Baldy Li had not misjudged Writer Liu. When he wasn't supposed to speak, you couldn't beat a word out of him with a stick; when he was, pearls streamed from his lips. When everyone was taking great delight in some sex scandal involving Baldy Li, Writer Liu came out and issued a correction: "Boss Li is a bachelor, and when a bachelor sleeps with a woman, that is not a scandal. What is a scandal? A scandal is when a husband sleeps with someone else's wife, or when a wife sleeps with someone else's husband."

Townspeople asked, "If someone else's wife sleeps with Baldy Li, does that count as a scandal?"

"That would indeed be a scandal." Writer Liu nodded. "But a scandal for someone else. Boss Li's hands would be clean."

Writer Liu's response on the scandal reached Baldy Li, who said approvingly, "That little bastard is absolutely right. For a bachelor like myself, even if I were to sleep with countless women from antiquity to the present, from China and abroad, it still wouldn't constitute a scandal."

After Writer Liu accepted his appointment as PR Liu, his first task was to deal with Baldy Li's vast mountain of mail. These letters came from every corner of the country and were all from self-avowed virgins. The thought of a multimillionaire who had never experienced love or met an honest-to-goodness virgin captured the imagination of countless women, leading them to write him letters professing their undying devotion. Young girls and young wives, mothers and prostitutes, city gals and country lasses, middle-school, high-school, and M.A. and Ph.D. students, even a lady professor all claimed to be virgins. Furthermore, they all either hinted or stated outright that they wanted to offer Baldy Li their hymens, which they had carefully preserved up to this point.

Every day the postman would deliver a huge sack of mail, and then a couple of burly young fellows from Baldy Li's company would drag the bag from the mailroom to Writer Liu's—or, rather, PR Liu's—office. PR Liu worked diligently. His office was right next door to Baldy Li's, and, like Baldy Li, he became so busy that he only had time to sleep two or three hours a night. He read through the vast pile of virgins' letters, selecting a few of the better ones to read out loud to Baldy Li.

Baldy Li was so busy that he barely had time to take a breath, so PR Liu had to seize whatever free moment Baldy Li happened to have. For instance, he would read a bit while Baldy Li was taking a piss, a bit more when he was taking a shit, and a bit more while he was having dinner. When Baldy Li went out, PR Liu followed behind, reading him a choice excerpt or two. When Baldy Li got into his sedan, Liu would also squeeze in and continue reading. When Baldy Li returned home in the middle of the night and lay down in bed, PR Liu would stand next to his bed reading; and when Baldy Li fell asleep, Liu would lie down at his feet and sleep as well. When Baldy Li woke up, PR Liu would immediately spring to his feet and continue reading as Baldy Li brushed his teeth, washed his face, and ate his breakfast. He continued reading right up until Baldy Li reached his office and became occupied with other matters, and only then would he rush off to brush his own teeth, wash his own face, and eat his own breakfast. Then he would bury himself again in the mountain of letters, struggling to get through each new batch that arrived with the day's mail.

PR Liu became Baldy Li's shadow, and the virgins' letters titillated Baldy Li to no end. When he thought of there being so many hymens throughout the country, lined up like a Great Wall of troops waiting for him, Baldy Li couldn't help excitedly scratching his thighs with both hands. The letters PR Liu picked were the most brilliant and moving ones, and Baldy Li's eyes would glitter as he listened to them. He was like a child in nursery school, crying out innocently at every turn, "Really? Really?"

Later Baldy Li found that he couldn't get away from these virgins' letters; they had become his spiritual sustenance. He became addicted to them as if they were amphetamines, and whenever he felt tired, he would have PR Liu read him a passage, after which he would immediately be able to throw himself back into his work. While he was being interviewed or was discussing business, he would often develop an irresistible craving and would have to sneak out and have PR Liu read him another letter. Only then would the reinvigorated Baldy Li be able to sit back down with the reporters or business partners. During that period, he would often forget that his public relations director was called PR Liu and instead would call him simply Virgin Letter. PR Liu was human, however, and therefore periodically also had to go to the bathroom to take a piss or shit. And if sometimes, when Baldy Li needed a hit of his spiritual heroin and couldn't immediately locate PR

Liu, he would stand in the middle of the hall and call out frantically, "Virgin Letter, where are you? Where the fuck have you gone?"

At that point, PR Liu would dash out of the bathroom, holding up his pants with one hand and a letter with the other, and start reading aloud.

CHAPTER 60

THE REPORTERS swept in and retreated like a tidal wave, all in the space of three months. During that time, Baldy Li flitted about like a social butterfly, until one day he suddenly noticed that the reporters were gone. Although there was still a steady stream of people coming to town to discuss business with him, suddenly there were no more reporters, and Baldy Li was finally able to relax a bit. Feeling as though he had been relieved of a heavy burden, he said that now he could finally sleep like a normal person. The first night, as soon as his head hit the pillow, he slept eighteen hours straight. Even after waking up when PR Liu called him on the phone, he complained that he hadn't slept enough. PR Liu himself had slept for seventeen hours and also complained that he hadn't slept enough. As both men lazed about in their beds, PR Liu read Baldy Li virgin letters for two hours until he heard thunderous snores on the other end of the line. Only then did Liu put down the virgin letters, and as soon as he closed his eyes he immediately started snoring as well. Baldy Li and PR Liu each slept for five more hours, and both sported puffy and bloodshot eyes when they saw each other at the office the next day.

For the next week, Baldy Li lounged on the couch in his office, listening to PR Liu's hoarse voice read more letters. Although the virgins' heartfelt letters still stimulated him like spiritual heroin, he found it hard to adjust to the reporters' sudden disappearance and became increasingly distracted. Interrupting PR Liu's reading, he wondered aloud, "Why did those bastards all vanish at the same time?"

PR Liu stood in front of Baldy Li's couch and explained that that was the nature of the media—bastards, each and every one of them, flocking en masse toward whatever happened to be the latest hot spot. Like dogs, they pounced wherever there were bones.

Baldy Li abruptly sat up and said, "And do you mean that I, Baldy Li, am no longer a bone?"

PR Liu stammered in response, "Boss Li, you shouldn't speak of yourself in that way."

Baldy Li lay down again on the couch and dispiritedly continued listening to the latest virgins' letters. He was lost in thought, and after listening to Liu read for a while, he suddenly sat up, face flushed with excitement, and cried out, "No, I insist on being a bone."

The continuous flow of virgin letters had given Baldy Li an inspiration, and he announced that he was going to host a National Hymen Olympic Games. When PR Liu heard this, his eyes opened wide in amazement, whereupon Baldy Li gushed ideas while walking back and forth through his office. He uttered the word *fucking* more than twenty times. He was going to make those fucking reporters come running back like mad dogs. He wanted the fucking television reporters to broadcast his Hymen Olympics live and also to have it streamed live on the fucking Internet. He wanted the fucking sponsors to open up their fucking checkbooks and take out their fucking money, and to have fucking ads for the games plastered all over the streets and alleys. He wanted to have those fucking beauties wear bikinis and sashay up and down the street, and to have the fucking townspeople of Liu feast their fucking eyes on the spectacle. He wanted to establish a fucking Hymen Games organizing committee, find some fucking political leaders to serve as fucking chairmen and fucking deputy chairmen, and find ten fuckers to come serve as fucking judges. Pausing briefly at this point, he specified that the ten judges must all be male. Finally, he told PR Liu, "And you will be my fucking spokesman."

With pen and paper in hand, PR Liu quickly recorded Baldy Li's fucking instructions. Only after Baldy Li sat down on the couch to catch his breath did PR Liu speak, singing the praises of Baldy Li's brilliant scheme and proposing two very minor suggestions. First, he volunteered that it seemed somewhat inappropriate to call it a Hymen Olympic Games and asked whether they could change the name to Inaugural National Virgin Beauty Competition.

Baldy Li nodded. "That is a good suggestion."

PR Liu then suggested that perhaps it was somewhat inappropriate for all the judges to be men. Shouldn't they also have some female judges? Baldy Li, however, disagreed, and said with a wave of his hand, "I don't want any women. It is ultimately us men who decide which women are pretty or not, so what point is there in including women?"

PR Liu considered for a moment and suggested that there might be unfortunate ramifications if all the judges were men, because this might lead to debates and criticism in the media, ultimately becoming a topic that people would discuss endlessly.

· "All the better!" Baldy Li shouted and added, "I want there to be controversy, and I want them to discuss this endlessly. That way I will always be a bone."

PR Liu sprang into action like a bolt of lightning, and the very next day he sent out press releases announcing the virgin competition. He spent the whole day on the phone placing calls to every corner of the country, confirming people to serve as chairmen and deputy chairmen of the organizing committee and also confirming the list of ten judges.

Baldy Li also called up a storm, phoning all those chairmen of the board and trustees who had previously discussed business with him in order to nail down sponsors and advertisers. Finally he called up County Governor Tao Qing and, after telling him about his glorious plan, asked Tao to make the main street of Liu Town available for hosting the proposed Inaugural National Virgin Beauty Competition. Nearly drooling, Baldy Li sketched out his vision: "More than a thousand beauties will come to Liu from throughout China to participate in the competition, and every fucking one of them will be a virgin. The biggest gathering place in the county is the movie theater, but it only has eight hundred fucking seats and therefore won't even be enough to hold all the beautiful virgins, much less us and the other political leaders. Even the judges wouldn't have seats. You wouldn't want us to have to sit in the virgins' laps, would you? And then there is the question of the fucking spectators who will want to come see the virgins. Naturally, the only option would be to hold it in the street."

Tao Qing was ecstatic about this proposal, immediately pronouncing it a major turning point in Liu Town's development and saying that if it was done well, it could increase the GDP of the entire county by 300 to 500 percent. He told Baldy Li, "Don't you worry. You are welcome to use two, three, or as many streets and alleys as you might need. Even if all of the beautiful virgins in the country end up here, we will still be able to accommodate them."

News of the Inaugural National Virgin Beauty Competition quickly spread throughout the country, and the reporters who had previously retreated like the tide now rushed back in. Baldy Li once again became the choice bone for the entire nation. His smiling face could once again be found in newspapers and on every television channel. PR Liu's boat also rose along with the tide, but he didn't forget to whom he owed his success. He knew if it hadn't been for Baldy Li's trust, he wouldn't be where he was now. Therefore, during the press conference for the competition, PR Liu took care to pepper his answers with "Boss Li."

One reporter asked, "Why is it necessary to host this National Virgin Beauty Competition?"

PR Liu replied evenly, "The competition will help promote traditional Chinese culture, increase the self-respect and ultimately the self-confidence of today's women, and at the same time support higher standards of health and hygiene. It is for these reasons that Boss Li has decided to organize this Inaugural National Virgin Beauty Competition—"

The reporter interrupted him to ask, "What do you mean by 'higher standards of health and hygiene'?"

PR Liu answered, "The hymen plays a crucial role in preventing the invasion of foreign microbes, protecting the internal reproductive system, and preserving the body's reproductive ability. This is what Boss Li means by 'higher standards of health and hygiene.'"

Another reporter asked, "What will be the entry requirements for prospective contestants?"

PR Liu responded as if reciting a tongue twister: "They must be beautiful and elegant, healthy and graceful, sociable and mature, accomplished and modest, respectful of elders and loving of the young, pure and chaste, and with no prior sexual experience."

The reporter then asked, "Will those women who may have torn their hymens while doing sports be permitted to compete? And how about those whose hymens have been breached as a result of sexual violence? Will they be allowed to participate?"

PR Liu answered, "Our Boss Li has the greatest respect for the two categories of women you mention and has given a great deal of thought to the question you have raised, losing appetite and sleep over the matter. In the end, however, he has decided to sacrifice those women to help preserve the integrity and authority of the competition as a whole. He explicitly asked, however, that I use this news conference to pay tribute to those women and exhort all Chinese men to lavish them with love and attention."

A female reporter asked, "Isn't this so-called Virgin Beauty Competition you are hosting actually an expression of feudal misogyny, which is to say a form of sexual discrimination?"

PR Liu shook his head and replied, "We are all our mothers' children, and we all love and respect our mothers. Our mothers are women, and therefore we love and respect women."

A final reporter asked, "Will the winner of the competition become your Boss Li's wife?"

PR Liu replied with a laugh, "Boss Li is hosting a beauty pageant, not a bridal pageant. Of course, you can't rule out the possibility that he might fall in love with one of the virgin beauties, but that would depend on whether or not she loved him. Love is inherently unpredictable."

When the news conference was televised, everyone in Liu watched it. PR Liu appeared with slick hair and smooth face, wearing a suit and leather shoes, and answered questions flawlessly. Baldy Li also watched the broadcast on television and was very satisfied with PR Liu's performance, remarking, "That old bastard is without question a genius."

Following the news conference, the Inaugural National Virgin Beauty Competition had its grand launch. The competition was divided into a preliminary round, semifinals, and a championship. The virgin beauties participating in the preliminary and semifinal rounds had to pay for their own room and board, and only the hundred finalists would have their food and board provided by the competition organizing committee. Out of those hundred finalists, a first-, second-, and third-place winner would be chosen, and their prizes would be one million, five hundred thousand, and two hundred thousand yuan, respectively. The organizing committee would then help launch the winners' Hollywood careers and groom them for international stardom.

A blizzard of application letters started arriving—the mail truck deposited a large sack of them at the front desk of Baldy Li's company headquarters every day. With virgins from all over the country applying, the homegrown virgins of Liu Town and the rest of the county didn't want to seem like slackers in comparison, so they all registered as well, declaring that local assets should be kept within the community. The top three prizes should definitely be kept in-house, they declared, and shouldn't be filched away by an outsider.

Of all those who registered, be they homegrown or from afar, most were actually no longer virgins. In fact, some were married, some had already been divorced, others were cohabiting with lovers, and there were even some who had lost count of how many men they had been with. Each of these women, however, had had their hymens reconstructed.

As usual, the townspeople of Liu were like frogs at the bottom of a well, with no perspective on the outside world. It was not until an itinerant charlatan by the name of Wandering Zhou arrived that they realized their competition, in placing such a high value on virgins, had spurred a rage for hymen-reconstruction surgery throughout China. Wandering Zhou told them that a Beijing economist had labeled this the age of the hymen economy. All across the country every medical facility from big-city hospitals to small rural clinics had started offering hymen recons. Wandering Zhou told the people of Liu that hymen-recon surgery had become China's most profitable industry and that, from an economist's perspective, "the entire hymen economy had its origins in Liu Town." Wandering Zhou concluded, "And that is why I have come."

Eventually the people of Liu came to appreciate the significance of the hymen economy. The county hospital, together with the rural clinics below it, was, of course, the first to benefit from the trend. Its hymen-recon ads could be found on bridge columns, electrical poles, roadside walls, even bathroom stalls. Everywhere you looked, you'd see an ad. You'd wake up in the morning to find one stuck to your front door; while you were eating lunch, more would be slipped under your door. When you went to the market to buy a pair of shoes, the salesman would hand you an advertisement, and the ticket seller would give you one when you went to buy a movie ticket. When you entered a restaurant and perused the menu, you would find an ad stuck inside it, and after ordering braised pig's feet, you would find that in the blink of an eye the dish had become hymen-recon—another flyer having been slipped onto your table and covering up your food.

Now that everyone in Liu—men and women, old and young—knew what hymen-recon surgery was, they said, "It is as simple as having double eyelid surgery."

Children would recite, "The operation lasts thirty minutes and requires only local anesthesia. Afterward there is no need to rest, and it won't affect your work or daily activities or even your menstrual cycle."

Pedicab drivers wore sandwich boards with ads from the county hospitals with a hole in the middle through which the driver could stick his head, as if it were a raincoat. On their chests and backs these drivers wore the following message, written in big yellow letters on a red background:

RECLAIM YOUR INTACT HYMEN! SUCCESS RATE OF THE OPERA-

TION: 100%. SATISFACTION RATE: 99.8%. PROBABILITY THAT YOU WILL BLEED DURING YOUR NEXT DEFLOWERING: 99.8%.

As the hymen economy sprang up it added fuel to Baldy Li's Inaugural National Virgin Beauty Competition. During that period, money from sponsorships and advertising companies flowed continuously into Baldy Li's accounts, and Baldy Li, his eyes completely bloodshot, continued furiously making phone calls, inviting new sponsors and advertisers to join. He spent the entire day hoarsely shouting into the receiver, "This is an opportunity that you simply can't pass up. This is a once-in-a-lifetime opportunity. Hurry, hurry, hurry!"

PR Liu became busier than he had ever been before, complaining that he was not only Baldy Li's fucking media spokesman but had to take care of all of Baldy Li's other fucking affairs as well. Baldy Li was concerned only with screaming into the telephone receiver like an executioner, asking everyone for money like a beggar, and couldn't trouble himself with other matters. PR Liu, therefore, had to delegate. He had to hire more assistants every day, and since his office had long been too small to accommodate everyone, he borrowed someone else's and eventually simply rented himself a small house, where he hung up a formal sign saying INAUGURAL NATIONAL VIRGIN BEAUTY COMPETITION ORGANIZING COMMITTEE. In the interest of both confidentiality and security, PR Liu asked Baldy Li to call the county division of armed police, and from that point on there were always two armed policemen standing guard at the entrance of the organizing committee building. Each of the committee's workers had to wear a badge with a photo ID, and anyone without this badge shouldn't even consider trying to get in.

After Baldy Li initially became famous, people started calling Liu Town Baldy Li Town, and now that his Virgin Beauty Competition became similarly well-known, everyone took to calling it Virgin Beauty Town instead. Virgin Beauty Town launched a series of beautification projects. The county government arranged to have all the houses along the road repainted and used all the county's radio and television broadcasts, as well as directives to each of its work units, to request that each family wash their windows so thoroughly that they appear invisible. They further requested that each family refrain from throwing garbage out and, especially after the competition began, that they hide their garbage under their beds. They enforced this ban by decreeing that anyone who threw out twenty *jin* of garbage would have to pay a fine equivalent to the price of twenty *jin* of pork. The government called on everyone to mobilize and asked that they help make Virgin Beauty Town as delicate and charming as the most exquisitely adorned woman, in order to put forward the most dazzling appearance while playing host for the Inaugural National Virgin Beauty Competition. Then the town decked itself out with lanterns and decorations, stringing banners along all the streets and from all the buildings. Giant billboard frames were erected along the street that was going to be used for the competition, and billboard advertisements that Baldy Li had secured with his screaming telephone calls started appearing in them one after another.

The week before the competition was set to begin, the town was already overflowing with visitors. The first to arrive were the reporters, with print journalists and broadcast journalists arriving in one clump after another. Next the television and radio trucks drove in, followed by the VIPs, who were Baldy Li's sponsors and advertisers, as well as political leaders and the judges for the event. The most luxurious hotel in Liu was one of Baldy Li's, and he crammed the reporters, friends, and VIPs into it, filling it to capacity.

Originally, more than twenty thousand beautiful virgins had registered for the event, but because they had to pay for their own room and board, in the end only three thousand showed up. They came from throughout China, and all the hotels and guesthouses in Liu were completely booked. What had originally been twin rooms were made into four-person rooms, and still they couldn't accommodate all the virgin beauties. In the interest of preserving Liu Town's upstanding image, the country government called on everyone to donate their beds for the virgin beauties to use. The reasoning was that it would not do to have the beauties camped out in the street, because what would happen if some of the local men couldn't control their urges and raped them in the middle of the night? Even if they didn't rape but just copped a feel or two, the entire town would still lose face. Fortunately, it was summertime, and everyone responded enthusiastically to the call, with the men of many households taking their bedrolls and sleeping outside in the streets and alleys, thereby allowing the visiting virgins to use their beds. Poet Zhao also slept in the streets and lent out his one-bedroom apartment to two virgin beauties, with each virgin paying him one hundred yuan a day in rent.

Song Gang and Lin Hong too lived in a one-bedroom apartment, and when Song Gang saw that Poet Zhao was earning two hundred yuan a day, Song Gang proposed that he sleep outside while Lin Hong remained at home, thereby at least allowing them to earn one hundred yuan a day hosting one virgin beauty. Lin Hong, however, vetoed the idea, noting that Song Gang was ill and shouldn't be sleeping outside. When he insisted, Lin Hong got angry, saying that now that he was going to the hospital every day for shots and treatment, his health was finally improving, but if he were to sleep outside, it would surely deteriorate, and the money they would waste on medical treatment would surely exceed any they might have earned from rent. Song Gang didn't know that Baldy Li was supporting them, since Lin Hong had told him that her parents and their friends were paying for the medical expenses. Song Gang had already placed his bedroll next to Poet Zhao's when he saw Lin Hong standing in the doorway weeping tears of fury. Therefore, he had no option but to roll up his bedroll and return home. Those days Song Gang would open his front door every morning and the first person he would see would be Poet Zhao stretching at his spot under the electrical pole. When Zhao saw Song Gang, he would sit up and start chatting animatedly, claiming that sleeping in the street was more comfortable than sleeping in his own bed, and pointing out that it was much cooler out here, not to mention that he was also earning two hundred yuan a day. Song Gang was very envious, but noticing that Poet Zhao's face was covered with mosquito bites, he asked, "What's wrong with your face?"

Poet Zhao answered proudly, "These are acne pimples."

CHAPTER 61

IT WAS at this juncture that the itinerant charlatan Wandering Zhou arrived in our Liu Town.

Wandering Zhou was a sight to behold: Like all con men these days, he had a movie star's good looks. He walked over from the bus depot with two twenty-nine-inch color television boxes and only five yuan in his pocket. Actually, apart from Chief Sub Song Gang, every man in Liu had more money in his pockets than did Wandering Zhou, yet they all felt poor. Even with only five yuan, however, Wandering Zhou had the air of someone who was on China's Forbes 400 list.

It was dusk and the moon had not yet come out, yet the lights from the streetlamps and the neon signs were already shimmering past one another on the streets. It was so muggy that the crowds wished they could simply run around naked. Wandering Zhou, however, was dressed formally in a suit and leather shoes. He set the two boxes down by his feet and stood on the street outside the bus depot, looking as cool and comfortable as if he were in an air-conditioned hall. Flashing a China Forbes 400 smile, he asked everyone walking back and forth, "Is this Virgin Beauty Town?"

Wandering Zhou asked five people in a row, but each time the passersby only nodded or grunted in response, and not a single one of them stopped to look at him carefully, much less came over to speak with him. Since no one would take his bait, Wandering Zhou did not know where to start. In the past, if such an unusual character had appeared on the street, everyone in Liu would have immediately crowded around curiously as if he were an ape. But he happened to show up at a moment when twenty-eight hundred out of an expected three thousand virgin beauties had already descended upon the town—not to mention the two-hundred-plus reporters, a famous announcer whom people previously had only seen on television, and various political leaders and celebrity judges—and as a result, the townspeople were suddenly as worldly and jaded as big-city folk. Wandering Zhou had thought that if he shouted "Virgin Beauty Town" a few times, he would surely get everyone's attention. What he didn't realize was that outsiders had already been calling this place Virgin Beauty Town for more than a week now and that even the people of Liu had begun referring to their own town that way.

Wandering Zhou stood in front of the bus depot until nightfall, but still no one came to speak to him, and consequently he had no opportunity to deploy his snake-oil-salesman routine. Just a few pedicab drivers looking for business approached him and asked, "Hey, mister, which hotel are you going to?"

Since Wandering Zhou had only five yuan in his pocket, if he were to take a pedicab, he would end up with no money at all. He knew that one shouldn't mess with these pedicab drivers—if he was short even a single yuan, they were liable to beat him to a pulp. Therefore, when they approached to vie for his business, he paid them no attention and instead took a toy cell phone from his suit pocket. This phone looked real and even had a triple-A battery inside, so that when he discreetly pushed a button, it would ring. When the pedicab drivers asked him which hotel he wanted to go to, his cell phone rang, and he pulled it out and shouted angrily into the receiver, "Why hasn't my exclusive-use car arrived yet?"

After night fell, Wandering Zhou realized that there was no point in continuing to stand there, so he had no alternative but to pick up his two enormous cardboard boxes and set off. No matter how hard he tried now, he couldn't maintain his China Forbes 400 gait but, rather, trudged along with a coolie's shuffle. The streets of Liu were chock-full of people. Wandering Zhou kept accidentally bumping his boxes into the thighs of visiting beauties, as well as the thighs of the townspeople of Liu. Under the twinkling of the streetlamps and the neon lights, amid the soaring melodies of foreign and Chinese songs, in the roar of jazz and rock and the melodic strains of foreign classical and Chinese folk music, Wandering Zhou walked and paused and walked and paused. When he paused, he would look around and admire the new Liu Town that Baldy Li had helped create. Along the old street adorned with traditional red lanterns there was now an eclectic mix of European classical architecture and American modernist architecture. Wandering Zhou spotted soaring Greek Doric columns belonging to Baldy Li's fanciest restaurant, the Roman-style red-walled atrium housing his brand-name clothing store, the Chinese-style slate-roofed courtyard of his Chinese restaurant, and the Japanese-style garden of his Japanese restaurant, as well as gothic windows and baroque roofs. Wandering Zhou said to himself, *This is a real mutt of a town.*

No one knows where this itinerant charlatan went that night, carrying those two large cardboard boxes, wearing his suit and dress shoes in the heat, and suffering from hunger, thirst, and overall fatigue. But one thing was certain: He must have been in excellent health, since he was able to continue walking around until eleven o'clock that night without collapsing from heatstroke. It seemed that this charlatan must have succeeded in tricking even his own body. He did a giant loop about town and noticed that the streets were full of sleeping men. From their discussions, he gathered that all of the town's hotels and guesthouses were completely booked and that even the private residences were packed full of virgin beauties.

Wandering Zhou finally stopped in front of Poet Zhao's straw mat. Zhao had not yet fallen asleep but was lying on his mat swatting at mosquitoes. Wandering Zhou nodded, but Zhao ignored him, wondering what this young man was doing here. Wandering Zhou's eyes wandered over to Mama Su's snack shop across the street, and he suddenly felt as famished as if his chest were plastered to his back. He realized that if he didn't eat something soon, he wouldn't be a charlatan as much as a starving ghost. Still carrying his two boxes, he crossed the street and, though he was still sporting his suit and dress shoes, his gait was now more like that of a refugee. He shuffled into the snack shop, where the air-conditioning instantly refreshed him, and sat down at a table near the door.

Because it was so late, there were just a couple of customers left. Mama Su had gone home and her daughter, Missy Su, was minding the cashier's counter, chatting with two waitresses. Missy Su was in her thirties but no one had any idea who her boyfriend was or if she had one at all—just as they never found out anything about who her father had been.

Missy Su saw the dashing Wandering Zhou walk in and sit down. The only things less than elegant about him were his two large boxes. On his part, Zhou immediately discerned that this eminently average-looking, and perhaps even a bit homely, Missy Su must be the proprietress. Therefore, with a handsome smile on his handsome face, he started gazing at her as if he were admiring a painting. Never having had a man admire her the way the charlatan Wandering Zhou was admiring her now, Missy Su felt her pulse start to race. Wandering

Zhou continued gazing at her until one of the waitresses handed him a menu, whereupon he finally tore his eyes away from her face and directed his attention to the menu. Seeing that a steamerful of mini–meat buns was five yuan, he ordered one. The waitress then brought over the drink menu and asked him what he wanted to drink. Wandering Zhou shook his head and said, "I have diabetes, so I'll just have a glass of water."

The waitress replied that they didn't have any tap water, only bottled mineral water. Wandering Zhou shook his head and repeated, "I don't drink mineral water. Mineral water is a swindle, since it doesn't actually contain any minerals. It is actually tap water which has the highest mineral content."

After saying this, Wandering Zhou continued admiring Missy Su, making her pulse race with excitement. He knew that she would surely bring him a glass of water. He then reached his hand into his pocket, and instantly his toy cell phone rang, whereupon he pulled it out and pretended to take a call. From his side of the conversation it appeared as if he was talking to his secretary. He complained that she had not reserved a room for him and now there were no rooms to be found. Unlike earlier with those pedicab drivers, this time in front of Missy Su he didn't make a show of losing his temper but, rather, complained very politely and concluded his call by uttering a few words of reassurance to the person on the other end of the line. When he finished and put his cell phone away, he turned back around and found Missy Su standing there with a glass of water. He knew that this was mineral water. By then he was as thirsty as if he had just come in from the desert, but he politely stood up to accept the water and politely thanked her for it. Then he sat back down and sipped it while nibbling on his steamed buns and began chatting with her.

He started talking about the buns, remarking how tasty they were, and then complimented Missy Su on how neat and clean her shop was. Missy Su, who had turned away, suddenly paused. Sensing an opening, Zhou then suggested that she should introduce the latest new thing in buns, whereupon she sat down across from him. Zhou continued, suggesting that she should introduce a kind of steamed meat bun that came with its own little straw. He described how in the top snack shops of Shanghai and Beijing all the mini-buns were served with tiny straws sticking out. Those buns had much lighter, thinner skins than regular mini-buns and therefore contained that much more meat juice. Customers first delicately sipped the flavorful juices through the straw, and only then did they eat the bun itself. Zhou said that these were currently considered the best buns; and moreover, they had become veritable symbols of our countrymen's new sophisticated lifestyles. Eating buns was no longer merely about eating meat filling wrapped in dough; rather, it was about savoring the juice. He said, "In fact, there are some customers who just sip the juice and don't even bother with the rest."

Missy Su's eyes started to gleam as she listened to Wandering Zhou's descriptions, and she promised she would immediately start developing this new kind of bun the very next day. Wandering Zhou took this opportunity to suggest that perhaps he could come by to assess her work. He said that he would gladly share his valuable experiences of sipping mini-bun juice if it could be of any help to her. He promised to help her make these straw-embedded mini-buns a runaway hit, one that would not only attract customers from one hundred *li* around but people from as far away as Beijing would fly down just to enjoy her specialty buns. Missy Su laughed delightedly at this and asked shyly, "Are you really willing to help me?"

"Of course," replied Wandering Zhou with a gracious wave.

Now that this charlatan had spent his final five yuan, his offer to be the official sampler of the straw-embedded buns turned out to be the perfect way to nab himself several days' worth of food. After he left the snack shop with his two cardboard boxes, his gait was much livelier than it had been when he had been so famished. Now he just needed to find a free place to sleep. He again walked up to Poet Zhao and came up with a plan to claim Zhao's straw mat.

Poet Zhao would have already been asleep by that point if it hadn't been for the mosquitoes. They had bitten him all over his body, driving him to distraction. When Wandering Zhou walked by, Zhao was slapping madly at the buzzing mosquitoes, his hands dotted with blood. As Wandering Zhou set down his piled-up boxes next to Poet Zhao's mat, Zhao peered down at his mosquito-blood dotted palms under the light of the streetlamps and showed Wandering Zhou, saying, "This is all *my* blood."

Wandering Zhou nodded politely, and then his toy cell phone rang. He took out his phone and said, *Hello,* followed by a string of foreign words Poet Zhao couldn't understand. Zhao looked at him curiously, waiting for him to finish, then asked cautiously, "Were you speaking American just now?"

"Yes." Wandering Zhou nodded. "I was discussing business with the manager of my American subsidiary."

Having guessed correctly that Wandering Zhou was speaking American, Poet Zhao said proudly, "I can also understand a little American."

Wandering Zhou looked at Poet Zhao, who was standing there impressed by his own brilliance, and realized that the telephone call had not sufficiently cowed him. Therefore, his toy cell naturally rang again, and he said, "*Buon giorno*," followed by a string of foreign words that Poet Zhao couldn't understand. Zhao waited until Wandering Zhou was finished and had put his cell phone back in his pocket, then again cautiously asked, "This time you weren't speaking American, were you?"

"It was Italian," Zhou replied. "I was discussing business with the manager of my Italian subsidiary."

Poet Zhao said proudly, "I knew it couldn't be American."

Since neither of these calls had been able to conquer this self-satisfied country bumpkin, Zhou's cell phone promptly rang a third time. He answered, "*Yeobo-seyo*."

This time Wandering Zhou finally succeeded in conquering Poet Zhao. Zhao didn't dare continue showing off but, rather, asked humbly, "What language were you speaking this time?"

Wandering Zhou smiled and said, "Korean. I was discussing business with the manager of my Korean subsidiary."

A look of respectful awe came over Poet Zhao's face, and he asked Wandering Zhou, "How many countries' languages *do* you know?"

Wandering Zhou held up three fingers and said, "Thirty."

Poet Zhao exclaimed in surprise, "That many!"

Wandering Zhou laughed modestly and said, "That includes Chinese, of course."

Poet Zhao was awestruck and said, "But that still leaves twenty-nine."

"Your math is very good," replied Wandering Zhou, then shook his head. "My businesses stretch worldwide, from the North to the South Pole, from Africa to Latin America, leaving me with no choice but to learn so many foreign languages."

Poet Zhao was completely taken in. He gazed at Zhou reverently and in a far more respectful tone of voice, asked, "May I inquire as to what line of business you might be in?"

Wandering Zhou replied, "Health products."

Wandering Zhou took off his jacket and set it down on the cardboard box. He then removed his tie and stuffed it into the jacket pocket. While he was undoing his shirt button, Poet Zhao asked cautiously, "What do you have in your boxes?"

Wandering Zhou answered, "Hymens."

With a look of astonishment, Poet Zhao watched as Wandering Zhou took off his shirt and placed it on top of the box, leaving him bare-chested like Poet Zhao. Seeing Zhao's astonished expression, Zhou said, "Haven't you ever heard of hymens?"

"Of course I've heard of hymens," Poet Zhao replied, still looking completely confused. "But hymens are located in women's bodies. How is it that you have them stored in boxes?"

Wandering Zhou laughed and said, "These are artificial hymens."

"Is there such a thing as an artificial hymen?" Poet Zhao was astonished.

"Of course."

Wandering Zhou sat on Poet Zhao's mat and removed his shoes and socks. He then removed his pants and placed them on the box. Now he was as undressed as Poet Zhao, who was also completely naked except for his underwear. Zhou told Poet Zhao, "There are artificial hearts, so why shouldn't there be artificial hymens? One uses these artificial hymens the same way one would a real one. There will certainly be real pain, and the first night they will bleed real blood."

As he was saying this Wandering Zhou lay down on Poet Zhao's mat, as if he were lying down in his own bed. He even nudged Poet Zhao over a little with his foot, but Zhao didn't budge, thinking to himself that this was his bed, and what right did this fellow have to kick him off? Poet Zhao began to get annoyed. Kicking Wandering Zhou back, he said, "Hey, this is my bed. What do you think you are doing, lying here?"

Lying on the mat, Wandering Zhou tapped his finger and asked disdainfully, "You call this a bed?"

Poet Zhao replied, "This straw mat is my bed. All that falls within the borders of this straw mat is my bed."

Wandering Zhou lay there comfortably with his eyes closed and yawned. "Okay, let's call it a bed. Isn't it appropriate to share one's bed with friends?"

Poet Zhao sat up on his mat, determined to push this fellow away before he fell asleep. "What do you mean, friends? We just met and exchanged a few words."

With his eyes closed, Wandering Zhou replied, "Some people become friends the instant they meet, while others may know each other for an entire lifetime without becoming friends."

Poet Zhao stood up and lifted his foot to kick Wandering Zhou, saying, "Get the fuck out of here. Who's friends with you?"

Poet Zhao kicked Wandering Zhou in the groin. Wandering Zhou immediately sat up, howling in pain. Holding his groin, he shouted at Poet Zhao, "You kicked me in the balls!"

Poet Zhao continued kicking him, saying, "Yes, I meant to kick you in the balls. If hymens can be replaced with artificial ones, then I want you to have to replace your balls with artificial balls."

Wandering Zhou jumped up and shouted at Poet Zhao, "I, Boss Zhou, always stay in the presidential suites of five-star hotels."

It was only then that Poet Zhao learned that Wandering Zhou's surname was Zhou. Paying no attention to what Wandering Zhou was saying, Poet Zhao said, "I don't care if you are a premier named Zhou, I wouldn't let you use my bed even if you were a chairman named Mao. Why don't you go stay in your presidential suite?"

Wandering Zhou stood next to Poet Zhao's mat and began to argue with him: "Here in your town they don't even have any ordinary rooms in ordinary hotels available, much less a presidential suite. Otherwise, why would I be lying down on your straw mat?"

Poet Zhao decided that Wandering Zhou had a point. It was true that all the hotels in Liu were booked solid. Otherwise, why would there be two virgin beauties sleeping in his own house? Zhao considered for a moment, then agreed to permit Wandering Zhou to sleep on his mat, but on the condition that he pay rent. "The lowest price I will charge for this bed is twenty yuan a night. Given that you are not from here, and furthermore can speak twenty-nine foreign languages in addition to Chinese, I won't overcharge you. The bed is twenty yuan a night, but since I, the owner, will be sleeping on half of it, I will only charge you, the customer, ten yuan."

"Okay, it's a deal," Wandering Zhou said quickly. "I'll pay you twenty yuan a day, and you can consider your half of the bed to be my treat."

Poet Zhao looked up with a smile and thought to himself that this fellow was truly a boss—no haggling over nickels and dimes. Reverting to his former polite tone of voice, he extended his hand and said, "If you could be so kind as to settle your account now. . . ."

Wandering Zhou had not expected Poet Zhao to pull this move, so he responded irritably, "When one stays at a hotel, it's customary to settle the bill upon checking out."

Wandering Zhou picked up his suit jacket from the box, and when he reached into his pocket, Poet Zhao thought that he was reaching for his money. At that moment Zhou's phone rang, and what he pulled out of his pocket, therefore, was not money but, rather, his cell. He yelled angrily into the receiver, lambasting the person on the other end of the line for not having reserved him a room, thereby making him sleep in the street. Hamming it up, he roared into the phone, "What? Go talk to their provincial governor? It's too late now. What? Tell their provincial governor to call up the county governor? What time do you think it is? It's past one o'clock in the morning! How the fuck do you want me to call him at this hour?"

When Poet Zhao heard this, his eyes grew wide with astonishment. After glancing over at Poet Zhao, Wandering Zhou changed his tone and, still speaking into the receiver, said, "Okay, let's leave aside the question of the room. But what about my salesmen? Why haven't they arrived? What? They had a car accident? They fucking totaled my Mercedes? . . . In any event, I can't be the one out on the streets selling my own products. Forget it, don't waste time apologizing. Just hurry to the hospital to look after the salesmen. I'll take care of things here on my own."

After Wandering Zhou closed his phone and put it back in his pocket, he looked at Poet Zhao and said, "My salesmen had a car accident and therefore won't be able to make it. Would you like to work for me?"

Poet Zhao had no way of knowing that Wandering Zhou didn't have a cent to his name. After Zhou put his phone back in his pocket and didn't take any money out, Poet Zhao assumed he had simply forgotten. When Zhou asked Poet Zhao if he wanted to work for him, Zhao himself also promptly forgot about the twenty-yuan bed fee and asked curiously, "What kind of work?"

Wandering Zhou pointed to the two boxes and replied, "Sales."

"You mean selling hymens?" Poet Zhao asked.

Wandering Zhou nodded. "I'll give you a salary of one hundred yuan a day, with additional bonuses based on performance."

A salary of one hundred yuan a day? Poet Zhao was delighted but cautiously asked Wandering Zhou, "When will you pay me my salary?"

Wandering Zhou replied, "After you have sold all the goods, of course."

Looking as though he couldn't care less whether Poet Zhao worked for him or not, Wandering Zhou had intimidated Poet Zhao so thoroughly Zhao didn't dare to ask about the salary again. Poet Zhao asked Zhou for his cell number, saying that an employee should know his boss's number. The number that Wandering Zhou then gave Poet Zhao left him dumbfounded, one starting with 000, followed by 88, and ending with a 123. This number was neither that of a Chinese cell phone nor that of a Chinese landline. Poet Zhao asked Wandering Zhou, "What kind of number is this?"

Wandering Zhou said, "It is a number from the British Virgin Islands."

Poet Zhao had never even heard of such a place, and in his astonishment he completely forgot about the twenty-yuan bed fee. Poet Zhao quickly squeezed his body over to the side, making every effort to give his temporary boss a little more room. He said, "Boss Zhou, please try to get some sleep."

Wandering Zhou was very satisfied with Poet Zhao's suggestion. He nodded, then lay down and immediately started snoring. At this point Poet Zhao suddenly remembered that Wandering Zhou had never paid his twenty-yuan bed fee, but he didn't dare kick him again.

The next morning, when Poet Zhao opened his eyes, his temporary boss had already put on his suit and tie. When Wandering Zhou saw that Poet Zhao had woken up, he feigned uncertainty and asked, "Did I hire you last night?"

"Yes," Poet Zhao answered, adding emphatically, "and at a salary of one hundred yuan a day."

Wandering Zhou nodded, then started issuing orders like a boss. The first thing he wanted Poet Zhao to do was to help him take the two boxes of artificial hymens to the warehouse. Poet Zhao looked at him blankly, not knowing where the warehouse was. Wandering Zhou saw Poet Zhao standing there without moving and barked, "Go, quick."

"Boss Zhou," Poet Zhao said, "where is your warehouse?"

"Where is your house?" Wandering Zhou asked in return, then added, "Your house is my warehouse."

Poet Zhao finally understood and thought that if this fellow wanted to use his house as a warehouse, that was fine, but he should pay for it.

Poet Zhao asked with a grin, "Boss Zhou, how much do you plan to pay to rent the warehouse?"

Wandering Zhou looked down at the straw mat on the ground and said, "Twenty yuan a day."

Poet Zhao happily agreed. When he picked up those two cardboard boxes and prepared to go, Wandering Zhou called out to him again, and from one of the boxes he took out two stacks of flyers for artificial hymens. One pile of ads was for domestic Lady Meng Jiang hymens, which sold for one hundred yuan apiece, and the other was for imported Joan of Arc ones, at three hundred yuan apiece. Wandering Zhou took the two thick stacks of ads and, looking around, said, "Originally I was supposed to have twenty salespeople here, but with the car accident they are now all laid up at the hospital. Now I just have you, and that is not going to be enough."

At this point Song Gang opened his door and walked out. Poet Zhao called out, "Song Gang, I'll hire you to be a salesman and will pay you eighty yuan a day. Are you interested?"

Song Gang had not yet had a chance to react when Wandering Zhou patted his suit and said to Poet Zhao, "So I hire you to work for me for one hundred yuan a day, and then you turn around and hire someone else to work for you for eighty yuan, allowing you to come out earning twenty yuan?"

"No." Poet Zhao shook his head. "You will be the one paying the salary, and you will give him eighty yuan and then give me twenty yuan more as my finder's fee."

Wandering Zhou continued patting his suit. "Then it would be me hiring him, not you."

Wandering Zhou saw that Song Gang was wearing a face mask despite the summer heat and asked curiously, "Is there something wrong with your mouth?"

"There's nothing wrong with my mouth," Song Gang replied, smiling behind his mask. "It's my lungs."

Wandering Zhou nodded. "I'll hire you, for one hundred yuan a day."

Song Gang didn't know what kind of work he was being hired for. He uncertainly mentioned his lung condition, but Wandering Zhou told him, "You won't need your lungs for this job. All you need is your mouth."

Wandering Zhou divided the flyers into two further piles and handed them to Poet Zhao and Song Gang, explaining that their assignment for the day was to distribute the flyers to every woman they saw. "Don't leave out anyone, not even the old ladies."

Wandering Zhou asked Poet Zhao and Song Gang to walk up and down the street distributing the flyers under the blazing sun. Meanwhile, he himself retreated to Missy Su's air-conditioned snack shop, from which he didn't emerge all day. He started helping Missy Su create the straw-embedded buns. That morning he ventured into the kitchen and, with the delighted Missy Su, started instructing the chef on how to prepare them. Mama Su sat at the cashier's counter, watching her daughter bustling through the shop with a rare look of delight on her face. She couldn't help feeling uneasy, unable to shake the feeling that this dapper young man was not to be trusted. When she herself was young, she had also been deceived by a handsome young man, who had left her pregnant with Missy Su. Though her handsome young man had sworn his eternal love and devotion, he soon disappeared, and she had never heard from him again.

Wandering Zhou spent the entire day sampling those straw-embedded buns, alternating between opining that they didn't contain enough juice, or that they were too bland. He began his taste-testing in the morning and continued right through to the afternoon, devouring seventy-two straw-embedded buns in all. He had so many of them that, by the end, he couldn't speak without burping. He had so many that Missy Su looked at him with concern, asking if they shouldn't rest for a bit and continue experimenting tomorrow. He rubbed his belly and readily agreed. Then, sipping the green tea that Missy Su brewed for him, he sat down in the seat nearest the air conditioner and launched into tall tales of his exploits.

Song Gang and Poet Zhao spent the entire day walking up and down the street, ending up completely covered in sweat. Even Song Gang's face mask became soaked. By this time virtually all of the virgin beauty contestants had arrived, and the streets of Liu were teeming with lovely and not-so-lovely women from all over the country. Accents ranging from the far north to the deep south mingled throughout town. Even though they were hot and tired, Song Gang and Poet Zhao were both upbeat—Song Gang was happy because he was earning one hundred yuan for such an easy day's work, while Poet Zhao was excited because never before had he seen so many comely young women gathered in the same place. Zhao whispered to Song Gang that he felt as though he had entered a women's bathhouse and only regretted that they still had on their blouses and skirts. The two distributed flyers for Wandering Zhou's artificial hymens to these virgin beauties, who would giggle as they stuffed them into their handbags, sniffing, "But of course *we* have no need for these."

When the two returned home at noon, Poet Zhao peeked into the snack shop across the street. Seeing Wandering Zhou sucking down his straw-embedded buns, Zhao handed Song Gang his remaining flyers, saying that he had other things to attend to that afternoon and asking Song Gang to distribute the remaining ads. Lin Hong was still working at the knitting factory, so Song Gang had lunch at home alone. After lunch he put on a new face mask, donned a straw hat, draped a towel around his neck, and filled a thermos with cold water before setting off again with his hymen ads. Song Gang could see that Wandering Zhou was still sampling straw-embedded buns in the snack shop and laughed. Wandering Zhou looked up and saw Song Gang about to go outside but didn't catch sight of Poet Zhao, and wondered what new trick that fellow was up to. He nodded to Song Gang, who nodded back before heading east down the street.

Poet Zhao snuck home to have lunch and, taking advantage of the fact that the two virgin beauties staying there were out, he lay down on the couch and took a nap. Zhao slept until evening, and when the two virgin beauties came home and saw him sleeping on the couch in his underwear, they cried out in alarm. Poet Zhao sprang up and rushed out the door. When he got downstairs, he saw that Wandering Zhou was still in the snack shop, waving his hands about and holding forth. A huge crowd had gathered around him, with some people sitting down and eating steamed buns and others standing around listening to his tall tales.

Poet Zhao quietly walked over to Song Gang's open door and saw that Lin Hong was inside cooking dinner and Song Gang was on the couch watching television. Poet Zhao asked him, "Did you distribute all of the flyers?"

Song Gang nodded, and Poet Zhao turned around and glanced over at the snack shop. Making sure that Wandering Zhou hadn't seen him, he sprinted across the street—covering the intervening 180 yards as though he were on a track and ending up bathed in sweat. He wiped the sleep from his eyes and, looking as if he had been diligently distributing hymen advertisements all day, trudged exhaustedly into the snack shop. When Wandering Zhou, in the middle of some tall tale, spotted him, he waved and told the people around him, "Exec. Asst. Zhao has arrived."

The crowd didn't know what "exec. asst." meant. Wandering Zhou explained that it was short for "executive assistant to the CEO." Poet Zhao therefore found himself suddenly promoted to executive assistant, having thought that he was merely a salesman, and as a result, he quickly shed his look of exhaustion, beamed happily, and proceeded to push aside the people who were standing in his way and walk over to Wandering Zhou. He bowed and announced that all the flyers had been distributed. Then, like a real assistant, he discreetly positioned himself behind Wandering Zhou. Zhou looked up and asked, "Have you been asleep all afternoon?"

"No." Poet Zhao shook his head emphatically. "I spent the entire afternoon walking through town distributing ads."

"Your breath smells like you just woke up," Wandering Zhou said.

The crowd erupted in laughter as Poet Zhao blushed furiously. He repeated that he had spent the entire afternoon distributing ads with Song Gang. Wandering Zhou replied with a slight smile, "I saw Song Gang but didn't see you."

Poet Zhao still wanted to defend himself, but Zhou gestured for him to be quiet. Then Zhou launched back into his account of his legendary exploits. Missy Su sat across from him, hanging onto his every word. Wandering Zhou saw that Poet Zhao's face and neck were covered in sweat, so he paused and thanked him for all his hard work. Then he returned to his account of his adventures in Africa: "African peasants are the most efficient workers in the world."

The crowd asked, "Why is that?"

Wandering Zhou replied, "They toil in the fields naked, and shit and piss as they work. That way, even as they are plowing the soil they are also fertilizing it."

The crowd marveled and sighed their approval, agreeing that this was indeed an ingenious approach. That way the peasants took care of two farming tasks at once, saving both time and energy. What's more, they added, those farmers wouldn't even need to wipe their bottoms, since they could just air-dry them as they worked.

Then Wandering Zhou pointed to the virgin beauties walking around outside and told the crowd, "If this handful of young women has already got you googly-eyed, how will you deal with having all three thousand of them here?"

Wandering Zhou said that he once traveled to an island in the Pacific. He uttered a few guttural sounds and said that this was the island's name, explaining that it literally meant "isle of woman." It was not until he had stepped onto the island that he realized he had entered a Country of Women. There were around 45,800 women there, and every one of them was as beautiful as a goddess. Only there were no men. One man before him had traveled to this island, but that had been eleven years earlier. Wandering Zhou looked straight at his audience and said, "Just think, they hadn't seen a single man in more than a decade, and then there I was."

He took a dramatic pause and slowly sipped some green tea, then asked the waitress for a refill. The men in the shop waited anxiously to hear the rest of his story, grumbling that the waitress was too slow. They waited for Zhou to take another sip of tea, then asked excitedly, "What did they do when they saw you?"

Wandering Zhou took a deep breath before continuing. "They lined up to gang-rape me. But of course my virginal night was to be spent with the ruler of the Country of Women."

Wandering Zhou explained that, contrary to what one might expect, the ruler was not an old lady. Instead, they had chosen the most beautiful woman in the land to be their ruler. Sighing, Wandering Zhou described at length the beauty of that eighteen-year-old queen: "Foreigners would call her a Venus, while the Chinese would compare her to the legendary beauty Xi Shi."

The crowd was now dying to know whether or not he ended up bedding this beautiful young queen. The men prompted, "Did you give her your virginity?"

"No." Wandering Zhou shook his head.

"Why not?" the men asked in astonishment.

Wandering Zhou said, "Although she was very beautiful, we were not in love."

The men shook their heads in disbelief, then asked, "What happened next?"

"Next?" Wandering Zhou answered casually. "Then I escaped."

The men asked, "How did you escape?"

"Very simple," Wandering Zhou said. "I used makeup to disguise myself as a woman."

The men heaved loud sighs of regret, and one complained, "Why did you want to escape? If it had been me, even if there had been a pis-

tol aimed at my head, a cannon aimed at my butt, and a fleet of Toma-
hawk cruise missiles aimed straight at my heart, I still wouldn't have
fucking left that island even if my life depended on it."

"That's right," the other men cried out.

"I beg to differ," Wandering Zhou said. "I definitely want to save my
virginity for a woman I truly love."

As he said this Wandering Zhou glanced at Missy Su, who blushed in
embarrassment. After listening to Zhou's adventures in the Country of
Women, several of the women in the crowd asked him, "How many
countries have you visited?"

Wandering Zhou made a show of calculating mentally, and then
replied, "Too many. I couldn't even count them with the help of a
calculator."

Poet Zhao's opportunity to brownnose had arrived, and he said,
"Boss Zhou can speak the languages of thirty different countries,
including of course that of our own China."

The crowd cried out in amazement, but Wandering Zhou shook his
head modestly. "That's a bit of an exaggeration. Of those thirty languages, there are only about ten that I know well enough to conduct
business. Another ten I know only well enough to carry on day-to-day
conversations, while the final ten I can only use for simple greetings."

"That's still amazing!" the crowd exclaimed.

Poet Zhao continued brownnosing, adding, "Everywhere Boss Zhou
goes, he always stays in the presidential suites of five-star hotels."

The crowd cried out in awe, but Wandering Zhou again waved modestly, saying, "Sometimes I don't stay in the presidential suite. For
instance, if a visiting president happened to be in the same hotel, then
I would stay in the business suite."

At this point, Wandering Zhou remembered that the previous night
he had slept with Poet Zhao on his straw mat on the side of the road,
and how some in the crowd might have seen him, so he decided to take
a different tack. He said that he was someone who knew both how to
stoop and how to hold his head high, someone who could stay in the
presidential suite of a five-star hotel but was equally content sleeping
by the side of the road. He added that he once slept for three days and
three nights in the Arabian desert, where the sun was so strong that he
was almost baked into a mummy. He also slept for a week in an Amazonian rain forest, where wild animals wandered by him as he slept.
Once a female tiger slept with him, and when he rested his head on a

fallen tree trunk, the tiger did the same, and so they spent the entire night sleeping face-to-face. The next morning the tiger's whiskers tickling his face woke him up, and only then did he realize that he and the tiger had spent the entire night sleeping together like husband and wife.

Poet Zhao continued his brownnosing, saying, "Boss Zhao's cell number is not even a Chinese number but, rather, it is from Britsomething or other."

Wandering Zhou corrected him, saying, "British Virgin Islands."

Some of the crowd asked in surprise, "Are you a citizen of those tiny islands?"

Wandering Zhou shook his head and said, "My company has registered there, thereby allowing it to be listed on the U.S. Nasdaq exchange."

The crowd cried out in surprise, "Your company is traded on the U.S. stock market?"

Wandering Zhou replied modestly, "Many Chinese companies are registered in the U.S."

Some of the townspeople bought and sold stocks, so they asked what his company's ticker symbol was. Wandering Zhou replied, "ABCD." Then he told them that if they had a chance to go to the United States, they should buy his stock—its performance had increased three years in a row. Everyone gasped in surprise and eagerly asked him for his cell number. When he told them, they stored it in their pockets as if it were a precious treasure, though he warned them that they shouldn't call without good reason. "Even if you just say hello three times, it could still cost you a full month's salary."

In this way, the charlatan Wandering Zhou succeeded in captivating the entire town. Everyone crowded around, gazing up at him admiringly and hanging on his every word, not dispersing until one in the morning. Executive Assistant to the CEO Poet Zhao followed Boss Zhou out of the air-conditioned snack shop and laid down his straw mat for the two of them in the muggy street. The thirty-something Missy Su, who had never been in love before, was now thoroughly captivated by Wandering Zhou. Seeing him and Poet Zhao lying down outside, she hesitantly walked over with a lit mosquito coil. Mosquitoes had also attacked Wandering Zhou the night before, leaving his face covered in so-called acne pimples. Missy Su placed the mosquito coil next to him, saying bashfully, "This was for the shop, but now that we have air-conditioning we don't need it anymore. You can use it."

Wandering Zhou stood up and politely gave his thanks. Missy Su gazed adoringly at him, then said to Poet Zhao, "Actually, it would be better if the two of you slept in the shop. There's air-conditioning, and no mosquitoes."

Poet Zhao was about to agree when Wandering Zhou politely declined, saying, "No need. This is far more comfortable than the Arabian desert or the Amazonian rain forest."

CHAPTER 62

WANDERING ZHOU enjoyed three days of free buns at Missy Su's snack shop. The day before the Virgin Beauty Competition formally began, however, this charlatan knew it was time for him to take over the reins of the operation. Taking advantage of Lin Hong's being at work, Zhou set up in Song Gang's apartment and spent two hours instructing Poet Zhao and Song Gang on how to sell his artificial hymens. Wandering Zhou was very disappointed to hear that Poet Zhao was unmarried and asked if at least he had a girlfriend. Poet Zhao first shook his head but then nodded. "I don't have a real-life girlfriend, but I do have many fantasy ones."

"Fantasy girlfriends?" Wandering Zhou shook his head. "We are selling real hymens, not fantasy ones. For that, you need a real girlfriend to serve as your talking point."

Wandering Zhou surveyed Song Gang, however, with a look of satisfaction. He remarked that Song Gang's wife, Lin Hong, was very beautiful and that he had heard she was once a well-known Liu Town beauty and something of a celebrity. Zhou then became very animated, exclaiming that they should definitely exploit this celebrity angle. He instructed Song Gang to stand on the side of the road and recount his own experiences, describing the various good, excellent, and truly miraculous aspects of Lin Hong's use of an artificial hymen. This was the first time Song Gang had heard Lin Hong talked about in this way, and he blushed bright red. He protested, "But Lin Hong hasn't ever used an artificial hymen."

"As long as you say that she's used one, then she has," Poet Zhao said. "Everyone will take you at your word."

Wandering Zhou nodded his approval and said to Song Gang, "Executive Assistant Zhao is absolutely right."

Song Gang shook his head. "I can't say that."

Poet Zhao said anxiously, "Boss Zhou pays you one hundred yuan a day, but you aren't willing to say one simple thing."

"I'm willing to say anything else, but I can't say that." Song Gang continued shaking his head.

Poet Zhao wanted to go on, but Wandering Zhou gestured for him to be quiet. Zhou thought for a moment, then suggested to Song Gang, "How about this? You don't need to say anything, just let Executive Assistant Zhao do the talking. All you need to do is stand next to him. You don't even need to nod; I just ask that you not shake your head."

Song Gang thought to himself that if he didn't need to speak or nod, then he could rest easy. Wandering Zhou had Poet Zhao and Song Gang scurry behind him like servants, each carrying one of his cardboard boxes. Song Gang's box even had a stool perched on top. Wandering Zhou, meanwhile, sauntered in front empty-handed.

The three of them reached the middle of the street that was to be used for the competition. Wandering Zhou stood on the stool and instructed Poet Zhao and Song Gang to open the two boxes and take out the two brands of imported and domestic artificial hymens. A crowd of virgin beauties and other onlookers gathered around, buzzing about like the mosquitoes that had swarmed around Wandering Zhou and Poet Zhao the night before. Wandering Zhou first took the imported Joan of Arc hymens, lifting them high above his head and shouting, "These are imported Joan of Arc artificial hymens, selling for three hundred yuan each. If you go to the hospital to have hymen-recon surgery, it will cost you three thousand yuan. At the hospital, furthermore, three thousand yuan will only allow you to be a virgin once, but if you buy my Joan of Arc hymens, for three thousand yuan you can be a virgin ten times over."

Wandering Zhou then explained how the hymens were to be used, illustrating the process with pantomime: "First, wash your hands well and dry them." He mimed washing and drying his hands. "Then take a hymen out of its vacuum-sealed aluminum-foil package and roll it up into a tight ball. Second, take this roll and place it in the deepest point of the vagina." He inserted his hand into his pants. "This should be done very quickly in order to prevent the hymen from sticking to your hands and being pulled back out." He immediately pulled his hand back out of his pants as though he had been burned. "Third, after the hymen has been in place for three to five minutes, you can engage in intercourse." This time he didn't perform the relevant action. "Fourth, after intercourse, you can go to the restroom and clean the bloody mucus from your genitals." He placed his hand in his pants and made scrubbing gestures. "When you begin intercourse, the woman should adjust her position as appropriate"—he twisted his own body—"in order to make it difficult for the man to enter her, and also should exhibit signs of pain to complement the rupture of the artificial hymen"—he furrowed his brows and adopted an agonized expression—"and if you add painful moans and a bashful expression"—he didn't moan, but he did offer a bashful look—"the effect will be even more realistic."

As the virgin beauties and other onlookers shouted in approval Wandering Zhou began to introduce his domestic hymens, saying, "These are my domestic Lady Meng Jiang hymens, which sell for one hundred yuan apiece. For the price of a single hymen-recon surgery in the hospital, you can be a virgin thirty times over."

Someone in the crowd shouted, "Why don't you demonstrate one for us?"

Wandering Zhou laughed and asked, "Is there a female comrade who would be willing to demonstrate for everyone?"

The virgin beauties and other onlookers erupted in laughter. The original questioner suggested, "Why don't you hold it in one hand and use a finger to pierce it?"

The crowd shouted their agreement, and Wandering Zhou laughed and said, "This costs one hundred yuan. There are more than one hundred of you, so if everyone contributes one yuan, I can demonstrate it for you."

Everyone took out one yuan, and Poet Zhao and Song Gang worked up heads full of sweat running back and forth until they had finally collected one hundred one-yuan bills. Wandering Zhou then began the demonstration, opening one of the Lady Meng Jiang brand boxes and removing an artificial hymen wrapped in aluminum foil. After ripping open the wrapper, he held the artificial hymen in his left hand and then tried to pierce it with his right index finger. The first time he failed to pierce it completely, and the second time he didn't pierce it either. The virgin beauties and other onlookers all laughed, and a man in the crowd shouted, "Is this an old virgin?"

"This is a Lady Meng Jiang brand hymen," Wandering Zhou said proudly. "Lady Meng Jiang's tears could topple the Great Wall, so naturally her hymen is sturdy."

In the ensuing peals of laughter, Wandering Zhou poked the hymen a third time and this time was finally able to puncture it, releasing a flood of blood-colored liquid. He proudly gestured and said, "Did you see? Did you see? This is wedding-night virgin blood!"

After the laughter died down, Wandering Zhou recommenced his original routine. Because Poet Zhao wasn't married, Wandering Zhou called out to Song Gang, "Song Gang, what brand of artificial hymen did your wife use last night?"

"An imported Joan of Arc one, of course," Poet Zhao replied on Song Gang's behalf. Then he added, in the same proud tone as Wandering Zhou, "Song Gang's wife wouldn't be using domestic products, would she?"

Wandering Zhou asked Song Gang again, "Last night when you made love, how did your wife feel?"

Again, it was Poet Zhao who replied, "She cried out in agony!"

Wandering Zhou nodded with satisfaction, then asked, "How did you feel?"

Again, it was Poet Zhao who replied, "Broke out in a cold sweat."

This response, however, displeased Wandering Zhou. He frowned and said, "It should have been warm sweat from all that happy exertion."

Poet Zhao immediately corrected himself. "First it was a cold sweat, and then—*a-one, a-two, a-three*—three seconds later, it turned into warm sweat!"

"Well said!" Wandering Zhou said loudly. "After three seconds of enjoyment, a polar chill becomes an African heat wave." Wandering Zhou was very pleased with Poet Zhao's rapid correction. He nodded approvingly, then confidently asked Song Gang, "Song Gang, in conclusion, what is the greatest advantage of artificial hymens?"

This time Song Gang blushed, blushing under his mask all the way from his neck to his forehead. He hadn't expected that he would still be placed in such a difficult position even if he didn't speak or nod. Now he wanted to find a hole in the ground to crawl into. In the end, it was again Poet Zhao who answered for him. Pointing at Song Gang, he said loudly, "Song Gang's wife is the only woman he has slept with in his entire life. But after she used an artificial hymen"—Poet Zhao held up two fingers—"Song Gang can say he has now slept with two virgins."

"You are absolutely right!" Wandering Zhou's eyes shimmered with excitement, and he shouted to everyone, "That is the advantage of artificial hymens. They not only allow women who have already lost their hymens to regain their self-confidence and self-respect, but furthermore help men to be even more faithful to their wives! Quick, come buy some. Women should buy them, and men need to buy them even more! For the price of a single operation in the hospital, with Joan of Arc hymens men can enjoy more than ten deflowerings with a single woman, and with Lady Meng Jiang hymens you'd be able to enjoy thirty deflowerings."

The virgin beauties and the Liu townspeople all laughed as they enjoyed this song-and-dance between Wandering Zhou and Poet Zhao. But as they watched they became somewhat confused. One man pointed at Song Gang and asked Poet Zhao, "He was clearly asking Song Gang, so why are you always the one who answers?"

"Would you be willing to talk openly about sleeping with your wife?" Poet Zhao retorted. "You wouldn't be, and neither is Song Gang. Therefore, he asked me to answer for him."

By this point Song Gang profoundly regretted having gotten himself into this situation and kept his head bowed low. Song Gang didn't say a word, neither nodding nor shaking his head. He just stood there, feeling extremely uncomfortable, as if there were a dull knife sawing away at his flesh. Wandering Zhou's sales pitch was extremely successful, and though no one bought a hymen on the spot, that night people kept waking Wandering Zhou and Poet Zhao as they slept next to the road, quietly asking to buy their artificial hymens. For several nights in a row, Wandering Zhou and Poet Zhao were woken by these hymen buyers even more often than by the mosquitoes. Most of the time it was virgin beauties who had come to take part in the competition, but sometimes it was young women from Liu Town. Of course, many men came to buy them as well, having all been affected by Poet Zhao's pitch and thinking to themselves that if they couldn't sleep with another woman, then at least they could experience several more first nights with their own wives.

All of this made Wandering Zhou look at Poet Zhao with new respect. He said, "You are truly a rare talent, and we should definitely collaborate in the future. This time your bonus will probably exceed your original salary."

When Poet Zhao heard this, he was delighted and asked, "How much of a bonus will I receive?"

Wandering Zhou replied, "You'll know when the time comes."

That same day, news of their performance made its way to Lin Hong, who became furious. She was about to erupt in anger when she returned home, but seeing Song Gang slumped on the couch with an uneasy, pathetic expression softened her heart, and she realized that he was merely trying to earn money for their household. Shaking her head, she walked to the outer room, but when she saw Poet Zhao, her anger immediately returned. She rushed at him furiously and, seeing that there was no one around, said in a low voice, "You bastard!"

CHAPTER 63

THE INAUGURAL National Virgin Beauty Competition finally began, attracting worldwide attention. In recognition of the fact that the event was being held in the street, and in consideration of both the blazing sun and the virgin beauties' delicate skin, the organizing committee decided to host the competition between afternoon and evening. The opening day was the most magnificent afternoon Liu Town had ever seen. Three thousand bikini-wearing virgin beauties—tall and short, fat and thin, beautiful and ugly—stood in a row stretching back more than a mile. Even the longest street in Liu Town was not long enough to hold them all, and therefore the line of virgin beauty troops turned a corner, extended over a bridge, and stretched down a second street.

The entire town turned out for the spectacle. The stores closed, all the factories stopped work, and all the other businesses also let their employees off early. As a result, everyone in town was crowded up and down both sides of the street, the wutong trees on the sides of the road were full of people who had clambered up them like monkeys, and all the electrical poles had men performing pole dances on them. The windows of the houses on both sides of the street were full of people, as were the rooftops. The doctors and nurses from the hospitals rushed out, explaining that if they didn't come see the spectacle, it would be a thousand years before a similar opportunity presented itself. The patients also came out, some using crutches and others with their arms in slings. Those who were in the process of having intravenous infusions came out holding their IV bottles, and those who had just had operations were carried out by their friends and relatives. Even if they had to be lying on a gurney or sitting on the backs of bicycles, everyone came out.

People from neighboring cities and counties spent up to five or six hours riding over on their bicycles, and then another five or six hours biking back after having caught a glimpse of the virgin beauties. Liu Town, which ordinarily had a population of about thirty thousand, more than tripled in size, to more than one hundred thousand. The streets with the virgin beauties standing in line were cleared out, and the traffic cops, armed police, and people's police were mobilized, forming a firewall to hold back the crowds. For the police, this was their happiest day, because they were able to see the virgin beauties more up close than anyone else. Even happier, however, were the reporters, since they were the only ones allowed to walk up and down the cleared-out streets. When they spotted a pretty woman, they would stop and interview her, carefully inspecting her heaving bosom and her belly button.

There was an enormous crowd of men behind the virgin beauties, and without exception, the bottoms of all three thousand virgin beauties ended up getting groped. Some of the men had taken off their shirts and were wearing only shorts, and they shouted out to the men behind them not to crowd too closely, while they shamelessly pressed their naked chests against the bikini-clad beauties. Some of the virgin beauties cried, some cursed, and others screamed in anger. With the air of innocent victims, the men in front would turn around and berate the crowds behind them, telling them not to push.

Baldy Li had repeated over and over again that the reason he was holding the beauty pageant in the street was in order to allow everyone to watch it for free. But after one of his trips to the restroom, he emerged with fresh inspiration on how to make money. He told PR Liu to immediately organize a team of people to publicize and sell "inspection" tickets. After a massive blitz of publicity, marketing, and sales, PR Liu sold more than five thousand inspection tickets. He rented all the trucks from Liu and neighboring cities and provinces for ticket holders to stand on—inspecting the virgin beauties as though they were inspecting military troops—but even then he couldn't accommodate all five thousand ticket holders. Finally, he also rented tractors from every farmer from one hundred *li* around. The line of virgin beauty troops extended more than a mile, while the line of cars and tractors carrying the inspectors stretched for two and a half miles.

Leading the way were twenty convertibles carrying Baldy Li and Tao Qing, the competition organizing committee, political leaders and judges, corporate sponsors and VIPs, with Popsicle Wang and Yanker Yu bringing up the rear in the final car. Yanker Yu had been on his way from Europe to Africa, but after Popsicle Wang called him up and told him about the Virgin Beauty Competition, he immediately changed plans and returned to Liu, deciding that, given the momentous occasion, it was high time for him to show his face. Yu stood in the open car wearing an exquisitely tailored suit with a perfectly matched shirt and tie. He looked so at home in his suit, it was as if he had never worn anything else in his entire life. He glanced over at Popsicle Wang standing next to him. Wang was also wearing a suit, but the sleeves were so long they covered the tips of his fingers, and the collar was so large that even buttoned up you could still see his collarbone. On top of that, he was wearing one of those cheap red ties that looked like an emergency pull tab. Disappointed by Popsicle Wang's attire, Yanker Yu shook his head and said, "You have no sense of style."

Behind the twenty sedan convertibles was a convoy of trucks. Leading the way was the truck for the VIPs, with tables, chairs, drinks, and fruits. Then came the truck for the A-list guests, which had everything the VIP truck had except for the tables. Next came the truck for the B-list guests, which lacked both tables and chairs and instead had the guests standing in two rows. The C-list truck had guests standing in four rows, and on the D-list truck the passengers were packed like sardines. Behind the trucks was an endless line of tractors for the regular ticket holders, on which people were packed like livestock on the way to market.

PR Liu was not riding in one of the sedans at the front but, rather, was standing at the entrance to the street with a starter gun in his hand, like an Olympic judge. The director of the organizing committee, who passed by in the first sedan, was a political leader Baldy Li had asked PR Liu to invite. He rambled into the microphone a lot of political pablum about how much Our Country had taken off thanks to the Reform and Opening Up Campaign, about how it had increased not only the national and provincial GDP but also that of the cities and towns. Just as he got around to speaking about Liu Town, he switched back to speaking about Our Country. After going on grandiosely for a while, he again turned back to Liu Town and specifically the Virgin Beauty Contest that was about to begin. He spoke about how the contest was evidence of the rise in both Our People's standard of living and China's international standing. The Virgin Beauty Competition not only would promote traditional Chinese culture but was also right on track with the tide of globalization. After going on in this fashion for more than half an hour, he finally cried out, "I hereby announce the beginning of the Inaugural National Virgin Beauty Competition!"

PR Liu fired his gun, and the sedans, trucks, and tractors full of inspectors coming to watch the virgin beauties ceremoniously filed in, as magnificent as a marathon. They rumbled along at a snail's pace, gradually making their way down the streets into the sunset. The three thousand virgin beauties, who had been pushed to their limits from the continual sexual harassment by the spectators, all sprang to attention at the sound of the starting gun. Each and every one of them stuck out their chests, swiveled their hips, and posed with smiles on their faces— composing a veritable gallery of three thousand different flirtatious expressions.

They watched as the political leaders and judges drove by in their convertibles, followed by an endless convoy of trucks and tractors full of inspectors. Still being groped by the men behind them, the contestants by now just wanted the competition to end so that they could go home and scrub themselves clean. But what kind of person was Baldy Li? He was always one step ahead of everyone and had already anticipated that the beauties would want to turn around and walk away as soon as the judges' sedans had passed, leaving the ticket holders in the trucks and tractors with nothing to see other than the setting sun, whereupon they would surely have rioted in front of the offices of the organizing committee. In order to avoid this problem, and also to increase people's interest in buying inspection tickets, Baldy Li arranged for the results of the first round of competition to be determined not by those first ten judges but, rather, by the five thousand ticket holders following behind.

Just think, with one hundred thousand sweaty people crowded together on a summer evening, how the stench of their sweat permeated the atmosphere of Liu. One hundred thousand people were exhaling carbon dioxide, and among them were five thousand who also had bad breath; one hundred thousand people meant two hundred thousand armpits, including six thousand armpits that reeked of BO; one hundred thousand people meant one hundred thousand assholes, of which at least seven thousand were farting, some more than once. The slower the cars drove, the more exhaust they emitted, but at least the car exhaust was gray and made the street look like a steam-filled sauna. Much worse were the streams of billowing black smoke coming from the tractors, as if they were burning houses.

The polluted atmosphere of Liu Town contaminated the three thousand beautiful virgins. For three hours they had to stand with their chests out and their hips swiveled, smiles plastered on their faces and flirtatious looks in their eyes, all in an attempt to have the country bumpkins riding in the trucks and tractors select them. Each of those five thousand bumpkins thought of himself as a competition judge. This was particularly true of those riding on the tractors, who, though they were crowded together like cattle, were actually the world's most conscientious judges. As soon as they pushed aside the heads in front of them, their own heads would be pushed aside by the people behind them, but they all nevertheless kept their eyes wide open, wanting to examine the virgin beauties carefully, and—holding their papers and pens above their heads—they recorded the pretty ones. They recommended and critiqued the virgins as earnestly as if they were investing in stocks. The spectators standing in the back were particularly conscientious, even though often, as soon as they glimpsed a virgin beauty with a decent face and physique, the tractor would drive past before they had a chance to see the number on her chest. Therefore, they would call out anxiously to the people in front and ask what was the number of the virgin who looked a certain way, acting as if they were afraid they might miss out on a stock that was about to open big the next day.

The three thousand virgin beauties had been standing all afternoon. They had spent about two hours simply lining up along the street and three hours more posing for the spectators. Whether they had started out wearing heavy or light makeup, by this point sweat had melted everything on their faces into a multicolored puddle. After the two-plus-mile caravan of convertibles, trucks, and tractors had driven by, the exhaust added a layer of black on top of the color. As a result, they were all as black as chimney sweeps, and the delighted crowds said that they looked like African virgin beauties.

The carnivalesque first round of competition finally concluded at nightfall, but the five thousand country bumpkins were still very excited as they went, with their sweat-drenched papers, to line up in front of the organizing committee's building and waited there until the middle of the night to turn in their ballots. They felt that they had purchased not merely inspection tickets but, rather, the opportunity to serve as judges for a national competition; this was an experience they planned to savor for the rest of their lives. PR Liu gazed out at the passionate and foolish lot of them and thought scornfully that bumpkins will be bumpkins, and even if you were to plop them down in New York or Paris, they would remain unqualified bumpkins. And it was precisely these bumpkin judges who eliminated two thousand of the virgin beauties, leaving only one thousand to enter the semifinals.

Of the two virgin beauties living in Poet Zhao's house, only one managed to qualify for the semifinals. Therefore, she happily checked into a hotel, now that they had some vacancies, while the other beauty packed her bags and left in a funk.

By this point Wandering Zhou had slept on the straw mat under the open sky for seven nights straight. He had managed to sell forty-three artificial hymens, and therefore now had some cash in his pocket. He paid Poet Zhao 140 yuan, explaining that it was his bed fee for the past seven nights, emphasizing the fact that he was treating Poet Zhao to his portion of the charges. Then he turned and walked into the snack shop across the street, sat down, and proceeded to chat intimately with Missy Su while sipping from his straw-embedded buns. The straw-embedded buns had been perfected, and consequently he couldn't continue sampling them for free on the pretense that he was testing them out. Therefore, he started to run up a tab at the snack shop, saying that it was too much trouble for him to pay such a small amount of money each day and that he would pay everything off when he left.

After Wandering Zhou emerged from the snack shop, Poet Zhao thought that he, too, was going to get a room in a hotel, but instead he came to stay at Poet Zhao's house. Upon entering he took one look at Poet Zhao's cramped home and said, his voice dripping with disdain, "Fine, I'll just sleep on your tattered couch."

Poet Zhao said, "This is simply too humiliating. You should go and stay in a hotel."

Wandering Zhou shook his head, crossed his legs and made himself comfortable on the old, tattered sofa, as if he were in his own home. He said, "I'm not used to sleeping in a regular hotel room. When I stay at hotels, the cheapest room I ever get is a suite, but the suites here have all been rented out to the political leaders and judges."

Poet Zhao suggested, "You could rent two rooms, and that would make a suite."

"Nonsense," Wandering Zhou replied. "How can you call two rooms a suite? How can I sleep in two rooms?"

Poet Zhao said, "You could sleep in one room the first half of the night, and in the other room the second half."

Wandering Zhou laughed out loud, saying, "To tell the truth, I'm not really comfortable in a regular suite. When I stay in hotels, I only use the presidential suites."

Poet Zhao said, "Then why don't you rent an entire floor? You could take a nap in every room. Wouldn't that be a presidential suite?

Wandering Zhou glared at Poet Zhao. "Don't start with me. I just want to sleep on your old, tattered couch. I've had my share of abalone and shark fin, and right now I'm in the mood for some pickled vegetables and rice gruel."

Though this charlatan was Poet Zhao's temporary boss, he hadn't yet paid him. If Zhou wanted to hang out in Poet Zhao's home, therefore, Poet Zhao had no choice but to grin and bear it. After all, if he were to shoo him away, he might also be shooing away his own wages.

CHAPTER 64

THE SEMIFINALS of the Inaugural National Virgin Beauty Competition were held two evenings later. Once again, tens of thousands of townspeople streamed into the streets to watch the excitement. This time, however, there weren't any trucks or tractors, nor were there any country bumpkins serving as judges. Instead, a giant platform covered with sponsors' ads had been erected in the middle of the street, which was lined with billboards advertising everything from cell phones to tourism, beauty products to laxatives, underwear to quilts, toys to health products. There were ads for things to eat, to play with, and to use; things for living people and dead people; things from China and things from abroad; things for people and things for pets. Even if you were to rack your brain like a high school student preparing for the college entrance exams, you wouldn't be able to come up with a product not covered by these ads.

Baldy Li and the organizing committee's political leaders and judges all sat on the platform, joined by Yanker Yu and Popsicle Wang. Under Yu's careful tutelage, Wang was now also dressed to the nines. Pop music blared from loudspeakers, but after every two lines or so the crooning would be interrupted by a commercial. After one ad concluded, the song would play for two more lines before being interrupted by another commercial. Each song would be interrupted at least four times, with the result that the famous stars singing through the loudspeakers were transformed into stuttering singers. One thousand virgins lined up, and each paraded back and forth three times in front of the platform to the beat of the stuttering music and the blaring commercials. This time the crowds were roped off, so the men couldn't grope the contestants' bottoms but could merely harass them from a distance with lecherous gazes and salacious comments. By the time each of the virgin beauties had paraded back and forth three times, the sun had set behind the mountains, thus concluding the semifinals of the competition. Baldy Li, the political leaders, and the judges all left, as did the one thousand virgin beauties and the tens of thousands of spectators. The loudspeakers, however, continued blaring commercials late into the night.

The semifinals eliminated nine hundred more contestants, leaving only one hundred to compete in the finals. The finals would be held in a movie theater, thereby allowing Baldy Li to sell more tickets and stuff his pockets with more wads of cash. Baldy Li had become a professional escort—escorting party leaders, judges, and sponsors to eat, play, and admire female beauty. As a result, the formerly awe-inspiring Baldy Li now simply spent the entire day smiling broadly as he escorted people around, to the point that he even began to resemble PR Liu.

The original three thousand virgin beauties had left him blurry-eyed and dizzy; the one thousand semifinalists had left him blurry-eyed but no longer dizzy; the one hundred finalists left him completely clear-eyed and clearheaded again. He summoned PR Liu, saying that if he didn't get his hands on some of these virgins now, he would lose his chance. He was sure that as soon as the competition concluded, they would disperse, and his only chance to bed one of them would be in his dreams. He remarked that all of the one hundred remaining beauties were quite fine, and he would be interested in sleeping with all of them; but since only a few days were left, he had to make some choices. The first one who caught his eye was contestant #1358—a beauty six feet two, perfectly proportioned, with a red-hot body. Baldy Li said that the tallest woman he had previously slept with had been just six feet, and therefore he was now in a position to break two personal Guinness records at once: his record for the tallest woman he had slept with, and also his first virgin.

Despite being busier than ever, PR Liu immediately made time to meet with contestant #1358. PR Liu, blurry-eyed and hoarse from overwork, had long since become inured to beautiful women, but the moment he saw the tall and sweet-faced #1358, his pulse started to race. Though he had been associating with the virgin beauties for quite a while by that point, he had never noticed this one. Liu decided that Baldy Li was truly formidable, being able to pick her out of a group of women more numerous than the hairs on a cow, thus demonstrating that Baldy Li's womanizing skills were truly in a class of their own.

PR Liu didn't arrange to meet contestant #1358 in the temporary office that the organizing committee was using. Instead they met in the company's café, the most ridiculously overpriced coffee shop in all of China. Naturally, PR Liu footed the bill. He first smiled and congratulated #1358 on reaching the finals, then began to beat around the bush. This being the first time he had acted as a pimp for someone, he didn't know how to get to the point. He couldn't speak too baldly, but at the same time he needed to make sure that she knew what he was getting at.

PR Liu didn't realize that Virgin Beauty #1358 wasn't actually a virgin anymore but was in fact already a mother. After spending three thousand yuan having hymen-recon surgery, she had traveled to Liu Town to participate in the competition. Upon arriving, she immediately figured out what the competition was really all about. Especially after they entered the semifinals, each of the contestants went and slept with the judges. There were only ten judges, so with several thousand virgin beauties vying to sleep with them, by the end the poor judges had been reduced to skin and bones. Contestant #1358 regretted that she had spent three thousand yuan on her surgery, feeling that that was a case of using an ox knife to slaughter a mere chicken. She realized now that she could have just gone to Wandering Zhou and bought either a Joan of Arc or a Lady Meng Jiang artificial hymen, and that would have done the trick. When she saw that the other contestants were using one artificial hymen after another to refashion themselves into born-again virgins to secure their positions with the judges, #1358 began to feel extremely anxious. Her own hymen, which she had spent good money to reconstruct, still had not been of any use, while the women with those cheap artificial hymens were all running wild. She felt that she needed to take some initiative and could no longer afford to wait for the judges to come to her. Those judges, their heads spinning from sleeping with so many women, were so exhausted that even if #1358 had been a goddess on earth, they wouldn't have had the energy to give her a second glance.

When PR Liu came for her, therefore, she was delighted. At first she thought that he himself had taken an interest in her. From all these days of observation she had deduced that he was certainly not a mere PR person but someone who could influence the outcome of the competition. Therefore, after she sat down in the café, she looked up at him with a charming smile. She never spoke first but only responded when he spoke to her, all the while secretly analyzing his every remark. From Liu's comments, she came to the realization that the person who was interested in her was not this man in front of her but, rather, his boss, Baldy Li. PR Liu repeatedly told her that Boss Li had a very high opinion of her and sincerely hoped that she would be one of the three finalists. Of course, she should work even harder. But how? PR Liu smiled but didn't answer; he was hoping that her increasing anxiety would leave her no choice but to guide the conversation to its ultimate point. As soon as he remarked that Boss Li liked her, she feigned bashfulness and demurred, "Why would Boss Li like me?"

PR Liu smiled and said, "Boss Li likes you a lot."

She acted as if she couldn't believe this and said, "He hasn't even said a single word to me."

PR Liu leaned forward and said, "Actually, Boss Li wants to speak to you tonight."

"Tonight?" she asked happily. "Where?"

PR Liu noticed her excitement and responded slowly, "At Boss Li's home."

She appeared even more pleased and said that she very much wanted to take a look at Boss Li's mansion, then asked whether he was hosting a large-scale event at his home. PR Liu shook his head, smiled mysteriously, and said, "No, this will be just an intimate affair, consisting only of yourself and Boss Li."

She wiped the smile from her face and sat without saying a word. PR Liu tapped the armrest of the couch with his finger and waited patiently for her decision. At this point she took her phone and stood up, explaining that she wanted to call her mother, then proceeded to walk out while dialing. PR Liu watched her as she paced back and forth, and eventually she shut her cell phone and walked back with a huge smile on her face. What she said next made PR Liu very happy: "My mother gave me permission to go to Boss Li's home."

That afternoon Baldy Li ceased work as a professional escort and, to prepare himself for an evening of carnal combat, spent the entire afternoon at home napping. When he woke up, PR Liu was standing there in his living room holding a bag. Baldy Li asked what he had in the bag, whereupon Liu carefully opened it and took out a magnifying glass, a telescope, and a microscope and explained, "I bought the magnifying glass and the telescope, but I borrowed the microscope from the hospital."

Baldy Li still didn't understand. He asked, "What do I need these for?"

Writer Liu answered, "They are for you to examine her hymen."

Baldy Li laughed, very satisfied with his PR chief. He patted Liu on the shoulder and said, "You're a fucking genius."

Baldy Li's praise made PR Liu glow with pride. He complimented Baldy Li's extraordinary eye and said that #1358 was not only unusually beautiful but furthermore was quite pure. He told Baldy Li that before Virgin Beauty #1358 had accepted the invitation to his home, she had first called her mother to ask permission. Baldy Li nodded and praised her mother, saying, "Her mother really knows what she is talking about."

At eight o'clock that night, PR Liu personally escorted Virgin Beauty #1358 to Baldy Li's mansion, taking her all the way to his bedroom before turning around and walking out.

Baldy Li had bathed and changed into his pajamas. When he saw #1358 come in, he thought that since she was a virgin, he should act like a gentleman. He turned off the television and stood up, nodding to her and bowing slightly. He wanted to say some romantic things but wasn't able to get anything out. Instead, he angrily pounded his bald head and said, "Fuck, I can't do the sweet talk."

Baldy Li saw #1358 standing there bashfully and thought that he shouldn't waste any time but should get directly to the point. He pointed to the bathroom and said gently, "Go wash up."

Virgin Beauty #1358 uneasily stood rooted there, as if she hadn't understood what Baldy Li had said. He realized that he had forgotten to say please and therefore quickly added, "Please go wash up."

Virgin Beauty #1358 asked bashfully, "Wash what?"

"Take a bath," Baldy Li replied.

Virgin Beauty #1358 again asked bashfully, "Why should I take a bath?"

"Why?" Baldy Li said. "Because I want to see your . . ."

Baldy Li didn't say the final word, *hymen,* but swallowed the end of his sentence. Virgin Beauty #1358 again asked bashfully, "See my what?"

Baldy Li stood there fidgeting for a while and finally had no option but to spit it out: "I want to see your hymen."

Virgin Beauty #1358 cried out in surprise when she heard this, and immediately her tears started flowing. She said, "How could you say something like that?"

"Fuck," Baldy Li cursed and pounded his head. "That's the only way I know how to talk."

Virgin Beauty #1358 was hurt and embarrassed. She looked at Baldy Li beseechingly, saying, "You shouldn't speak to women that way."

Baldy Li felt that he had in fact been too coarse, and therefore he bowed to Virgin Beauty #1358 and offered his apologies. "I'm sorry."

Virgin Beauty #1358 still stood there, tears running down her face as she stared dolefully at Baldy Li. Meanwhile, he continued to apologize, saying, "I'm sorry. I've never been with a virgin before, and therefore I don't know how to speak to one."

After wiping away her tears, Virgin Beauty #1358 took out her cell phone and again said that she needed to ask her mother. While saying this, she walked into the bathroom and shut the door. Baldy Li heard her saying something, and after a while he heard the sound of water splashing. Baldy Li laughed, thinking that her mother must have agreed to let him look at her hymen, thereby sparing him the trouble of a whole lot of persuasion. He said to himself, *Her mother is truly a sensible person.*

When Virgin Beauty #1358 emerged from the bathroom, she was also wearing pajamas, like Baldy Li. She went directly to Baldy Li's bed, lay down, and buried her head in a pillow. Baldy Li removed his own pajamas and, bare-bottomed and holding his magnifying glass, telescope, and microscope, he too crawled onto the bed. He lifted her nightgown as if he were raising her skirt and enjoyed the sight of the virgin beauty's round and plump butt, exclaiming delightedly, "Nice ass."

First he grabbed her butt and kissed it four times, then he bit it four times, making Virgin Beauty #1358 cry out so hard that her entire body trembled. Next he began to use his magnifying glass and telescope. Realizing that the microscope was of no use whatsoever, he threw it under the bed. Because the angle was too flat, Baldy Li couldn't see her hymen, and therefore he asked her to turn over so that she was lying on her back. She, however, refused by wiggling her butt. Baldy Li ultimately had no choice but to compromise and asked her to lift her butt up. She, however, again refused. Baldy Li couldn't help cursing, "Damn it. Virgins are such trouble."

He thought to himself that even saints can be tempted, so he promised, "If you lift up your butt, I'll guarantee that you'll be one of the three finalists."

Virgin Beauty #1358 wiggled her butt again, as though she was still unwilling, but while wiggling it she gradually lifted it up. With her face still buried in the pillow, she mumbled, "My mother said that I could only let you look at it. Nothing more."

Baldy Li was elated. He took his magnifying glass and inspected the hymen for a while, then switched over to the telescope. Deciding that the telescope wasn't clear enough, he switched back to the magnifying glass. After he had inspected the hymen as carefully as his own hand, he again took the telescope. This time, however, he turned the telescope around to look through it in reverse. The hymen now seemed far away, as though he were glimpsing flowers through the mist, only in this case it was a hymen in the mist. He became profoundly confused and muttered to himself, "This hymen looks rather ridiculous. Regardless of whether I look at it from close up or far away, it doesn't look at all innocent or cute."

Virgin Beauty #1358 asked in a quivering voice, "Are you done?"

"Not yet," Baldy Li said.

Baldy Li then set down his magnifying glass and proceeded to do precisely what the virgin beauty's mother had said he shouldn't. He immediately stuck it in, thereby ripping the hymen. Virgin Beauty #1358 let out a shriek of pain and cried out, "My mother said not to."

"Fuck your mother."

While pounding her, Baldy Li happily told #1358, "You should give your mother a call, because now you are the champion. You have won the million-yuan prize."

The virgin beauty's sobs gradually died away, but her painful moans continued. She cried out in a wavering voice, "Mama, mama . . ."

Baldy Li did it from behind for a while, then asked her to turn over, explaining that he wanted to switch positions. She, however, adamantly refused to turn over. Baldy Li therefore forcibly turned her over, and she again began to cry and beg him, saying that this was her first time and she was very scared and therefore didn't dare look at him. Baldy Li eventually took pity on her, having no choice but to continue taking her from behind while at the same time cursing, "Virgins are truly a fucking pain."

That night Baldy Li fucked Virgin Beauty #1358 nearly to death. She had thought that after doing it once he would let her go. She hadn't expected that he would keep her there and do her over and over again all night—four times in all. The first two times she insisted on lying facedown, adamantly refusing to turn over. She was afraid that as soon as she turned over, Baldy Li would see her stretch marks. By the time she finally fell asleep from pain and exhaustion, Baldy Li had fallen asleep as well. She didn't expect that he would wake up after two hours and, while she was still asleep, turn her over and take her a third time. It was then that Baldy Li noticed that she had some marks on her stomach. When she woke up and noticed him looking at them, she immediately rolled back over, leaving him no choice but to continue taking her from behind. While pounding her, Baldy Li asked why she had these marks. Moaning, she explained that they were scars from a skin condition she had as a child. Baldy Li didn't ask again, and after taking her the third time, he fell asleep once more, but she didn't dare, afraid that if he had a chance to examine her stretch marks again, he would guess the truth and her secret would be revealed. Therefore she continued lying facedown hugging a pillow. At daybreak, Baldy Li took her a fourth time, from behind again. Then he slept for five more hours, and by the time he awoke, she was dressed and sitting on the couch.

After sending Virgin Beauty #1358 away, Baldy Li was jubilant for a couple of hours. When PR Liu came, Baldy Li still had a broad smile on his face. Liu was pleased to see this, thinking that Baldy Li must have had a brilliant time in bed that night. He grinned and said, "I just saw #1358 limping away. I imagine that last night you must have swept her off her feet."

Baldy Li held up four fingers and said, "I swept her four times."

PR Liu jumped in surprise, holding up four fingers, said, "If I could sweep someone once every four weeks, I would consider myself to be doing well."

"I have finally known a hymen." Baldy Li laughed proudly, then added with disappointment, "That fucking hymen wasn't what I had expected. It wasn't at all innocent and romantic."

He pointed to the magnifying glass, telescope, and microscope and continued, "I couldn't use the microscope, and it was only when I turned the telescope around that it showed me something interesting, as though I were peeking at a hymen from across the street. The magnifying glass was the most useful, allowing me to see everything clearly.

"My biggest regret," he concluded, "was that all four times I had to do it from behind."

Suddenly Baldy Li frowned, remembering the marks on #1358's belly. He was reminded of how, when doing this kind of thing with young mothers, he had seen similar marks on their bellies as well. Suddenly realizing why Virgin Beauty #1358 had insisted on lying face-down, refusing to turn over, he cried out, "Damn it, I've been had!"

PR Liu stared at Baldy Li, who exclaimed, "She's had a baby! That's why she had stretch marks on her belly. She must have fucking had her hymen reconstructed. She wasn't an out-of-the-box virgin. She was a fucking refurbished one."

PR Liu stared at Baldy Li for a long time before finally understanding what had happened. Very uneasily he said, "I'm sorry, Boss Li. This is my fault, it's my fault that you didn't break your record."

"It wasn't your fault," said Baldy Li. "I was the one who picked her." Then he laughed magnanimously and said, "She did have a great body, though—a round ass, thin shoulders, long, plump legs, not to mention a pretty face. At the very least, I broke my height record."

PR Liu swore that he would go and find someone else, and this time he would make sure she was a real virgin. Before the Virgin Beauty Competition concluded, he promised, he was going to make sure Baldy Li broke his personal record.

Now that PR Liu had a sense of Baldy Li's type, he carefully inspected each of the finalists and found #864, who was also over six feet tall and who also had a round ass and long, plump legs, though her face wasn't as pretty as the first one's. PR Liu decided that that she would do.

What PR Liu didn't know, however, was that not only was contestant #864 not an original virgin; she wasn't even a refurbished one—at most she was just unassembled parts. In order to secure the championship, #864 had already slept with six of the judges and had already bought six Joan of Arc artificial hymens from that charlatan Wandering Zhou in order to have six bloody deflowerings. Therefore, all six judges were tricked into thinking that they had slept with a virgin. This #864, therefore, was even worse than #1358, because at least #1358 was a refurbished virgin who had maintained her secondary virginity until she went to bed with Baldy Li.

When PR Liu went to find #864, this unpackaged virgin was in the process of flirting with the seventh judge and was about to go to bed with him.

PR Liu met #864 in the café. He was quite pleased by this virgin beauty's bold and frank manner, which was quite different from #1358's false modesty. She snuggled up to Liu and spoke warmly. PR Liu was much more relaxed with her and didn't feel the need to beat around the bush. He started by explaining that they had discovered that many of the contestants were no longer virgins, and furthermore that some, in order to gain an unfair advantage, had tried to win over the judges.

PR Liu didn't specify that the contestants had actually *slept* with the judges, instead using the euphemism *win over*. When #864 heard PR Liu speak this way, she became very nervous and thought that someone had ratted her out to Baldy Li. Blushing furiously, she denounced women for falsely accusing innocent contestants of sleeping with the judges after doing precisely that themselves. Tears streamed down her face, as she repeatedly insisted on her own purity, saying that she was willing to submit to a medical examination. "You are welcome to take me to the hospital for an examination, or even examine me yourself."

PR Liu had not expected the conversation to go so smoothly or to have reached this point so quickly. He laughed cordially and told her, "In order to prove your purity, you must be inspected, and furthermore you must be inspected personally by our Boss Li."

After Virgin Beauty #864 and PR Liu parted, she immediately went to find Wandering Zhou. By that point, Wandering Zhou had only a single Lady Meng Jiang domestic hymen left. He was sitting in the snack shop flirting with Missy Su. Virgin Beauty #864 sent Wandering Zhou a glance from the doorway, and he knew immediately that she needed another artificial hymen. She was Wandering Zhou's old customer, but he pretended that he didn't see her and continued flirting with Missy Su. Virgin Beauty #864 acted as if her house were on fire, but Zhou still waited until Missy Su got up to go check on the kitchen before walking slowly to the door. Virgin Beauty #864 urgently asked him for a Joan of Arc hymen, but he took out his last Lady Meng Jiang and said, "I don't have any more Joan of Arcs, just this final Lady Meng Jiang."

She accepted the hymen, handed over the money, and cursed, "That bunch of whores!"

At eight o'clock that night, PR Liu brought Virgin Beauty #864 to Baldy Li's bedroom, where Baldy Li was again watching television in his pajamas. While #864 stood there bashfully, Baldy Li didn't say anything romantic but simply turned off the television and stood up. This time he first bowed and apologized, then pointed to the bathroom and said gently, "Please go wash up."

Beauty #864 just stood there without moving, saying that she wanted to say something first. Baldy Li couldn't imagine what she would want to say and thought to himself yet again that virgins truly are a pain and that he wouldn't attempt to screw any more of them after this batch. He felt that he simply didn't have the patience to deal with them.

She began to go on and on about how much she admired Baldy Li and how the first time she read an article about him in the paper, she told herself that if she was going to give herself to anyone, she should give herself to a man like Baldy Li. Having said that, she turned around and walked into the bathroom.

Baldy Li was elated, thinking that this #864 was certainly much more straightforward than #1358. He thought to himself that if he had realized this from the beginning, he would never have bothered to bow to her. After she finished washing up, she secretly inserted the artificial hymen into her vagina.

When she walked in wearing her nightgown, she saw that Baldy Li had already undressed and was sitting there butt-naked and grinning. She gasped in surprise and immediately covered her face with her hands. Baldy Li then removed her nightgown and pushed her down onto the bed. During the entire process, she never removed her hands from her face.

Baldy Li took his magnifying glass and first examined her stomach but didn't see any stretch marks. Very pleased, he then examined her hymen. He could see it clearly but felt it looked somewhat different from #1358's. He didn't think much about this, telling himself that it must be normal that there would be different kinds of hymens. In fact, even a woman's two breasts could be of different sizes.

As Baldy Li took his magnifying glass and telescope and excitedly began to examine her, #864 continued to cover her face, but her body began to sway suggestively. She lay on the bed in a bashful manner, delighting Baldy Li to no end and making him lose interest in continuing his examination. Therefore, he threw down his magnifying glass and telescope and climbed onto her. She took her hands from her eyes and used one to grasp his neck. They went at it for a while, #864 moaning softly as Baldy Li panted, but not only did the Lady Meng Jiang hymen not bleed; eventually Baldy Li even managed to accidentally poke it out.

In this way, Wandering Zhou's cheap counterfeit merchandise

almost destroyed #864's beautiful future. When Baldy Li picked up the artificial hymen and stared at it with a look of bewilderment, #864 thought to herself that this was it. She trembled and watched Baldy Li with a look of genuine fear. He finally realized what he was holding in his hands and began to curse, "Damn it, another fake virgin."

Seeing Baldy Li furiously throw the artificial hymen away, #864 burst into tears. She begged him to allow her to explain. As she was in the process of trying to figure out what kind of explanation to give him, Baldy Li waved her away, indicating that he had neither the interest nor the patience to hear her stories. "Don't fucking cry, and also don't fucking try to explain. Given that you are not a virgin, then just be a whore. If you can please me, you can still take third place."

At first #864 stared at him in surprise, then she quickly wiped away her tears, turned over, and positioned Baldy Li beneath her. Baldy Li was astonished to discover how strong she was. She mounted him and began fucking him, moaning and twisting her body. She looked as though she was dancing the world's most erotic dance, and even a jaded old bastard like Baldy Li could only stare in amazement. Previously without rival in bed, Baldy Li had finally met his match. He gave it all he had, and so did she, as the two engaged in endless rounds of battle.

When PR Liu saw Baldy Li the next day, he noted his look of satisfaction and assumed it was because the night before he had finally encountered an authentic product. Baldy Li, however, told him, "She was also a fake. The fucking thing even fell out." Baldy Li said that as soon as he stuck his thing in, he felt that something wasn't right. "It was like when you have a sock in your shoe, so when you stick your foot in, you feel something."

Horrified, PR Liu again blamed himself, saying that he had handled things poorly. Liu cursed himself repeatedly and said, with a sigh, "Everything else I can try out for you first, but if I try out a virgin first, even if she were real, she would thereby become fake."

Baldy Li waved him away, saying that even though the previous night he didn't encounter a virgin, #864 still placed him on cloud nine. In all the years he had been whoring around, he had never before encountered a woman as wild and crazy and as fond of attack as #864. As they say, *it's enough in life to meet one true friend*, though in this case that true friend was a wild and crazy sex partner. He said that the two of them had gone back and forth, with one blowing the spring winds and the other playing war drums. The East Wind did indeed blow away the West Wind, but then the West Wind blew it right back. He said that even calling her a whore was too fucking refined; instead she was the World Wide Whoring Federation Champion. He said that the previous night the two of them had fought endless rounds of an extraordinary carnal battle, and finally both ended up so wounded that they had to call it a draw.

Then Baldy Li instructed PR Liu to go find the ten judges and tell them not to select a champion or a third-place finalist, just a second-place finalist. He said that the champion would be #1358 and the third-place award would go to #864. Even though neither of them was a virgin, both of them had gone to bed with him. While in bed Baldy Li had made certain promises, and now he patted his chest as he announced, "I, Baldy Li, am someone whose word is as good as gold."

The curtain finally fell on the Inaugural National Virgin Beauty Competition. PR Liu completed the task Baldy Li had given him in instructing the ten judges to award first place to #1358 and third place to #864. Second place, meanwhile, went to #79. This #79 was Wandering Zhou's best customer. She wasn't like #864, buying a new artificial hymen each time she slept with a different judge. Instead, she bought ten Joan of Arc hymens all at once and then proceeded to systematically devour all ten judges.

The festivities wrapped up quickly, with the one hundred finalists departing on the same day. Baldy Li stood in front of his company all day bidding farewell to the virgin beauties, to the political leaders of the organizing committee, as well as to the judges. While shaking hands with #1358, Baldy Li quietly asked her, "How old is your child?"

At first she looked confounded, but then she laughed knowingly and whispered back, "She's two."

When he shook hands with #864, Baldy Li leaned up to her ear and said, "I bow to my superior."

The ten judges were helped onto the bus like so many elderly cripples, all of them completely depleted. Two were running a low-grade fever, three could no longer keep food down, and four complained that their eyesight had degraded dramatically; only one still looked normal. He climbed aboard the bus himself, and while bidding goodbye to Baldy Li, he still had strength to speak. Baldy Li asked quietly whether this time he had eaten his fill. The judge sighed and replied that he didn't even like women anymore.

After the competition concluded, a chorus of criticism emerged in the papers, radio, and television, complaining that this Virgin Beauty Competition represented a return of feudal values, that it trampled on women's self-confidence and self-esteem, and so forth. The focus of the criticisms was ultimately on the competition's creator, Baldy Li, though PR Liu was also implicated. The initial critiques were then followed by a flurry of rumors. Some of the beauties who weren't selected among the top three couldn't contain their fury and proceeded to anonymously leak the fact that the judges had accepted sexual bribes from some of the virgin contestants. Of course, the biggest scandal was the fact that the grand winner of the Virgin Beauty Competition was already a mother. This news immediately circulated throughout the country. But in dealing with the press, #1358 turned out to be a veritable female Baldy Li. She repeatedly stated her views and accepted all invitations for interviews. She admitted that, indeed, she had a two-year-old daughter, but she nevertheless insisted that she was still a virgin. She explained that, spiritually, she would always be a virgin, because she had maintained her spiritual purity. Contestant #1358 gave virginity a new definition, which in turn inspired wide-ranging social commentary. She had her detractors as well as her supporters, and they argued back and forth for more than half a year.

During that half year, Baldy Li was delighted. As long as discussions about him continued he would remain a choice bone. He fully supported #1358's new definition of virginity and told PR Liu that, ultimately, the most important thing was spiritual purity. Baldy Li sighed over how times had changed, complaining that today's women were all unreliable and that in a mere twenty years social mores had been turned upside down. Twenty years earlier, 90 percent of unmarried women were still virgins, but now at most one out of every ten was. Baldy Li immediately corrected himself, saying that out of every ten women today, there wasn't even half a virgin. Of the women strolling out on the streets, not a single one is a virgin. Nowadays, the only place one can still find virgins might be in preschool! Outside preschool, finding a virgin is harder than finding a needle in a haystack.

"But," Baldy Li added, changing the subject, "spiritual virgins can still be found everywhere."

Then he extended Virgin Beauty #1358's spiritology to himself. He knew that those doglike reporters would forget him very quickly, but he no longer minded. He said philosophically, "At a spiritual level, I, Baldy Li, will always be a bone."

CHAPTER 65

WANDERING ZHOU sold his last artificial hymen before the Virgin Beauty Competition had even concluded. As the final round was about to begin the charlatan was prepared to bid farewell to our Liu Town, to the straw-embedded buns in Missy Su's snack shop, and to the virgin beauties who bought his artificial hymens. He also bid farewell to Poet Zhao, noting that he owed Zhao one thousand yuan for working for him for ten days, plus two hundred yuan for letting Zhou use his house as a warehouse, and two thousand yuan as a bonus for good performance. Zhou licked his finger and counted out Zhao's thirty-two hundred yuan. Then he licked his finger again and counted out five hundred yuan more, saying that this was for Missy Su, to pay for the buns. He couldn't remember how much exactly he owed her but said that five hundred yuan should definitely be enough and asked Poet Zhao to pass it on to her.

Wandering Zhou didn't say goodbye to Song Gang, although he did give him one thousand yuan in wages and two thousand yuan as a bonus. Then he sat down on the couch in Song Gang's home. The enormous success of his artificial-hymen sales in Liu Town made Wandering Zhou very ambitious, and he expansively sketched out a glorious future. He told Song Gang he needed an assistant, and this assistant would be Song Gang. When it came to work ability, Poet Zhao was much stronger than Song Gang, but Zhao was unreliable and was capable at any point of selling him out. Wandering Zhou said that after working together for ten days, he felt that Song Gang was a friend he could trust implicitly.

"You are the kind of person," Wandering Zhou said as he sat on Song Gang's couch with his legs crossed, "that even if I were to leave you all my money and go away for a year, when I returned, I'd find that you wouldn't have spent a single cent."

Then Wandering Zhou exclaimed passionately, "Song Gang, come with me!"

Song Gang was excited by this opportunity. He knew that he didn't have a future in Liu Town, where he would never be more than "chief sub." If he went with Wandering Zhou to make a living away from home, however, he might be able to establish a career. He shuddered to think how much money Lin Hong had already spent on his medical bills, not realizing that it was actually all Baldy Li's money. Lin Hong had told him that her parents, friends, and relatives had supplied the money, but he knew that none of them was rich. He suspected that she had borrowed money from someone, and if things continued like this, she would be crushed by the burden of supporting him. Song Gang nodded to Wandering Zhou and said with determination, "I'll go with you."

That evening, when Song Gang gave Lin Hong the three thousand yuan he had earned selling artificial hymens, she was flabbergasted, never having expected that he could earn so much in ten days simply following that Wandering Zhou character up and down the street. Seeing her surprise, Song Gang stammered out a long explanation about how he felt much better after his treatment, sighing over how much money that treatment must have cost, and finally rambling on about how *if there's a will, there's a way, and great rewards come at great risk,* and so on. His ramblings left her completely in a fog as to what he was trying to get at. Finally, he told her straight out that he was planning to go out into the world with Wandering Zhou and try to make a career for himself. He then related to her word for word what Wandering Zhou had discussed with him. Then Song Gang earnestly asked her, "Do you agree to let me go?"

"No, I don't agree." Lin Hong shook her head emphatically. "You must first finish your treatment, and after you are better, we can discuss it."

Song Gang said sorrowfully, "But I'm afraid that by that point it may be too late."

"Too late for what?"

Song Gang sighed as he explained, "We don't have enough money to pay for my treatment, and your friends and relatives don't have that much money either. I know that you have borrowed the money from someone, and even if I am cured, we still won't be able to pay back the money we owe."

"You don't need to worry about the money." Lin Hong understood his concerns. "Just concentrate on getting better."

Song Gang shook his head and didn't respond. He knew that even if he continued to insist, Lin Hong wouldn't agree. During their twenty years of marriage, whenever she hadn't agreed to something, Song Gang hadn't done it. So when he fell silent, Lin Hong assumed that he wouldn't continue to press his point. What she didn't realize, however, was that Song Gang had already made up his mind to follow Wandering Zhou on the road. She had forgotten about Song Gang's capacity for stubbornness. When she went to bed as usual, Song Gang lay at her feet unable to sleep. As he listened to her rhythmic breathing, he gently caressed her calves, and countless memories came flooding back to him. When he thought of how he would have to leave Lin Hong the next day, he suddenly felt a pang of sorrow. This would be the first time since they were married that they would be separated.

The next morning, when Lin Hong left for the knitting factory, Song Gang stood at the doorway and watched her ride away down the street. Then he went back inside and sat down at the table, got out a sheet of paper, and wrote her a letter. Song Gang wrote very simply, first asking that she forgive him for leaving, and then asking that she trust him, promising that this time he would definitely make something of himself. Even though he couldn't compete with Baldy Li, he would earn enough money to allow her to live comfortably for the rest of her life. Finally, he told her that he was taking with him a photograph of the two of them and a house key. He would look at the photograph every night before going to bed, and the key signified that he would return home as soon as he earned enough money.

When Song Gang finished writing the letter, he got up and went to find the photograph. It was taken just after they bought the shiny new Eternity brand travel bicycle and captured the two of them smiling happily as they stood beside it. Song Gang examined the photograph for a long time, then placed it in his breast pocket. Next he ransacked the room looking for the travel bag with SHANGHAI printed on the side—the only artifact of his father's he had in his possession. He filled the bag with several sets of clothing for all seasons, as well as his unfinished medicine. Deciding he still had some time, he took the clothing Lin Hong had just worn and washed it in the washing machine. Then, his face covered in sweat, Song Gang cleaned the house to the point that not a speck of dust remained and wiped the windows to the point that they were as bright as mirrors.

Around noon, he and Wandering Zhou snuck out of town like two thieves. Wandering Zhou was very dissatisfied with Song Gang's old-fashioned travel bag. He said that it looked like something from the old society and that they wouldn't be able to do any business while he was carrying it. He therefore put Song Gang's clothing into a cardboard box and threw the travel bag into a trash can on the side of the road. Seeing Song Gang looking back longingly, Wandering Zhou consoled him and said that after they reached Shanghai, he would buy him a suitcase with foreign words on it.

Then Song Gang and Wandering Zhou hurried toward the bus depot, their heads bowed under the noon sun, with Song Gang carrying his cardboard box and Wandering Zhou carrying his large black bag. Song Gang didn't know that Wandering Zhou had one hundred thousand yuan in cash in his bag. When he arrived in Liu Town, Wandering Zhou had only five yuan left in his pocket, having invested all his money in artificial hymens. His gamble had paid off. When their bus pulled out of the depot, Wandering Zhou turned and said to Liu Town, "We'll meet again someday."

Song Gang also turned back and looked at Liu Town, and upon seeing the familiar faces in the street fade away in the distance, followed by the familiar houses and streets, he felt a pang of sorrow. He thought about how, in a few hours, Lin Hong would ride home through those familiar streets and, upon discovering that he had left, become angry or start weeping. In his mind, Song Gang told her he was sorry. As the bus drove away Liu Town faded into the distance, eventually disappearing behind the wide-open fields. Song Gang turned back around and saw that Wandering Zhou had fallen asleep, still grasping his black bag. Song Gang felt tears run down his face and into his face mask.

When Lin Hong rode her bike home that evening, she opened the door and noticed that the house was all clean. She smiled and called out, remarking on how neat the house was. Then she walked into the kitchen calling out to Song Gang, but there was no sign of him. Normally at this time he would be cooking dinner, and Lin Hong wondered where he could have gone. When she passed by the living-room table, she failed to notice the letter Song Gang had left for her. Instead she went and stood outside for a while. People wandered up and down the street in the twilight, and the lights in Mama Su's snack shop across the street were already on. Lin Hong went back inside, then went into the kitchen and began to prepare dinner. She thought she heard the sound of a key opening the door and thought it was Song Gang returning home. She went to the kitchen doorway but didn't see any movement in the rest of the house, so she continued fixing dinner.

When Lin Hong finished, she carried the food out to the table. By this point it was dark, and when she turned on the light, she noticed the paper on the table but didn't pay any attention to it. She sat down at the table and watched the doorway, waiting for Song Gang to return home. Suddenly she noticed that there were several lines of writing on the paper. With a sense of trepidation she grabbed it and hurriedly read it, only then understanding that Song Gang had left. His letter in hand, she rushed out the door toward the bus depot, as though determined to catch up with him. After she had run one hundred yards or so down the street lined with lights and neon signs, she began to slow down, realizing that by now he was already far away. She stopped in confusion and, watching the people and cars going up and down the street, glanced down at the sheet of paper in her hand, then slowly headed home again.

That night Lin Hong sat under her lamp and read Song Gang's letter over and over again, and it wasn't until her tears had made the writing virtually illegible that she finally put the letter down. She didn't blame Song Gang, because she knew that he was doing this for her. Instead, she blamed herself for not realizing his determination to leave. The next several days seemed like an eternity. At the factory she continued to endure the chain-smoking Director Liu's harassment, and each evening she returned home to an empty house. In her loneliness, she had no choice but to spend countless hours in front of the TV, which merely made her miss Song Gang even more desperately. Before falling asleep at night, she would feel a twinge of anguish as she remembered how, when he left, he hadn't taken a single cent of their money.

Lin Hong didn't tell anyone that Song Gang had left with Wandering Zhou, saying only that he had gone to Canton to do business. When Wandering Zhou first arrived in Liu, Lin Hong had sensed that he was up to no good. Assuming that Wandering Zhou and Song Gang would continue selling artificial hymens when they reached Canton, Lin Hong couldn't bring herself to tell people what Song Gang would be doing.

Lin Hong waited every day for a letter from Song Gang, and every day at noon she would go to the reception office of her factory and watch as the postman threw a bundle of letters onto the counter. She would urgently open the bundle and search for a letter with her name on it. Song Gang didn't write her, but a month later he did call her. It was nighttime, and he called Mama Su's snack shop. Mama Su rushed across the street and knocked on Lin Hong's door. Lin Hong rushed back across the street into the snack shop and picked up the phone. On the other end of the line, Song Gang asked, "Lin Hong, are you well?"

When Lin Hong heard Song Gang's voice, her eyes teared up and she yelled into the receiver, "Come back, you must come back immediately!"

On the other end of the line, Song Gang said, "I will come back—"

Lin Hong continued to shout, "You must return right away!"

The two continued on in this way for a while, with Lin Hong demanding that Song Gang return immediately and Song Gang saying that he would. At first, Lin Hong issued her cry to return as an imperative, but later she began to plead with him. As for Song Gang, he initially insisted that he would definitely return but eventually said that he was going to have to hang up, since this was a very expensive long-distance call. Lin Hong, however, continued to plead with him, "Song Gang, come back. . . ."

Song Gang finally hung up as Lin Hong was still speaking into the receiver. When she heard the dial tone, she disappointedly put the phone down. Then it occurred to her that she hadn't asked Song Gang how or what he was doing but had only repeated "Come back" over and over again. She bit her lip in frustration, then looked at Missy Su, who was sitting somberly at the counter. Lin Hong laughed bitterly in Missy Su's direction, and Missy Su laughed bitterly in response. When Lin Hong left the snack shop, she wanted to say something to Missy Su but couldn't think of what to say. Therefore, she merely bowed her head and walked out.

For the next several months, Missy Su and Lin Hong were similarly depressed. Five months after the charlatan Wandering Zhou left without saying goodbye, Missy Su's growing belly began to show, leading everyone to speculate who might be responsible. As their imaginations ran wild the number of suspects increased until they finally reached a list of 101. Poet Zhao was also a suspect, and in fact he was the 101st. Poet Zhao swore high and low that he had nothing to do with it, but this only made everyone even more convinced that he was the one. He bitterly told everyone that, even though Missy Su was not terribly pretty, it was common knowledge that she was loaded. Therefore, if he had been the one responsible for making her belly grow big, why would he still be living in his dilapidated old house? "I would have moved long ago into the snack shop across the street and become its boss."

Everyone then realized that Poet Zhao must be innocent of this whole affair and therefore once again started suspecting others, but during the entire process no one thought of Wandering Zhou. Zhou was an extraordinary charlatan. He arrived in Liu Town at the same time as the three thousand virgin beauties, who had slept with the judges, with the political leaders, with Baldy Li, with PR Liu— essentially with everyone. The judges, political leaders, Baldy Li, and PR Liu were all hoodwinked, having slept with women who either had surgically reconstructed hymens or were using artificial ones. Wandering Zhou, meanwhile, was the only one who slept with an authentic virgin, transforming the only genuine virgin in Liu Town, Missy Su, into an ex-virgin.

Missy Su still sat at the cashier's counter every day, but now she no longer chatted with the waitresses or customers. Wandering Zhou's unannounced departure had left her heartbroken, and from that point on she was somber and grim. Mama Su would often stare off into space and sigh, and sometimes she would secretly cry. What she couldn't figure out was why her fate was now being repeated by her daughter. At first everyone was curious and excited, but gradually they got used to the situation, pointing out that the same thing had happened to Mama Su and that no one knew who had gotten her knocked up—they only knew that she subsequently gave birth to Missy Su. Now Missy Su's belly was made big by a mysterious man, and nine months later she too gave birth to a daughter. Missy Su named her Su Zhou, but even then no one suspected that the itinerant charlatan Wandering Zhou was the father. By this point everyone had lost interest in speculating and shifted their attention to divination: They predicted that after this girl grew up, her belly would also mysteriously get large, just like that of her grandmother and mother. They concluded confidently, "That is fate."

CHAPTER 66

WHEN WANDERING ZHOU left our Liu Town for Shanghai with Song Gang, he headed south along the railway system and hoped to repeat his enormous success, this time selling male virility-enhancing pills. Zhou and Song Gang got off the train at a couple of midsize cities along the railroad and hawked their male-potency pills at the train station, at the wharf, and in the commercial districts. The neatly dressed Wandering Zhou held up a vial of imported Apollo pills in his right hand and one of domestic Fierce Zhang Fei pills in his left, announcing dramatically, "Every man wants to have a hard erection and fully display his virility. For many reasons, however, men often develop erectile problems as they grow older. This is very common."

Wandering Zhou shook the vials, letting the people crowded around hear the pills rattling inside. The Fierce Zhang Fei pills, he said, were made from a treasured formula of traditional Chinese medicine, originating in the imperial medical files of the Ming and Qing dynasties preserved in the Forbidden City's Palace Museum and created from a synthesis of the best concoctions used at the time. As for the imported Apollo ones, he said that they were the pride of foreigners, formulated on the basis of the American company Pfizer's Viagra but with additional genetic engineering and nanotechnology. Wandering Zhou was like a street vendor with his peddler's drum, waving the vials around and cordially telling everyone that their formal name was Virility Enhancing Pills but colloquially they were called Bigger, Thicker, Longer Lasting Pills. Wandering Zhou patted his chest and guaranteed that just two to three doses could make you a "real macho man."

By this point Song Gang had realized that Wandering Zhou was a charlatan. As their long-distance bus left Liu Town and set off toward Shanghai, Zhou pulled off Song Gang's face mask and threw it out the window into some tree branches. Wandering Zhou told Song Gang that now no one knew of his illness and therefore his lungs could be considered cured. Song Gang breathed the Shanghai air, then turned around and looked back at his face mask hanging from the branch. When the bus turned a corner, the mask disappeared from view.

It was a few days into their journey, though, that Song Gang really understood what kind of person Wandering Zhou was. After traveling down many dark alleys, they arrived at an underground warehouse full of counterfeit tobacco and liquor. In a dark corner of the warehouse, Wandering Zhou bought two boxes of virility-enhancing pills. Then he and Song Gang, carrying their boxes of Fierce Zhang Fei and Apollo pills, hopped aboard a train headed south and embarked on an excruciatingly long and unsuccessful year trying to sell them off.

The cheap "hard seat" rail compartment they rode in was full of itinerant workers heading south, speaking a wide variety of dialects. Some were going to Canton, and others planned to take the ferry to Hainan Island. All of them were young bachelors hoping to earn some money and then return home, get married, and have a child. Wandering Zhou sat among them, a smile plastered on his face, occasionally striking up a conversation with some of the laborers and periodically glancing up at the two boxes of virility-enhancing pills up in the luggage rack. Song Gang felt that Wandering Zhou looked quite comical, dressed so nicely and sitting among all of these itinerant laborers. Two laborers asked Wandering Zhou what he did for a living, and Zhou glanced at Song Gang and casually answered, "Health products." Zhou knew that these laborers didn't have any money to be swindled out of and therefore didn't even bother trying to make a sales pitch.

Song Gang realized that everything Wandering Zhou had said in Liu Town was a complete lie. He looked sadly out the window at the endless fields, feeling very agitated. What prospects did he have following this charlatan around? Song Gang didn't know. But when he remembered that Wandering Zhou had, in fact, earned a huge sum of money in Liu, Song Gang began to be feel more hopeful. He hoped that he could quickly earn a fortune and then return home. The sum he set his sights on was one hundred thousand yuan, because with that Lin Hong wouldn't have to worry about anything. *For Lin Hong*, Song Gang told himself, *I'd be willing to do anything.*

For several years, Song Gang had been breathing through a saliva-soaked face mask, so during the first few days without a mask he felt that the air had become unusually dry. While Song Gang was fairly quiet to begin with, after following Wandering Zhou on his swindles, he became even more silent. Often he would wake up in the middle of the night and recall his departure from Liu Town, imagining how Lin Hong must have ridden her bike home from the factory and found the house empty, and his eyes would tear up. Many mornings, when he would walk out of an unfamiliar hotel and into the streets of an unfamiliar part of the country, he would feel a strong urge to return to Liu Town, to Lin Hong's side. But the die was cast, and he told himself that he couldn't return empty-handed. Now he had to grin and bear it and follow Wandering Zhou on the road.

Song Gang would often take out that picture of himself and Lin Hong and examine it closely. Their lives had been so perfect, and that Eternity bicycle had been a symbol of their happiness. For the first few months, the photograph served as Song Gang's spiritual support, but after half a year he couldn't bring himself to even look at it. At the mere sight of Lin Hong's smiling face, he would begin to feel uneasy and be overcome by a wave of homesickness. Therefore, from that point on he left the photograph locked up in his luggage and struggled to forget it existed.

The two traveled to five cities over the course of the next two months. Zhou's method of hawking his virility-enhancing pills resembled that of a highway bandit: He would grab a passerby by the shoulder and begin speaking nonstop. He shouted himself hoarse but during those two months only managed to sell ten vials of medicine, five each of the Apollo and Fierce Zhang Fei brands. Song Gang also tried to sell the pills but proceeded much as he had when selling the little magnolia flowers in Liu Town—politely inquiring of middle-aged men as they walked by, "Do you need enhancing pills?"

"Enhancing *what* pills?"

Song Gang would smile, hand them the instructions to the Apollo and Fierce Zheng Fei pills, and patiently wait while they read them and decided whether they wanted to buy some or not. Some people read the instructions over and over again but in the end left empty-handed. Wandering Zhou felt that Song Gang missed out on a lot of good opportunities, but Song Gang disagreed. He felt that the efficacy of these pills was very dubious to begin with, and a hard sell would only make people more suspicious. He said that when selling something, one should use reverse psychology. After two months, Song Gang had sold twenty-three vials of virility-enhancing pills. His reverse-psychology business model turned out to be twice as effective as Wandering Zhou's highway-bandit approach.

Wandering Zhou began to look at Song Gang with newfound respect. He no longer regarded Song Gang as his assistant but, rather, as a partner, saying that they would divide their profits 80/20, with Wandering Zhou taking 80 percent and Song Gang 20 percent. Furthermore, from here on out he would make his financial operations completely transparent. That night they stayed in a small town in Fujian, in the basement of a small hotel. Wandering Zhou had a worried look and said that even though they had stayed in the cheapest hotels and eaten the cheapest food, they nevertheless had sold only thirty-three vials over the past two months, and consequently all of their revenue had been spent on room and board. Song Gang didn't respond for a long time, since his thoughts had once again wandered to Lin Hong all alone in Liu Town.

After he returned to the present, with some hesitation he told Wandering Zhou that when he was selling magnolia blossoms in Liu Town, he discovered that it was easier to sell them when standing in the door of a clothing store rather than in the street. Why was that? Because young women who are fond of beauty go to clothing stores, and after buying clothing they were likely to buy a string of magnolia blossoms.

"You have a point." Wandering Zhou nodded and asked Song Gang, "Where do men tend to congregate? Particularly those who aspire to become 'real macho men'?"

"In bathhouses," Song Gang replied after considering for a moment. "Plus, there you can tell at a glance who is somewhat on the small side."

"You have a point." Wandering Zhou's eyes brightened. "That is called targeted marketing."

"But," Song Gang said hesitantly, "in order to get into the bathhouses, we would need to spend more money."

"We will spend what we need to spend," Wandering Zhou said firmly. "As they say, *if you can't bear to sacrifice the child, you won't be able to lure the wolf into the trap.*"

The two of them decided to go with this plan, so they took ten vials each of the Apollo and Fierce Zhang Fei pills and went to a bathing center near the hotel. They left the pills in their locker, took off their clothes, and ventured inside. This bathhouse was not very fancy, but it was enough to astonish Song Gang. Inside there were three large pools: the middle one filled with water, a second filled with milk, and the third filled with roses. Wandering Zhou led the way to the milk pool, where he was joined by Song Gang. Zhou saw several men taking showers and whispered to Song Gang that, given that they had spent the money to get in, they might as well enjoy themselves. Song Gang nodded and submerged his body in the pool, then asked Wandering Zhou in a low voice, "Is this really milk?"

"It is made from powdered milk," Wandering Zhou responded knowingly. "Low-quality powdered milk."

The two sat soaking in the low-quality powdered-milk pool for half an hour. Then Wandering Zhou got up, walked past the clear-water bath, and, with a comfortable look on his face, submerged himself in the rose-petal pool. Song Gang remained in the milk bath but felt somewhat uneasy hanging out there alone, so he went and sat in the rose-petal bath. He grabbed a fistful of petals and, seeing the red water, remarked with surprise, "The color has seeped out."

"It is red dye," Wandering Zhou told Song Gang calmly. "They pour in a few bottles of dye and then toss in a few rose petals."

When Song Gang heard that it was red dye, he quickly stood up. Wandering Zhou pulled him back down and made him sit next to him, saying that even if it was merely red dye, it was still more expensive than plain water. Wandering Zhou smelled the steam rising from the rose petals and announced with satisfaction, "They also throw in several drops of perfume."

Both of them closed their eyes and lay soaking in the red-dye bath. At that point, a well-built man with an enormous member walked by, leading a German shepherd. Wandering Zhou glanced at the man's crotch and said quietly, "A real macho man." The man heard Wandering Zhou and, standing next to the clear-water bath, shouted, "What did you say?"

As the man shouted his dog also barked a couple of times. Song Gang began to tremble, and Wandering Zhou, a smile plastered on his face, lifted his hand from the rose water, pointed at the man's crotch, and repeated, "I said that you are a real macho man."

The man glanced down and chuckled with satisfaction, then he jumped into the clear-water pool like a cannonball, splattering clear water into the rose-petal bath and splashing water all over Wandering Zhou's and Song Gang's faces. Soaking in the pool as his dog lay next to him, the man rubbed his chest with his right hand and scratched the dog's back with his left. The dog's eyes looked like those of a professional assassin as he stared at Zhou and Song Gang, making their hearts pound in fear. Song Gang asked with a quavering voice, "How can dogs come in here?" The dog immediately started barking and snarling at him, terrifying Song Gang and Wandering Zhou so much that they didn't dare say anything else, instead simply lying there without moving.

At this point several naked men walked in carrying white towels. When they entered, they were talking and laughing, planning on soaking in the clear-water bath. When they saw the German shepherd lying beside it, however, they turned pale and beat a hasty retreat. Outside in the changing room they angrily asked the attendant what the hell a dog—and what's more, a fucking German shepherd—was doing in the bathing room. The dog, hearing the commotion outside, for a second stopped watching Wandering Zhou and Song Gang and instead turned around and barked a couple of times in the direction of the changing room, making the changing room become as still as death. Then an attendant carefully walked in and stood about five yards away from the dog and said quietly, "Excuse me, mister. . . ."

This attendant had originally planned to convince the well-endowed man to take his dog outside, but when the dog lunged at him, he quickly retreated in terror back to the dressing room. Wandering Zhou took this opportunity to move to the side of the rose pool, but as soon as he stood up, the dog turned around and resumed snarling at him. Wandering Zhou couldn't decide whether to advance or retreat, so just stood there staring at the man with a broad smile on his face. The man petted his dog and told it to lie down. Zhou held his breath and, feigning calmness, climbed down the stairs. Then, seeing a door, he pushed it open and walked inside. Song Gang also began to move slowly toward the side of the pool. The dog stared at him the entire time, and he continued staring at the dog with a kind smile. As soon as he stood up at the side of the pool, the dog also stood up and barked. The man again patted the dog and made it lie down, whereupon Song Gang jumped down the stairs. He also saw the wooden door and rushed in.

One after the other, Wandering Zhou and Song Gang entered the sauna. When Song Gang entered, he saw that Zhou was sitting in the sweltering wooden room with a dazed look on his face. Song Gang asked him, "What is this place?"

Wandering Zhou immediately assumed a calm expression and replied, "A sauna."

Song Gang breathed heavily as he sat down next to Wandering Zhou. Zhou picked up a wooden spoon and splashed water onto the stove, generating a cloud of steam. Song Gang felt it was becoming hard to breathe and said, "It's too hot in here."

Wandering Zhou replied proudly, "That's what a sauna is."

At that point the wooden door opened and the brawny man entered. Wandering Zhou and Song Gang jumped in surprise, but when they saw that the German shepherd wasn't following him in, they breathed a sigh of relief. As the man prepared to lie down Wandering Zhou and Song Gang jumped up to give him room. He nodded with satisfaction and lay down on the very top step of the wooden steps while Wandering Zhou and Song Gang sat on the lower steps. After sitting in the steam for a while, Wandering Zhou felt that he couldn't endure it anymore and stood up and announced that he was leaving. When he opened the door, the dog lunged at him through the doorway. Zhou slammed the door shut in terror, turned around, and muttered to himself, "I might as well steam for a little while longer."

He sat down next to Song Gang, and the man lying above them gestured and said, "Add some more water."

"Okay," Wandering Zhou replied, then he poured more water onto the stove and white steam again billowed forth. Song Gang felt that he was about to pass out from the heat and said to Wandering Zhou, "I think I'm going to be sick."

"Then leave." Zhou pushed him toward the door.

Song Gang stood up. Knowing that the dog was lying in the doorway like a tiger eyeing its prey, he gathered his courage and pushed the door open. The dog stood up and started barking as if he were about to bite Song Gang in the crotch. Song Gang shut the door again and retreated, reflexively holding his crotch. He smiled helplessly as he sat back down next to Wandering Zhou. The two felt as though they were about to pass out, but they were more terrified by the dog in the doorway. Therefore, they had no alternative but to continue sitting there, enduring the heat of the steam and hoping that the man lying above them would soon get up and leave, taking his dog with him. But the man seemed to be getting increasingly comfortable and after a while even started whistling. Wandering Zhou felt that if he stayed a moment longer, he would almost certainly pass out and die. Therefore, he staggered over to the man, leaned over, and called out into his ear, "Excuse me, mister. . . ."

The whistling man opened his eyes and looked at Wandering Zhou, who said feebly, "Your bodyguard . . ."

"What bodyguard?" The man didn't know what Wandering Zhou was talking about.

"Your canine bodyguard is guarding the door," Zhou said. "We can't get out."

The man laughed and said, "Add some more water."

Wandering Zhou wiped the sweat from his face, then headed over to the stove to add more water, producing another cloud of steam. Song Gang seemed about to topple over, and Wandering Zhou staggered forward and said to the man, "I added the water."

"Good," the man said. "You can leave."

"But," Wandering Zhou said, "your canine bodyguard . . ."

The man laughed as he got up and climbed down. He opened the door and pulled the dog to one side, allowing Wandering Zhou and Song Gang to exit safely, then lay back down in the sauna and left the dog standing guard by the door. Zhou and Song Gang returned to the dressing room, feeling that they had just had a close brush with death. Zhou immediately drank eight cups of distilled water, and Song Gang drank seven. The two sat in the changing room for more than ten minutes, their heads hanging down, before finally recovering. Then they put on their robes and, looking halfway human again, strutted into the rest hall with the virility-enhancing pills in the black bag.

There were about twenty customers lounging about. Some of them were getting pedicures, and others were getting foot massages. A soccer game was playing on the projection TV. Wandering Zhou signaled Song Gang with a look, and the two proceeded to opposite sides of the hall. Song Gang lay down next to a middle-aged man who was watching the soccer game, patiently waited until halftime, then took out the instruction booklet and handed it to the man, asking politely, "Sir, do you have a moment to look at this?"

The man stared in surprise, then took the booklet and began to read it intently. When he finished reading the booklet for the domestic Fierce Zhang Fei pills, Song Gang handed him the one for the imported Apollo pills. After the man finished reading both, he looked around at the other men resting in the hall and whispered, "How much for a bottle?"

Wandering Zhou, meanwhile, was much more direct with his sales pitch. With imported and domestic vials in either hand, he smiled and asked the man next to him, "Do you want to be a real macho man?"

"What do you mean by 'real macho man'?"

Zhou then launched into a long, complicated explanation, until finally the young man took the two vials to have a look and even opened his robe to glance down at his member. Wandering Zhou took the opportunity to take a peek as well and told him, "You are already a macho man, but unfortunately you are not yet a top-quality real macho man."

The young man asked Wandering Zhou skeptically, "These aren't counterfeit, are they?"

"You will know as soon as you try them," Wandering Zhou replied with a smile.

When the brawny man and his German shepherd arrived, panic swept through the hall. Several attendants politely intervened, and the man agreed not to bring the dog in. Therefore, the dog lay down in the doorway, as though he were guarding a pass to prevent a thousand enemies from getting through. As a result, none of the customers in the rest hall dared leave, having no choice but to wait for the dog's owner to leave first. Wandering Zhou and Song Gang were now in their element like fish in water and methodically spoke with each member of their captive audience, cajoling them into buying the pills. The dog's owner noticed that they were whispering to all the other customers but hadn't said a word to him. Curious, he pulled Wandering Zhou aside and asked him what they were doing. Zhou handed him the Apollo and Fierce Zhang Fei booklets, adding, "But you don't need these."

When the man finished reading the instruction booklets, he said loudly, "Who says I don't need this? The strong can always get even stronger."

"Well said!" Wandering Zhou exclaimed. He pointed to the other men in the hall and added quietly, "For them, these pills would be like an emergency shot to the arm, but for you they would be like a bonus."

The dog's owner laughed with satisfaction, then held up two fingers and said, "I'll take two vials."

"Two vials is one dose," Wandering Zhou explained patiently. "You need at least two or three doses to see results."

The dog's master said brightly, "In that case, I want eight vials."

"Okay." Wandering Zhou nodded, then asked him, "Do you want imported or domestic ones?"

The dog's master said, "Four of each."

Wandering Zhou hesitated, then, in a expert tone, said, "These imported ones are made with genetic engineering and nanotechnology, while the domestic ones are made from Ming-Qing dynastic medical files from the Palace Museum. If you mix them together, their effectiveness will be compromised."

"The imported ones are for me," the man explained, then pointed to his dog lying in the doorway. "The domestic ones are for him."

CHAPTER 67

WANDERING ZHOU and Song Gang continued strolling through Fujian, stopping at one bathhouse after another to sell their virility-enhancing pills. Whenever they spotted someone who appeared underendowed, they would recommend a remedy, patiently pique their interest, and describe extravagant results. By the time they left Fujian for Canton, they had managed to sell the entire two boxes of pills. Wandering Zhou summed up what they had learned from their experiences when he noted that it had taken them nearly five months to sell the two boxes of pills, meaning that their revenue was much too low and they hadn't earned a trace of profit. In fact, after factoring in their living expenses, they had actually lost money. Wandering Zhou recalled wistfully his glorious experience selling artificial hymens in our Liu Town and decided that he would stop selling men's health products, because women were much more willing to spend money on these sorts of things. Therefore, when they reached Canton, the two began to sell a bust-enhancing cream called Boobs.

By this point Song Gang had been away from home for half a year. While in Fujian he had called Lin Hong three times—each time he called her in the evening while standing in front of the convenience store, with dust blowing through the streets and passersby talking loudly in the local Minnan dialect. Song Gang would grab the receiver tightly with both hands, as if he were afraid someone would come and snatch it from him. His palms wet with sweat, he stammered softly, completely incoherent. At the other end of the line, Lin Hong's voice sounded half-crazed with anxiety as she entreated him to return immediately. Repeating "Come home" over and over, she asked Song Gang how he had been feeling, and Song Gang replied that his health had been good and his lung disease was cured. Then, in a voice as soft as a mosquito, he added, "I don't cough anymore."

Song Gang had to repeat himself several times before Lin Hong understood. Then she hollered, "Are you still taking your medicine?"

At this point Song Gang hung up the phone and, as he was putting it down, said softly, "I've stopped taking it."

Then he stood, confused, on the lamplit street, watching one stranger after another pass by and listening to their voices. Finally he shook his head and slowly began to make his way back to the cheap hotel where they were staying.

When he arrived, Wandering Zhou was sitting cross-legged on the bed, wiping his tears as he watched a Korean soap opera on television. While in Fujian, Wandering Zhou had watched three and a half Korean miniseries, and after arriving in Canton he searched through all the television channels but couldn't find the second half of the last miniseries. He proceeded to curse all of Canton and then, when he finally calmed down, went out to peddle his Boobs cream.

For the next several months, the Minnan dialect they heard in Fujian was replaced by Cantonese, and although they went to fifteen different locations, they managed to sell only ten or so vials of the cream. In a moment of despair, Wandering Zhou suddenly had an inspiration and decided to sell the cream to beauty salons at a discount, but he discovered that all the salons were already selling bust-enhancing creams of their own. Wandering Zhou then investigated the pharmacies and department stores and discovered that they too were selling their own bust-enhancing creams. They saw more than a hundred brands of breast creams, and all of them were cheaper than their own Boobs brand. Zhou found himself at an impasse as he and Song Gang wandered aimlessly like headless flies trying to sell their Boobs cream on unfamiliar streets. The two looked around depressed, asking each other what they should do next. Wandering Zhou had lost confidence in selling the Boobs cream, so whenever he saw a young woman walk by, he pushed Song Gang to go speak to her while he stood behind him like a sentry. Song Gang would walk over with a bowed head and respectfully ask the young women, "Do you need bust-enhancing cream?"

The women always looked as if they had been accosted by a thief and scurried away while tightly grasping their purses. One pretty young woman didn't hear clearly and therefore paused and asked, "What?"

Song Gang gestured at his own chest, saying, "Bust-enhancing cream, in order to make your breasts bigger and firmer."

"You hooligan!" The woman backed away as she cursed them. Other passersby also stopped and stared at Song Gang, who started blushing and went back to Wandering Zhou, standing as though nothing was happening.

Around this time, Zhou had found a new Korean soap opera on a local television station, so he would spend the entire day being frustrated at every turn but at night would recover his spirits. During the first hour of the Korean drama he sat attentive on the edge of the bed with the remote control in his hand and asked Song Gang to take a walk outside so as not to interrupt his viewing pleasure. He added that if Song Gang didn't want to leave, he could stay, but "you mustn't make a sound."

Song Gang didn't stay in the room but wandered aimlessly through this foreign city, staring through countless windows of countless buildings. Eventually he stopped under a tree by the side of the road and watched spellbound through some family's window as a young husband and wife walked around inside. Sometimes a single shadow would appear in front of the window, sometimes there would be two, and sometimes there would be only the light of a lamp. Song Gang stood staring for a long time, until the husband and wife walked up to the window together and lowered the curtain, kissing each other as they did so. This scene brought tears to Song Gang's eyes. At that moment he yearned so intensely for Lin Hong and wanted more than anything to soar directly back to Liu Town. But he didn't know when he would start making some money. Dejected, he felt that the day he would finally be able to return to Liu Town was retreating further and further into the distance.

While they were in Canton, Wandering Zhou watched four entire Korean miniseries. Eventually, he became irritated to discover that he could no longer find any new ones. At that point they were on the coast, staying in a second-floor room of a dilapidated old hotel. Across the street was a billboard advertising bust-enhancing cream. Rather than a pretty young woman, however, the billboard featured a muscular hunk. This hunk was wearing a red bra over enormous breasts and a red G-string below. Wandering Zhou hadn't noticed this billboard, but after he calmed down and reconciled himself to the fact that there were no more Korean series to watch, he sat downcast on the bed, and his thoughts eventually returned to the bust-enhancing cream. The charlatan took out his calculator and started furiously punching in numbers. Half an hour later he looked up with an aggrieved expression and said simply, "We're fucked!"

Song Gang already knew that they were fucked. After six months of running around they had succeeded in selling only ten vials of the cream, during which time Wandering Zhou had become addicted to Korean melodramas the way a decadent ruler might become addicted to women. Now that there weren't any more melodramas to watch, Wandering Zhou had to face reality. He told Song Gang that if they couldn't sell all of the remaining vials within a month, they would have no alternative but to go to court. When Song Gang asked him what the point of going to court would be, Zhou tugged at his tie and, sounding like a boss of a State factory that was about to close, replied, "To apply for bankruptcy protection."

Song Gang laughed bitterly, wondering how Wandering Zhou found it in him to speak so grandly when they had fallen so low. Just as the two felt that they had reached a dead end, Zhou suddenly noticed the bust-enhancing-cream billboard across the street. He stared at the image of the magnificent hunk wearing bikini briefs and cried out in astonishment, "Bikinis!"

Song Gang also saw it, and his jaw dropped. Even in his wildest dreams he had never imagined such an advertisement. Wandering Zhou again muttered to himself, "I never imagined that men could also have a pair of plump breasts."

It was then that Wandering Zhou had his inspiration. After his eyes left the billboard, he began to stare lecherously at Song Gang. Song Gang felt very uneasy with Wandering Zhou looking at him like that and asked, "What are you thinking?"

Wandering Zhou sighed. "If only you had a pair of plump breasts, we would certainly be able to sell out our entire stock of Boobs bust-enhancing cream in no time."

Song Gang blushed to the roots. When Wandering Zhou saw Song Gang's face assume a sort of feminine bashfulness, his eyes lit up, and he enthusiastically began to lay out his plan. They would give Song Gang a boob job, and after he had an impressive pair of knockers, he would look as attractive as that hunk in the billboard. Zhou patiently explained that breast-enlargement surgery was just minor surgery and could be done in an outpatient clinic. He said, "It's as simple as hymen-recon surgery."

Song Gang gazed blankly out the window. He looked at the billboard, then the building behind it, and finally at the sky above it. His sorrow and hopelessness flew out his eyes into the distance. Then he turned around and nodded with determination, saying, "As long as it will help us earn money, I'm willing to do anything."

Wandering Zhou hadn't expected Song Gang to agree so easily. He excitedly jumped up and began pacing back and forth across the room, searching for the most effusive language with which to praise Song Gang. He announced that the money they earned would no longer be divided 20/80 but, rather, would be split evenly, 50/50. He then concluded emotionally, "When we were in Liu Town, I knew that you would be willing to take two for the team."

"This isn't for you." Song Gang shook his head. "I'm doing it for Lin Hong."

Having been entranced by Korean soap operas the entire year they spent traveling from Fujian to Canton, Wandering Zhou, when he took Song Gang to the cosmetic surgery clinic, rejected out of hand all but the Korean-style breast-enlargement surgeries. The doctor recommended three kinds: Korean no-scar breast enlargement, Korean breast enlargements with silicone implants, and Korean natural breast enlargement using the body's own fat. He explained that the no-scar surgery used a patented new Korean "UNTOUCH" technology, which used tiny incisions, that was guaranteed to leave no scars. After the operation, even those with whom you are most intimate wouldn't be able to tell the difference. Furthermore, after they take shape, the breasts look completely natural and realistic, feel as soft and smooth as dripping water, and follow the rhythm of your steps with a tiny natural jiggle, making you look sexy and charming. When Wandering Zhou heard this introduction, he smiled and said, "We'll take the Korean no-scar breasts."

That afternoon was the most embarrassing and uncomfortable one of Song Gang's life. He sat with his head bowed, not saying a word as Wandering Zhou made up a tearjerking story about how Song Gang had dreamed his entire life of being able to become a woman. While the doctor was speaking to Wandering Zhou, he kept looking over at Song Gang. Song Gang's face alternated between beet red and deathly pale as he listened to them discuss how to give him large breasts and how after the surgery they would remove his penis and testicles, reroute his urinary tract, and make him an artificial vagina. The doctor guaranteed that the shape and feel of the exterior of the vagina would be completely realistic. The vagina would be comfortably wide and deep, and the clitoris would be sexually sensitive. When Song Gang heard this, he felt nauseated, whereas Wandering Zhou appeared elated, nodding enthusiastically to the doctor while looking happily at

Song Gang, as if he really was going to become a woman. Finally, the doctor carefully examined Song Gang and said that he would also have to give him a nose job and a chin job and alter the shape of his cheekbones to make his face look more feminine.

Wandering Zhou made an appointment with the doctor for them to return three days later to have the breast surgery. After the two left the clinic, Wandering Zhou gazed at Song Gang delightedly and said, "If you really did become a woman, I'd marry you, and I'd love you like the male leads in Korean soaps love their women. I'd love you like life itself."

Song Gang, who usually never cursed, glared at Wandering Zhou with an ashen face and screamed, "Go fuck yourself!"

Then, one drizzly morning, Song Gang followed behind Wandering Zhou as they left their old, rundown hotel and walked out into the wet street. Zhou waved at the taxis that drove by, and Song Gang gazed out at the misty ocean. He could hear the cries of the seagulls but couldn't see them. Three hours later he was lying on the operating table as the doctor drew two purple ovals on his chest. He closed his eyes under the spotlight, and when he received the full-body anesthesia, a single seagull suddenly appeared in his mind's eye, soaring in the dense fog over the ocean, but he couldn't hear the gull's cry.

Although the doctor told Wandering Zhou that men's and women's chests have certain anatomical and physiological differences and therefore Song Gang's operation would be more complicated than a standard breast enhancement, the operation was nevertheless very successful, and within two hours it was all finished. Song Gang stayed in the hospital for observation, and when he left the next day it was still drizzling. He endured the pain of the incisions under his armpits as he and Wandering Zhou took a taxi back to the little hotel by the ocean. When he got out of the taxi, as Zhou was paying the driver, Song Gang once again gazed spellbound at the misty ocean, but nothing was there—neither gull cries nor the gulls themselves.

Song Gang spent six days recuperating in the hotel, during which time it drizzled continuously. The bra-wearing hunk on the billboard flickered in and out of view in the rain. Every time Song Gang saw the image he felt a rush of shame, as if the man in the billboard were himself. Wandering Zhou meticulously looked after Song Gang. Every day he would conscientiously ask what kind of food he wanted to eat, then would go out to several nearby restaurants, copy out their menus, and take them back to Song Gang, telling him to order whatever he wanted. Song Gang would always select only the cheapest dishes. Wandering Zhou would then call the restaurant on the phone and ask them to deliver to the hotel room. On the phone, Wandering Zhou would always roar vigorously, "Our Boss Song is tired of eating abalone and shark fin, so please send us some tofu and vegetables."

Song Gang thus became Boss Song, a Boss Song with a pair of women's breasts. After Song Gang had his stitches removed, Wandering Zhou happily went out to buy him a bra. He told Song Gang that this was a D-cup bra, and those able to wear a D cup were genuine Boobs Queens. Then he told Song Gang ingratiatingly, "You are also a Boobs Queen."

Song Gang saw that Wandering Zhou had bought him a red bra just like the one on the billboard. He took it and threw it to the floor. Wandering Zhou picked it up and said, "The red one is so good, it really catches the eye."

Song Gang said, "Fuck your mother!"

"I'll exchange it immediately," Wandering Zhou replied. "Song Gang, I know that you are a low-key person, so I'll exchange it for a white one right away."

Five days later the rain finally stopped and the sun came out. Song Gang wore a white bra under his shirt, and he and Wandering Zhou took a ferry to Hainan Island. Having sold so little Boobs cream in more than seven months wandering through Canton, Wandering Zhou had decided that Canton was an inauspicious place and resolved to travel to Hainan Island to make a new beginning. With his new fake breasts, Song Gang would often lose his balance while walking, as his body would pitch forward, to the point that he gradually became hunchbacked. When Song Gang climbed aboard the ferry, he stood on the deck gripping the railing, feeling the weight of his fake breasts. He gazed out at the Canton coast, feeling empty inside and not knowing what the future would bring. Amid the sounds of the waves and the rays of the sun, between the sky and the ocean, he saw a seagull soaring and heard its cries. He thought of Lin Hong's exhortations over the phone that he return home immediately. As the waves jostled the ferry, and with the breeze blowing through his hair, he began to hear Lin Hong's exhortations in the seagull's cries. As they gradually faded away Song Gang couldn't help weeping, out of a sense of desolation. It had already been a year since he left home. When he left Liu Town, he imagined that he would be home by now, but instead he was traveling farther and farther away.

On Hainan Island, Wandering Zhou and Song Gang once again began selling their bust-enhancing cream. As they had done while selling artificial hymens in Liu Town a year earlier, the two stood on the street surrounded by men and women. Song Gang stood there like a model, without saying a word—his shirt unbuttoned, revealing his white bra and D-cup breasts. Wandering Zhou kept wagging his tongue, tirelessly singing the praises of their Boobs cream, saying that it was made up of 35 percent natural vitamins and 65 percent genetically engineered human growth hormone. The growth agent could make breasts mature X times over the course of just a few days, X times faster than weeds. The vitamins not only helped make the breasts supple but also kept the skin soft and tender, and furthermore, "it doesn't contain any steroids and is completely safe and reliable."

When Wandering Zhou finished introducing the bust-enhancing cream, he then turned to Song Gang's breasts. He introduced Song Gang to the men and women crowded around them as Boss Song. Wandering Zhou expounded on how, in the city, breast-enlargement creams were as plentiful as the hairs on a cow, but truly effective ones were as rare as a single hair out of every nine cows. Therefore, in order to determine whether or not the cream was truly effective, Boss Song used some himself, never expecting that two months later . . . Wandering Zhou then pointed to Song Gang's chest and said, "As a result, our Boss Song now no longer has a man's strapping build but, rather, the supple and graceful figure of a young woman."

The crowds started laughing uncontrollably, crowding around and staring at Song Gang curiously as though he were an alien. As Song Gang blushed with embarrassment, a petite young woman pinched his nipples. Song Gang angrily swatted her hand away, and one of the men reprimanded her, saying, "Where do you get off, thinking that you can fondle a man's sexual organs?"

"You call this a sexual organ?" the woman asked in surprise.

"As long as it is a breast and fondling it can bring on an orgasm, then it is a sexual organ." The man pointed at the woman's petite breasts and added, "I assume you consider these to be sexual organs, don't you?"

As he was speaking the man also pinched Song Gang's nipples, and Song Gang exploded. He grabbed the man's hand and pushed it away. The women in the crowd were pleased, saying that anyone with such big breasts must be considered a woman. Therefore, they collectively criticized that man, saying, "Who do you think you are, fondling a woman's breasts like that?"

"Is he a woman?" the man asked in surprise.

"If she weren't a woman, how could she have such big breasts?" the women all replied in unison.

"Regardless of whether you're a man or a woman"—Wandering Zhou lifted his Boobs bust-enhancing cream high in the air—"the important thing is that whoever uses this will become a modern-day Queen Boobs."

The petite woman who had fondled Song Gang's fake breasts was the first to come forward. She bashfully paid for two vials of the cream and hurried away. Several middle-aged women then came forward and bought several vials, explaining that they were buying them for their daughters. Some young women also bought some, saying that the cream was for their friends. Finally, some men came forward, explaining that they were buying it for the girlfriends of their girlfriends, or for their wives' sisters. Wandering Zhou was all smiles as he raked in the money with one hand and handed out the vials of bust-enhancing cream with the other. Within an hour he had managed to sell thirty-seven vials. He then proudly lifted up a box of Boobs bust-enhancing cream, announcing loudly, "Thirty-seven vials of Boobs cream have already found owners. Who will these last ones go to?"

After Wandering Zhou put the box down, a man crowded forward and pointed at Wandering Zhou's crotch, whispering, "Will it have any effect if you apply it there?"

"You mean on your penis?" Wandering Zhou replied in a loud voice. "Of course it will."

"Hey, hey," that man whispered. "Please lower your voice."

"I understand." Wandering Zhou nodded to the man, then held up the bust-enhancing cream and said to the men who were crowded around, "This Boobs cream can also serve as a penis enlarger, making your erections bigger, longer, and longer-lasting. But when you use it, you must be very careful to follow doctor's orders. Otherwise, it might end up so big that it will no longer be a penis."

"If it's no longer a penis, what will it be?" some of the men asked laughing.

"If it becomes too big"—Wandering Zhou thought for a moment—then "it will become a breast."

Wandering Zhou was blessed with beginner's luck, and the first day he sold fifty-eight vials of the cream. For Song Gang, however, that day was like the seventh circle of hell. Having to unbutton his shirt and let all these unknown men and women admire his fake breasts, and to listen to some of them even debate whether he was a man or a woman, was enough to make him feel as though he was about to go insane. However, he gritted his teeth and collected himself. As the sun went down Wandering Zhou gathered the boxes. Song Gang, looking like a woman who had just been sexually brutalized, shamefully buttoned his shirt back up and, with an ashen face, followed Zhou back to the hotel. Wandering Zhou knew that Song Gang was distressed and therefore comforted him, saying, "No one knows you here."

The next day, the two returned to the same street and continued their performance. This time, Wandering Zhou managed to sell sixty-four vials of the cream. According to Zhou's custom, the third day they should have moved to a new location, but their success up to that point made him reluctant to leave and therefore they once again returned to the same street corner. By noon, the petite woman who had pinched Song Gang's nipple the first day came forward with a big, burly man. The man, who looked like a butcher, walked right up to Song Gang and carefully examined his fake breasts. At the time Wandering Zhou was energetically hawking his wares and didn't notice that this man's lips were swollen to an enormous size. When the man was finished examining Song Gang's breasts, he grabbed Zhou by the collar and started cursing up a storm, saying that the breast-enlargement cream he was selling contained poison. This man caught Zhou by surprise, and at first all Zhou heard was a buzzing sound coming from the man's swollen lips. Eventually he understood that the man had applied the cream to his lips. Wandering Zhou forcefully pushed away the man's hand and reprimanded him, "Why did you use the cream on your lips? That was an idiotic thing to do—"

"Fuck you!" The man with the swollen lip became furious. "Why would I want to use your cream?"

"Then what did you use?" Wandering Zhou was confused.

"I . . ."

The man didn't know what to say, and so his wife blushed and said, "I was the one who used it."

Not allowing her to finish, Wandering Zhou cried out, "How could you apply the bust-enhancing cream to his lips?"

"I didn't!" By this point even her neck was blushing red. She pointed to her chest and said, "I applied it here, but I didn't tell him, so he—"

All the men and women crowded around immediately broke into uproarious laughter. Even Song Gang couldn't help laughing, and Wandering Zhou was even more delighted. He repeated over and over again, "I understand, I understand. . . ."

"You tell me," the man howled, "isn't this poison?"

"It's not poison, it's a kind of growth agent." Wandering Zhou pointed to the man's swollen lip and told the crowd, "Do you see? His lips grew this much in just two days and have even started to develop a red nipple!"

The man's wife protested quietly, "But I myself haven't gotten any bigger."

"Of course you haven't. All the growth agent was rubbed off on him!" Zhou pointed to her husband's swollen lip and didn't pass up this opportunity to make another pitch to the crowd, saying, "Do you see? He was only exposed to it indirectly, so just imagine what would have happened if he had applied it directly—his lips would have grown into two ears!"

As the crowd laughed, the man with the swollen lips went from embarrassment to fury and proceeded to punch Wandering Zhou in the face, leaving him staggering. This punch was like the one Blacksmith Tong gave the young Baldy Li so many years earlier, and like Baldy Li's, Wandering Zhou's ears also buzzed for several days afterward.

In business terms, this man with the swollen lips ended up helping Wandering Zhou immeasurably: That day he sold ninety-seven vials of the cream. The morning of the fourth day, Wandering Zhou held his buzzing ears and quietly snuck off with Song Gang. For the next ten days, their sales on Hainan Island were extraordinarily successful. They were like dragonflies treading water, not staying in any one place for more than two or three days, promptly moving on before anyone saw through their act. Song Gang gradually became accustomed to unbuttoning his shirt in public and began to feel less and less ashamed. Seeing the pile of cash in Wandering Zhou's black bag grow, Song Gang felt reassured. Each night, Zhou sat on the hotel room bed, listening to the buzzing sound in his head and counting their day's earnings. When he told Song Gang how much they had made, a smile appeared on Song Gang's face, as he was convinced that he would soon be able to return home.

At that point, Wandering Zhou discovered a Korean soap that he hadn't watched before. Therefore, every night he would sit on the end of his bed and warmly invite Song Gang to join him, helpfully explaining the plot to him. Song Gang hadn't spoken with Lin Hong for a long time, so he went out to call her. Wandering Zhou told him to use the phone in the room. Song Gang said it was very expensive to make calls from the hotel, but Wandering Zhou replied that they had money now, so it was okay to spend it. Song Gang then said that if he called from the room, he might disturb Wandering Zhou watching his Korean soaps, but Wandering Zhou said not to worry. Therefore, the two sat together on the bed—one absorbed by the Korean miniseries, and the other placing a long-distance call to Mama Su's snack shop.

Song Gang held the receiver with both hands, and as Mama Su ran across the street to get Lin Hong, he heard a tumult in the snack shop, including the crying of a newborn baby. When he heard the sound of footsteps on the other end of the line, he knew that Lin Hong had arrived. His hand began to tremble, and then he heard her eager voice, saying, "Hello . . ."

Song Gang's eyes filled with tears, and Lin Hong said hello several more times before he could gather himself together enough to sob, "Lin Hong, I miss you."

Lin Hong became silent for a moment, then sobbed back, "Song Gang, I miss you, too."

The two spoke for a long time. Song Gang told Lin Hong that he was in Hainan, but he didn't tell her that he was selling bust-enhancing cream, merely saying that business was going very well. Lin Hong told him some of the things that had happened in Liu Town. As the sound of the baby's crying grew louder and louder, Lin Hong quietly told Song Gang that Missy Su had had a daughter and had named her Su Zhou but that no one knew who the father was. As the two spoke they lost all track of time. Wandering Zhou watched two entire episodes of his Korean soap while Song Gang and Lin Hong were still pouring their hearts out to each other. Song Gang saw Zhou sitting there watching him and realized it was time to hang up. At that point Lin Hong cried out to him, "When will you be coming home?"

Song Gang replied emotionally, "Soon. I'll be home soon."

After Song Gang put down the phone, he looked at Wandering Zhou with downcast eyes. Wandering Zhou also looked depressed—depressed that he didn't know what was going to happen in the next episode. Song Gang laughed bitterly, then felt an urge to talk. He muttered miserably that he didn't know how Lin Hong had gotten on that past year while he was away. Wandering Zhou was still mulling over the Korean drama that just ended and didn't register what Song Gang was saying. After a while, Song Gang asked Zhou whether he remembered Missy Su from the Liu Town snack shop. Zhou nodded and looked at Song Gang with alarm. Song Gang then told Zhou that Missy Su had had a daughter and had named her Su Zhou but that no one in Liu Town knew who the father was. When he heard this, Wandering Zhou's jaw dropped in astonishment.

That night both of them tossed and turned in bed. Song Gang missed Lin Hong's every little gesture, her smile, and her temperament. Wandering Zhou, meanwhile, kept thinking about Missy Su's smile and imagining the baby girl's smile. Even after Song Gang finally fell asleep, Wandering Zhou continued to stare straight ahead, imagining Missy Su's and the baby's smiles. Song Gang woke up the next morning at dawn and saw that Zhou was already dressed and had placed two piles of bills on the bed. Zhou announced proudly, "I am Su Zhou's father."

At first Song Gang didn't understand what he was saying. Wandering Zhou pointed to the pile of cash on the bed and said that their entire earnings were there—45,000 yuan in all. Divided 50/50, they each got 22,500 yuan. Wandering Zhou took one pile of bills and put it in his pocket then pointed to the other pile and said, "This is yours."

Song Gang stared at Wandering Zhou with a look of profound skepticism. Wandering Zhou said that they also had more than two-hundred vials of the bust-enhancing cream left over, and he was leaving all of that to Song Gang as well. Then Wandering Zhou passionately declared that he had been wandering through the region of rivers and lakes like a knight-errant for more than fifteen years and that the dangers and travails of life on the road had made him profoundly weary and left him longing for a stable resting place. Therefore, he had decided to bid farewell to all this and return to settle down in Liu Town, where he would enjoy being a family man as Missy Su's husband and Su Zhou's father.

When he finished, Wandering Zhou picked up his black bag and walked out. Only then did Song Gang finally understand that it was Zhou who had gotten Missy Su pregnant and that Wandering Zhou's breast-enlargement business was being abruptly terminated. He called out to Wandering Zhou, pointing at his own fake breasts and asked, "If you leave, what about me?"

Wandering Zhou looked at Song Gang's fake breasts with profound sympathy and said, "You'll have to figure that out for yourself."

CHAPTER 68

ABOUT TEN MONTHS after Song Gang left our Liu Town with Wandering Zhou, there was a new hubbub in town concerning the Russian painter Baldy Li hired to come paint his portrait. It was said that the resulting painting was as big as Mao's portrait in Tiananmen Square. Legend had it that this particular artist had just spent three months living it up in the Kremlin while painting Putin's portrait. After Yeltsin stepped down from power and became a stale flower, he wanted to hire this same artist, but since he wasn't able to offer as high a price as Baldy Li, the painter came to Liu Town instead. The townspeople all saw him with their own eyes, with his white hair and white beard, his big nose and blue eyes. He loved to eat Chinese snacks, so every day he would walk happily to Mama and Missy Su's snack shop to have steamed mini-buns.

What this Russian artist liked best were the straw-embedded buns, and each time he came, he would order five steamer trays of them, with three buns in each tray. With fifteen buns and fifteen miniature straws in front of him like a birthday cake with fifteen candles, he carefully sipped the juices out of each bun, then ate the buns themselves. This was the delicacy the charlatan Wandering Zhou had introduced to Liu Town. He had personally taught Missy Su how to make the buns and also personally made her belly grow big. He had left abruptly, but the straw-embedded buns he brought to Liu Town not only took root but even became famous. Everyone would line up each day to have them, and the snack shop was full of a sound like suckling infants.

The famous Russian painter ate straw-embedded buns at Missy Su's snack shop for three straight months, until he finally finished his portrait of Baldy Li. The day he finished, he dragged his luggage to the snack shop, and as he ate, everyone learned that he was about to return to Russia. They all assumed that he was finally going to get to work on Yeltsin. Just as the painter finished eating his buns, Baldy Li's sedan pulled up in front of the snack shop. At that moment Lin Hong was standing outside her apartment building. Baldy Li was not in the sedan, but his chauffeur took the artist's luggage and placed it in the trunk. The artist then walked out, wiping his mouth, and got in the car. Lin Hong watched as they drove away.

Lin Hong and Song Gang had now been separated for more than a year. Lin Hong was alone with her shadow. She would bike to work every morning and return every evening. With Song Gang gone, their home, which had originally seemed small and cramped, now appeared enormous, cavernous, and deathly still. It was only when she turned on the television that Lin Hong had a chance to hear other people's voices. Ever since the first time Song Gang called the snack shop across the street, Lin Hong had taken to standing in the doorway of her apartment building in the evening, expectantly watching the people walking in and out of the snack shop. At first she was waiting for Song Gang to call, but since his calls were few and far between, she no longer knew what she was waiting for.

Lin Hong felt extremely ashamed. After the chain-smoking Factory Director Liu learned that Song Gang had left, he became even bolder in his advances. Once he called Lin Hong into his office and, after shutting the door, pushed her onto the couch. This time he succeeded in ripping her shirt as well as her bra. Lin Hong struggled and screamed, eventually frightening him to the point that he didn't dare continue. After that, she never returned to his office, and when Director Liu told her workshop leader to send her in, she would shake her head firmly and state, "I won't go."

The workshop leader didn't want to let Director Liu down and therefore stood entreating Lin Hong, but she repeated, "I won't go. He doesn't keep his hands to himself."

After Lin Hong stopped going to Director Liu's office, he began coming to her workshop every day to observe her. He would silently sneak up behind her like a ghost and pinch her butt. Because the machinery obstructed the view of the other female workers, he would sometimes also pinch her breasts. Each time he did this, Lin Hong would angrily pry his hand off. Once he grabbed her from behind and began fiercely kissing her neck. This time Lin Hong simply couldn't take it anymore and pushed him away, screaming, "Keep your hands off me!"

The other workers heard her scream and ran over. Director Liu's embarrassment turned to anger, and he proceeded to reprimand them, "What are you staring at? Go back to work."

Lin Hong went home and cried over and over again, particularly distraught that there was no one she could talk to about her humiliation. Several times when Song Gang called, she considered telling him, but each time there were people around, and therefore she bit her tongue. After hanging up the phone and returning home, she would again cry all alone, thinking that even if she did tell Song Gang what was happening, what could he do about it?

While standing in her doorway in the evening, she would often see Baldy Li drive by in his sedan. One day, two months after Song Gang left, the sedan stopped in front of her house. Baldy Li emerged and, smiling, walked up to her. Lin Hong blushed and, as she was standing there unsure what to do, he peered around her into the house, muttering, "And where is Song Gang?"

When Baldy Li learned that Song Gang had gone away with someone else to do business, he became so furious he could barely stand straight. He cursed over and over again, "That bastard, that fucking bastard . . ."

After calling him a bastard five times in succession, Baldy Li told Lin Hong angrily, "That bastard has hurt me deeply. He is willing to do business with anyone but me."

"It's not like that," Lin Hong quickly explained. "Song Gang has always regarded you as the person closest to him in the world."

Baldy Li was already walking back toward the sedan. When he opened the door, he turned around and asked sympathetically, "How could you marry such a bastard?"

After Baldy Li's sedan drove away into the sunset, Lin Hong was filled with mixed emotions. She remembered how Song Gang and Baldy Li, when they were young, would walk together down the streets of Liu, one tall figure and one short one. Lin Hong had never imagined that, twenty years later, they would end up with such different fates. Even after Song Gang had been away from home for more than a year, Baldy Li kept his promise and every six months would deposit another hundred thousand yuan into Lin Hong's bank account. Lin Hong had spent more than twenty thousand yuan on Song Gang's medical expenses and left the remaining balance completely untouched. Although Song Gang insisted over the phone that his business was taking off, Lin Hong didn't dare touch the money in her account. That was money for Song Gang's medical treatment, to support him in his old age and possibly save his life. Lin Hong knew that Song Gang was not a businessman, and she was afraid that he would return empty-handed.

With the chain-smoking Director Liu still eyeing her covetously, she knew that, sooner or later, she would have to leave the knitting factory and therefore would find herself unemployed. This realization made her even less willing to touch the money in her account. She would wander aimlessly through the clothing stores and see many outfits that would suit her, but wouldn't buy a single one.

Whenever Baldy Li saw Lin Hong standing in her doorway, he would roll down the window of his sedan and ask her whether or not Song Gang had returned. When she responded that he hadn't, he would invariably curse, "That bastard!" Once, after inquiring about Song Gang, Baldy Li suddenly expressed concern for Lin Hong herself, asking, "Are you doing okay?"

Lin Hong's heart skipped a beat. She was accustomed to Baldy Li's filthy mouth, so his gentle inquiry took her breath away. Tears welled up in her eyes.

That afternoon Director Liu had told Lin Hong that her name was on the next list of workers to be laid off, and that the list would be made public in a week's time. After the incident when Lin Hong had cried out and told him to keep his hands to himself, the director didn't return to Lin Hong's workshop for a full three months. This time, when he entered, he didn't seem like a ghost but, rather, marched right up to Lin Hong and quietly informed her that she would be unemployed within a week. Director Liu didn't make any advances this time but, rather, coldly reminded her that if she didn't want to be laid off, she should go to his office after work. Lin Hong bit her lip and didn't say anything. After work, she continued biting her lip as she rode her Eternity bicycle home. Once home, she stood woodenly in the doorway, and when Baldy Li asked her how she was doing, she burst into tears at the mere thought of the humiliation she had endured from Director Liu.

When he saw Lin Hong crying, Baldy Li got out of the sedan and rushed over to her, asking, "Did something happen to Song Gang?"

Lin Hong shook her head and for the first time spoke of her humiliation at Director Liu's hands. She then wiped her tears and entreated Baldy Li, "Could you please say something to Director Liu?"

Baldy Li gave the heartbroken Lin Hong a confused look and asked, "Do you mean the chain-smoking Director Liu?"

Lin Hong nodded, and after a brief hesitation she told him the entire story of her humiliation, concluding, "Could you speak to him, and ask him to leave me alone?"

"That fucking bastard!" When Baldy Li finally understood, he gritted his teeth in anger and cursed. Then he told Lin Hong, "Give me three days, and then you will be able to rest easy."

Three days later someone came from the county government to announce that they were relieving Director Liu of his duties, on the ground that he had allowed productivity at the factory to fall three years in a row. Before he had a chance to announce the new list of layoffs he himself was fired. With a somber expression, Director Liu collected his belongings and trudged out the factory door with his tail between his legs. On the day he received the news, he went a full two hours without smoking a single cigarette and didn't even have one as he walked out the door. The workers at the knitting factory all laughed, remarking that if Director Liu had forgotten to smoke, he must indeed be at his wit's end.

The first thing the new director did was to promote Lin Hong from her former position in the workshop to the factory office. When the new director saw Lin Hong, he greeted her with a smile, then added quietly that if she didn't like this new position, she could have her pick of any position in the factory.

Never having expected things to work out this way, Lin Hong was extremely grateful. A situation that had caused her such hardship had been resolved easily as soon as Baldy Li learned of it. By this point, she had nothing but goodwill for Baldy Li and felt that her previous hatred of him had been without merit. From then on, when Lin Hong stood in her doorway in the evening, she was no longer certain whether she was waiting for Song Gang's call or for Baldy Li to drive by.

When the famous Russian painter departed, everyone in Liu knew that Baldy Li's enormous portrait had been completed. It was said that he had hung it in his thousand-square-foot office and covered it with a red velvet drape, and that no one other than Baldy Li had even seen it. The people working in Baldy Li's company told everyone in town that Baldy Li wanted to invite a VIP to come and unveil his portrait, and everyone starting speculating as to who that might be. At first, they thought it might be County Governor Tao Qing. For a month Tao Qing didn't go anywhere but waited around every day for Baldy Li to call him up and invite him to host the ceremony. But the portrait still remained covered by the red velvet drape, and Baldy Li still hadn't organized an unveiling ceremony. Baldy Li's underlings reported that the ceremony had not been held yet because Baldy Li was waiting for his new car to be delivered, since he wanted to pick the host up in it. Therefore, everyone began to suspect that the host must be someone even more important than the county governor; otherwise, why would Baldy Li need a new car to pick him up?

From that point on, rumors spread like wildfire. First people speculated that it would be a national Party leader. Then someone suggested that Baldy Li would invite the secretary-general of the United Nations to host the ceremony. Some people started watching the news on television, listening to the radio, and reading the newspaper, and after a few days began to ask themselves, "Why is it that there isn't any news about the secretary-general coming to visit China?"

Others responded, "That explains why Baldy Li is still waiting!"

Some people went to ask PR Liu, who by this point had been promoted to the position of executive deputy to the president. The townspeople of Liu at first called him Boss Liu, but he felt that Boss Liu sounded too much like Boss Li and therefore asked people to call him Executive Deputy Liu instead. Everyone, however, felt that that was too much trouble and therefore settled for Deputy Liu. It was as if Deputy Liu's mouth had grown a hymen, so absolute was his discretion. Even if his friends and relatives came to ask him the question, he would always give the same response: "No comment."

Two months later, the two cars Baldy Li had ordered finally arrived. One was a black Mercedes-Benz, and the other was a white BMW. Why had he suddenly bought two new sedans? Baldy Li announced that he wanted to become one with nature, sitting in his white BMW during the day and in his black Mercedes at night. These were the first high-end sedans to arrive in Liu Town, and when they were parked in front of Baldy Li's company, everyone crowded around to marvel at them. They all agreed that the Mercedes was exceedingly black and the BMW exceedingly white. The Mercedes was even blacker than the skin of Africans, and the BMW was whiter than that of Europeans; the Mercedes was blacker than coal and the BMW whiter than freshly driven snow; the Mercedes was blacker than ink and the BMW whiter than paper. Everyone concluded that the Mercedes was blacker than night and the BMW was whiter than day. The whitest BMW sedan in the world drove two loops around Liu Town during the day, and the blackest Mercedes sedan drove two loops around town at night. While the cars were making their loops, Baldy Li was not inside, only his driver. The Santana driver had been promoted to be the Mercedes and BMW chauffeur.

Everyone was convinced that now that Baldy Li's new sedans had arrived, the host of his unveiling ceremony would somehow mysteriously appear as well. They started speculating again about who that important personage would be. Having eliminated County Governor Tao Qing from consideration, they started with the mayor and again worked their way up to the secretary-general of the United Nations.

One evening Lin Hong ate dinner all alone and was standing alone in her doorway when Deputy Liu appeared. He hurried forward, with someone panting along behind him with a red carpet on his shoulders. Deputy Liu marched up to Lin Hong and very politely asked her to get out of the way. With a look of bewilderment, she stepped aside and let him in, then watched as he directed the man behind him to unroll the red carpet from Lin Hong's front door all the way to the street. The bystanders stared in astonishment, completely at a loss. Lin Hong also stared in astonishment, having no idea what was going on. Deputy Liu smiled and said to Lin Hong as though he were speaking with reporters, "Boss Li has requested that you go to unveil his portrait."

Lin Hong continued staring in astonishment, convinced that she must have misunderstood. The crowds around her were initially speechless with surprise and then exploded into a cacophonous roar. Deputy Liu lowered his voice and whispered to Lin Hong, "Quick, go change your clothes."

Lin Hong finally realized why he was here. She looked blankly at the crowds surrounding her and heard their buzzing voices and thought she heard someone say that an ugly ducking had turned into a beautiful swan. She laughed bitterly and stared at Deputy Liu, not knowing what to do. Deputy Liu again quietly urged her to go change her clothes, but she only registered that his mouth was moving, without understanding what he was saying.

She stood in the Liu Town twilight, looking as if she had fallen into a stupor. She stared blankly at the crowds that kept accumulating in the street. At one point she appeared to forget what was happening, but then she furrowed her brow and finally seemed to remember. She shook her head hesitantly and nervously looked behind her. She didn't see Song Gang but just her empty house. When she turned around again, a white BMW sedan was slowly coming up the street, followed by a black Mercedes, and the crowd cried out, "Baldy Li has arrived!"

Baldy Li had, in fact, arrived, together with his two new cars, for which he had hired two drivers. First the white BMW drove up and stopped in front of the red carpet. Then the black Mercedes pulled up behind it, and as Deputy Liu ran to open the door, an impeccably dressed Baldy Li emerged, smiling. He was carrying a single red rose and had a rose boutonniere in his front pocket. He walked up to the baffled Lin Hong, and when he handed her the rose he was holding, this local moneybags looked like a genuine foreign gentleman. First he delicately sniffed the rose, then he handed it to Lin Hong. He then held her hand as he led her onto the red carpet and started walking back to the BMW. Extending his hand, he gestured gallantly for her to get in. Lin Hong looked back nervously but saw only the empty doorway of her house. She then looked at the crowds, saw the strange expressions on their faces, and heard their dull roar. Suddenly she wanted to get away as quickly as possible, and therefore she climbed into the BMW—never having ridden in a sedan before, she didn't get in so much as *crawl* in. The crowd saw her wiggle her butt as though she were trying to climb into a foxhole. Then they watched as Baldy Li waved at them and lowered himself into his seat.

After Deputy Liu helped close the door, the white BMW drove away, with the black Mercedes following behind. Deputy Liu's underling rolled the red carpet back up and once again loaded it onto his shoulder, then followed Deputy Liu as he began to walk away. One of the bystanders asked, "After Lin Hong unveils the portrait, will she spend the night with Baldy Li?"

Deputy Liu answered without turning around, "No comment."

CHAPTER 69

THE WHITE BMW and the black Mercedes slowly drove through Liu. When the sun was about to set, the BMW stopped at a curve in the road and Baldy Li announced, "It has gotten dark," then opened the door and pulled Lin Hong out of the white BMW. The instant night fell he pulled her into the black Mercedes, blending into the night. Lin Hong was grasping her rose, still so completely bewildered by what had just transpired that she didn't even realize they had switched cars. Baldy Li just gazed at her with a chivalrous smile on his face.

When the black Mercedes drove up to the entrance to Baldy Li's company, he leapt out and opened the door for Lin Hong, then gallantly led her into his brightly illuminated office. Baldy Li took Lin Hong by the hand, led her over to the couch and, gazing at her tenderly, said, "I've been waiting for this day for twenty years."

Lin Hong stared at him, perplexed, and laughed noncommittally. Baldy Li took the rose she was holding and tossed it onto the coffee table, then reached out and began caressing her face. Lin Hong began to tremble as Baldy Li's hands slid down to her shoulders, from her shoulders on down her arms, and finally to her hands, waiting patiently for her to stop trembling. He felt that he had a million things to tell her but didn't know where to begin. He shook his head, and said unhappily, "Lin Hong, please understand. . . ."

Lin Hong looked at him in confusion, not knowing what she was supposed to understand. Baldy Li said pathetically, "I have forgotten how to court someone. I hope you'll understand. . . ."

"Understand what?" Lin Hong asked quietly.

"Fuck," Baldy Li cursed. "I don't know how to talk about love. I only know how to make love."

Then he became a bandit. As Lin Hong stared at him in bewilderment, not having the slightest idea what he was talking about, he grabbed her and stuck his hand into her underpants. He did this lightning-fast, and by the time she realized what had happened, she was already pinned down on the couch with her pants pulled down to her knees. She grabbed her pants with both hands and cried out, "Stop, stop! Stop doing that!"

Baldy Li, however, was like a wild animal. Within two minutes he had stripped her naked, and within another minute he had stripped off his own clothes. Lin Hong fought him off with all her strength, while imploringly crying out her husband's name, "Song Gang, Song Gang . . ."

Baldy Li pinned Lin Hong down on the sofa, held her hands and feet down with his, and shouted, "Song Gang, forgive me!"

Baldy Li then entered her. Since Song Gang had been ill so long, it had been several years since a man had touched her like this, and while she cried out in terror, the subsequent pleasurable sensation almost made her pass out. As Baldy Li began to thrust she started to cry out again. Not having done this kind of thing for such a long time, she was like a piece of dry kindling exposed to a flame. She cried out, but it was unclear whether it was from shame or pleasure. After more than ten minutes, her cries became moans. As Baldy Li happily carried on she lost track of time, fully absorbed with her body's rapid contractions. Baldy Li and Lin Hong did it for more than an hour, during which time Lin Hong experienced countless orgasms—even having three in a row, each one following on the heels of the previous one, making her body tremble like the engines of Baldy Li's BMW and Mercedes and making her cry out like the cars' horns.

When they were done, Lin Hong lay exhausted on the couch with Baldy Li on top of her, panting heavily. She remembered how she and Song Gang had never lasted more than two minutes. Even when Song Gang was healthy they would do it very perfunctorily, and after he became ill he could not manage even that. Lin Hong caressed Baldy Li's body, thinking, *So this is what a real man is like.*

After lying on top of her for a few minutes, Baldy Li excitedly jumped up and ran into the bathroom to rinse himself off. After he had dressed, he saw that Lin Hong had draped her clothing over her naked body. He told her to go rinse herself as well, but she merely lay on the couch, exhaustedly shaking her head and unwilling to move.

Baldy Li didn't say anything else to her but sat down at his desk and started making business calls. Lin Hong lay there, delirious—her mind in a tumult, like a boat buffeted by the waves—thinking back over what had just happened. It had all been very sudden, like a flash of lightning, starting abruptly, and concluding equally abruptly. Then in a flash of sudden clarity she realized that she was lying naked on Baldy Li's couch. Using her clothing to cover her herself, she got up and walked unsteadily to the bathroom to wash up. As she dressed she gradually revived. When she looked at herself in the mirror, she immediately blushed with embarrassment. She couldn't quite muster the courage to leave the bathroom because she didn't know how she would face Baldy Li when she did.

After Baldy Li finished his phone calls, he pushed open the bathroom door, and, announcing loudly that he was hungry, he reached in and pulled Lin Hong out into the office. Lin Hong confusedly followed Baldy Li into the Mercedes—both having completely forgotten about the unveiling ceremony—and they proceeded to a private room of a restaurant owned by Baldy Li's company. For the first time in her life Lin Hong ate abalone and shark fin. She had heard of these delicacies but knew that her annual salary at the knitting factory was enough for only a couple of servings, and therefore she had never tasted them.

Lin Hong assumed that after dinner she would be allowed to return home. What she didn't realize was that the evening had just begun. After eating, Baldy Li remained excited and proceeded to take her to a nightclub also owned by his company. She sat bewildered in a private karaoke room as Baldy Li sang her three love songs. He then asked Lin Hong to also sing a song, but she said she didn't know how. Baldy Li then pushed her down onto the couch and started to remove her pants. She struggled to pull them back up and cried out, "Don't! Don't do that!"

Baldy Li repeatedly nodded his head and said, "Just take off your trousers," then proceeded to remove them. This time she didn't cry out Song Gang's name. She lay on the couch, hugging Baldy Li while he jerked up and down on her body as though he were being shocked, continuing in this way for an hour. Lin Hong felt another orgasm coming on. This time she didn't have three in a row but only one. Then, with weak knees, she followed Baldy Li out of the nightclub and confusedly went home with him.

The two lay in bed and watched a Hong Kong movie. By this point it was three in the morning, and Lin Hong, who was accustomed to going to bed early, was so tired that she could barely keep her eyes open. When Baldy Li rolled over and again began making love to her, she no longer struggled to push him away but quietly acceded. This time she didn't have an orgasm, but she still got excited, though toward the end her vagina started to hurt. Baldy Li finally finished an hour later, whereupon Lin Hong fell sound asleep.

She had slept for only two hours when Baldy Li woke her up. It had occurred to him that they had never unveiled his portrait, so she had to get up and follow him unsteadily to his office. By the time they got there she had managed to wake up somewhat and noticed how dignified the office was. She walked over to the enormous portrait so big that it covered virtually the entire wall. Pulling away the satin drape that was covering it, she saw that the figure of Baldy Li was so immense that he resembled Atlas, wearing fancy dress clothes and smiling. Lin Hong looked at the image, then back at Baldy Li, and was about to remark that the portrait really looked like him when Baldy Li abruptly pushed her down and took her again on the red velvet cloth lying on the floor. This was the fourth time in ten hours that they had made love. This time, however, Lin Hong didn't feel anything other than excruciating pain, as though he were whipping her genitals. As she gritted her teeth Baldy Li thought that her cries of pain were moans of ecstasy. More than an hour later, when it seemed as if he had no intention of stopping, Lin Hong couldn't help but sigh. When Baldy Li asked why she was sighing, she confessed that she was in agony. He immediately stopped and, inspecting her genitals, discovered that they were red and swollen. He chastised her for not saying something sooner, saying that if he had known she was in pain, he would certainly not have continued. Even if he had been about to establish a Guinness World Record, he would still not have continued. Then he wrapped himself and Lin Hong in the red satin cloth, saying that they would stop and sleep for a while. They slept there on the floor until noon, when Deputy Liu came knocking on the door.

Baldy Li cried out, "Who is it? What do you want?"

Terrified, Deputy Liu said he didn't want anything in particular, just that he was worried because he hadn't seen Boss Li all morning. Baldy Li grunted and said, "I'm fine. I'm still sleeping with Lin Hong."

When Lin Hong finally emerged from Baldy Li's office soon after, Baldy Li wanted her to go home in his white BMW. Lin Hong, however, declined, afraid that would attract more attention and make her a laughingstock in the community. She said that she would walk home instead. She slowly trudged home, her genitals throbbing with every step. Lin Hong finally believed the rumors that Baldy Li was a beast of a man and that every woman left his bed more dead than alive.

When she finally got home, several neighbors looked at her curiously, but she pretended not to notice as she proceeded into the house and shut the door. She lay in bed fully clothed; by evening she still had not gotten up. Her thoughts in a jumble, she spent a long time thinking back over the events of the night before, with every detail appearing clearly in her mind's eye. She also recalled her twenty years living with Song Gang, as well as Song Gang's departure more than a year earlier. After he left she felt that their shared experiences became more and more distant, whereas her memories of her night with Baldy Li were indelibly printed on her brain. At the thought of Song Gang, Lin Hong began to cry, but she understood that, after having spent the night with Baldy Li, she was now entangled with him, regardless of how guilty and humiliated she felt.

News of the scandal involving Baldy Li and Lin Hong circulated throughout the town. From Baldy Li's appearance in court, followed by the Virgin Beauty Competition, the Russian painter's arrival, and Lin Hong's unveiling of the portrait, Baldy Li had provided the townspeople with four consecutive surprises, making every day seem as fresh as the morning sun. Even in their wildest dreams, the people of Liu had never imagined that the host of Baldy Li's portrait unveiling ceremony would be not the secretary-general of the United Nations, but, rather, Liu Town's own homegrown beauty, Lin Hong. Everyone was shocked—this was truly an unexpected development. Then they remembered how Baldy Li, in a fit of anger, had gone to the hospital and had a vasectomy, thereby cutting off the possibility of having descendants—and hadn't that been done for the sake of this very same Lin Hong? What did it matter that the portrait unveiling ceremony hadn't turned out as expected? The truth is, Baldy Li had gotten what he had wanted from the very start: He had succeeded in bedding her. His lightning-fast seduction of Lin Hong was just as he always said: One should get up right from wherever one has fallen down—that is the only way to succeed. When everyone thought of it this way, the entire situation began to make perfect sense. They concluded, "This was unexpected yet perfectly understandable."

CHAPTER 70

BALDY LI let Lin Hong rest for four days, but by the third night her body had become excited again. She tossed and turned, yearning for Baldy Li to come and press his body down on hers. Her desire had lain dormant for the entire two decades of her marriage to Song Gang, and now that it had suddenly been roused by Baldy Li at the age of forty, it started to surge. For the first time in her life, she discovered her body and the fact that she had a strong libido. On the fourth night, when Baldy Li's black Mercedes drove up to her door, her entire body started to tremble as soon as she heard the honking of the horn. She walked out the front door with quivering legs and climbed into the car.

In the days that followed, Baldy Li's Mercedes and BMW shuttled Lin Hong back and forth every day. Sometimes the BMW would come in the middle of the day, and sometimes it would be the Mercedes in the middle of the night. Baldy Li had countless affairs to attend to and therefore didn't always have free time. When he was free, however, he would sleep with Lin Hong. She was no longer bashful, and whenever she hugged Baldy Li, it seemed as if she wanted to suffocate him. She would even undress him. Baldy Li had never expected that Lin Hong would be so passionate, and he remarked in surprise, "Fuck, you're even hornier than I am."

Lin Hong had learned her lesson that first night and knew that she couldn't endure Baldy Li's lovemaking three or four times in a row. Therefore, she made a pact with him that they would not have sex more than twice in any twenty-four-hour period—and ideally no more than once. Lin Hong then said something that made Baldy Li burst out laughing: "Let me live a few more years."

For the next three months Lin Hong made love to Baldy Li virtually every day—in his bed, on the couch in his office, in the private room of the restaurant, and in the private room of the nightclub. In the Mercedes one night Baldy Li suddenly became aroused and wanted neither to go home and do it in bed nor to go to his office and do it on the couch but, rather, to do it right there in the car. He asked the driver to go to the restroom and stay there for an hour and a half, regardless of whether or not he needed to piss or shit. Then Baldy Li and Lin Hong intertwined their limbs in the back of the car and moaned and cried as they got it on for more than an hour.

After Baldy Li had had crazy sex with Lin Hong for three months, he suddenly felt that the sex had become stale. They had done it on the bed, on the couch, on the floor, in the bath, in the car; they had done it standing, sitting, kneeling, missionary and doggy style, sideways and up and down. In short, they had tried every position imaginable, and Lin Hong had cried out every imaginable sound. After the lovemaking lost its freshness for Baldy Li, he began to reminisce and remarked that it would have been perfect if only they had been able to make love twenty years earlier. Baldy Li told her that back then, as soon as it got dark, he would always fantasize about those three parts of her body as he masturbated. He asked her, "Do you know how many days a year I masturbated to you?"

Lin Hong shook her head. "No."

"Three hundred sixty-five days a year. I didn't even take time off for New Year's or other holidays."

Then Baldy Li's eyes grew bright as he cried out, "And to think that at the time you were still a virgin!"

After he had repeated this three times, he decided to send Lin Hong to a hospital in Shanghai to have hymen-recon surgery. Once she became a virgin again, he would make love to her once more and pretend that it was taking place twenty years earlier. After that they would never do it again. "With that, I'll return you to Song Gang!"

Realizing that their time together was about to be up, Lin Hong became very depressed. She had fully indulged her own craziness, and during this period her heart and body had become increasingly separated from each other, as if countless mountains and rivers had come between them. Her heart longed every day for Song Gang, but her body lusted for Baldy Li. She didn't know how, without the powerful Baldy Li, she would ever make it through the interminable nights. Her desire was like a forest fire, and once it started burning, it was almost impossible to extinguish. She realized sadly that she could never return to her former state of abstinence. She hated herself for this, but there was nothing she could do about it.

At this point, Lin Hong began to sense that Song Gang was about to return home to Liu. Wandering Zhou, who had led him away in the first place, had suddenly reappeared in Missy Su's snack shop a month earlier. Lin Hong had heard about this and also seen him with her own eyes. At that moment she had felt a jolt of surprise and wanted to rush over to him and ask about Song Gang, but just then Baldy Li's white BMW had driven up, and she lost her courage. Afterward she sent Deputy Liu to ask Wandering Zhou on her behalf, and she learned that Song Gang was temporarily unable to return. Wandering Zhou told Deputy Liu that Song Gang was still selling health products in Hainan, where he had already made a considerable profit, and therefore had no interest in coming home.

Lin Hong was still uneasy and worried every day that Song Gang might suddenly show up. This anxiety gradually began to take its toll on her libido. Whenever she thought of Song Gang, she would burst into tears and feel that she was committing a crime. As a result, her frenzied desire for Baldy Li began to ebb. She felt that for her and Baldy Li to have had these three months was more than enough; this way, when Song Gang returned home, she would be able to love and cherish him with renewed intensity. She understood Song Gang and knew that he was the kindest man in the world, and that no matter what she might do to betray him, he would continue to love her as before. Therefore, she hoped to break off her relationship with Baldy Li before Song Gang returned and agreed to travel to Shanghai for the hymen-recon surgery.

The next day Baldy Li and Lin Hong took the white BMW to Shanghai. Baldy Li needed to go to Beijing and the northeast to do business and would be gone for half a month. He knew that the hymen-recon surgery would take less than an hour. Therefore, he asked Lin Hong to wait for him in Shanghai. He would leave the BMW and a driver for her and told her to use her time in Shanghai to wine, dine, and shop.

When Wandering Zhou reappeared in Liu Town in October, he looked just as he had the first time he arrived—carrying two large cardboard boxes. This time, however, the boxes were not filled with artificial hymens but, rather, with children's toys. And this time, instead of walking over from the bus depot, Wandering Zhou hailed a pedicab and returned in glory. Seeing the men and women along the road, he remarked regretfully to the driver, "Not much has changed. It's still the same people as before."

After the pedicab delivered him to Missy Su's snack shop, Wandering Zhou paid the driver three yuan and asked him to carry his two cardboard boxes for him. Zhou then strutted into the snack shop, and when he saw Missy Su sitting at the cashier's counter, he acted as though he hadn't disappeared without a word for an entire year but, rather, had merely gone on a short business trip. He said warmly, "My dear, I'm home."

Missy Su looked as though she had seen a ghost. Her entire body began to tremble, and she immediately scurried off into the kitchen. Wandering Zhou smiled as he looked around. Noticing some people eating steamed buns staring at him, he asked them, as if he were the restaurant's proprietor, "Taste good, don't they?"

Then he noticed Mama Su sitting there flabbergasted, holding a four- or five-month-old infant. Zhou smiled at her and said sweetly, "Ma, I'm back."

Mama Su didn't know how to respond and, like her daughter, started trembling from head to toe. Wandering Zhou took the infant from her and kissed it repeatedly, saying affectionately, "Daughter, did you miss your daddy?"

Zhou asked the pedicab driver to open the two boxes, and then he put all the toys on the table. He placed his daughter in the middle of the toys, and started playing with her as if no one else were around. The soft-spoken Mama Su stared in astonishment at how easily Wandering Zhou was bantering with everyone, as if he had never left. The other customers finally came to their senses and realized that he was the one who had gotten Missy Su knocked up. Everyone began to laugh and chatter all at once, pointing at the infant playing with the toys on the table and asking Zhou, "Is this your daughter?"

"Of course," Wandering Zhou answered without hesitation.

Everyone looked around and asked again, "Are you and Missy Su married?"

"Of course," Wandering Zhou answered again without equivocation.

"When?" they asked, trying to get to the bottom of things.

"Earlier," Wandering Zhou replied simply.

"Earlier?" Everyone was confused. "How is it that we didn't know?"

"Why would you have known?" Wandering Zhou also looked confused.

This charlatan played happily with his daughter while exchanging nonsensical remarks with the customers, making them more and more confused until in the end some actually believed him and told each other, "They are really married."

Mama Su shook her head repeatedly, thinking that he was a bald-faced liar. Missy Su, meanwhile, never reemerged after having fled into the kitchen. Even after the sun had gone down, she could still hear Wandering Zhou chatting with the customers, but she was simply too embarrassed to come out and face everyone. Eventually she ended up sneaking out the side door. At eleven o'clock the snack shop closed for the night, and Wandering Zhou picked up the sleeping infant and calmly followed Mama Su home. He chatted warmly with Mama Su the entire way home, but she merely bowed her head and refused to answer. She tried several times to take her granddaughter away from him, but each time he politely declined, saying, "Ma, I'll hold her."

When they reached home, she didn't immediately close the door but stood looking at Wandering Zhou. She hesitated a moment but in the end couldn't bring herself to send him away. He slept on the couch in the living room for three days, and during that time, whenever he was in the house, Missy Su would lock herself in her room and refuse to come out. Wandering Zhou, however, acted as though nothing was out of the ordinary. He happily went to the snack shop with Mama Su every morning and every night happily followed her home. During those three days, Missy Su didn't go to the snack shop at all but instead stayed home with her daughter. Wandering Zhou was very tactful: Although he wasn't able to see his daughter during the days and every night when he returned home she was in Missy Su's room, he'd never-theless go to sleep on the couch without saying a word. On the fourth evening, however, Mama Su went into her daughter's room and sat on her bed for about half an hour, softly repeating one thing over and over: "No matter how much he may have done wrong, at the very least your man knew to come back."

Missy Su lay on the bed sobbing. Her mother sighed, picked up the sleeping infant, and walked out of the room. She took the baby to Wan-dering Zhou, who was sleeping soundly on the couch. Zhou immedi-ately sprang up, wanting to take the infant from her, but Mama Su shook her head and pointed toward Missy Su's room. Wandering Zhou saw that her door was ajar, so he kissed his daughter on the forehead and marched into the bedroom. After shutting the door, he walked toward the bed as if he slept in this room every night, then climbed under the covers and turned off the light. Missy Su was lying with her back to him, and he casually leaned over and hugged her. She struggled briefly but then let him. After hugging her, he didn't take the next step but simply said, "I don't intend to go away on any more business trips."

CHAPTER 71

THAT AUTUMN Song Gang continued wandering through Hainan, carrying with him the remaining vials of Boobs cream. Without Wandering Zhou by his side, he didn't know what to do. He didn't have the courage to unbutton his shirt and flaunt his fake breasts and therefore simply stood on street corners with a dull look in his eyes, as silent as a bump on a log, with his vials of bust-enhancing cream arranged neatly in the cardboard box. The people walking by stared at him curiously, seeing that big-breasted man standing there motionless, hour after hour. A few women leaned over and looked at the vials of bust-enhancing cream, then took them out to inspect them more carefully. Noticing Song Gang's huge breasts under his shirt, they would cover their mouths and chortle. Initially too embarrassed to ask about them, the women would look down at the cream in their hands, then up at Song Gang's breasts, struggling to understand the relationship between the two. Finally, lifting the bust-enhancing cream, they would point first at the cream, then at his breasts, and ask Song Gang, "Did you use this to make those so big?"

Song Gang would blush and, out of habit, look around for Wandering Zhou, only to find himself surrounded by strange faces. Now he had to answer the questions Zhou would normally have answered on his behalf. He nodded uneasily and, lowering his head in shame, would say softly, "Uh-huh."

His shame moved many of the women and made them think that this man looked honest and reliable. Therefore, even without Wandering Zhou's clever talk and ingratiating manner, Song Gang continued to sell vial after vial of the cream. The male passersby were not as tactful as the women, and when they saw Song Gang's breasts, they would respond as if they were drugged, their eyes glued to Song Gang's chest as if they were staring through a microscope.

Song Gang didn't know, as he wandered through Hainan, that the silicone implants had begun to harden. He just knew that the breasts were beginning to feel as hard as stones. At the same time, his lung disease staged a comeback. Before he quit taking his medicine, he had stopped coughing, but now, exhausted from traveling continuously, he often felt that he was suffocating and would wake up coughing in the middle of the night. Song Gang was worried not so much about his body as about the future. He saw the box of bust-enhancing cream become emptier and emptier, until finally there were only five vials left. He was disconsolate, because he didn't know what he would sell after the Boobs cream was gone. Without Zhou, Song Gang was adrift, like a leaf fluttering aimlessly after leaving the tree. It was then that he came to understand what solitude was, the only thing keeping him company being the photograph of himself and Lin Hong. He carried it with him wherever he went, but he couldn't bring himself to actually look at it. He wanted desperately to go home but hadn't yet earned enough money to provide for Lin Hong for the rest of her life. Therefore, he had no choice but to continue wandering aimlessly, like a solitary leaf.

Song Gang was standing in the marketplace of some small town, trying to sell the final five vials of bust-enhancing cream. A fifty-year-old man was shouting himself hoarse hawking cutlery. This man had more than ten kinds of knives spread out on the ground, including kitchen knives, cleavers, fruit knives and paring knives, as well as bayonets, throwing knives, and daggers. Holding a cleaver in his hand, he cried out, "This is forged from tungsten steel and can cut through carbon steel, cold-pressed steel, stainless steel, cast steel, and titanium alloy. Every cleaver here is guaranteed to draw blood without a single nick in the blade."

As he spoke the man knelt down and demonstrated, with one blow slicing through a thick metal wire. After he stood up, he lifted the cleaver and walked around, asking the onlookers to inspect the blade to see if it had gotten chipped. After all the onlookers confirmed that it was not chipped, he squatted down again, rolled up his pants, and then began using the blade to shave off his leg hair as though he were shaving his beard. He then stood up with a fistful of leg hair in his hand and walked around, letting the onlookers get a good look.

"Do you see?" he cried out. "This is a legendary precious blade, which can slice through steel as through clay and shaves hair as if with a mere breath." Then he explained, "What is tungsten steel? It is the world's hardest and most precious metal and is used not only for blades but also for expensive watches. Tungsten-steel watches are even more valuable than gold ones. The two Swiss 'Ni brands and the Chinese Yibo brand are all tungsten-steel watches."

"What do you mean by the two Swiss 'Ni brands and the Chinese Yibo brand?" the onlookers asked in confusion.

"The two Swiss 'Ni brands are Genie and Rossini, both of which are known around the world." He added, "Yibo watches are China's own famous brand."

That afternoon Song Gang sold three vials of Boobs cream. He stood at a distant point in the market and couldn't see the knife seller's face, though he heard his hoarse shouts for three hours straight. Song Gang estimated that, at most, the man had sold five or six knives before placing his unsold merchandise into a canvas bag and walking toward Song Gang, his knives rattling over his shoulder. As he was passing Song Gang the enormous pair of breasts caught his attention. He peered down, glanced up at Song Gang, then with a look of utter astonishment said, "You are obviously a man. . . ."

Song Gang was already used to this sort of remark, so he merely smiled and looked at the man, then looked away. He suddenly felt that this man looked very familiar, but when he turned back, the man laughed and walked away. After he'd walked about ten yards, the knife seller stopped, turned around, and looked at Song Gang more carefully, then tentatively asked, "Song Gang?"

Song Gang then asked in surprise, "Are you Little Scissors Guan?"

In this way, two Liu Town sojourners met up in a distant province. Little Guan walked up to Song Gang and looked him over as though he were inspecting a knife blade. He looked at Song Gang's face, then at his fake breasts. He seemed to want to say something but then stopped himself and instead looked up at Song Gang's face and said, "Song Gang, you have aged."

"You have also aged," Song Gang said.

"It's been more than ten years." Little Guan laughed bitterly. "I haven't seen anyone from Liu Town for more than ten years. I never expected that I would run into you here. How long have you been away?"

"Over a year," Song Gang said sadly.

"Why did you leave?" Little Guan shook his head. "What did you come to do?"

"I sell health products," Song Gang stammered.

Little Guan reached for the last two vials of Boobs cream and looked at them, then couldn't help but look at Song Gang's breasts. Song Gang blushed and said softly, "These are fake."

Little Guan nodded. He pulled Song Gang's arm, inviting him to come sit for a while at the place where he was staying. Song Gang put the remaining two vials of Boobs cream into his pocket, then walked a long way with Little Guan. By dusk they had arrived at an area full of itinerant workers on the edge of the city. Little Guan led Song Gang along a muddy road lined with decrepit shacks. The shacks all had clothes hanging out in front, with women cooking on coal stoves in the doorways and men standing around smoking, chatting lazily with one another. Children were running around crazily, each dirty from head to toe. Little Guan told Song Gang that he would generally stay in a place for about a month before moving on, because if he stayed any longer, it became difficult to continue selling his cutlery. He explained that he was now about to move again. Little Guan brought Song Gang to a dilapidated shack, where a dark-skinned woman in her forties was standing in the doorway hanging up clothes. Little Guan called out to her, "We're leaving tomorrow, so why are you washing clothes?"

The woman turned around and replied tartly, "It's precisely because we are leaving tomorrow that I need to wash clothes today."

Little Guan replied angrily, "We're taking the bus early tomorrow morning. What will we do if the clothes aren't dry yet?"

The woman replied confidently, "Then you can go first and I'll wait behind for the clothes."

"Fuck," Little Guan said, "I must have been blind when I married you."

"I was blind to have married you," she replied.

Little Guan angrily turned to Song Gang and explained, "This is my wife."

Song Gang nodded and smiled at the woman, and she looked quizzically at Song Gang's enormous breasts. Little Guan pointed to Song Gang and said, "This is Song Gang, from my hometown."

Little Guan noticed his wife staring at Song Gang's breasts and said unhappily, "What are you looking at? These are fake, he needed them for business."

Little Guan's wife nodded, then smiled at Song Gang. Little Guan led Song Gang into a hundred-square-foot room containing a bed, a cabinet, a table, and four chairs. Little Guan took out the knives he was carrying and placed them in a corner, then invited Song Gang to sit down. He then sat himself and called out to his wife, "Quick, fix us some food."

The woman yelled back, "Can't you see that I'm hanging out clothes?"

"Fuck," Little Guan cursed, then continued to call out, "Song Gang and I haven't seen each other for more than ten years. Quick, go buy us a bottle of *baijiu* liquor, a chicken, and a fish."

"*Quick, go!*" the woman snorted. "Are you going to come hang out the clothes?"

Little Guan pounded the table with his fist. Noticing Song Gang's uneasy expression, he shook his head, saying, "Miserable wench."

After the woman finished hanging the clothes, she took her apron from the window ledge, then turned to Little Guan and cursed, "You're the miserable wench."

"Fuck." Little Guan watched his wife walk away, then turned and said to Song Gang, "Don't mind her."

Then he urgently asked Song Gang after many of their mutual acquaintances from Liu Town, including Baldy Li, Yanker Yu, Popsicle Wang, Blacksmith Tong, Tailor Zhang, and Mama Su. Song Gang slowly told Little Guan about each of them, inserting bits of his own story. As Song Gang was speaking Little Guan's wife came back with the liquor and fish and placed them on the table. Then she put on her apron and began cooking on the coal stove just outside the door. Little Guan opened the bottle but noticed that they didn't have any glasses, so he shouted, "What about glasses? Quick, bring us some fucking glasses."

"Don't you have hands?" Little Guan's wife hollered from outside. "Get them yourself."

"Fuck that."

Little Guan cursed as he stood up and went to find two shot glasses for the *baijiu*. He drank a swallow and wiped his mouth, then noticed that Song Gang hadn't picked up his glass. Little Guan said, "Drink."

Song Gang shook his head and said, "I can't drink."

"Drink!" Little Guan ordered.

As he was saying this he lifted his own cup and waited for Song Gang. Therefore, Song Gang had no choice but to pick up his glass and toast Little Guan, then take a little sip. As the strong *baijiu* went down his throat Song Gang started to cough. This was the first time he had ever drunk *baijiu*. Little Guan ended up downing seven shots, and Song Gang three. As the two drank and chatted, their conversation gushed forth like a river. When Little Guan heard about Baldy Li's vast fortune, how Yanker Yu and Popsicle Wang had gotten rich along with him, how Blacksmith Tong had gotten rich independently, and how Tailor Zhang and Mama Su were also getting along increasingly well, Little Guan, who had endured countless hardships, did not have any complaints or envy but calmly nodded and smiled. Then Song Gang carefully brought up Old Scissors Guan, saying he hadn't seen him for a long time, but he had heard that the old man was sick and bedridden. When Little Guan heard this, his eyes filled with tears. He recalled how, when he had excitedly left Liu Town, his father had followed behind him with his cane, hollering. Little Guan wiped away his tears and said, "Let's not speak of that. I'm too ashamed to go back and face him."

Song Gang described how he had lost his job, looked everywhere for work, ruined his lungs, and subsequently left Liu Town with a certain Wandering Zhou to seek his fortune. Now, however, Zhou had returned to Liu Town but Song Gang was still wandering aimlessly through distant provinces while Lin Hong waited in Liu Town for him to return. Profoundly moved by Song Gang's account, Little Guan sighed repeatedly and muttered to himself, "I know how hard it can be to leave home. I myself have been away for more than ten years, and if I had known that it would be like this, I certainly would never have left."

Song Gang lowered his head and also muttered to himself, "If I had known it would be like this, I would never have left either."

"This is fate," said Little Guan. "Neither of us was fated to have wealth." He looked at Song Gang sympathetically. "My father would often say: If you are fated to have only fifteen ounces of rice in this life, then even if you go away to seek your fortune, you still won't end up with a full pound."

Song Gang drank a sip of *baijiu* and coughed fiercely. Little Guan took a big gulp of the liquor and waited for Song Gang's coughing fit to subside. He then urged Song Gang, "You should go home. Lin Hong is back in Liu Town waiting for you."

Little Guan told Song Gang that during the first two years he spent wandering abroad, not a day went by that he didn't yearn to return home, but he lacked the courage. Four or five years later, he found that it had become impossible for him to do so. He said, "You've only been away for a year, so you are still able to go back. After a few years, your very desire to return will die."

As the two sat drinking and recounting their difficulties, Little Guan's wife cooked dinner. She hurriedly wolfed down her share, then began to pack, repeatedly walking in and out of the room but completely uninterested in what the men were saying. After she had neatly arranged all the belongings in a corner, it was well past eleven o'clock. Without saying a word, she lay down in bed, pulled up the covers, and went to sleep. Song Gang then got up and bid Little Guan farewell, noting that it was quite late and he needed to go back to his room at the hotel. Little Guan wouldn't let him leave, saying plaintively, "I haven't seen anyone from Liu Town for more than ten years and have no idea when I'll get another chance."

Song Gang sat back down, and the two continued to exchange accounts of the sufferings they had each endured. After coming to Hainan Island, Little Guan had, like Song Gang, worked the docks. After a year he went on to Canton and Fujian, where he worked as a construction worker for several years. He was traveling with five contractors, but at the end of the year, when it was time to hand out wages, all five disappeared without a trace. It was then that he started his current job selling cutlery. Little Guan smiled bitterly, noting that back in Liu Town he had sharpened blades for a living and now he sold them— it seemed he was fated to keep coming back to blades. Later they began to laugh happily as they reminisced about their childhoods. Little Guan began to cheer up, then turned and looked at his sleeping wife with a grateful expression. He said that, though he still hadn't found his fortune, at the very least he had had some luck in love, and found himself a good woman. He said, "I would never have found such a good woman back in Liu Town."

Then Little Guan described their wedding. It had taken place thirteen years earlier. Little Guan had first seen his future wife when he was in Fujian selling cutlery. She was squatting by the side of the river, wiping away her tears as she washed her clothes. This sight broke Little Guan's heart, and he stood watching her for a long time without her noticing. He eventually let out a long sigh, but she didn't hear him, engrossed in her own sorrow. Finally he turned and walked away.

His years of solitary existence had left Little Guan feeling lonely and desolate, and he couldn't get her sorrowful image out of his mind. After he had walked several *li*, he suddenly turned and headed back to the riverbank. She was still squatting there, wiping away her tears and washing clothes. Little Guan walked down the steps to the riverbank and sat down beside her. The two began to talk, and Little Guan learned that her parents had both passed away and her husband had run off with another woman. She also got to know Little Guan, about his solemn pledge as he left Liu Town and how miserable he had been, encountering obstacles at every turn. They were both far from home and immediately felt as though they had known each other for a long time. Little Guan told her earnestly, "Come with me. I'll take care of you."

By this point she had finished washing her clothes and was about to get up, but when she heard Little Guan say this, she plopped back down again. She stared vacantly at the river for a while before finally gathering up the clothes and proceeding up the steps. Little Guan followed her all the way home and watched as she hung the clothes out on the line. He repeated, "Come away with me."

She stared at him blankly and said the first thing that came to her mind: "My clothes aren't dry yet."

Little Guan nodded and said, "I'll return when your clothes are dry."

He then turned around and left. That night he stayed in that small town in Fujian, and the next morning when he arrived at her front door, she was standing there with a large suitcase, waiting. Little Guan realized that she had agreed to leave with him, so he simply walked up to her and asked, "Are your clothes dry?"

"They are dry," she said, nodding.

"Let's go," Little Guan replied with a wave.

Pulling her suitcase along, she followed Little Guan as they left the province, and at that point she began a different but equally hard life on the road.

By the time Little Guan finished recounting the story of his marriage, the sun had started to come up. His wife woke up and got out of bed and did not appear at all surprised to see the two of them still talking. She simply turned off the lights and left the house. After a while she returned with ten piping-hot steamed buns, and as Little Guan and Song Gang ate breakfast she collected the clothes outside, folded them on the bed, and packed them in the large suitcase. She then took a steamed bun and ate it as she surveyed the room to see if she had forgotten anything. Little Guan ate four buns in one gulp, while Song

Gang ate only one before announcing that he was full. Little Guan's wife then put the remaining four buns back in the bag and carefully placed it in a backpack. Then, hoisting the large backpack on her back, carrying a travel bag in her right hand, and pulling her suitcase with her left, she walked out the door and waited for Little Guan to come out. He emerged carrying his bag of knives and pulling a large suitcase. As he walked by Song Gang, Little Guan patted him on the shoulder and said, "Song Gang, go back! Listen to me and go back to Liu Town, because in a few years you will no longer be able to return."

Song Gang nodded. He patted Little Guan on the shoulder and said, "I know."

Little Guan's wife smiled at Song Gang, and Song Gang smiled back. He stood there watching that adversity-ridden couple walking into the sunrise. After Little Guan's wife put on the big backpack, Song Gang could no longer see her form but could see only the suitcase and travel bag in either hand. As the couple left they were arguing loudly. Little Guan, with his bag of cutlery and pulling his smaller suitcase, was insisting on taking the large travel bag his wife was carrying, but she adamantly refused to give it to him. Then he tried to take the large suitcase she was pulling, but she refused to hand over anything. The two argued furiously, and Little Guan roared at her, "Damn it, I have an empty hand."

"Your hand? Hmmm," she said loudly. "You are rheumatic and arthritic."

"Fuck." Little Guan cursed her again. "I must have been blind when I married you."

"I was the one who was blind to have married you," she cursed right back.

CHAPTER 72

ON HAINAN ISLAND that morning, Song Gang waved goodbye to Little Guan and his wife and then stood, dazed and alone, in the market where he first saw Little Guan, and sold off his final two vials of Boobs cream.

He finally decided to go home. Little Guan's remarks had made him miss Lin Hong terribly, and he was worried that if he waited too long he would become like Little Guan and his very desire to return would fade. He stayed at the little hotel one final night, and the next day he went to the plastic surgery clinic to have his breast implants removed. By this point the implants had become stiff, and the doctor, when he saw this silent patient, assumed that this was why he was having them removed. The doctor therefore asked if he had had his breasts massaged regularly, but Song Gang just shook his head. The doctor left it at that and concluded that the implants had hardened because Song Gang hadn't received his massages. After the operation, the doctor told him to return in six days to have the stitches removed, then warmly recommended his own hospital, telling Song Gang that if he ever wanted to have a sex-change operation, this hospital should be his first choice. Song Gang nodded as he took the anti-inflammatory medicine and left the clinic.

That afternoon he took a bus to the seaport. As the bus was driving up the coast, he again saw the gulls soaring between the sun and the waves. This time, however, his ears were so full of the noise of the bus engine that he couldn't hear the gulls' cries. When he boarded the ferry to cross over to Canton, he was finally able to make out the gulls' cries in the sound of the waves. At that point he was standing on deck, watching the gulls chase the boat's eddies as though they too were eddies. As the sun set below the horizon, the gulls all soared away together, rising up like a cloud of smoke and gradually disappearing into the horizon.

As Song Gang rode the train from Canton to Shanghai, the gulls had disappeared. He once again put on a face mask, feeling that his lungs were getting progressively worse. Each time he coughed, he felt shooting pains in the wounds under his armpits. He would often take out the sweet photograph of himself and Lin Hong when they were young. At that point, even the Eternity bicycle was still young. Song Gang hadn't looked at the photograph in more than half a year, having been afraid that, upon seeing it, he would feel heartbroken for days on end, or that he would want to drop what he was doing and rush back to our Liu Town. Now, however, he had no misgivings. He looked repeatedly at the picture of Lin Hong, occasionally also glancing at his own young, smiling face, but his thoughts were still soaring with the shadows of the gulls.

As the autumn wind blew up the leaves Song Gang walked out of Liu Town's bus depot, pulling his suitcase. This mask-wearing man returned in the evening. Treading on the fallen leaves, he walked home with a swishing sound accompanying every step. The sound of his breath behind the face mask also made a swishing sound every time he inhaled. Excited at the thought of finally seeing Lin Hong again, he began coughing fiercely. This time, however, the wound under his armpits did not hurt. He quickly walked down the main street of Liu, and the neon lights and raucous music faded away like mist. When he finally glimpsed his house from far away, his eyes grew moist. He removed his glasses as he proceeded forward, pulling his suitcase with one hand and wiping the lenses of his glasses with the other.

Song Gang walked up to his front door. While still on the bus, he had taken out his key and held it in his hand, and now it was in the hand with which he was pulling his suitcase. As he put the suitcase down and inserted the sweaty key into the keyhole he hesitated a moment and then decided to knock instead. He knocked three times, and three more times, then stood there eagerly waiting for Lin Hong to open the door. But inside there was no hint of movement, and finally Song Gang had no choice but to use his key. As he opened the door and went in he called out with a trembling voice, "Lin Hong."

Hearing no response, he put down his suitcase and walked into the bedroom, then into the bathroom, but both were empty. He stood for a while in the living room at a complete loss, and then it occurred to him that Lin Hong might still be on her way home from the factory. He went to stand in the doorway, looking down the road, bathed in the light of the setting sun. As people and cars bustled back and forth Song Gang stood excitedly in the doorway until the light had completely died away, but still there was no sign of Lin Hong. Instead, a few passersby stopped when they saw Song Gang and remarked in surprise, "Song Gang? You've returned?"

Song Gang nodded blankly. Even as he saw these familiar faces his thoughts remained absorbed with Lin Hong, to the point that he couldn't remember these people's names. After he had stood in front of his house for more than an hour, he happened to glance at the snack shop across the street and noted in surprise that the neon sign above the store had changed. It no longer read SU FAMILY SNACK SHOP but, rather, had been changed to WANDERLESS ZHOU'S SNACK SHOP. Then Song Gang saw Wandering Zhou's bobbing face in the window. Song Gang crossed the street and entered the shop.

He saw Missy Su sitting behind the cashier's counter and Wandering Zhou chattering with several customers as they ate. Song Gang nodded to Missy Su and smiled. When she saw him with his face mask, she stared in alarm, at first not knowing how to respond. Song Gang then turned to the charlatan and called out, "Wandering Zhou."

Like Missy Su, Zhou also stared in alarm when he saw Song Gang, until he finally recognized who he was. Wandering Zhou warmly called out to him, "Song Gang, it's you. You've returned?"

As Wandering Zhou walked up to Song Gang he suddenly remembered something and corrected him, "I've changed my name to Wanderless Zhou."

Song Gang remembered the neon sign outside the snack shop and smiled behind his face mask. He noticed a little girl sitting in a high chair and asked Wandering Zhou—or, rather, Wanderless Zhou—"Is this Su Zhou?"

Wanderless Zhou gestured vigorously and again corrected him, "The other way around—Zhou Su."

Missy Su walked over and, seeing Song Gang coughing, asked solicitously, "Song Gang, did you just return? Have you had dinner yet?"

Wanderless Zhou immediately stepped into his role as restaurant proprietor and instructed a waitress, "Bring us a menu."

The waitress brought the menu, and Zhou signaled for her to hand it to Song Gang, saying, "Song Gang, please eat as much as you like. It's on the house."

Song Gang coughed as he gestured, saying, "I won't eat here. I'm waiting for Lin Hong to come home and eat with me."

"Lin Hong?" When Wanderless Zhou heard this, he jumped with

surprise. "Don't bother waiting. She's gone off to Shanghai with Baldy Li."

Missy Su anxiously warned him, "Watch what you say."

"Who should watch what they say?" Zhou countered. "Everyone has seen it with their own eyes."

Seeing Missy Su signaling furiously at him, he didn't continue but, rather, looked with concern at Song Gang's chest and smiled mysteriously. "You had them removed?"

Song Gang nodded, bewildered by Wanderless Zhou's earlier comment. Zhou pulled Song Gang into a seat, then crossed his legs and proudly said, "After leaving the health-products business to you, I turned my attention to the restaurant business. Soon I will open two more Wanderless Zhou Snack Shops in Liu Town, and within three years I plan to open a chain of one hundred stores throughout the country—"

Missy Su interrupted him, saying, "But the two Liu Town stores haven't even opened yet."

Wanderless Zhou glanced at her with annoyance but didn't respond and instead said to Song Gang, "Do you know who my primary rival is? It's not Baldy Li—he's too small. My primary rival is McDonald's. I want my Wanderless Zhou restaurants to dominate McDonald's throughout the land and in the process make McDonald's stock drop by fifty percent."

Missy Su said unhappily, "I get embarrassed just listening."

Zhou again glanced at her, then, after looking down at his watch, he stood up anxiously and said, "Song Gang, let's continue this some other time. I'm going home to watch my Korean soaps."

After Wanderless Zhou left, Song Gang also walked out of the snack shop to return to his empty house. There he turned on all the lights, took off his face mask, stood for a while in the bedroom, then proceeded to the kitchen, where he also stood for a while. Next he stood for a while in the bathroom, then returned to the living room, where he started to cough fiercely. His wounds began to throb, as if his sutures had torn. Song Gang was in such agony that tears streamed down his face. He doubled up in pain, then sat down in a chair, gripping his chest with both hands as he waited for the coughing fit to subside. After the pain had diminished, he lifted his head and discovered that everything was blurred. He blinked several times, but his vision remained blurry, and he had no idea why. After a while he realized that his glasses were completely smeared with tears, so he took them off and wiped them with his shirt, then put them back on and found he could see clearly again.

Song Gang put the face mask back on, stood up, and returned to the front of the house. He was still fantasizing that Lin Hong would suddenly walk up. He looked at the crowds in the street, which appeared distorted and grotesque by the light of the streetlamps and neon signs. At this point Poet Zhao appeared. He walked right up to Song Gang and inspected his face mask, then took a step back and called out, "Song Gang."

As Poet Zhao had emerged from the crowd and walked up Song Gang had belatedly recognized him and replied quietly. Poet Zhao laughed and said, "I didn't even need to see your face. I recognized you from your face mask."

Song Gang nodded, coughed a few times, and gripped his chest wounds in anguish. Poet Zhao looked at him sympathetically and asked, "Are you waiting for Lin Hong?"

Song Gang nodded and then shook his head, once again looking confusedly toward the crowd. Poet Zhao softly patted his shoulder and consoled him. "You needn't wait for her. She ran off with Baldy Li."

Song Gang's entire body shuddered, and he gazed at Poet Zhao with a look of terror. Zhao laughed mysteriously, then patted him again on the shoulder, saying, "You would have found out sooner or later."

Still smiling mysteriously, Poet Zhao walked up the steps and returned to his own apartment. Song Gang remained in the doorway, his emotions in tumult. He couldn't see anything clearly and continued coughing nonstop behind his face mask, though now he no longer felt any pain from his wounds. He stood woodenly by the side of the road until the crowds began to diminish and the neon lights were gradually turned off. As everything quieted down he finally turned around and stumbled like an old man back into his house—his house without Lin Hong.

Song Gang endured an excruciating night. Lying alone on the bed he formerly shared with Lin Hong, he felt frigid underneath the covers, and the covers themselves also felt frigid. Even the room felt frigid. Although his thoughts were in a tumult, Wanderless Zhou's and Poet Zhao's comments made Song Gang feel that something momentous had taken place. He realized that that "something" had to do with his brother whom he trusted with his life, and Song Gang's wife, who had pledged to love him till death did them part. At this point, however, he lacked the courage to pursue this line of thought any further. Terrified, he tossed and turned all night, unable to fall asleep.

The next morning Song Gang, again wearing his face mask, walked with an empty heart through the streets of Liu, having no idea where to go. His feet, however, knew, and they led him straight to the entrance-way of Baldy Li's company headquarters, but after they stopped, he didn't have any idea what to do next. At that point he saw Popsicle Wang rush excitedly out of the reception room and call out warmly, "Song Gang, Song Gang. You've returned."

After Popsicle Wang became one of Liu Town's tycoons, he spent every day wandering the streets like a vagabond. After several years, however, he grew tired of wandering and began going to the office every day, like a vice president. While everyone else rushed around busily, he sat there idly with nothing to do. After another year, he grew fed up with sitting in the office and therefore volunteered to work as the building's doorman. This way, at least, he would be able to speak to people as they came and went.

Given that Popsicle Wang was the company's third-biggest share-holder, Deputy Liu didn't dare complain. Therefore, Liu ordered that the former security guard shack be torn down and a newer, much more dignified "reception room" be built in its place, complete with a large living room, a large bedroom, a large kitchen, and a large bathroom for Wang, all built in accordance with the standards of a five-star hotel. In summer it had central air, and in winter it used geothermal heat. It had a sofa imported from Italy, a bed imported from Germany, a cabinet imported from France, as well as an executive desk and chair set. After Wang moved into his five-star-hotel doorman's room, he was as happy as a clam, and from that point on he never again returned home. Every time they saw each other, he would praise Deputy Liu to the skies, and Liu would be elated.

Popsicle Wang was most satisfied with his hi-tech TOTO toilet, because after you used it to take a shit, you didn't even have to wipe your ass; instead, a spurt of water would immediately rinse it clean, and a jet of air would blow it dry for you. Deputy Liu even installed five satellite dishes on the roof and told Popsicle Wang that with them, he would be able to watch all the television channels of the countries richer than China, all the channels of the countries as wealthy as China, and even some of the channels of the countries poorer than

China. Therefore, all day long Wang's reception area echoed with all sorts of accents and languages, as if he were hosting a meeting of the United Nations.

At that point, Popsicle Wang's most intimate comrade in arms, Yanker Yu, decided to upgrade the quality of his world travels. He now felt that both following a tour group and traveling on his own had gotten old. Therefore, each time he arrived at a new location, he would hire a female interpreter. He was bored with traveling to scenic points; his interests now lay entirely with demonstrations and mass rallies. He participated in rallies in more than a dozen European and American cities. He didn't differentiate based on politics—as long as something was a demonstration or a rally, he would excitedly rush over to participate. If he found two demonstrations taking place at the same time, he would join the larger one. Yanker Yu learned marching slogans in more than ten different languages, and he would often call Popsicle Wang and randomly shout out these foreign slogans while speaking to him.

When Popsicle Wang heard of these rallies and demonstrations, he assumed Yanker Yu was participating in Great Cultural Revolutions in other parts of the world, and every time Yu would call and tell Wang that he was joining a protest march in some foreign city, Wang would immediately call Deputy Liu and tell him which city was currently staging a Great Cultural Revolution.

Yanker Yu was very displeased with Popsicle Wang's explanation, and he upbraided him long-distance, saying, "You country bumpkin, you just don't understand. This is politics."

Yanker Yu explained why he had become so passionate about politics: "This can be explained by the principle that comfortable circumstances breed freethinking, which is why the rich love politics."

Popsicle Wang at first wasn't at all convinced, but one day he happened to glimpse Yanker Yu on a foreign television channel. The left side of his face appeared briefly as he marched. Wang stared in amazement, and from that point on he became extremely respectful of Yu. When Yanker Yu called him up, Popsicle Wang told him he had seen him on television but was so excited he started to stutter. On the other end of the line, Yanker Yu also began to stutter with excitement, and they both shrieked and cawed like exotic birds. Then Yu immediately asked Wang whether he had recorded the segment. Popsicle Wang replied that he hadn't, and Yanker Yu began to blow a gasket right there on the phone, calling Popsicle Wang a son of a gun, son of a bitch, son of a dirty rotten stinking scoundrel. Then he complained sadly that his dearest friend had failed to record his moment of celebrity. Popsicle Wang felt terrible and repeatedly promised Yanker Yu that the next time he would be sure to record any scene in which Yu happened to appear. From that point on, Popsicle Wang's television channels tracked Yanker Yu's every step. Every time Yu arrived in a new country, Wang would lock on to that country's television channels, then conscientiously search for images of protest marches. When he found one, he would stare at the television like a cat watching a mouse, remote control in his hand, on the off chance that Yanker Yu might appear.

When Popsicle Wang saw Song Gang standing outside the building, Yanker Yu happened to be flying from Madrid to Toronto, and therefore Wang had a temporary reprieve from watching the television. Seeing Song Gang reappear after such a long absence, he rushed over and dragged him inside. Wang asked him to sit down on the Italian couch and then started relating various fantastic stories about Yanker Yu. Finally he sighed and said, "How did Yanker Yu become so courageous? He doesn't know a single word of any foreign language, and yet there is nowhere he doesn't dare to go."

Song Gang hadn't heard a word Popsicle Wang had said. In agony, his chest throbbing, and sunk in confusion, he simply peered over his face mask at Wang. When Song Gang realized that Baldy Li wasn't there and that Lin Hong wasn't there either, he no longer knew what he himself was doing there. He sat for half an hour without saying a word. Then, still without saying a word, he stood up and walked out of Popsicle Wang's extravagant reception area. Wang followed him out, rattling on nonstop. When he reached the entranceway, however, Popsicle Wang stood still. He was still talking, but Song Gang didn't hear a word. Song Gang stared vacantly at the streets of Liu and, with a heavy heart, returned home.

CHAPTER 73

AFTER SONG GANG returned to our Liu Town, he went six days without receiving any news of his wife. During those six days, he cooked six meals, but each day he ate only a single bowl of rice. He kept his door shut and went out only to buy vegetables. He encountered many people he knew, and their brief remarks gave him the vague understanding that something had transpired between Baldy Li and Lin Hong. He looked apathetic and listless. On the evening of the seventh day, Song Gang took out the family photo album and looked at each of the portraits of himself and Lin Hong; then sighed and closed the album. He found the photograph of himself; his father, Song Fanping; his mother, Li Lan; and his brother, Baldy Li. This black-and-white photograph was already turning yellow with age. Song Gang again sighed, put it into the photo album as well, and lay back in his bed with tears streaming down his face.

After mucking about for seven days, Song Gang finally recovered his senses. All the memories of his history with Baldy Lin and Lin Hong came rushing back to him, twenty years passing in the blink of an eye. Now he understood that Lin Hong should never have married him but rather should have married Baldy Li. When he saw things this way, Song Gang suddenly felt relieved, as if a heavy weight had been lifted from his heart.

At sunrise on the eighth morning, Song Gang sat at the dining table and started earnestly writing two letters, one to Lin Hong and the other to Baldy Li. Though he wrote painstakingly, there were a lot of sentences he wasn't sure he had written correctly and a lot of characters he wasn't sure how to write. He remembered how, when he was twenty, he had been so fond of reading and of literature. He recalled how he had written a story and how Baldy Li had praised it highly. During the intervening years, however, life had borne down on him mercilessly, to the point that he could barely breathe. He had stopped reading books and newspapers, with the result that now he realized he couldn't even write a simple letter.

Song Gang therefore made a mental note of the characters he didn't know how to write, then wore his face mask to the bookstore, where he looked them up in a dictionary. Then he returned home and continued writing his letters. He couldn't bring himself to buy a dictionary, though he had brought thirty thousand yuan back for Lin Hong. He felt that the entire time they had been together, he had never been able to provide for her, and therefore he was determined to leave her this money he had finally earned. Over the next several days, he went to and from the bookstore more than ten times, and every time the clerks saw him they would laugh, remarking to each other that Song Gang used to be Chief Sub but now had become the town's chief scholar. One day the clerks couldn't help calling him first Chief Scholar, then Chief Dictionary. When Song Gang heard this, he laughed but didn't respond; instead he simply lowered his head and diligently looked up the characters he didn't know. Chief Dictionary Song Gang spent five days writing his letters, alternating between composing, looking up characters in the dictionary, and correcting his writing. When he finally finished the two letters, he carefully copied them over, then stood up as if relieved of a heavy burden and went to the post office to buy two envelopes and two stamps. After addressing the envelopes and putting on the stamps, he hid both letters in his breast pocket.

The pain in Song Gang's chest had become increasingly severe. Confused by the binding pain, he slowly opened his shirt and found that it had become stuck to the open wounds under his armpits. As he removed the shirt he felt as though he was ripping away his flesh. The searing pain made his entire body shudder. He waited for it to subside, then lifted his arms and saw that his wounds had become swollen and infected, with the black stitches now stretched tight over them. He remembered that he was supposed to have removed the stitches six days after the operation but now thirteen days had passed. The pain had become virtually unbearable.

Song Gang got up and went to look for a pair of scissors and then, with a mirror, prepared to take out his own stitches. Worried that the scissors weren't clean, he lit a flame and placed them over it for five minutes to sterilize them. He patiently waited another ten minutes for the scissors to cool off, then finally began to carefully clip away until the scissors were covered with bits of black thread. He felt the throbbing pain in his chest gradually subside, as though his entire body had been released from immense tension.

That evening Song Gang used an old newspaper to wrap up the money he had brought home and placed the bundle under his pillow, leaving aside only ten yuan for himself. He took his key out and inspected it carefully, then lay it on the table, put on his face mask, and walked to the front door. When he opened it, he turned and looked back at his home and at the key on the table: Everything in his house seemed to be in sharp focus, but the key was a blur in his vision. He carefully closed the door, then stood there for a while. It occurred to him that the key was inside, that he would never be coming back.

Song Gang turned and walked down the street, proceeding on into Wanderless Zhou's Snack Shop. He had never eaten straw-embedded buns, and now he wanted to try some. When he went in, he didn't see Zhou or Missy Su. He looked around and noticed that Mama Su wasn't there either. As it turned out, Zhou had succeeded in converting both of them into fans of Korean soaps, and therefore every weekday at this time the three of them would sit at home, staring intently at the television screen. Song Gang hesitated in the doorway for a moment. Seeing a strange waitress sitting at the cashier's counter, he approached her and, after pondering for a moment, mumbled vaguely, "How do you eat . . ."

The cashier had no idea what he was talking about "How do you eat what?"

Song Gang realized he had misspoken but couldn't think of the proper way to phrase the question. He pointed to some customers eating the straw-embedded buns and said, "These straw-embedded buns. . . ."

The customers laughed out loud, and one of them asked him, "Did you suckle at your mother's breast as a child?"

Song Gang felt that this person was making fun of him, and therefore he replied smartly, "We all did."

"Did you eat buns after you grew up?"

"We all did."

"Good," that person said. "I'll teach you. First, you suck it like you did your mother's breast, sucking out the juice, then you eat the remaining bun the way you would eat any bun."

All the customers laughed uncontrollably, and even the waitress at the cashier's counter couldn't help laughing. Song Gang, however, didn't laugh. The customer's response allowed him to regain some clarity of mind, so he turned back to the waitress and said, "I was asking how much they cost?"

Understanding him now, the waitress took Song Gang's money and gave him a receipt. Song Gang then took his receipt and continued standing in front of the counter. The waitress suggested that he sit down, because it would be ten minutes before the buns were ready. Song Gang eyed the laughing customers, then sat at a table as far from them as possible. With an expressionless gaze, he sat there patiently like a student, waiting for his straw-embedded buns.

Song Gang's buns were finally brought out and, faced with this wave of hot steam, Song Gang slowly lowered his face mask, put the straw in his mouth, and immediately sucked out the meat sauce. Those customers who had been making fun of him jumped in surprise, because the sauce was at least 175 degrees Fahrenheit. Song Gang, however, sipped it up as though he were sipping cold water. After finishing one bun, he proceeded to another. In all, he sipped the sauce out of three buns, then looked up at the astonished customers and smiled. His smile sent shivers down their spines, making them suspect that he was somewhat deranged. He then lowered his head again and placed one of the buns in his mouth. After he had eaten the three buns, Song Gang put his face mask back on, stood up, and walked out of the snack shop.

By this point it was evening, and Song Gang set off toward the setting sun. He didn't walk down the street with his head bowed, as he used to. Instead, he walked with his head up and looked back and forth at the stores and the pedestrians on either side of the street. When people called out his name, he no longer mumbled in reply but, rather, waved at them amicably. When he walked past a shop window, he stopped to look at the products on display inside. Many of the townspeople of Liu saw Song Gang stroll by that evening. Later they recalled how, in the past, every time he appeared he was always hurrying to get somewhere; this was the only evening they had seen him just strolling. They said he stopped to look in every shop window, turned to greet every person he passed, even displayed considerable interest in the wutong trees on either side of the street. He stood outside a music store for five or six minutes listening to two pop songs, turning to someone walking by and saying, "These two songs sound really good."

When he passed the post office, he took Lin Hong's and Baldy Li's letters from his breast pocket and, after putting them in the mailbox, squatted down and peered inside to make sure that they had gone all the way in. Then he continued walking in the direction of the setting sun.

Song Gang walked out of Liu Town to where the railroad tracks were. He sat down on a rock next to the tracks, took off his face mask, and contentedly inhaled the evening air. He looked around at the fields full of grain waiting to be harvested. There was a stream not far from him, and the setting sun tinted the water crimson. That made him look up, and he felt that the evening sky was even more beautiful than the earth. The sun glowed crimson, and the clouds shimmered brightly, with layer upon layer of colors pouring in like the tide. As the multi-hued rays shuttled unpredictably through the sky he felt as if he had seen the light. Then he lowered his gaze and once again looked at the fields of grain stretching in every direction, reflecting the evening light like fields full of red roses, he felt as if he were sitting in the middle of a million blooming flowers.

Hearing the sound of a train whistle approaching, he took off his glasses, wiped them, and put them back on. He saw that the sun had sunk halfway below the horizon and that a train was approaching from the same direction as the setting sun. He stood up and told himself it was time to bid farewell to the world of the living. He couldn't bear to part with his glasses but was afraid that the train would crush them. Therefore, he took them off and placed them on the stone where he had been sitting, and again felt everything become blurred. He removed his jacket, folded it, and lay it on the same stone, placing his glasses on top. Then he took a deep breath and put his face mask back on. He forgot that dead people couldn't breathe, and was afraid that his lung illness would be transmitted to the mortician. He walked forward four paces, then lay facedown on the tracks with both arms extended. His chest pressing against the tracks was excruciatingly painful, so he crawled forward until his abdomen was resting on the tracks and immediately felt much more comfortable. The approaching train made the tracks under him tremble, and as a result his body also started to tremble. He raised his head to look at the distant sky, feeling it was truly beautiful. He then turned his head and looked at the fields of roselike grain in front of him and felt they too were quite beautiful. At this point he noticed with delight a seagull flying overhead. The seagull was crying out, flapping its wings as it flew from far away. As the train rumbled over his back the last thing he saw was the solitary seagull soaring among the million blooming flowers.

CHAPTER 74

BALDY LI and Lin Hong rode into our Liu Town in the white Mercedes just before dusk, driving right into Baldy Li's mansion. Lin Hong had had her hymen surgically reconstructed, and Baldy Li had done a lot of business in Beijing and the northeast. When they got out of the car, it was as if they were making a triumphant return. As soon as they walked into the living room, Baldy Li's phone rang. It was Deputy Liu telling him that dinner was prepared, and that he could come eat whenever he wished. Baldy Li closed his cell phone and said, "That bastard definitely thinks of everything."

Baldy Li and Lin Hong deposited their luggage in the living room, then glided into the dining room. By that point, night had fallen, so Baldy Li turned on the chandelier. He saw that the dinner was laid out and that a bouquet of roses had been placed in the middle of the table. A bottle of French red wine was sitting in a stainless-steel ice bucket. The bottle had been opened and the cork reinserted. Baldy Li and Lin Hong sat down across from each other. Baldy Li was very satisfied with Deputy Liu, telling Lin Hong, "That bastard has arranged everything very romantically."

Lin Hong glanced over at the dinner and the roses and began to giggle, remarking that it was as if they were foreigners sitting down to a meal. Like a foreign gentleman, Baldy Li took the wine out of the ice bucket, and after removing the cork, he poured a little into his glass. Then he put down the bottle, raised his glass, swished it around, sniffed it, and drank a sip. He said approvingly, "This wine is not bad at all."

After he got up, he placed his left hand on his back and used his right hand to elegantly fill Lin Hong's glass. At the sight of the uncouth, foul-mouthed Baldy Li acting with such refinement, Lin Hong couldn't help laughing. This being the first time Lin Hong had seen such elegance, she asked Baldy Li, "Where did you learn this?"

"From TV," Baldy Li replied graciously, then lifted his glass and waited for Lin Hong to lift hers and toast with him. She took a tiny sip of her wine, then put her glass down. Baldy Li, by contrast, immediately downed his entire glass, as if he were engaged in a drinking competition. He was an old dog who couldn't be taught new tricks, and he called out to Lin Hong, "Eat quickly, then go wash up. When you're done, go to the bed and wait for me."

At that moment, Song Gang was sitting in Wanderless Zhou's Snack Shop eating straw-embedded buns for the first time in his life. The piping-hot juice was scalding the inside of his mouth, but he couldn't feel a thing. By the time he walked out of the snack shop and headed toward the railroad tracks to the east of town, Baldy Li had wolfed down his dinner and was urging Lin Hong to finish hers. Thus was life: Someone who was walking toward death might linger over the setting sun's glorious rays, while two others who were hedonistically pursuing pleasure might be completely oblivious to the beauty of the sunset.

The setting sun finally vanished, and a heavy night sky enveloped Liu Town. As Song Gang lay down on the railroad tracks under the faint light of the moon, Lin Hong was sitting on the bed with her pants off, waiting for Baldy Li to emerge from the bathroom. He dawdled for a long time, and just as he turned on the faucet Deputy Liu called again. Liu had figured that Baldy Li would have gone to the restroom and conscientiously told him that in the cabinet there were two new instruments for inspecting hymens. Baldy Li warmly called Deputy Liu a bastard, and after he washed up, he hurriedly dried himself off, then opened the cabinet to see what kind of instruments they were. Surprised to discover miner's implements, Baldy Li stared in astonishment, then once again affectionately called Deputy Liu a bastard.

Lin Hong heard Baldy Li mumbling in the bathroom but didn't know what he was saying. When he finally emerged, she stared at him in astonishment. He had his pants off but was wearing a miner's hat with a lamp. Around his waist he had a leather belt with a battery in back, and a cord ran like a Qing dynasty queue from the hat down to the belt. Noticing Lin Hong staring in astonishment, Baldy Li turned on the lamp on the miner's hat, and a beam of light suddenly shone directly on her crotch. He announced proudly that this time he wanted to appreciate her hymen. Looking like a miner crawling into a cave, Baldy Li chortled as he crawled into bed. Lin Hong finally reacted and let out a huge laugh, never having imagined that Baldy Li would have accoutered himself in this way. She laughed so hard that she couldn't catch her breath and began to cough. Baldy Li was very displeased by her reaction and lifted his head so that his light shone on her chest, then asked, "In what way is this supposed to resemble a virgin?"

Lin Hong was laughing so hard tears came to her eyes, and she said, "You're killing me. I'm going to die laughing. . . ."

Baldy Li angrily sat down next to her, with his searchlight shining on the wall. He waited for her to finish, then exclaimed, "Damn it, you look like a slut. In what way do you resemble a virgin?"

After Lin Hong covered her mouth to smother her last few guffaws, she adopted a serious demeanor and asked Baldy Li, "How should a virgin act?"

Baldy Li instructed her: "The first time you see a naked man, you should cover your face."

Lin Hong laughed under her breath, then covered her face with both hands but still kept her legs spread wide. Baldy Li was not pleased and said, "Only sluts would spread their legs upon seeing a naked man. What kind of virgin would do that?"

Lin Hong locked her legs together and asked, "How's this?"

Baldy Li continued to instruct her: "You should also cover that area with your hands and not let the man see."

Lin Hong replied unhappily, "First you ask me to cover my face with my hands, and then you tell me to cover that area. Does it look to you like I have four hands?"

Baldy Li thought that Lin Hong had a point. He sought her advice, asking, "What were you like when you did it with Song Gang for the first time?"

Lin Hong replied, "It was under the covers, with the light off."

Baldy Li quickly got out of bed and turned off the lights, making the spotlight on his head appear to shine even brighter, so bright that Lin Hong couldn't keep her eyes open. Lin Hong told him to turn the miner's light off, but he refused, saying that if he did, he wouldn't be able to see her hymen. He then asked her, "How did Song Gang look at your hymen?"

Lin Hong replied, "He didn't look. He was too embarrassed."

"That idiot," Baldy Li said. "I want to look. It would be a waste not to."

Baldy Li then crawled between Lin Hong's thighs, wanting to peer at her hymen. She used both hands to cover herself, not letting him see. He struggled to pull her hands away, but she twisted herself to the side. When he managed to straighten her butt, she once again covered

herself with both hands. After several rounds Baldy Li still had not succeeded in seeing anything and complained, "Let me fucking see!"

Lin Hong replied, "But you told me to cover myself with my hands."

"Fuck," Baldy Li said. "It's true that you should cover yourself, but
you should resist and acquiesce at the same time."

"Okay," Lin Hong said. "I'll both resist and acquiesce."

After Baldy Li struggled a couple more times, Lin Hong removed
her hands and squealed as she flailed her limbs, parting her legs
reluctantly. Baldy Li was very pleased and said, "Good! Excellent
performance!"

Baldy Li peered in with the miner's lamp, and Lin Hong again pretended to be embarrassed and covered herself with her hands. Baldy
Li happily called out his approval, "That's great! Really realistic."

At this point Lin Hong became displeased, asking, "In what way do
you resemble a man doing it for the first time? With that ridiculous
lamp, you look like an old whoremonger. Men, when they do it the
first time, should also be somewhat shy. Song Gang, for instance, was
very shy."

Baldy Li decided that Lin Hong had a point, so he turned off the
lamp, unfastened his belt, and threw the entire contraption under the
bed, saying, "Now it's dark. We are now a pair of virgins."

The two hugged in the darkness, and after they caressed each other
for a while, Baldy Li inserted himself. Lin Hong uttered a cry, and this
cry was one of genuine pain. When Baldy Li heard it, he trembled with
excitement. In all the times he and Lin Hong had done it, this was the
first time he had heard her cry out like this. She then started to moan—
a moan of agony, but also of ecstasy. Her entire body was bathed in
sweat, and her ecstasy was gradually catching up with her agony. Her
body had never before experienced this sort of stimulation as she felt
her intense agony propelling her sense of ecstasy, like a rocket propelling the space shuttle. Then her orgasm exploded like a tsunami, the
wave of pleasure that swept over her making her tremble from head to
toe. She cried out hoarsely, "That hurts. . . ."

By that point, Baldy Li felt that he had gone back in time twenty
years. Despite having been on the meat market for so long, he had also
never experienced such intense thrill. Their bodies mutually stimulated each other, and as Lin Hong clasped Baldy Li, Baldy Li clapsed
her back. As Lin Hong's body started to tremble, so did Baldy Li's. As
Lin Hong's orgasm approached, her entire body started to shudder,

and Baldy Li felt that he had his arms around an earthquake. At that point his own orgasm came screaming out.

Afterward, the two lay motionless on the bed, their hearts pounding, Lin Hong breathing feebly and Baldy Li gasping for air. Both had experienced mind-blowing orgasms, which had taken them to unprecedented peaks of pleasure. Now it was as if they were fluttering down from the peak of Mount Everest, surrounded by white snow on all sides. Both of them felt that their bodies were like paper fluttering back down to earth.

CHAPTER 75

THAT EVENING, after Lin Hong experienced her unprecedented orgasm, she closed her eyes and lay in bed utterly exhausted. Then, like a lamb to the slaughter, she allowed Baldy Li to vigorously do it a second, a third, and even a fourth time. In Baldy Li's bed Lin Hong experienced over and over again a feeling of narrowly escaping death. The third time she didn't agree and said exhaustedly that they had made a pact to do it no more than twice a day. Baldy Li boldly said that today he considered himself a male virgin who was tasting the flavor of woman for the first time, like a dog falling into a pile of shit and eating to its heart's content. Therefore, how could a mere two times suffice? Lin Hong had no choice but to lie there numbly and allow him to do it a third time, after which he wanted to do it yet again. She almost cried, but he told her that this would be the last time the two of them would ever make love, because after this, he would return her to Song Gang.

When Deputy Liu called at two in the morning, Baldy Li was in the process of having sex with Lin Hong that fourth time, and she was enduring the agony of doing it with this beastlike man. When Baldy Li's cell phone rang, he continued to thrust as he checked the phone. Noticing that it was Deputy Liu's number, he cursed and didn't answer. After a while the phone rang again, and Baldy Li cursed again but still didn't answer. Then the cell started ringing continuously, and Baldy Li, absolutely furious, flipped it open and screamed, "I'm fucking in the middle of something!" Baldy Li then heard what Deputy Liu was trying to say and cried out like a bomb exploding, "*What?*"

In a state of shock, Baldy Li jumped off the bed, then stood there like an idiot, naked, holding his cell phone, with his mouth hanging open. Every time Deputy Liu said something, Baldy Li would shudder. When Liu finished and hung up the phone, Baldy Li still stood there with the phone to his ear, completely immobile, as if he had lost his mind. After a while he dropped the phone to the floor and was then startled when it started to ring. When he recovered his senses, he began to curse himself tearfully, saying, "I should fucking die. I don't deserve to die well, and if I'm not run over by a car, I should be burned to death. If I'm not burned to death, I should drown in freezing water or be run over by a car. . . . I'm such a bastard. . . ."

Lin Hong was bone tired. She vaguely perceived that Baldy Li was on top of her, then answered a telephone call. Like a spring, this telephone call catapulted Baldy Li right off her. Then there was no sound, after which Baldy Li started shaking his fist and cursing himself as he pounded his head. Lin Hong opened her eyes but couldn't understand what was happening. She nervously sat up and saw that Baldy Li's phone had fallen to the floor while he himself was crying as though his heart were broken, wiping at his tears with both fists like a child. Lin Hong had a vague feeling and asked uneasily, "Did something happen?"

With tears streaming down his face, Baldy Li told her, "Song Gang is dead. That bastard killed himself by lying across the train tracks."

Her mouth hanging open, Lin Hong stared at Baldy Li in terror. Looking as if Baldy Li had just raped her, she leapt off the bed and quickly got dressed. Then she didn't know what to do next. She had a look of absolute bafflement on her face, as though a doctor had informed her that she was terminally ill. After a while, tears began to stream down her face. She bit her lip but couldn't stop the flow of tears. She noticed that Baldy Li was standing there naked and suddenly felt a wave of revulsion sweep over her. She spat at him, "Why don't you die?"

"You whore." Baldy Li finally found an enemy on whom to vent his fury. He thundered, "Song Gang's corpse has been lying at your front door for more than three hours, waiting for you to open the door! But you're out whoring around!"

"If I am a filthy whore," Lin Hong said furiously, "then what does that make you? You are a fucking bastard!"

"If I am a fucking bastard," Baldy Li responded, equally furiously, "then you are a fucking dirty slut!"

"If I am a dirty slut," Lin Hong said with bitter fury, "then you are worse than a beast."

"If I am worse than a beast"—Baldy Li's eyes glinted bright red—"then what the fuck are you? You fucking killed your own husband!"

"If I killed my own husband," Lin Hong screamed, "then you killed your own brother!"

After she said this, Baldy Li again began to cry. Suddenly pathetic, he walked toward Lin Hong with his arms extended, exclaiming sorrowfully, "We both killed Song Gang, and therefore neither of us deserves to die well."

Lin Hong pushed away Baldy Li's hand and shouted with disgust, "Get away from me!"

She walked out of Baldy Li's bedroom and down the stairs. When she arrived in the living room, she noticed that Baldy Li, still bucknaked, was following her. When she opened the front door, a naked Baldy Li followed her out. Lin Hong then stopped and said, "Don't follow me!"

"Who is fucking following you?" the naked Baldy Li asked as he walked up to her. "I'm going to see Song Gang!"

"Stop!" Lin Hong cried. "You have no face to go see Song Gang."

"If I have no face to go see Song Gang," Baldy Li said as he sorrowfully came to a halt and then turned around and thrust a finger in Lin Hong's direction, "you, whore, also have no face to go see him."

"I may not have any face to see him"—Lin Hong nodded somberly, as if agreeing with Baldy Li—"but he is this whore's husband."

Baldy Li cried, "He is my brother."

He cried as he beat his breast and stamped his feet, whereupon he suddenly realized that he was completely naked. He stood there, not knowing what to do. When Lin Hong walked up from behind, he bashfully covered his crotch with his hands. She felt a jolt of pity and said softly, "You should go home."

Baldy Li nodded like an obedient child, and when Lin Hong walked past him she heard him mumbling, "I will receive my retribution, as will you."

Lin Hong nodded and, wiping her tears from her eyes, said, "I will certainly receive my retribution."

That night the autumn wind blew and the moon shone brightly. Someone walking along the railroad tracks collecting stray pieces of coal discovered Song Gang's body, and he told two people living near the tracks. The body didn't have a single bloodstain on it. The train had ridden over Song Gang's waist, and while his body was sliced clean in half, his clothing hadn't even been torn. At eleven o'clock that night, the two people living near the tracks transported Song Gang in a pullcart to the front door of his house. Former workmates of his from the docks, they recognized Song Gang under the face mask and saw his clothes and glasses lying on the stone. After discussing the situation, they found a pullcart and put Song Gang in it, then placed his glasses in his jacket pocket and draped the jacket over his body. Song Gang was very tall, so as his body lay in the cart his head stuck out and his feet dragged on the ground. Therefore, one of the workers walked in front pulling the cart while the other walked behind, holding up Song Gang's legs. In this way they walked through the deathly quiet streets of Liu Town. The autumn leaves rustled beneath the wheels, and occasionally a few passersby would stop and watch them curiously. Neither of the two workmates said anything as they walked, hunched over, returning Song Gang to his door.

After they put the cart down, they pulled Song Gang's body a little so that his head was no longer hanging over the side, and folded up his legs so that his feet rested on the ground. Then they gently knocked on the door, called out softly, and waited silently for more than half an hour before realizing that Lin Hong was not home. One of them sat on the pullcart's handlebars watching over Song Gang while the other walked along the empty streets, trying to find someone from Baldy Li's company. The dockworker knew that Baldy Li was Song Gang's brother and had heard the rumors about Lin Hong and Baldy Li.

The dead Song Gang had been brought home, but they couldn't get him through his own front door; instead, he was lying faceup in the flatbed of a pullcart in front of the house. The worker sitting on the handlebars watched blankly as the wind blew leaves onto Song Gang's body. Some of the leaves came from the tree overhead, and some were blown up from the ground. Around two o'clock in the morning, the worker finally saw his workmate coming back with Deputy Liu.

Deputy Liu stood in front of the pullcart looking at Song Gang. After shaking his head, he stepped aside to call Baldy Li, then walked back to the pullcart, and the three of them waited there in front of Song Gang's house. At around three, they saw Lin Hong appear in the empty street, and as she approached she passed in and out of the light from the streetlamps. She walked solemnly with her head bowed and hugging her shoulders, looking as if she were walking in and out of life itself.

Lin Hong walked up to the pullcart, avoiding the three men's gazes, then turned and walked away. As she was opening the front door she looked back at Song Gang's body lying in the pullcart, covered with leaves. She opened the door and found complete darkness inside. Lin Hong looked back at Song Gang and couldn't help going back and leaning over the pullcart to clean off the leaves that were covering his body. What she saw was not Song Gang's face but his face mask. She knelt down and began to cry, her entire body shuddering, as she pulled off the mask. Under the moonlight she was able to make out his peaceful expression. As she cried her trembling hands caressed his face. This face that once had so many happy smiles, that not so long before was full of yearning as Song Gang rode the train back to Liu, was now lifeless, as cold as the dark night.

CHAPTER 76

L IN HONG experienced a silent dawn. After Song Gang was carried to his bed by his former workmates, she realized that his body had been virtually sliced in two. As the two men lifted the tenuously connected halves of Song Gang by his arms and legs and walked toward the bed, Song Gang's body looked as though it had been folded in half. His posterior dragged against the concrete floor, as leaves fell from his body. After they lay Song Gang down, his folded body was once again stretched flat, and a few remaining leaves fell onto the bed. After Deputy Liu and Song Gang's two former workmates left, predawn Liu Town was absolutely silent. Lin Hong sat on the bed hugging her knees to her chest, gazing at the peaceful Song Gang and the peaceful leaves as tears streamed down her face, her thoughts alternating between utter confusion and utter clarity.

In her periods of confusion, she felt as lonely as the depth of night. In her periods of clarity, it seemed as if Song Gang were speaking, smiling, walking, and tenderly caressing her. These were sweet secrets that the two of them shared and that no one could intrude upon. Now the twenty years they had shared had been brought to an end, and they would never again share any experience together. Lin Hong felt a chill run through her body, a chill of loneliness and solitude. She told herself over and over that it was she who killed Song Gang; as a result, she hated herself and wanted to scream. She didn't scream but instead silently grabbed a clump of her hair and pulled it with all her might. Her hair sliced open her fingers, leaving them red with blood. She gazed abjectly at Song Gang, lying there in eternal rest, and asked over and over again, "Why did you have to leave?"

Then she felt a wave of humiliation sweep over her as she remembered how lonely she had been after he left and all she had suffered at the hands of the chain-smoking Director Liu, and she couldn't help sobbing, "You left before I had a chance to tell you about all the humiliation I endured."

The next morning Lin Hong received the letter Song Gang had sent her before committing suicide. The letter was six pages long, and each line was deeply moving. Song Gang told her that he had been very happy all these years together and thanked her for always being at his side. He said that ever since his lungs went bad, he had considered separating from her, but she had told him that, no matter what happened, she would never leave him. He said that, knowing this, he could die without regrets. He asked that she forgive him for taking his own life and that she not feel bad because of him. He said that being with her those twenty years was better than spending twenty lifetimes with any other woman, and therefore he had no regrets. Song Gang also told her very apologetically that when he left without saying goodbye more than a year earlier, it was only in order to earn enough money so that she would be able to live without worries. He regretted, however, that he was not very talented at earning money and had been able to bring back only thirty thousand yuan, which he had stuffed under the pillow. He hoped that, after she rid herself of this burden, she could live comfortably, relying on her own abilities. Finally, he emphasized that he didn't hate Baldy Li and certainly didn't hate Lin Hong, nor did he hate himself. He had just taken a first step and would look for Lin Hong in the next world. He was confident that they would have an opportunity to be together again, and after that they would be together forever.

Lin Hong read Song Gang's letter over and over again, crying so much that the pages became soaked with tears. Then, still crying, she got up, removed Song Gang's clothes, and began washing his body. When she noticed the two red swellings on his chest, she gripped the towel in terror, wiped at the red swellings, and uncovered the festering wounds under his armpits. Her entire body began to tremble. She looked at Song Gang's wounds over and over again, and each time her tears started to blur her vision, she would wipe them away and continue looking carefully at the wounds, until her eyes would again blur over. She couldn't understand what these wounds were from, or what had happened to Song Gang while he was away traveling. She stood blankly for a long time, still holding the towel. She cried, she shook her head, she became confused, she couldn't understand.

Finally, she unwrapped the thirty thousand yuan that Song Gang had carefully wrapped in newspaper and placed under the pillow, and she nearly fainted. Her legs gave out as she knelt, looking at the bills scattered across the bed, and it was then that she understood their significance. She picked up every bill and carefully folded it. From Song

Gang's swellings on his chest and the wounds under his armpits, she knew that every one of these bills was soaked with his sweat and blood.

When they cremated Song Gang's corpse five days later, the people of Liu saw Lin Hong again and noticed that her eyes were red and swollen. By that time she didn't have any tears left, and her expressionless gaze seemed oddly detached. When Song Gang's corpse was pushed into the cremation furnace she didn't wail in grief as people expected she would but, rather, closed her eyes and silently told Song Gang, "Regardless of what I might have done, you are the only person I have ever loved."

Baldy Li also received Song Gang's letter, and tears also streamed down his face as he read it. In his letter, Song Gang recalled their tragic childhood and how they had relied on each other for survival. He mentioned how, after he went to the countryside, he had taken long bus rides to come back and see Baldy Li; how, when he came back to Liu Town at the age of eighteen to work, Baldy Li had happily gone to make him a spare key; as well as the happiness they had both felt the first time they received their wages. Then he mentioned Lin Hong, and at this point Song Gang's tone became joyful as he recalled with something resembling pride how Lin Hong had not fallen in love with Baldy Li but instead had fallen in love with him. Song Gang told Baldy Li that he had always been secretly happy for each of Baldy Li's successes. He said that, before their mother died, she had urged him to look after Baldy Li, and therefore he was happy that, when he saw their mother, he would have no regrets and could tell her how great Baldy Li was. Song Gang once again became sorrowful as he described how he still very much missed their father, Song Fanping, and how, if it weren't for that family portrait, he probably wouldn't even be able to remember what Papa looked like. He hoped that, after all these years, Papa's appearance would not have changed, and when he encountered him in the netherworld, he would be able to recognize him at once. In the final page of the letter Song Gang encouraged Baldy Li to look out for Lin Hong, in consideration of their brotherly love. The last line of Song Gang's letter read: "Baldy Li, you once said to me: 'Even if heaven and earth were to be turned upside down, we would still be brothers.' Now I say to you: 'Even if we are separated by life and death, we will still be brothers.'"

Like Lin Hong, Baldy Li read Song Gang's letter over and over again, and each time he finished, he would slap his own face and cry out in anguish. Since Song Gang's death, Baldy Li had become a different person. He no longer went to work and instead spent the entire day sitting silently in his mansion. Deputy Liu was the only person permitted to enter. As Liu reported the company's operations Badly Li would stare at him like a kindergartner staring at his teacher, and when Liu finished his report and stood waiting for his instructions, Baldy Li would look out the window and say with a sigh, "It's almost dark."

After a while Deputy Liu would have no choice but to prompt Baldy Li, "Boss Li, it is your intention that I . . ."

Baldy Li would turn around and pathetically say to Deputy Liu, "I am now an orphan."

As Lin Hong was sorting through Song Gang's remains, she discovered two things she needed to give Baldy Li: the family portrait and Baldy Li's appointment letter as factory director, which Song Gang had carefully copied out by hand. She placed the documents into two envelopes and asked Deputy Liu to deliver them. As Baldy Li accepted the envelopes from Deputy Liu the family portrait slipped out and fell to the floor. Baldy Li knelt down and picked it up, then walked toward his desk carrying the photograph and the other envelope. After sitting down, he opened a drawer and started rustling through it, eventually finding another family portrait. He looked at the two photographs, then carefully placed them together in the drawer. As he walked back to Deputy Liu he opened the other envelope and saw the appointment letter that Baldy Li had copied out by hand. He stopped walking and stared in confusion at the words on the page, and when he saw the seal that Song Gang had drawn with red ink, Baldy Li finally realized what it was. His body started to sway, and he collapsed to the floor.

Baldy Li didn't leave his mansion until the day they cremated Song Gang's remains. When he left, he didn't want his BMW or his Mercedes but walked alone, teary-eyed, to the crematorium. As Song Gang was being inserted into the furnace Lin Hong didn't cry but Baldy Li wept silently. Then, Baldy Li, tears streaming down his face, walked out of the crematorium. The black BMW and white Mercedes followed him slowly, but he flew into a rage and told both cars to get out of his sight. Then he wiped his tears and continued walking on alone. The onlookers were astounded, saying, "Who knew that Baldy Li was such a sentimental heroine under all that bluster?"

Baldy Li did not return to the office but, rather, went to the Good Works Factory—now his Liu Town Economic Research Business Corporation. The appointment letter Song Gang had meticulously copied out brought back many memories for Baldy Li. He hadn't seen his fourteen loyal minions for years, and now he missed them terribly.

When Baldy Li suddenly showed up, he startled the two cripples, who were still playing chess and cursing each other. They immediately cried out, "Director Li!" and excitedly ran over, one of them tumbling to the ground and the other slamming into the door frame. Baldy Li treated them as if they were his own sons, helping the one who had fallen down get back to his feet and massaging the head of the one who had run into the door frame. Then he took both cripples by the hand and walked toward his other twelve loyal minions. The cripples cried out excitedly, "Director Li has come! Director Li has come!"

The three idiots and four blind men heard this, but the five deaf men couldn't hear anything. The four blind men reacted faster than the three idiots, and they hurried outside, tapping the ground with their canes. Only one, however, succeeded in getting out, while the other three all ended up jammed in the doorway, none of them willing to give way for anyone else. They kept shouting, "Director Li!" and their eyes narrowed to mere slits, making their mouths seem obscenely large. The three idiots also reacted, and simultaneously rushed toward the door. When they saw Baldy Li, they all shouted "Director Li!" but the doorway was already blocked by the three blind men. The three idiots nevertheless crowded forward at the same time, pushing the three blind men in front of them to the ground. Again, it was Baldy Li who picked each of them up, after which the crippled, idiot, and blind loyal minions delightedly crowded around him as he walked into the meeting hall. The five deaf men sitting in the meeting hall finally realized what the excitement was about, and each of them leapt up from their chairs. The two deaf men who were able to speak also called out "Director Li!" while the three deaf-mutes opened and closed their mouths. Baldy Li stood among them and heard one "Director Li!" after another. After he felt he had heard enough, he gestured toward the seats and invited them to sit down. After the fourteen loyal minions sat, they started twittering away, until one of the crippled men called out and asked them to be quiet. The other cripple, meanwhile, faced the five deaf men and repeatedly opened and closed his mouth. In this way, the meeting hall immediately quieted down, and the former crippled factory director told the other thirteen loyal minions, "Let us welcome Director Li, who has come to speak to us."

The fourteen loyal minions all applauded, but when Baldy Li gestured, they immediately stopped. Baldy Li looked at each of his followers and sighed. "You have all aged," he said. "I too have aged."

When the three idiots heard Baldy Li say this, they immediately applauded, afraid of being beaten to the punch. The five deaf men didn't know what Baldy Li had said, but when the idiots started clapping, they quickly joined in. The four blind men then blindly joined in the excitement and started applauding as well. The two cripples felt that it was somewhat inappropriate to applaud what Baldy Li had said, but since everyone else was already doing so, they had no choice but to join in. Baldy Li again gestured for them to be quiet and said, "It is not appropriate to applaud what I just said."

The two cripples immediately stopped applauding, as did the four blind men. The five observant deaf men followed suit. The three idiots continued applauding, but when they saw that everyone else had ceased, they lost confidence and stopped as well. Baldy Li looked up at the conference room, then out the window at the trees, and sighed repeatedly. His loyal minions all grew somber. Then Baldy Li emotionally recalled the first time he came to the Good Works Factory, more than twenty years earlier. As he was speaking he pulled Song Gang's copy of his appointment letter out of his breast pocket, opened it up, and read it out loud. When he was finished, he lifted it up for the fourteen loyal minions to see, and as they gazed up at it he laughed bitterly, saying, "This is a handwritten copy. The original is in a file at the county's Civil Affairs Bureau. The seal on the front used to be red but now has turned yellow. Song Gang copied this out by hand, and he drew the seal by hand as well. He carefully kept it all this time because he was happy for me. He even knitted me a Great Prospects Ship sweater. . . ."

Baldy Li became so choked up he couldn't continue. The two cripples and four blind men waited anxiously, while the three idiots, not understanding what was going on, saw that Baldy Li had stopped talking and immediately burst into applause. The five deaf men were more careful this time, noticing Baldy Li's heartbroken expression. The two cripples whispered to the three enthusiastically applauding idiots, "It's not appropriate to applaud."

The idiots looked around and, feeling that the situation had become awkward, stopped applauding. At this point Baldy Li, with an anguished look on his face, began to relate his and Song Gang's history together. When he described Song Fanping's tragic death in front of the bus depot and how he and Song Gang were later left all alone, he found himself unable to continue. The two cripples wiped away their tears, and the four blind men gripped their canes, tears flowing from their sightless eyes. When the five deaf men saw Baldy so miserable, his sorrow was transmitted from their eyes to their hearts, and they too began to cry as sorrowfully as the two cripples. The three idiots, seeing the great Director Li looking so devastated and their workmates sobbing as if their hearts were breaking, also began bawling thunderously, quickly drowning out the sound of their workmates' sobs.

For the next ten days Baldy Li came every day to the so-called Liu Town Economics Research Business Corporation, recounting over and over stories from the past. Baldy Li himself no longer wept, but his tragic stories caused tears to stream down the faces of his loyal minions. The sorrow of the handicapped workers was a source of great consolation for Baldy Li, as if his own sorrow had somehow been transmitted to them. While recounting his stories of the past, Baldy Li told the workers not to be upset, but the more he tried to reassure them, the more upset they became and the harder they cried. Baldy Li felt that, in all the world, only his fourteen loyal minions were able to share in the sorrow and misery that he felt.

At last Baldy Li returned to work in order to make good on Song Gang's last request. Baldy Li asked Deputy Liu to call his business partners and all the other rich people he knew and invite them to attend a three-day tofu banquet in the restaurant he had founded. After Liu drew up a list of invitees, he spent a day on the phone, telling everyone that Baldy Li's brother, Song Gang, had died and inviting them to commemorate him by attending a tofu banquet in his honor. After a day of nonstop calling, Deputy Liu lost his voice, but he nevertheless managed to invite Baldy Li's business associates throughout China, together with all the important people from the city and province, but no one who was poor or unknown.

Baldy Li's tofu banquet began with breakfast and continued through lunch and dinner. Some guests had sat in an airplane for several hours, then spent another couple of hours on the bus, in order to arrive that evening; therefore Baldy Li extended the banquet late into the night. At Song Gang's cremation Baldy Li and Lin Hong had seen each other once again, but they simply looked past each other as if they were strangers. Both wore mourning shrouds of white hemp and black armbands as they stood in the doorway of the restaurant for three days. Each of the VIPs who attended gave Lin Hong a thick envelope containing anywhere from several thousand to tens of thousands of yuan. The people at the bank saw Lin Hong come by every day to make a deposit, and each time she would arrive carrying a huge sack of bills. In three days she received more than one hundred envelopes, and people estimated that she had received several million yuan. It was said that her fingers had gotten shredded, her wrists cramped, and her eyes bloodshot from counting so much money.

After the conclusion of the tofu banquet, Baldy Li said to Lin Hong, "Song Gang asked that I make sure you are well taken care of. What else would you like me to do?"

Lin Hong said, "This is enough."

THREE YEARS ELAPSED, during which time some people died and others were born. Old Scissors Guan departed from the world, as did Tailor Zhang, but during those same three years three infants named Guan and nine infants named Zhang arrived. Day in and day out, our Liu Town was constantly replenishing itself.

No one knew the impact that Song Gang's death had had on Lin Hong's heart; they knew only that she had quit her job at the knitting factory and moved out of the building where they had lived together. She used the money from the tofu banquet to buy a new apartment, then stayed there by herself, living in complete seclusion for half a year. The people of Liu Town rarely saw her, and when they did, she would always have a cold expression—everyone called it a widow's expression. There were just a handful of observant people who noticed her gradual transformation, and they pointed out that her clothing was becoming increasingly fashionable. After her old place had been vacant for half a year, she started to appear in public more and more frequently, thereby bringing to an end her period of isolation. She renovated her old place and made it into a beauty salon, then became the salon's proprietor. From then on, music emanated from the salon, a neon sign flickered overhead, and business boomed. When the men of Liu arrived at her beauty salon, they wouldn't use the rustic phrase *cut their hair* but, rather, would speak more fashionably of *styling their hair*. Even those who were always cursing like sailors wouldn't say *cut their hair* but rather, *style their fucking hair*.

During this period, Wanderless Zhou in the snack shop across the street continued to proclaim that within three years' time he would open one hundred Wanderless Zhou chain stores throughout China. But after repeating this boast for three straight years, not only did he not open a single store outside of Liu Town; he didn't even make any progress on the two proposed stores within Liu Town itself. Wanderless Zhou continued to boast wildly that he would make the price of McDonald's stock drop by half. Missy Su had grown accustomed to his boasts and knew that if he didn't boast during the day and watch his

Korean soaps at night, he would be reduced to a state worse than death. Consequently, she had long since lost the capacity of being embarrassed for him.

Wanderless Zhou's Snack Shop continued on as before, but Lin Hong's beauty salon was quietly changing. At first there were three male hair stylists and three female hair washers. Within a year, one girl after another began to arrive from all over. Regardless of whether they were tall or short, fat or thin, pretty or homely, they all nevertheless wore the same décolleté tops and superminiskirts. There were twenty-three of them in all, and after they arrived in Liu Town, they moved into the same six-story building. One after another, the families originally living in the building moved out, and Poet Zhao moved out with them. Then Lin Hong rented each of the one-bedroom apartments and, after renovating them, housed two girls in each apartment, whereupon the entire building rang out with accents and dialects from throughout China.

These girls would sleep peacefully during the day but then become active each night, when these twenty-three heavily made-up and gaudily attired girls would crowd into the beauty salon, brightly soliciting customers like twenty-three red lanterns at New Year's. The men would stand outside and furtively peer in as the girls would glance seductively back out at them. Then the beauty salon began to resemble a black market, abuzz with the sounds of people bargaining. The men would speak carefully, as if they were buying drugs, while the girls would speak boldly, as though they were selling cosmetics. After finding a girl and agreeing on a price, the men and their chosen girls would walk up the stairs, bantering lewdly. After entering a room, they would produce all kinds of sounds imaginable, transforming the six-floor building into a virtual zoo, a veritable encyclopedia of men and women's lovemaking noises.

Everyone in Liu Town referred to the building as the town's red-light district, and since Wanderless Zhou's Snack Shop was directly across the street, his business also increased impressively. In the past, the snack shop would close its doors at eleven each night, but now it stayed open twenty-four hours a day. From one till four or five o'clock each morning, the constant stream of men and young women emerging from the building would pour across the street and into the snack shop, where they would sit and suck down their straw-embedded mini-buns.

Was there anyone in Liu Town who could have accurately predicted Lin Hong's life trajectory? Beginning as a pure and easily embarrassed young girl, she was transformed into a sweet young woman in love, a virtuous wife completely devoted to Song Gang, a crazy lover who made crazy love to Baldy Li for three months, a solitary widow, an expressionless single woman living in complete isolation, a beauty salon proprietess, and finally this business-minded madam who always had a smile for her clients. After those heavily made-up young women started appearing in Liu, Lin Hong became smoother and warmer in her social interactions. The young women didn't call her Lin Hong but, rather, Madam Lin, and gradually the people of Liu started calling her that as well. Lin Hong became a Janus-like figure: Whenever a prospective customer walked in the door, she would break out into a radiant smile and speak to him sweetly, yet when she ran into a man unrelated to her business, she would look at him with eyes as cold as ice.

Although, by that time, Madam Lin's eyes and forehead were full of wrinkles, she was nevertheless very fashionable and wore tight-fitting black clothes, showing off her curvy breasts and buttocks. She always carried a cell phone, grasping it tightly as though it were a strand of gold. Her cell rang throughout the day and night, and she would smile into it, addressing people as Bureau Director, Manager, and Brother, then saying, "A few older ones have left, and some new ones have arrived, each of whom is young and pretty."

If she then said, "I'll send one over for you to take a look," that meant that the person on the other end of the line was a VIP customer— either a powerful provincial official or a rich provincial businessman. If it was a working stiff who had called, however, she would still smile, but in a very different tone of voice would simply say, "Our girls are all very pretty."

BLACKSMITH TONG was one of Madam Lin's VIP customers. He was now more than sixty years old, and his wife a year older than he. Tong had opened three stores of his supermarket chain. Everyone addressed him as Boss Tong, but he wouldn't let his workers call him this, insisting that they continue calling him Blacksmith Tong, since he thought that sounded more vigorous.

The sixty-something Blacksmith Tong was still as randy as a young man, and when he saw a young woman, his eyes would light up like a thief spotting money. When she was in her fifties, his formerly plump wife had two major operations, one that removed half her stomach and the other, her entire uterus. After his wife's body collapsed and she became reduced to skin and bones, her libido also completely collapsed. Blacksmith Tong, however, still full of vitality, needed to have sex at least twice a week and invariably would leave his wife so anguished that she no longer wanted to live. She said that each time they finished, she felt as though she had just had another hysterectomy, and it would take her at least half a month to recover, but within a few days Blacksmith Tong was raring to go again.

In order to survive, Blacksmith Tong's wife resolved not to let him have sex with her anymore, leading him to develop a temper like a boar in heat unable to find a sow. He smashed dishes while at home and cursed his employees at the supermarkets. Once he even came to blows with a customer. His wife felt that if he continued to throw these tantrums, sooner or later something would happen—either another woman would seduce him or else he would take a handful of mistresses, but either way the money he had painstakingly earned and couldn't bring himself to spend would all be taken away by some other woman. After considering every possibility, his wife finally decided to send him over to Madam Lin's and have one of her girls cure his explosive temper. The girls would want a tip, and Madam Lin would charge an administrative fee, all of which wouldn't come cheap, but though it distressed Tong's wife to have to part with all that money, she preferred to think of it as medical expenses for her husband. In this way she was able to put her mind at rest, telling herself that this was well-spent preventive care.

Every time Blacksmith Tong came to Madam Lin's place, he would enter boldly, his wife at his side. His wife was afraid that he would get cheated and therefore insisted on helping him pick the girls herself and negotiate a good price. She would leave only after having settled the bill and go home to wait for Blacksmith Tong to return with his report.

The first time he returned home after going whoring, his wife was very critical of the fact that he and the girl had carried on for more than an hour and demanded to know whether or not he had fallen in love with that slut. Blacksmith Tong retorted that, given that they had already spent the money, why shouldn't he reap the benefits? "This is called having the return be proportional to the investment."

Blacksmith Tong's wife felt that her husband had a point, and therefore each time she would always want to make sure that the girl had done it long enough. Despite his age, Tong was still indomitable, and each time he visited a prostitute, he would go on for more than an hour. His wife was very pleased, feeling they were getting a good return on their investment. Occasionally he would fail to give a good performance, and a few times he finished up after just half an hour, making his wife feel that they weren't getting a good enough return. Therefore, she adjusted her strategy and, rather than allowing him to go whoring twice a week, she switched to a once-a-week plan.

Blacksmith Tong felt humiliated because, in order to save money, his wife would always pick relatively homely girls for him. At first he felt that they were all right and told himself that, although they weren't very pretty, at least they were young. Gradually, however, he began to lose interest in girls who weren't pretty, and therefore the number of rounds he could rouse himself for carnal battle also diminished. In Madam Lin's building there were some very pretty girls whom Blacksmith Tong lusted after with all his heart. He would beg his wife to pick him a pretty one, but she would refuse on the ground that the pretty ones were more expensive and therefore her cost would dramatically increase. Blacksmith Tong swore that if he got a pretty girl, he would definitely do her for at least two hours and therefore make good on their investment.

During the several decades they had been married, Blacksmith Tong had always strutted about proudly in front of his wife. Especially since he opened his store, then his chain of supermarkets, his success in business made him even prouder, and he would often reprimand and curse her. Now, however, he frequently implored her to find him a pretty girl and didn't hesitate to kneel with tears streaming down his face. When his wife saw him like this and remembered his former cockiness, she couldn't help but shake her head and, sighing, ask, "Why are men such losers?"

She then agreed to find him a pretty girl for holidays and festivals. Blacksmith Tong reacted as though he had just received a royal blessing and immediately rushed off to find a calendar and make a list of all of the holidays. Starting with the Chinese Lunar New Year, he first wrote down the traditional Chinese holidays, including the Mid-Autumn Festival, the Duanwu Dragon Boat Festival, the Chongyang Double Ninth Festival, the Qingming Ancestors' Festival, and so forth. Then he added Labor Day, Youth Day, Army Building Day, and

National Day, together with Teachers' Day, Valentine's Day, Bachelors' Day, and Elders' Day, as well as the foreigners' holidays of Halloween, Thanksgiving, and Christmas, and finally added Women's Day and Children's Day as well. When Blacksmith Tong told his wife all of the holidays he had found, she jumped in alarm and cried out hoarsely, "Oh, my God!"

Then the two started bargaining feverishly. Blacksmith Tong's wife first tried to eliminate all the foreigners' holidays, declaring nationalistically, "We are Chinese and don't observe foreigners' holidays."

Blacksmith Tong didn't agree. He had worked in business for more than ten years and naturally knew more than his wife, and therefore he admonished her, "What era do we live in? This is the age of globalization. Our refrigerator, television, and washing machine are all foreign brands. Can you possibly claim that, because you are Chinese, therefore you won't use foreign brands?"

His wife opened her mouth, but no words came out. Finally, she simply said, "I'm no match for you."

After the foreigners' holidays were preserved, Blacksmith Tong's wife picked out the Qingming Ancestors' Festival from among the traditional Chinese holidays and said, "This is a festival of the dead, and therefore you can't count it among your own."

Blacksmith Tong didn't agree with that either and said, "The Qingming festival is for the living to mourn the deceased, and therefore it is actually a holiday for the living. On that day every year, we first go visit my parents' graves and then visit yours. Why wouldn't this count?"

His wife pondered for a long time and finally again conceded, "I'm no match for you."

Therefore, the Qingming festival was also preserved. Next, his wife firmly opposed his inclusion of Youth Day, Teachers' Day, and Children's Day. Blacksmith Tong agreed to leave out Teachers' Day but insisted that he be allowed to keep the others. He said that it was only after having experienced his own childhood and youth that he was able to have his current old age, and he declared boldly, "Comrade Lenin taught us: *To forget the past is to betray it.*"

The two continued going back and forth, and after they had argued for more than an hour, Blacksmith Tong's wife once again gave in, saying, "I'm no match for you."

Finally, the dispute came down to Women's Day, and Blacksmith Tong's wife asked him, "What does Women's Day have to do with you?"

Blacksmith Tong replied, "Precisely because it *is* Women's Day, one must go find oneself a woman."

His wife suddenly became downcast and, wiping her tears, said, "No matter what I say, I'll never be a match for you."

Buoyed by his success, Blacksmith Tong thought of two more holidays. "There are two more: your birthday and mine."

His wife finally became infuriated and cried out, "So you want to go find a prostitute even on my birthday?"

Blacksmith Tong realized his mistake and immediately corrected himself. He shook his head and waved away the thought. "No, no, of course not! I won't go anywhere on your birthday but will spend the entire day with you. I won't go anywhere on my birthday either and will spend that entire day with you as well. Our two birthdays count as my Chastity Days, and not only will I not sleep with other women on either of those days, I won't even look in their direction."

Blacksmith Tong's last concession made his simpleminded wife believe that she had finally achieved a victory. Gratified, she said, "At any rate, I'm no match for you."

Blacksmith Tong's wife continued to personally escort him to Madam Lin's, and every holiday and festival he received a bonus allowing him to hire a more expensive girl. All the married men in Liu Town were extremely envious and remarked that this proved that Blacksmith Tong was indeed born lucky, to have such a sensible and enlightened wife who supported him when he went whoring while she herself remained chaste. They decided that, even if Tong were reduced to a pile of dog shit, he would still manage to find some dog-shit fortune—he was *that* lucky. They then looked again at their own wives, each of whom was unreasonable and had a rigid way of thinking, grasping their husbands' wallets with one hand and their belts with the other. The men sighed, and when they ran into Blacksmith Tong they would ask quietly, "How did you manage to have such good fortune?"

With a pleasant expression, Tong would say modestly, "I simply had the fortune to find a good wife."

If his wife was by his side, he would add, "This good wife of mine is one of a kind, and even if you took a red lantern to search heaven, hell, and the bottom of the sea, you still wouldn't find another like her."

From the time Blacksmith Tong's wife started accompanying him to Madam Lin's to hire girls, his tantrums abruptly disappeared. The cockiness his wife had endured for decades disappeared too, and he stopped cursing his employees, becoming instead as polite and refined as an intellectual, always smiling and not uttering a single curse word when he spoke. His wife was very pleased with his transformation, because not only did he abandon his cocky attitude but he furthermore became quite subservient when he was with her. Before, he wasn't even willing to go shopping with her, and now he would carry her bag; previously he refused to discuss anything with her, but now he asked her permission for everything. Blacksmith Tong even dismissed the chairman of his company's board of directors and appointed his wife in his place, and he himself settled for being company president. Therefore, his wife had to sign all the company's papers—she had no understanding of what was going on, she just knew that she had to sign everything her husband brought her. When other people brought her documents, she would categorically refuse to sign anything she didn't fully understand—unless she saw that her husband had signed it before her. Blacksmith Tong's wife was no longer a housewife and instead went to work with her husband every day. As a result, she began to pay more attention to her dress and makeup, to the point of wearing name-brand clothing and name-brand lipstick. The company's employees would nod and bow when they saw her, making her feel as if she had a successful career. She liked to lecture others, and whenever she ran into women who had been housewives for several decades, like herself, she would try to enlighten them, saying that women shouldn't rely entirely on men but, rather, should have their own careers. At the end of her lecture, she would add a fashionable phrase: "They should find their own self-worth."

Blacksmith Tong now had each holiday and festival etched in his memory and therefore became Liu Town's own living calendar. When the women of Liu wanted their husbands to let them buy some new outfit, they would call out to Blacksmith Tong, "Are there any holidays coming up?"

When the men of Liu wanted to find an excuse for their wives to let them spend the night out playing mahjong, they too would ask Blacksmith Tong, "What holiday is it today?"

When children were harassing their parents to purchase them a toy, if Blacksmith Tong happened to walk by, they would ask him, "Blacksmith Tong, is there a kid's holiday today?"

After Tong became Liu Town's famous King of Holidays, he attacked his work with increased vigor, and not only did business at his supermarkets continue to improve but he expanded into a wholesale business in household products. Many of the shops in Liu Town bought their goods through Blacksmith Tong's company, and therefore his profits increased each quarter. His wife decided that this was due to her brilliant tactics, because ever since she made her timely intervention to resolve Blacksmith Tong's libido crisis, his vigor increased dramatically and his company's fortunes rose day by day. Compared with the rise in his profits, the money they spent on girls didn't amount to much. Blacksmith Tong's wife felt that their rewards already far outweighed her investment, and occasionally she would splurge and hire her husband a pretty, high-class call girl even when it wasn't a holiday or a festival.

Twice each week this sixty-something couple would climb up the stairs of Madam Lin's bordello—Blacksmith Tong glowing and his wife panting heavily, the two speaking to each other heedless of who might be listening. After the first time Tong was allowed to hire a pretty call girl even though it wasn't a holiday, he wanted to do so every time. He would stand in front of the building entreating his wife like a child begging his parents to buy him a toy, saying pathetically, "Darling, please find me a high-class call girl."

His wife would say firmly, like the chairman of the board, "No, today is not a holiday, and neither is it a festival."

Like one of the chairman's subordinates, he would reply, "Today an account receivable was deposited to our account."

When his board-chairman wife heard this, she would smile and nod and say, "Okay, I'll find you a high-class call girl."

None of the girls working there liked Blacksmith Tong, and in fact they all agreed they couldn't stand him, because once he got started, there was no stopping him. Tong already had gray hair and a gray beard, but when he got into bed, he was like a man in his twenties, though afterward he would leave a smaller tip than anyone else. Furthermore, his invalid wife would always accompany him and insist on receiving a discount, leading to an exhausting, teeth-grinding negotiation that could last up to an hour. After his wife had spoken for a few minutes, she would have to take a drink of water and catch her breath for a few minutes, and only after resting for a while would she be able to continue to bargain down the girl's asking price. The girls all felt that servicing Blacksmith Tong was more exhausting than servicing any four other men combined, but with him they received payment for only a single customer and even had to grant him a discount. Therefore, they were all unwilling to service Blacksmith Tong, but since he was an important figure in Liu and furthermore was one of Madam Lin's VIPs, they couldn't refuse. Whenever Tong and his wife picked out a girl, she would laugh bitterly and sigh, saying, "That's it. I will need to imitate the revolutionary martyr, Lei Feng."

SUCCESS LIU—a.k.a. Writer Liu, a.k.a. PR Liu, a.k.a. Deputy Liu—was now CEO Liu and also one of Madam Lin's VIPs. After Song Gang's death, Baldy Li gave Liu the position of company president, and after Executive Deputy Liu became President Liu, he decided he didn't like people calling him President Liu and instead asked them to call him CEO Liu. The people of Liu Town decided that pronouncing four syllables was altogether too much trouble and furthermore said that it sounded more like a Japanese name than a Chinese one; therefore they shortened it to C Liu. In this way, Success Liu was transformed from the poor bachelor Writer Liu to the tycoon C Liu. He wore Italian name-brand suits, rode in the white BMW sedan Baldy Li had given him, and spent a million yuan buying his way out of his marriage, saying that this was compensation for his wife's loss of her youthful innocence. In this way he was finally able to rid himself of the woman he had tried to abandon twenty years earlier, and then proceeded to find one, two, three, four, even five pretty girls to be his girlfriends. As he put it, these girlfriends were sunshine girls. His house was already filled with spring beauty, but often he still couldn't resist coming over to Madam Lin's to roam. He said that after eating in most nights, he needed to drop by Madam Lin's and tickle his palate with some exotic flavors.

By this point C Liu had become more disdainful than ever toward Poet Zhao. Zhao still boasted about his constant toiling at his craft, while C Liu said that Zhao's playing around with words was a form of suicide, and that he might as well tie a noose around his neck and hang himself. C Liu held up four fingers and enumerated Poet Zhao's failings: "He has been writing for almost thirty years, starting with that early mimeographed magazine in which he published those four lines of poetry. But after all these years he hasn't published even a single punctuation mark. And he still calls himself Poet Zhao! Wouldn't it be more appropriate if he called himself Mimeographed Magazine Poet Zhao?"

Poet Zhao, who had been laid off and unemployed for several years, was equally disdainful toward C Liu. When he heard that Liu was enumerating his failings and calling him a mimeographed magazine poet, he initially became furious but then laughed disdainfully and said that he didn't even need to hold up four fingers in appraising an opportunist like C Liu, since even one finger would be more than he deserved. Poet Zhao held up one finger and said simply, "He has sold his soul."

After Poet Zhao moved out of his house in Liu Town's red-light district, he rented a cheap room next to the railroad tracks on the west side of town. Every day more than a hundred trains would rumble by, making his room tremble as though it had been hit by an earthquake. His table, chairs, and bed would also tremble, as would his cabinet, dishes, and chopsticks and even his ceiling and floor. Zhao would compare the trembling of his cheap room to contractions from an electrical shock, and this metaphor pleased him to no end. At night, when the trains passing by made his room go into tremors, he would frequently dream that he was sitting in an electric chair and, his face full of tears, bidding farewell to the mortal world.

The abjectly poor Poet Zhao depended for his survival on the rent Madam Lin paid him every month, and although he continued to wear a suit every day, it was now all wrinkled and dirty. The people of Liu had been watching color television for more than twenty years and now were beginning to switch over to high-definition rear-projection and plasma units, while Poet Zhao was still watching his fourteen-inch black-and-white television, which frequently would go blank. Zhao would carry it around throughout the town's streets and alleys but couldn't find anyone able to fix a black-and-white television, so in the end he had no choice but to fix it himself. Therefore, the next time the picture went out, he hit it as if he were slapping someone across the face, and sure enough the picture reappeared. Sometimes, however, the picture wouldn't reappear even after he had hit it several times, and he would have to resort to the leg-sweeping kick of his youth and sweep-kick the picture back on.

The formerly polite and refined Poet Zhao had become angry and cynical, always cursing up a storm. While C Liu was living amid a bevy of beauties, Zhao didn't have a single woman in his life and had to settle for hanging an old pinup poster on the crumbling wall of his dilapidated apartment and staring at it ravenously, like a man who paints a cake to assuage his hunger. There was not a living woman who was willing to look him in the eye, and even when he once tried to chat up some old widows, they saw through his ruse and told him straight up that he should first figure out how to provide for himself before entertaining thoughts of finding a companion. Zhao became extremely depressed. Many years earlier he had had an elegant and attractive girlfriend, and the two had enjoyed a yearlong loving relationship, but then he tried to straddle two boats simultaneously as he pursued Lin Hong, and as a result, not only did he not secure Lin Hong but his girlfriend ran off with someone else.

Meanwhile, after C Liu's former wife was cast off, although she was very satisfied with the million yuan she had in her bank account, she would nevertheless stand in the street crying woefully, complaining that C Liu was heartless and cruel. She would again hold up all ten fingers, though now of course what she was counting was not the number of times they had slept together but, rather, the matrimonial bliss they had shared over twenty years of marriage. She said that over the past twenty years she had cooked for C Liu and washed his clothes and looked after him through good times and bad. After C Liu was laid off and became unemployed, she didn't leave him but, rather, cared for him even more considerately. She said that her body was like a stove in winter, warming him up, and like an ice cube in the summer, cooling him down. She tearfully complained that his entire being was obsessed with money, just as his mind was obsessed with sex. She said that, in the past, he had been a high-minded writer, walking elegantly and speaking with refinement. She had fallen in love with him and married him because he was Writer Liu, but now that Writer Liu no longer existed, her husband no longer existed either.

At that point, one of her listeners remembered Poet Zhao and, in an attempt to play the role of a pimp, said, "Although it's true that Writer Liu doesn't exist anymore, there is still Poet Zhao, who has not yet married. He's a bachelor about to approach his diamond anniversary— a rare gem."

"Poet Zhao? A rare gem?" She snorted a couple of times. "He wouldn't even stand out in a bachelor remainder sale."

Liu's wife considered herself one of Liu Town's rich maidens, and for someone to mention her and that poor bachelor Zhao in the same breath was profoundly humiliating for her. She angrily added, "Even an old hen wouldn't deign to give him a second glance."

Poet Zhao, to whom even an old hen wouldn't give a second glance, would often come in and out of Popsicle Wang's five-star reception booth and sit on Wang's Italian sofa, caress his French cabinet, and lie down in the German bed, and if he happened to have a chance to wash and dry his butt in the TOTO toilet, he naturally wouldn't pass that up either. Zhao was very complimentary of the giant high-definition plasma television Wang had hung on the wall. He said that it was several millimeters thinner than the poetry collection he was preparing to publish and that the number of television programs it played was even greater than the number of poems in that forthcoming collection. When Popsicle Wang heard Poet Zhao speaking of his forthcoming publication, he sent Zhao a congratulatory card and asked where it would be published. "You wouldn't be publishing it in Liu Town, would you?"

"Of course not," Zhao replied. He recalled how, at the Virgin Beauty Competition, Wandering Zhou had mentioned a place-name and, impulsively borrowing it, he said, "It's being published in the British Virgin Islands."

POPSICLE WANG led a luxurious and boring life. Day after day he used his television channels to pursue traces of Yanker Yu's political activities, continuously regaling people with tales of them. The people of Liu eventually grew tired of hearing these tales and began calling Popsicle Wang Brother Xianglin, after Sister Xianglin, the compulsively repetitive protagonist of that Lu Xun story. In the end, Poet Zhao was the only one who did not grow weary of Wang's stories; each time he would listen attentively, looking completely entranced and making Popsicle Wang believe that it was enough to have just one true friend in life. In fact, what Poet Zhao did not tire of was all the drinks in Wang's giant refrigerator, the empty bottles from which would pile into a mountain that scraped the sky.

At this point, a wave of anti-Japanese sentiment swept through the nation, and the anti-Japanese parades in Shanghai and Beijing could be seen on television, in the newspapers, and all over the Web. Seeing Japanese stores in Shanghai being destroyed and Japanese cars in Shanghai being burned, a crowd of townspeople from Liu didn't want to miss out on the action, so they also went marching with big banners, looking for something to destroy or burn. When they came upon Baldy Li's sushi shop, they spiritedly walked up and smashed the windows, then brought the chairs out and burned them for two hours, though they refrained from destroying the other installations. Blacksmith Tong saw them and decided that things were not looking good, so he immediately threw out all the Japanese goods in his supermarkets and hung a huge banner in the entranceway saying: WE REFUSE TO SELL JAPANESE PRODUCTS!

After Yanker Yu returned from his globe-trotting pursuit of political hotspots, Popsicle Wang promptly lost interest in Poet Zhao now that his *real* best friend had returned. Wang closed the door to the luxurious reception booth, shutting out Poet Zhao, who gazed through the window at Popsicle Wang's giant refrigerator, swallowing his saliva and sighing as he thought of the refreshments inside it.

Wang devoutly followed Yanker Yu everywhere he went, leaving early each morning and not returning until late each evening; each night he would even yearn to share a bed with Yu. Liu Town's anti-Japanese demonstrations had in fact run their course, but after Yanker Yu returned, they again picked up steam. Whenever he spoke, political slogans in ten different languages would stream out of his mouth, which the people of Liu then learned by heart, and within ten days or so they too could utter this string of foreign slogans as needed. Yanker Yu was no longer the best tooth-yanker within one hundred *li;* now, having experienced political disturbances around the world, he returned to Liu Town looking and sounding like a true political leader. As he put it, "I have weathered countless political storms."

Yanker Yu decided to take Popsicle Wang to Tokyo in order to oppose Japanese prime minister Junichiro Koizumi's annual visit to the Yasukuni shrine. When Popsicle Wang heard this, he muttered, "I could count on the fingers of one hand the number of times I have left Liu Town, much less left the country, and now he wants me to go to someone else's country and protest against their prime minister?" Popsicle Wang really had his doubts. He suggested delicately, "How about if we continue our protests here in Liu Town?"

"If we protest in Liu Town, you will merely be one of the masses." Yanker Yu had political ambitions, and he directed Popsicle Wang, "But if we go to Tokyo to protest, you will truly be a politician."

Wang couldn't care less about either the masses or politicians; all he cared about was Yanker Yu. He idolized him and knew that Yu's horizons were much broader than his own; therefore, as long as he followed Yanker Yu, he couldn't go wrong. Popsicle Wang looked at his aged face in the mirror and thought to himself that his life was almost

over and he had not visited a single foreign country. He therefore gritted his teeth and resolved to accompany Yanker Yu to Tokyo, and while
Yu was carrying out his political activities, Wang could do some foreign
touring.

C Liu took very seriously the company's second- and third-largest
shareholders' upcoming trip to Tokyo and arranged for a newly arrived
Toyota Crown sedan to take them to the Shanghai airport. C Liu was
full of good intentions. He said this was a brand-new sedan that no one
had ever ridden in before and therefore Yu and Wang would be riding
in a virgin car.

Yanker Yu and Popsicle Wang sat on the Italian sofa in the luxurious
reception area, waiting. When Yu saw that it was a Japanese sedan that
had arrived to pick them up, he waved the chauffeur over and in an
even tone told him, "Go and bring me a big iron hammer."

The chauffeur was completely baffled. He looked at Yanker Yu and
then at Popsicle Wang, but Wang was similarly baffled. Yanker Yu continued urging the chauffeur, "Go on."

Popsicle Wang didn't know what the hammer was for but figured
that whatever Yanker Yu said must be correct, so he too urged the
chauffeur, "Go, quickly!"

The chauffeur left stupidly, and Popsicle Wang asked Yanker Yu,
"What is the hammer for?"

"This is a Japanese product." Yu pointed at the Toyota Crown sedan
outside and, crossing his legs on the Italian sofa, said, "If we ride a
Japanese sedan to protest in Japan, it would become politically very
sensitive."

Wang finally understood and nodded repeatedly. He thought that
Yanker Yu was truly impressive and a born politician, and that C Liu
was genuinely confused. Liu knew full well that they were going to
Japan to protest but still sent a Japanese sedan to pick them up, indicating that he didn't have any understanding of politics whatsoever.

At this point the chauffeur showed up with the hammer and stood at
the door of the reception area waiting for Yanker Yu's instructions. Yu
gestured and said, "Smash it."

"Smash what?"

"Smash the Japanese product," said Yanker Yu, still speaking in an
even tone of voice.

"What Japanese product?"

Yu pointed at the sedan outside the window and said, "That car."

The chauffeur jumped in astonishment and stared at these two stockholders. He slowly backed out until he was standing in front of the Toyota Crown sedan, then he dropped the hammer and ran away. After a while, C Liu came over, all smiles, and explained to the two stockholders that this Toyota Crown sedan was actually not a Japanese product but, rather, a Chinese-Japanese joint venture product, and therefore at least 50 percent of it belonged to China. Popsicle Wang had always trusted C Liu and said to Yanker Yu, "That's right, it's not a Japanese product."

Yanker Yu replied very deliberately, "All political matters are of paramount importance and can't be treated haphazardly. We should retain the fifty percent that belongs to China and destroy the fifty percent that is Japanese."

Popsicle Wang immediately sided with Yanker Yu and said, "That's right. We should destroy fifty percent."

C Liu became livid and thought to himself that what he should be smashing with that iron hammer were those two bastards' thick skulls. He didn't dare lose his temper in front of the stockholders, so he turned and charged toward the chauffeur, shouting, "Smash it! Quick, smash it!"

C Liu stalked away furiously while the chauffeur lifted his hammer and, after a long hesitation, brought it down on the windshield. Yanker Yu stood up with satisfaction and, taking Popsicle Wang by the hand, said, "Let's go."

"If we don't have a car, how are we going to get there?"

"We'll hitch a ride," Yanker Yu replied. "We'll hitch a ride in a German sedan to go to Shanghai."

Therefore, these two seventy-year-old tycoons walked down the street pulling their suitcases and tried to hail a taxi. Popsicle Wang was very complimentary of Yanker Yu's calm manner. Yanker Yu hadn't uttered a single vicious word, but what he had accomplished was extremely vicious. Yanker Yu nodded and said to Wang, "Politicians don't need to utter vicious words. It is only little hooligans fighting among themselves that need to use vicious language."

Popsicle Wang nodded repeatedly, and upon remembering that he was soon going to accompany this extraordinary Yanker Yu to Japan, he couldn't help but feel a rush of pride. But when he thought the situation over again, he again became anxious and softly asked Yanker Yu, "When we go to Japan to protest, won't the Japanese police arrest us?"

"They won't," Yu assured him, then added, "though actually, in my heart of hearts I wish they would."

"Why?" Popsicle Wang jumped in alarm.

Yanker Yu looked around to make sure no one was listening, then said quietly, "If we are arrested by the Japanese police, China would certainly protest and negotiate on our behalf, the United Nations would mediate, and newspapers throughout the world would print our pictures, because aren't we world-famous celebrities?"

Seeing Popsicle Wang's confused expression, Yanker Yu said in a voice dripping with pity, "You just don't understand politics, do you?"

BALDY LI was not one of Madam Lin's VIP customers. More than three years elapsed, and Baldy Li hadn't seen Lin Hong a single time, nor did he see any other women. The last time he and Lin Hong made love had become their eternal elegy. The news of Song Gang's death had made Baldy Li leap away from Lin Hong as though she were on fire, and that instant of surprise followed by remorse left Baldy Li at a point of complete collapse. From that point on, he became impotent or, to use his own words, "I've lost all my superpowers."

After Baldy Li lost all his superpowers, his ambition also disappeared. When he went to work at the company, it was completely routine, like casting and then drying his nets, and he increasingly resembled a decadent emperor who had lost interest in ruling. After organizing the tofu banquet for Lin Hong, Baldy Li had handed over the position of company president to Deputy Liu.

The day Baldy Li handed over his presidency was April 28, 2001. That night he sat on the gold-plated toilet in his bathroom as the plasma television on the wall showed an image of a Russian Federation rocket taking off. Having bought a ticket for $20 million, the American businessman Dennis Tito was wearing a space suit with an astronaut's expression to match, proudly departing on a space tour. When Baldy Li turned to look at his own reflection in the mirror and saw his pissing and shitting expression, he felt as though he had just seen a fresh flower followed by a pile of cow dung. Baldy Li was very dissatisfied by his reflection and thought how this American was traveling into space to eat, drink, piss, and shit, while here he was, wasting away his years on this toilet in this tiny town. He told himself, "I want to go, too."

More than a year later, the South African Internet tycoon Mark

Shuttleworth also spent $20 million to hitch a ride on a Russian Federation rocket. He said that they orbited the earth sixteen times a day, and therefore every day he could see sixteen sunrises and sixteen sunsets. Next the American pop star Lance Bass announced that he too would fly into space. By this point Baldy Li was as anxious as an ant on a hot frying pan and said impatiently, "There have already been three bastards who have jumped ahead of me."

Baldy Li hired foreign students from Russia to eat and live with him and teach him Russian. To help improve his Russian faster, he vowed that he would speak only Russian in his mansion and no Chinese. This rule caused C Liu considerable distress, since when he came to report on the company's business every month, it would take him more than three hours to say what he should have been able to cover in twenty minutes. Baldy Li obviously understood everything he said but pretended he didn't understand Chinese and therefore asked the two Russian students to translate everything into Russian. After hearing the Russian, Baldy Li would shake his head pensively and would search his extremely limited Russian vocabulary for the appropriate word to respond. Unable to find the correct word, he would instead come up with some rough approximations, which the Russian students would then translate back into Chinese; but when C Liu heard the translation he would merely stare in bewilderment, having no idea what Baldy Li was trying to say. Baldy Li would also realize it hadn't come out right, but he couldn't allow himself to correct it, on account of his vow not to speak Chinese. Therefore, he would continue fruitlessly searching for the appropriate Russian words. In the end, C Liu was exhausted and felt that he was trying to speak human language with an animal, or animal language with a human, and would silently curse Baldy Li, *This fucking fake foreigner!*

As Baldy Li was struggling to learn Russian he also started to train his body. First he would train in the gym, and then he started running and swimming, followed by Ping-Pong, badminton, basketball, tennis, soccer, bowling, and golf. His training routine was constantly changing—he would grow tired of each new routine before two weeks had elapsed. By this point Baldy Li was leading a pure and celibate existence, having even become a vegetarian, like a monk. Apart from his Russian studies and his physical training, he would often reminisce about the excellent rice Song Gang had cooked when they were young. At the mention of Song Gang, Baldy Li would forget to speak Russian and, with an orphan's pathos, he would burst into Liu Town vernacular and recite that final line of Song Gang's suicide note: "Even if we are parted by death, we will still be brothers."

Baldy Li owned eleven restaurants in Liu Town, so he tried out each of them but couldn't find in any of them rice as good as that first successful pot of rice that Song Gang made. Baldy Li also went to other people's restaurants but couldn't find any there either. Being a generous tipper, he would still place one hundred yuan on the table before getting up and walking out when each time he found that it wasn't Song Gang rice. The people of Liu would all cook rice at home and invite Baldy Li to come over and see if it compared to the legendary Song Gang rice. For a while he went from house to house trying them out, but after a while he could tell at a glance that it wasn't Song Gang rice. He would then leave the money on the table, stand up shaking his head, and say, "It's not Song Gang rice."

Seeing how much Baldy Li reminisced about his Song Gang rice, a few townspeople with a nose for business saw an opportunity. Like archeologists, they unearthed Song Gang's relics and tried to sell them to Baldy Li for a good price. One lucky youngster even found the travel bag with SHANGHAI printed on the side that Song Gang was carrying when he left Liu Town with Wandering Zhou but that Wandering Zhou had thrown in the garbage. When Baldy Li saw the travel bag, he recognized it right away, and memories started rushing back to him. He felt a wave of loneliness as he grasped the bag and then bought it back for twenty thousand yuan.

With that, Liu Town exploded, and countless Song Gang relics, both real and counterfeit, were quickly unearthed. Poet Zhao found a Song Gang relic and carried an old, tattered pair of yellow sneakers to all sorts of different ball courts until he finally found Baldy Li training at the tennis courts. Zhao devoutly held out the sneakers and warmly called out, "Boss Li, Boss Li. Please come take a look."

Baldy Li stopped and glanced at the tattered yellow sneakers, asking, "What is the meaning of this?"

Poet Zhao said ingratiatingly, "This is a Song Gang relic!"

Baldy Li took the shoes and studied them for a second, then handed them back to Poet Zhao, saying, "Song Gang never wore these sneakers."

"It's true that Song Gang never wore them," Poet Zhao hurried to explain. "I wore them, don't you remember? When we were little and I gave the two of you my leg-sweeping kicks, I was wearing these shoes. I primarily leg-swept Song Gang and secondarily leg-swept you, and therefore these shoes also count as Song Gang relics."

When Baldy Li heard this, he cried out in fury and proceeded to give Poet Zhao eighteen leg-sweeping kicks right there on the court. The fifty-something Poet Zhao tumbled head over heels eighteen times, leaving his entire body racked with pain. Baldy Li kicked him until he was breathing heavily and covered with sweat and kept shouting out, "Damn, that feels good!"

In the process, Baldy Li unexpectedly discovered that leg-sweeping kicks were actually his favorite form of physical training. He looked down at Poet Zhao moaning in the grass and gestured for him to get up. Zhao didn't stand but sat up, moaning, and Baldy Li asked him, "Would you like to work for me?"

When Poet Zhao heard this, he stopped moaning, jumped up, and asked delightedly, "Boss Li, what kind of work?"

"Physical trainer," Baldy Li replied. "You would receive the salary of a mid-rank employee in my company."

Therefore, while Poet Zhao didn't succeed in selling off his old shoes, he did manage to secure a high-paying position as Baldy Li's personal trainer. From then on, Poet Zhao would wear knee and elbow pads and even on hot days would wear a padded jacket and pants. Rain or shine, he would stand in the grass of the tennis court and obediently wait for Baldy Li to come and leg-sweep him.

Baldy Li studied Russian for three years, during which time his Russian improved dramatically. During his three years of physical training, his physical fitness also improved daily. In six months he would go to the Russian space-training center to receive the basic training to be a cosmonaut. The day he would get to see outer space grew closer and closer, and Baldy Li began to let his thoughts run wild. Often, while sitting on the sofa in his living room, he would forget his own rule and begin alternating between speaking in Russian and in the Liu Town vernacular.

As garrulous as an old man, he began addressing the two Russian students as though they were both Song Gang. Counting on his fingers, he said, "When that American, Tito, went into space, he took with him a camera, a video recorder, a laser disc, and pictures of his wife and children. When Shuttleworth went into orbit, he took with him photos of his family and friends, together with a microscope, a notebook computer, and a disc." Then Baldy Li held out one finger and said that the Chinese Baldy Li would take only one thing into space with him. And what was that? It was Song Gang's ashes. Baldy Li looked through his french windows, saw the bright, distant sky, and, with a romantic look in his eyes, declared that he wanted to place Song Gang's ashes in orbit, so that every day they could see sixteen sunrises and sixteen sunsets. That way Song Gang would perpetually be traveling between the moon and the stars.

"From that point on," Baldy Li suddenly declared in Russian, "my brother Song Gang will be a space alien!"